THE ANATOMY OF MEMORY

THE ANATOMY OF
MEMORY

AN ANTHOLOGY

Edited by

James McConkey

New York   Oxford
OXFORD UNIVERSITY PRESS
1996

Oxford University Press

Oxford   New York
Athens   Auckland   Bangkok   Bombay
Calcutta   Cape Town   Dar es Salaam   Delhi
Florence   Hong Kong   Istanbul   Karachi
Kuala Lumpur   Madras   Madrid   Melbourne
Mexico City   Nairobi   Paris   Singapore
Taipei   Tokyo   Toronto

and associated companies in
Berlin   Ibadan

Library of Congress Cataloging-in-Publication Data
The anatomy of memory : an anthology / edited by James McConkey.
p.   cm.   Includes index.
ISBN 0-19-507841-1
1. Memory.   I. McConkey, James.
BF371.A52   1996
153.1'2—dc20   95-33727

1 3 5 7 9 8 6 4 2

Printed in the United States of America
on acid-free paper

Preface

The invitation to me from Linda Halvorson Morse, editor of the trade reference department of Oxford University Press in New York City, to compile this anthology about memory couldn't have arrived at a more propitious time. I was almost seventy, and about to become an emeritus professor of English at Cornell; and I was nearing the completion of the final volume of my *Court of Memory*, the third volume of an autobiographical work. For more than thirty years, that exploration of personal memory had permitted me (for reasons known to other memoirists, some of whom discuss the issue in essays that follow) a distance necessary for whatever self-understanding I possess; my discoveries led to thoughts and observations separate from my own experiences, where they became the seeds for all my other writing, whether fiction or nonfiction. Apparently, I was finished with all that, and had no sense of how I might concentrate my future energies. Still, I hesitated for some months before accepting the invitation, partly because the subject seemed to require a double focus difficult to obtain: one broad enough to encompass the capabilities of the human mind—for memory is not to be distinguished from them—and yet detailed enough to permit a close observation of memory's specific attributes.

I saw the subject not only as ambitious but as important as any I could imagine. We are a single human race, whatever our cultural or ethnic differences; and yet, as we approach the end of the millennium, we seem to be splintering into fragments, each with its own political agenda. We seem to be losing a spiritual awareness of who and what we are, either as individuals or as societies. Memory is responsible for our identity; it is the faculty whereby we perceive connections between past and present, thus enabling us to make sense of our surroundings; it underlies our creative achievements. As the source of whatever unitary apprehensions we have, memory surely is at least as important a subject as that to be found in any of the many anthologies devoted to a single agenda or social goal.

My enthusiasm for the project soon became as boundless as my initial concept of the subject, one that didn't emphasize nonfictional prose at the expense of more imaginative work: I wanted a selection of the material that throughout the ages has been directed either to the nature of memory or to the values it can provide us with. As a consequence, my desk, file cabinets, and bookcases are littered with marvelous choices and notes about them; but it soon became clear that if I continued in such a fashion I would end up with a volume comparable in bulk to my copy of *The Compact Oxford English Dictionary*, whose more than two thousand pages are so reduced in type size that one needs a bright light and a magnifying glass to read them. Gone from the present volume are Plato, Aristotle, Cicero; gone, too, are Pascal, Rousseau, Locke, Hume. As for the poets and fiction writers who have been excised, their names are so numerous that my memory rebels from compiling that tiresome list.

Nonfictional prose dominates the selections I ultimately made, for it is the genre that most readily permits observation, description, and direct comment about the nature and qualities of memory. Poetry from the Romantic period to the present now serves to introduce the sections of the anthology, where its function is anything but decorative: I depend upon it for the special kind of illumination (intense and concentrated) poetry can cast upon any given subject. Short stories with a clear autobiographical basis occasionally augment the nonfiction. While the anthology includes some salient work from the past, the majority of the prose was written in the century now ending.

Given my reason for wanting to edit this anthology—that is, my sense of the special importance of memory to us today—it probably was predetermined that I would incorporate the insights of the past mainly through modern eyes and minds. Some (but clearly not all) of the earlier assumptions about the nature and value of memory have only historical merit, the insights they led to now disqualified by our growing knowledge about both memory and ourselves. That growing knowledge is very much a part of our present-day spiritual problem, as I recognized from the beginning. Whatever integrity this anthology has is a consequence of the integrity of its component parts: essays and imaginative works that reflect, in large measure, both those older truths that remain undiminished and those newer truths that we have come to accept, either willingly or unwillingly; prose and poems that show the uses to which memory can be put in the struggles of our daily lives, however painful or anguished those struggles may be; and, finally, literature of various kinds that without sentimentality points to those attributes of memory that still can participate in our redemption.

The categories into which the selections in this book are divided were not established in advance; I let the material itself determine them. The introductions I have written for each section constitute the substance of whatever general introduction I might otherwise have written here. I have also provided headnotes for the individual selections. Some of these introductory notes, particularly to selections excerpted from larger works, may be longer than customary: as one who always has been wary of excerpts, I wished to put the selection in the context of the larger work and sometimes in the context of a specific writer's entire output.

At least two of the essayists included here—Vladimir Nabokov and Toni Morrison—are novelists who have referred to the crucial role that combinations play in the creative process: Nabokov elsewhere, and Morrison in the essay I have selected. Combinations form the structure—the anatomy—of a work of fiction, becoming an integral aspect of its meaning. The combinations I have discerned in the diverse pieces that make up this anthology serve in much the same anatomical way, as the titles to the various sections may suggest: "The Nature of Memory," "The Memory of Nature," "Memory and Creativity," "Memory, Culture, and Identity," "Perspectives of Memory," and (finally) "Beyond Memory." Those who read the selections in this order will find, I think, that they show a certain progression. The introduction to the final section summarizes major themes underlying the entire collection; the selections so introduced are attempts to reach beyond conscious formulations, beyond the categories of this or any book.

In his *Aspects of the Novel,* the English writer E. M. Forster says of expansion that it "is the idea the novelist must cling to. Not completion. Not rounding off but opening out. When the symphony is over we feel that the notes and tunes composing it have been liberated, they have found in the rhythm of the whole their individual freedom. Cannot the novel be like that?" Upon bringing this anthology to a close, I felt much happiness in the thought that I had managed (through the assistance of all the contributors to *The Anatomy of Memory*) to achieve something of that sort.

I am fortunate that Gladys McConkey shares not only her life but her professional expertise with me; as an editor capable of making scientific research accessible to intelligent nonspecialists, she has kept my language from being more recalcitrant to understanding than it might otherwise have been. I am obligated to the many colleagues at Cornell, and to other friends elsewhere, who responded to my request for suggestions of material; and I am especially grateful to the four Cornell doctoral candidates who, for two summers, provided research assistance, a younger perspective, and sensitive advice about selections. They are Elizabeth Davey and Elizabeth Graver (summer 1992) and Susan Choi and Daniel Coleman (summer 1993).

Ithaca, N.Y.   J. M.
February 1995

Contents

I. The Nature of Memory

Emily Dickinson, "The Brain—is wider than the sky—"
Introductory Essay
3

II. The Memory of Nature

Walt Whitman, *from* "Out of the Cradle Endlessly Rocking"
Introductory Essay
65

Contents

III. Memory and Creativity
William Butler Yeats, "Leda and the Swan"
Introductory Essay
123

IV. Memory, Culture, and Identity
Langston Hughes, "Theme for English B"
Introductory Essay
227

Contents

∽

V. Perspectives of Memory
Introductory Essay
311

Childhood and the Middle Years
William Wordsworth, *from* "The Two-Part Prelude"
Introductory Essay   313

Other Dimensions
Marianne Moore, "What Are Years?"
Introductory Essay   380

Contents

THE ANATOMY OF MEMORY

The Brain—is wider than the sky—
For—put them side by side—
The one the other will contain
With ease—and You—beside—

The Brain is deeper than the sea—
For—hold them—Blue to Blue—
The one the other will absorb—
As Sponges—Buckets—do—

The Brain is just the weight of God—
For—Heft them—Pound for Pound—
And they will differ—if they do—
As Syllable from Sound—

—Emily Dickinson,
"The Brain—is wider than the sky"

The Nature of Memory

By "Brain," Emily Dickinson is referring to "mind"—and to the faculty of memory that is its distinguishing characteristic. In giving the qualities of human consciousness, including its spiritual dimension, to the brain (a biological organism), she shows a grand insouciance to the philosophical dualism—the split between mind and body, between soul and matter—that has existed in, and haunted, Western thought ever since Descartes.

Current research by neuroscientists—including Gerald Edelman, Stephen Rose, and Antonio R. Damasio, whose writings close this initial section of *The Anatomy of Memory*—indicates that the dualism was a fallacy all along: when we speak of "mind" (of learning and memory), we are speaking of activities of the brain. Such activities or processes (complex changes in the properties of specific cells of the central nervous system when learning takes place, for example) can be scientifically observed, through laboratory dissection of animal brains—the method used by Rose—and increasingly through the techniques of brain imaging in humans—such as PET scans and magnetic resonance imaging.

But to see the mind as a process of the brain is not to make it simply an aspect of matter. As Edelman suggests, the most recent research into the complex operations of the brain intensifies our awareness that each of us is individual, each possessed of her or his unique spirit or soul, and each of us capable (within limits) of free will. Rose remarks that this research also has made simplistic the old determinist view that personality is a consequence of nothing more than nature and nurture, with either genes or upbringing given the greater emphasis according to the bias of the investigator. For Damasio, the brain is "body-minded"; emotion—feelings that originate in the body—helps to inform and direct our mental decisions.

Dickinson's little poem may foreshadow, in its implications, some of the most recent scientific studies of the brain, but my major reason for choosing it to introduce this opening section of the faculty of memory is for the way it mirrors insights from a much earlier period. As the reader will discover from the headnote to, as well as the brief excerpt from, Book X of St. Augustine's *Confessions,* the poem bears a surprising kinship with the marvels, spiritual dimensions, and apparent paradoxes of memory described by Augustine in that chapter.

I have chosen to open this section with material from Augustine and two others who are not professional scientists. (I have quite arbitrarily limited my selections by nonscientists in this section to a few with an active interest in describing the phenomenon of memory itself.) Frances Yates, a scholar, uses Roman texts to reveal the techniques discovered by the Greeks for improving—often to a remarkable degree—their "artificial" (as opposed to their innate or natural) memories; such techniques depend upon the associations, or groupings, so essential to remembering. Diane Ackerman is a poet and essayist. The three brief segments I have selected from her *A Natural History of the Senses* indicate the importance of one of those senses—smell—to memory.

Ackerman's lively interest in contemporary science permits these segments to serve as a bridge to the essays given the majority of space in this section— essays all written by scientists, each of whom is exploring one or more of the many facets that constitute the faculty of memory. Among those facets are the genetic memories that still are part of our human response (René Dubos' essay in particular emphasizes this aspect), collective or social memories transmitted by language and custom (Lewis Thomas and Rose both stress these memories), and the psychological dimension of memory (Freud). The three scientists whose writings conclude this section comment separately upon the general signifi- cance of the most recent research on the brain. This research represents work in progress, and much of it remains speculative, the various neuroscientists not always in agreement with each other. The selections I have chosen from their writings *do* represent, however, a commonality of belief, a view of mind and brain based on a shared foundation of scientific evidence too persuasive to be dismissed. Indeed, what has been most recently revealed by neuroscience is in keeping with what we have already come to know about ourselves—in keeping, that is, with all that we have come to understand about the evolutionary processes involved in our development as a sentient species, a species whose biological origin (like that of all creatures and plants on Earth) lies within the workings of nature.

Taken together, the selections in this section give credence to Dickinson's view that the brain "is wider than the sky" and "deeper than the sea." Instead of denying or limiting the attributes ascribed to memory by Augustine as well as Dickinson, scientific research augments them, showing how astonishing the faculty of memory is—and how intricately its components are interrelated. That research makes no claim of solving our deepest metaphysical questions, most of which begin with the interrogative *Why?* The growing knowledge of our- selves—of our intricate brain processes—should increase rather than diminish our innate capacity for wonder.

from *Confessions*

St. Augustine (354–430)

For about a decade I taught a course at Cornell called "The Modern European Novel"—a course made famous by Vladimir Nabokov, from whom I inherited it, if at second remove. The first text that the students and I read each semester was St. Augustine's *Confessions,* which is neither "modern" nor a "novel"—nor is Augustine a native European. (It was written around 397, a few years after Augustine had become bishop of Hippo, in a Roman province of his native Africa.) As an autobiography that is both spiritual and psychological, though, it does foreshadow the modern European novel in so many ways that it became a measure—in style, structure, and subject matter—for the actual novels we later discussed; indeed, the course came to be informally identified with his name. Especially from the Romantic period to the present day, his book has been a great influence upon Western literature, in poetry and fiction as well as autobiography. Indeed, in planning the contents of this anthology, Augustine's *Confessions* was the first title to come to my mind.

For the final selection of *The Anatomy of Memory,* I have chosen a portion of the *Confessions* that is one of the most moving autobiographical narratives—containing both visionary insight and grief at the death of a beloved mother—I know of; here I present a chapter from Book X that commences Augustine's lengthy struggle to comprehend, to define, what his memory contains. It is part of a still greater struggle—to find an answer to the grand question "What, then, do I love when I love my God?" (He already knows he loves God, and he knows, too, that God is not a substance and hence not to be recalled as a material image. Influenced by the Neoplatonists, Augustine perceives of God as a divine emanation, everywhere present in the universe. Evil is not a palpable presence or antithetical force to God, but simply a willful turning away from the divine illumination. Our memories do not contain God, but they do contain a memory of "a state of blessed happiness," a state that must contain an awareness of Truth; we all desire such happiness, and can approach it by grateful and willing acceptance of His radiant will. One can, of course, connect such a view with certain aspects of Catholic doctrine, including the fall from divine grace in the garden. Many writers since Augustine—including a number who have explicitly rejected religious doctrine—have explored the spiritual dimension of memory, finding in it a lost happiness and a truth beyond time and mundane reality: other selections in this anthology that have affinities with Augustine include those by Proust, Woolf, Agee, and Chekhov.)

Neuroscientists today—as evidenced by other selections in this opening section—may have an insight into the processes of the brain that was unavailable to Augustine, but I know of no later account that better describes the rich complexities of memory than that offered by Augustine in Book X of his *Confessions.*

5

So I must also go beyond this natural faculty [bodily life] of mine, as I rise by stages towards the God who made me. The next stage is memory, which is like a great field or a spacious palace, a storehouse for countless images of all kinds which are conveyed to it by the senses. In it are stored away all the thoughts by which we enlarge upon or diminish or modify in any way the perceptions at which we arrive through the senses, and it also contains anything else that has been entrusted to it for safe keeping, until such time as these things are swallowed up and buried in forgetfulness. When I use my memory, I ask it to produce whatever it is that I wish to remember. Some things it produces immediately; some are forthcoming only after a delay, as though they were being brought out from some inner hiding place; others come spilling from the memory, thrusting themselves upon us when what we want is something quite different, as much as to say "Perhaps we are what you want to remember?" These I brush aside from the picture which memory presents to me, allowing my mind to pick what it chooses, until finally that which I wish to see stands out clearly and emerges into sight from its hiding place. Some memories present themselves easily and in the correct order just as I require them. They come and give place in their turn to others that follow upon them, and as their place is taken they return to their place of storage, ready to emerge again when I want them. This is what happens when I recite something by heart.

In the memory everything is presented separately, according to its category. Each is admitted through its own special entrance. For example, light, colour, and shape are admitted through the eyes; sound of all kinds through the ears; all sorts of smell through the nostrils; and every kind of taste through the mouth. The sense of touch, which is common to all parts of the body, enables us to distinguish between hard and soft, hot and cold, rough and smooth, heavy and light, and it can be applied to things which are inside the body as well as to those which are outside it. All these sensations are retained in the great storehouse of the memory, which in some indescribable way secretes them in its folds. They can be brought out and called back again when they are needed, but each enters the memory through its own gateway and is retained in it. The things which we sense do not enter the memory themselves, but their images are there ready to present themselves to our thoughts when we recall them.

We may know by which of the senses these images were recorded and laid up in the memory, but who can tell how the images themselves are formed? Even when I am in darkness and in silence I can, if I wish, picture colours in my memory. I can distinguish between black and white and any other colours that I wish. And while I reflect upon them, sounds do not break in and confuse the images of colour, which reached me through

6

the eye. Yet my memory holds sounds as well, though it stores them separately. If I wish, I can summon them too. They come forward at once, so that I can sing as much as I want, even though my tongue does not move and my throat utters no sound. And when I recall into my mind this rich reserve of sound, which entered my memory through my ears, the images of colour, which are also there in my memory, do not interfere or intrude. In the same way I can recall at will all the other things which my other senses brought into my memory and deposited in it. I can distinguish the scent of lilies from that of violets, even though there is no scent at all in my nostrils, and simply by using my memory I recognize that I like honey better than wine and smooth things better than rough ones, although at that moment I neither taste nor touch anything.

All this goes on inside me, in the vast cloisters of my memory. In it are the sky, the earth, and the sea, ready at my summons, together with everything that I have ever perceived in them by my senses, except the things which I have forgotten. In it I meet myself as well. I remember myself and what I have done, when and where I did it, and the state of my mind at the time. In my memory, too, are all the events that I remember, whether they are things that have happened to me or things that I have heard from others. From the same source I can picture to myself all kinds of different images based either upon my own experience or upon what I find credible because it tallies with my own experience. I can fit them into the general picture of the past; from them I can make a surmise of actions and events and hopes for the future; and I can contemplate them all over again as if they were actually present. If I say to myself in the vast cache of my mind, where all those images of great things are stored, "I shall do this or that," the picture of this or that particular thing comes into my mind at once. Or I may say to myself "If only this or that would happen!" or "God forbid that this or that should be!" No sooner do I say this than the images of all the things of which I speak spring forward from the same great treasure-house of the memory. And, in fact, I could not even mention them at all if the images were lacking.

The power of the memory is prodigious, my God. It is a vast, immeasurable sanctuary. Who can plumb its depths? And yet it is a faculty of my soul. Although it is part of my nature, I cannot understand all that I am. This means, then, that the mind is too narrow to contain itself entirely. But where is that part of it which it does not itself contain? Is it somewhere outside itself and not within it? How, then, can it be part of it, if it is not contained in it?

I am lost in wonder when I consider this problem. It bewilders me. Yet men go out and gaze in astonishment at high mountains, the huge waves of the sea, the broad reaches of rivers, the ocean that encircles the world, or the stars in their courses. But they pay no attention to themselves. They do not marvel at the thought that while I have been mentioning all these things, I have not been looking at them with my eyes, and that I could not even speak of mountains or waves, rivers or stars, which are things that I have seen, or of the ocean, which I know only on the evidence of others, unless I could see them in my mind's eye, in my memory, and with the same vast spaces between them that would be there if I were looking at them in the world outside myself. When I saw them with the sight of my eyes, I did not draw them bodily into myself. They are not inside me themselves, but only their images. And I know which of my senses imprinted each image on my mind.

from *The Art of Memory*

Frances A. Yates (1899–1981)

Though it is obvious that Homer had found his own method several centuries before, the Greek poet Simonides of Ceos (c.556–468) is acknowledged as the founder of the art—that is to say, the training—of memory. Much of our knowledge of what the Greeks had to say about memory comes to us from the Romans. In the opening chapter of her *The Art of Memory,* "The Three Latin Sources for the Classical Art of Memory," Frances A. Yates turns to Cicero, Quintilian, and the anonymous author of the influential *Ad Herennium* to describe the principles used by the Greeks for improving their "artificial" (as distinct from their innate) memories. The Greeks realized the importance of visual images to memory and the need to find some visual method of organizing the material that one wishes to remember.

The techniques described in the following selection from "The Three Latin Sources for the Classical Art of Memory" are of more than antiquarian interest. Yates' own concern is their relationship with "the astonishing developments of the art of memory in the sixteenth century." (Jonathan Spence, in *The Memory Palace of Matteo Ricci*—an intriguing account of a sixteenth-century Italian missionary's encounters in China—remarks that Simonides' system, as elaborated upon over the centuries, became "a way for ordering all one's knowledge of secular and religious subjects.")

As an innate faculty, memory permits the recall of certain images or things, but beyond this conscious use it also easily, in what seems an involuntary manner, associates one thing with another, often through images; the classical techniques for strengthening the "artificial" memory, then, can be seen as a conscious attempt to use the dual aspects of that faculty for particular ends (such as clarity and order in speechmaking.) Yates remarks that the classical techniques rely upon the use of places and images. Most commonly, the individual desirous of improving his memory for the purposes of a speech will reconstruct in his mind all the rooms and other architectural features of a specific building, placing in each of these rooms or features specific material he wishes to remember; he will assign to each chamber or object an image designed to reveal the contents held within it. (Unconsciously, perhaps—and certainly in a less rigorous manner—many of us employ elements of that system in our attempts at recall.)

Of particular interest is the recommendation that the images chosen for remembering in proper order the elements of (say) a reasoned argument should be striking or unusual—images with an emotional appeal. Some of these suggested images—for example, the figure "stained with blood or soiled with mud or smeared with red paint"—would seem to appeal to dark regions of the human psyche; the use of such figures as an assistance to order is, perhaps, an example of the balance between reason and emotions frequently attributed to the classical period.

9

At a banquet given by a nobleman of Thessaly named Scopas, the poet Simonides of Ceos chanted a lyric poem in honour of his host but including a passage in praise of Castor and Pollux. Scopas meanly told the poet that he would only pay him half the sum agreed upon for the panegyric and that he must obtain the balance from the twin gods to whom he had devoted half the poem. A little later, a message was brought in to Simonides that two young men were waiting outside who wished to see him. He rose from the banquet and went out but could find no one. During his absence the roof of the banqueting hall fell in, crushing Scopas and all the guests to death beneath the ruins; the corpses were so mangled that the relatives who came to take them away for burial were unable to identify them. But Simonides remembered the places at which they had been sitting at the table and was therefore able to indicate to the relatives which were their dead. The invisible callers, Castor and Pollux, had handsomely paid for their share in the panegyric by drawing Simonides away from the banquet just before the crash. And this experience suggested to the poet the principles of the art of memory of which he is said to have been the inventor. Noting that it was through his memory of the places at which the guests had been sitting that he had been able to identify the bodies, he realised that orderly arrangement is essential for good memory.

> He inferred that persons desiring to train this faculty (of memory) must select places and form mental images of the things they wish to remember and store those images in the places, so that the order of the places will preserve the order of the things, and the images of the things will denote the things themselves, and we shall employ the places and images respectively as a wax writing-tablet and the letters written on it.

The vivid story of how Simonides invented the art of memory is told by Cicero in his *De oratore* when he is discussing memory as one of the five parts of rhetoric; the story introduces a brief description of the mnemonic of *places* and *images* (*loci* and *imagines*) which was used by the Roman rhetors. Two other descriptions of the classical mnemonic, besides the one given by Cicero, have come down to us, both also in treatises on rhetoric when memory as a part of rhetoric is being discussed; one is in the anonymous *Ad C. Herennium libri IV*; the other is in Quintilian's *Institutio oratoria*.

The first basic fact which the student of the history of the classical art of memory must remember is that the art belonged to rhetoric as a technique by which the orator could improve his memory, which would enable him to deliver long speeches from memory with unfailing accuracy. And it was as a part of the art of rhetoric that the art of memory travelled down through the European tradition in which it was never forgotten, or not forgotten until comparatively modern times, that those infallible guides in all human activities, the ancients, had laid down rules and precepts for improving the memory. It is not difficult to get hold of the general principles of the mnemonic. The first step was to imprint on the memory a series of *loci* or places. The commonest, though not the only, type of mnemonic place system used was the architectural type. The clearest description of the process is that given by Quintilian. In order to form a series of places in memory, he says, a building is to be remembered, as spacious and varied a one as possible, the forecourt, the living room, bedrooms, and parlours, not omitting statues and other ornaments with which the rooms are decorated. The images by which the speech is to be remembered—as an example of these Quintilian says one may use an anchor or a weapon—are then placed in imagination on the places which have been memorised in the building. This done, as soon as the memory of the facts requires to be revived, all these places are visited in turn and the various deposits demanded of the custodians. We have to think of the ancient orator as moving in imagination through his memory building *whilst* he is making his speech, drawing from the memorised places the images he has placed on them. The method ensures that the points are remembered in the right order, since the order is fixed by the sequence of places in the building. Quintilian's examples of the anchor and the weapon as images may suggest that he had in mind a speech which dealt at one point with naval matters (the anchor), at another with military operations (the weapon).

There is no doubt that this method will work for anyone who is prepared to labour seriously at these mnemonic gymnastics. I have never attempted to do so myself but I have been told of a professor who used to amuse his students at parties by asking each of them to name an object; one of them noted down all the objects in the order in which they had been named. Later in the evening the professor would cause general amazement by repeating the list of objects in the right order. He performed his little memory feat by placing the objects, as they were named, on the window sill, on the desk, on the wastepaper basket, and so on. Then, as Quintilian advises, he revisited those places in turn and demanded from them their deposits. He had never heard of the classical mnemonic but had discovered his technique quite independently. Had he extended his efforts by attaching notions to the objects remembered on the places he might have caused still greater amazement by delivering his lectures from memory, as the classical orator delivered his speeches.

Whilst it is important to recognise that the classical art is based on workable mnemotechnic principles it may be misleading to dismiss it with the label "mnemotechnics." The classical sources seem to be describing inner techniques which depend on visual impressions of almost incredible intensity. Cicero emphasises that Simonides' invention of the art of memory rested, not only on his discovery of the importance of order for memory, but also on the discovery that the sense of sight is the strongest of all the senses.

> It has been sagaciously discerned by Simonides or else discovered by some other person, that the most complete pictures are formed in our minds of the things that have been conveyed to them and imprinted on them by the senses, but that the keenest of all our senses is the sense of sight, and that consequently perceptions received by the ears or by reflexion can be most easily retained if they are also conveyed to our minds by the mediation of the eyes.

The word "mnemotechnics" hardly conveys what the artificial memory of Cicero may have been like, as it moved among the buildings of ancient Rome, *seeing* the places, *seeing* the images stored on the places, with a piercing inner vision which immediately brought to his lips the thoughts and words of his speech. I prefer to use the expression "art of memory" for this process.

We moderns who have no memories at all may, like the professor, employ from time to time some private mnemotechnic not of vital importance to us in our lives and professions. But in the ancient world, devoid of printing, without paper for note-taking or on which to type lectures, the trained memory was of vital importance. And the ancient memories were trained by an art which reflected the art and architecture of the ancient world, which could depend on faculties of intense visual memorisation which we have lost. The word "mnemotechnics," though not actually wrong as a description of the classical art of memory, makes this very mysterious subject seem simpler than it is.

An unknown teacher of rhetoric in Rome compiled, *circa* 86–82 B.C., a useful text-book for his students which immortalised, not his own name, but the name of the man to whom it was dedicated. It is somewhat tiresome that this work, so vitally important for the history of the classical art of memory and which will be constantly referred to in the course of this book, has no other title save the uninformative *Ad Herennium*. The busy and efficient teacher goes through the five parts of rhetoric (*inventio, dispositio, elocutio, memoria, pronuntiatio*) in a rather dry text-book style. When he comes to memory as an essential part of the orator's equipment, he opens his treatment of it with the words: "Now let us turn to the treasure-house of inventions, the custodian of all the parts of rhetoric, memory." There are two kinds of memory, he continues, one natural, the other artificial. The natural memory is that which is engrafted in our minds, born simultaneously with thought. The artificial memory is a memory strengthened or confirmed by training. A good natural memory can be improved by this discipline and persons less well endowed can have their weak memories improved by the art.

After this curt preamble the author announces abruptly, "Now we will speak of the artificial memory."

An immense weight of history presses on the memory section of *Ad Herennium*. It is drawing on Greek sources of memory teaching, probably in Greek treatises on rhetoric all of which are lost. It is the only Latin treatise on the subject to be preserved, for Cicero's and Quintilian's remarks are not full treatises and assume that the reader is already familiar with the artificial memory and its terminology. It is thus really the main source, and indeed the only complete source, for the classical art of memory both in the Greek and in the Latin world. Its rôle as the transmitter of the classical art to the Middle Ages and the Renaissance is also of unique importance. The *Ad Herennium* was a well known and much used text in the Middle Ages when it had an immense prestige because it was thought to be by Cicero. It was therefore believed that the precepts for the artificial memory which it expounded had been drawn up by "Tullius" himself.

In short, all attempts to puzzle out what the classical art of memory was like must be mainly based on the memory section of *Ad Herennium*. And all attempts such as we are making in this book to puzzle out the history of that art in the Western tradition must refer back constantly to this text as the main source of the tradition. Every *Ars memorativa* treatise, with its rules for "places," its rules for "images," its discussion of "memory for things" and "memory for words," is repeating the plan, the subject matter, and as often as not the actual words of *Ad Herennium*. And the astonishing developments of the art of memory in the sixteenth century, which it is the chief object of this book to explore, still preserve the "Ad Herennian" outlines below all their complex accretions. Even the wildest flights of fancy in such a work as Giordano Bruno's *De umbris idearum* cannot conceal the fact that the philosopher of the Renaissance is going through yet once again the old, old business of rules for places, rules for images, memory for things, memory for words.

Evidently, therefore, it is incumbent upon us to attempt the by no means easy task of trying to understand the memory section of *Ad Herennium*. What makes the task by no means easy is that the rhetoric teacher is not addressing us; he is not setting out to explain to people who know nothing about it what the artificial memory was. He is addressing his rhetoric students as they congregated around him *circa* 86–82 B.C., and *they* knew what he was talking about; for *them* he needed only to rattle off the "rules" which they would know how to apply. We are in a different case and are often somewhat baffled by the strangeness of some of the memory rules.

13

In what follows I attempt to give the content of the memory section of *Ad Herennium,* emulating the brisk style of the author, but with pauses for reflection about what he is telling us.

The artificial memory is established from places and images (*Constat igitur artificiosa memoria ex locis et imaginibus*), the stock definition to be forever repeated down the ages. A *locus* is a place easily grasped by the memory, such as a house, an intercolumnar space, a corner, an arch, or the like. Images are forms, marks or simulacra (*formae, notae, simulacra*) of what we wish to remember. For instance if we wish to recall the genus of a horse, of a lion, of an eagle, we must place their images on definite *loci.*

The art of memory is like an inner writing. Those who know the letters of the alphabet can write down what is indicated to them and read out what they have written. Likewise those who have learned mnemonics can set in places what they have heard and deliver it from memory. "For the places are very much like wax tablets or papyrus, the images like the letters, the arrangement and disposition of the images like the script, and the delivery is like the reading."

If we wish to remember much material we must equip ourselves with a large number of places. It is essential that the places should form a series and must be remembered in their order, so that we can start from any *locus* in the series and move either backwards or forwards from it. If we should see a number of our acquaintances standing in a row, it would not make any difference to us whether we should tell their names beginning with the person standing at the head of the line or at the foot or in the middle. So with memory *loci.* "If these have been arranged in order, the result will be that, reminded by the images, we can repeat orally what we have committed to the *loci,* proceeding in either direction from any *locus* we please."

The formation of the *loci* is of the greatest importance, for the same set of *loci* can be used again and again for remembering different material. The images which we have placed on them for remembering one set of things fade and are effaced when we make no further use of them. But the *loci* remain in the memory and can be used again by placing another set of images for another set of material. The *loci* are like the wax tablets which remain when what is written on them has been effaced and are ready to be written on again.

In order to make sure that we do not err in remembering the order of the *loci* it is useful to give each fifth *locus* some distinguishing mark. We may for example mark the fifth *locus* with a golden hand, and place in the tenth the image of some acquaintance whose name is Decimus. We can then go on to station other marks on each succeeding fifth *locus.*

It is better to form one's memory *loci* in a deserted and solitary place for crowds of passing people tend to weaken the impressions. Therefore the student intent on acquiring a sharp and well-defined set of *loci* will choose an unfrequented building in which to memorise places.

Memory *loci* should not be too much like one another, for instance too many intercolumnar spaces are not good, for their resemblance to one another will be confusing. They should be of moderate size, not too large for this renders the images placed on them vague, and not too small for then an arrangement of images will be overcrowded. They must not be too brightly lighted for then the images placed on them will glitter and dazzle; nor must they be too dark or the shadows will obscure the images. The intervals between the *loci* should be of moderate extent, perhaps about the thirty feet, "for like the external eye, so the inner eye of thought is less powerful when you have moved the object of sight too near or too far away."

A person with a relatively large experience can easily equip himself with as many suitable *loci* as he pleases, and even a person who thinks that he does not possess enough sufficiently good *loci* can remedy this. "For thought can embrace any region whatsoever and in it and at will construct the setting of some locus." (That is to say, mnemonics can use what were afterwards called "fictitious places," in contrast to the "real places" of the ordinary method.)

Pausing for reflection at the end of rules for places I would say that what strikes me most about them is the astonishing visual precision which they imply. In a classically trained memory the space between the *loci* can be measured, the lighting of the *loci* is allowed for. And the rules summon up a vision of a forgotten social habit. Who is that man moving slowly in the lonely building, stopping at intervals with an intent face? He is a rhetoric student forming a set of memory *loci*.

"Enough has been said of places," continues the author of *Ad Herennium*, "now we turn to the theory of images." Rules for images now begin, the first of which is that there are two kinds of images, one for "things" (*res*), the other for "words" (*verba*). That is to say "memory for things" makes images to remind of an argument, a notion, or a "thing"; but "memory for words" has to find images to remind of every single word.

I interrupt the concise author here for a moment in order to remind the reader that for the rhetoric student "things" and "words" would have an absolutely precise meaning in relation to the five parts of the rhetoric. Those five parts are defined by Cicero as follows:

> Invention is the excogitation of true things (*res*), or things similar to truth to render one's cause plausible; disposition is the arrangement in order of the things thus discovered; elocution is the accommodation of

suitable words to the invented (things); memory is the firm perception in the soul of things and words; pronunciation is the moderating of the voice and body to suit the dignity of the things and words.

"Things" are thus the subject matter of the speech; "words" are the language in which that subject matter is clothed. Are you aiming at an artificial memory to remind you only of the order of the notions, arguments, "things" of your speech? Or do you aim at memorising every single word in it in the right order? The first kind of artificial memory is *memoria rerum*; the second kind is *memoria verborum*. The ideal, as defined by Cicero in the above passage, would be to have a "firm perception in the soul" of both things and words. But "memory for words" is much harder than "memory for things"; the weaker brethren among the author of *Ad Herennium*'s rhetoric students evidently rather jibbed at memorising an image for every single word, and even Cicero himself, as we shall see later, allowed that "memory for things" was enough.

To return to the rules for images. We have already been given the rules for places, what kind of places to choose for memorising. What are the rules about what kind of images to choose for memorising on the places? We now come to one of the most curious and surprising passages in the treatise, namely the psychological reasons which the author gives for the choice of mnemonic images. Why is it, he asks, that some images are so strong and sharp and so suitable for awakening memory, whilst others are so weak and feeble that they hardly stimulate memory at all? We must enquire into this so as to know which images to avoid and which to seek.

Now nature herself teaches us what we should do. When we see in every day life things that are petty, ordinary, and banal, we generally fail to remember them, because the mind is not being stirred by anything novel or marvellous. But if we see or hear something exceptionally base, dishonourable, unusual, great, unbelievable, or ridiculous, that we are likely to remember for a long time. Accordingly, things immediate to our eye or ear we commonly forget; incidents of our childhood we often remember best. Nor could this be so for any other reason than that ordinary things easily slip from the memory while the striking and the novel stay longer in the mind. A sunrise, the sun's course, a sunset are marvellous to no one because they occur daily. But solar eclipses are a source of wonder because they occur seldom, and indeed are more marvellous than lunar eclipses, because these are more frequent. Thus nature shows that she is not aroused by the common ordinary event, but is moved by a new or striking occurrence. Let art, then, imitate nature, find what she desires, and follow as she directs. For in invention nature is never last, education never first; rather the beginnings of things arise from natural talent, and the ends are reached by discipline. We ought, then, to set up images of a kind that can adhere longest in memory. And we shall do so if we establish similitudes as striking as possible; if we set up images that are not many or vague but active (*imagines agentes*); if we assign to them exceptional beauty or singular ugliness; if we ornament some of them, as with crowns or purple cloaks, so that the similitude may be more distinct to us; or if we somehow disfigure them, as by introducing one stained with blood or soiled with mud or smeared with red paint, so that its form is more striking, or by assigning certain comic effects to our images, for that, too, will ensure our remembering them more readily. The things we easily remember when they are real we likewise remember without difficulty when they are figments. But this will be essential—again and again to run over rapidly in the mind all the original places in order to refresh the images.

Our author has clearly got hold of the idea of helping memory by arousing emotional affects through these striking and unusual images, beautiful or hideous, comic or obscene. And it is clear that he is thinking of human images, of human figures wearing crowns or purple cloaks, bloodstained or smeared with paint, of human figures dramatically engaged in some activity—doing something. We feel that we have moved into an extraordinary world as we run over his places with the rhetoric student, imagining on the places such very peculiar images. Quintilian's anchor and weapon as memory images, though much less exciting, are easier to understand than the weirdly populated memory to which the author of *Ad Herennium* introduces us.

from *A Natural History of the Senses*

Diane Ackerman (1948–)

Diane Ackerman's *A Natural History of the Senses* is a lively and encyclopedic celebration of the faculties through which we apprehend the world. The exuberance of the style—its playfulness, even its excesses—is one with its call for us to respond more fully to life: "We need to return to feeling the textures of life," she says in her introduction. "Much of our experience in twentieth-century America is an effort to get away from those textures, to fade into a stark, simple, solemn, puritanical, all-business routine that doesn't have anything so unseemly as sensuous zest."

Despite our belief that our minds exist in our heads, we should be aware, she goes on to tell us, that "the latest findings in physiology suggest that *the mind* doesn't really dwell in the brain but travels the whole body on caravans of hormone and enzyme, busily making sense of the compound wonders we catalogue as touch, taste, smell, hearing, vision."

"Mind," that thinking and perceiving part of consciousness, encompasses memory—memory that is genetically inherited as well as that which comes from experience, through our senses. In regard to genetic or biological memories, Ackerman says, "We like to think that we are finely evolved creatures, in suit-and-tie or pantyhose and chemise, who live many millennia and mental detours away from the cave, but that's not something our bodies are convinced of." Our genetic past influences our senses today: "We still stake out or mark our territories, though sometimes now it is with the sound of radios. . . . And we still perceive the world, in all its gushing beauty and terror, right on our pulses." In regard to our personal memories, she, like Proust, is aware of how fully a present aroma can carry us into a past experience, recreating it as if it were new; like Wordsworth and other poets, she is also aware of how memory—through habit, repetition—can dull sensation. In her "Postscript," she remarks that the "senses crave novelty. Any change alerts them, and they send a signal to the brain. . . . There is that unique moment when one confronts something new and astonishment begins. . . . But the second time one sees it, the mind says, Oh, that again, another wing walker, another moon landing." Since her purpose is to awaken us to freshness of response, to prevent us from passing our lives "in a comfortable blur," she is drawn to memories that recapture an initial sensation; she resists our human tendency to turn daily experiences into commonplace events. ("Living on the senses requires an easily triggered sense of marvel, a little extra energy, and most people are lazy about life," she scolds, hoping to wake up the lazy majority. "Life is something that happens to them while they wait for death.")

"Buckets of Light," "The Winter Palace of the Monarchs," and "The Oceans Inside Us" are consecutive segments, each of them brief, from the first chapter—"Smell"—of *A Natural History of the Senses*. The initial segment is a selective listing, with pertinent quotations, of the use of smell in literature, from

18

"The Song of Solomon" to a contemporary novel; the second employs a vivid example from Ackerman's own memory to show how an aroma can connect past with present; and the third discusses our biological inheritance from our salty and fishy origins in the sea.

BUCKETS OF LIGHT

Much of life becomes background, but it is the province of art to throw buckets of light into the shadows and make life new again. Many writers have been gloriously attuned to smells: Proust's lime-flower tea and madeleines; Colette's flowers, which carried her back to childhood gardens and her mother, Sido; Virginia Woolf's parade of city smells; Joyce's memories of baby urine and oilcloth, holiness and sin; Kipling's rain-damp acacia, which reminded him of home, and the complex barracks smells of military life ("one whiff . . . is all Arabia"); Dostoevsky's "Petersburg stench"; Coleridge's notebooks, in which he recalled that "a dunghill at a distance smells like musk, and a dead dog like elder flowers"; Flaubert's rhapsodic accounts of smelling his lover's slippers and mittens, which he kept in his desk drawer; Thoreau's moonlight walks through the fields when the tassels of corn smelled dry, the huckleberry bushes oozed mustiness, and the berries of the wax myrtle smelled "like small confectionery"; Baudelaire's plunges into smell until his "soul soars upon perfume as the souls of other men soar upon music"; Milton's description of the odors God finds pleasing to His divine nostrils and those preferred by Satan, an ace sniffer-out of carrion ("Of carnage, prey innumerable . . . scent of living carcasses"); Robert Herrick's fetishistic and intimate sniffing of his sweetheart, whose "breast, lips, hands, thighs, legs . . . are all/richly aromatical," indeed "All the spices of the East/Are circumfused there"; Walt Whitman's praise of sweat's "aroma finer than prayer"; François Mauriac's *La Robe Prétexte,* which is adolescence remembered through its smells; Chaucer's "The Miller's Tale," where we find one of the first mentions in literature of breath deodorants; Shakespeare's miraculously delicate flower similes (to the violet he says: "Sweet thief, whence didst thou steal the sweet, if not from my love's breath?"); Czeslaw Milosz's linen closet, "filled with the mute tumult of memories"; Joris-Karl Huysmans's obsession with nasal hallucinations, and the smell of liqueurs and women's sweat that fills his lush, almost unimaginably decadent, hedonistic novel, *A Rebours.* About one character, Huysmans explained that she was "an ill-balanced, nerve-ridden woman, who loved to have her nipples macerated in scents, but who really experienced a genuine and overmastering ecstasy when her head was tickled with a comb and she could, in the act of being caressed by a lover, breathe the smell of the chimney soot, of wet from a house building in rainy weather, or of dust of a summer storm."

The most scent-drenched poem of all time, "The Song of Solomon," avoids talk of body or even natural odors, and yet weaves a luscious love story around perfumes and unguents. In the story's arid lands, where water was rare, people perfumed themselves often and well, and this betrothed couple, whose marriage day approaches, in the meantime converse amorously in poetry, sweetly dueling with compliments lavish and ingenious. When he dines at her table he is "a bundle of myrrh" or "a cluster of camphire in the vineyards of En-ge-di," or muscular and sleek as a "young gazelle." To him, her robust virginity is a secret "garden . . . a spring shut up, a fountain sealed." Her lips "drop as the honeycomb: honey and milk are under thy tongue; and the smell of thy garments is like the smell of Lebanon." He tells her that on their wedding night he will enter her garden, and he catalogues all the fruits and spices he knows he'll find there: frankincense, myrrh, saffron, camphire, pomegranates, aloes, cinnamon, calamus, and other treasures. She will weave a fabric of love around him, and fill his senses until they brim with oceanic extravagance. So stirred is she by this loving tribute and so wild with desire that she replies yes, she will throw open the gates of her garden to him: "Awake, O north wind; and come, thou south; blow upon my garden, that the spices thereof may flow out. Let my beloved come into his garden, and eat his pleasant fruits."

In the macabre contemporary novel *Perfume,* by Patrick Süskind, the hero, who lives in Paris in the eighteenth century, is a man born without any personal scent whatsoever, although he develops prodigious powers of smell: "Soon he was no longer smelling mere wood, but kinds of wood: maple wood, oak wood, pinewood, elm wood, pearwood, old, young, moldering, mossy wood, down to single logs, chips, and splinters—and could clearly differentiate them as objects in a way that other people could not have done by sight." When he drinks a glass of milk each day, he can smell the mood of the cow it has come from; out walking, he can easily identify the origin of any smoke. His lack of human scent frightens people, who treat him badly, and this warps his personality. He ultimately creates personal odors for himself that other people aren't aware of per se, but which make him appear more normal, including such delicacies as "an odor of inconspicuousness, a mousey, workaday outfit of odors with the sour, cheesy smell of humankind still present." In time, he becomes a murderer-perfumer, who seeks to distill the fragrant essence from certain people as if they were flowers.

Many writers have written of how smells trigger flights of comprehensive remembrance. In *Swann's Way*, Proust, that great blazer of scent trails through the wilderness of luxury and memory, describes a momentary whirlwind in his day:

> I would turn to and fro between the prayer-desk and the stamped velvet armchairs, each one always draped in its crocheted antimacassar, while the fire, baking like a pie the appetizing smells with which the air of the room was thickly clotted, which the dewy and sunny freshness of the morning had already "raised" and started to "set," puffed them and glazed them and fluted them and swelled them into an invisible though not impalpable country cake, an immense puff-pastry, in which, barely waiting to savor the crustier, more delicate, more respectable, but also drier smells of the cupboard, the chest-of-drawers, and the patterned wall-paper I always returned with an unconfessed gluttony to bury myself in the nondescript, resinous, dull, indigestible, and fruity smell of the flowered quilt.

Throughout his adult life, Charles Dickens claimed that a mere whiff of the type of paste used to fasten labels to bottles would bring back with unbearable force all the anguish of his earliest years, when bankruptcy had driven his father to abandon him in a hellish warehouse where they made such bottles. In the tenth century, in Japan, a glitteringly talented court lady, Lady Murasaki Shikibu, wrote the first real novel, *The Tale of Genji,* a love story woven into a vast historical and social tapestry, the cast of which includes perfumer-alchemists, who concoct scents based on an individual's aura and destiny. One of the real tests of writers, especially poets, is how well they write about smells. If they can't describe the scent of sanctity in a church, can you trust them to describe the suburbs of the heart?

THE WINTER PALACE OF MONARCHS

We each have our own aromatic memories. One of my most vivid involves an odor that was as much vapor as scent. One Christmas, I traveled along the coast of California with the Los Angeles Museum's Monarch Project, locating and tagging great numbers of overwintering monarch butterflies. They prefer to winter in eucalyptus groves, which are deeply fragrant. The first time I stepped into one, and every time thereafter, they filled me with sudden tender memories of mentholated rub and childhood colds. First we reached high into the trees, where the butterflies hung in fluttering gold garlands, and caught a group of them with telescoping nets. Then we sat on the ground, which was densely covered with the South African ice plant, a type of succulent, and one of the very few plants that can tolerate the heavy oils that drop from the trees. The oils kept crawling insects away, too, and, except for the occasional Pacific tree frog croaking like someone working the tumblers of a safe, or a foolish blue jay trying to feed on the butterflies (whose wings contain a digitalis-like poison), the sunlit forests were serene, otherworldly, and immense with quiet. Because of the eucalyptus vapor, I not only smelled the scent, I felt it in my nose and throat. The loudest noise was the occasional sound of a door creaking open, the sound of eucalyptus bark peeling off the trees and falling to the ground, where it would soon roll up like papyrus. Everywhere I looked, there seemed to be proclamations left by some ancient scribe. Yet, to my nose, it was Illinois in the 1950s. It was a school day; I was tucked in bed, safe and cosseted, feeling my mother massage my chest with Vicks Vapo-Rub. That scent and memory brought an added serenity to the hours of sitting quietly in the forest and handling the exquisite butterflies, gentle creatures full of life and beauty who stalk nothing and live on nectar, like the gods of old. What made this recall doubly sweet was the way it became layered in my senses. Though at first tagging butterflies triggered memories of childhood, afterward the butterfly-tagging *itself* became a scent-triggerable memory, and, what's more, it replaced the original one: In Manhattan one day, I stopped at a flower-seller's on the street, as I always do when I travel, to choose a few flowers for the hotel room. Two tubs held branches of round, silver-dollar-shaped eucalyptus, the leaves of which were still fresh—bluish-green with a chalky surface; a few of them had broken, and released their thick, pungent vapor into the air. Despite the noise of Third Avenue traffic, the drilling of the City Works Department, the dust blowing up off the streets and the clotted gray of the sky, I was instantly transported to a particularly beautiful eucalyptus grove near Santa Barbara. A cloud of butterflies flew along a dried-up riverbed. I sat serenely on the ground, lifting yet another gold-and-black monarch butterfly from my net, carefully tagging it and tossing it back into the air, then watching for a moment to make sure it flew safely away with its new tag pasted like a tiny epaulet on one wing. The peace of that moment crested over me like a breaking wave and saturated my senses. A young Vietnamese man arranging his stock looked hard at me, and I realized that my eyes had suddenly teared. The whole episode could not have taken more than a few seconds, but the combined scent memories endowed eucalyptus with an almost savage power to move me. That afternoon, I went to one of my favorite shops, a boutique in the Village, where they will compound a bath oil for you, using a base of sweet almond oil, or make up shampoos or body lotions from other fragrant ingredients. Hanging from my bathtub's shower attachment is a blue net bag of the sort Frenchwomen use when they do their daily grocery shopping; I keep in it a wide variety of bath potions, and eucalyptus is one of the most calming. How is it possible that Dickens's chance encounter with a few molecules of glue, or mine with eucalyptus, can transport us back to an otherwise inaccessible world?

THE OCEANS INSIDE US

Driving through farm country at summer sunset provides a cavalcade of smells: manure, cut grass, honeysuckle, spearmint, wheat chaff, scallions, chicory, tar from the macadam road. Stumbling on new smells is one of the delights of travel. Early in our evolution we didn't travel for pleasure, only for food, and smell was essential. Many forms of sea life must sit and wait for food to brush up against them or stray within their tentacled grasp. But, guided by smell, we became nomads who could go out and search for food, hunt it, even choose what we had a hankering for. In our early, fishier version of humankind, we also used smell to find a mate or detect the arrival of a barracuda. And it was an invaluable tester, allowing us to prevent something poisonous from entering our mouths and the delicate, closed system of our bodies. Smell was the first of our senses, and it was so successful that in time the small lump of olfactory tissue atop the nerve cord grew into a brain. Our cerebral hemispheres were originally buds from the olfactory stalks. We *think* because we *smelled*.

Our sense of smell, like so many of our other body functions, is a throwback to that time, early in evolution, when we thrived in the oceans. An odor must first dissolve into a watery solution our mucous membranes can absorb before we can smell it. Scuba-diving in the Bahamas some years ago, I became aware of two things for the first time: that we carry the ocean within us; that our veins mirror the tides. As a human woman, with ovaries where eggs lie like roe, entering the smooth, undulating womb of the ocean from which out ancestors evolved millennia ago, I was so moved my eyes teared underwater, and I mixed my saltiness with the ocean's. Distracted by such thoughts, I looked around to find my position vis-à-vis the boat, and couldn't. But it didn't matter: Home was everywhere.

That moment of mysticism left my sinuses full, and made surfacing painful until I removed my mask, blew my nose in a strange two-stage snite, and settled down emotionally. But I've never forgotten that sense of belonging. Our blood is mainly salt water, we still require a saline solution (salt water) to wash our eyes or put in contact lenses, and through the ages women's vaginas have been described as smelling "fishy." In fact, Sandor Ferenczi, a disciple of Freud's, went so far as to declare, in *Thalassa: A Theory of Genitality,* that men only make love to women because women's wombs smell of herring brine, and men are trying to get back to the primoridal ocean—surely one of the more remarkable theories on the subject. He didn't offer an explanation for why women have intercourse with men. One researcher claims that this "fishiness" is due not to anything intrinsic to the vagina, but rather to poor hygiene after intercourse, or vaginitis, or stale sperm. "If you deposit semen in the vagina and leave it there, it comes out smelling fishy," he argues. This has a certain etymological persuasiveness to it, if we remember that in many European languages the slang names for prostitutes are variations on the Indo-European root *pu*, to decay or rot. In French, *putain*; to the Irish, *old put*; in Italian *putta*; *puta* in both Spanish and Portuguese. Cognate words are putrid, pus, suppurate, and putorius (referring to the skunk family). *Skunk* derives from the Algonquin Indian word for polecat; and during the sixteenth and seventeenth centuries in England polecat was a derogatory term for prostitute. Not only do we owe our sense of smell and taste to the ocean, but we smell and taste *of* the ocean.

from *So Human an Animal*

René Dubos (1901–1982)

Born in France, René Dubos emigrated to the United States at the age of twenty-four; he became an eminent microbiologist. Concerned with destructive processes at work within civilization, he set out to define, in his *So Human an Animal,* the qualities that make us human—qualities that both contribute to the present quandary and suggest possible solutions to it. A lengthy chapter is entitled "Biological Remembrance of Things Past"; the subject here is the buried memory that through genetic evolution connects us to the distant past of our race. "Considered broadly," he says at the outset of the chapter section called "The Genetic Record of Past Experiences," "evolution always involves learning by experience." In this section, he explores the related genetic responses of humans and other animals; all species demonstrate historical determinants in their patterns of response. One ancient biological trait common to humankind and the other animals is the "urge to control property and to dominate one's peers." He adds that within "the deepest layers of man's nature" lies the call of "the mysterious and wonderful world of the past"—a "call of the wild" which, while dangerous for us unconsciously to yield to, is "perhaps destructive to ignore."

Since 1968, the publication date of *So Human an Animal,* scientific research no doubt has modified some of its views, but the book remains a graceful and illuminating account of who and what we are—human animals, who for the sake of the future must not ignore the past.

In its most general sense, the word "evolution" means the progressive transformations of a system in the course of time. When biologists or sociologists use the word, they usually have in mind the long-range molding of living organisms or institutions by the environment. Biological species, individual persons, societies or their institutions are indeed molded by the environment as a result of the adaptive responses that they make to its stimuli. Considered broadly, evolution always involves learning from experience. The learning may take place by storage of genetic information in the chromosomes, by accumulation of knowledge and skills in the individual organism, or by transmission of practices and wisdom in institutions or in society as a whole.

Neo-Darwinian biologists give to the word evolution a more precise but narrower meaning. For them, it denotes the transformations of a species resulting from spontaneous mutations in its genetic equipment and from the selection of mutants by environmental forces. Darwinians regard natural selection as the agency that translates environmental challenges into the genetic alterations of the species and thus brings about the evolutionary changes which improve its fitness to the environment. Since the following discussion is focused on Darwinian evolution, it may be helpful to define briefly some of the determinants of the evolutionary process.

The amazing ability of living organisms to learn from experience and to transmit this learning to their progeny is greatly facilitated by certain peculiar characteristics of their genetic equipment. On the whole, genes are very stable structures and thus they usually transfer the hereditary attributes of the organism from one generation to the next in an unaltered form. But equally important is the fact that genes are not completely stable. As they spontaneously undergo alterations now and then, the species can respond adaptively to environmental changes by using the mutant forms thus produced. Sexual reproduction also facilitates the evolutionary process. Sexual union results in a shuffling of the two different gene arrays contributed by the two mating organisms and thereby brings about the emergence of new characteristics through new combinations of genes. The availability of these combinations in turn enlarges the range of adaptability of the species to changing environmental conditions.

Heredity does not determine fixed characters or traits; it only controls developmental processes. Furthermore, the path followed by any developmental process can in principle be modified by both genetic and environmental variables. However, the degree of modifiability or plasticity is quite different for different processes. As a general rule, the processes essential for survival and reproduction are buffered against environmental and genetic disturbances; in other words, they are not readily affected by the environment. Two eyes, a four-chambered heart, the ability to maintain an approximately stable body temperature, the suckling instinct in the infant, sexual drive in the adult, the capacity to think symbolically and to learn a symbolic language are all characters that develop in almost every human being irrespective of the environment in which he lives. Their development is coded in the genetic constitution in such a manner as to be little affected by external factors. In contrast, less stable characters are generally those for which variability is advantageous. For example, sun tanning and shade bleaching are obviously brought about by environmental factors.

Under natural circumstances, mutations are spontaneous events, shuffling of genes during sexual reproduction is accidental, and the selection of new genetic assortment by environmental forces occurs blindly. Genetic evolution is therefore an unconscious process. The interplay between organism and environment, however, is far more subtle than is indicated by this simple formulation, particularly in the case of the higher animals and man.

It is a truism that a given environment can act as a selective agent, and thus govern evolutionary changes, only if the animal elects to stay in it long enough to reproduce. In general, an animal occupies a given site and continues to function there because forced to do so by external forces. Commonly also, the animal reaches a new environment accidentally in the course of exploration and elects to remain in it. Such choice implies a preadaptation which can be either genetically determined or the result of prior individual experience. In any case an important aspect of the preadaptive state is that the natural selection exerted by the environment is preceded by some kind of choice, not necessarily conscious, by the animal. Whatever the precise mechanisms of this ill-defined situation, common sense indicates that animals and men do not behave as passive objects when they become established in a given environment.

Eventually a change of environment leads to a change in habits, which in turn modifies certain characteristics of the organism. Even when repeated for several generations, such modifications are not truly inheritable, but they may nevertheless foster evolutionary changes. The reason is that continued residence in a particular environment tends to favor the selection of mutants adapted to it. Eventually, such mutations are incorporated into the genetic structure of the species involved.

The preceding inadequate statement of an immensely complex problem will suffice to indicate that the evolutionary system comprises not only the mutations, genetic recombinations, and selective processes of classical neo-Darwinism, but also the processes by which animals, and especially men, choose and modify one particular habitat out of all the environmental possibilities available to them. This view of biological evolution does not imply acceptance of the discredited Lamarckian hypothesis, according to which changes in physical or mental activity, if continued long enough, eventually bring about corresponding changes in the body or the mind that are genetically transmissible from parent to offspring. Biological evolution always takes place through the spontaneous production of genetic mutants which are then selected by environmental forces. But the actual selective mechanisms are extremely complicated; they always involve uninterrupted feedback processes between the organism, its environment, and its ways of life.

The exquisite adjustment between the shape of flowers and of the birds or insects that pollinate them by feeding on them beautifully illustrates the place of the feedback concept in the theory of evolution. From the comparative study of fossils, it has become apparent that primitive forms of the flowers evolved simultaneously with primitive forms of their bird or insect visitors. Mutual anatomical adaptations developed progressively through countless small adaptive changes occurring over millions of years of continuous interplay.

The evolutionary development of most animals has certainly been profoundly influenced by their ability to move, to learn and to establish social structures. While this is difficult to demonstrate convincingly, observations on birds and mammals in the wild and in the laboratory point to a variety of mechanisms that may have a bearing on human evolution.

Certain evolutionary changes probably had their primary origin in an exploratory curiosity that made animals discover new ways of sustenance and of life. In Great Britain during the past few years, the birds known as tits have developed the habit of pecking through the cardboard tops of milk bottles delivered in the morning at doorsteps. Apparently, the birds open the bottles to get at the cream. As one tit tends to imitate another, the habit has progressively spread from a few centers in Britain to other parts of Europe. It does not seem unreasonable to postulate that individual members of this species endowed with a gene complex preadapted to bottle opening would have a better chance of survival in urban environments, and thus would initiate an evolutionary trend. Through selection of mutants, a new shape of beak might evolve as a result of the change of habit, provided milk containers and the practices of milk distribution remained the same long enough to continue favoring the birds which have become specialists in bottle opening.

Field studies and unpublished experiments by my colleague Peter Marler provided another intriguing suggestion for the possible role of learning in the evolution of birds.

Under natural conditions, birds learn their song patterns from their parents and from other birds of the same species around them. In the laboratory, newly hatched birds can also learn from playbacks of recorded songs. When male white-crowned sparrows are raised in isolation and exposed to sequences of two recorded songs, one of their own species and one of another species, they invariably learn their species song. This selectivity explains why most birds in the wild learn only one kind of song and why the songs of all male birds of one species living in the same area are almost identical. The selectivity, however, is not absolute. Striking differences in vocalization patterns occur consistently among birds of the same species from one area to another, even within small distances. These differences are so stable from year to year that ornithologists are wont to speak of bird song "dialects."

Young white-crowned sparrows can learn a dialect other than that of their parents if they are raised in isolation and exposed early in life to the song of adult birds of their species obtained from another area or to recorded playbacks of such songs. In the wild, the variations in vocalizing patterns must be transmitted from generation to generation, young birds learning from their parents.

No anatomical differences have been recognized among birds obtained from different dialect areas. The stability of the dialects in nature suggests that, despite the mobility of birds, little exchange of individuals between populations occurs after the vocalizing patterns have been acquired. If males are more likely to settle in an area where their dialect is heard, and if females are more likely to mate with a male living in their own dialect area, the population will be progressively fragmented into small local subgroups and inbreeding will occur. Inbreeding continued over long periods of time almost inevitably brings about hereditary changes. Thus, as small a behavioral difference as bird song dialects, first entirely under environmental control, may eventually be incorporated in the genetic endowment of the isolated populations.

Populations of primates have been repeatedly observed in nature to learn entirely new habits from one of their members—for example, washing food or unwrapping and eating caramels. Changes in habit may eventually alter the structure of animal societies and affect genetic constitution through selective processes. Because the diet of chimpanzees consists largely of large fruit, in the wild they must move over wide areas to find enough food and therefore cannot live in stable social groupings. In contrast, gorillas eat almost any plant food at hand in the rich and varied vegetation of their tropical environment; since they need not move far from their home base they can form permanent family groups. It has been suggested that the differences in food habits and social structure between these two primate species have influenced their genetic evolution.

The environments into which man's precursors moved during the Paleolithic periods naturally conditioned the activities in which they engaged, and this in turn must have contributed to determining the genetic endowment which defines mankind. Similarly, the habits introduced by modern civilization are now acting as selective forces and guiding human evolution toward new forms of adaptation to the technicized urban environment.

Under certain conditions, in contrast, cultural attitudes can oppose the selective effects of the physical environment. In the Indian city of Cochin, for example, the famous street of the White Jews harbors a Jewish population that has lived there for nearly 2,000 years. In contrast to the rest of the Cochin population, these Jews have retained skins as white as those of their ancestors who migrated from Palestine, the reason being that they have carefully kept themselves out of the sun's direct rays under roofs and lattices. At the present time, only 150 Jews out of a former population of 1,500 still exist in Cochin, but despite their small numbers, they have retained their biological identity through environmental protection, choice of occupation, and a breeding pattern of their own choosing enforced by religious sanctions. They illustrate the fact that culture is as much a part of the total environment as solar radiation, temperature, rainfall, or altitude.

All living organisms retain structural and functional evidences of their distant evolutionary past. Whatever the conditions under which they are born and develop, their responses to stimuli are always affected by the experiences of the past which are incorporated in their genetic make-up. The evolutionary steps through which man reached the level of *Homo sapiens* explain, for example, why the structure of his backbone can be traced to the early fishes, or why the salinity of his blood still reflects the composition of sea water from which terrestrial life originally emerged.

The thickening of the sole of the foot relative to the rest of the skin probably constitutes an expression of biological remembrance of the past, since this process starts before the body experiences any frictional stimulus and is detectable even within the womb. It seems legitimate to assume that, as the protoamphibian ancestors of man occasionally came out of water and pushed themselves on land with their fin lobes, these organs responded by a minor thickening of the part of the skin that came in contact with the ground, much as our skin thickens whenever it is subjected to friction. When locomotion on land became more common and the ability to develop calluses on the feet thereby became important for biological success, the individuals best endowed with this ability probably had a better chance of survival. The tendency to develop callus thus became inscribed in the genetic code.

Many other types of anatomical and physiological attributes now considered characteristic of certain human races also demonstrate the persistence of the biological past. In the highlands of East Africa, where the fossils of early man are found in greatest profusion and where *Homo sapiens* probably emerged as a distinct species, the climate is moderate and provides a physical environment very similar to that which most human beings generally consider desirable for health, comfort, and activity. Granted this general preference for a temperate climate, certain adaptations have naturally occurred among the various sub-races of men under the influence of the local conditions prevailing in the regions where they settled over long periods of time. The fact that men who hunted on the grasslands and deserts must have been rigorously selected for speed may explain why a light, lean body build is still prevalent in the desert countries. In contrast, speed over long distances is of little use in a forest. Whereas the Arabs of the desert are likely to be tall and lean, typical forest dwellers are short-legged, long-trunked, barrel-chested, and broad-handed.

Subcutaneous fat is most abundant in people who have evolved in cold regions; differences are also found in the number of sweat glands per unit of skin area. Pigmentation of the skin is a function of exposure to light. While skin pigments are of particular importance for protection against ultraviolet light, it is also possible that the capacity of black skin to absorb visible light rather than reflect it, and to convert this light into heat, may also lower the heating threshold of dark-skinned races.

In many animal species, the chemical changes in the sex glands that occur as a response to the environmental changes associated with spring initiate the process of courting and display. In birds, for example, this process is followed by nest-building, which begins at the proper time with the choice of the right material. Mating and egg-laying follow, then breeding and the feeding of the young. All these behavioral patterns are under the control of hormonal secretions which must be closely integrated with seasonal changes in the environment if the biological functions are to be successful. Such integration—the outcome of long evolutionary adaptation—has been most extensively studied in birds and in a few other animal species. In human life also, many physiological processes are still linked to cosmic events.

Modern man is wont to boast that he can control his external environment and has thereby become independent of it. He can illuminate his rooms at night, heat them during the winter, and cool them during the summer; he can secure an ample and varied supply of food throughout the year; he can if he wishes to make each day like every other day. But even when he elects to follow unchangeable ways of life in an environment which appears uniform, all the functions of his body continue to fluctuate according to certain rhythms linked to the movements of the earth and of the moon with respect to each other and to the sun. His hormonal activities in particular exhibit marked diurnal and seasonal rhythms, and probably other rhythms also linked to those of the cosmos.

Man's physiological and behavioral responses to any situation are different in the morning from what they are at night, and different in the spring from what they are in the autumn. The writers of Western stories have a sound biological basis when they recount that the Indians always attacked at dawn, because they knew that the spirits of the white men were then at a low ebb. Napoleon is reported to have said that few are the soldiers who are brave at three o'clock in the morning. The wild imaginings of the night and the fears they engender are indirectly the effects of earth movements, because the human organism readily escapes from the control of reason under the influence of the physiological changes associated with darkness.

The lunar cycles are also reflected in the physiology and behavior of animals and probably therefore of man. It would not be surprising if moon worshipers—as well as "lunatics," as the term suggests—were really affected by lunar forces to which all of us are somewhat sensitive.

Seasonal changes certainly affect most living things, including man, even when the temperature and illumination are artificially maintained at a constant level. In the most mechanized, treeless, birdless, and air-conditioned city, just as in the hills of Arcadia long ago, men and women perceive in their senses and reveal by their behavior that the exuberance of springtime and the despondency of late fall have origins more subtle than the mere change in temperature. It is for good biological reasons that Carnival and Mardi Gras are celebrated when the sap starts running up the trees, and that Europeans commemorate their dead in late fall when nature is dying. Modern man in his sheltered environment continues to be under the influence of cosmic forces even as he was when he lived naked in direct contact with nature.

The view that all aspects of life have historical determinants applies also to patterns of behavior that cannot yet be traced to hormonal activities or other physiological processes. Even the simplest organism differs from inanimate matter by virtue of the fact that all its activities are conditioned by its past. For example, the sea urchin displays a manifestation of biological remembrance when it responds to a sudden shadow falling upon its body by pointing its spines in the direction from which the shadow originates. Such response has a defensive value which is potentially useful because it helps in protecting the animal from enemies that might have cast the shadow. But in reality it refers to a past experience symbolized by the shadow—the possible approach of a predator—rather than the actual presence of a predator. The sea urchin's response to a shadow illustrates that even in the case of relatively primitive animals much of behavior is conditioned by ancient experiences of the species that have generated instinctive reaction patterns.

In the usual events of daily life, man continues to react physiologically to the presence of strange living things, and especially of human competitors, as if he were in danger of being physically attacked by them. The fight-or-flight response, with all its biochemical, hormonal, and other physiological accompaniments is a carryover from the time when the survival of primitive man encountering a wild animal or a human stranger depended upon his ability to mobilize the body mechanisms that enabled him either to engage effectively in physical struggle or to flee as rapidly as possible.

On the other hand, man evolved as a social animal, and he can neither develop normally nor long function successfully except in association with other human beings. All social stimuli that man experiences elicit physiological and mental processes which in their turn condition his responses to the situations that evoke them. Thus crowding, isolation, challenge of any sort have effects that have their origin in the evolutionary past and that tend to imitate the kind of response then favorable for biological success, even when such a response is no longer suitable to the conditions of the modern world.

Many aspects of human behavior which appear incomprehensible or even irrational become meaningful when interpreted as survivals of attributes that were useful when they first appeared during evolutionary development and that have persisted because the biological evolution of man was almost completed about 100,000 years ago. Phenomena ranging all the way from the aberrations of mob psychology to the useless disturbances of metabolism and circulation that occur during verbal conflicts at the office or at a cocktail party are as much the biological expressions of the distant past as they are direct consequences of the stimuli of which the person is aware.

The urge to control property and to dominate one's peers is also an ancient biological trait that exists in the different forms of territoriality and dominance among most if not all animal societies. The lust for political power independent of any desire for financial or other material rewards, which is so common among men, has likewise prototypes in animal behavior. Even the play instinct and certain kinds of aesthetic expression correspond to derivative but nevertheless important biological needs that exist in one form or another among animal species and that have always been part of man's nature.

Jack London's story *The Call of the Wild* (1903) probably owed part of its popular success to its evocation of ancient precivilized traits that persist in man's nature. The actual story tells of a dog, Buck, taken from civilized life in California to be used as a sled dog in the Klondike. Jack London clearly intended to express through the dog's behavior his own protest against the constraints of civilized life. Some of the most beguiling moments of the story dramatize the power of the racial past, as Buck instinctively follows the lure of a wolf howl and finds a satisfying companionship among wolves far from men or dogs. The story ends with Buck plunging joyfully into the primeval forest to join the wolf pack, "leaping gigantic above his fellows, his great throat a bellow as he sings a song of the younger world." Many psychologists interpret this story as advocating psychological regression, but it can be read with equal justice as a song celebrating the mysterious and wonderful world of the past which survives in the deepest layers of man's nature. It is dangerous to yield without thought to the call of the wild, but perhaps destructive to ignore it altogether. While the voices of the deep may seem strange and at times frightening, they are the expressions of forces that must be reckoned with, because inherent in the human race and influential in all aspects of human behavior.

from *The Lives of a Cell: Notes of a Biology Watcher*

Lewis Thomas (1913–1993)

Lewis Thomas, a biologist, was president of the Memorial Sloan-Kettering Cancer Center in New York—and one of the most humane essayists of our time. By implication, and occasionally by direct reference, nearly all of the brief essays that constitute *The Lives of a Cell* are concerned with memory, often at its most basic level of cells with their special genomes. But Thomas has the ability to see the large in the small as well as the small in the large; I am aware at all times of his own marvelous human memory at work, making associations and analogies from all the material held in one capacious storeroom.

I have chosen two essays from *The Lives of a Cell*. The first, "On Societies as Organisms," perceives likenesses between ants and bees, on the one hand, and humans, on the other, so far as "the storage, processing, and retrieval of information" is concerned. While no doubt a corrective to human pride, the essay is less unsettling than one might expect, for it is written with humor, respect for the social achievements of the insects, and an awareness of the biological connection among all living things on this planet. He remarks that it is considered in biological circles "quite bad form . . . to imply that the operation of insect societies has any relation at all to human affairs," but then goes on to demonstrate the affinity between the collective intelligence found in, say, the termite organism and that found in scientific groups, dependent as these groups are on the transmission by individuals of fragments of information to build their corporate structures. Though in this essay Thomas makes no reference to memory as such, it is clear that past research constitutes a kind of collective memory necessary for the advancement of science.

The other essay, "Information," *does* acknowledge a difference between us and the other animals—a difference based on our unique ability to construct language. All animals have lymphocytes which, while varying in the range of their information, are all capable of replicating themselves into new colonies or clusters. "The new cluster," Thomas says, "is a memory, nothing less." But "speechless animals . . . are limited to single-stage transactions" and cannot "drift away in the presence of locked-on information, straying from each point in a hunt for a better, different point." Our species has apparently been granted "strands of special, peculiarly human DNA" which permit us to communicate meanings not only through words but through music and paintings. Interestingly enough, Thomas extols the ambiguity in language (and the nonverbal art forms) that certain contemporary theorists decry. Such ambiguity is necessary for creativity—it provides for new meanings and their communication, it gives us new directions; it is as crucial to science as it is to art.

All of the essays in *The Lives of a Cell* originally appeared in the *New England Journal of Medicine*.

ON SOCIETIES AS ORGANISMS

Viewed from a suitable height, the aggregating clusters of medical scientists in the bright sunlight of the boardwalk at Atlantic City, swarmed there from everywhere for the annual meetings, have the look of assemblages of social insects. There is the same vibrating, ionic movement, interrupted by the darting back and forth of jerky individuals to touch antennae and exchange small bits of information; periodically, the mass casts out, like a trout-line, a long single file unerringly toward Childs's. If the boards were not fastened down, it would not be a surprise to see them put together a nest of sorts.

It is permissible to say this sort of thing about humans. They do resemble, in their most compulsively social behavior, ants at a distance. It is, however, quite bad form in biological circles to put it the other way round, to imply that the operation of insect societies has any relation at all to human affairs. The writers of books on insect behavior generally take pains, in their prefaces, to caution that insects are like creatures from another planet, that their behavior is absolutely foreign, totally unhuman, unearthly, almost unbiological. They are more like perfectly tooled but crazy little machines, and we violate science when we try to read human meanings in their arrangements.

It is hard for a bystander not to do so. Ants are so much like human beings as to be an embarrassment. They farm fungi, raise aphids as livestock, launch armies into wars, use chemical sprays to alarm and confuse enemies, capture slaves. The families of weaver ants engage in child labor, holding their larvae like shuttles to spin out the thread that sews the leaves together for their fungus gardens. They exchange information ceaselessly. They do everything but watch television.

What makes us most uncomfortable is that they, and the bees and termites and social wasps, seem to live two kinds of lives: they are individuals, going about the day's business without much evidence of thought for tomorrow, and they are at the same time component parts, cellular elements, in the huge, writhing, ruminating organism of the Hill, the nest, the hive. It is because of this aspect, I think, that we most wish for them to be something foreign. We do not like the notion that there can be collective societies with the capacity to behave like organisms. If such things exist, they can have nothing to do with us.

Still, there it is. A solitary ant, afield, cannot be considered to have much of anything on his mind; indeed, with only a few neurons strung together by fibers, he can't be imagined to have a mind at all, much less a thought. He is more like a ganglion on legs. Four ants together, or ten, encircling a dead moth on a path, begin to look more like an idea. They fumble and shove, gradually moving the food toward the Hill, but as though by blind chance. It is only when you watch the dense mass of thousands of ants, crowded together around the Hill, blackening the ground, that you begin to see the whole beast, and now you observe it thinking, planning, calculating. It is an intelligence, a kind of live computer, with crawling bits for its wits.

At a stage in the construction, twigs of a certain size are needed, and all the members forage obsessively for twigs of just this size. Later, when outer walls are to be finished, thatched, the size must change, and as though given new orders by telephone, all the workers shift the search to the new twigs. If you disturb the arrangement of a part of the Hill, hundreds of ants will set it vibrating, shifting, until it is put right again. Distant sources of food are somehow sensed, and long lines, like tentacles, reach out over the ground, up over walls, behind boulders, to fetch it in.

Termites are even more extraordinary in the way they seem to accumulate intelligence as they gather together. Two or three termites in a chamber will begin to pick up pellets and move them from place to place, but nothing comes of it; nothing is built. As more join in, they seem to reach a critical mass, a quorum, and the thinking begins. They place pellets atop pellets, then throw up columns and beautiful, curving, symmetrical arches, and the crystalline architecture of vaulted chambers is created. It is not known how they communicate with each other, how the chains of termites building one column know when to turn toward the crew on the adjacent column, or how, when the time comes, they manage the flawless joining of the arches. The stimuli that set them off at the outset, building collectively instead of shifting things about, may be pheromones released when they reach committee size. They react as if alarmed. They become agitated, excited, and then they begin working, like artists.

Bees live lives of organisms, tissues, cells, organelles, all at the same time. The single bee, out of the hive retrieving sugar (instructed by the dancer: "south-southeast for seven hundred meters, clover—mind you make corrections for the sundrift") is still as much a part of the hive as if attached by a filament. Building the hive, the workers have the look of embryonic cells organizing a developing tissue; from a distance they are like the viruses inside a cell, running off row after row of symmetrical polygons as though laying down crystals. When the time for swarming comes, and the old queen prepares to leave with her part of the population, it is as though the hive were involved in mitosis. There is an agitated moving of bees back and forth, like granules in cell sap. They distribute themselves in almost precisely equal parts, half to the departing queen, half to the new one. Thus, like an egg, the great, hairy, black and golden creature splits in two, each with an equal share of the family genome.

The phenomenon of separate animals joining up to form an organism is not unique in insects. Slimemold cells do it all the time, of course, in each life cycle. At first they are single amebocytes swimming around, eating bacteria, aloof from each other, untouching, voting straight Republican. Then, a bell sounds, and acrasin is released by special cells toward which the others converge in stellate ranks, touch, fuse together, and construct the slug, solid as a trout. A splendid stalk is raised, with a fruiting body on top, and out of this comes the next generation of amebocytes, ready to swim across the same moist ground, solitary and ambitious.

Herring and other fish in schools are at times so closely integrated, their actions so coordinated, that they seem to be functionally a great multifish organism. Flocking birds, especially the seabirds nesting on the slopes of offshore islands in Newfoundland, are similarly attached, connected, synchronized.

Although we are by all odds the most social of all social animals—more interdependent, more attached to each other, more inseparable in our behavior than bees—we do not often feel our conjoined intelligence. Perhaps, however, we are linked in circuits for the storage, processing, and retrieval of information, since this appears to be the most basic and universal of all human enterprises. It may be our biological function to build a certain kind of Hill. We have access to all the information of the biosphere, arriving as elementary units in the stream of solar photons. When we have learned how these are rearranged against randomness, to make, say, springtails, quantum mechanics, and the late quartets, we may have a clearer notion how to proceed. The circuitry seems to be there, even if the current is not always on.

The system of communications used in science should provide a neat, workable model for studying mechanisms of information-building in human society. Ziman, in a recent *Nature* essay, points out, "the invention of a mechanism for the systematic publication of *fragments* of scientific work may well have been the key event in the history of modern science." He continues:

> A regular journal carries from one research worker to another the various . . . observations which are of common interest. . . . A typical scientific paper has never pretended to be more than another little piece in a larger jigsaw—not significant in itself but as an element in a grander scheme. *This technique, of soliciting many modest contributions to the store of human knowledge, has been the secret of Western science since the seventeenth century, for it achieves a corporate, collective power that is far greater than one individual can exert* [italics mine].

With some alternation of terms, some toning down, the passage could describe the building of a termite nest.

It is fascinating that the word "explore" does not apply to the searching aspect of the activity, but has its origins in the sounds we make while engaged in it. We like to think of exploring in science as a lonely, meditative business, and so it is in the first stages, but always, sooner or later, before the enterprise reaches completion, as we explore, we call to each other, communicate, publish, send letters to the editor, present papers, cry out on finding.

INFORMATION

According to the linguistic school currently on top, human beings are all born with a genetic endowment for recognizing and formulating language. This must mean that we possess genes for all kinds of information, with strands of special, peculiarly human DNA for the discernment of meaning in syntax. We must imagine the morphogenesis of deep structures, built into our minds, for coding out, like proteins, the parts of speech. Correct grammar (correct in the logical, not fashionable, sense) is as much a biologic characteristic of our species as feathers on birds.

If this is true, it would mean that the human mind is preset, in some primary sense, to generate more than just the parts of speech. Since everything else that we recognize as human behavior derives from the central mechanism of language, the same sets of genes are at least indirectly responsible for governing such astonishing behavior as in the concert hall, where hundreds of people crowd together, silent, head-tilted, mediating, listening to music as though receiving instructions, or in a gallery, moving along slowly, peering, never looking at each other, concentrating as though reading directions.

This view of things is compatible with the very old notion that a framework for meaning is somehow built into our minds at birth. We start our lives with templates, and attach to them, as we go along, various things that fit. There are neural centers for generating, spontaneously, numberless hypotheses about the facts of life. We store up information the way cells store energy. When we are lucky enough to find a direct match between a receptor and a fact, there is a deep explosion in the mind; the idea suddenly enlarges, rounds up, bursts with new energy, and begins to replicate. At times there are chains of reverberating explosions, shaking everything: the imagination, as we say, is staggered.

This system seems to be restricted to human beings, since we are the only beings with language, although chimpanzees may have the capability of manipulating symbols with a certain syntax. The great difference between us and the other animals may be the qualitative difference made by speech. We live by making transformations of energy into words, storing it up, and releasing it in controlled explosions.

Speechless animals cannot do this sort of thing, and they are limited to single-stage transactions. They wander, as we do, searching for facts to fit their sparser stock of hypotheses, but when the receptor meets its match, there is only a single thud. Without language, the energy that is encoiled, springlike, inside information can only be used once. The solitary wasp, Sphex, nearing her time of eggs, travels aloft with a single theory about caterpillars. She is, in fact, a winged receptor for caterpillars. Finding one to match the hypothesis, she swoops, pins it, paralyzes it, carries it off, and descends to deposit it precisely in front of the door of the round burrow (which, obsessed by a different version of the same theory, she had prepared beforehand). She drops the beast, enters the burrow, inspects the interior for last-minute irregularities, then comes out to pull it in for the egg-laying. It has the orderly, stepwise look of a well-thought-out business. But if, while she is inside inspecting, you move the caterpillar a short distance, she has a less sensible second thought about the matter. She emerges, searches for a moment, finds it, drags it back to the original spot, drops it again, and runs inside to check the burrow again. If you move the caterpillar again, she will repeat the program, and you can keep her totally preoccupied for as long as you have the patience and the heart for it. It is a compulsive, essentially neurotic kind of behavior, as mindless as an Ionesco character, but the wasp cannot imagine any other way of doing the thing.

Lympocytes, like wasps, are genetically programmed for exploration, but each of them seems to be permitted a different, solitary idea. They roam through the tissues, sensing and monitoring. Since there are so many of them, they can make collective guesses at almost anything antigenic on the surface of the earth, but they must do their work one notion at a time. They carry specific information in their surface receptors, presented in the form of a question: is there, anywhere out there, my particular molecular configuration? It seems to be in the nature of biologic information that it not only stores itself up as energy but also instigates a search for more. It is an insatiable mechanism.

Lymphocytes are apparently informed about everything foreign around them, and some of them come equipped for fitting with polymers that do not exist until organic chemists synthesize them in their laboratories. The cells can do more than predict reality; they are evidently programmed with wild guesses as well.

Not all animals have lymphocytes with the same range of information, as you might expect. As with language, the system is governed by genes, and there are genetic differences between species and between inbred animals of the same species. There are polymers that will fit the receptors of one line of guinea pigs or mice but not others; there are responders and nonresponders.

When the connection is made, and a particular lymphocyte with a particular receptor is brought into the presence of the particular antigen, one of the greatest small spectacles in nature occurs. The cell enlarges, begins making new DNA at a great rate, and turns into what is termed, appropriately, a blast. It then begins dividing, replicating itself into a new colony of identical cells, all labeled with the same receptor, primed with the same question. The new cluster is a memory, nothing less. For this kind of mechanism to be useful, the cells are required to stick precisely to the point. Any ambiguity, any tendency to wander from the matter at hand, will introduce grave hazards for the cells, and even more for the host in which they live. Minor inaccuracies may cause reactions in which neighboring cells are recognized as foreign, and done in. There is a theory that the process of aging may be due to the cumulative effect of imprecision, a gradual degrading of information. It is not a system that allows for deviating.

Perhaps it is in this respect that language differs most sharply from other biologic systems for communication. Ambiguity seems to be an essential, indispensable element for the transfer of information from one place to another by words, where matters of real importance are concerned. It is often necessary, for meaning to come through, that there be an almost vague sense of strangeness and askewness. Speechless animals and cells cannot do this. The specifically locked-on antigen at the surface of a lymphocyte does not send the cell off in search of something totally different; when a bee is tracking sugar by polarized light, observing the sun as though consulting his watch, he does not veer away to discover an unimaginable marvel of a flower. Only the human mind is designed to work in this way, programmed to drift away in the presence of locked-on information, straying from each point in a hunt for a better, different point.

If it were not for the capacity for ambiguity, for the sensing of strangeness, that words in all languages provide, we would have no way of recognizing the layers of counterpoint in meaning, and we might be spending all our time sitting on stone fences, staring into the sun. To be sure, we would always have had some everyday use to make of the alphabet, and we might have reached the same capacity for small talk, but it is unlikely that we would have been able to evolve from words to Bach. The great thing about human language is that it prevents us from sticking to the matter at hand.

"My Contact with Josef Popper-Lynkeus"

Sigmund Freud (1856–1939)

Sigmund Freud believed that his *Interpretation of Dreams* (1899) was his "most significant work"; like Charles Darwin's *Origin of Species* (1859), it has had an incalculable effect upon the way we continue to look upon ourselves. Like Augustine's *Confessions* fifteen hundred years earlier, *Interpretation of Dreams* is an innovative foray into the subjective genre of autobiography; wishing to avoid the complications of abnormal psychic behavior illustrated in case histories, Freud primarily depends upon his own dreams and their causes as a means of illustrating the rules underlying dream interpretation. Memory is crucial to his investigations—memory as instinct, as part of what he calls, in the essay that follows, our "primitive, ungovernable nature" and memory of actual experiences and desires, particularly from early childhood, that we distort or repress.

I have spent much of my career as a writer in pursuit of the meanings of my own memories, including those that are reflected in dreams; unlike Freud, my interest in such matters is nonscientific, and my own subjectivity no doubt influences my response to his insights. It would take an unusually persuasive psychoanalyst to convince me (given all that I do remember along these lines) that I have repressed painful events or shameful desires. Personal experience causes me to doubt that hostility between father and son is caused by sexual rivalry for the affections of wife and mother. Finally, my most vivid dreams seem to have been offered up by my unconscious either as a warning against my excesses or as an active help to a sometimes despairing conscious mind, and hence have little in common with the dreams that Freud describes. But my response to Freud over the years has been more a response to what is current in our culture about him than to a close reading of what he actually wrote; hence I am grateful that my responsibility as editor of this anthology has caused me to be engrossed for some weeks in his own, sometimes difficult, writings. Though his scientific methods have been attacked in recent years as self-serving and lacking adequate objectivity, I have come to admire him for his courage and tenacity, the breadth of his learning, and his insight into the tensions of our obviously flawed nature. Often for better, though on occasion for worse, he has given us the terms that describe our psychology.

The essay that follows is one of the short papers written in his later years. "My Contact with Josef Popper-Lynkeus" (1932) is a tribute (of sorts) to a deceased author he respected, despite their obvious differences, but never knew. I have chosen it for Freud's engaging simplicity in describing the motives and purposes of his complex *Interpretation of Dreams* as well as for the despairing fatalism that seems to underlie his response to the idealism of Popper, that "simple-minded great man" who believed—despite the sufferings inflicted upon him as a fellow Jew, despite his knowledge of "the hollowness of the ideals of present-day civilization"—in the possibility of humanitarian reforms simply because he was that rarity (the innocent exception that proves the rule), a person without need of repression.

Freud and his family found refuge from the Nazis at the last moment, escaping Austria for England in 1938; he died in 1939, shortly after the commencement of the Second World War.

It was in the winter of 1899 that my book on the *Interpretation of Dreams* (though its title-page was post-dated into the new century) at length lay before me. This work was the product of the labours of four or five years and its origin was unusual. Holding a lectureship in Nervous Diseases at the University, I had attempted to support myself and my rapidly increasing family by a medical practice among the so-called "neurotics" of whom there were only too many in our society. But the task proved harder than I had expected. The ordinary methods of treatment clearly offered little or no help: other paths must be followed. And how was it remotely possible to give patients any help when one understood nothing of their illness, nothing of the causes of their sufferings or of the meaning of their complaints? So I eagerly sought direction and instruction from the great Charcot in Paris and from Bernheim at Nancy; finally, an observation made by my teacher and friend, Josef Breuer of Vienna, seemed to open a new prospect for understanding and therapeutic success.

For these new experiments made it a certainty that the patients whom we described as neurotic were in some sense suffering from *mental* disturbances and ought therefore to be treated by psychological methods. Our interest therefore necessarily turned to psychology. The psychology which ruled at that time in the academic schools of philosophy had very little to offer and nothing at all for our purposes: we had to discover afresh both our methods and the theoretical hypotheses behind them. So I worked in this direction, first in collaboration with Breuer and afterwards independently of him. Finally I hit upon the technical device of requiring my patients to tell me without criticism whatever occurred to their minds, even if they were ideas which did not seem to make sense or which it was distressing to report.

When they fell in with my instructions they told me their dreams, amongst other things, as though they were of the same kind as their other thoughts. This was a plain hint that I should assign as much importance to these dreams as to other, intelligible, phenomena. They, however, were *not* intelligible, but strange, confused, absurd: like dreams, in fact—which for that very reason, were condemned by science as random and senseless spasms of the organ of the mind. If my patients were right—and they seemed only to be repeating the ancient beliefs held by unscientific men for thousands of years—I was faced by the task of "interpreting dreams" in a way that could stand up against scientific criticism.

To begin with, I naturally understood no more about my patients' dreams than the dreamers did themselves. But by applying to these dreams, and more particularly to my own dreams, the procedure which I had already used for the study of other abnormal psychological structures, I succeeded in answering most of the questions which could be raised by an interpretation of dreams. There were many such questions: What do we dream about? Why do we dream at all? What is the origin of all the strange characteristics which distinguish dreams from waking life?—and many more such questions besides. Some of the answers were easily given and turned out to confirm views that had already been put forward; but others involved completely new hypotheses with regard to the structure and functioning of the apparatus of the mind. People dream about the things that have engaged their minds during the waking day. People dream in order to allay impulses that seek to disturb sleep, and in order to be able to sleep on. But why should the dream seem so strange, so confusedly senseless, so obviously contrasted with the content of waking thought in spite of being concerned with the same material? There could be no doubt that the dream was only a substitute for a rational process of thought and could be interpreted—that is to say, translated into a rational process. But what needed explaining was the fact of the distortion which the work of dreaming had carried out upon the rational and intelligible material.

Dream-distortion was the profoundest and most difficult problem of dream life. And in order to elucidate it I reached the conclusions that follow, which placed the dream in a class along with other psychopathological formations and revealed it, as it were, as the normal psychosis of mankind. Our mind, that precious instrument by whose means we maintain ourselves alive, is no peacefully self-contained unity. It is rather to be compared with a modern State in which a mob, eager for enjoyment and destruction, has to be held down forcibly by a prudent superior class. The whole flux of our mental life and everything that finds expression in our thoughts are derivations and representatives of the multifarious instincts that are innate in our physical constitution. But these instincts are not all equally susceptible to direction and education, or equally ready to fall in with the demands of the external world and of human society. Many of them have retained their primitive, ungovernable nature; if we let them have their way, they would infallibly bring us to ruin. Consequently, made wise by our sufferings, we have developed organizations in our mind which, in the form of inhibitions, set themselves up against the direct manifestations of the instincts. Every impulse in the nature of a wish that arises from the sources of instinctual energy must submit itself to examination by the highest agencies of our mind, and, if it is not approved, is rejected and restrained

*memories that make us
displease us or make us
look bad work same
way* 43

from exercising any influence upon our movements, that is, from coming into execution. Often enough, indeed, such wishes are even forbidden to enter consciousness, which is habitually unaware even of the existence of these dangerous instinctual sources. We describe such impulses as being *repressed* from the point of view of consciousness, and as surviving only in the unconscious. If what is repressed contrives somehow to force its way into consciousness or into movement or into both, we are no longer normal: at that point the whole range of neurotic and psychotic symptoms arise. The maintenance of the necessary inhibitions and repressions imposes upon our mind a great expenditure of energy, from which it is glad to be relieved. A good opportunity for this seems to be offered at night by the state of sleep, since sleep involves a cessation of our motor functions. The situation seems safe, and the severity of our internal police-force may therefore be relaxed. It is not entirely withdrawn, since one cannot be certain: may be the unconscious never sleeps at all. And now the reduction of pressure upon the repressed unconscious produces its effect. Wishes arise from it which during sleep might find the entrance to consciousness open. If we were to know them we should be appalled, alike by their subject-matter, their immense extent and indeed the mere possibility of their existence. This, however, occurs but seldom, and when it does we awake as speedily as may be, overcome by fear. But as a rule our consciousness does not experience the dream as it really was. It is true that the inhibitory forces (the dream censorship, as we may call them) are not completely awake, but neither are they wholly asleep. They have had an influence on the dream while it was struggling to find an expression in words and pictures, they have got rid of what was most objectionable, they have altered other parts of it till they are unrecognizable, they have severed real connections while introducing false ones, until the honest but brutal phantasy of a wish fulfilled which lay behind the dream has turned into the manifest dream as we remember it—more or less confused and almost always strange and incomprehensible. Thus the dream (or the distortion which characterizes it) is the expression of a compromise, the evidence of a conflict between the mutually incompatible impulses and strivings of our mental life. And do not let us forget that the same process, the same interplay of forces, which explains the dreams of a normal sleeper, gives us the key to understanding all the phenomena of neurosis and psychosis.

I must apologize if I have hitherto talked so much about myself and my work upon the problems of the dream; but it was a necessary preliminary to what follows. My explanation of dream-distortion seemed to me new: I had nowhere found anything like it. Years later (I can no longer remember when) I came across Josef Popper-Lynkeus' book *Phantasien eines Realisten*. One of the stories contained in it bore the title of "Träumen wie Wachen" ["Dreaming like Waking"], and it could not fail to arouse my deepest interest. There was a description in it of a man who could boast that he had never dreamt anything senseless. His dreams might be fantastic, like fairy tales, but they were not enough out of harmony with the waking world for it to be possible to say definitely that "They were impossible or absurd in themselves." Translated into my manner of speech this meant that in the case of this man no dream-distortion occurred; and the reason produced for its absence put one at the same time in possession of the reason for its occurrence. Popper allowed the man complete insight into the reasons for his peculiarity. He made him say: "Order and harmony reign both in my thoughts and in my feelings, nor do the two struggle with each other. . . . I am one and undivided. Other people are divided and their two parts—waking and dreaming—are almost perpetually at war with each other." And again, on the question of the interpretation of dreams: "That is certainly no easy task; but with a little attention on the part of the dreamer himself it should no doubt always succeed.—You ask why it is that for the most part it does *not* succeed? In you other people there seems always to be something that lies concealed in your dreams, something unchaste in a curious way, a certain secret quality in your being which it is hard to express. And that is why your dreams so often seem to be without meaning or even to be nonsense. But in the deepest sense this is not in the least so; indeed, it cannot be so at all—for it is always the same man, whether he is awake or dreaming."

Now, if we leave psychological terminology out of account, this was the very same explanation of dream-distortion that I had arrived at from my study of dreams. Distortion was a compromise, something in its very nature disingenuous, the product of a conflict between thought and feeling, or, as I had put it, between what is conscious and what is repressed. Where a conflict of this kind was not present and repression was unnecessary, dreams could not be strange or senseless. The man who dreamed in a way no different from that in which he thought while awake was granted by Popper the very condition of internal harmony which, as a social reformer, he aimed at producing in the body politic. And if Science informs us that such a man, wholly without evil and falseness and devoid of all repressions, does not exist and could not survive, yet we may guess that, so far as an approximation to this ideal is possible, it had found its realization in the person of Popper himself.

Overwhelmed by meeting with such wisdom, I began to read all his works—his books on Voltaire, on Religion, on War, on State Provision of Subsistence, etc.—till there was built up clearly before my eyes a picture of this simple-minded, great man, who was a thinker and a critic and at the same time a kindly humanitarian and reformer. I reflected much over the rights of the individual which he advocated and to which I should gladly have added my support had I not been restrained by the thought that neither the process of Nature nor the aims of human society quite justified such claims. A special feeling of sympathy drew me to him, since he too had clearly had painful experience of the bitterness of the life of a Jew and of the hollowness of the ideals of present-day civilization. Yet I never saw him in the flesh. He knew of me through common acquaintances, and I once had occasion to answer a letter from him in which he asked for some piece of information. But I never sought him out. My innovations in psychology had estranged me from my contemporaries, and especially from the older among them: often enough when I approached some man whom I had honoured from a distance, I found myself repelled, as it were, by his lack of understanding for what had become my whole life to me. And after all Josef Popper had been a physicist: he had been a friend of Ernst Mach. I was anxious that the happy impression of our agreement upon the problem of dream-distortion should not be spoilt. So it came about that I put off calling upon him till it was too late and I could now only salute his bust in the gardens in front of our Rathaus.

from *Bright Air, Brilliant Fire: On the Matter of the Mind*
Gerald M. Edelman (1929–)

In *Bright Air, Brilliant Fire,* Gerald M. Edelman, a neuroscientist, summarizes for a general audience the theory of the human mind that he has developed from years of research—a theory comprehensive enough to include all the diverse observations of brain function that presently exist and to serve as a basis for future investigations. Though I find it impossible to make a single generalization that is capable of summarizing this ambitious undertaking, I think it fair to say that Edelman rescues mind from the dilemmas of philosophical dualism, putting it firmly back in nature, while denying that it can be reduced to the present laws of physics: unlike physics, which concerns itself with inanimate matter, the mind (in its historical development, and at each and every moment for the living individual) is a biological process, a process that demonstrates an intentionality not found elsewhere in nature.

Edelman's theory—known by its acronym TNGS—is one of neuronal group selection. It consists of three major tenets; these tenets "are concerned with how the anatomy of the brain is first set up during development, how patterns of responses are then selected from this anatomy during experience, and how reentry, a process of signaling between the resulting maps of the brain, gives rise to behaviorally important functions." (The emphasis on selection depends upon the insights of Darwin; indeed, one of the trilogy of books for specialists that Edelman has written on his research is called *Neural Darwinism.*) My own mind, forced to contemplate itself from my reading and rereading of *Bright Air, Brilliant Fire,* ached from complex abstractions until it made certain neuronal adjustments—a new map, perhaps?—that enabled me to respond with pleasure to the theory's underlying beauty. In a lengthy review of *Bright Air, Brilliant Fire* in the April 8, 1993, issue of the *New York Review of Books,* Oliver Sacks remarks that the theory "coincides with our sense of 'flow,' that feeling we have when we are functioning optimally, of a swift, effortless, complex, ever-changing, but integrated and orchestrated stream of consciousness"—a response to it by another scientist in the field that is in keeping with that of a general reader like myself.

I have selected a chapter from "Harmonies," the final section of the book—a section concerned less with the scientific basis of the theory than with its implications for all of us. In "Memory and the Individual Soul," Edelman, after demonstrating the inability of the Enlightenment adequately to describe an individual person within its view of a mechanistic universe, shows how memory—that "key element in consciousness"—is connected with intentionality, enabling us (within limits) to have the freedom to determine our future; in its moving concluding paragraphs, the chapter suggests that we can rebound from the successive losses of value inflicted upon us by our growing scientific knowledge since Copernicus.

∞

From the last quarter of the seventeenth century to the last decade of the eighteenth, an explosion of creativity called the Enlightenment changed the history of ideas. Its reigning views were many, but above all it was dedicated to reason, to science, and to human freedom and individuality. Its underlying science was physics, the system of Newton, and its philosophy of society was, in large measure, that of Locke. Yet the Enlightenment ideas of causality and determinism, along with its mechanistic view of science, undermined hopes for a theory of human action based on freedom. If we are determined by natural forces—by mechanism—we cannot easily put together a consistent picture in which a free individual makes moral choices. Moreover, while the ideas of the Enlightenment paid much attention to the role of reason and culture in such choices, there was no general notion of how deeply the minds of all humans (including those of "reasonable" human beings—that is, the "cultured") were influenced by unconscious forces and by emotion.

Whatever forms it took at various times and places, the overriding Enlightenment view was a secular one that forged many of the ideas underlying modern democracy. But despite its valuable heritage, the Enlightenment is over. The first great blow to its ideas came with Hume's damaging attacks on both rationalism and the notion of human progress as linked to natural science. Its major fault was its inability to create an adequate scientific description of a human individual to accompany its description of a machinelike universe. Its social failure was its inability to go beyond the concept of a society composed of self-seeking, commercially successful individuals with a shallow view of "humanism." Certainly, Enlightenment thinkers attempted to provide us with a larger, more inspiring view of ourselves. But its science was a mechanistic physics and it had no body of data or ideas with which to link the world, the mind, and society in the style of scientific reason to which it aspired. Whatever the Enlightenment's failures and inconsistencies, however, it left us with high hopes for the place of the individual in society.

Can we expect to do better with a sound scientific view of mind? In this chapter I hope to show that the kind of reductionism that doomed the thinkers of the Enlightenment is confuted by evidence that has emerged both from modern neuroscience and from modern physics. I have argued that a person is not explainable in molecular, field theoretical, or physiological terms alone. To reduce a theory of an individual's behavior to a theory of molecular interactions is simply silly, a point made clear when one considers how many different levels of physical, biological, and social interactions must be put into place before higher-order consciousness emerges. The brain is made up of 10^{11} cells with at least 10^{15} connections. Each cell has a fantastically intricate regulatory biochemistry constrained by particular sets of genes. These cells come together during morphogenesis and exchange signals in a place-dependent fashion to make a body and a brain with enormous numbers of control loops, all obeying the homeostatic mechanisms that govern survival. Selection on neuronal repertoires leads to changes in myriad synapses as cells die or differentiate. An animal's survival and motion in the world allow perceptual and conceptual categorization to occur continually in global mappings. Memory dynamically interacts with perceptual categorization by reentry. Learning involving the connection of categorization to value (in its most subtle form within a speech community) links symbolic and semantic abilities to conceptual centers that already provide embodied structures for the building of meaning.

A calculation of the significant molecular combinations of such a sequence of events, even in identical twins, is almost impossible, and in any case, useless. The mappings are many—many, and the processes are individual and irreversible. I wonder what Enlightenment humanists would have made of all this. Diderot, who . . . speculated about the nervous system of his friend in *Le Rêve de d'Alembert,* might have been pleased. Diderot's view of human consciousness opened up the possibility that to be human was to go beyond mere physics.

I have taken the position that there can be no complete science, and certainly no science of human beings, until consciousness is explained in biological terms. Given our view of higher-order consciousness, this also means an account that explains the bases of how we attain personhood or selfhood. By selfhood I mean not just the individuality that emerges from genetics or immunology, but the person individuality that emerges from developmental and social interactions.

Selfhood is of critical philosophical importance. Some of the problems related to it may be sharpened by the selectionist view I have taken on the matter of mind. Please remember, however, that no scientific theory of an individual self can be given. . . . Nonetheless, I believe that we can progress toward a more complete notion of the free individual, a notion that is essential to any philosophical theory concerned with human values.

The issues I want to deal with are concerned with the relationship between consciousness and time, with the individual and the historical aspects of memory, and with whether our view of the thinking conscious subject alters our notion of causality. I also want to discuss briefly the connection between emotions and our ideas of embodied meaning. All of these issues ultimately bear upon the matter of free will and therefore upon morality under mortal conditions.

According to the extended TNGS, memory is the key element in consciousness, which is bound up with continuity and different time scales. There is a definite temporal element in perceptual categorization, and a more extended one in setting up a conceptually based memory. The physical movements of an animal drive its perceptual categorization, and the creation of its long-term memory depends on temporal transactions in its hippocampus. As we have seen, the Jamesian properties of consciousness may be derived from the workings of such elements. But in human beings, primary consciousness and higher-order consciousness coexist, and they each have different relations to time. The sense of time past in higher-order consciousness is a *conceptual* matter, having to do with previous orderings of categories in relation to an immediate present driven by primary consciousness. Higher-order consciousness is based not on ongoing experience, as is primary consciousness, but on the ability to model the past and the future. At whatever scale, the sense of time is first and foremost a conscious event.

The ideas of consciousness and "experienced" time are therefore closely intertwined. It is revealing to compare the definition of William James, who stated that consciousness is something the meaning of which "we know as long as no one asks us to define it," with the reflections of St. Augustine, who wrote in his *Confessions,* "What then is time? If no one asks me, I know what it is. If I wish to explain to him who asks me, I do not know." The notion of continuity in personal, historical, and institutional time was a central one in Augustine's thought.

Time involves succession. An intriguing suggestion about the connection between time and the ideas of numbers has come from L. E. J. Brouwer, a proponent of intuitionism in mathematics. He suggests that all mathematical elements (and particularly the sequence of natural numbers) come from what he calls "two-icity." Two-icity is the contrast between ongoing conscious experience (with primary consciousness as a large element) and the direct awareness of past experience (requiring higher-order consciousness). What is intriguing about this is that it suggests that one's concept of a number may arise not simply from perceiving sets of things in the outside world. It may also come from inside—from the intuition of two-ness or two-icity plus continuity. By recursion, one may come to the notion of natural numbers.

Whatever the origins of such abstractions, the personal sense of the sacred, the sense of mystery, and the sense of ordering and continuity all have connections to temporal continuity as we experience it. We experience it as individuals, each in a somewhat different way.

Indeed, the flux of categorization, whether in primary or higher-order consciousness, is an individual and irreversible one. It is a history. Memory grows in one direction; with verbal means, the sense of duration is yet another form of categorization. This view of time is distinguishable from the relativistic notion of clock time used by physicists, which is, in the microscopic sense, reversible. Aside from the variation and irreversibility of *macroscopic* physical events recognized by physicists, a deep reason for the irreversibility of individually experienced time lies in the nature of selective systems. In such systems, the emergence of pattern is *ex post facto*. Given the diversity of the repertoires of the brain, it is extremely unlikely that any two selective events, even apparently identical ones, would have identical consequences. Each individual is not only subject, like all material systems, to the second law of thermodynamics, but also to a multilayered set of irreversible selectional events in his or her perception and memory. Indeed, selective systems are by their nature irreversible.

This "double exposure" of a person—to real-world alterations affecting nonintentional objects as well as to individual historical alterations in his or her memory as an intentional subject—has important consequences. The flux of categorizations in a selective system leading to memory and consciousness alters the ordinary relations of causation as described by physicists. A person, like a thing, exists on a world line in four-dimensional spacetime. But because individual human beings have intentionality, memory, and consciousness, they can sample patterns at one point on that line and on the basis of their personal histories subject them to plans at other points on that world line. They can then enact these plans, altering the causal relations of objects in a definite way according to the structures of their memories. It is as if one piece of spacetime could slip and map onto another piece. The difference, of course, is that the entire transaction does not involve any unusual piece of physics, but simply the ability to categorize, memorize, and form plans according to a conceptual model. Such an historical alteration of causal chains could not occur in so rich a way in any combination of inanimate nonintentional objects, for they lack the appropriate kind of memory. This is an important point in discriminating biology from physics. . . .

In certain memorial systems, unique historical events at one scale have causal significance at a very different scale. If the sequence of an ancient ancestor's genetic code was altered as a result of that ancestor's travels through a swamp (driven, say, by climatic fluctuations), the altered order of nucleotides, if it contributed to fitness, could influence present-day selectional events and animal function. Yet the physical laws governing the actual *chemical* interaction of the genetic elements making up the code (the nucleotides) are deterministic. No deterministic laws at the chemical level could alone, however, explain the *sustained* code change that was initiated then stabilized over long periods as a result of complex selectional events on whole animals in unique environments.

Memorial events in brains undergoing selectional events are of the same ilk. Because the environment being categorized is full of novelty, because selection is *ex post facto,* and because selection occurs on richly varied historical repertoires in which different structures can produce the same result, many degrees of freedom exist. We may safely conclude that, in a multilevel conscious system, there are even greater degrees of freedom. These observations argue that, for systems that categorize in the manner that brains do, there is macroscopic indeterminacy. Moreover, given our previous arguments about the effects of memory on causality, consciousness permits "time slippage" with planning, and this changes how events come into being.

Even given the success of reductionism in physics, chemistry, and molecular biology, it nonetheless becomes silly reductionism when it is applied exclusively to the matter of the mind. The workings of the mind go beyond Newtonian causation. The workings of higher-order memories go beyond the description of temporal succession in physics. Finally, individual selfhood in society is to some extent an historical accident.

These conclusions bear on the classical riddle of free will and the notion of "soft determinism," or compatibilism, as it was called by James Mill. If what I have said is correct, a human being has a degree of free will. That freedom is not radical, however, and it is curtailed by a number of internal and external events and constraints. This view does not deny the influence of the unconscious on behavior, nor does it underestimate how small biochemical changes or early events can critically shape an individual's development. But it does claim that the strong psychological determinism proposed by Freud does not hold. At the very least, one freedom is in our grammar.

These reflections, and the relationship of our model of consciousness to evolved values bear also on our notion of meaning. Meaning takes shape in terms of concepts that depend on categorizations based on value. It grows with the history of remembered body sensations and mental images. The mixture of events is individual and, in large measure, unpredictable. When, in society, linguistic and semantic capabilities arise and sentences involving metaphor are linked to thought, the capability to create new models of the world grows at an explosive rate. But one must remember that, because of its linkage to value and to the concept of self, this system of meaning is almost never free of affect; it is charged with emotions. This is not the place to discuss emotions, the most complex of mental objects, nor can I dedicate much space to thinking itself. I consider them in the next chapter. But it is useful to mention them here in connection with our discussion of free will and meaning. As philosophers and psychologists have often remarked, the range of human freedom is restricted by the inability of an individual to separate the consequences of thought and emotion.

Human individuals, created through a most improbable sequence of events and severely constrained by their history and morphology, can still indulge in extraordinary imaginative freedom. They are obviously of a different order than nonintentional objects. They are able to refer to the world in a variety of ways They may imagine plans, propose hopes for the future, and causally affect world events by choice. They are linked in many ways, accidental and otherwise, to their parents, their society, and the past. They possess "selfhood," shored up by emotions and higher-order consciousness. And they are tragic, insofar as they can imagine their own extinction.

Often it is said that modern humans have suffered irreversible losses from several episodes of decentration, beginning with the destruction of earlier cosmologies placing human beings at the center of the universe. The first episode, according to Freud, however, took place when geocentrism was displaced by heliocentrism. The second was when Darwin pointed out the descent of human beings. And the third occurred when the unconscious was shown to have powerful effects on behavior. Well before Darwin ad Freud, however, the vision of a Newtonian universe led to a severe fatalism, a view crippling to the societal hopes of Enlightenment thought. Yet we can now see that if new ideas of brain function and consciousness are correct, this fatalistic view is not necessarily justified. The present is not pregnant with a fixed programmed future, and the program is not in our heads. The theories of modern physics and the findings of neuroscience rule out not only a machine model of the world but also such a model of the brain.

We may well hope that if sufficiently general ideas synthesizing the discoveries that emerge from neuroscience are put forth, they may contribute to a second Enlightenment. If such a second coming occurs, its major scientific underpinning will be neuroscience, not physics.

The problem then will be not the existence of souls, for it is clear that each individual person is like no other and is not a machine. The problem will be to accept that individual minds are mortal. Given the secular views of our time, inherited from the first Enlightenment, how can we maintain morality under mortal conditions? Under present machine models of the mind this is a problem of major proportions, for under such models it is easy to reject a human being or to exploit a person as simply another machine. Mechanism now lives next to fanaticism: Societies are in the hands either of the commercially powerful but spiritually empty or, to a lesser extent, in the hands of fanatical zealots under the sway of unscientific myths and emotion. Perhaps when we understand and accept a scientific view of how our mind emerges in the world, a richer view of our nature and more lenient myths will serve us.

How would humankind be affected by beliefs in a brain-based view of how we perceive and are made aware? What would be the result of accepting the ideas that each individual's "spirit" is truly embodied; that it is precious *because* it is mortal and unpredictable in its creativity; that we must take a skeptical view of how much can know; that understanding the psychic development of the young is crucial; that imagination and tolerance are linked; that we are at least all brothers and sisters at the level of evolutionary values; that while moral problems are universal, individual instances are necessarily solved, if at all, only by taking local history into account? Can a persuasive morality be established under mortal conditions? This is one of the largest challenges of our time.

What will remain unclear until neuroscience grows more mature is how any of these issues can be linked to our history as individuals in a still-evolving species. In any case, silly reductionism and simple mechanism are out. A theory of action based on the notion of human freedom—just what was missing in the days of the Enlightenment—appears to be receiving more and more support from the scientific facts. We may now examine the connection of these facts to thought itself.

from *The Making of Memory*

Steven Rose (1938–)

To Steven Rose, the investigation of memory offers the best chance we have of reconciling the disparate but equally objective languages descriptive of, and underlying research in, the faculties of mind and brain. Mind—the mental or psychic faculty—is a subject for scientific scrutiny by psychologists and others; the brain—a biological faculty—a subject for neurobiologists and other neuroscientists. His analogy for the crucial role that memory can play in reconciling the languages is that of the Rosetta stone: if Greek can be said to be the language of mind, and Egyptian hieroglyphs that of the brain, then memory—so essential to mind, yet created within the brain—may offer the code enabling us to understand the rules necessary for the translation of these parallel languages, each of which is "describing the same unitary phenomena of the material world."

Rose is director of the Brain and Behaviour Research Group at the Open University in London. His *The Making of Memory* is intended, in part, "to demystify [for the layperson] the workings of my sort of science" through descriptions of "what it feels like to be a neuroscientist, to design experiments, to train animals, to build—and reject—theories." Concerned with the subject of memory throughout his professional career, for the last half of that span he has been investigating, in his laboratory, the processes of "learning, memory, and remembering" in the brains of chicks who have been given beads to peck at, some of the beads having been given a chemical that imparts a bitter taste to them. In 1990, as Rose begins to write, he is engaged in a laboratory experiment with his chicks; in 1992, as he is completing the book, the experiment, which at first produced some mysterious (and hence unsatisfactory) results, is such a success that he is elated. Within the limitations of this headnote, I cannot describe that experiment, except to say that it proves that the epithet "birdbrain" is unduly pejorative. Like the human brain, the chick's is "an open learning system"; it "remembers not 'the bead' but a series of cues as to its characteristics," cues that are stored in more than one site. (Humans, in trying to remember a name, rely on similar cues, Rose suggests.)

Future research must emphasize the process of "re-membering," Rose says. (He follows the African American novelist Toni Morrison's use in inserting the hyphen in that word, to demonstrate "that it is an active, not a passive process"; his research on the brains of chicks is, of course, in service of an initial understanding of that process.) The book is unusual in its attempt to describe Rose himself, his own memories and crucial elements of his own biography—in a way, he is describing his personal mental processes—as well as for its illumination into the politics that both abet and hamper scientific discovery. (This latter concern is connected with his awareness that memory has a collective, or social, dimension as well as one that centers on the individual.) Such a scope makes it difficult to choose excerpts that will be both representative and self-contained. "Plasticity and Specificity," which follows, describes general characteristics of all brains —ones necessary for the survival of chick as well as human. The other excerpt, which comes from his final chapter, discusses the differences that separate human memory from that of other animals.

PLASTICITY AND SPECIFICITY

Experience is a term in the behavioural lexicon. Its translation into the language of biology is *plasticity*. To function effectively—that is, to respond appropriately to their environment—all living organisms must show two contradictory properties. They must retain stability—*specificity*—during development and into adult life, resisting the pressures of the endless buffeting of environmental contingency, both day-to-day and over a lifetime. And they must show plasticity—that is, the ability to adapt and modify this specificity in the face of repeated experience. Whereas once biologists used to speak of organisms as the product of the interplay of *nature* and *nurture,* or, in modern language, genes and environment, today this dichotomy is recognized as simplistic, for it is an individual's genes, expressed during development, which provide the basis for both specificity and plasticity. If we didn't have the genes which are instrumental in producing a brain which could learn by experience, we wouldn't survive. But equally, if we didn't have the genes which ensure that our brains become wired up correctly, so to say, during development, we also would fail to survive. To unravel the dialectic between specificity and plasticity and to understand its mechanisms form some of the major tasks of modern biology. The changes that occur in the brain as a result of experience are a form of plasticity, and memory is one major aspect of that experience. So it turns out that to understand the mechanisms of memory, of plasticity, it is also necessary to understand the mechanisms of specificity. If the brain were not, most of the time, invariant, unmoved by experience, we would be unable to survive. . . .

THE UNIQUENESS OF HUMANS

I have insisted on the commonality between human and animal memory. But there is of course more to it than this, for there are profound ways in which human memory is very different from that of non-human animals. The first, and perhaps the least important, is that because humans are the only speaking animals, we must presume that we are the only ones to possess a verbal memory. Such a verbal memory means the possibility of learning and re-membering without manifest behaviour. Insofar as we can even begin to imagine what it could be like *not* to have such a verbal memory, it must mean that our powers of memory are overwhelmingly richer than those of other animals. Whereas procedural memory dominates the lives of non-human animals, it is declarative memory which profoundly shapes our every act and thought. Nonetheless, I see no reason to believe that in principle the cellular mechanisms which have been found to operate in nonhuman declarative memory should not operate in human verbal memory too. The richness of our linguistic recall may be biologically no more mysterious than the capacity of a homing pigeon to navigate precisely over hundreds of kilometers or a dog to distinguish and remember thousands of different odours at almost infinitesimally low concentration.

What does much more to distinguish our specific human from non-human memory is our social existence, and the technological facility which has created a world in which memories are transcribed onto papyrus, wax tablets, paper or electronic screens; that is, a world of artificial memory. It is artificial memory which means that whereas all living species have a past, only humans have a history. Although the biological mechanisms of each human's individual memory may be the same as those of our fellow vertebrates, artificial memory is profoundly liberatory, transforming both what we need to and what we are able to remember. The multimedia of modern memory devices free us of the necessity to remember vast areas of facts and processes, liberating, presumably, great numbers of neurons and their synapses to other purposes.

And it is the existence of artificial memory too which makes possible the third great difference between human and non-human memory, the importance to all our lives of what I have called collective memory. Where there is no artificial memory, each individual animal lives in its own unique and personal set of memories, memories which begin with its birth and end with its death and can represent only its own experience. Each human, just like each non-human animal, experiences the world and remembers it uniquely, yet artificial memory presents the same picture, set of words, video image to many hundreds, thousands or millions of us, resetting, training and hence limiting our own individual memories, creating instead a mass consensus about what is to be remembered and how it is to be remembered.

Thus whilst for each of us the experience of collective memory is an individual biological and psychological one, its existence serves purposes which transcend the individual, welding together human societies by imposing shared understandings, interpretations, ideologies. It is no wonder that at any time the dominant social group endeavours to impose its own interpretation of this collective memory on the rest of society. Think about Britain in the last half-century, and you may recall images ranging from the camaraderie of London under the Blitz to the piles of rubbish in the street during the "winter of discontent" in 1979. For very few of

57

us are these images and their interpretation our own; each has been in some measure manufactured in the effort to create a certain type of social cohesion and viewpoint about the world and how we could and should live in it.

If this is hard to think about in the context of our own society, we might ask instead what part such imposed collective memories play in the current conflicts between, say, Serbs and Croatians, populations which have lived together in something like harmony for more than the individual lifetimes of most of those currently killing one another, yet whose national passions are rooted in images which run back through hundreds of years, before fascist/communist, Ustashi/Chetnik to catholic/orthodox and beyond. The present events are incomprehensible unless we take into account this collective memory.

Memories of this type are no part of our biology, yet they dominate our lives. Which is why each new social movement needs to begin with the hard work of creating its own collective memories. Socialism has struggled to recreate the submerged memories of working-class people, black movements have rediscovered their roots, feminists the suppressed history of women. These collective memories, whether imposed from above as ruling ideologies or forged from below by the struggle of emerging social movements, are the means whereby we re-member the past, our history, and therefore they both guide our present actions and shape our futures. Nothing in biology in general, or in our own human life in particular, makes sense except in the context of memory, of history.

Do we need to understand the intricate cellular and biochemical processes which have been the major theme of this book in order to make such sense? I believe we do. Let me revert to a more domestic example. Understanding the biochemistry of cooking and the physiology of digestion will surely never reduce the enjoyment of the meal to "mere" biology—but it undoubtedly enriches and improves both our cooking and our eating. Those dimensions of understanding which depend on social ambience, on the company in which we eat, on our own subjective states, are never thus reducible even though they too have their biological correspondents. A commitment to a belief in the ontological unity of the biological and social dimensions of our world never reduces the social to the biological, never privileges one type of explanation over another, but continues to search for ways of learning the translation rules between the two languages.

The search for the Rosetta stone and the effort to decode it which have formed the themes of this book are for me ways of integrating my day-to-day activity as a neuroscientist with my own intense personal memories of early childhood, of air-raid shelters or of birthday parties. At its best, research on memory may help heal the split in our lives between subjectivity and objectivity, reduce the fractures in our own personae. As we face the challenge of a new millennium in an increasingly fragmented world, this goal seems not abstract but urgent.

But psychobiology and neuroscience are never going to replace the equally hard work of the novelist or poet in exploring this subjectivity, in re-membering and re-creating the foreign country which is the past. Here, to end with, is the playwright Brian Friel, working at this re-membering in the closing mediation of his hero, now adult, recalling his childhood in the play *Dancing at Lughnasa*:

> And so, when I cast my mind back to that summer of 1936, different kinds of memory offer themselves to me. But there is one memory of that Lughnasa time that visits me most often, and what fascinates me about the memory is that it owes nothing to fact. In that memory atmosphere is more real than incident and everything is simultaneously actual and illusory. In that memory, too, the air is nostalgic with the music of the thirties. It drifts in from somewhere far away—a mirage of sound—a dream music that is both heard and imagined; that seems to be both itself and its own echo . . .

"Descartes' Error and the Future of Human Life"

Antonio R. Damasio (1944–)

In "Descartes' Error and the Future of Human Life," Antonio R. Damasio, head of the neurology department at the University of Iowa College of Medicine, summarizes some of the implications of his research into the nature and operations of the human brain—research that is the subject of his book, *Descartes' Error: Emotion, Reason, and the Human Brain.* (The essay appeared in *Scientific American* shortly after the publication of the book.) Like Gerald Edelman and Steven Rose, then, Damasio has written a a book for a general audience about his investigations as a neuroscientist; he joins them in celebrating the growing scientific knowledge of the intimate connections between brain and mind, between body and consciousness, that has led to the rejection both of Descartes' separation of mind from matter and the deterministic view that suggests humanity's helplessness to influence its future. While in general agreement on such matters, each of these three neuroscientists has his own emphasis; Damasio emphasizes the importance of emotion and feeling to our ability to reason properly and to plan for the future. ("Images of something that has not yet happened and that may in fact never happen," Damasio remarks in his book, "are no different in nature from the images you hold of something that has already happened. They constitute the memory of a possible future rather than of the past that was.")

Damasio's laboratory is a major center for the study of patients affected by brain damage. In *Descartes' Error,* Damasio discusses patients who have lost the capacity for effective decision making because of damage to portions of their brains necessary for emotion but apparently not for normal recall or adequate performance on intelligence tests. Effective decision making requires rational thought—deliberation—but is facilitated by feelings about "good" or "bad" outcomes engendered in the body as a consequence of past learning: in a sense, these sensations constitute a memory (the "gut feeling" that we experience while making a sudden judgment) that can "assist the process of sifting through . . . a wealth of detail." Indeed, without such feelings the details would overwhelm the mind, as they do for Damasio's patients. Somatic states (the signals created by the body's feelings) can be overt—available to consciousness—or covert, existing separately from consciousness; the latter "would be the source of what we call intuition." (Though it was written early in this century, Henri Poincaré's "Mathematical Creation," the opening essay of a later section of this anthology, "Memory and Creativity," has elements in common with some of the results of Damasio's research into decision making, particularly in regard to the role ascribed by Poincaré to the unconscious; and Damasio, aware of that connection, quotes a passage from the essay.)

Memory is not specifically referred to in this brief essay, nor is it addressed at much length in the book. Its importance can be inferred, however, from the descriptions in *Descartes' Error* of the neurological means by which the "key elements in an individual's autobiography," as well as her or his primordial and recent body states, are represented within the brain—all of them constituting representations crucial to emotion.

At the beginning of the 1950s, in an impassioned speech inspired by the threat of nuclear destruction, William Faulkner warned his fellow writers that they had "forgotten the problems of the human heart in conflict with itself." He asked them to leave no room in their workshops "for anything but the old verities and truths of the heart, the old universal truths lacking which any story is ephemeral and doomed—love and honor and pity and pride and compassion and sacrifice."

Although the towering nuclear threat of four decades ago has assumed a less dramatic posture, it is apparent to all but the most absent-minded optimists that other clear and present dangers confront us. The world population is still exploding; air, water and food are still being polluted; ethical and educational standards are still declining; violence and drug addiction are still rising. Many specific causes are at work behind all these developments, but through all of them runs the irrationality of human behavior, spreading like an epidemic, and no less threatening to our future than was the prospect of nuclear holocaust when Faulkner was moved to speak.

I have always taken his words to mean that the rationality required for humans to prevail and endure should be informed by the emotion and feeling that stem from the core of every one of us. This view strikes a sympathetic chord, because my research has persuaded me that emotion is integral to the process of reasoning. I even suspect that humanity is not suffering from a defect in logical competence but rather from a defect in the emotions that inform the deployment of logic.

What evidence can I produce to back these seemingly counterintuitive statements? The evidence comes from the study of previously rational individuals who, as a result of neurological damage in specific brain systems, lose their ability to make rational decisions along with their ability to process emotion normally. Their instruments of rationality can still be recruited; the knowledge of the world in which they must operate remains available; and their ability to tackle the logic of a problem remains intact. Yet many of their personal and social decisions are irrational, more often than not disadvantageous to the individual and to others. I have suggested that the delicate mechanism of reasoning is no longer affected by the weights that should have been imparted by emotion.

The patients so affected usually have damage to selected areas of the frontal, temporal and right parietal regions, but there are other conditions for which a neurological cause has not yet been identified, whose characteristics are similar in many respects. The sociopaths about whom we hear in the daily news are intelligent and logically competent individuals who nonetheless are deprived of normal emotional processing. Their irrational behavior is destructive to self and society.

Thus, absence of emotion appears to be at least as pernicious for rationality as excessive emotion. It certainly does not seem true that reason stands to gain from operating without the leverage of emotion. On the contrary, emotion probably assists reasoning, especially when it comes to personal and social matters, and eventually points us to the sector of the decision-making space that is most advantageous for us. In brief, I am not suggesting that emotions are a substitute for reason or that they decide for us. Nor am I denying that excessive emotion can breed irrationality. I am saying only that new neurological evidence suggests that no emotion at all is an even greater problem. Emotion may well be the support system without which the edifice of reason cannot function properly and may even collapse.

The idea that the bastion of logic should not be invaded by emotion and feeling is well established. You will find it in Plato as much as in Kant, but perhaps the idea would never have survived had it not been expressed as powerfully as it was by Descartes, who celebrated the separation of reason from emotion and severed reason from its biological foundation. Of course, the Cartesian split is not the cause of the contemporary pathologies of reason, but it should be blamed for the slowness with which the modern world has recognized their emotional root. When reason is conceptualized as free of biological antecedents, it is easier to overlook the role emotions play in its operation, easier not to notice that our purported rational decisions can be subtly manipulated by the emotions we want to keep at bay, easier not to worry about the possible negative consequences of the vicarious emotional experiences of violence as entertainment, easier to overlook the positive effect that well-tuned emotions can have in the management of human affairs.

It is not likely that reason begins with thought and language, in a rarefied cognitive domain, but rather that it originates from the biological regulation of a living organism bent on surviving. The brain core of complex organisms such as ours contains, in effect, a sophisticated apparatus for decisions that concern the maintenance of life processes. The responses of that apparatus include the regulation of the internal milieu, as well as drives, instincts and feelings. I suspect that rationality depends on the spirited passion for reason that animates such an apparatus.

It is intriguing to realize that Pascal prefigured this idea within the same 17th century that brought us Cartesian dualism, when he said, "It is on this knowledge of the heart and of the instincts that reason must establish itself and create the foundation for all its discourse." We are beginning to uncover the pertinent neurobiological facts behind Pascal's profound insight, and that may be none too soon. If the human species is to prevail, physical resources and social affairs must be wisely managed, and such wisdom will come most easily from the knowledgeable and thoughtful planning that characterizes the rational, self-knowing mind.

Out of the cradle endlessly rocking,
Out of the mocking-bird's throat, the musical shuttle,
Out of the Ninth-month midnight,
Over the sterile sands and the fields beyond, where the child leaving
his bed
    wander'd alone, bareheaded, barefoot,
Down from the shower'd halo,
Up from the mystic play of shadows twining and twisting as if they
were alive,
Out from the patches of briers and blackberries,
From the memories of the bird that chanted to me . . .
A man, yet by these tears a little boy again,
Throwing myself on the sand, confronting the waves,
I, chanter of pains and joys, uniter of here and hereafter, . . .
A reminiscence sing.

        —Walt Whitman, from "Out of the Cradle Endlessly Rocking"

The Memory of Nature

In Walt Whitman's famous poem, he is reliving an episode of his childhood on Long Island during which he heard a bird near the seashore lamenting the loss of his mate. The "cradle," of course, is the sea—the source of all life: what Diane Ackerman in the previous section refers to as our "home." While the bird sings of his grief, the waves of the sea are carrying their own whispered refrain: "Hissing melodious, neither like the bird nor like my arous'd child's heart," the waves "[L]isp'd to me the low and delicious word death/And again death, death, death, death . . ." The eternal sea—the mother of life, a spiritual agent as well as a natural phenomenon—reclaims all her children, and the boy's intimation that this is so makes the bird his "brother." "My own songs awaked from that hour," the adult poet tells us—and surely the unifying insight that he imputes to his childhood self is in keeping with the meaning implicit in *Leaves of Grass,* the inclusive title he gave to his ever-growing body of work.

While the seas (despite their growing pollution) can continue to remind us of our origin in uncorrupted nature—and also to remind us (as does the movement of sun and stars) of infinitude and the recurrent natural cycles in which each of us participates—civilization has increasingly moved us farther and farther from our beginnings and from a spiritual basis found in our relationship to the natural environment.

On an intellectual level, nature has lost none of its crucial importance: the exploration of nature is the very subject of science. And regardless of our increasing distance from it, the natural world remains embedded in our psyches, as a number of the essays in the opening section indicate. Sometimes "nature" now seems of concern only to a select number of our poets; but a reading of this anthology reveals nature's significance to many prose writers, present as well as past—they include Chekhov, Agee, Momaday, Dillard, and Morris. For this brief section devoted to the subject, I have chosen work in which nature is clearly the dominant concern.

In reviewing selections I had chosen for the present category, I was surprised that three of them dealt with walking, with sojourns into the natural world—and that the other three also concern journeying. I shouldn't have been surprised, of course: in the modern world, such excursions are necessary, if one wishes to escape the confines of civilization. To judge from some of these essays, one who is seeking to discover—or to rediscover—the natural reality must escape more than crowded streets, overheated apartment buildings, and industrial pollution. Jean-Jacques Rousseau, the eighteenth-century French philosopher, holds that society inevitably turns the twin qualities of human goodness that once marked us as inhabitants of a natural world—a love of self that caused us to seek our preservation, and a pity for the suffering and death of others—into a self-love that leads us into envy, aggression, and a consequent social inequality

unknown to our distant forbears. Until he is caught up in that society, the child instinctively remains responsive to the earlier, more generous vision. I have excluded Rousseau from this anthology because his autobiography suggests to me that he is too unreliable a witness, his philosophy possibly serving (at least in part) as justification for his own indulgences; still, he makes clear that the atmosphere—the very assumptions—of modern civilization alienate us from our roots, whatever the genetic heritage that may underlie (say) the competitive nature of our economic system. In any event, the essayists in this section are, more often than not, seeking an insight for which an escape from society in nearly all its ramifications is required.

The ambiguity toward memory expressed in several of these essays is more than an interesting phenomenon. (For Thoreau in particular, not only is history—civilization's memory of itself—suspect, but one's personal memory as well.) The desire to reach beyond memory (to achieve what John Haines calls "the endless present") may reflect a spiritual desire for unity with the natural world that is innate to human memory itself—a view to be explored in the final section of this anthology. It is a state or condition obtainable only in vision for inhabitants of the modern-day world—time-bound citizens that we are. Logically, of course, it represents an impossibility. William James, in his chapter "Memory" in *Principles of Psychology,* speaks of "the specious present," our intuition of living in the present moment of time. "Beyond its borders," he says, "extends the immense region of *conceived* time, past and future, into one direction or another of which we mentally project all the events which we think of as real." Our apprehension of any "real" event of the passing moment is given coherence, made acceptable rather than fantastic, by the memories we impose upon it. Movies depend on the human mind to participate with the projector not only in giving the illusion of motion to a series of static images but in granting depth to images that are two-dimensional. Anticipation based on experience—that is, a dual awareness of past and future—gives "reality" to whatever it is that we perceive; in this sense, the present reality is always subjective.

For individuals who wish to capture the essential reality of any aspect of nature, to connect their time-bound consciousness to the timelessness of nature itself, the attempt must be, then, to *try* to view it as if they were seeing it for the first time—one reason, perhaps, that essayists on nature are likely to cherish habitats not already hopelessly colored by conventional or habitual responses: Thoreau, for example, places a high value on desolate swamps, Kim Stafford (in a conscious attempt to strip himself to his essence) wanders in a remote California region without a goal in mind, Haines is drawn to snowy Arctic vistas, and John Landretti is fascinated by a small piece of urban wasteland.

The final essayists in this section, Esther Warner and Loren Eiseley, may seem somewhat more conventional, at least in the manner of their respective tellings; but they, too, would bring us home again.

"Walking"

Henry David Thoreau (1817–1862)

Thoreau's essay "Walking" is a call to us to respond to the "absolute freedom and wildness" of our heritage in the natural world, qualities which are restrained, if not extinguished, by society with its rules and collective memory—and by our individual memories, as well. Nature itself exists always in the present moment while ceaselessly moving into the future. Our freedom comes from living in a similar way, always responsive to nature's wildness, always forgetful of the past; like material possessions, much that we carry in memory constitutes a burden of useless baggage. In *Walden*, his most famous book, Thoreau urges us not to seize the day, but to seize the morning, to be as close as possible to the eternal rebirth that occurs in nature; the sense of being newly awake should mark our experiences all day long. "Walking," a later work, was published in the *Atlantic Monthly* in 1862, the year of his death, and the sunset, the daily migration of the sun over the horizon, now takes precedence over the dawn, though the vaporous beauty of the sunset foreshadows not death but an imagined future—a "terrestrial paradise" whose promise is akin to that underlying Greek myth. Our desires lead us westward; to the east is history, the Old World that has corrupted the original promise. Memory looks eastward, to the past, and must be jettisoned with all the other debris.

His is, Thoreau acknowledges, an "extreme statement," one intended to oppose the many "champions of civilization" by demonstrating that each of us is "an inhabitant, or part and parcel of Nature." He would redress the balance, since we can be stifled by social convention and bias, by dependence upon memory. (And, as an American, he wishes to establish his independence from a tamed or spiritually enervated European culture.) If Thoreau had been able to renounce his own memory in anything but the most relative way, he would have found it impossible, of course, to compose his essay. One notices, for example, the degree to which his heightened responses to nature—including that marvelous depiction of invisible presences on Spaulding's Farm, difficult to remember though they may be—remain as feelings within his memory; and one notices, too, the references (scattered through *Walden* as well as this essay) to an instinctive, or genetic, memory: to a time when people lived within the natural environment, their fresh and uncorrupted responses to it transmitted to us through mythology as well as instinct. The very desire for freedom, which gives Thoreau his dislike of memory and other accumulated burdens from the past, is in this sense a desire that comes from memory itself—from a genetic inheritance at odds with the cultural accretions and other artifices of an established civilization.

In a measured tribute to Thoreau following his death in his forty-fourth year, Emerson, after describing his younger friend's "wonderful fitness of body and mind," adds, "And the relation of body to mind was still finer than we have indicated. He said he wanted every stride his legs made. The length of his walk

67

uniformly made the length of his writing. If shut up in the house, he did not write at all." The walk that resulted in "Walking" was apparently an extensive one; so lengthy, in fact, that for the purposes of this anthology I found it necessary on occasion to leave the attractive meanders of his prose path for a shortcut across the field.

I wish to speak a word for Nature, for absolute freedom and wildness, as contrasted with a freedom and culture merely civil,—to regard man as an inhabitant, or a part and parcel of Nature, rather than a member of society. I wish to make an extreme statement, if so I may make an emphatic one, for there are enough champions of civilization: the minister and the school-committee and every one of you will take care of that.

I have met with but one or two persons in the course of my life who understood the art of Walking, that is, of taking walks,—who had a genius, so to speak, for *sauntering*: which word is beautifully derived "from idle people who roved about the country, in the Middle Ages, and asked charity, under pretense of going *à la Sainte Terre*," to the Holy Land, till the children exclaimed, "There goes a *Sainte-Terrer*," a Saunterer, a Holy-Lander. They who never go to the Holy Land in their walks, as they pretend, are indeed mere idlers and vagabonds; but they who do go there are saunterers in the good sense, such as I mean. Some, however, would derive the word from *sans terre*, without land or home, which, therefore, in the good sense, will mean, having no particular home, but equally at home everywhere. For this is the secret of successful sauntering. He who sits still in a house all the time may be the greatest vagrant of all; but the saunterer, in the good sense, is no more vagrant than the meandering river, which is all the while sedulously seeking the shortest course to the sea. But I prefer the first, which, indeed, is the most probable derivation. For every walk is a sort of crusade, preached by some Peter the Hermit in us, to go forth and reconquer this Holy Land from the hands of the Infidels.

It is true, we are but faint-hearted crusaders, even the walkers, nowadays, who undertake no persevering, never-ending enterprises. Our expeditions are but tours, and come round again at evening to the old hearth-side from which we set out. Half the walk is but retracing our steps. We should go forth on the shortest walk, perchance, in the spirit of undying adventure, never to return,—prepared to send back our embalmed hearts only as relics to our desolate kingdoms. If you are ready to leave father and mother, and brother and sister, and wife and child and friends, and never see them again,—if you have paid your debts, and made your will, and settled all your affairs, and are a free man, then you are ready for a walk.

To come down to my own experience, my companion and I, for I sometimes have a companion, take pleasure in fancying ourselves knights of a new, or rather an old, order,—not Equestrians or Chevaliers, not Ritters or Riders, but Walkers, a still more ancient and honorable class, I trust. The chivalric and heroic spirit which once belonged to the Rider seems now to reside in, or perchance to have subsided into, the Walker,— not the Knight, but Walker, Errant. He is a sort of fourth estate, outside of Church and State and People.

We have felt that we almost alone hereabouts practiced this noble art; though, to tell the truth, at least, if their own assertions are to be received, most of my townsmen would fain walk sometimes, as I do, but they cannot. No wealth can buy the requisite leisure, freedom, and independence which are the capital in this profession. It comes only by the grace of God. It requires a direct dispensation from Heaven to become a walker. You must be born into the family of the Walkers. *Ambulator nascitur, non fit.* Some of my townsmen, it is true, can remember and have described to me some walks which they took ten years ago, in which they were so blessed as to lose themselves for half an hour in the woods; but I know very well that they have confined themselves to the highway ever since, whatever pretensions they may make to belong to this select class. No doubt they were elevated for a moment as by the reminiscence of a previous state of existence, when even they were foresters and outlaws. . . .

When we walk, we naturally go to the fields and woods: what would become of us, if we walked only in a garden or a mall? Even some sects of philosophers have felt the necessity of importing the woods to themselves, since they did not go to the woods. "They planted groves and walks of Platanes," where they took *subdiales ambulationes* in porticos open to the air. Of course it is of no use to direct our steps to the woods, if they do not carry us thither. I am alarmed when it happens that I have walked a mile into the woods bodily, without getting there in spirit. In my afternoon walk I would fain forget all my morning occupations and my obligations to society. But it sometimes happens that I cannot easily shake off the village. The thought of some work will run in my head and I am not where my body is,—I am out of my senses. In my walks I would fain return to my senses. What business have I in the woods, if I am thinking of something out of the woods? I suspect myself, and cannot help a shudder, when I find myself so implicated even in what are called good works,—for this may sometimes happen.

My vicinity affords many good walks; and though for so many years I have walked almost every day, and sometimes for several days together, I have not yet exhausted them. An absolutely new prospect is a great happiness, and I can still get this any afternoon. Two or three hours' walking will carry me to as strange a country as I expect ever to see. A single farm-house which I had not seen before is sometimes as good as the dominions of the King of Dahomey. There is in fact a sort of harmony discoverable between the capabilities of the landscape within a circle of ten miles' radius, or the limits of an afternoon walk, and the threescore years and ten of human life. It will never become quite familiar to you.

Nowadays almost all man's improvements, so called, as the building of houses, and the cutting down of the forest and of all large trees, simply deform the landscape, and make it more and more tame and cheap. A people who would begin by burning the fences and let the forest stand! I saw the fences half consumed, their ends lost in the middle of the prairie, and some worldly miser with a surveyor looking after his bounds, while heaven had taken place around him, and he did not see the angels going to and fro, but was looking for an old post-hole in the midst of paradise. I looked again, and saw him standing in the middle of a boggy stygian fen, surrounded by devils, and he had found his bounds without a doubt, three little stones, where a stake had been driven, and looking nearer, I saw that the Prince of Darkness was his surveyor.

I can easily walk ten, fifteen, twenty, any number of miles, commencing at my own door, without going by any house, without crossing a road except where the fox and the mink do: first along by the river, and then the brook, and then the meadow and the woodside. There are square miles in my vicinity which have no inhabitant. From many a hill I can see civilization and the abodes of man afar. The farmers and their works are scarcely more obvious than woodchucks and their burrows. Man and his affairs, church and state and school, trade and commerce, and manufactures and agriculture, even politics, the most alarming of them all,—I am pleased to see how little space they occupy in the landscape. Politics is but a narrow field, and that still narrower highway yonder leads to it. I sometimes direct the traveler thither. If you would go to the political world, follow the great road,—follow that marketman, keep his dust in your eyes, and it will lead you straight to it; for it, too, has its place merely, and does not occupy all space. I pass from it as from a bean-field into the forest, and it is forgotten. In one half-hour I can walk off to some portion of the earth's surface where a man does not stand from one-year's end to another, and there, consequently, politics are not, for they are but as the cigarsmoke of a man. . . .

What is it that makes it so hard sometimes to determine whither we will walk? I believe that there is a subtle magnetism in Nature, which, if we unconsciously yield to it, will direct us aright. It is not indifferent to us which way we walk. There is a right way; but we are very liable from heedlessness and stupidity to take the wrong one. We would fain take that walk, never yet taken by us through this actual world, which is perfectly symbolical of the path which we love to travel in the interior and ideal world; and sometimes, no doubt, we find it difficult to choose our direction, because it does not yet exist distinctly in our idea.

When I go out of the house for a walk, uncertain as yet whither I will bend my steps, and submit myself to my instinct to decide for me, I find, strange and whimsical as it may seem, that I finally and inevitably settle southwest, toward some particular wood or meadow or deserted pasture or hill in that direction. My needle is slow to settle,—varies a few degrees, and does not always point due southwest, it is true, and it has good authority for this variation, but it always settles between west and south-southwest. The future lies that way to me, and the earth seems more unexhausted and richer on that side. The outline which would bound my walks would be, not a circle, but a parabola, or rather like one of those cometary orbits which have been thought to be non-returning curves, in this case opening westward, in which my house occupies the place of the sun. I turn round and round irresolute sometimes for a quarter of an hour, until I decide, for a thousandth time, that I will walk into the southwest or west. Eastward I go only by force; but westward I go free. Thither no business leads me. It is hard for me to believe that I shall find fair landscapes or sufficient wildness and freedom behind the eastern horizon. I am not excited by the prospect of a walk thither; but I believe that the forest which I see in the western horizon stretches uninterruptedly toward the setting sun, and there are no towns nor cities in it of enough consequence to disturb me. Let me live where I will, on this side is the city, on that the wilderness, and ever I am leaving the city more and more, and withdrawing into the wilderness. I should not lay so much stress on this fact, if I did not believe that something like this is the prevailing tendency of my countrymen. I must walk toward Oregon, and not toward Europe. And that way the nation is moving, and I may say that mankind progress from east to west. Within a few years we have witnessed the phenomenon of a southeastward migration, in the settlement of Australia; but this affects us as a retrograde movement, and, judging from the moral and physical character of the first generation of Australians, has not yet proved a successful experiment. The eastern Tartars think that there is nothing west beyond Thibet. "The world ends there," say they; "beyond there is nothing but a shoreless sea." It is unmitigated East where they live.

We go eastward to realize history and study the works of art and literature, retracing the steps of the race; we go westward as into the future, with a spirit of enterprise and adventure. The Atlantic is a Lethean stream, in our passage over which we have had an opportunity to forget the Old World and its institutions. If we do not succeed this time, there is perhaps one more chance for the race left before it arrives on the banks of the Styx; and that is in the Lethe of the Pacific, which is three times as wide.

I know not how significant it is, or how far it is an evidence of singularity, that an individual should thus consent in his pettiest walk with the general movement of the race; but I know that something akin to the migratory instinct in birds and quadrupeds,—which, in some instances, is known to have affected the squirrel tribe, impelling them to a general and mysterious movement, in which they were seen, say some, crossing the broadest rivers, each on its particular chip, with its tail raised for a sail, and bridging narrower streams with their dead,—that something like the *furor* which affects the domestic cattle in the spring, and which is referred to a worm in their tails,—affects both nations and individuals, either perennially or from time to time. Not a flock of wild geese cackles over our town, but it to some extent unsettles the value of real estate here, and, if I were a broker, I should probably take that disturbance into account.

> "Than longen folk to gon on pilgrimages,
> And palmeres for to seken strange strondes."

Every sunset which I witness inspires me with the desire to go to a West as distant and as fair as that into which the sun goes down. He appears to migrate westward daily, and tempt us to follow him. He is the Great Western Pioneer whom the nations follow. We dream all night of those mountain-ridges in the horizon, though they may be of vapor only, which were last gilded by his rays. The island of Atlantis, and the islands and gardens of the Hesperides, a sort of terrestrial paradise, appear to have been the Great West of the ancients, enveloped in mystery and poetry. Who has not seen in imagination, when looking into the sunset sky, the gardens of the Hesperides, and the foundation of all those fables? . . .

The West of which I speak is but another name for the Wild; and what I have been preparing to say is, that in Wildness is the preservation of the World. Every tree sends its fibres forth in search of the Wild. The cities import it at any price. Men plough and sail for it. From the forest and wilderness come the tonics and barks which brace mankind. Our ancestors were savages. The story of Romulus and Remus being suckled by a wolf is not a meaningless fable. The founders of every state which has risen to eminence have drawn their nourishment and vigor from a similar wild source. It was because the children of the Empire were not suckled by the wolf that they were conquered and displaced by the children of the northern forests who were.

I believe in the forest, and in the meadow, and in the night in which the corn grows. We require an infusion of hemlock-spruce or arbor-vitæ in our tea. There is a difference between eating and drinking for strength and from mere gluttony. The Hottentots eagerly devour the marrow of the koodoo and other antelopes raw, as a matter of course. Some of our Northern Indians eat raw the marrow of the Arctic reindeer, as well as the various other parts, including the summits of the antlers, as long as they are soft. And herein, perchance, they have stolen a march on the cooks on Paris. They get what usually goes to feed the fire. This is probably better than stall-fed beef and slaughter-house pork to make a man of. Give me a wildness whose glance no civilization can endure,—as if we lived on the marrow of koodoos devoured raw.

There are some intervals which border the strain of the wood-thrush, to which I would migrate,—wild lands where no settler has squatted; to which, methinks, I am already acclimated. . . .

Life consists with wildness. The most alive is the wildest. Not yet subdued to man, its presence refreshes him. One who pressed forward incessantly and never rested from his labors, who grew fast and made infinite demands on life, would always find himself in a new country or wilderness, and surrounded by the raw material of life. He would be climbing over the prostrate stems of primitive forest-trees.

Hope and the future for me are not in lawns and cultivated fields, not in towns and cities, but in the impervious and quaking swamps. When, formerly, I have analyzed my partiality for some farm which I had contemplated purchasing, I have frequently found that I was attracted solely by a few square rods of impermeable and unfathomable bog,—a natural sink in one corner of it. That was the jewel which dazzled me. I derive more of my subsistence from the swamps which surround my native town than from the cultivated gardens in the village. There are no richer parterres to my eyes than the dense beds of dwarf andromeda *(Cassandra calyculata)* which cover these tender places on the earth's surface. Botany cannot go farther than tell me the names of the shrubs which grow there,—the high-blueberry, panicled andromeda, lamb-kill, azalea, and rhodora,—all standing in the quaking sphagnum. I often think that I should like to have my house front on this mass of dull red bushes, omitting other flower plots and borders, transplanted spruce and trim box, even graveled walks,— to have this fertile spot under my windows, not a few imported barrow-fulls of soil only to cover the sand which was thrown out in digging the cellar. Why not put my house, my parlor, behind this plot, instead of behind that meagre assemblage of curiosities, that poor apology for a Nature and Art, which I call my front yard? It is an effort to clear up and make a decent appearance when the carpenter and mason have departed, though done as much for the passer-by as the dweller within. The most tasteful front-yard fence was never an agreeable object of study to me; the most elaborate ornaments, acorn-tops, or what not, soon wearied and disgusted me. Bring your sills up to the very edge of the swamp, then (though it may not be the best place for a dry cellar), so that there be no access on the side to citizens. Front yards are not made to walk in, but, at most, through, and you could go in the back way.

Yes, though you may think me perverse, if it were proposed to me to dwell in the neighborhood of the most beautiful garden that ever human art contrived, or else of a Dismal Swamp, I should certainly decide for the swamp. How vain, then, have been all your labors, citizens, for me!

My spirits infallibly rise in proportion to the outward dreariness. Give me the ocean, the desert, or the wilderness! In the desert, pure air and solitude compensate for want of moisture and fertility. The traveler Burton says of it: "Your *morale* improves; you become frank and cordial, hospitable and single-minded. . . . In the desert, spirituous liquors excite only disgust. There is a keen enjoyment in a mere animal existence." They who have been traveling long on the steppes of Tartary say: "On reëntering cultivated lands, the agitation, perplexity, and turmoil of civilization oppressed and suffocated us; the air seemed to fail us, and we felt every moment as if about to die of asphyxia." When I would recreate myself, I seek the darkest wood, the thickest and most interminable and, to the citizen, most dismal swamp. I enter a swamp as a sacred place,—a *sanctum sanctorum*. There is the strength, the marrow of Nature. The wild-wood covers the virgin-mould,—and the same soil is good for men and for trees. A man's health requires as many acres of meadow to his prospect as his farm does loads of muck. There are the strong meats on which he feeds. A town is saved, not more by the righteous men in it than by the woods and swamps that surround it. A township where one primitive forest waves above while another primitive forest rots below,—such a town is fitted to raise not only corn and potatoes, but poets and philosophers for the coming ages. In such a soil grew Homer and Confucius and the rest, and out of such a wilderness comes the Reformer eating locusts and wild honey. . . .

In literature it is only the wild that attracts us. Dullness is but another name for tameness. It is the uncivilized free and wild thinking in "Hamlet" and the "Iliad," in all the Scriptures and Mythologies, not learned in the schools, that delights us. As the wild duck is more swift and beautiful than the tame, so is the wild—the mallard—thought, which 'mid falling dews wings its way above the fens. A truly good book is something as natural, and as unexpectedly and unaccountably fair and perfect, as a wild flower discovered on the prairies of the West or in the jungles of the East. Genius is a light which makes the darkness visible, like the lightning's flash, which perchance shatters the temple of knowledge itself,—and not a taper lighted at the hearthstone of the race, which pales before the light of common day. English literature, from the days of the minstrels to the Lake Poets,— Chaucer and Spenser and Milton, and even Shakespeare, included,— breathes no quite fresh and, in this sense, wild strain. It is an essentially tame and civilized literature, reflecting Greece and Rome. Her wilderness is a greenwood, her wild man a Robin Hood. There is plenty of genial love of Nature, but not so much of Nature herself. Her chronicles inform us when her wild animals, but not when the wild man in her, became extinct. The science of Humboldt is one thing, poetry is another thing. The poet to-day, notwithstanding all the discoveries of science, and the accumulated learning of mankind, enjoys no advantage over Homer.

Where is the literature which gives expression to Nature? He would be a poet who could impress the winds and streams into his service, to speak for him; who nailed words to their primitive senses, as farmers drive down stakes in the spring, which the frost has heaved; who derived his words as often as he used them,—transplanted them to his page with earth adhering to their roots; whose words were so true and fresh and natural that they would appear to expand like the buds at the approach of spring, though they lay half-smothered between two musty leaves in a library,—ay, to bloom and bear fruit there, after their kind, annually, for the faithful reader, in sympathy with surrounding Nature.

I do not know of any poetry to quote which adequately expresses this yearning for the Wild. Approached from this side, the best poetry is tame. I do not know where to find in any literature, ancient or modern, any account which contents me of that Nature with which even I am acquainted. You will perceive that I demand something which no Augustan nor Elizabethan age, which no *culture,* in short, can give. Mythology comes nearer to it than anything. How much more fertile a Nature, at least, has Grecian mythology its root in than English literature! Mythology is the crop which the Old World bore before its soil was exhausted, before the fancy and imagination were affected with blight; and which it still bears, wherever its pristine vigor is unabated. All other literatures endure only as the elms which overshadow our houses; but this is like the great dragontree of the Western Isles, as old as mankind, and, whether that does or not, will endure as long; for the decay of other literatures makes the soil in which it thrives.

The West is preparing to add its fables to those of the East. The valleys of the Ganges, the Nile, and the Rhine having yielded their crop, it remains to be seen what the valleys of the Amazon, the Plate, the Orinoco, the St. Lawrence, and the Mississippi will produce. Perchance, when, in the course of ages, American liberty has become a fiction of the past,—as it is to some extent a fiction of the present,—the poets of the world will be inspired by American mythology.

The wildest dreams of wild men, even, are not the less true, though they may not recommend themselves to the sense which is most common among Englishmen and Americans to-day. It is not every truth that recommends itself to the common sense. Nature has a place for the wild clematis as well as for the cabbage. Some expressions of truth are reminiscent,—others merely *sensible,* as the phrase is,—others prophetic. Some forms of disease, even, may prophesy forms of health. The geologist has discovered that the figures of serpents, griffins, flying dragons, and other fanciful embellishments of heraldry, have their prototypes in the forms of fossil species which were extinct before man was created, and hence "indicate a faint and shadowy knowledge of a previous state of organic existence." The Hindoos dreamed that the earth rested on an elephant, and the elephant on a tortoise, and the tortoise on a serpent; and though it may be an unimportant coincidence, it will not be out of place here to state, that a fossil tortoise has lately been discovered in Asia large enough to support an elephant. I confess that I am partial to these wild fancies, which transcend the order of time and development. They are the sublimest recreation of the intellect. The partridge loves peas, but not those that go with her into the pot.

In short, all good things are wild and free. There is something in a strain of music, whether produced by an instrument or by the human voice,—take the sound of a bugle in a summer night, for instance,—which by its wildness, to speak without satire, reminds me of the cries emitted by wild beasts in their native forests. It is so much of their wildness as I can understand. Give me for my friends and neighbors wild men, not tame ones. The wildness of the savage is but a faint symbol of the awful ferity with which good men and lovers meet. . . .

I would not have every man nor every part of a man cultivated, any more than I would have every acre of earth cultivated: part will be tillage, but the greater part will be meadow and forest, not only serving an immediate use, but preparing a mould against a distant future, by the annual decay of the vegetation which it supports. . . .

We have heard of a Society for the Diffusion of Useful Knowledge. It is said that knowledge is power; and the like. Methinks there is equal need of a Society for the Diffusion of Useful Ignorance, what we will call Beautiful Knowledge, a knowledge useful in a higher sense: for what is most of our boasted so-called knowledge but a conceit that we know something, which robs us of the advantage of our actual ignorance? What we call knowledge is often our positive ignorance; ignorance our negative knowledge. By long years of patient industry and reading of the newspapers,—for what are the libraries of science but files of newspapers?—a man accumulates a myriad facts, lays them up in his memory, and then when in some spring of his life he saunters abroad into the Great Fields of thought, he, as it were, goes to grass like a horse and leaves all his harness behind in the stable. I would say to the Society for the Diffusion of Useful Knowledge, sometimes,—Go to grass. You have eaten hay long enough. The spring has come with its green crop. The very cows are driven to their country pastures before the end of May; though I have heard of one unnatural farmer who kept his cow in the barn and fed her on hay all the year round. So, frequently, the Society for the Diffusion of Useful Knowledge treats its cattle.

A man's ignorance sometimes is not only useful, but beautiful,—while his knowledge, so called, is oftentimes worse than useless, besides being ugly. Which is the best man to deal with,—he who knows nothing about a subject, and, what is extremely rare, knows that he knows nothing, or he who really knows something about it, but thinks that he knows all?

My desire for knowledge is intermittent; but my desire to bathe my head in atmospheres unknown to my feet is perennial and constant. The highest that we can attain to is not Knowledge, but Sympathy with Intelligence. I do not know that this higher knowledge amounts to anything more definite than a novel and grand surprise on a sudden revelation of the insufficiency of all that we called Knowledge before,—a discovery that there are more things in heaven and earth than are dreamed of in our philosophy. It is the lighting up of the mist by the sun. Man cannot *know* in any higher sense than this, any more than he can look serenely and with impunity in the face of the sun: 'Ως τί νοῶν, οὐ χεῖνον νοῆσεις,— "You will not perceive that, as perceiving a particular thing," say the Chaldean Oracles.

There is something servile in the habit of seeking after a law which we may obey. We may study the laws of matter at and for our convenience, but a successful life knows no law. It is an unfortunate discovery certainly, that of a law which binds us where we did not know before that we were bound. Live free, child of the mist,—and with respect to knowledge we are all children of the mist. The man who takes the liberty to live is superior to all the laws, by virtue of his relation to the law-maker. "That is active duty," says the Vishnu Purana, "which is not for our bondage; that is knowledge which is for our liberation: all other duty is good only unto weariness; all other knowledge is only the cleverness of an artist.". . .

While almost all men feel an attraction drawing them to society, few are attracted strongly to Nature. In their reaction to Nature men appear to me for the most part, notwithstanding their arts, lower than the animals. It is not often a beautiful relation, as in the case of the animals. How little appreciation of the beauty of the landscape there is among us! We have to be told that the Greeks called the world *Κόσμος*, Beauty, or Order, but we do not see clearly why they did so, and we esteem it at best only a curious philological fact.

For my part, I feel that with regard to Nature I live a sort of border life, on the confines of a world into which I make occasional and transient forays only, and my patriotism and allegiance to the State into whose territories I seem to retreat are those of a moss-trooper. Unto a life which I call natural I would gladly follow eve a will-o'-the-wisp through bogs and sloughs unimaginable, but no moon nor firefly has shown me the causeway to it. Nature is a personality so vast and universal that we have never seen one of her features. The walker in the familiar fields which stretch around my native town sometimes finds himself in another land than is described in their owners' deeds, as it were in some far-away field on the confines of the actual Concord, where her jurisdiction ceases, and the idea which the word Concord suggests ceases to be suggested. These farms which I have myself surveyed, these bounds which I have set up, appear dimly still as through a mist; but they have no chemistry to fix them; they fade from the surface on the glass; and the picture which the painter painted stands out dimly from beneath. The world with which we are commonly acquainted leaves no trace, and it will have no anniversary.

I took a walk on Spaulding's Farm the other afternoon. I saw the setting sun lighting up the opposite side of a stately pine wood. Its golden rays straggled into the aisles of the wood as into some noble hall. I was impressed as if some ancient and altogether admirable and shining family had settled there in that part of the land called Concord, unknown to me,—to whom the sun was servant,—who had not gone into society in the village,—who had not been called on. I saw their park, their pleasure-ground, beyond through the wood, in Spaulding's cranberry-meadow. The pines furnished them with gables as they grew. Their house was not obvious to vision; the trees grew through it. I do not know whether I heard the sounds of a suppressed hilarity or not. They seemed to recline on the sunbeams. They have sons and daughters. They are quite well. The farmer's cart-path, which leads directly through their hall, does not in the least put them out, as the muddy bottom of a pool is sometimes seen through the reflected skies. They never heard of Spaulding, and do not know that he is their neighbor,—notwithstanding I heard him whistle as he drove his team through the house. Nothing can equal the serenity of their lives. Their coat of arms is simply a lichen. I saw it painted on the pines and oaks. Their attics were in the tops of the trees. They are of no politics. There was no noise of labor. I did not perceive that they were weaving or spinning. Yet I did detect, when the wind lulled and hearing was done away, the finest imaginable sweet musical hum,—as of a distant hive in May, which perchance was the sound of their thinking. They had no idle thoughts, and no one without could see their work, for their industry was not as in knots and excrescences embayed.

But I find it difficult to remember them. They fade irrevocably out of my mind even now while I speak, and endeavor to recall them and recollect myself. It is only after a long and serious effort to recollect my best thoughts that I become again aware of their cohabitancy. If it were not for such families as this, I think I should move out of Concord.

We are accustomed to say in New England that few and fewer pigeons visit us every year. Our forests furnish no mast for them. So, it would seem, few and fewer thoughts visit each growing man from year to year, for the grove in our minds is laid waste,—sold to feed unnecessary fires of ambition, or sent to mill, and there is scarcely a twig left for them to perch on. They no longer build nor breed with us. In some more genial season, perchance, a faint shadow flits across the landscape of the mind, cast by the *wings* of some thought in its vernal or autumnal migration, but, looking up, we are unable to detect the substance of the thought itself. Our winged thoughts are turned to poultry. They no longer soar, and they attain only to a Shanghai and Cochin-China grandeur. Those *gra-a-ate thoughts,* those *gra-a-ate men* you hear of!

We hug the earth,—how rarely we mount! Methinks we might elevate ourselves a little more. We might climb a tree, at least. I found my account in climbing a tree once. It was a tall white-pine, on the top of a hill; and though I got well pitched, I was well paid for it, for I discovered new mountains in the horizon which I had never seen before,—so much more of the earth and the heavens. I might have walked about the foot of the tree for three-score years and ten, and yet I certainly should never have seen them. But, above all, I discovered around me,—it was near the end of June,—on the ends of the topmost branches only, a few minute and delicate red cone-like blossoms, the fertile flower of the white pine looking heavenward. I carried straightway to the village to the topmost spire, and showed it to stranger jurymen who walked the streets,—for it was court-week,—and the farmers and lumber-dealers and wood-choppers and hunters, and not one had ever seen the like before, but they wondered as at a star dropped down. Tell of ancient architects finishing their works on the tops of columns as perfectly as on the lower and more visible parts! Nature has from the first expanded the minute blossoms of the forest only toward the heavens, above men's heads and unobserved by them. We see only the flowers that are under our feet in the meadows. The pines have developed their delicate blossoms on the highest twigs of the wood every summer for ages, as well over the heads of Nature's red children as of her white ones; yet scarcely a farmer or hunter in the land has ever seen them.

Above all, we cannot afford not to live in the present. He is blessed over all mortals who loses no moment of the passing life in remembering the past. Unless our philosophy hears the cock crow in every barn-yard within our horizon, it is belated. That sound commonly reminds us that we are growing rusty and antique in our employments and habits of thought. His philosophy comes down to a more recent time than ours. There is something suggested by it that is a newer testament,—the gospel according to this moment. He has not fallen astern; he has got up early and kept up early, and to be where he is is to be in season, in the foremost rank of time. It is an expression of the health and soundness of Nature, a brag for all the world,—healthiness as of a spring burst forth, a new fountain of the Muses, to celebrate this last instant of time. Where he lives no fugitive slave laws are passed. Who has not betrayed his master many times since last he heard that note?

The merit of this bird's strain is in its freedom from all plaintiveness. The singer can easily move us to tears or to laughter, but where is he who can excite in us a pure morning joy? When, in doleful dumps, breaking the awful stillness of our wooden sidewalk on a Sunday, or, perchance, a watcher in the house of mourning, I hear a cockerel crow far or near, I think to myself, "There is one of us well, at any rate,"—and with a sudden gush return to my senses.

We had a remarkable sunset one day last November. I was walking in a meadow, the source of a small brook, when the sun at last, just before setting, after a cold gray day, reached a clear stratum in the horizon, and the softest, brightest morning sunlight fell on the dry grass and on the stems of the trees in the opposite horizon and on the leaves of the shrub-oaks on the hillside, while our shadows stretched long over the meadow eastward as if we were the only motes in its beams. It was such a light as we could not have imagined a moment before, and the air also was so warm and serene that nothing was wanting to make a paradise of that meadow. When we reflected that this was not a solitary phenomenon, never to happen again, but that it would happen forever and ever an infinite number of evenings, and cheer and reassure the latest child that walked there, it was more glorious still.

The sun sets on some retired meadow, where no house is visible, with all the glory and splendor that it lavishes on cities, and perchance as it has never set before,—where there is but a solitary marsh-hawk to have his wings gilded by it, or only a musquash looks out from his cabin, and there is some little black-veined brook in the midst of the marsh, just beginning to meander, winding slowly round a decaying stump. We walked in so pure and bright a light, gilding the withered grass and leaves, so softly and serenely bright, I thought I had never bathed in such a golden flood, without a ripple or a murmur to it. The west side of every wood and rising ground gleamed like the boundary of Elysium, and the sun on our backs seemed like a gentle herdsman driving us home at evening.

So we saunter toward the Holy Land, till one day the sun shall shine more brightly than ever he has done, shall perchance shine into our minds and hearts, and light up our whole lives with a great awakening light, as warm and serene and golden as on a bankside in autumn.

"A Walk in Early May"

Kim R. Stafford (1949–)

The Kwakiutl—an Indian tribe along the northwest coast dispossessed by white settlers in the last decades of the nineteenth century—used happenings or stories as place names, Kim R. Stafford, an Oregon writer, tells us in the introduction to a collection of his essays. The title of that collection—*Having Everything Right*—is a transcription of the Kwakiutl word for "a place where people gather abundant berries and make a good life." That word, Stafford says, "is a portable name, an expandable place," since the Kwakiutl gave it to every place appropriate to its meaning. The word *could* apply to "what we call earth. But it will not, unless we sift from our habits the nourishing ways: listening, remembering, telling, weaving a rooted companionship with home ground."

The essays are held together by his conscious attempt to achieve such a companionship; he desires "to *make* my place upriver deserve that name." In one of the accounts, "The Story that Saved Life," listening and telling are woven into a single fabric through memory: "Memory," the essay begins, "is made as a quilt is made. From the whole cloth of time, frayed scraps of sensation are pulled apart and pieced together in a pattern that has a name." Another essay, "The Separate Hearth," refers to memory as like the little screw-top match safe he carried in his pocket as a child, one whose matches can rekindle the past.

I had the good fortune to read this collection while it was still in manuscript; I was asked to comment on it prior to the citation for excellence given it in 1986 by the Western States Book Awards. Most of the essays are held in my own memory from that first reading, but none more strongly than "A Walk in Early May," Stafford's recollection of an afternoon, night, and morning spent many years earlier along the shores and up the cliffs of coastal northern California, not far from Eureka. It describes his sensations while wandering about, and spending the night, in a remote natural area—alone, without map, food, bedding, or conscious destination. Indeed, it is the memory of a time in which he divested himself as fully as he could from memory itself. The essay reminds me of Thoreau's "Walking"; here, though, is a more concise, more dramatic rendition of what it means to exist each moment within nature—Stafford's is an essay devoid of philosophical speculation, one brave enough to court the vision of what it is to be a skeleton, or to be one with the vultures attacking his corpse.

"A Walk in Early May" is frightening—to the degree that one wants to hold onto the preciousness of one's unique and wholly mortal self by separating it from the impersonal processes of the natural world. And yet this essay is part of the attempt to be both alive and at home on our planet—and within a universe whose constellations, in the human mind, trace the very objects and life forms encountered on Earth. In her "Teaching a Stone to Talk," Annie Dillard says, "We are here to witness. There is nothing else to do with those mute materials we do not need." Near the end of his essay, Stafford says much the same; and, given what he has told us, he can note, without any risk of sentimentality, that his experience ended with his viewing of a rainbow.

Solitude is the scientific method of the human spirit. If you decide to fast, a full day and its night will be one arc of experience. If you decide not to take a map or to follow a trail, the path you make through broken country will be a chain of sensations. If you decide to take no warm covering for the night, you will change with the world, from warm and light, to cold.

South of Eureka lies a coastal country now dangerous with marijuana farmers and their guerrilla ways, with federal agents marauding in infrared helicopters and armored jeeps. But that was years away. I was there without a map, without food. I left the car and walked out onto the beach. The air was hot and still. The waves were an old rhythm beside me. I knelt over flat sand, where the tallest wave had sorted a ribbon of shell. Some four-footed creature had been along, leaving a trail that turned aside, as mine did, for every cluster of debris, every drift-bundle in the sand. One clear print told me it had been a coon, with two little ones. Inside the print, a gray scorpion the size of a ladybug was turning in a pirouette with its hands together. I was already hungry enough to understand that much.

In the midday shimmer, two women were talking in the waves. I turned: two seals, their eyes and whiskers level with the slick pelt of the water that rose and fell, rose and fell with a whisper. Not fear or purpose: a gentle curiosity came between us. An invitation to know. When they disappeared, kelp swirled from rocks that punctured the surface. I sat on the hot sand a long time. Then they came up, one little one bobbing behind them. This time they did not look at me. In seal, this was a compliment. The swell rose and they were gone again. Like the rocks, they had shown between waves; like the water, they had flowed away.

I walked south from the car, because it was easier to walk than decide. After a time, it was easier to stop. The inland dune glittered white above the tide-line. I held my hand above my eyes. It was a midden, a packed hill of rotted shell where the Indians had opened clams together. Generations of cockles to make one human life; generations of those lives to make a low hill waves had begun to carve. When I climbed it, deer in the meadow beyond bounded away into the blue-flowered scrub.

The hillside where the deer had fled was steep above the cove. The old ones had a narrow place to be happy together. Rocks clucked at the sliding water, the seals spoke now and then. There was a great distance in a small space. Before my face where I lay down, wind made the tiny seed of the grass sway where it was tethered.

I walked south in the trance of heat, at the rim of hunger. Walking was what the wind did, the sun. It had nothing to do with destination. Not a plan, but a way of being. Where I stopped, the seals were clustered offshore, bobbing in the water between two arms of rock. I was a stranger. They were older with the place. I lay down on the sand, my arms tight to my sides, my feet together. Became a shape for water. They murmured and came closer. They climbed onto the rocks. The curiosity came between us. All about me on the sand were the curved prints of their bodies where the tide had beached them high, where they had slept a while, then elbowed down to the water. Now they said one syllable with all its inflections—*oh, oh, oh, oh*—from deep in the body. The seals go down into another world, then come back to tell that.

Behind the beach was another midden, the white strata of shell deep in the bank waves had opened, had spilled. The bright slope I climbed was littered with whole abalone shell, each moonshape just shy of full, with a curved line of bubbles spiraling out from where it began. Clamshell crumbled like ash under my feet, and the white bone too long to not be whale-rib flaked away when I bent to touch it.

My hand closed over a hammerstone: a cylindrical shape with a rim at the top for my first finger to curve under. The striking face at the bottom was worn down by shell of clam and shattered acorn. It was heavy, hot like the sand it came from, just the blunt, thick shape of a man. It was a tool of abundance even as it opened a hull or shell. The works of food and pleasure had a single way in this stone; each motion with it was a blessing.

Somewhere up the hill, in a private midden of their own, the bones of the maker lay. I climbed the white slope, my shoes filling with sand. Above, on the uneroded midden roof, a fawn lay still, bunched on its side as if running, the small black hooves joined to the leg-bones in a white articulation repeated in the multiple curve of rib, the compact flex of spine, in the skull turned back over the shoulder, the small jaw open. It moved yet it did not. It slept, more than slept. Coyote would have scattered the bones. It must have been vulture or crow pared away all color from it, all flesh.

Where I knelt in the grass to know this, at the tip of a stem the flat, round body of the tick reached yearning toward me. I held my finger out. She clung to the grass with two feet, the other six flailing the air. I was the prey, she the predator courting me, embrace aching in her arms. In the old tale it was Coyote who heard the tick call, "Darling, darling, will you marry me?" And then the tick climbed onto his back and they walked away. Soon, the tick was the greater of the two. Soon, Coyote clung to a twig and called to travelers, "Darling, darling, will you marry me?" Things are powerful in proportion to their smallness. This one came blindly onto my finger, not now in haste, having found the broad landscape of desire, to begin the deep kiss that fulfills her life. There is one feast; all are invited. The clam, the fawn, the crow. The tick, the shaper of the stone.

But the two of us would be hungry for a time. With a buttercup leaf I brushed her gently to the ground, still thin, still stirring her eight short filaments for knowing. She found the base of a tall stem and began to climb. The sun was hot on my shoulders. I felt the cramp in my knees and stood.

To the north, my car was a grain of light. The sun had gone into mist over the long waves, a haze that rose up in plumes of gray. I sat a while by a drift log above the water. Far up past the beach, over the ridgetop a hawk was hovering low. Maybe, if I climbed there and lay in the grass, the hawk would come back along the spine of meadow, unsuspecting, and be close above my face, its wings just over my mouth. I had learned to stand up slowly now.

The slope was steep, perhaps dangerous to one in a hurry. There was no path at first, and I climbed with the speed of the blind. My feet had to know first, and balance was more than direction. Where the slope quickened, I hunched aside into a small cave. On the ceiling, swallows had made their nests of mud like beaded bags against damp rock. They were absent this season, and the nest-shapes were crooked throats. A bit of swallow-down flickered at the mud rim of one. There was a line across the cave mouth: water's blue horizon.

The open slope narrowed to a slot between spicy bushes of a small blue flower, then to a thistle-arroyo, then to poison oak in a broad band, the blond flowers clustered on it sweet, its green leaves bright with oil. Where deer had shouldered through that thicket, I turned aside, went down on all fours under a wind-flattened fir, into the aisle of its shade so dark nothing grew. One tree was braided to the next, the lowest limbs shade-killed and rotten, dropping from my lightest touch as I crawled the dark tunnel upward. In this thicket of limbs, to be straight, to aspire, was death by wind. Side-limbs fattened into trunks, until the trees joined by the rub and link of long limbs, their pitch-wounds sealed in the cambium weld.

Smaller than aphids, red bugs dusted my hand. A centipede, stone-gray, flowed over a crumpled limb, the lashes of its feet automatic as water. I crouched to watch its grace in the impossible maze of duff. It was the must of travel, the patron saint of complexity. Past this solitude, beyond the dark interlace limbs in silhouette, a meadow hummed with sunlight. Flattened on belly and knee, I flowed out from under the last limbs sweeping into the grass and rose up, vacant in the heat.

Steeper, but impossibly open and easy, the slope of grass and fern led me higher, as I switched back and forth along the quilted trails of the deer to stretch the muscles on either side. Wind hit the slope full force, gleaning away every loose crumb of soil or rock. Rain, frost-clench, seismic nudge made me a participant in scree. I balanced on a pebble, a tuft.

At the blunt brow of the ridge, I crept low to the peak; the wind was behind me, but my scent would be baffled by the updraft, and there could be deer or coyote dozing on the far falling slope. As I peered over, the wind snatched back my breath. Beyond, through the tears buffeted from my eyes, was green, all green, a variety of shape and tone to hills and cleft ravines dividing them.

I rolled back into calmer air, spread my cramped legs and arms. Would the hawk swing down now? I sprawled on my back in the deep grass and slept.

I was a shape stunned by sunlight, inert, compact, my motive exhaled and done. The sun spun through my head and chest; my four limbs lay flung out in limp vines, a dumb warmth in each leafy palm; my eyes were blank slots of sunlight. The sky hung above in a red dome. One shadow, another, crossed the dome in a flicker of blue. When I cracked open my eyelids, the air above me was thick with vultures wheeling close from the pivot of myself. I did not want to frighten them.

Be still. Know this as they do: first the eyes—by them confirm possession—then the softer flesh about the mouth, and then the rest with time as rot makes easy. I was afraid only of myself for thinking this—that I might scare them off by moving too soon, too soon to fully live out in mind the necessary accomplishment of my bones, as the fawn had lived it out, the abalone pried from certainty, the hand that made the round stone and left it.

But then of itself, my left hand twitched, and the broad forms of the vultures—nine, I counted now—rose from me, still silent as wind, and drifted off when my eyes came wider. Their calm was mine; we were patient with each other. Our etiquette was to have no fear. I was now awake.

I had never seen the world. I was alive. Down the eastern slope air was cooler, and light in a slant made every leaf testify, every stick and pebble stand bright as witness to itself. Where poison oak seemed to close my way, there was a ravine beckoning to the side. I sat on the shoulder of it, tried to know its poise. From the redwood to the bay tree, a bluebird made of song and flight one motion. There was a water-sound. The honey-colored ant explored my sleeve, slowing to a crawl at my wrist-fur. Inland, the great blue hills, the sky, loomed in a single color beyond the slot of the canyon where the ground dropped away. Tumbling from my finger, the ant set off through the grass with something white between its jaws.

On the east slope I was now in shadow, and as I drifted across a steep meadow I saw the doe, curled asleep, twenty yards below me. I was blessed to see this. I had seen the bones of the fawn lie still. I had slept. I watched over the doe. After a time, she lifted her head slowly to watch the open country below, her wide ears spread away from where I crouched in fern. The wind was toward me, and only a sound or flicker of movement could startle her. A jay cried; the ears swiveled like broad leaves. A small bird sang long and easy; the doe's ears folded back behind her slender head.

She rose up, watched a moment for any response to her rising, then stretched and stepped out onto the open slope. Beside her, another doe rose up from the shade. The two stood, slightly oblique to one another, divided as the one's ears had been, to listen. They did not look my way, only below into the brushy ravines between shoulders of clear ground.

As they began to feed, their lips had the touch of small hands reaching into bunched leaves at the ground. The head of the first swung up toward me, as the other browsed. There was a design for knowing: the round eyes sprang open to each side, the nostrils flared forward, while the ears, veined and gray, spread like moth wings for flight. Her tail flashed white, then again, pleading with a predator to lunge. I let my gaze drift slowly from that signal to a distant leaf: be native to this place, be harmless—a stump hunched gray, solid in the fern, with a wisp of lichen at the top. I had been here a century alive and twenty winters after, stripped by fire, wind-shattered, whitened in the sun. Fern spore had fallen into the rotted hollow of my throat, and moss held to the cool north side of my face, always damp, shaggy with dew. An ant crept across my rooted hand.

When my eyes, released from their trance, drifted into focus on the deer, they both were feeding. Soon, they had worked their way around the hill and were out of sight. Wind skittered through the ferns.

The bedded circles of the deer in shade were no longer warm to my hand, but the grass lay flat. Here, the morning sun would strike, the afternoon be cool; rising air all day would bring living scents from below, and uphill was nothing but open ground. This place was safe, for no one of this country crossed open ground in daylight. I sat a while myself there, looking over the world; the sun was low, and this slope was all bright shade. Bay trees in the ravine passed the wind one to another. The moon, in half, hung straight above. With the deer, it was time for me to move away into the evening. As I walked I began to break off the unraveled brush of the fern. I would need a bed somewhere. The deer was gone; I would not disturb them with my noise.

At the peak of the ridge again, under a fir I spread my armload of fern, then leaned branches from a windfall against each other to make a roof. Crooked sticks were best for this. They were strong two ways at once. In the thin grass at the hilltop was a bronze survey-marker, a ring of numbers and words too dark to read. Four fallen fenceposts and a tangled strand of wire. I sat down. The sun had gone but the sky was bright. I would be warm for a time; a mosquito came singing.

With the first stars came the light-points of eight fishing boats far below on the flat Pacific. Some were anchored still; others wandered across the darkness. There in the sky above rambled the round constellation of the tick, its eight arms glimmering; there the starlight cluster of the fawn's bones. There among stars the vacant sack of the swallow's nest. There the alert triangle of the deer's head, listening. Slowly, the deer's face slid to the horizon; it became a curve, a seal diving without a word. A star fell burning across the west. The wind began to touch me with cold.

I turned toward my shelter of branches. Far to the east, too far for sound, above the distant light of a farm a human flare burned sudden in the sky, scattering out in fragments as it flashed and went dark. In both worlds, a disintegration by fire. Because I was awake with hunger and vulnerable with cold, I was afraid.

My body had four sides. The side toward earth was warm. I lay on my back this time in the seventh turning. The crushed fern was soft, the wind cold. Moon was moving west, toward water, where it would make a path. Later, maybe, there would be an owl calling.

If I had rounded a stone with my hands I would hold it now. The stone would not be mine, but its shape would belong in my hands. The stone would be cold as I was—not quite cold enough to shake. I was still; it was the tree that moved. An owl did call. I was not shaking yet. I had four sides, and one was warm. If I began to shake, I would turn part way. The seasons pass to keep the Earth alive. The owl was calling for this. I was cold now. Even the tree was still.

Something touched the earth—I felt it. Down the slope two deer were feeding; the darker clusters of their bodies moved against moonlit grass. I lay back. The sky. The tree. The owl calling. Something comes to one alone, not a song like honey is sweet. A song like water. I was cold and had not eaten; this was a part of it. How does the tree stand, even after it has died? We both lived. The moon was there; a moth flew toward it. The owl made a sound. A song is given in the place one lives. Even the tick, wordless with desire, knew this. The tree has a way, a secret way. Sometimes another may hear it. The seal dives to find out. I was cold; I was spared the fullness of it, knowing then my own. Something came to me shapeless. Then it had a shape and I belonged.

When I had turned twenty-eight times, the fern grew thin and the darkness softened. These ways are nocturnal: the full blossoming of stars; a pilgrim's true solitude. As light came on, a clarity retreated from the world. A small bird was telling what it knew.

By the time I had picked my way downslope for an hour, the sun came to me and I was warm again, so filled with waking I felt no hunger. When I would eat, sometime soon, the precision to my witness of the earth would dwindle, as the tones of darkness dwindle at first light and are hard to remember. I lived on hunger for the time, and all forms lived with me—dew on the bay leaf swiveling from its twig, the vines of position oak braided by light on a trunk of fir.

I came to a stream, then to the road. I saw the car at a great distance, a white glint of modern time. Beyond it, the waves came silently. I perched on a boulder broken from the road-cut. Soon I would balance on one foot beside the car and shed my clothes—the ones with poison oak brushed into them—and stand naked a moment. I would be cold. Then I would dress and it would go away.

Rain was driving in toward land, but where I stood was still. If this were a story, no rainbow could hang clean and various over the road; but this was my life, and the arc of the storm was there.

"Moments and Journeys"

John Haines (1924–)

In "Moments and Journeys," John Haines remarks that the Yuma Indians who once inhabited the shores of the Colorado River were reported to have "moved without effort from waking into dreaming life; life and dream were bound together. And in this must be a kind of radiance, a very old and deep assurance that life has continuity and meaning, that things are somehow in place. It is the journey resolved into one endless present."

Known primarily as a poet, Haines, who now lives in Fairbanks, has been a sculptor as well, and lived from 1954 to 1969 as a homesteader in Alaska; few of us have existed so closely within the elemental forces as he, and fewer yet have had the ability or desire to report upon what they found in their solitude among vistas of snow, ice, and ocean waters. "When life is simplified," Haines says, no doubt basing such a generalization on his own experiences, "its essence becomes clearer, and we know our lives as part of some ancient human activity in a time measured not by clocks and calendars but by the turning of a great wheel, the positions of which are not wage-hours, nor days and weeks, but immense stations called Spring, Summer, Autumn, and Winter." During the cycles of these stations, we make our individual forays, our journeys. One who lives not within the multitudes but within nature gains the perspective to see the importance of life, human and animal and vegetable; even the perspective provided by a modest hill in Scotland enabled the young John Muir to ask the question—Haines here quotes Muir's own words—"Why, seen from a distance, do the casual journeys of men and women, perhaps going on some trivial errand, take on the appearance of a pilgrimage? I can only explain it by some deep archetypal image in our minds of which we become conscious only at the rare moments when we realize that our own life is a journey."

The essay holds our interest not for its narrative power but for its description of simple and highly evocative moments—mainly, images of individuals within a natural environment—that are held in Haines' memory; it ends with an excursion that is charged with the past, with representations of an older way of life. Though Haines doesn't directly say so, it is as if the three participants of this journey have been granted an intimation—at least a hint—of what it would mean to live in the "endless present"; the experience, in any event, makes them "strangely happy."

The movement of things on this earth has always impressed me. There is a reassuring vitality in the annual rise of a river, in the return of the Arctic sun, in the poleward flight of spring migrations, in the seasonal trek of nomadic peoples. A passage from Edwin Muir's autobiography speaks to me of its significance.

I remember . . . while we were walking one day on the Mönchsberg—a smaller hill on the opposite side of the river—looking down on a green plain that stretched away to the foothills, and watching in the distance people moving along the tiny roads. Why do such things seem enormously important to us? Why, seen from a distance, do the casual journeys of men and women, perhaps going on some trivial errand, take on the appearance of a pilgrimage? I can only explain it by some deep archetypal image in our minds of which we become conscious only at the rare moments when we realize that our own life is a journey.

[Edwin Muir, *An Autobiography* (Sommers, Conn.: Seabury, 1968), p. 217.]

This seems to me like a good place to begin, not only for its essential truth, but because it awakens in me a whole train of images—images of the journey as I have come to understand it, moments and stages in existence. Many of these go back to the years I lived on my homestead in Alaska. That life itself, part of the soil and weather of the place, seemed to have about it much of the time an aura of deep and lasting significance. I wasn't always aware of this, of course. There were many things to be struggled with from day to day, chores of one sort or another—cabins to be built, crops to be looked after, meat to kill, and wood to cut—all of which took a kind of passionate attention. But often when I was able to pause and look up from what I was doing, I caught brief glimpses of a life much older than mine.

Some of these images stand out with great force from the continual coming and going of which they were part—Fred Campbell, the old hunter and miner I had come to know, that lean, brown man of patches and strange fits. He and I and my first wife, Peg, with seven dogs—five of them carrying packs—all went over Buckeye Dome one day in the late summer of 1954. It was a clear, hot day in mid-August, the whole troop of us strung out on the trail. Campbell and his best dog, a yellow bitch named Granny, were in the lead. We were in a hurry, or seemed to be, the dogs pulling us on, straining at their leashes for the first two or three miles, and then, turned loose, just panting along, anxious not to be left behind. We stopped only briefly that morning, to adjust a dog pack and to catch our wind. Out of the close timber with its hot shadows and swarms of mosquitoes, we came into the open sunlight of the dome. The grass and low shrubs on the treeless slopes moved gently in the warm air that came from somewhere south, out of the Gulf of Alaska.

At midday we halted near the top of the dome to look for water among the rocks and to pick blueberries. The dogs, with their packs removed, lay down in the heat, snapping at flies. Buckeye Dome was the high place nearest to home, though it was nearly seven miles by trail from Richardson. It wasn't very high, either—only 3,000 feet—but it rose clear of the surrounding hills. From its summit you could see in any direction, as far west as Fairbanks when the air was clear enough. We saw other high places, landmarks in the distance, pointed out to us and named by Campbell: Banner Dome, Cockscomb, Bull Dome, and others I've forgotten. In the southeast, a towering dust cloud rose from the Delta River. Campbell talked to us of his trails and camps, of years made of such journeys as ours, an entire history told around the figure of one man. We were new to the North and eager to learn all we could. We listened, sucking blueberries from a tin cup.

And then we were on the move again. I can see Campbell in faded jeans and red felt hat, bending over one of the dogs as he tightened a strap, swearing and saying something about the weather, the distance, and himself getting too old to make such a trip. We went off down the steep north slope of the dome in a great rush, through miles of windfalls, following that twisting, root-grown trail of his. Late in the evening, wading the shallows of a small creek, we came tired and bitten to his small cabin on the shore of a lake he had named for himself.

That range of images is linked with another at a later time. By then I had my own team, and with our four dogs we were bound uphill one afternoon in the cool September sunlight to pick cranberries on the long ridge overlooking Redmond Creek. The tall, yellow grass on the partly cleared ridge bent over in the wind that came easily from the west. I walked behind, and I could see, partly hidden by the grass, the figures of the others as they rounded the shoulder of a little hill and stopped to look back toward me. The single human figure there in the sunlight under moving clouds, the dogs with their fur slightly ruffled, seemed the embodiment of an old story.

And somewhere in the great expanse of time that made life in the wilderness so open and unending, other seasons were stations on the journey. Coming across the Tanana River on the midwinter ice, we had three dogs in harness and one young female running loose beside us. We had been three days visiting a neighbor, a trapper living on the far side of the river, and were returning home. Halfway across the river we stopped to rest; the sled was heavy, the dogs were tired and lay down on the ice.

Standing there, leaning on the back of the sled, I knew a vague sense of remoteness and peril. The river ice always seemed a little dangerous, even when it was thick and solid. There were open stretches of clear, blue water, and sometimes large, deep cracks in the ice where the river could be heard running deep and steady. We were heading downriver into a cloudy December evening. Wind came across the ice, pushing a little dry snow, and no other sound—only the vast presence of snow and ice, scattered islands, and the dark crest of Richardson Hill in the distance.

To live by a large river is to be kept in the heart of things. We become involved in its life, the heavy sound of it in the summer as it wears away silt and gravel from its cutbanks, pushing them into sandbars that will be islands in another far off year. Trees are forever tilting over the water, to fall and be washed away, to lodge in a drift pile somewhere downstream. The heavy gray water drags at the roots of willows, spruce, and cotton-woods; sometimes it brings up the trunk of a tree buried in sand a thousand years before, or farther back than that, in the age of ice. The log comes loose from the fine sand, heavy and dripping, still bearing the tunnel marks made by the long dead insects. Salmon come in midsummer, then whitefish, and salmon again in the fall; they are caught in our nets and carried away to be smoked and eaten, to be dried for winter feed. Summer wears away into fall; the sound of the river changes. The water clears and slowly drops; pan ice forms in the eddies. One morning in early winter we wake to a great and sudden silence: the river is frozen.

We stood alone there on the ice that day, two people, four dogs, and a loaded sled, and nothing before us but land and water into Asia. It was time to move on again. I spoke to the dogs and gave the sled a push.

Other days. On a hard-packed trail home from Cabin Creek, I halted the dogs part way up a long hill in scattered spruce. It was a clear evening, not far below zero. Ahead of us, over an open ridge, a full moon stood clear of the land, enormous and yellow in the deep blue of the Arctic evening. I recalled how Billy Melvin, an old miner from the early days at Richardson, had once described to me a moonrise he had seen, a full moon coming up ahead of him on the trail, "big as a rain barrel." And it was very much like that—an enormous and rusty rain barrel into which I looked, and the far end of the barrel was open. I stood there, thinking it might be possible to go on forever into that snow and yellow light, with no sound but my own breathing, the padding of the dog's feet, and the occasional squeak of the sled runners. The moon whitened and grew smaller; twilight deepened, and we went on to the top of the hill.

What does it take to make a journey? A place to start from, something to leave behind. A road, a trail, or a river. Companions, and something like a destination: a camp, an inn, or another shore. We might imagine a journey with no destination, nothing but the act of going, and with never an arrival. But I think we would always hope to find *something* or *someone,* however unexpected and unprepared for. Seen from a distance or taken part in, all journeys may be the same, and we arrive exactly where we are.

One late summer afternoon, near the road to Denali Park, I watched the figures of three people slowly climb the slope of a mountain in the northeast. The upper part of the mountain was bare of trees, and the small alpine plants there were already red and gold from the early frost. Sunlight came through broken rain clouds and lit up the slope and its three moving figures. They were so far away that I could not tell if they were men or women, but the red jacket worn by one of them stood out brightly in the sun. They climbed higher and higher, bound for a ridge where some large rocks broke through the thin soil. A shadow kept pace with them, slowly darkening the slope below them, as the sun sank behind another mountain in the southwest. I wondered where they were going—perhaps to hunt mountain sheep—or they were climbing to a berry patch they knew. It was late in the day; they would not get back by dark. I watched them as if they were figures in a dream, who bore with them the destiny of the race. They stopped to rest for a while near the skyline, but were soon out of sight beyond the ridge. Sunlight stayed briefly on the high rock summit, and then a rain cloud moved in and hid the mountaintop.

When life is simplified, its essence becomes clearer, and we know our lives as part of some ancient human activity in a time measured not by clocks and calendars but by the turning of a great wheel, the positions of which are not wage-hours, nor days and weeks, but immense stations called Spring, Summer, Autumn, and Winter. I suppose it will seem too obvious to say that this sense of things will be far less apparent to people closed off in the routine of a modern city. I think many people must now and then be aware of such moments as I have described, but do not remember them, or attach no special significance to them. They are images that pass quickly from view because there is no place for them in our lives. We are swept along by events we cannot link together in a significant pattern, like a flood of refugees pushed on by the news of a remote disaster. The rush of conflicting impressions keeps away stillness, and it is in stillness that the images arise, as they will, fluently and naturally, when there is nothing to prevent them.

There is the dream journey and the actual life. The two seem to touch now and then, and perhaps when men lived less complicated and distracted lives the two were not separate at all, but continually one thing. I have read somewhere that this was once true for the Yuma Indians who lived along the Colorado River. They dreamed at will, and moved without effort from waking into dreaming life; life and dream were bound together.

And in this must be a kind of radiance, a very old and deep assurance that life has continuity and meaning, that things are somehow in place. It is the journey resolved into one endless present.

And the material is all around us. I retain strong images from treks with my stepchildren: of a night seven years ago when we camped on a mountaintop, a night lighted by snow patches and sparks from a windy fire going on. Sleeping on the frozen ground, we heard the sound of an owl from the cold, bare oak trees above us. And there was a summer evening I spent with a small class of schoolchildren near Painted Rock in central California. We had come to learn about Indians. The voices of the children carried over the burned fields under the red glare of that sky, and the rock gave back heat in the dusk like an immense oven. There are ships and trains that pull away, planes that fly into the night; or the single figure of a man crossing an otherwise empty lot. If such moments are not as easily come by, as clear and as resonant as they once were in the wilderness, it may be because they are not so clearly linked to the life that surrounds them and of which they are part. They are present nonetheless, available to imagination, and of the same character.

One December day a few years ago, while on vacation in California, I went with my daughter and a friend to a place called Pool Rock. We drove for a long time over a mountain road, through meadows touched by the first green of the winter rains, and saw few fences or other signs of people. Leaving our car in a small campground at the end of the road, we hiked four miles up a series of canyons and narrow gorges. We lost our way several times but always found it again. A large covey of quail flew up from the chaparral on a slope above us; the tracks of deer and bobcat showed now and then in the sand under our feet. An extraordinary number of coyote droppings scattered along the trail attracted our attention. I poked one of them with a stick, saw that it contained much rabbit fur and bits of bone. There were patches of ice in the streambed, and a few leaves still yellow on the sycamores.

We came to the rock in mid-afternoon, a great sandstone pile rising out of the foothills like a sanctuary or a shrine to which one comes yearly on a pilgrimage. There are places that take on symbolic value to an individual or a tribe, "soul-resting places," a friend of mine has called them. Pool Rock has become that to me, symbolic of that hidden, original life we have done so much to destroy.

We spent an hour or two exploring the rock, a wind and rain-scoured honeycomb stained yellow and rose by a mineral in the sand. Here groups of the Chumash Indians used to come, in that time of year when water could be found in the canyons. They may have come to gather certain foods in season, or to take part in magic rites whose origin and significance are no longer understood. In a small cave at the base of the rock, the stylized figures of headless reptiles, insects, and strange birdmen are painted on the smoke-blackened walls and ceiling. These and some bear paw impressions gouged in the rock, and a few rock mortars used for grinding seeds, are all that is left of a once-flourishing people.

We climbed to the summit of the rock, using the worn footholds made long ago by the Chumash. We drank water from the pool that gave the rock its name, and ate our lunch, sitting quietly in the cool sunlight. And then the wind came up, whipping our lunchbag over the edge of the rock; a storm was moving in from the coast. We left the rock by the way we had come, and hiked down the gorge in the windy, leaf-blown twilight. In the dark, just before the rain, we came to the campground, laughing, speaking of the things we had seen, and strangely happy.

"On Waste Lonely Places"

John Landretti (1958–)

"On Waste Lonely Places" gives a sharp focus to areas of the landscape that normally are given no value by our past experiences or our expectations. Americans, John Landretti says, tend to be inattentive to their surroundings, reserving their awe—or their expectations of awe—for the grand natural vistas of the national parks in the West. Such inattentiveness, of course, is not limited to Americans; the English Romantic poets, for example, were aware that habitude, familiarity with a landscape, dulls the fresh responses to nature that we feel in childhood. Still, Americans have a particular cultural problem, for, as Landretti says, we "live in a country so lathered by dreams" that anticipation—desire—can negate what is currently everywhere about us. (The discontent so prevalent in the final years of this century may be a consequence of the fact that the ingrained dreaming is accompanied by a sometimes bitter awareness of the likely impossibility of its attainment.) Crowded together at "a scenic turnoff at the Great Divide," Americans on vacation in their Winnebagos gaze at the glaciers that are their goal but "remain as spiritually distanced as they were the day they left home."

How can we overcome expectation—the promise of tomorrow—enough to gain a "keener seeing," and respond with awe to our present habitat? Choose to spend the night, as a hitchhiker must often of necessity do, at any of the waste places that are surrounded by highway cloverleafs or that are simply a part of the detritus at the edges of urban sprawl—choose any such place ignored for its apparent spiritual barrenness, for its separation from promise and memory, and permit it to become "a place of its own knowing." Landretti evokes the specialness of such waste areas through specific description; in "the quiet of ditch and litter and grass and self," he remarks, "you begin to see your place in a different way, from the ground up."

The essay opens with a present experience—the adult Landretti is sitting on something as prosaic as a toilet seat in his downtown second-story apartment, looking out at the "unextraordinary horizon of roots, wires and trees." Using memory, he reconstructs pertinent moments of his childhood before turning to his experiences as a hitchhiker, in the period following his college graduation. Here he became acquainted with those waste places—"islands," he calls them—that in memory still serve to remind him of a reality impervious to habit and expectation, an insight permitting him to acknowledge how extraordinary the ordinary always is.

I have gone into the waste lonely places
Behind the eye; the lost acres at the edge of smoky cities.

—Theodore Roethke

I live in an old neighborhood near a small downtown, just beyond the reach of the last parking meters. Any of the houses here would look stately and haunted perched on a hill somewhere, but as it is they're all serried together down the long city blocks: most gables and bay windows look out on the bay windows and gables of one's immediate neighbor. I've given up a country view for convenience; the university I attend is just a half mile away—and five hundred feet up—at rest on a stack of sea bottoms some three hundred and fifty million years old. From that height the view affords a wilderness of hanging valleys and dramatic clouds that typify the Finger Lakes region of central New York. But at my home in the lowlands, where I occupy a second story flat, I must content myself with a more modest vista: that meager scrap of landscape as seen from a small window in the back bathroom. You work with what you've got. Using the toilet as a chair I'll occasionally ponder that unextraordinary horizon of roofs, wires and trees. The best viewing occurs at dusk, especially after a rain, when the sky is red and newly washed, when the clouds reflect on the wet glass of old garages and in the watery sheen of gardens.

Years passed by before I realized that the quality of awe I sometimes felt among grandeur (the peaks of mountains, say) was really no different from the awe available to me in places as prosaic as the view from a bathroom window. It all seems to be a matter of keener seeing, of opening oneself to a degree of perception that Rilke suggests is not simply an aesthetic consideration, but an issue of personal responsibility: "All this was mission./But could you accomplish it? Weren't you always distracted by expectation, as if every event announced a beloved?"

I certainly know that hindsight marks *me* as distracted, a person so given to introspection that I've slid through countless days announcing beloveds left and right. To be sure, nobody could possibly devote all attention to every thing encountered—we would go mad—but it could be argued, successfully, I think, that as a culture we Americans, most of us, trend too far in the other direction, toward inattention, and if this is taken to be true we might do well to reconnoiter our aesthetic prejudices, especially those that shape our definitions of what we call "ugly" and even more so, "mundane."

As a kid I believed the only sights that deserved my undivided attention, simply because they were places, were those bastions of grandeur, our national parks. A national park was the high art of topography. Its ascribed purpose was to inspire, the way we're told that a symphony is supposed to awe and edify. This I learned from the adults that populated my childhood, well-meaning small town folks who once or twice a year approached national parks the way they might attend a big-city concert: dressed for the occasion, they bought tickets and arrived with programs and an air of reverent uncertainty. Meanwhile the rest of their world, all those rural and urban scrapscapes that circumfused their days, received for the balance of the year that glazy attention generally applied to music at supermarkets. In those years of growing up, at the end of every spring, many of the families in my old neighborhood loaded their cars and headed west. Yosemite, Death Valley, Yellowstone—all through the summer and until the leaves dropped, they rolled out of the suburbs toward the geysers, the mesas and peaks. During this collective absence I ran a profitable traffic in yard work; on those long afternoons of high summer I'd watch my reflection pacing a lawn mower in their vacant windows, and I'd wonder about the world they were bound for. What were they seeing and feeling in the presence of those topographical icons? In our kitchen my mother kept a nature calendar; occasionally I'd touch the picture (a split rail fence before a mountain, a whale breaching at dusk) as if those images alone could charge my blood with a moment of "real" living.

When the families returned, their cars were always dusty, the windshields plastered with stickers. Though the kids had a lot to say, I no longer recall their stories. What stays in my mind is the parents, how so many of those good people returned spent of language, how wearily they unpacked their luggage. Far from revitalized, they shuffled with the slump-backed, long-throated look of pilgrims returning from exile. While the wife implored after the kids, the husband would take me aside and press some cash into my hand—often with an appreciative, if perfunctory, compliment, one that rarely followed any sort of inspection.

How was the trip, I'd say. Some husbands murmured about the expense, while others said "Fine." A few winked and told me to stay single. Most simply rubbed their faces and said they were glad to be back.

When I finished college I went west myself, finally passing through those majestic places encapsulated on the bumpers of my neighbors' station wagons. I travelled as a hitchhiker, musing the whole way; headed nowhere special, I was pacing on a continental scale. At first I made a point to tramp through every national park in my path. A time or two I got into back country, but most often I simply glimpsed the grandeur from the edge of a park road, or the lip of a scenic overlook. Usually I shared the view with a host of other tourists, and I recall that of the more congested overlooks, as time passed and more people arrived, these crowds always seemed to enact a common dynamic: they became a sort of microcosm, one that in a curious way acted out the whole of our moiled and imploring immigrant history.

Imagine a scenic turnoff at the Great Divide. Beyond the pay binoculars the view is magnificent, striated with glaciers and peppered with hawks. Say it's July Fourth, the dawn's early light. For a while the turnoff is unoccupied, save for a few orbiting flies and perhaps a marmot at rest on the base of its elongated shadow. Then a Winnebago sails in with flapping flags. These new arrivals dock near the edge and gape from stickered windows, bringing to this solitary view a sense of wonder and privilege. Then others begin to arrive; they park their RV's and stake places along the stone fence. Kids eye one another from the safety of parental legs. Animals mull in the dust and people walk around with pop cans and cigars. Still more arrive, and eventually the little overlook becomes as crowded as a steerage deck drawing up to Ellis Island. A line of people flute the line of the fence, and as they vie for a private audience, there grows among them a sense of burgeoning annoyance and polite restraint. As the group continues to swell, so does the general uneasiness. The old timers feel entitled to the spot they had claimed; the newcomers feel the pie ought to be shared. The very latest arrivals sense this, as much as they note the lack of space, and grimly press on.

The worst aspect of this crowding is not the hostility or desperation, but the collective embarrassment. It's present in the flinching eye contact, in the contrast between the bright cheery clothes and that tight-lipped bumping around with cameras. Crowded as they are, they understand that something is amiss, that though they are physically close to the object of their journey, they remain as spiritually distanced as they were the day they left home. Despite all the gaping, the glaciers retain their cool and fragrant secrets and the hawks circle away out of sight. From high above, those turnoffs must be quite a view: each a little bump off a road where a crowd of tiny hands flail like cilia at time immemorial. It was during moments like these that I began to understand the why of that devitalized look which had marred the faces of so many of my childhood neighbors just back from grandeur.

As interactive an enterprise as hitchhiking can be, it is also a study in solitude. Often it is life on a desert island. Check out the guard rails near Gillette Wyoming, Altoona Pennsylvania, El Paso Texas and you will find home states scratched into the steel; you will see the hours tallied and crossed out, the names of lovers cut in with nubs of shale. This is the archaeology of the stranded. Perhaps it's more accurate to say that as the hitchhiker's day passes, his or her life is lived out on a string of desert islands—an archipelago of crossroads and on-ramps. It was this solitary aspect of hitchhiking, more than anything, that led me to reconsider the way I measured the worth of a place.

During all that "island hopping," with hours and sometimes days to kill in a single spot, I found myself forced to acknowledge, and later to admire, that meager terrain upon which I was so repeatedly stranded. I refer to those places we pass every day: our interstate weed beds and chemical sloughs; the cinder narrows of our commuter tracks; the hard yellow fields around our tank farms; the industrial fairways and caged waterfalls of power plants; our pits of kudzu and piss elm; our dump-edge wallows with stumps and tires nested in ponds of green oatmeal. These are our other parks, our marginalized and unnoticed acres, grandeur's doppelganger, with a doppelganger's disturbing wisdom and equivocal hospitality.

The places I came to know best were the ones in which I found myself at dusk. I'd have travelled all night if I'd been assured safe passage, but it was too violent and unreliable a time, and so I would head for the margins, throw my hat to the ground and call it home. When I began to take these places into account, when I acknowledged that every such place was not mere background music between topographical symphonies, but that any patch of ground was special all to itself and worthy of consideration—then a curious reciprocation occurred: these places began to notice me.

What occurs is a kind of situational coalescence. As the taillights of that last ride grow small and wink out, the horizon gathers itself to your singular perspective. There is no grandeur to bait expectation, no promise to invite distraction, only the quiet of ditch and litter and grass and self; without preconceptions you begin to see your place in a different way, from the ground up. You warm to how consummate this place is in its becoming: the perfect pattern of stones along the shoulder; the fast food wrappers, their logos clinging just so to the sage; there at long rest in the shadows, that old trilobite of the highway, the fallen muffler. And so you become consummate yourself; instead of a face lost in an embarrassed crowd, you become unique and necessary to that moment, your perspective creating, for better or worse, this one place in the world. It is a time to whistle.

I recall a night in Ohio spent in the loop of a cloverleaf. The grass was tall and as I lay on my back, it rose up around me and created an intimacy of panicles and thistles that in their complete stillness seemed to touch against the stars. Meanwhile the trucks moaned around me, each executing in that curve of sound a profound change of course, from dead south to due east.

That circle of earth is named somewhere on a map; like all our land it is endowed with coordinates. Yet no traveler would have cause to set a course for such a place, and so its representation gathers dust somewhere—in a library perhaps, or among some courthouse archive—of interest only to civil engineers and road crews. Offering your attention to a waste place is like finding a book in the library, a book nobody reads. Or perhaps a book harboring a single due date, one purple smudge thirty years old. And there it is in your hand by the effortless design of coincidence. You look over its pages and before you is effort and presence; whether the contents have appeal is another matter, but the book does exist and is open before you, full of its telling. And so it is with these shelves and sheaves of world that daily surround us: every rock, blade, and bottle, every leaf, an invitation to an understanding.

Keep in mind, lolling in a waste place will perplex and even disturb those who catch you at it. Once some time ago I was travelling back east when dusk came and I made camp just outside a large city, near the end of a runway. I sat in the sooty, blown down grass and watched the jets rush through the fields and lift away. Behind me was a road and beyond that the backwash of an industrial park. In the distance, lights strobed on a smokestack and powerline scaffolds marshalled along an oily black slough. I left my camp to wander along the slough. I counted box turtles, submerged appliances, watched the tiny shadow of a jet slide across the polished sludge. Meanwhile the cars shot by, one after the other, every driver staring at me, askance. What in God's name, they seemed to wonder, was that man doing out there without a vehicle? Some bowed toward the other land, giving me plenty of room. It was a sobering observation, to see that there are places in our cities so completely dismissed of our consideration that when one of us finally stops to poke around, the spectacle invites puzzlement and even alarm.

In my earlier days as a hitchhiker, when I was still inclined to grumble while stranded on my desert islands, I found myself, one evening, waylaid on a patch of Nebraska hardpan. There were train tracks along the road, and I remember how faraway and straight they went. Stuck for four hours, I was forced finally to give up any hope of a night camped in full view of the Rockies. Wearily, I climbed the bank and tossed my hat on the ground. It was a five star waste place, with beer cans at rest in the ditch and old cattails crippled against the sky. I chewed on some wheat bread and morosely watched as hundreds of small birds gathered on the powerlines across the road. After dusk I crawled into my tent to wait out the night.

Some time later, when I was asleep, my tent brightened, became a sort of nylon membrane shaking with light. I sat up, bolt straight, still half in a dream. The ground was trembling along my legs. There was an explosion and the light vanished. Another explosion, then a third. Following this came a bombardment of noise so loud and relentless that in my fright I believed the noise alone would kill me. It went on for ten minutes, a flash flood of axles and bed springs slamming down an iron coulee.

When it quieted I crawled from my tent, bewildered. I watched the caboose retreating, a speedy clickety-clack with a red light low at the terminus. That freighter must have been doing eighty. I went the five feet over to the tracks and grasped the rail still ringing and warm. From far away came a mournful whistle, then the child's play of a passing semi. A quarter moon was just up, lifting its hooks through those powerlines of sleeping birds. This is what I am it all seemed to say; now let's review.

I was not quick to go back to sleep. Instead I lowered myself onto the edge of that humming rail and stared a while at the moon in the powerlines.

Here was not the grandeur of glaciers and massifs. But neither was it void space, a mere window blur from which to bounce a cigarette. It was *somewhere*, a place full of its own knowing, and it had shaken me to the core. I sat quietly for a long while, feeling the incredible reach of silence around me. It is a sobering thing, and strange, to live in a country so lathered with dreams and to find yourself in a place where nothing, absolutely nothing, is promised. I drew a breath and then for a long while looked out on all the different darknesses. By noon the next day I was among the mountains, among the aspens and snow and alpine light; all that grandeur seen from a new perspective, seen walking as if walking anywhere, dazzling in its own place in the world.

from *The Crossing Fee*

Esther Warner (1910–)

Long ago, in response to something I had written, Esther Warner sent me a copy of *The Crossing Fee,* an autobiographical account of her experiences in Liberia. It happened to arrive on the day that Robert Kennedy was assassinated; that night, unable to sleep, I read every word in Warner's book, and at dawn wrote her a note of gratitude for a gift that had helped me through those hours of darkness. I liked it for the simple clarity of its prose, for the modesty of its author, for its awareness of the preciousness of memory (not only to her but to the Mano tribesmen with whom she had lived), and for its appreciation of an African way of life that gives a spiritual meaning to daily experience. In rereading that book today, I realize that its appeal to me then must also have come from its elegiac quality (for it celebrates a culture in the process of vanishing) and from the reversal enacted in my own mind of the metaphor underlying such a well-known story as Conrad's "Heart of Darkness": in *The Crossing Fee,* Warner provided me an African light during a period of assassinations of major American figures that showed the extent of darkness in our "civilized" country.

The title is itself a metaphor: the "crossing fee" is a chicken sacrificed on the grave of one whose "unseen and unseeable spirit" is carried across the river by a ferryman as part of a mourning ritual enabling that spirit to join the spirits of all others of the community who have died; the chicken is given to the ferryman for his necessary service. *The Crossing Fee* is divided into two sections: the first, "Discovery," describes Warner's experiences on the five-day journey that brought her to a remote Mano village to attend the funeral of its chief, Old One, and it also is a narrative of her life in that village for some months afterward; the second, "Return," describes what she found upon her return to the village, this time with her husband, twenty years later. Central to both sections is Konsuo, an English-speaking Mano who became Warner's close friend during her first visit; by the time of her return, he has become chief of the village.

In the chapter from "Return" that I have chosen, "This Old and Thingless World," Warner and her husband are taken by Konsuo to his village, which he has had moved to a new location. They are introduced to his wife, Fanta, who, twenty years earlier, he had been planning to marry. Nyama, one of their daughters, has recently come back to the village, having graduated from high school; as we know from a previous chapter, she wishes to continue her educa-tion in college, so that she may become a nurse. Konsuo, who long ago received her "bride price" from a village farmer, thinks it is time she married, to give him grandchildren before his death. Of the others mentioned in this chapter, Yoda is perhaps the most important, for Warner has ties with him that go back to his childhood: she bandaged the sores of his leprosy then, and now Western medicine has stopped further ravages of his disease. (One of the virtues of the autobiography is its awareness of the benefits—for Nyama, for Yoda—of the same cultural and technological changes that are bringing devastation to the former way of life, and are turning Konsuo's village into a kind of "museum.")

In "This Old and Thingless World," the illiterate Konsuo defends his refusal to attend literacy classes for adults by saying to Warner, "I got too plenty things, it be my work to remember, Ma," and in support of his view he adds an objection to reading and writing that is similar to the one that Plato ascribes to Socrates in the Phaedrus: "When a person writes his thinks in a book," Konsuo tells her, "it breaks the remembers." This chapter is intimately concerned with the need for remembering. The "thinking stone" that Konsuo gives Warner so that she will remember his objection to the Christian God, whatever the good brought him by that God, affords her a memento for always recalling the spiritual values that for the Mano underlie materiality and connect them to the past and their natural environment.

As we walked with Konsuo to his town, the smart slap of his sandals on the path kept us up to pace. We crossed a little stream where the women beat their clothing on the rocks and hang it on the bushes to dry. The bushes were abloom with yards of bright cloth.

"More cloth past the old days, Ma." He paused so we could admire the sight. I was remembering the time we could not find even one additional little rag to dip in Bidu's dye pot. I asked Konsuo whether the women still make their laundry soap out of palm oil and leached wood ashes.

"Same way, Ma. Only thing, they like sweet soap from the store for take-bath."

Konsuo said that the cloth had come from the coffee they had marketed. They had planted coffee several years ago for the government (to pay taxes), but after the last crop was sold enough money was left over to buy a new *lappa* and headcloth for every woman in the village.

As the path wound up the hill to the town, it became an aisle between wild bushes. I wondered whether this might be Konsuo's snake preserve. We were soon out of the bushes and at the entrance to the town. On our right, sheep and goats were penned in a compound of their own by a stick fence. The goats and sheep were mottled creatures and difficult to distinguish except for their tails. The tail of a sheep droops. A goat wears his tail as though he is ready at any moment to fly Satan's own flag from the mast on his rear. The goats are fenced, not because I had advocated it two decades earlier, but because the people now have clothing which they do not wish to have eaten. Konsuo pointed to the fence and giggled. He, too, was remembering my feud with the nanny I tried to milk for my baby chimpanzees.

"No leopards come for the goats, Ma. Same like you said, first time." This was a generous concession on his part. I thought I ought to make one of my own.

"I suppose there are not so many leopards, now, Konsuo."

"True, Ma. Too plenty guns live here now. Soon-time, all leopards can finish."

We had to detour around clusters of ducks who refused to budge from the path. There were many chickens, too, but there were scratching in the dirt, looking for spilled grains of rice, pecking at fallen avocado fruit. Before us we saw a pleasant place of about twenty thatched huts, all of them facing an open-sided palaver house. When I complimented Konsuo on the neatness of his village, he said that every bit of earth is swept every morning unless rain is pouring down. The tracks of the women's brooms were visible in the soft earth. Tribesmen tend to judge one another by the way they maintain the houses they have built. Scraggly thatch and leaky roofs or any litter on the ground make a village a "bad place without take-care" and is a disgrace to everyone living there.

Liberian chicken coops are built into the clay foundations of the huts. Each one is a little bulge in the wall large enough for one hen, and it has a door which may be closed. Konsuo lifted one of the doors to show me a hen setting on eggs. The evil-eyed old biddy jabbed her beak toward his hand, and he barely evaded her thrust. Konsuo grimaced toward the door which he quickly closed. "Old, mad woman chicken! She thinks she will get chicken babies. Hah! She will get duck babies. Some time the stupid, old woman chicken will not know what thing she has got until her *pickin* make a walk to the waterside." Konsuo was jerking his neck hen-fashion as he spoke. "Well, Ma, it is more past [other things besides] chickens that don't know what thing their young can do."

Obviously, he was thinking that an eighteen-year-old girl who wanted additional schooling more than she wanted a husband and babies was as far outside the natural order of things as a chickenlike ball of fuzz which suddenly takes to the water and swims.

As I entered Konsuo's small chiefdom with him, I was thrilled in every nerve to be standing once again in what seemed an almost perfect tiny town. One has the knowledge that rural village life is doomed by change, that it is only a matter of time until places like this will be a thing of the past. It seemed to me like a museum piece, something already under a roof where tourists may see it, much as they may see an Indian village, complete with all the utensils once used in daily life, in a museum in Santa Fe. A layer of fog above our heads shut off the blue sky as effectively as a flat roof. Every house in the village glistened with fresh thatch, every stick of cooking wood was corded under the overhanging eaves, and every duck was as quiet as a painted decoy. A number of women were gathered in the palaver house around a big clay cooking pot. They were statue-still, staring at us, and might have been modeled by Malvina Hoffman, perfect tribal types cast into bronze for the Museum of Natural History. One of the statues detached herself from the group and walked toward us, arms outstretched, palms up, in the ancient African expression of welcome. She wore a tightly stretched *lappa,* knotted under her right arm, which fell smoothly to her ankles. The fabric had a burnt-orange design over a dark blue background.

"Ma, this be Fanta, *my wife.*" Konsuo identified her with pride.

Konsuo's emphasis took me back to the night when Kekle wanted to help "English the elders" so that everyone might know that *wife* is a word above all others. "*W* is for weaver bird, Wele, water, and wife."

Fanta is of a size which would block the better part of an ordinary doorway, but when she moved she did not waddle or wobble in any part. One knew her to be field-hand hard before feeling the callouses on her hands. I understood why big old Kekle had to be the one to charge up the bank of the waterside with Konsuo's bride on his shoulders.

Fanta stood in front of me and ran her hands along my arms. She was looking at me with rapt attention. If one were to flinch or shrink back from that kind of steady gaze, he would do well to leave at once.

It was typical in Fanta to want to set up something alive between us by running her hands along my arms. This is part of the wordless conversation one may learn in Africa. Different degrees of relationship require differing amounts of space between persons. Fanta was making it known that she wanted to be spiritually close to me, that she wanted each of us to participate in the life of the other.

One trait emanated in force from Fanta—the fierce pride and strength of her motherhood. Looking at her, one could almost subscribe to the earth-mother belief of African men who say that seed from their hands would be wasted in the soil, that only the life force of a woman will cause seed to germinate and grow. Fanta seems a graver person than Konsuo. In him there is a hilarity bubbling just beneath the surface, ready to break forth in laughter at anything which amuses him. Fanta is more likely to smile quietly.

Fanta and Konsuo led us to their hut. They have four handmade rattan chairs. There is no table or bed or any other furniture in their house except for two small wooden trunks for clothing. Nyama's little bamboo valise was sitting beside the trunks. The cooking pots, the mortar for beating rice, the fanner for tossing rice to rid it of chaff—these things were outside under the eaves. The straw mats and the blankets on which the family sleeps at night are rolled up and placed in the roof poles during the day. After the chairs had been set outside for us, there was nothing left to show that six persons (now that Nyama was home) had their home under this roof.

I knew, without being shown, how almost completely thingless a tribal home is, but I was impressed and amazed anew after the years lived away and in the midst of a welter of things. It has never seemed to me that a mud hut is bleak because it is bare. I am sure that Konsuo has never thought of his way of life as a hardness of condition. He may have an extra robe or two in his wooden box, but his house is no larger than the others just because he is the chief or because he is one of the Poro master's stalwarts in the entire area or because he is perhaps as high in the secret Snake Society as a man may go.

I missed seeing the radio he had mentioned during one of our earlier conversations. I felt unsure whether to ask concerning it. I wondered where it was, but I did not want to listen to it instead of him.

"Oh, the radio lives in the palaver house, Ma. I set him down there so all could hear."

Konsuo went on to say with beaming pride that in his town a man could leave a radio out, or anything else for that matter, and no one would think of stealing it. This was not true in Ganta town or anywhere that the road passed. He reminded me that in olden days if one left the smallest thing behind in a village, the chief sent a runner after one with the forgotten object. Not even my money chest needed a lock after we left the coast behind us.

"Ma, the old country way was to give things. The new way is to rogue [steal] things." Konsuo said that this was one of the reasons he wanted his own village. He wanted the children away from the hateful trend of wanting a thing enough to steal it.

He gestured us out of the hut as soon as we had seen it. I think he wanted the village people to see us sitting down together.

Konsuo set out the rattan chairs one at a time, and with great deliberation, in front of his house. He declined our help; he must serve us himself. He made a sweeping gesture inviting us to sit. There was something ritual and ceremonious about that simple act of sitting down together.

Konsuo told us, then, that when he decided to "make the town," he and Kekle had gone on a journey to visit the villages scattered throughout Manoland. They wanted to see which town was the finest and to ask what medicine man had made the medicine to keep it fine. To their surprise, the medicine man most in demand was not a Mano man at all, but a Gio man named Gbo. It was this same Gbo who had recently made himself famous by making medicine which enabled soldiers to take a killer—Yakpawolo by name. Konsuo was certain that Yakpawolo would have been on the loose and murdering more people that very moment had it not been for the powerful medicine of Gbo.

Everytime Konsuo said something to us in English, Fanta bobbed her head and smiled as though she understood. Perhaps some of this was to impress her watching comrades in the palaver house, but I had more the feeling that her uncritical approval of unknown things being said came from her pride in her husband. We would have been more comfortable inside the hut. The sun was burning through patches of high fog and we were stickily hot, but I did not suggest that we move until Konsuo mentioned that he had a "small book" in his wooden chest that he wanted us to read.

Under his neatly folded robes were two mimeographed pages stapled together bearing the banner of the *Sanniquellie Sun*. It was printed January 18, 1964, and was priced at three cents. An editorial by Sekou A. Seesee, Jr., editor-in-chief, announced 1964 as the year when every individual must produce something beyond his own needs, something to sell. The article stressed that "this is a material world," and people have got to realize it. Wise old Konsuo, who cannot read, knew exactly what the article said because Nyama had read it to him and explained it to him many times. He realized that I would be deeply interested in this new way in which people were being urged to think—the world as a material place. Mekula had thought of the world that way, but none of us had liked Mekula.

Fanta glanced out of the door now and then toward the entrance to the town. I thought she must be worrying, as I was, about how Nyama was making out in her courtesy call to the intended sister-wives.

I asked Konsuo whether his town had a medicine hut, a separate place where the sacred objects of ritual are kept. He escorted us then to a hut with a gable roof. It had no door except in the peak of the loft. Getting in or out of it would have necessitated the use of a ladder. There was a chain across the door and a large padlock in place. I thought it quite likely that Konsuo had the key to that lock in the pocket of his robe, but I had little hope that he would fit the key to the lock while the village women watched. Since he had no problem of thieves, the lock must have been set in place to discourage curiosity. Had one been allowed to inspect them, the sacred objects might well have included some carved wooden fetishes, perhaps the one Fanta had worn when she bathed in the sacred pool before Nyama was born. Daisy-chains of snake bones. A few oracle sticks. Cowrie shells to toss when asking questions at the graves of ancestors. These and other objects whose functions we would not have known. Perhaps there were a few ancient spears flaking with rust, now that tribal wars are no longer waged.

When I asked Konsuo where the graveyard was, he said, "No graves here, Ma. Each person, when he die, we carry to the place he got born. When Yoda dies, we will carry him to the town where he buries Kekle tomorrow."

As he talked, Konsuo caressed the walls of the medicine hut. Inside this hut were the really important things of the village, the ritual objects which made possible an access to the world of spirit. All the foolish talk about the world being a *material place*! Indeed! Konsuo snorted whenever he thought of it.

Konsuo said that he and Kekle both wanted to make the village farther away from the road than it is, but they knew it had to be within walking distance of the mission school. I asked him whether he had gone to any of the literacy classes held for adults. He shook his head.

"I got too plenty things, it be my work to remember, Ma. When a person writes his thinks in a book, it breaks the remembers."

Konsuo then showed us the one sad thing in his town, the two empty huts abandoned by two young men who wanted to make rum. They wanted money for things, things they did not intend to share with others. Konsuo considers that it is worse to be selfish than to accidentally kill a man. A selfish deed draws something precious out of the cosmos and spoils that particle of good forever.

Only the day before, Yoda had elected to hobble a long way on his toeless feet in great danger of damaging them since he has no feeling in them. He could have gone "like the wind" on a bike, but he did not wish to seem superior to his people in any way. The bike is a thing and makes a separation between himself and others. Things, when there are any, are for presents and the great joy of giving. I understood why Konsuo was so pleased because Nyama had brought her mother a new orange *lappa,* himself a money bill, each of her aunts a bar of store soap.

Konsuo's face seemed to sag into deeper lines as he opened and then closed the door of one vacated house after the other. Fanta patted his shoulder tenderly. I could not endure to see his face so crumpled. I recalled my desire to make a pot.

"Where's the woman that makes the pots, Konsuo?"

"There the woman. She sits in the palaver house."

We walked back toward the central compound. As we approached them, the women in the palaver house giggled and nudged one another. No matter which of them was the potter, I knew she was not going to lead me to her clay. I had been through this before. Clay is sacred stuff which only certain of the most respected elderly women may handle. Even though I was Konsuo's friend and had known him before he knew his wife, the clay might not "agree for me."

Konsuo introduced me to the potter and made my request in Mano. The woman did not look at me. She ran to her hut and came back out with a large black pot which she pushed into my arms.

"No, no. I mean, thank you, but I want to make a pot of my own, please. It is the clay I ask."

She shook her old head in a stubborn wagging. Konsuo had to translate her refusal. "The clay don't know English. I sorry too much, Ma."

Konsuo and Fanta walked us to the stream and beyond. Perhaps Konsuo would have been amazed had he known at that moment how highly I esteemed him and all the good old ways he embodied. I did not know how to tell him how much I hoped that the new chicks of his people would know how to hold tight to this genuine goodness. They were getting themselves hatched into a large and changing world. I hoped they would treasure memories of his ancient, thingless world, where the clay does not speak English and writing a thought down on paper breaks the remembers.

My husband carried the pot in his arms, and I carried the camera as we walked back to our house. We had not taken a single picture. Our visit had assumed, through Konsuo's and Fanta's dignity, the antique quality of a formal call. Both of us had felt it had been unwilling to break the spell by attempting to use the camera.

As we left the village, we met a few men coming home from work. We stopped to meet them and to snap fingers. There was a certain awkwardness about meeting on that narrow path. The sun was aslant toward the west, and our shadows were long. We had to take care not to step on any person's shadow-self. Also, each time we stopped, my husband had to set the big clay pot down in order to properly front the new acquaintance. Konsuo took great pride in introducing us. At one spot where the path was especially narrow, Fanta picked up the pot to show us how it could be carried with complete convenience on top of the head, leaving both hands free. My husband told her, through Konsuo, that he is like the schoolboys who have not yet learned to carry head loads, a wobbleneck.

After one of our ceremonious pauses for introductions Konsuo said that some of the men we had met had jobs at the Mission, that his town had "one part, Christian quarter" and he liked that. "Christian people not agree for get drunk." All villages seem to have areas which are called quarters, but this does not mean that they are divided like a piece of pie. I have never been able to tell where one quarter leaves off and another begins.

I asked him whether he had become a Christian. He shook his head, he had not, but he stopped walking in order to attend to his answer with all of his faculties. His manner indicated that I had asked a serious question which deserved a serious answer. He looked down at the pebbles at our feet. Seeing none there which suited his purposes, he circled us and came back with a little white rock of a proper size to fit in my palm. It was thinned at the edges and smoothly rounded as though it had been polished in the bed of some ancient stream.

"Ma, I give you this so that you are holding a think."

I nodded. He had given me thinking stones in the past. Their purpose is to focus concentration. One associates a certain thought with the stone and carries it about in a pocket when it is not in the hand. If the stone has been taken from the belly of a crocodile, it carries an especial magical weight quite out of proportion to the physical weight. "This stone stands behind the remembers."

The first time he had given me a stone to hold, we were making ready to cross a rain-swollen stream. The men who carried my loads were lined up along the bank. Each of them had a small, personal mask carved to resemble his facial features, carried in an underarm raffia bag, slung at the side. Each man removed his mask from the covering raffia, spit on the forehead of the image, and rubbed it vigorously with his thumbs. I stood with them. My hands were empty. Seeing that I was shaking with fear, Konsuo picked up a pebble and pressed it in my hands. "Hold tight, Ma. No fear." I had to put the pebble in my pocket when I climbed up on Kekle's shoulders to be piggy-backed across the water, but I confess that I had comfort from that something to hold.

As Konsuo pressed this new rock in my hands, I looked at it carefully. There was nothing special about it, at least not then. After I had the thought he was preparing to give me, the rock might (and did) come to seem special, indeed. The top side of the pebble is milk-white. On the bottom side, where it has lain in contact with the red earth, it is stained a dark rust.

I knew that the acceptable thing to do with the pebble was to rub it vigorously with both thumbs in a circular motion. The "think" Konsuo was about to give me would enter into the stone through my thumbs. When I wished to recall it back out of the stone, I must rub it in the same manner; the thought could be summoned into my body through the contact made by my thumbs. I would be able to warm the thought and nurse it alive by the warmth of my blood.

I stood on the path waiting, savoring the sheer delight of being told something in this manner. The waiting, the pause is necessary. When a tribal African speaks to you of his religion, it is no surface matter. He is speaking of what is deepest and most important in his life.

Konsuo looked into my eyes to see whether I was ready to receive his thought. "Ma, if every person take the Christian God, then all the stones, they die, all dead."

I thought that he was trying to say that something mysterious and wonder-charged would go out of his life and that he would yearn and long for it if he gave up his ancient African religion in which spirit lives in every stick and stone, in every river and tree.

I rubbed the stone as he expected me to do. He went on to say that the Christian God had sent the school and the hospital, good, good people to run them. He thanked them plenty for that.

In the old days of our trekking together, it seemed to me that Konsuo had what Wordsworth called the *primal sympathy*. I recall especially one morning when I stood beside him beneath a sacred tree. When I spoke to him, he did not hear. He had become totally deaf to my voice. It was as though his consciousness had passed over into the tree.

Konsuo had less English then than he has now. He tried when he "had ear for me" again to explain something which is highly difficult to get into words no matter how many of them one may have. He said that the tree had water inside and he had blood inside and that the water and the blood ran together.

I believe that when Konsuo placed his hand on the bark of the sacred tree, he not only knew that the sap was flowing beneath the bark; he felt himself flowing with it, pumping toward the farthest twiggy branch.

Perhaps Konsuo now thought that the Christians in his village, good sober citizens though they are, have lost the ability to share in the life of natural objects, and that to the extent that they have lost this, they, too, seem to have less life. At the time, I had not read *The Primal Vision*. Now that I have read it, the thoughts of John V. Taylor who wrote it have gathered around, have snowballed around, the thought from Konsuo.

I thanked Konsuo for the stone and told him that I would carry it for a long time and "hang head" on all that he had said.

"Yeah, Ma. I go now." The little old man taking his leave from us did a sort of pirouette so that his robe whirled out away from him, and the swirl of disturbed cloth loosened fumes of indigo dye from the fabric, causing him to smell more than ever like a bottle of new ink.

Fanta said good-bye in her own language. The phrase means "my back is toward you now." The implications go beyond translation. It implies that after parting we are no longer intensely in one another's presence; our presence together has been broken.

After Konsuo and Fanta turned back, we met another group of home-ward-bound men. They were younger than the others and took no care for shadows, ours or theirs. They greeted us pleasantly in English but without curiosity. The heated subject of their conversation was an athletic event between the Ganta Mission School Lions and the Lamco Trolls.

As we walked on alone, my husband and I talked about the things which had changed in twenty years and the things which had not. The yards of bright new cloth blooming on the bushes by the waterside was a new sight. The cash crop which had made the cloth possible was a new phenomenon. Marketing additional crops for cash would not be much of a problem. The Liberian Information Service had just made an attempt to get more palm kernels to market. They pointed out in a press release that tons of palm kernels go to waste in Liberia, that the current price of $7.75 is the highest price ever offered for palm kernels. One might quote other factual information regarding imports and exports, tons of iron ore shipped, pounds of rubber and grades. And it was plain to see how increases in these figures are reflected in the miles of road that have been built, the cars and buses running on the roads, the bank about to be built in Ganta.

At first thought, it would seem that the great difference in the country is in the proliferation of material things. Second thoughts suggest that the great difference is that *there are more things which have within them no gods, no meaning.*

The Mano tribesman's God is *Wala Va,* God-there. *There* is far, far away. The distance is so great that it is seldom spanned by a prayer. In some cases a man's mother may be considered holy enough to try to talk directly to God. Therefore, the felt need for magic. The unseen is highly real. As for the seen, there are many ways of looking.

We paused once to rest in a spot where we could look back at Konsuo's village on the hill. We saw smoke filtering through the thatch of one of the roofs. Some woman had decided to cook inside of her house instead of in the palaver house. When the door of a hut is closed and the smoke from the fire in the center of the floor filters up and out, it appears from the outside that the entire roof is breathing. This is not like breath made visibly white by frost. Rather, it is the soft breath of crooning. Snatches of lullaby stir in the mind and drift off into forgotten endings and nothingness like the smoke.

"The Brown Wasps"

Loren Eiseley (1907–1977)

Though some scientists, such as Fred Hoyle and Carl Sagan, have written science fiction, the great majority of them—as their contributions to this anthology indicate—choose the personal essay as the genre for their literary efforts. The personal essay permits them to remain in close contact with physical phenomena while allowing them to comment on those phenomena from a wholly human position; it enables them to connect the objectivity of scientific study to insights that, being subjective, lie beyond demonstrable proof. Too, the essay (unlike the poem, story, or novel) permits scientists to satisfy their requirement for analysis: whenever they wish to, they can summarize the meanings they have abstracted from the connections offered them by memory.

Once said, such a generalization seems obvious; it occurred to me, however, only after I'd read a number of essays by Loren Eiseley, an anthropologist and naturalist whose fusion of the personal with the scientific made him an influence upon many later scientist-writers of our century. "The Brown Wasps" offers a particularly clear illustration of Eiseley's use of memory in his prose. It is difficult to know the genesis—the particular present-day experience—of this essay; conceivably, the sight of homeless people in the railroad station brought into his mind their likeness to the "old brown wasps" he previously had observed "creep[ing] slowly over an abandoned wasp nest" in midwinter. If so, memory soon gave him the analogous image necessary to his autobiographical narrative—that of a cottonwood sapling he transplanted to his yard as a child, shortly before moving from his Nebraska home.

"I have spent a large portion of my life in the shade of a non-existent tree," he writes, early in the essay; much later, after reflecting first upon a particular field mouse that came into his apartment and then upon the behavior of pigeons following the dismantlement of the Philadelphia El, he explains the meaning of his striking paradox. For sixty years the "tree had taken root in his mind" as an image of home—even though, as he ultimately discovers, the sapling never grew into the large tree he had envisioned. Wasps, field mice, pigeons, and homeless people, like Eiseley himself, carry in their memories an attachment to nonexistent places. As part of the abstraction that he draws from such attachments, Eiseley separates himself (and presumably the destitute people in the train station) from the other forms of conscious life: his memory of the tree "was part of my orientation in the universe and I could not survive without it. There was more than an animal's attachment to a place. There was something else, the attachment of the spirit to a grouping of events in time; it was part of our morality."

There is a corner in the waiting room of one of the great Eastern stations where women never sit. It is always in the shadow and overhung by rows of lockers. It is, however, always frequented—not so much by genuine travelers as by the dying. It is here that a certain element of the abandoned poor seeks a refuge out of the weather, clinging for a few hours longer to the city that has fathered them. In a precisely similar manner I have seen, on a sunny day in midwinter, a few old brown wasps creep slowly over an abandoned wasp nest in a thicket. Numbed and forgetful and frost-blackened, the hum of the spring hive still resounded faintly in their sodden tissues. Then the temperature would fall and they would drop away into the white oblivion of the snow. Here in the station it is in no way different save that the city is busy in its snows. But the old ones cling to their seats as though these were symbolic and could not be given up. Now and then they sleep, their gray old heads resting with painful awkwardness on the backs of the benches.

Also they are not at rest. For an hour they may sleep in the gasping exhaustion of the ill-nourished and aged who have to walk in the night. Then a policeman comes by on his round and nudges them upright.

"You can't sleep here," he growls.

A strange ritual then begins. A old man is difficult to waken. After a muttered conversation the policeman presses a coin into his hand and passes fiercely along the benches prodding and gesturing toward the door. In his wake, like birds rising and settling behind the passage of a farmer through a cornfield, the men totter up, move a few paces and subside once more upon the benches.

One man, after a slight, apologetic lurch, does not move at all. Tubercularly thin, he sleeps on steadily. The policeman does not look back. To him, too, this has become a ritual. He will not have to notice it again officially for another hour.

Once in a while one of the sleepers will not awake. Like the brown wasps, he will have had his wish to die in the great droning center of the hive rather than in some lonely room. It is not so bad here with the shuffle of footsteps and the knowledge that there are others who share the bad luck of the world. There are also the whistles and the sounds of everyone, everyone in the world, starting on journeys. Amidst so many journeys somebody is bound to come out all right. Somebody.

Maybe it was on a like thought that the brown wasps fell away from the old paper nest in the thicket. You hold till the last, even if it is only to a public seat in a railroad station. You want your place in the hive more than you want a room or a place where the aged can be eased gently out of the way. It is the place that matters, the place at the heart of things. It is life that you want, that bruises your gray old head with the hard chairs; a man as a right to his place.

But sometimes the place is lost in the years behind us. Or sometimes it is a thing of air, a kind of vaporous distortion above a heap of rubble. We cling to a time and place because without them man is lost, not only man but life. This is why the voices, real or unreal, which speak from the floating trumpets at spiritualist seances are so unnerving. They are voices out of nowhere whose only reality lies in their ability to stir the memory of a living person with some fragment of the past. Before the medium's cabinet both the dead and the living revolve endlessly about an episode, a place, an event that has already been engulfed by time.

This feeling runs deep in life; it brings stray cats running over endless miles, and birds homing from the ends of the earth. It is as though all living creatures, and particularly the more intelligent, can survive only by fixing or transforming a bit of time into space or by securing a bit of space with its objects immortalized and made permanent in time. For example, I once saw, on a flower pot in my own living room, the efforts of a field mouse to build a remembered field, I have lived to see this episode repeated in a thousand guises, and since I have spent a large portion of my life in the shade of a nonexistent tree, I think I am entitled to speak for the field mouse.

One day as I cut across the field which at that time extended on one side of our suburban shopping center, I found a giant slug feeding from a runnel of pink ice cream in an abandoned Dixie cup. I could see his eyes telescope and protrude in a kind of dim, uncertain ecstasy as his dark body bunched and elongated in the curve of the cup. Then, as I stood there at the edge of the concrete, contemplating the slug, I began to realize it was like standing on a shore where a different type of life creeps up and fumbles tentatively among the rocks and sea wrack. It knows its place and will only creep so far until something changes. Little by little as I stood there I began to see more of this shore that surrounds the place of man. I looked with sudden care and attention at things I had been running over thoughtlessly for years. I even waded out a short way into the grass and the wild-rose thickets to see more. A huge black-belted bee went droning by and there were some indistinct scurryings in the underbrush.

Then I came to a sign which informed me that this field was to be the site of a new Wanamaker suburban store. Thousands of obscure lives were about to perish, the spores of puffballs would go smoking off to new fields, and the bodies of little white-footed mice would be crunched under the inexorable wheels of the bulldozers. Life disappears or modifies its appearances so fast that everything takes on an aspect of illusion—a momentary fizzing and boiling with smoke rings, like pouring dissident chemicals into a retort. Here man was advancing, but in a few years his plaster and bricks would be disappearing once more into the insatiable maw of the clover. Being of an archaeological cast of mind, I thought of this fact with an obscure sense of satisfaction and waded back through the rose thickets to the concrete parking lot. As I did so, a mouse scurried ahead of me, frightened of my steps if not of that ominous Wanamaker sign. I saw him vanish in the general direction of my apartment house, his little body quivering with fear in the great open sun on the blazing concrete. Blinded and confused, he was running straight away from his field. In another week scores would follow him.

I forgot the episode then and went home to the quiet of my living room. It was not until a week later, letting myself into the apartment, that I realized I had a visitor. I am fond of plants and had several ferns standing on the floor in pots to avoid the noon glare by the south window.

As I snapped on the light and glanced carelessly around the room, I saw a little heap of earth on the carpet and a scrabble of pebbles that had been kicked merrily over the edge of one of the flower pots. To my astonishment I discovered a full-fledged burrow delving downward among the fern roots. I waited silently. The creature who had made the burrow did not appear. I remembered the wild field then, and the flight of the mice. No house mouse, no *Mus domesticus,* had kicked up this little heap of earth or sought refuge under a fern root in a flower pot. I thought of the desperate little creature I had seen fleeing from the wild rose thicket. Through intricacies of pipes and attics, he, or one of his fellows, had climbed to this high green solitary room. I could visualize what had occurred. He had an image in his head, a world of seed pods and quiet, of green sheltering leaves in the dim light among the weed stems. It was the only world he knew and it was gone.

Somehow in his flight he had found his way to this room with drawn shades where no one would come till nightfall. And here he had smelled green leaves and run quickly up the flower pot to dabble his paws in common earth. He had even struggled half the afternoon to carry his burrow deeper and had failed. I examined the hole, but no whiskered twitching face appeared. He was gone. I gathered up the earth and refilled the burrow. I did not expect to find traces of him again.

Yet for three nights thereafter I came home to the darkened room and my ferns to find the dirt kicked gaily about the rug and the burrow reopened, though I was never able to catch the field mouse within it. I dropped a little food about the mouth of the burrow, but it was never touched. I looked under beds or sat reading with one ear cocked for rustlings in the ferns. It was all in vain; I never saw him. Probably he ended in a trap in some other tenant's room.

But before he disappeared I had come to look hopefully for his evening burrow. About my ferns there had begun to linger the insubstantial vapor of an autumn field, the distilled essence, as it were, of a mouse brain in exile from its home. It was a small dream, like our dreams, carried a long and weary journey along pipes and through spider webs, past holes over which loomed the shadows of waiting cats, and finally, desperateley, into this room where he had played in the shuttered daylight for an hour among the green ferns on the floor. Every day these invisible dreams pass us on the street, or rise from beneath our feet, or look out upon us from beneath a bush.

Some years ago the old elevated railway in Philadelphia was torn down and replaced by a subway system. This ancient El with its barnlike stations containing nut-vending machines and scattered food scraps had, for generations, been the favorite feeding ground of flocks of pigeons, generally one flock to a station along the route of the El. Hundreds of pigeons were dependent upon the system. They flapped in and out of its stanchions and steel work or gathered in watchful little audiences about the feet of anyone who rattled the peanut-vending machines. They even watched people who jingled change in their hands, and prospected for food under the feet of the crowds who gathered between trains. Probably very few among the waiting people who tossed a crumb to an eager pigeon realized that this El was like a food-bearing river, and that the life which haunted its banks was dependent upon the running of the trains with their human freight.

I saw the river stop.

The time came when the underground tubes were ready; the traffic was transferred to a realm unreachable by pigeons. It was like a great river subsiding suddenly into desert sands. For a day, for two days, pigeons continued to circle over the El or stand close to the red vending machines. They were patient birds, and surely this great river which had flowed through the lives of unnumbered generations was merely suffering from some momentary drought.

They listened for the familiar vibrations that had always heralded an approaching train; they flapped hopefully about the head of an occasional workman walking along the steel runways. They passed from one empty station to another, all the while growing hungrier. Finally they flew away.

I thought I had seen the last of them about the El, but there was a revival and it provided a curious instance of the memory of living things for a way of life or a locality that has long been cherished. Some weeks after the El was abandoned workmen began to tear it down. I went to work every morning by one particular station, and the time came when the demolition crews reached this spot. Acetylene torches showered passersby with sparks, pneumatic drills hammered at the base of the structure, and a blind man who, like the pigeons, had clung with his cup to a stairway leading to the change booth, was forced to give up his place.

It was then, strangely, momentarily, one morning that I witnessed the return of a little band of the familiar pigeons. I even recognized one or two members of the flock that had lived around this particular station before they were dispersed into the streets. They flew bravely in and out among the sparks and the hammers and the shouting workmen. They had returned—and they had returned because the hubbub of the wreckers had convinced them that the river was about to flow once more. For several hours they flapped in and out through the empty windows, nodding their heads and watching the fall of girders with attentive little eyes. By the following morning the station was reduced to some burned-off stanchions in the street. My bird friends had gone. It was plain, however, that they retained a memory for an insubstantial structure now compounded of air and time. Even the blind man clung to it. Someone had provided him with a chair, and he sat at the same corner staring sightlessly at an invisible stairway where, so far as he was concerned, the crowds were still ascending to the trains.

I have said my life has been passed in the shade of a nonexistent tree, so that such sights do not offend me. Prematurely I am one of the brown wasps and I often sit with them in the great droning hive of the station, dreaming sometimes of a certain tree. It was planted sixty years ago by a boy with a bucket and a toy spade in a little Nebraska town. That boy was myself. It was a cottonwood sapling and the boy remembered it because of some words spoken by his father and because everyone died or moved away who was supposed to wait and grow old under its shade. The boy was passed from hand to hand, but the tree for some intangible reason had taken root in his mind. It was under its branches that he sheltered; it was from this tree that his memories, which are my memories, led away into the world.

After sixty years the mood of the brown wasps grows heavier upon one. During a long inward struggle I thought it would do me good to go and look upon that actual tree. I found a rational excuse in which to clothe this madness. I purchased a ticket and at the end of two thousand miles I walked another mile to an address that was still the same. The house had not been altered.

I came close to the white picket fence and reluctantly, with great effort, looked down the long vista of the yard. There was nothing there to see. For sixty years that cottonwood had been growing in my mind. Season by season its seeds had been floating farther on the hot prairie winds. We had planted it lovingly there, my father and I, because he had a great hunger for soil and live things growing, and because none of these things had long been ours to protect. We had planted the little sapling and watered it faithfully, and I remembered that I had run out with my small bucket to drench its roots the day we moved away. And all the years since it had been growing in my mind, a huge tree that somehow stood for my father and the love I bore him. I took a grasp on the picket fence and forced myself to look again.

A boy with the hard bird eye of youth pedaled a tricycle slowly up beside me.

"What'cha lookin' at?" he asked curiously.

"A tree," I said.

"What for?" he said.

"It isn't there," I said, to myself mostly, and began to walk away at a pace just slow enough not to seem to be running.

"What isn't there?" the boy asked. I didn't answer. It was obvious I was attached by a threat to a thing that had never been there, or certainly not for long. Something that had to be held in the air, or sustained in the mind, because it was part of my orientation in the universe and I could not survive without it. There was more than an animal's attachment to a place. There was something else, the attachment of the spirit to a grouping of events in time; it was part of our morality.

So I had come home at last, driven by a memory in the brain as surely as the field mouse who had delved long ago into my flower pot or the pigeons flying forever amidst the rattle of nut-vending machines. These, the burrow under the greenery in my living room and the red-bellied bowls of peanuts now hovering in midair in the midst of pigeons, were all part of an elusive world that existed nowhere and yet everywhere. I looked once at the real world about me while the persistent boy pedaled at my heels.

It was without meaning, though my feet took a remembered path. In sixty years the house and street had rotted out of my mind. But the tree, the tree that no longer was, that had perished in its first season, bloomed on in my individual mind, umblemished as my father's words. "We'll plant a tree here, son, and we're not going to move any more. And when you're an old, old man you can sit under it and think how we planted it here, you and me, together."

I began to outpace the boy on the tricycle.

"Do you live here, Mister?" he shouted after me suspiciously. I took a firm grasp on airy nothing—to be precise, on the bole of a great tree. "I do," I said. I spoke for myself, one field mouse, and several pigeons. We were all out of touch but somehow permanent. It was the world that had changed.

A sudden blow: the great wings beating still
Above the staggering girl, her thighs caressed
By the dark webs, her nape caught in his bill,
He holds her helpless breast upon his breast.

How can those terrified vague fingers push
The feathered glory from her loosening thighs?
And how can body, laid in that white rush,
But feel the strange heart beating where it lies?

A shudder in the loins engenders there
The broken wall, the burning roof and tower
And Agamemnon dead.
               Being so caught up,
So mastered by the brute blood of the air,
Did she put on his knowledge with his power
Before the indifferent beak could let her drop?

—William Butler Yeats, "Leda and the Swan"

Memory and Creativity

Countless poems contain references to the creative process or are about the nature of creativity itself. I considered many of them—from the Romantic period onward—before choosing Yeats' "Leda and the Swan" as epigraph for this section. Based on the Greek myth of the rape of Leda by Zeus, who has taken on the shape of a swan for this particular conquest, it refers to what is destined to occur as a consequence of this mating of divine with human: Helen and Clytemnestra are one of the two pairs of offspring hatched from the eggs. Whatever else this sensuous poem is, it is first and foremost about creativity, a fact so obvious it is often ignored. Yeats initially intended the poem to be political in nature. "My fancy," he remarks in a note, "began to play with Leda and the Swan for metaphor, and I began this poem; but as I wrote, bird and lady took such possession of the scene that all politics went out of it." In a way, then, the writing of the poem is an illustration of its very subject—the power of some presence (imaginative or divine) to possess the self.

As Clara Claiborne Park remarks in one of the essays included in this section, what we now call *creativity* was once referred to as *inspiration*—a term that implied a truth given us through the mysterious agency of the gods. (It is a view that Yeats uses to his advantage.) Inspiration is still a useful term in some contexts; while creativity usually refers to the whole process involved in discovery or invention, inspiration remains a word to describe the sudden illumination that sets the process in motion. The gods (and the derangement they bring to our normal mental activities) are absent from this modern usage without detracting from the unique and apparently mysterious nature of these unexpected illuminations: the source of them is now accorded to the human unconscious. The essay by Henri Poincaré that opens this section explores the relationship between conscious and unconscious thought through his own experience in mathematical discovery. His emphasis upon an esthetic filter or screen as a requirement for inspiration is only one of the reasons that his self-exploration into the nature of creativity has an applicability to artists as well as abstract thinkers.

Imagination is another word frequently used in descriptions of creativity. As part of my reading for this anthology, I have come across much that I admire but have been unable to use, sometimes because of the length of a piece, sometimes because its insights are so sensible they are common to a number of texts. Early on, I read a couple of slim and lucid volumes—one titled *Imagination* and a later one called *Memory*—by the Cambridge philosopher Mary Warnock. Although I have not included anything from these books, they encouraged me in the belief that an anthology such as this one might be not only possible but also of some assistance in our quest for an insight into ourselves that would include the necessary dimension of nonmaterial values. *Memory* was written, Warnock tells us, as an attempt "to suggest an answer to a particular and limited question: why do we value memory so highly?" In the course of her investigation, she admits—something perhaps implicit in the first volume—that the "two powers" of imagination and memory "are impossible to separate. . . . For, whether we are imagining or recalling, we are thinking of something that is not before our eyes and ears, and of something that has meaning for us, and may be imbued with strong emotions. We could say that, in recalling something, we are employing imagination; and that, in imagining something, exploring it imaginatively, we use memory."

Current investigations by neuroscientists appear to reinforce Warnock's position—as the headnote to Damasio's essay in the opening section indicates. Since imagination and memory are so interconnected (PET scans, for example, show that the same areas of the brain are affected, whether we imagine or experience something), it might at first glance seem handy to connect the two names with a hyphen, in the manner of certain present-day marriage partners. But in this case memory (the chief element of consciousness) is no doubt the dominant partner, and must provide the family name. Still, there is a dalliance between the pair, one necessary for literature. (As the excerpt from Marcel Proust's *Time Regained* suggests, memory, through imagination, can impose a value beyond that of the actual experience.) The introduction to the previous section demonstrates the role of memory in giving an apparent—or imagined—"reality" to any passing moment of time. Here, while we remain under the influence of Yeats' gorgeous poem, it may be helpful to visualize memory and imagination as entwined and necessary lovers: the images of memory are colored, viewed obliquely, sometimes even transformed, by the beloved. The memory of an event, then, is never identical with the event itself, which sometimes is a blessing and sometimes a curse. (The question of the trustworthiness of memory—an issue of particular importance today in reference to repressed memories of childhood abuse—is raised in the essay by Patricia Hample.)

Poincaré's "Mathematical Creation" is the only essay in this section that makes no mention of literature. With the exception of Poincaré, William James, Carl Jung, and Park, all of the authors are imaginative writers—and the last-named, though not a poet or fiction writer, is one whose professional life (as teacher and critic) has been devoted to literature. (That so many included here write fiction or verse is not simply a consequence of my bias or inadequate knowledge of fields other than literature: not only do poets and novelists often contemplate—sometimes with joy, sometimes with despair—their creative abilities while engaged in their work, they are normally the ones most capable of writing about creativity in a manner that engages the nonspecialist.)

In addition to referring to inspiration, imagination, and both conscious and unconscious processes of thought, the authors in this section frequently imply or assert the power of memory to find likenesses, to join together disparate experiences, concepts, or physical facts. (Indeed, that unifying quality is usually equated with the power of imagination itself, as is apparent in any number of Romantic poems.) The impulse to search for a synthesis, for a unity beyond difference, connects scientific investigations of physical phenomena with literary explorations of human experience. (The essays by James and Wordsworth separate poetry, or art generally, from science on the basis that the former is intuitive—often immediately unitary—while the latter is analytical, based on the deliberate comparison of parts; the generalization is valid enough and helps to distinguish the pursuit of subjective truth from that of objective truth. Synthesis, though, remains the goal of each.)

Other than to say that I found it fitting to open this section with essays by Poincaré and James and end it with excerpts from Eudora Welty's *One Writer's Beginnings,* I have little to say about the order of the essays between—except that I intentionally followed Jung's "Psychology and Literature" with E. M. Forster's "Anonymity: an Enquiry." In Jung's essay, the unconscious—here the collective unconscious—is not so much the cause of a sudden inspiration that creates the greatest (or visionary) literature as it is the force that both propels and consumes it. One can be both fascinated and appalled by Jung's views; I find Forster's essay helpful in dampening a conflagration that could consume a world.

"Mathematical Creation"

Henri Poincaré (1854–1912)

According to Henri Poincare, a French mathematician best known for his work in the theory of functions, a strong memory is not the crucial requirement for creation in his field of expertise. What *is* essential is "a special esthetic sensibility"; the creator possesses a kind of "delicate sieve" that permits only the combinations of the greatest elegance and beauty to pass from the subliminal to the conscious self.

Though physicists as well as pure mathematicians commonly refer to the "elegance" of particular theories, it is surprising that a mathematician would give priority to an intuitive, esthetic response for creation—and acknowledge as well the role played by the unconscious or subliminal self. It is a brave admission, with unsettling implications, for someone engaged in an intellectual enterprise. But having made such an acknowledgment, Poincare emphasizes thought—rationality—as crucial for both the groundwork of creativity and the final result. Inspiration, he says, depends upon conscious thought that then is transmitted to the underlying memory-bank of the unconscious where the "mobilized atoms" of that thought are assembled into an almost infinite number of combinations; the "delicate sieve" permits certain combinations—the ones most beautiful and normally (but not always) true—to be accessible to the reactivated consciousness for refinement and proof. (Since memory is, after all, our faculty for perceiving likenesses and connections, it seems to me that the "delicate sieve" is actually memory's own filter. As a writer, I know that my mind and viscera alike respond with what seems pure happiness to an unexpected synthesis or harmony of complex and apparently antithetical elements that my memory, set to its explorations by a conscious thought, has been in pursuit of.)

At the beginning of the essay in which he discusses the subject, Poincare suggests that mathematical creation "is the activity in which the human mind seems to take least from the outside world," and that in studying "the procedure of geometrical thought we may hope to reach what is most essential in man's mind." The essay demonstrates the interpenetrations of thought, subliminal memory, and emotion in achieving inspiration. It has remained in my own memory ever since I first read it, almost forty years ago—suggesting its appeal to my own mind.

The genesis of mathematical creation is a problem which should intensely interest the psychologist. It is the activity in which the human mind seems to take least from the outside world, in which it acts or seems to act only of itself and on itself, so that in studying the procedure of geometric thought we may hope to reach what is most essential in man's mind.

126

This has long been appreciated, and some time back the journal called *L'Enseignement Mathématique,* edited by Laisant and Fehr, began an investigation of the mental habits and methods of work of different mathematicians. I had finished the main outlines of this article when the results of that inquiry were published, so I have hardly been able to utilize them and shall confine myself to saying that the majority of witnesses confirm my conclusions; I do not say all, for when the appeal is to universal suffrage unanimity is not to be hoped.

A first fact should surprise us, or rather would surprise us if we were not so used to it. How does it happen there are people who do not understand mathematics? If mathematics invokes only the rules of logic, such as are accepted by all normal minds; if its evidence is based on principles common to all men, and that none could deny without being mad, how does it come about that so many persons are here refractory?

That not every one can invent is nowise mysterious. That not every one can retain a demonstration once learned may also pass. But that not every one can understand mathematical reasoning when explained appears very surprising when we think of it. And yet those who can follow this reasoning only with difficulty are in the majority: that is, undeniable, and will surely not be gainsaid by the experience of secondary-school teachers.

And further: how is error possible, in mathematics? A sane mind should not be guilty of a logical fallacy, and yet there are very fine minds who do not trip in brief reasoning such as occurs in the ordinary doings of life, and who are incapable of following or repeating without error the mathematical demonstrations which are longer, but which after all are only an accumulation of brief reasonings wholly analogous to those they make so easily. Need we add that mathematicians themselves are not infallible?

The answer seems to me evident. Imagine a long series of syllogisms, and that the conclusions of the first serve as premises of the following: we shall be able to catch each of these syllogisms, and it is not in passing from premises to conclusion that we are in danger of deceiving ourselves. But between the moment in which we first meet a proposition as conclusion of one syllogism, and that in which we reëncounter it as premise of another syllogism occasionally some time will elapse, several links of the chain will have unrolled; so it may happen that we have forgotten it, or worse, that we have forgotten its meaning. So it may happen that we replace it by a slightly different proposition, or that, while retaining the same enunciation, we attribute to it a slightly different meaning, and thus it is that we are exposed to error.

Often the mathematician uses a rule. Naturally he begins by demonstrating this rule; and at the time when this proof is fresh in his memory he understands perfectly its meaning and its bearing, and he is in no danger of changing it. But subsequently he trusts his memory and afterward only applies it in a mechanical way; and then if his memory fails him, he may apply it all wrong. Thus it is, to take a simple example, that we sometimes make slips in calculation because we have forgotten our multiplication table.

According to this, the special aptitude for mathematics would be due only to a very sure memory or to a prodigious force of attention. It would be a power like that of the whist-player who remembers the cards played; or, to go up a step, like that of the chess-player who can visualize a great number of combinations and hold them in his memory. Every good mathematician ought to be a good chess-player, and inversely; likewise he should be a good computer. Of course that sometimes happens; thus Gauss was at the same time a geometer of genius and a very precocious and accurate computer.

But there are exceptions; or rather I err; I cannot call them exceptions without the exceptions being more than the rule. Gauss it is, on the contrary, who was an exception. As for myself, I must confess, I am absolutely incapable even of adding without mistakes. In the same way I should be but a poor chess-player; I would perceive that by a certain play I should expose myself to a certain danger; I would pass in review several other plays, rejecting them for other reasons, and then finally I should make the move first examined, having meantime forgotten the danger I had foreseen.

In a word, my memory is not bad, but it would be insufficient to make me a good chess-player. Why then does it not fail me in a difficult piece of mathematical reasoning where most chess-players would lose themselves? Evidently because it is guided by the general march of the reasoning. A mathematical demonstration is not a simple juxtaposition of syllogisms, it is syllogisms *placed in a certain order,* and the order in which these elements are placed is much more important than the elements themselves. If I have the feeling, the intuition, so to speak, of this order, so as to perceive at a glance the reasoning as a whole, I need no longer fear lest I forget one of the elements, for each of them will take its allotted place in the array, and that without any effort of memory on my part.

It seems to me then, in repeating a reasoning learned, that I could have invented it. This is often only an illusion; but even then, even if I am not so gifted as to create it by myself, I myself re-invent it in so far as I repeat it.

We know that this feeling, this intuition of mathematical order, that makes us divine hidden harmonies and relations, cannot be possessed by every one. Some will not have either this delicate feeling so difficult to define, or a strength of memory and attention beyond the ordinary, and then they will be absolutely incapable of understanding higher mathematics. Such are the majority. Others will have this feeling only in a slight degree, but they will be gifted with an uncommon memory and a great power of attention. They will learn by heart the details one after another; they can understand mathematics and sometimes make applications, but they cannot create. Others, finally, will possess in a less or greater degree the special intuition referred to, and then not only can they understand mathematics even if their memory is nothing extraordinary, but they may become creators and try to invent with more or less success according as the intuition is more or less developed in them.

In fact, what is mathematical creation? It does not consist in making new combinations with mathematical entities already known. Any one could do that, but the combinations so made would be infinite in number and most of them absolutely without interest. To create consists precisely in not making useless combinations and in making those which are useful and which are only a small minority. Invention is discernment, choice.

How to make this choice I have before explained; the mathematical facts worthy of being studied are those which, by their analogy with other facts, are capable of leading us to the knowledge of a mathematical law just as experimental facts lead us to the knowledge of a physical law. They are those which reveal to us unsuspected kinship between other facts, long known, but wrongly believed to be strangers to one another.

Among chosen combinations the most fertile will often be those formed of elements drawn from domains which are far apart. Not that I mean as sufficing for invention the bringing together of objects as disparate as possible; most combinations so formed would be entirely sterile. But certain among them, very rare, are the most fruitful of all.

To invent, I have said, is to choose; but the word is perhaps not wholly exact. It makes one think of a purchaser before whom are displayed a large number of samples, and who examines them, one after the other, to make a choice. Here the samples would be so numerous that a whole lifetime would not suffice to examine them. This is not the actual state of things. The sterile combinations do not even present themselves to the mind of the inventor. Never in the field of his consciousness do combinations appear that are not really useful, except some that he rejects but which have to some extent the characteristics of useful combinations. All goes on as if the inventor were an examiner for the second degree who would only have to question the candidates who had passed a previous examination.

But what I have hitherto said is what may be observed or inferred in reading the writings of the geometers, reading reflectively.

It is time to penetrate deeper and to see what goes on in the very soul of the mathematician. For this, I believe, I can do best by recalling memories of my own. But I shall limit myself to telling how I wrote my first memoir on Fuchsian functions. I beg the reader's pardon; I am about to use some technical expressions, but they need not frighten him, for he is not obliged to understand them. I shall say, for example, that I have found the demonstration of such a theorem under such circumstances. This theorem will have a barbarous name, unfamiliar to many, but that is unimportant; what is of interest for the psychologist is not the theorem but the circumstances.

For fifteen days I strove to prove that there could not be any functions like those I have since called Fuchsian functions. I was then very ignorant; every day I seated myself at my work table, stayed an hour or two, tried a great number of combinations and reached no results. One evening, contrary to my custom, I drank black coffee and could not sleep. Ideas rose in crowds; I felt them collide until pairs interlocked, so to speak, making a stable combination. By the next morning I had established the existence of a class of Fuchsian functions, those which come from the hypergeometric series; I had only to write out the results, which took but a few hours.

Then I wanted to represent these functions by the quotient of two series; this idea was perfectly conscious and deliberate, the analogy with elliptic functions guided me. I asked myself what properties these series must have if they existed, and I succeeded without difficulty in forming the series I have called theta-Fuchsian.

Just at this time I left Caen, where I was then living, to go on a geologic excursion under the auspices of the school of mines. The changes of travel made me forget my mathematical work. Having reached Coutances, we entered an omnibus to go some place or other. At the moment when I put my foot on the step the idea came to me, without anything in my former thoughts seeming to have paved the way for it, that the transformations I had used to define the Fuchsian functions were identical with those of non-Euclidean geometry. I did not verify the idea; I should not have had time, as, upon taking my seat in the omnibus, I went on with a conversation already commenced, but I felt a perfect certainty. On my return to Caen, for conscience's sake, I verified the result at my leisure.

Then I turned my attention to the study of some arithmetical questions apparently without much success and without a suspicion of any connection with my preceding researches. Disgusted with my failure, I went to spend a few days at the seaside, and thought of something else. One morning, walking on the bluff, the idea came to me, with just the same characteristics of brevity, suddenness and immediate certainty, that the arithmetic transformations of indeterminate ternary quadratic forms were identical with those of non-Euclidean geometry.

Returned to Caen, I mediated on this result and deduced the consequences. The example of quadratic forms showed me that there were Fuchsian groups other than those corresponding to the hypergeometric series; I saw that I could apply to them the theory of theta-Fuchsian series and that consequently there existed Fuchsian functions other than those from the hypergeometric series, the ones I then knew. Naturally I set myself to form all these functions. I made a systematic attack upon them and carried all the outworks, one after another. There was one however that still held out, whose fall would involve that of the whole place. But all my efforts only served at first the better to show me the difficulty, which indeed was something. All this work was perfectly conscious.

Thereupon I left for Mont-Valérien, where I was to go through my military service; so I was very differently occupied. One day, going along the street, the solution of the difficulty which had stopped me suddenly appeared to me. I did not try to go deep into it immediately, and only after my service did I again take up the question. I had all the elements and had only to arrange them and put them together. So I wrote out my final memoir at a single stroke and without difficulty.

I shall limit myself to this single example; it is useless to multiply them. In regard to my other researches I would have to say analogous things and the observations of other mathematicians given in *L'Enseignement Mathématique* would only confirm them.

Most striking at first is this appearance of sudden illumination, a manifest sign of long, unconscious prior work. The rôle of this unconscious work in mathematical invention appears to me incontestable, and traces of it would be found in other cases where it is less evident. Often when one works at a hard question, nothing good is accomplished at the first attack. Then one takes a rest, longer or shorter, and sits down anew to the work. During the first half-hour, as before, nothing is found, and then all of a sudden the decisive idea presents itself to the mind. It might be said that the conscious work has been more fruitful because it has been interrupted and the rest has given back to the mind its force and freshness. But it is more probable that this rest has been filled out with unconscious work and that the result of this work has afterward revealed itself to the geometer just as in the cases I have cited; only the revelation, instead of coming during a walk or a journey, has happened during a period of conscious work, but independently of this work which plays at most a rôle of excitant, as if it were the goad stimulating the results already reached during rest, but remaining unconscious, to assume the conscious form.

There is another remark to be made about the conditions of this unconscious work: it is possible, and of a certainty it is only fruitful, if it is on the one hand preceded and on the other hand followed by a period of conscious work. These sudden inspirations (and the examples already cited sufficiently prove this) never happen except after some days of voluntary effort which has appeared absolutely fruitless and whence nothing good seems to have come, where the way taken seems totally astray. These efforts then have not been as sterile as one thinks; they have set agoing the unconscious machine and without them it would not have moved and would have produced nothing.

The need for the second period of conscious work, after the inspiration, is still easier to understand. It is necessary to put in shape the result of this inspiration, to deduce from them the immediate consequences, to arrange them, to word the demonstrations, but above all is verification necessary. I have spoken of the feeling of absolute certitude accompanying the inspiration; in the cases cited this feeling was no deceiver, nor is it usually. But do not think this is a rule without exception; often this feeling deceives us without being any the less vivid, and we only find it out when we seek to put on foot the demonstration. I have especially noticed this fact in regard to ideas coming to me in the morning or evening in bed while in a semi-hypnagogic state.

Such are the realities; now for the thoughts they force upon us. The unconscious, or, as we say, the subliminal self plays an important rôle in mathematical creation; this follows from what we have said. But usually the subliminal self is considered as purely automatic. Now we have seen that mathematical work is not simply mechanical, that it could not be done by a machine, however perfect. It is not merely a question of applying rules, of making the most combinations possible according to certain fixed laws. The combinations so obtained would be exceedingly numerous, useless and cumbersome. The true work of the inventor consists in choosing among these combinations so as to eliminate the useless ones or rather to avoid the trouble of making them, and the rules which must guide this choice are extremely fine and delicate. It is almost impossible to state them precisely; they are felt rather than formulated. Under these conditions, how imagine a sieve capable of applying them mechanically?

A first hypothesis now presents itself: the subliminal self is in no way inferior to the conscious self; it is not purely automatic; it is capable of discernment; it has tact, delicacy; it knows how to choose, to divine. What do I say? It knows better how to divine than the conscious self, since it succeeds where that has failed. In a word, is not the subliminal self superior to the conscious self? You recognize the full importance of this question. Boutroux in a recent lecture has shown how it came up on a very different occasion, and what consequences would follow an affirmative answer.

Is this affirmative answer forced upon us by the facts I have just given? I confess that, for my part, I should hate to accept it. Reëxamine the facts then and see if they are not compatible with another explanation.

It is certain that the combinations which present themselves to the mind in a sort of sudden illumination, after an unconscious working somewhat prolonged, are generally useful and fertile combinations, which seem the result of a first impression. Does it follow that the subliminal self, having divined by a delicate intuition that these combinations would be useful, has formed only these, or has it rather formed many others which were lacking in interest and have remained unconscious?

In this second way of looking at it, all the combinations would be formed in consequence of the automatism of the subliminal self, but only the interesting ones would break into the domain of consciousness. And this is still very mysterious. What is the cause that, among the thousand products of our unconscious activity, some are called to pass the threshold, while others remain below? Is it a simple chance which confers this privilege? Evidently not; among all the stimuli of our senses, for example, only the most intense fix our attention, unless it has been drawn to them by other causes. More generally the privileged unconscious phenomena, those susceptible of becoming conscious, are those which, directly or indirectly, affect most profoundly our emotional sensibility.

It may be surprising to see emotional sensibility invoked *à propos* of mathematical demonstrations which, it would seem, can interest only the intellect. This would be to forget the feeling of mathematical beauty, of the harmony of numbers and forms, of geometric elegance. This is a true esthetic feeling that all real mathematicians know, and surely it belongs to emotional sensibility.

Now, what are the mathematic entities to which we attribute this character of beauty and elegance, and which are capable of developing in us a sort of esthetic emotion? They are those whose elements are harmoniously disposed so that the mind without effort can embrace their totality while realizing the details. This harmony is at once a satisfaction of our esthetic needs and an aid to the mind, sustaining and guiding. And at the same time, in putting under our eyes a well-ordered whole, it makes us foresee a mathematical law. Now, as we have said above, the only mathematical facts worthy of fixing our attention and capable of being useful are those which can teach us a mathematical law. So that we reach the following conclusion: The useful combinations are precisely the most beautiful, I mean those best able to charm this special sensibility that all mathematicians know, but of which the profane are so ignorant as often to be tempted to smile at it.

What happens then? Among the great numbers of combinations blindly formed by the subliminal self, almost all are without interest and without utility; but just for that reason they are also without effect upon the esthetic sensibility. Consciousness will never know them; only certain ones are harmonious, and, consequently, at once useful and beautiful. They will be capable of touching this special sensibility of the geometer of which I have just spoken, and which, once aroused, will call our attention to them, and thus give them occasion to become conscious.

This is only a hypothesis, and yet here is an observation which may confirm it: when a sudden illumination seizes upon the mind of the mathematician, it usually happens that it does not deceive him, but it also sometimes happens, as I have said, that it does not stand the test of verification; well, we almost always notice that this false idea, had it been true, would have gratified our natural feeling for mathematical elegance.

Thus it is this special esthetic sensibility which plays the rôle of the delicate sieve of which I spoke, and that sufficiently explains why the one lacking it will never be a real creator.

Yet all the difficulties have not disappeared. The conscious self is narrowly limited, and as for the subliminal self we know not its limitations, and this is why we are not too reluctant in supposing that it has been able in a short time to make more different combinations than the whole life of a conscious being could encompass. Yet these limitations exist. Is it likely that it is able to form all the possible combinations, whose number would frighten the imagination? Nevertheless that would seem necessary, because if it produces only a small part of these combinations, and if it makes them at random, there would be small chance that the *good*, the one we should choose, would be found among them.

Perhaps we ought to seek the explanation in that preliminary period of conscious work which always precedes all fruitful unconscious labor. Permit me a rough comparison. Figure the future elements of our combinations as something like the hooked atoms of Epicurus. During the complete repose of the mind, these atoms are motionless, they are, so to speak, hooked to the wall; so this complete rest may be indefinitely prolonged without the atoms meeting, and consequently without any combination between them.

On the other hand, during a period of apparent rest and unconscious work, certain of them are detached from the wall and put in motion. They flash in every direction through the space (I was about to say the room) where they are enclosed, as would, for example, a swarm of gnats or, if you prefer a more learned comparison, like the molecules of gas in the kinematic theory of gases. Then their mutual impacts may produce new combinations.

What is the rôle of the preliminary conscious work? It is evidently to mobilize certain of these atoms, to unhook them from the wall and put them in swing. We think we have done no good, because we have moved these elements a thousand different ways in seeking to assemble them, and have found no satisfactory aggregate. But, after this shaking up imposed upon them by our will, these atoms do not return to their primitive rest. They freely continue their dance.

Now, our will did not choose them at random; it pursued a perfectly determined aim. The mobilized atoms are therefore not any atoms whatsoever; they are those from which we might reasonably expect the desired solution. Then the mobilized atoms undergo impacts which make them enter into combinations among themselves or with other atoms at rest which they struck against in their course. Again I beg pardon, my comparison is very rough, but I scarcely know how otherwise to make my thought understood.

However it may be, the only combinations that have a chance of forming are those where are least one of the elements is one of those atoms freely chosen by our will. Now, it is evidently among these that is found what I called the *good combination*. Perhaps this is a way of lessening the paradoxical in the original hypothesis.

Another observation. It never happens that the unconscious work gives us the result of a somewhat long calculation *all made,* where we have only to apply fixed rules. We might think the wholly automatic subliminal self particularly apt for this sort of work, which is in a way exclusively mechanical. It seems that thinking in the evening upon the factors of a multiplication we might hope to find the product ready made upon our awakening, or again that an algebraic calculation, for example a verification, would be made unconsciously. Nothing of the sort, as observation proves. All one may hope from these inspirations, fruits of unconscious work, is a point of departure for such calculations. As for the calculations themselves, they must be made in the second period of conscious work, that which follows the inspiration, that in which one verifies the results of this inspiration and deduces their consequences. The rules of these calculations are strict and complicated. They require discipline, attention, will, and therefore consciousness. In the subliminal self, on the contrary, reigns what I should call liberty, if we might give this name to the simple absence of discipline and to the disorder born of chance. Only, this disorder itself permits unexpected combinations.

I shall make a last remark: when above I made certain personal observations, I spoke of a night of excitement when I worked in spite of myself. Such cases are frequent, and it is not necessary that the abnormal cerebral activity be caused by a physical excitant as in that I mentioned. It seems, in such cases, that one is present at his own unconscious work, made partially perceptible to the over-excited consciousness, yet without having changed its nature. Then we vaguely comprehend what distinguishes the two mechanisms or, if you wish, the working methods of the two egos. And the psychologic observations I have been able thus to make seem to me to confirm in their general outlines the views I have given.

Surely they have need of it, for they are and remain in spite of all very hypothetical: the interest of the questions is so great that I do not repent of having submitted them to the reader.

from *The Principles of Psychology*

William James   (1842–1900)

In the introduction to the section "The Memory of Nature," I refer to William James' views on memory, which constitute the concluding chapter of the first volume of his *The Principles of Psychology*. For the present section, I have chosen a segment, "Different Orders of Human Genius," from the lengthy account of reasoning found in the second volume of that work. In this segment, James makes no reference to memory, and it is not central to his description of reasoning in the fuller account. I include it here for James' well-known definition of genius, and for the classification he then makes of genius into two types, the intuitive and the analytical. "Genius," he says *"is identical with the possession of similar association to an extreme degree."* The artist intuitively apprehends analogies and other likenesses; the scientist or philosopher, on the other hand, not only consciously notices the connections but abstracts significance from them. As a consequence, the latter kind of individual—the abstract reasoner—represents the higher form, even though he or she may have chosen to enter (say) a scientific field through "an *absence* of certain emotional sensibilities." And it follows that "[a] certain richness of the aesthetic nature may . . . easily keep one in the intuitive stage."

In his earlier chapter on memory, James remarks that "the *object* of memory . . . is a synthesis of parts thought of as related together, perception, imagination, comparison and reasoning being analogous syntheses of parts into complex objects"; perhaps, then, he feels no need in "Different Orders of Human Genius" to emphasize the crucial role of memory in the ability to perceive likenesses among objects that at first glance may appear dissimilar. In my own thinking about the creative process over the years, "Different Orders of Human Genius"—like Poincaré's "Mathematical Creation"—has played an influential role. Its very importance requires me to indicate what I take to be its limitations. For example, it ignores the "special esthetic sensibility" so important to Poincaré's own abstract thinking as well as to artistic discovery. Nor does it acknowledge the possibility that the artist can have a considerable awareness of the abstraction underlying the likenesses he or she employs. While a creative writer like Shakespeare (or William James' novelist brother, Henry, for that matter) might be as capable as a philosopher like James himself in abstracting a meaning from the likenesses offered up by memory, he or she normally chooses not to do so partly to make the reader an active participant in the creative work, partly because (given the spiritual dimensions of that work, its sometimes almost infinite implications) any single statement of its meaning—of the "theme" to be abstracted from its parts—would hopelessly reduce it. Whatever James' sensitive appreciation of the likenesses to be found in Homer and Shakespeare, his own predisposition for analysis seems here to have interfered with his full understanding of the requirements of esthetic forms.

My final reservation concerns James' use of the term *savages*. While he admits that "[o]ver immense departments of our thought we are still, all of us, in the savage state," James' separation of savages (and artists) from analytical thinkers—with the latter representing a higher state of civilization—carries assumptions that belong to an age at once more biased, more innocent, and more optimistic than our own.

The excerpt begins with a portion of James' own transition to his topic.

Another of the great capacities in which man has been said to differ fundamentally from the animal is that of possessing self-consciousness or reflective knowledge of himself as a thinker. But this capacity also flows from our criterion, for (without going into the matter very deeply) we may say that the brute never reflects on himself as a thinker, because he has never clearly dissociated, in the full concrete act of thought, the element of the thing thought of and the operation by which he thinks it. They remain always fused, conglomerated—just as the interjectional vocal sign of the brute almost invariably merges in his mind with the thing signified, and is not independently attended to *in se*.

Now, the dissociation of these two elements probably occurs first in the child's mind on the occasion of some error or false expectation which would make him experience the shock of difference between merely imagining a thing and getting it. The thought experienced once with the concomitant reality, and then without it or with opposite concomitants, reminds the child of other cases in which the same provoking phenomenon occurred. Thus the general ingredient of error may be dissociated and noticed *per se,* and from the notion of his error or wrong thought to that of his thought in general the transition is easy. The brute, no doubt, has plenty of instances of error and disappointment in his life, but the similar shock is in him most likely always swallowed up in the accidents of the actual case. An expectation disappointed may breed dubiety as to the realization of that particular thing when the dog next expects it. But that disappointment, that dubiety, while they are present in the mind, will *not* call up other cases, in which the material details were different, but this feature of possible error was the same. The brute will, therefore, stop short of dissociating the general notion of error *per se,* and *a fortiori* will never attain the conception of Thought itself as such.

We may then, we think, consider it proven that *the most elementary single difference between the human mind and that of brutes lies in this deficiency on the brute's part to associate ideas by similarity*—characters, the abstraction of which depends on this sort of association, must in the brute always remain drowned, swamped in the total phenomenon which they help constitute, and never used to reason from. If a character stands out alone, it is always some obvious sensible quality like a sound or a smell which is instinctively exciting and lies in the line of the animal's propensities; or it is some obvious sign which experience has habitually coupled with a consequence, such as, for the dog, the sight of his master's hat on and the master's going out.

DIFFERENT ORDERS OF HUMAN GENIUS

But, now, since nature never makes a jump, it is evident that we should find the lowest men occupying in this respect an intermediate position between the brutes and the highest men. And so we do. Beyond the analogies which their own minds suggest by breaking up the literal sequence of their experience, there is a whole world of analogies which they can appreciate when imparted to them by their betters, but which they could never excogitate alone. This answers the question why Darwin and Newton had to be waited for so long. The flash of similarity between an apple and the moon, between the rivalry for food in nature and the rivalry for man's selection, was too recondite to have occurred to any but exceptional minds. *Genius, then,* as has been already said, *is identical with the possession of similar association to an extreme degree.* Professor Bain says:"This I count the leading fact of genius . . . I consider it quite impossible to afford any explanation of intellectual originality, except on the supposition of an unusual energy on this point." Alike in the arts, in literature, in practical affairs, and in science, association by similarity is the prime condition of success.

But as, according to our view, there are two stages in reasoned thought, one where similarity merely *operates* to call up cognate thoughts, and another farther stage, where the bond of identity between the cognate thoughts is *noticed;* so *minds of genius may be divided into two main sorts, those who notice the bond and those who merely obey it.* The first are the abstract reasoners, properly so called, the men of science, and philosophers—the analysts, in a word; the latter are the poets, the critics—the artists, in a word, the men of intuitions. These judge rightly, classify cases, characterize them by the most striking analogic epithets, but go no further. At first sight it might seem that the analytic mind represented simply a higher intellectual stage, and that the intuitive mind represented an arrested stage of intellectual development; but the difference is not so simple as this. Professor Bain has said that a man's advance to the scientific stage (the stage of noticing and abstracting the bond of similarity) may often be due to an *absence* of certain emotional sensibilities. The sense of color, he says, may no less determine a mind away from science than it determines it towards painting. There must be a penury in one's interest in the details

138

of particular forms in order to permit the forces of the intellect to be concentrated on what is common to many forms. In other words, supposing a mind fertile in the suggestion of analogies, but, at the same time, keenly interested in the particulars of each suggested image, that mind would be far less apt to single out the particular character which called up the analogy than one whose interests were less generally lively. A certain richness of the æsthetic nature may, therefore, easily keep one in the intuitive stage. All the poets are examples of this. Take Homer:

> Ulysses, too, spied round the house to see if any man were still alive and hiding, trying to get away from gloomy death. He found them all fallen in the blood and dirt, and in such number as the fish which the fishermen to the low shore, out of the foaming sea, drag with their meshy nets. These all, sick for the ocean water, are strewn around the sands, while the blazing sun takes their life from them. So there the suitors lay strewn round on one another.

Or again:

> And as when a Mæonian or a Carian woman stains ivory with purple to be a cheek-piece for horses, and it is kept in the chamber, and many horsemen have prayed to bear it off; but it is kept a treasure for a king, both a trapping for his horse and a glory to the driver—in such wise were thy stout thighs, Menelaos, and legs and fair ankles stained with blood.

A man in whom all the accidents of an analogy rise up as vividly as this, may be excused for not attending to the ground of the analogy. But he need not on that account be deemed intellectually the inferior of a man of drier mind, in whom the ground is not as liable to be eclipsed by the general splendor. Rarely are both sorts of intellect, the splendid and the analytic, found in conjunction. Plato among philosophers, and M. Taine, who cannot quote a child's saying without describing the *"voix chantante, étonnée, heureuse"* in which it is uttered, are only exceptions whose strangeness proves the rule.

An often-quoted writer has said that Shakespeare possessed more *intellectual power* than anyone else that ever lived. If by this he meant the power to pass from given premises to right or congruous conclusions, it is no doubt true. The abrupt transitions in Shakespeare's thought astonish the reader by their unexpectedness no less than they delight him by their fitness. Why, for instance, does the death of Othello so stir the spectator's blood and leave him with a sense of reconcilement? Shakespeare himself could very likely not say why: for his invention, though rational, was not ratiocinative. Wishing the curtain to fall upon a reinstated Othello, that speech about the turbaned Turk suddenly simply flashed across him as the right end of all that went before. The dry critic who comes after can, however, point out the subtle bonds of identity that guided Shakespeare's pen through that speech to the death of the Moor. Othello is sunk in ignominy, lapsed from his height at the beginning of the play. What better way to rescue him at last from this abasement than to make him for an instant identify himself in memory with the old Othello of better days, and then execute justice on his present disowned body, as he used then to smite all enemies of the State? But Shakespeare, whose mind supplied these means, could probably not have told why they were so effective.

But though this is true, and though it would be absurd in an absolute way to say that a given analytic mind was superior to any intuitional one, yet it is none the less true that the former *represents* the higher stage. Men, taken historically, reason by analogy long before they have learned to reason by abstract characters. Association by similarity and true reasoning may have identical results. If a philosopher wishes to prove to you why you should do a certain thing, he may do so by using abstract considerations exclusively; a savage will prove the same by reminding you of a similar case in which you notoriously do as he now proposes, and this with no ability to state the *point* in which the cases are similar. In all primitive literature, in all savage oratory, we find persuasion carried on exclusively by parables and similes, and travellers in savage countries readily adopt the native custom. Take, for example, Dr. Livingstone's argument with the negro conjuror. The missionary was trying to dissuade the savage from his fetichistic ways of invoking rain. "You see," said he, "that, after all your operations, sometimes it rains and sometimes it does not, exactly as when you have not operated at all." "But," replied the sorcerer, "it is just the same with you doctors; you give your remedies, and sometimes the patient gets well and sometimes he dies, just as when you do nothing at all." To that the pious missionary replied: "The doctor does his duty, after which God performs the cure if it pleases Him." "Well," rejoined the savage, "it is just so with me. I do what is necessary to procure rain, after which God sends it or withholds it according to His pleasure."

This is the stage in which proverbial philosophy reigns supreme. "An empty sack can't stand straight" will stand for the reason why a man with debts may lose his honesty; and "a bird in the hand is worth two in the bush" will serve to back up one's exhortations to prudence. Or we answer the question: "Why is snow white?" by saying, "For the same reason that soap-suds or whipped eggs are white"—in other words, instead of giving the *reason* for a fact, we give another *example* of the same fact. This offering a similar instance, instead of a reason, has often been criticised as one of the forms of logical depravity in men. But manifestly it is not a perverse act of thought, but only an incomplete one. Furnishing parallel cases is the necessary first step towards abstracting the reason embedded in them all.

As it is with reason, so it is with words. The first words are probably always names of entire things and entire actions, of extensive coherent groups. A new experience in the primitive man can only be talked about by him in terms of the old experiences which have received names. It reminds him of certain ones from among them, but the *points* in which it agrees with them are neither named nor dissociated. Pure similarity must work before the abstraction can work which is based upon it. The first adjectives will therefore probably be total nouns embodying the striking character. The primeval man will say, not "the bread is hard," but "the bread is stone"; not "the face is round," but "the face is moon"; not "the fruit is sweet," but "the fruit is sugar-cane." The first words are thus neither particular nor general, but *vaguely* concrete; just as we speak of an "oval" face, a "velvet" skin, or an "iron" will, without meaning to connote any other attributes of the adjective-noun than those in which it *does* resemble the noun it is used to qualify. After a while certain of these adjectively-used nouns come only to signify the particular quality for whose sake they are oftenest used; the *entire thing* which they originally meant receives another name, and they become true abstract and general terms. Oval, for example, with us suggests *only* shape. The first abstract qualities thus formed are, no doubt, qualities of one and the same sense found in different objects—as big, sweet; next analogies between different senses, as "sharp" of taste, "high" of sound, etc.; then analogies of motor combinations, or form of relation, as simple, confused, difficult, reciprocal, relative, spontaneous, etc. The extreme degree of subtlety in analogy is reached in such cases as when we say certain English art critics' writing reminds us of a close room in which pastilles have been burning, or that the mind of certain Frenchmen is like old Roquefort cheese. Here language utterly fails to hit upon the basis of resemblance.

Over immense departments of our thought we are still, all of us, in the savage state. Similarity operates in us, but abstraction has not taken place. We know what the present case is like, we know what it reminds us of, we have an intuition of the right course to take, if it be a practical matter. But analytic thought has made no tracks, and we cannot justify ourselves to others. In ethical, psychological, and æsthetic matters, to give a clear reason for one's judgment is universally recognized as a mark of rare genius. The helplessness of uneducated people to account for their likes and dislikes is often ludicrous. Ask the first Irish girl why she likes this country better or worse than her home, and see how much she can tell you. But if you ask your most educated friend why he prefers Titian to Paul Veronese, you will hardly get more of a reply; and you will probably get absolutely none if you inquire why Beethoven reminds him of Michael Angelo, or how it comes that a bare figure with unduly flexed joints, by the latter, can so suggest the moral tragedy of life. His thought obeys a *nexus,* but cannot name it. And so it is with all those judgments of *experts,* which even though unmotived are so valuable. Saturated with experience of a particular class of materials, an expert intuitively feels whether a newly-reported fact is probable or not, whether a proposed hypothesis is worthless or the reverse. He instinctively knows that, in a novel case, this and not that will be the promising course of action. The well-known story of the old judge advising the new one never to give reasons for his decisions, "the decisions will probably be right, the reasons will surely be wrong," illustrates this. The doctor will feel that the patient is doomed, the dentist will have a premonition that the tooth will break, though neither can articulate a reason for his foreboding. The reason lies embedded, but not yet laid bare, in all the countless previous cases dimly suggested by the actual one, all calling up the same conclusion, which the adept thus finds himself swept on to, he knows not how or why.

judge / dentist different reasons for gut feeling
judge because emotionally he knows it's right
dentist because logically / from memory he knows it's right

from "Preface to *Lyrical Ballads*"

William Wordsworth (1770–1850)

In the preceding essay, William James puts philosophy on the side of science, both of them representing the kind of investigation that is based on analysis. Less than ninety years earlier, Wordsworth assumed philosophy to be on the side of poetry, both of them in pursuit of general and universal truth—of the spiritual reality underlying the phenomenal one. In his "Preface to *Lyrical Ballads*," Wordsworth (wrongly, as it turns out) attributes to Aristotle his own view that "poetry is the most philosophic of writing." That Wordsworth and James have opposing assumptions about the nature of philosophy accounts for much of what separates them, in their respective discussions of the differences between poetry and science.

The following excerpt from Wordsworth's "Preface" begins with his definition of a poet, continues that definition by distinguishing poet from scientist, and concludes with his famous statement about poetic creativity as "the spontaneous overflow of powerful feelings . . . recollected in tranquility." The importance of memory to creativity is apparent from the beginning, in the reference to the poet's "disposition to be affected more than other men by absent things as if they were present." The poet "is a man speaking to other men," but one in whom the shared qualities of humanity are intensified, permitting him to look with particular sympathy—and with "an overbalance of enjoyment"—upon man and environment.

In the concluding book of his long autobiographical poem, *The Prelude,* Wordsworth finds that the final development of his growth as a poet is the realization that the love of nature leads to the love of man. But more than nature itself is responsible for this achievement: "The spiritual love acts not nor can exist/ Without imagination, which in truth/Is but another name for absolute power/And clearest insight, amplitude of mind,/And reason in her most exalted mood." For Wordsworth, our responses to the natural world become the images upon which memory's power is based—images less factual, less objectively true, than they are subjective, transformed by the imagination. "Reason in her most exalted mood" is thought infused by feeling, by imagination; in that credo about poetic creativity that closes this excerpt from his "Preface," the relation of thought to feeling is everywhere apparent, with the emotional value that immediately surrounds the recalled image or experience given the crucial role.

What is a poet? To whom does he address himself? And what language is to be expected from him? He is a man speaking to men: a man, it is true, endued with more lively sensibility, more enthusiasm and tenderness, who has a greater knowledge of human nature, and a more comprehensive soul, than are supposed to be common among mankind; a man pleased

143

with his own passions and volitions, and who rejoices more than other men in the spirit of life that is in him; delighting to contemplate similar volitions and passions as manifested in the goings-on of the universe, and habitually impelled to create them where he does not find them. To these qualities he has added a disposition to be affected more than other men by absent things as if they were present; an ability of conjuring up in himself passions, which are indeed far from being the same as those produced by real events, yet (especially in those parts of the general sympathy which are pleasing and delightful) do more nearly resemble the passions produced by real events, than anything which, from the motions of their own minds merely, other men are accustomed to feel in themselves; whence, and from practice, he has acquired a greater readiness and power in expressing what he thinks and feels, and especially those thoughts and feelings which, by his own choice, or from the structure of his own mind, arise in him without immediate external excitement. . . .

Aristotle, I have been told, hath said, that poetry is the most philosophic of all writing: it is so: its object is truth, not individual and local, but general, and operative; not standing upon external testimony, but carried alive into the heart by passion; truth which is its own testimony, which gives strength and divinity to the tribunal to which it appeals, and receives them from the same tribunal. Poetry is the image of man and nature. The obstacles which stand in the way of the fidelity of the biographer and historian, and of their consequent utility, are incalculably greater than those which are to be encountered by the poet who has an adequate notion of the dignity of his art. The poet writes under one restriction only, namely, that of the necessity of giving immediate pleasure to a human being possessed of that information which may be expected from him, not as a lawyer, a physician, a mariner, an astronomer or a natural philosopher, but as a man. Except this one restriction, there is no object standing between the poet and the image of things; between this, and the biographer and historian there are a thousand.

Nor let this necessity of producing immediate pleasure be considered as a degradation of the poet's art. It is far otherwise. It is an acknowledgment of the beauty of the universe, an acknowledgment the more sincere, because it is not formal, but indirect; it is a task light and easy to him who looks at the world in the spirit of love: further, it is a homage paid to the native and naked dignity of man, to the grand elementary principle of pleasure, by which he knows, and feels, and lives, and moves. We have no sympathy but what is propagated by pleasure: I would not be misunderstood; but wherever we sympathize with pain it will be found that the sympathy is produced and carried on by subtle combinations with pleasure. We have no knowledge, that is, no general principles drawn from the contemplation of particular facts, but what has been built up by pleasure, and exists in us by pleasure alone. The man of science, the chemist and mathematician, whatever difficulties and disgusts they may have had to struggle with, know and feel this. However painful may be the objects with which the anatomist's knowledge is connected, he feels that his knowledge is pleasure; and where he has no pleasure he has no knowledge. What then does the poet? He considers man and the objects that surround him as acting and re-acting upon each other, so as to produce an infinite complexity of pain and pleasure; he considers man in his own nature and in his ordinary life as contemplating this with a certain quantity of immediate knowledge, with certain convictions, intuitions, and deductions which by habit become of the nature of intuitions; he considers him as looking upon this complex scene of ideas and sensations, and finding everywhere objects that immediately excite in him sympathies which, from the necessities of his nature, are accompanied by an overbalance of enjoyment.

To this knowledge which all men carry about with them, and to these sympathies in which without any discipline than that of our daily life we are fitted to take delight, the poet principally directs his attention. He considers man and nature as essentially adapted to each other, and the mind of man as naturally the minor of the fairest and most interesting qualities of nature. And thus the poet, prompted by this feeling of pleasure which accompanies him through the whole course of his studies, converses with general nature with affections akin to those, which, through labor and length of time, the man of science has raised up in himself, by conversing with those particular parts of nature which are the objects of his studies. The knowledge both of the poet and the man of science is pleasure; but the knowledge of the one cleaves to us as a necessary part of our existence, our natural and unalienable inheritance; the other is a personal and individual acquisition, slow to come to us, and by no habitual and direct sympathy connecting us with our fellow-beings. The man of science seeks truth as a remote and unknown benefactor; he cherishes and loves it in his solitude: the poet, singing a song in which all human beings join with him, rejoices in the presence of truth as our visible friend and hourly companion. Poetry is the breath and finer spirit of all knowledge; it is the impassioned expression which is in the countenance of all science. Emphatically may it be said of the poet, as Shakespeare hath said of man, "that he looks before and after." He is the rock of defense of human nature; an upholder and preserver, carrying everywhere with him relationship and love. In spite of difference of soil and climate, of language and manners, of laws and customs, in spite of things silently gone out of mind and things violently destroyed, the poet binds together by passion and knowledge the vast empire of human society, as it is spread over the whole earth, and over all time. The objects of the poet's thoughts are everywhere; though the eyes and senses of man are, it is true, his favorite guides, yet

145

he will follow wheresoever he can find an atmosphere of sensation in which to move his wings. Poetry is the first and last of all knowledge—it is as immortal as the heart of man. If the labors of men and science should ever create any material revolution, direct or indirect, in our condition, and in the impressions which we habitually receive, the poet will sleep then no more than at present, but he will be ready to follow the steps of the man of science, not only in those general indirect effects, but he will be at his side, carrying sensation into the midst of the objects of the science itself. The remotest discoveries of the chemist, the botanist, or mineralogist, will be as proper objects of the poet's art as any upon which it can be employed, if the time should ever come when these things shall be familiar to us, and the relations under which they are contemplated by the followers of these respective sciences shall be manifestly and palpably material to us as enjoying and suffering beings. If the time should ever come when what is now called science, thus familiarized to men, shall be ready to put on, as it were, a form of flesh and blood, the poet will lend his divine spirit to aid the transfiguration, and will welcome the being thus produced, as a dear and genuine inmate of the household of man. . . .

Among the qualities which I have enumerated as principally conducing to form a poet, is implied nothing differing in kind from other men, but only in degree. The sum of what I have there said is, that the poet is chiefly distinguished from other men by a greater promptness to think and feel without immediate external excitement, and a greater power in expressing such thoughts and feelings as are produced in him in that manner. But these passions and thoughts and feelings are the general passions and thoughts and feelings of men. And with what are they connected? Undoubtedly with our moral sentiments and animal sensations, and with the causes which excite these; with the operations of the elements and the appearances of the visible universe; with storm and sunshine, with the revolutions of the seasons, with cold and heat, with loss of friends and kindred, with injuries and resentments, gratitude and hope, with fear and sorrow. These, and the like, are the sensations and objects which the poet describes, as they are the sensations of other men, and the objects which interest them. The poet thinks and feels in the spirit of the passions of men. . . .

I have said that poetry is the spontaneous overflow of powerful feelings: it takes its origin from emotion recollected in tranquility: the emotion is contemplated till by a species of reaction the tranquility gradually disappears, and an emotion, kindred to that which was before the subject of contemplation, is gradually produced, and does itself actually exist in the mind. In this mood successful composition generally begins, and in a mood similar to this it is carried on. . . .

146

"Psychology and Literature"

Carl Gustav Jung (1875–1961)

In "Psychology and Literature," Carl Jung explicitly separates himself from Freud by his own refusal to explain—reduce—the psychical or visionary elements of literature by making of them symptoms of, say, a concealed childhood experience.

Jung divides works of literature into two categories or modes, one psychological and the other visionary; it is clear that his preference is for the latter, in which "the divine gift of the creative fire" most intensely glows—indeed, the visionary mode soon becomes the only subject of interest to him. It is not paradoxical to Jung that the professional psychologist would find less of interest in the psychological mode (writers who use this mode, he says, deal with consciousness, with "the vivid foreground of life," surfaces which are accessible to reason and to the writers' own psychologizing) than in the visionary mode, the material for which is timeless and primordial and beyond the reach of consciousness. In literature of this sort, the subject is actually the "collective unconscious, a certain psychic disposition shaped by the forces of heredity; from it consciousness has developed." The authors of the great works of literature are ruled "by the unconscious as against the active will"; for this reason, their works are objective and wholly impersonal.

To Jung, the "manifestations of the collective unconscious," which can "range from the ineffably sublime to the perversely grotesque," are compensatory to a specific historical period or epoch (which, like a person, can suffer from bias and psychic ills), providing it with a necessary psychical adjustment. This adjustment "is effected by the collective unconscious in that a poet, a seer or a leader allows himself to be guided by the unexpressed desire of his times and shows the way, by word or deed, to the attainment of that which everyone blindly craves and expects—whether this attainment results in good or evil, the healing of an epoch or its destruction." While recognizing that Jung is describing, not advocating, a psychical state in which morality is rendered meaningless, and that the "adjustment" sought by Jung's collective unconscious has nothing whatsoever to do with proportion or balance—what we would think of as mental health—the reader may feel the need to resist the argument. Most assuredly, *this* reader feels such a need. It strikes me as a virulent romantic exaggeration, one that obliterates responsibility or will to author and dictator alike, cloaks "the primordial vision" in a mystical fabric decorated with demonic and angelic figures, and invokes an attitude conducive to blind faith and warfare.

To counter Jung's hypothesis—for it is only that—let me construct (much too briefly) one of my own. As the selections that precede and follow this one suggest, memory searches for likenesses, affinities. No doubt such an impulse goes far back, far into the human past when we lived intimately within the natural world; perhaps it represents in part a way of coping with our terror of the unknown. From such an impulse, both science and religion have developed—both in pursuit of an ultimate synthesis or unity that remains a metaphysical ideal. Normally, today, we recognize that encompassing unity as something we simply desire; but in periods of social stress or illness, in times of a widely shared and ever-intensifying psychosis, a recognizable part (a particular nation, a particular race, a particular belief) can represent—be mistaken for—the invisible and elusive whole.

I include "Psychology and Literature" in this anthology because it has become an influential essay on the subject of buried memory—and because of my own struggles with a thesis that takes some views I accept but carries them off into a Valhalla from which I am happy to be excluded. For comparison purposes, a reader of Jung's essay might want to turn back to some of the essays in the opening section that concern genetic memories—and to read the essay that immediately follows this one.

It is obvious enough that psychology, being the study of psychic processes, can be brought to bear upon the study of literature, for the human psyche is the womb of all the sciences and arts. We may expect psychological research, on the one hand, to explain the formation of a work of art, and on the other to reveal the factors that make a person artistically creative. The psychologist is thus faced with two separate and distinct tasks, and must approach them in radically different ways.

In the case of the work of art we have to deal with a product of complicated psychic activities—but a product that is apparently intentional and consciously shaped. In the case of the artist we must deal with the psychic apparatus itself. In the first instance we must attempt the psychological analysis of a definitely circumscribed and concrete artistic achievement, while in the second we must analyse the living and creative human being as a unique personality. Although these two undertakings are closely related and even interdependent, neither of them can yield the explanations that are sought by the other. It is of course possible to draw inferences about the artist from the work of art, and *vice versa,* but these inferences are never conclusive. At best they are probable surmises or lucky guesses. A knowledge of Goethe's particular relation to his mother throws some light upon Faust's exclamation: "The mothers—mothers—how very strange it sounds!" But it does not enable us to see how the attachment to his mother could produce the Faust drama itself, however unmistakably we sense in the man Goethe a deep connection between the two. Nor are we more successful in reasoning in the reverse direction. There is nothing in *The Nibelungenring* that would enable us to recognize or definitely infer the fact that Wagner occasionally liked to wear womanish clothes, though hidden connections exist between the heroic masculine world of the Nibelungs and a certain pathological effeminacy in the man Wagner.

The present state of development of psychology does not allow us to establish those rigorous causal connections which we expect of a science. It is only in the realm of he psychophysiological instincts and reflexes that we can confidently operate with the idea of causality. From the point where psychic life begins—that is, at a level of greater complexity—the psychologist must content himself with more or less widely ranging descriptions of happenings and with the vivid portrayal of the warp and weft of the mind in all its amazing intricacy. In doing this, he must refrain from designating any one psychic process, taken by itself, as "necessary." Were this not the state of affairs, and could the psychologist be relied upon to uncover the causal connections within a work of art and in the process of artistic creation, he would leave the study of art no ground to stand on and would reduce it to a special branch of his own science. The psychologist, to be sure, may never abandon his claim to investigate and establish causal relations in complicated psychic events. To do so would be to deny psychology the right to exist. Yet he can never make good this claim in the fullest sense, because the creative aspect of life which finds its clearest expression in art baffles all attempts at rational formulation. Any reaction to stimulus may be causally explained; but the creative act, which is the absolute antithesis of mere reaction, will for ever elude the human understanding. It can only be described in its manifestations; it can be obscurely sensed, but never wholly grasped. Psychology and the study of art will always have to turn to one another for help, and the one will not invalidate the other. It is an important principle in the study of art that a psychic product is something in and for itself—whether the work of art or the artist himself is in question. Both principles are valid in spite of their relativity.

THE WORK OF ART

There is a fundamental difference of approach between the psychologist's examination of a literary work, and that of the literary critic. What is of decisive importance and value for the latter may be quite irrelevant for the former. Literary products of highly dubious merit are often of the greatest interest to the psychologist. For instance, the so-called "psychological novel" is by no means as rewarding for the psychologist as the literary-minded suppose. Considered as a whole such a novel explains itself. It has done its own work of psychological interpretation, and the psychologist can at most criticize or enlarge upon this. The important question as to how a particular author came to write a particular novel is of course left unanswered, but I wish to reserve this general problem for the second part of my essay.

The novels which are most fruitful for the psychologist are those in which the author has not already given a psychological interpretation of

149

his characters, and which therefore leave room for analysis and explanation, or even invite it by their mode of presentation. Good examples of this kind of writing are the novels of Benoît, and English fiction in the manner of Rider Haggard, including the vein exploited by Conan Doyle which yields that most cherished article of mass-production, the detective story. Melville's *Moby Dick,* which I consider the greatest American novel, also comes within this class of writings. An exciting narrative that is apparently quite devoid of psychological exposition is just what interests the psychologist most of all. Such a tale is built upon a groundwork of implicit psychological assumptions, and, in the measure that the author is unconscious of them, they reveal themselves, pure and unalloyed, to the critical discernment. In the psychological novel, on the other hand, the author himself attempts to reshape his material so as to raise it from the level of crude contingency to that of psychological exposition and illumination—a procedure which all too often clouds the psychological significance of the work or hides it from view. It is precisely to novels of this sort that the layman goes for "psychology"; while it is novels of the other kind that challenge the psychologist, for he alone can give them deeper meaning.

I have been speaking in terms of the novel, but I am dealing with a psychological fact which is not restricted to this particular form of literary art. We meet with it in the works of the poets as well, and are confronted with it when we compare the first and second parts of the *Faust* drama. The love-tragedy of Gretchen explains itself; there is nothing that the psychologist can add to it that the poet has not already said in better words. The second part, on the other hand, calls for explanation. The prodigious richness of the imaginative material has so overtaxed the poet's formative powers that nothing is self-explanatory and every verse adds to the reader's need of an interpretation. The two parts of *Faust* illustrate by way of extremes this psychological distinction between works of literature.

In order to emphasize the distinction, I will call the one mode of artistic creation *psychological,* and the other *visionary.* The psychological mode deals with materials drawn from the realm of human consciousness—for instance, with the lessons of life, with emotional shocks, the experience of passion and the crises of human destiny in general—all of which go to make up the conscious life of man, and his feeling life in particular. This material is psychically assimilated by the poet, raised from the commonplace to the level of poetic experience, and given an expression which forces the reader to greater clarity and depth of human insight by bringing fully into his consciousness what he ordinarily evades and overlooks or senses only with a feeling of dull discomfort. The poet's work is an interpretation and illumination of the contents of consciousness, of the ineluctable experiences of human life with its eternally recurrent sorrow and joy. He leaves nothing over for the psychologist, unless, indeed, we expect the latter to expound the reasons for which Faust falls in love with Gretchen, or which drive Gretchen to murder her child! Such themes go to make up the lot of humankind; they repeat themselves millions of times and are responsible for the monotony of the police-court and of the penal code. No obscurity whatever surrounds them, for they fully explain themselves.

Countless literary works belong to this class: the many novels dealing with love, the environment, the family, crime and society, as well as didactic poetry, the larger number of lyrics, and the drama, both tragic and comic. Whatever its particular form may be, the psychological work of art always takes its materials from the vast realm of conscious human experience—from the vivid foreground of life, we might say. I have called this mode of artistic creation psychological because in its activity it nowhere transcends the bounds of psychological intelligibility. Everything that it embraces—the experience as well as its artistic expression—belongs to the realm of the understandable. Even the basic experiences themselves, though non-rational, have nothing strange about them; on the contrary, they are that which has been known from the beginning of time—passion and its fated outcome, man's subjection to the turns of destiny, eternal nature with its beauty and its horror.

The profound difference between the first and second parts of *Faust* marks the difference between the psychological and the visionary modes of artistic creation. The latter reverses all the conditions of the former. The experience that furnishes the material for artistic expression is no longer familiar. It is a strange something that derives its existence from the hinterland of man's mind—that suggests the abyss of time separating us from pre-human ages, or evokes a super-human world of contrasting light and darkness. It is a primordial experience which surpasses man's understanding, and to which he is therefore in danger of succumbing. The value and the force of the experience are given by its enormity. It arises from timeless depths; it is foreign and cold, many-sided, demonic and grotesque. A grimly ridiculous sample of the eternal chaos—a *crimen laesae majestatis humanae,* to use Nietzsche's words—it bursts asunder our human standards of value and of aesthetic form. The disturbing vision of monstrous and meaningless happenings that in every way exceed the grasp of human feeling and comprehension makes quite other demands upon the powers of the artist than do the experiences of the foreground of life. These never rend the curtain that veils the cosmos; they never transcend the bounds of the humanly possible, and for this reason are readily shaped to the demands of art, no matter how great a shock to the individual they may be. But the primordial experiences rend from top to bottom the curtain upon which is painted the picture of an ordered world, and allow a glimpse into the unfathomed abyss of what has not yet become. Is it a vision of other worlds, or of the obscuration of the spirit, or of the beginning of things before the age of man, or of the unborn generations of the future? We cannot say that it is any or none of these.

> Shaping—re-shaping—
> The eternal spirit's eternal pastime.

We find such vision in *The Shepherd of Hermas,* in Dante, in the second part of *Faust,* in Nietzsche's Dionysian exuberance, in Wagner's *Nibelungenring,* in Splitteler's *Olympischer Frühling,* in the poetry of William Blake, in the *Ipnerotomachia* of the monk Francesco Colonna, and in Jacob Boehme's philosophic and poetic stammerings. In a more restricted and specific way, the primordial experience furnishes material for Rider Haggard in the fiction-cycle that turns upon *She,* and it does the same for Benoit, chiefly in *L'Atlantide,* for Kubin in *Die andere Seite,* for Meyrink in *Das grüne Gesicht*—a book whose importance we should not undervalue—for Goetz in *Das Reich ohne Raum,* and for Barlach in *Der tote Tag.* This list might be greatly extended.

In dealing with the psychological mode of artistic creation, we never need ask ourselves what the material consists of or what it means. But this question forces itself upon us as soon as we come to the visionary mode of creation. We are astonished, taken aback, confused, put on our guard or even disgusted—and we demand commentaries and explanations. We are reminded in nothing of everyday, human life, but rather of dreams, nighttime fears and the dark recesses of the mind that we sometimes sense with misgiving. The reading public for the most part repudiates this kind of writing—unless, indeed, it is coarsely sensational—and even the literary critic feels embarrassed by it. It is true that Dante and Wagner have smoothed the approach to it. The visionary experience is cloaked, in Dante's case, by the introduction of historical facts, and, in that of Wagner, by mythological events—so that history and mythology are sometimes taken to be the materials with which these poets worked. But with neither of them does the moving force and the deeper significance lie there. For both it is contained in the visionary experience. Rider Haggard, pardonably enough, is generally held to be a mere inventor of fiction. Yet even with him the story is primarily a means of giving expression to significant material. However much the tale may seem to overgrow the content, the latter outweighs the former in importance.

The obscurity as to the sources of the material in visionary creation is very strange, and the exact opposite of what we find in the psychological mode of creation. We are even led to suspect that this obscurity is not unintentional. We are naturally inclined to suppose—and Freudian psychology encourages us to do so—that some highly personal experience underlies this grotesque darkness. We hope thus to explain these strange

152

glimpses of chaos and to understand why it sometimes seems as though the poet had intentionally concealed his basic experience from us. It is only a step from this way of looking at the matter to the statement that we are here dealing with a pathological and neurotic art—a step which is justified in so far as the material of the visionary creator shows certain traits that we find in the fantasies of the insane. The converse also is true; we often discover in the mental output of psychotic persons a wealth of meaning that we should expect rather from the works of a genius. The psychologist who follows Freud will of course be inclined to take the writings in question as a problem in pathology. On the assumption that an intimate, personal experience underlies what I call the "primordial vision"—an experience, that is to say, which cannot be accepted by the conscious outlook—he will try to account for the curious images of the vision by calling them cover-figures and by supposing that they represent an attempted concealment of the basic experience. This, according to his view, might be an experience in love which is morally or aesthetically incompatible with the personality as a whole or at least with certain fictions of the conscious mind. In order that the poet, through his ego, might repress this experience and make it unrecognizable (unconscious), the whole arsenal of a pathological fantasy was brought into action. Moreover, this attempt to replace reality by fiction, being unsatisfactory, must be repeated in a long series of creative embodiments. This would explain the proliferation of imaginative forms, all monstrous, demonic, grotesque and perverse. On the one hand they are substitutes for the unacceptable experience, and on the other they help to conceal it.

Although a discussion of the poet's personality and psychic disposition belongs strictly to the second part of my essay, I cannot avoid taking up in the present connection the Freudian view of the visionary work of art. For one thing, it has aroused considerable attention. And then it is the only well-known attempt that has been made to give a "scientific" explanation of the sources of the visionary material or to formulate a theory of the psychic processes that underlie this curious mode of artistic creation. I assume that my own view of the question is not well known or generally understood. With this preliminary remark, I will now try to present it briefly.

If we insist on deriving the vision from a personal experience, we must treat the former as something secondary—as a mere substitute for reality. The result is that we strip the vision of its primordial quality and take it as nothing but a symptom. The pregnant chaos then shrinks to the proportions of a psychic disturbance. With this account of the matter we feel reassured and turn again to our picture of a well-ordered cosmos. Since we are practical and reasonable, we do not expect the cosmos to be perfect; we accept these unavoidable imperfections which we call abnormalities and diseases, and we take it for granted that human nature is not exempt from them. The frightening revelation of abysses that defy the human understanding is dismissed as illusion, and the poet is regarded as a victim and perpetrator of deception. Even to the poet, his primordial experience was "human—all too human," to such a degree that he could not face its meaning but had to conceal it from himself.

We shall do well, I think, to make fully explicit all the implications of that way of accounting for artistic creation which consists in reducing it to personal factors. We should see clearly where it leads. The truth is that it takes us away from the psychological study of the work of art, and confronts us with the psychic disposition of the poet himself. That the latter presents an important problem is not to be denied, but the work of art is something in its own right, and may not be conjured away. The question of the significance to the poet of his own creative work—of his regarding it as a trifle, as a screen, as a source of suffering or as an achievement—does not concern us at the moment, our task being to interpret the work of art psychologically. For this undertaking it is essential that we give serious consideration to the basic experience that underlies it—namely, to the vision. We must take it at least as seriously as we do the experiences that underlie the psychological mode of artistic creation, and no one doubts that they are both real and serious. It looks, indeed, as if the visionary experience were something quite apart from the ordinary lot of man, and for this reason we have difficulty in believing that it is real. It has about it an unfortunate suggestion of obscure metaphysics and of occultism, so that we feel called upon to intervene in the name of a well-intentioned reasonableness. Our conclusion is that it would be better not to take such things too seriously, lest the world revert again to a benighted superstition. We may, of course, have a predilection for the occult; but ordinarily we dismiss the visionary experience as the outcome of a rich fantasy or of a poetic mood—that is to say, as a kind of poetic license psychologically understood. Certain of the poets encourage this interpretation in order to put a wholesome distance between themselves and their work. Spitteler, for example, stoutly maintained that it was one and the same whether the poet sang of an Olympian spring or to the theme: "May is here!" The truth is that poets are human beings, and that what a poet has to say about his work is often far from being the most illuminating word on the subject. What is required of us, then, is nothing less than to defend the importance of the visionary experience against the poet himself.

It cannot be denied that we catch the reverberations of an initial love-experience in *The Shepherd of Hermas*, in the *Divine Comedy* and in the *Faust* drama—an experience which is completed and fulfilled by the vision.

There is no ground for the assumption that the second part of *Faust* repudiates or conceals the normal, human experience of the first part, nor are we justified in supposing that Goethe was normal at the time when he wrote *Part I*, but in a neurotic state of mind when he composed *Part II*. Hermas, Dante and Goethe can be taken as three steps in a sequence covering nearly two thousand years of human development, and in each of them we find the personal love-episode not only connected with the weightier visionary experience, but frankly subordinated to it. On the strength of this evidence which is furnished by the work of art itself and which throws out of court the question of the poet's particular psychic disposition, we must admit that the vision represents a deeper and more impressive experience than human passion. In works of art of this nature—and we must never confuse them with the artist as a person—we cannot doubt that the vision is a genuine, primordial experience, regardless of what reason-mongers may say. The vision is not something derived or secondary, and it is not a symptom of something else. It is true symbolic expression—that is, the expression of something existent in its own right, but imperfectly known. The love-episode is a real experience really suffered, and the same statement applies to the vision. We need not try to determine whether the content of the vision is of a physical, psychic or metaphysical nature. In itself it has psychic reality, and this is no less real than physical reality. Human passion falls within the sphere of conscious experience, while the subject of the vision lies beyond it. Through our feelings we experience the known, but our intuitions point to things that are unknown and hidden—that by their very nature are secret. If ever they become conscious, they are intentionally kept back and concealed, for which reason they have been regarded from earliest times as mysterious, uncanny and deceptive. They are hidden from the scrutiny of man, and he also hides himself from them out of *deisidaemonia*. He protects himself with the shield of science and the armour of reason. His enlightenment is born of fear; in the day-time he believes in an ordered cosmos, and he tries to maintain this faith against the fear of chaos that besets him by night. What if there were some living force whose sphere of action lies beyond our world of every day? Are there human needs that are dangerous and unavoidable? Is there something more purposeful than electrons? Do we delude ourselves in thinking that we possess and command our own souls? And is that which science calls the "psyche" not merely a question-mark arbitrarily confined within the skull, but rather a door that opens upon the human world from a world beyond, now and again allowing strange and unseizable potencies to act upon man and to remove him, as if upon the wings of the night, from the level of common humanity to that of a more than personal vocation? When we consider the visionary

155

mode of artistic creation, it even seems as if the love-episode had served as a mere release—as if the personal experience were nothing but the prelude to the all-important "divine comedy."

It is not alone the creator of this kind of art who is in touch with the nightside of life, but the seers, prophets, leaders and enlighteners also. However dark this nocturnal world may be, it is not wholly unfamiliar. Man has known of it from time immemorial—here, there, and everywhere; for primitive man today it is an unquestionable part of his picture of the cosmos. It is only we who have repudiated it because of our fear of superstition and metaphysics, and because we strive to construct a conscious world that is safe and manageable in that natural law holds in it the place of statute law in a commonwealth. Yet, even in our midst, the poet now and then catches sight of the figures that people the night-world—the spirits, demons and gods. He knows that a purposiveness out-reaching human ends is the life-giving secret for man; he has a presentiment of incomprehensible happenings in the pleroma. In short, he sees something of that psychic world that strikes terror into the savage and the barbarian.

From the very first beginnings of human society onward man's efforts to give his vague intimations a binding form have left their traces. Even in the Rhodesian cliff-drawings of the Old Stone Age there appears, side by side with the most amazingly lifelike representations of animals, an abstract pattern—a double cross contained in a circle. This design has turned up in every cultural region, more or less, and we find it today not only in Christian churches, but in Tibetan monasteries as well. It is the so-called sunwheel, and as it dates from a time when no one had thought of wheels as a mechanical device, it cannot have had its source in any experience of the external world. It is rather a symbol that stands for a psychic happening; it covers an experience of the inner world, and is no doubt as lifelike a representation as the famous rhinoceros with the tick-birds on its back. There has never been a primitive culture that did not possess a system of secret teaching, and in many cultures this system is highly developed. The men's councils and the totem-clans preserve this teaching about hidden things that lie apart from man's daytime existence—things which, from primeval times, have always constituted his most vital experiences. Knowledge about them is handed on to young men in the rites of initiation. The mysteries of the Graeco-Roman world performed the same office, and the rich mythology of antiquity is a relic of such experiences in the earliest stages of human development.

It is therefore to be expected of the poet that he will resort to mythology in order to give his experience its most fitting expression. It would be a serious mistake to suppose that he works with materials received at second-hand. The primordial experience is the source of his creativeness; it cannot be fathomed, and therefore requires mythological imagery to give it form.

analogies

In itself it offers no words or images, for it is a vision seen "as in a glass, darkly." It is merely a deep presentiment that strives to find expression. It is like a whirlwind that seizes everything within reach and, by carrying it aloft, assumes a visible shape. Since the particular expression can never exhaust the possibilities of the vision, but falls far short of it in richness of content, the poet must have at his disposal a huge store of materials if he is to communicate even a few of his intimations. What is more, he must resort to an imagery that is difficult to handle and full of contradictions in order to express the weird paradoxicality of his vision. Dante's presentiments are clothed in images that run the gamut of Heaven and Hell; Goethe must bring in the Blocksberg and the infernal regions of Greek antiquity; Wagner needs the whole body of Nordic myth; Nietzsche returns to the hieratic style and recreates the legendary seer of prehistoric times; Blake invents for himself indescribable figures, and Spitteler borrows old names for new creatures of the imagination. And no intermediate step is missing in the whole range from the ineffably sublime to the perversely grotesque.

Psychology can do nothing towards the elucidation of this colorful imagery except bring together materials for comparison and offer a terminology for its discussion. According to this terminology, that which appears in the vision is the collective unconscious. We mean by collective unconscious, a certain psychic disposition shaped by the forces of heredity; from it consciousness has developed. In the physical structure of the body we find traces of earlier stages of evolution, and we may expect the human psyche also to conform in its make-up to the law of phylogeny. It is a fact that in eclipses of consciousness—in dreams, narcotic states and cases of insanity—there come to the surface, psychic products or contents that show all the traits of primitive levels of psychic development. The images themselves are sometimes of such a primitive character that we might suppose them derived from the ancient, esoteric teaching. Mythological themes clothed in modern dress also frequently appear. What is of particular importance for the study of literature in these manifestations of the collective unconscious is that they are compensatory to the conscious attitude. This is to say that they can bring a one-sided, abnormal, or dangerous state of consciousness into equilibrium in an apparently purposive way. In dreams we can see this process very clearly in its positive aspect. In cases of insanity the compensatory process is often perfectly obvious, but takes a negative form. There are persons, for instance, who have anxiously shut themselves off from all the world only to discover one day that their most intimate secrets are known and talked about by everyone.

If we consider Goethe's *Faust*, and leave aside the possibility that it is compensatory to his own conscious attitude, the question that we must answer is this: In what relation does it stand to the conscious outlook of *collective memory / individual memory* (handwritten)

universality (handwritten, left margin)

his time? Great poetry draws its strength from the life of mankind, and we completely miss its meaning if we try to derive it from personal factors. Whenever the collective unconscious becomes a living experience and is brought to bear upon the conscious outlook of an age, this event is a creative act which is of importance to everyone living in that age. A work of art is produced that contains what may truthfully be called a message to generations of men. So *Faust* touches something in the soul of every German. So also Dante's fame is immortal, while *The Shepherd of Hermas* just failed of inclusion in the New Testament canon. Every period has its bias, its particular prejudice and its psychic ailment. An epoch is like an individual; it has its own limitations of conscious outlook, and therefore requires a compensatory adjustment. This is effected by the collective unconscious in that a poet, a seer or a leader allows himself to be guided by the unexpressed desire of his times and shows the way, by word or deed, to the attainment of that which everyone blindly craves and expects—whether this attainment results in good or evil, the healing of an epoch or its destruction.

It is always dangerous to speak of one's own times, because what is at stake in the present is too vast for comprehension. A few hints must therefore suffice. Francesco Colonna's book is cast in the form of a dream, and is the apotheosis of natural love taken as a human relation; without countenancing a wild indulgence of the senses, he leaves completely aside the Christian sacrament of marriage. The book was written in 1453. Rider Haggard, whose life coincides with the flowering-time of the Victorian era, takes up this subject and deals with it in his own way; he does not cast it in the form of a dream, but allows us to feel the tension of moral conflict. Goethe weaves into the theme of Gretchen-Helen-Mater Gloriosa like a red thread into the colourful tapestry of Faust. Nietzsche proclaims the death of God, and Spitteler transforms the waxing and waning of the gods into a myth of the seasons. Whatever his importance, each of these poets speaks with the voice of thousands and ten thousands, foretelling changes in the conscious outlook at his time.

THE POET

Creativeness, like the freedom of the will, contains a secret. The psychologist can describe both these manifestations as processes, but he can find no solution of the philosophical problems they offer. Creative man is a riddle that we may try to answer in various ways, but always in vain, a truth that has not prevented modern psychology from turning now and again to the question of the artist and his art. Freud thought that he had found a key in his procedure of deriving the work of art from the personal experiences of the artist. It is true that certain possibilities lay in this direction, for it was conceivable that a work of art, no less than a neurosis,

memory (handwritten, bottom margin)

might be traced back to those knots in psychic life that we call the complexes. It was Freud's great discovery that neuroses have a causal origin in the psychic realm—that they take their rise from emotional states and from real or imagined childhood experiences. Certain of his followers, like Rank and Stekel, have taken up related lines of enquiry and have achieved important results. It is undeniable that the poet's psychic disposition permeates his work root and branch. Nor is there anything new in the statement that personal factors largely influence the poet's choice and use of his materials. Credit, however, must certainly be given to the Freudian school for showing how far-reaching this influence is and in what curious ways it comes to expression.

Freud takes the neurosis as a substitute for a direct means of gratification. He therefore regards it as something inappropriate—a mistake, a dodge, an excuse, a voluntary blindness. To him it is essentially a shortcoming that should never have been. Since a neurosis, to all appearances, is nothing but a disturbance that is all the more irritating because it is without sense or meaning, few people will venture to say a good word for it. And a work of art is brought into questionable proximity with the neurosis when it is taken as something which can be analysed in terms of the poet's repressions. In a sense it finds itself in good company, for religion and philosophy are regarded in the same light by Freudian psychology. No objection can be raised if it is admitted that this approach amounts to nothing more than the elucidation of those personal determinants without which a work of art is unthinkable. But should the claim be made that such an analysis accounts for the work of art itself, then a categorical denial is called for. The personal idiosyncrasies that creep into a work of art are not essential; in fact, the more we have to cope with these peculiarities, the less is it a question of art. What is essential in a work of art is that it should rise far above the realm of personal life and speak from the spirit and heart of the poet as man to the spirit and heart of mankind. The personal aspect is a limitation—and even a sin—in the realm of art. When a form of "art" is primarily personal it deserves to be treated as if it were a neurosis. There may be some validity in the idea held by the Freudian school that artists without exception are narcissistic—by which is meant that they are undeveloped persons with infantile and auto-erotic traits. The statement is only valid, however, for the artist as a person, and has nothing to do with the man as an artist. In his capacity of artist he is neither auto-erotic, nor hetero-erotic, nor erotic in any sense. He is objective and impersonal—even inhuman—for as an artist he is his work, and not a human being.

Every creative person is a duality or a synthesis of contradictory aptitudes. On the one side he is a human being with a personal life, while on the other side he is an impersonal, creative process. Since as a human

Art not related to human experience or memory!?

being he may be sound or morbid, we must look at his psychic make-up to find the determinants of his personality. But we can only understand him in his capacity of artist by looking at his creative achievement. We should make a sad mistake if we tried to explain the mode of life of an English gentleman, a Prussian officer, or a cardinal in terms of personal factors. The gentleman, the officer and the cleric function as such in an impersonal role, and their psychic make-up is qualified by a peculiar objectivity. We must grant that the artist does not function in an official capacity—the very opposite is nearer the truth. He nevertheless resembles the types I have named in one respect, for the specifically artistic disposition involves an overweight of collective psychic life as against the personal. Art is a kind of innate drive that seizes a human being and makes him its instrument. The artist is not a person endowed with free will who seeks his own ends, but one who allows art to realize its purposes through him. As a human being he may have moods and a will and personal aims, but as an artist he is "man" in a higher sense—he is "collective man"—one who carries and shapes the unconscious, psychic life of mankind. To perform this difficult office it is sometimes necessary for him to sacrifice happiness and everything that makes life worth living for the ordinary human being. *Sacrifices himself - no!*

higher responsibility as man, he to whole, what does not matter

All this being so, it is not strange that the artist is an especially interesting case for the psychologist who uses an analytical method. The artist's life cannot be otherwise than full of conflicts, for two forces are at war within him—on the one hand the common human longing for happiness, satisfaction and security in life, and on the other a ruthless passion for creation which may go so far as to override every personal desire. The lives of artists are as a rule so highly unsatisfactory—not to say tragic—because of their inferiority on the human and personal side, and not because of a sinister dispensation. There are hardly any exceptions to the rule that a person must pay dearly for the divine gift of the creative fire. It is as though each of us were endowed at birth with a certain capital of energy. The strongest force in our make-up will seize and all but monopolize this energy, leaving so little over that nothing of value can come of it. In this way the creative force can drain the human impulses to such a degree that the personal ego must develop all sorts of bad qualities—ruthlessness, selfishness and vanity (so-called "auto-erotism")—and even every kind of vice, in order to maintain the spark of life and to keep itself from being wholly bereft. The auto-erotism of artists resembles that of illegitimate or neglected children who from their tenderest years must protect themselves from the destructive influence of people who have no love to give them— who develop bad qualities for that very purpose and later maintain an invincible egocentrism by remaining all their lives infantile and helpless or by actively offending against the moral code or the law. How can we

creativity and the drive for art enriches life and makes living more worth living - Jung is cold

160

art is all so like is
defined by art

doubt that it is his art that explains the artist, and not the insufficiencies and conflicts of his personal life? These are nothing but the regrettable results of the fact that he is an artist—that is to say, a man who from his very birth has been called to a greater task than the ordinary mortal. A special ability means a heavy expenditure of energy in a particular direction, with a consequent drain from some other side of life.

It makes no difference whether the poet knows that his work is begotten, grows and matures with him, or whether he supposes that by taking thought he produces it out of the void. His opinion of the matter does not change the fact that his own work outgrows him as a child its mother. The creative process has feminine quality, and the creative work arises from unconscious depths—we might say, from the realm of the mothers. *Goethe* Whenever the creative force predominates, human life is ruled and moulded by the unconscious as against the active will, and the conscious ego is swept along on a subterranean current, being nothing more than a helpless observer of events. The work in process becomes the poet's fate and determines his psychic development. It is not Goethe who creates *Faust,* but *Faust* which creates Goethe. And what is *Faust* but a symbol? By this I do not mean an allegory that points to something all too familiar, but an expression that stands for something not clearly known and yet profoundly alive. Here it is something that lives in the soul of every German, and that Goethe has helped to bring to birth. Could we conceive of anyone but a German writing *Faust* or *Also sprach Zarathustra?* Both play upon something that reverberates in the German soul—a "primordial image," as Jacob Burckhardt once called it—the figure of a physician or teacher of mankind. The archetypal image of the wise man, the saviour or redeemer, lies buried and dormant in man's unconscious since the dawn of culture; it is awakened whenever the times are out of joint and a human society is committed to a serious error. When people go astray they feel the need of a guide or teacher or even of the physician. These primordial images are numerous, but do not appear in the dreams of individuals or in works of art until they are called into being by the waywardness of the general outlook. When conscious life is characterized by one-sidedness and by a false attitude, then they are activated—one might say, "instinctively"—and come to light in the dreams of individuals and the visions of artists and seers, thus restoring the psychic equilibrium of the epoch.

In this way the work of the poet comes to meet the spiritual need of the society in which he lives, and for this reason his work means more to him than his personal fate, whether he is aware of this or not. Being essentially the instrument for his work, he is subordinate to it, and we have no reason for expecting him to interpret it for us. He has done the best that in him lies in giving it form, and he must leave the interpretation to others and to the future. A great work of art is like a dream; for all its

mor (margin)

cultural memory (margin)

sacrificing self for sake of the common good....

yet these conclusions are foregone; determined by collective memory that prompted them

apparent obviousness it does not explain itself and is never unequivocal. A dream never says: "You ought," or: "This is the truth." It presents an image in much the same way as nature allows a plant to grow, and we must draw our own conclusions. If a person has a nightmare, it means either that he is too much given to fear, or else that he is too exempt from it; and if he dreams of the old wise man it may mean that he is too predagogical, as also that he stands in need of a teacher. In a subtle way both meanings come to the same thing, as we perceive when we are able to let the work of art act upon us as it acted upon the artist. To grasp its meaning, we must allow it to shape us as it once shaped him. Then we understand the nature of his experience. We see that he has drawn upon the healing and redeeming forces of the collective psyche that underlies consciousness with its isolation and its painful errors; that he has penetrated to that matrix of life in which all men are embedded, which imparts a common rhythm to all human existence, and allows the individual to communicate his feeling and his striving to mankind as a whole.

The secret of artistic creation and of the effectiveness of art is to be found in a return to the state of *participation mystique*—to that level of experience at which it is man who lives, and not the individual, and at which the weal or woe of the single human being does not count, but only human existence. This is why every great work of art is objective and impersonal, but none the less profoundly moves us each and all. And this is also why the personal life of the poet cannot be held essential to his art—but at most a help or a hindrance to his creative task. He may go the way of a Philistine, a good citizen, a neurotic, a fool or a criminal. His personal career may be inevitable and interesting, but it does not explain the poet.

"Anonymity: An Enquiry"

E. M. Forster (1879–1970)

In his introductory talk to the series of Clark lectures at Trinity College, Cambridge, that the English writer E. M. Forster gave in 1924 and later published as *Aspects of the Novel,* he says that he is going to forgo history with its chronology in order to visualize all novelists "as seated together in a room, a circular room, a sort of British Museum reading-room—all writing their novels simultaneously." Critics and theorists of a later day, concerned as they are less with essences and universals than they are with limitations, differences, and the relationship of literature to its specific culture, reject that hypothetical proposition with contempt; that he would make it, one of them has said, means that Forster as critic must be dismissed as having nothing of significance to offer us.

But to Forster, who always takes the larger view, it is the human soul or spirit that finally matters in the creation of all forms of art, giving to each work its measure of autonomy; and that essential spirit has not changed much—he refers somewhere to its progress as sideways, crablike—whatever the particulars of a specific time, whatever the rise and fall of societies. Within each of us is a deeper personality, an unconscious self—it is a kind of subterranean pool in which the commonality of all individuals past and present is to be found. In "Anonymity: An Enquiry," he says that the creator of a worthwhile work of art—one that remains accessible to succeeding generations—must now and then dip a bucket into that timeless region lying deep beneath his or her upper (or social) personality. To the mystic, Forster comments, this deeper region or "common quality is God . . . and . . . here, in the obscure recesses of our being, we near the gates of the Divine." (In his finest novel, *A Passage to India,* an elusive spiritual truth or mystery is the basis not only of a haunting atmospheric strangeness but of the occasionally sensed mutuality that underlies the misunderstandings between individuals and the conflict of cultures.)

The essay that immediately precedes this one, Jung's "Psychology and Literature," also deals with a subterranean memory shared by all humans, and puts an equal emphasis upon the impersonal nature of great works of art. Forster's distinction between the upper and lower personalities is similar to the distinction Jung makes between psychological and visionary modes. And finally, in speaking of the reader's ability to approximate the author's creative state, Forster seems in agreement with Jung in the latter's reference to "the state of *participation mystique*" linking reader with author. The great difference between the two has something to do with a difference in the value implied by each to the unconscious and a difference of immersion: Forster's visionary writer drops buckets into an inner well, suggesting that part of him remains outside where the sun sometimes shines; Jung's is submerged and carried along within the dark subterranean currents. (I have no conjecture of the influence, if any, of Jung upon Forster. Actually, Forster's essay predates the volume in which Jung's essay was brought to the attention of the general reader. "Anonymity: An Enquiry" first appeared in the December 17, 1925 issue of the *Times Literary Supplement; Modern Man in Search of a Soul,* which included "Psychology and Literature," was published in 1933, though Jung's interest in the unconscious traces at least as far back as his *Psychology of the Unconscious,* published in 1916.)

Do you like to know who a book's by?

The question is more profound than may appear. A poem for example: do we gain more or less pleasure from it when we know the name of the poet? The *Ballad of Sir Patrick Spens,* for example. No one knows who wrote *Sir Patrick Spens.* It comes to us out of the northern void like a breath of ice. Set beside it another ballad whose author is known—*The Rime of the Ancient Mariner.* That, too, contains a tragic voyage and the breath of ice, but it is signed Samuel Taylor Coleridge, and we know a certain amount about this Coleridge. Coleridge signed other poems and knew other poets; he ran away from Cambridge; he enlisted as a Dragoon under the name of Trooper Comberback, but fell so constantly from his horse that it had to be withdrawn from beneath him permanently; he was employed instead upon matters relating to sanitation; he married Southey's sister, and gave lectures; he became stout, pious and dishonest, took opium and died. With such information in our heads, we speak of the *Ancient Mariner* as "a poem by Coleridge," but of *Sir Patrick Spens* as "a poem." What difference, if any, does this difference between them make upon our minds? And in the case of novels and plays—does ignorance or knowledge of their authorship signify? And newspaper articles—do they impress more when they are signed or unsigned? Thus—rather vaguely—let us begin our quest.

Books are composed of words, and words have two functions to perform: they give information or they create an atmosphere. Often they do both, for the two functions are not incompatible, but our enquiry shall keep them distinct. Let us turn for our next example to Public Notices. There is a word that is sometimes hung up at the edge of a tramline: the word "Stop." Written on a metal label by the side of the line, it means that a tram should stop here presently. It is an example of pure information. It creates no atmosphere—at least, not in my mind. I stand close to the label and wait and wait for the tram. If the tram comes, the information is correct; if it doesn't come, the information is incorrect; but in either case it remains information, and the notice is an excellent instance of one of the uses of words.

Compare it with another public notice which is sometimes exhibited in the darker cities of England: "Beware of pickpockets, male and female."

Here, again, there is information. A pickpocket may come along presently, just like a tram, and we take our measures accordingly. But there is something else besides. Atmosphere is created. Who can see those words without a slight sinking feeling at the heart? All the people around look so honest and nice, but they are not, some of them are pickpockets, male or female. They hustle old gentlemen, the old gentleman glances down, his watch is gone. They steal up behind an old lady and cut out the back breadth of her beautiful sealskin jacket with sharp and noiseless pairs of scissors. Observe that happy little child running to buy sweets. Why does he suddenly burst into tears? A pickpocket, male or female, has jerked his halfpenny out of his hand. All this, and perhaps much more, occurs to us when we read the notice in question. We suspect our fellows of dishonesty, we observe them suspecting us. We have been reminded of several disquieting truths, or the general insecurity of life, human frailty, the violence of the poor, and the fatuous trustfulness of the rich, who always expect to be popular without having done anything to deserve it. It is a sort of *memento mori,* set up in the midst of Vanity Fair. By taking the form of a warning it has made us afraid, although nothing is gained by fear; all we need to do is to protect our precious purses, and fear will not help us to do this. Besides conveying information it has created an atmosphere, and to that extent is literature. "Beware of pickpockets, male and female," is not good literature, and it is unconscious. But the words are performing two functions, whereas the word "Stop" only performed one, and this is an important difference, and the first step in our journey.

Next step. Let us now collect together all the printed matter of the world into a single heap; poetry books, exercise books, plays, newspapers, advertisements, street notices, everything. Let us arrange the contents of the heap into a line, with the works that create pure information at one end, and the works that create pure atmosphere at the other end, and the works that do both in their intermediate positions, the whole line being graded so that we pass from one attitude to another. We shall find that at the end of the pure information stands the tramway notice "Stop," and that at the extreme other end is lyric poetry. Lyric poetry is absolutely no use. It is the exact antithesis of a street notice, for it conveys no information of any kind. What's the use of "A slumber did my spirit seal" or "Whether on Ida's snowy brow" or "So we'll go no more a roving" or "Far in a western brookland"? They do not tell us where the tram will stop or even whether it exists. And, passing from lyric poetry to ballad, we are still deprived of information. It is true that the *Ancient Mariner* describes an antarctic expedition, but in such a muddled way that it is no real help to the explorer, the accounts of the polar currents and winds being hopelessly inaccurate. It is true that the *Ballad of Sir Patrick Spens* refers to the bringing home of the Maid of Norway in the year 1285, but the reference is so vague and confused that the historians turn from it in despair. Lyric poetry is absolutely no use, and poetry generally is almost no use.

But when, proceeding down the line, we leave poetry behind and arrive at the drama, and particularly at those plays that purport to contain normal human beings, we find a change. Uselessness still predominates, but we begin to get information as well. *Julius Caesar* contains some reliable information about Rome. And when we pass from the drama to the novel, the change is still more marked. Information abounds. What a lot we learn from *Tom Jones* about the west countryside! And from *Northanger Abbey* about the same countryside fifty years later! In psychology too the novelist teaches us much. How carefully has Henry James explored certain selected recesses of the human mind! What an analysis of a country rectory in *The Way of All Flesh!* The instincts of Emily Brontë—they illuminate passion. And Proust—how amazingly does Proust describe not only French Society, not only the working of his characters, but the personal equipment of the reader, so that one keeps stopping with a gasp to say "Oh! how did he find that out about me? I didn't even know it myself until he informed me, but it is so!" The novel, whatever else it may be, is partly a notice-board. And that is why many men who do not care for poetry or even for the drama enjoy novels and are well qualified to criticise them.

Beyond the novel we come to works whose avowed aim is information, works of learning, history, sociology, philosophy, psychology, science, etc. Uselessness is now subsidiary, though it still may persist as it does in the *Decline and Fall* or the *Stones of Venice*. And next come those works that give, or profess to give, us information about contemporary events: the newspapers. (Newspapers are so important and so peculiar that I shall return to them later, but mention them here in their place in the procession of printed matter.) And then come advertisements, time tables, the price list inside a taxi, and public notices: the notice warning us against pickpockets, which incidentally produced an atmosphere, though its aim was information, and the pure information contained in the announcement "Stop." It is a long journey from lyric poetry to a placard beside a tramline, but it is a journey in which there are no breaks. Words are all of one family, and do not become different because some are printed in a book and others on a metal disc. It is their functions that differentiate them. They have two functions, and the combination of those functions is infinite. If there is on earth a house with many mansions, it is the house of words.

Looking at this line of printed matter, let us again ask ourselves: Do I want to know who wrote that? Ought it to be signed or not? The question is becoming more interesting. Clearly, in so far as words convey information, they ought to be signed. Information is supposed to be true. That is its only reason for existing, and the man who gives it ought to sign his name, so that he may be called to account if he has told a lie. When I have waited for several hours beneath the notice "Stop," I have the right to suggest that it be taken down, and I cannot do this unless I know who put it up. Make your statement, sign your name. That's common sense. But as we approach the other function of words—the creation of atmosphere—the question of signature surely loses its importance. It does not matter who wrote "A slumber did my spirit seal" because the poem itself does not matter. Ascribe it to Ella Wheeler Wilcox and the trams will run as usual. It does not matter much who wrote *Julius Caesar* and *Tom Jones*. They contain descriptions of ancient Rome and eighteenth-century England, and to that extent we wish them signed, for we can judge from the author's name whether the description is likely to be reliable; but beyond that, the guarantee of Shakespeare or Fielding might just as well be Charles Garvice's. So we come to the conclusion, firstly, that what is information ought to be signed; and, secondly, that what is not information need not be signed.

The question can now be carried a step further.

What is this element in words that is not information? I have called it "atmosphere," but it requires stricter definition than that. It resides not in any particular word, but in the order in which words are arranged—that is to say, in style. It is the power that words have to raise our emotions or quicken our blood. It is also something else, and to define that other thing would be to explain the secret of the universe. This "something else" in words is undefinable. It is their power to create not only atmosphere, but a world, which, while it lasts, seems more real and solid than this daily existence of pickpockets and trams. Before we begin to read the *Ancient Mariner* we know that the Polar Seas are not inhabited by spirits, and that if a man shoots an albatross he is not a criminal but a sportsman, and that if he stuffs the albatross afterwards he becomes a naturalist also. All this is common knowledge. But when we are reading the *Ancient Mariner,* or remembering it intensely, common knowledge disappears and uncommon knowledge takes its place. We have entered a universe that only answers to its own laws, supports itself, internally coheres, and has a new standard of truth. Information is true if it is accurate. A poem is true if it hangs together. Information points to something else. A poem points to nothing but itself. Information is relative. A poem is absolute. The world created by words exists neither in space nor time though it has semblances of both, it is eternal and indestructible, and yet its action is no stronger than a flower; it is adamant, yet it is also what one of its practitioners thought it to be, namely, the shadow of a shadow. We can best define it by negations. It is not this world, its laws are not the laws of science or logic, its conclusions not those of common sense. And it causes us to suspend our ordinary judgments.

Now comes the crucial point. While we are reading the *Ancient Mariner* we forget our astronomy and geography and daily ethics. Do we not also forget the author? Does not Samuel Taylor Coleridge, lecturer, opium eater, and dragoon, disappear with the rest of the world of information? We remember him before we begin this poem and after we finish it, but during the poem nothing exists but the poem. Consequently while we read the *Ancient Mariner* a change takes place in it. It becomes anonymous, like the *Ballad of Sir Patrick Spens*. And here is the point I would support: that all literature tends towards a condition of anonymity, and that, so far as words are creative, a signature merely distracts us from their true significance. I do not say literature "ought" not to be signed, because literature is alive, and consequently "ought" is the wrong word to use. It wants not to be signed. That puts my point. It is always tugging in that direction and saying in effect: "I, not my author, exist really." So do the trees, flowers and human beings say "I really exist, not God," and continue to say so despite the admonitions to the contrary addressed to them by clergymen and scientists. To forget its Creator is one of the functions of a Creation. To remember him is to forget the days of one's youth. Literature does not want to remember. It is alive—not in a vague complementary sense—but alive tenaciously, and it is always covering up the tracks that connect it with the laboratory.

It may here be objected that literature expresses personality, that it is the result of the author's individual outlook, that we are right in asking for his name. It is his property—he ought to have the credit.

An important objection; also a modern one, for in the past neither writers nor readers attached the high importance to personality that they do today. It did not trouble Homer or the various people who were Homer. It did not trouble the writers in the Greek Anthology, who would write and re-write the same poem in almost identical language, their notion being that the poem, not the poet, is the important thing, and that by continuous rehandling the perfect expression natural to the poem may be attained. It did not trouble the mediaeval balladists, who, like the Cathedral builders, left their works unsigned. It troubled neither the composers nor the translators of the Bible. The Book of Genesis today contains at least three different elements—Jahvist, Elohist and Priestly—which were combined into a single account by a committee who lived under King Josiah at Jerusalem and translated into English by another committee who lived under King James I at London. And yet the Book of Genesis is literature. These earlier writers and readers knew that the words a man writes express him, but they did not make a cult of expression as we do today. Surely they were right, and modern critics go too far in their insistence on personality.

They go too far because they do not reflect what personality is. Just as words have two functions—information and creation—so each human mind has two personalities, one on the surface, one deeper down. The upper personality has a name. It is called S. T. Coleridge, or William Shakespeare, or Mrs. Humphry Ward. It is conscious and alert, it does things like dining out, answering letters, etc., and it differs vividly and amusingly from other personalities. The lower personality is a very queer affair. In many ways it is a perfect fool, but without it there is no literature, because unless a man dips a bucket down into it occasionally he cannot produce first-class work. There is something general about it. Although it is inside S. T. Coleridge, it cannot be labelled with his name. It has something in common with all other deeper personalities, and the mystic will assert that the common quality is God, and that here, in the obscure recesses of our being, we near the gates of the Divine. It is in any case the force that makes for anonymity. As it came from the depths, so it soars to the heights, out of local questionings; as it is general to all men, so the works it inspires have something general about them, namely beauty. The poet wrote the poem, no doubt, but he forgot himself while he wrote it, and we forget him while we read. What is so wonderful about great literature is that it transforms the man who reads it towards the condition of the man who wrote, and brings to birth in us also the creative impulse. Lost in the beauty where he was lost, we find more than we ever threw away, we reach what seems to be our spiritual home, and remember that it was not the speaker who was in the beginning but the Word.

If we glance at one or two writers who are not first class this point will be illustrated. Charles Lamb and R. L. Stevenson will serve. Here are two gifted, sensitive, fanciful, tolerant, humorous fellows, but they always write with their surface-personalities and never let down buckets into their underworld. Lamb did not try: bbbbuckets, he would have said, are bbeyond me, and he is the pleasanter writer in consequence. Stevenson was always trying oh ever so hard, but the bucket either stuck or else came up again full of the R. L. S. who let it down, full of the mannerisms, the self-consciousness, the sentimentality, the quaintness which he was hoping to avoid. He and Lamb append their names in full to every sentence they write. They pursue us page after page, always to the exclusion of higher joy. They are letter writers, not creative artists, and it is no coincidence that each of them did write charming letters. A letter comes off the surface: it deals with the events of the day or with plans: it is naturally signed. Literature tries to be unsigned. And the proof is that, whereas we are always exclaiming "How like Lamb!" or "How typical of Stevenson!" we never say "How like Shakespeare!" or "How typical of Dante!" We are conscious only of the world they have created, and we are in a sense co-partners in it. Coleridge, in his smaller domain, makes us co-partners too. We forget for ten minutes his name and our own, and I contend that this temporary forgetfulness, this momentary and mutual anonymity, is sure evidence of good stuff. The demand that literature should express personality is far too insistent in these days, and I look back with longing to the earlier modes of criticism where a poem was not an expression but a discovery, and was sometimes supposed to have been shown to the poet by God.

The personality of a writer does become important after we have read his book and begin to study it. When the glamour of creation ceases, when the leaves of the divine tree are silent, when the co-partnership is over, then a book changes its nature, and we can ask ourselves questions about it such as "What is the author's name?" "Where did he live?" "Was he married?" and "Which was his favourite flower?" Then we are no longer reading the book, we are studying it and making it subserve our desire for information. "Study" has a very solemn sound. "I am studying Dante" sounds much more than "I am reading Dante." It is really much less. Study is only a serious form of gossip. It teaches us everything about the book except the central thing, and between that and us it raises a circular barrier which only the wings of the spirit can cross. They study of science, history, etc., is necessary and proper, for they are subjects that belong to the domain of information, but a creative subject like literature—to study that is excessively dangerous, and should never be attempted by the immature. Modern education promotes the unmitigated study of literature and concentrates our attention on the relation between a writer's life—his surface life—and his work. That is one reason why it is such a curse. There are no questions to be asked about literature while we read it because "la paix succède à la pensée," in the words of Paul Claudel. An examination paper could not be set on the *Ancient Mariner* as it speaks to the heart of the reader, and it was to speak to the heart that it was written, and otherwise it would not have been written. Questions only occur when we cease to realise what it was about and become inquisitive and methodical.

A word in conclusion on the newspapers—for they raise an interesting contributory issue. We have already defined a newspaper as something which conveys, or is supposed to convey, information about passing events. It is true, not to itself like a poem, but to the facts it purports to relate— like the tram notice. When the morning paper arrives it lies upon the breakfast table simply steaming with truth in regard to something else. Truth, truth, and nothing but the truth. Unsated by the banquet, we sally forth in the afternoon to buy an evening paper, which is published at midday as the name implies, and feast anew. At the end of the week we buy a weekly, or a Sunday paper, which as the name implies has been written on the Saturday, and at the end of the month we buy a monthly. Thus do we keep in touch with the world of events as practical men should.

And who is keeping us in touch? Who gives us this information upon which our judgments depend, and which must ultimately influence our characters? Curious to relate, we seldom know. Newspapers are for the most part anonymous. Statements are made and no signature appended. Suppose we read in a paper that the Emperor of Guatemala is dead. Our first feeling is one of mild consternation; out of snobbery we regret what has happened, although the Emperor didn't play much part in our lives, and if ladies we say to one another "I feel so sorry for the poor Empress." But presently we learn that the Emperor cannot have died, because Guatemala is a Republic, and the Empress cannot be a widow, because she does not exist. If the statement is signed, and we know the name of the goose who made it, we shall discount anything he tells us in the future. If—which is more probable—it is unsigned or signed "Our Special Correspondent"—we remain defenceless against future misstatements. The Guatemala lad may be turned on to write about the Fall of the Franc and mislead us over that.

It seems paradoxical that an article should impress us more if it is unsigned than if it is signed. But it does, owing to the weakness of our psychology. Anonymous statements have, as we have seen, a universal air about them. Absolute truth, the collected wisdom of the universe, seems to be speaking, not the feeble voice of a man. The modern newspaper has taken advantage of this. It is a pernicious caricature of literature. It has usurped that divine tendency towards anonymity. It has claimed for information what only belongs to creation. And it will claim it as long as we allow it to claim it, and to exploit the defects of our psychology. "The High Mission of the Press." Poor Press! as if it were in a position to have a mission! It is we who have a mission to it. To cure a man through the newspapers or through propaganda or any sort is impossible: you merely alter the symptoms of his disease. We shall only be cured by purging our minds of confusion. The papers trick us not so much by their lies as by their exploitation of our weakness. They are always confusing the two functions of words and insinuating that "The Emperor of Guatemala is dead" and "A slumber did my spirit seal" belong to the same category. They are always usurping the privileges that only uselessness may claim, and they will do this as long as we allow them to do it.

This ends our enquiry. The question "Ought things to be signed?" seemed, if not an easy question, at all events an isolated one, but we could not answer it without considering what words are, and disentangling the two functions they perform. We decided pretty easily that information ought to be signed: common sense leads to this conclusion, and newspapers which are largely unsigned have gained by that device their undesirable influence over civilisation. Creation—that we found a more difficult matter. "Literature wants not to be signed," I suggested. Creation comes from the depths—the mystic will say from God. The signature, the name, belongs to the surface-personality, and pertains to the world of information, it is a ticket, not the spirit of life. While the author wrote he forgot his name; while we read him we forget both his name and our own. When we have finished reading we begin to ask questions, and to study the book and the author, we drag them into the realm of information. Now we learn a thousand things, but we have lost the pearl of great price, and in the chatter of question and answer, in the torrents of gossip and examination papers we forget the purpose for which creation was performed. I am not asking for reverence. Reverence is fatal to literature. My plea is for something more vital: imagination. Imagination is as the immortal God which should assume flesh for the redemption of mortal passion (Shelley). Imagination is our only guide into the world created by words. Whether those words are signed or unsigned becomes, as soon as the imagination redeems us, a matter of no importance, because we have approximated to the state in which they were written, and there are no names down there, no personality as we understand personality, no marrying or giving in marriage. What there is down there—ah, that is another enquiry, and may the clergymen and the scientists pursue it more successfully in the future than they have in the past.

"The Mother of the Muses: In Praise of Memory"

Clara Claiborne Park (1923–)

Since I was hoping to find an essay for this anthology that referred to the high value assigned by the Greeks to memory, I was delighted to come across Clara Claiborne Park's "The Mother of the Muses: In Praise of Memory." It makes a companion piece to the selection from Frances A. Yates' *The Art of Memory* included in the opening section. If any justification is needed for an emphasis on memorization in contemporary as well as classical times, surely Park's essay—which gives us a capsule history of the effects, both good and bad, of written communication since the days of Plato—provides it. Today, as she says, we denigrate the need to hold material in our personal memories, preferring to rely on books, calculators, prompt boards. Yet from the knowledge provided by one's own memory comes the needed substance of inspiration (now handled more comfortably under the category of creativity), of thought itself.

I don't think I've ever read such a gracefully written defense of the need for committing material to memory, and not simply for its own sake (valuable though that may be), but so that it remains waiting—as Park says in her conclusion—"in the unconscious, where the Muses sing to us darkling, and all the richness of what we know and value can come together in unexpected, unheard-of combinations."

Sing, goddess, the anger of Peleus' son Achilles . . .

Tell me, Muse, of the man of many turnings . . .

Yours am I, holy Muses, Calliope, rise . . .

Of man's first disobedience, and the fruit
Of that forbidden tree, whose mortal taste
Brought death into the world, and all our woe.
With loss of Eden, till one greater man
Restore us, and regain the blissful seat.
Sing, Heav'nly Muse. . .

     —& THERE ARE GOLDEN
CONTAINERS LABELED CLIO ERATO CALLIOPE
& OF THESE 9 WE KNOW ONLY THE RUSHING OF THEIR WINGS. . .

The Muses, these goddesses who span so many centuries, whose presence, real or allegorical, has carried meaning for so many poets, who survive in our own mouths whenever we say "music"—who are they? Hesiod begins his account of the genesis of the gods by showing the Muses dancing with soft feet by a spring of violet water, then rising in mist to talk in the night, singing. They are indeed a seductively lovely assembly, if we ignore the forbidding classical polysyllables and listen to their names with a Greek ear. Calliope of the beautiful voice, Euterpe in whom we well delight, Erato the desirable, Melpomene who sings and dances, Thalia the blooming, Terpsichore who delights in the dance, Polyhymnia of the many songs, Clio the glory giver, Urania the heavenly. Who are these lovely ladies, or—since we no longer so easily personify the forces that are important to us—what are they? What are Homer and Hesiod talking about, and Dante and Milton, and James Merrill in a poem no older than yesterday? For whatever we may think about Homer and Hesiod, we know quite well that Dante and Milton and Merrill do not believe in the literal reality of the heavenly Nine. And yet if we are sensitive to when a poet's words grow warm with meaning, we know just as well that they do not invoke the Muses for mere decoration. The important place given these invocations confirms the message of the words and rhythms. To call on the Muses is a way of talking about what are, if not actual presences, still realities which poets take utterly seriously—as must many of us who have found words taking shape in our heads, and wondered where on earth (on earth?) they were coming from.

What do the Muses do? Milton continues:

> . . . Sing, Heav'nly Muse, that on the secret top
> Of Oreb, or of Sinai, didst *inspire*
> That shepherd who first taught the chosen seed . . .

They sing and they *inspire*. And most of us would agree that if they mean anything at all, the Muses are a way of talking about what we call Inspiration. For want of a better word. And when we are impelled into reaching for abstractions "for want of a better word" so we can name forces we don't understand, we would do well to wonder if what the Greeks would have called a god is hovering in the offing, and if we can explain what we are talking about any better than they did.

Or perhaps there is a better word—we could use the twentieth-century name for Inspiration: Creativity. We are just as interested in Creativity as Homer and Dante and Milton were in the Muses. "Inspiration" sounds old-fashioned, but psychological studies are made, tests are devised, books are written on Creativity. Advertising agencies have Creative Directors. Invisible as she is, Creativity must be real.

So let's strip off their gauzy robes down to the bare abstraction and say that the Muses represent Inspiration or Creativity. And then let's robe them again and recall that Hesiod gave them a parentage, as was his habit when seeking to explain his world. They are the daughters of almighty

Zeus, father of gods and men, and—who? What goddess is powerful enough, full enough, fecund enough to give birth to the Muses—to music and dance and poetry and drama, to history and astronomy, even to the eloquence that a ruler needs so sorely in order to govern and that our own rulers so sorely lack? The Muses, for Hesiod, inspire all those arts of communication that inform, delight, civilize, and link us with the past and with our fellows. *And the Muses are the daughters of Mnemosyne, Memory.* It is my antique conviction that the Greeks knew what they were talking about, that to make the Muses the daughters of Memory is to express a fundamental perception of the way in which Creativity operates.

Yet it doesn't suit us at all. Heirs of the Romantics whether we know it or not, we are more likely to think of Memory and Inspiration as enemies than as mother and daughter. Blake, for instance—in the same long poem in which he called for his bow of burning gold to build Jerusalem in England—proclaimed a new age in which "the daughters of Memory" (and of course he knew quite well they were the Muses) "shall become the daughters of Inspiration." For Blake, out of Memory could come only a cold and abstract art: "Mathematic," not "Living Form." And hordes of us agree. We ask ourselves, and our children, to remember nothing these days: not the multiplication table, for we have calculators; not the presidents or the periodic table or the great dates of history; not 1066, not 1453, not 1517, not 1789, not even, perhaps, 1914 and 1917 and 1939. We may make an exception for things we really care about—baseball statistics, for instance. The educated man, however, need not burden his memory. He has learned how to look things ups. And if we do not expect to remember the facts, which after all, we respect, we certainly do not expect to remember those rhythmic evocations of meaning that we call poetry.

In fact, over the years I have noticed a curious transmogrification in the spelling of the word *memory.* It now begins with an R, and it is pronounced "rotememory"—one word. Students say it that way, but not students only. One college president, talking to a *Times* reporter, called rotelearning, memorization, "the lowest form of human intellectual activity." All of us resist the work of memory, which holds so large a place in the educational practice of so many cultures and until only yesterday held so large a place in our own. We have come a long way from Hesiod's Muses; from Saint Thomas Aquinas and Albertus Magnus, for whom the cultivation of Memory was part of Prudence, one of the four cardinal virtues; from the elaborate Renaissance methods of memory training; even from the illiterate Vermont countryman of a hundred years ago who took the orders of isolated farm wives on back country roads and brought back from town unerringly the three spools of thread, the packet of embroidery needles, the pound of tea. Memory now is the marker of outmoded and sterile education. What is important, after all? Not, surely, meaningless cultural facts, still less the great stories of the past or the great weighted sentences and phrases. What is important is to *learn to think*. As for carrying around something in your head to think *about*, to think *with*, a range of language to think and speak *in*—well, what we learn today will be obsolete tomorrow; nobody can hope to keep up with the present explosion of knowledge; the task of education is not to teach us to hold on to the old stuff but to adapt to the new. And the prophecy fulfills itself as our educational practice changes to reflect our convictions. Papers substitute for examinations; exam questions are given out in advance; exams are written at home; teachers discover that they can grade their students just as readily if they give no exams at all. We license ourselves to forget. Who needs memory? Those who live by the word—politicians, commentators, TV ministers, professors—speak from prompt boards or read their texts.

But the Muses are the daughters of Memory. Hear Homer, as he prepares to sing that curious catalogue of ships in the second book of the *Iliad*—261 long lines crammed with 509 discrete facts which in a nonliterate culture he had no way of looking up:

> Tell me now, you Muses who have your homes on Olympos,
> for you, who are goddesses, are there and you know all
>   things,
> and we have heard only the rumour of it and know nothing.
> Who then of those were the chief men and lords of the
>   Danaans?
> I could not tell over the multitude of them nor name them,
> not if I had ten tongues and ten mouths, not if I had
> a voice never to be broken and a heart of bronze within me,
> not unless the Muses of Olympia, daughters
> of Zeus of the aegis, remembered all those who came
>   beneath Ilion.

Not alone, not unassisted could such a catalogue be composed and transmitted, or the almost sixteen thousand lines of the *Iliad*—not without the help of the Muses, the daughters of Memory, who know all things. And what could they do for Homer? What is he talking about?

Well, what can they do for us, on the rare occasions when we ask their assistance? How do we remember the number of days in the months? "Thirty days hath September, / April, June, and November," the rhymes and strong fourfold beat combining to give us instant recall of needed facts we might otherwise have to figure out on our knuckles? How did my mother remember the kings of England, so surely that she still knew them at eighty?

First William the Norman, then William his son,
Henry, Stephen, and Henry, then Richard and John.
Next Henry Third, Edwards One, Two, and Three;
Again, after Richard, three Henrys we see.
Two Edwards, third Richard, if rightly I guess,
Two Henrys, Sixth Edward, Queen Mary, Queen Bess,
Next Jamie the Scot; then Charles, whom they slew,
Then Oliver Cromwell, another Charles too;
Then James, called the Second, ascended the throne;
Then William and Mary, and William alone;
Then Anne, Georges four, Fourth William, all passed—
God sent then Victoria—may she long be the last!

Homer remembers in the same way. It's much more elaborate, of course.
The Homeric poems are freely composed out of thousands of rhythmic
verbal formulas; to quote Denys Page, "about nine tenths of the Iliad's
language was supplied by memory in ready-made verses or parts of verses."

Leitos and Peneleos were leaders of the Boiotians,
with Arkesilaos and Prothoenor and Klonios;
they who lived in Hyria and in rocky Aulis,
in the hill-bends of Eteonos, and Schoinos, and Skolos, . . .
they who held Koroneia, and the meadows of Haliartos, . . .
they who held Arne of the great vineyards, and Mideia,
with Nisa the sacrosanct, and uttermost Anthedon.

Not if he had ten tongues and ten mouths would Homer be able to tell
his story without the Muses to remember for him all those who came
beneath Ilion and what they did there. If he is to keep all that information
in mind, and transmit it to others, it must be by *mousike,* music, by the
beating, measured, repetitive sound patterns that preserve. "Not marble,
nor the gilded monuments / Of princes shall outlive this powerful rhyme."

The Muses remember for Homer all that he knows. The bard's essential
skill is to have mastered those traditional verse formulas and the information
they contain so well that he can create within and around and with them
as spontaneously as if the Muses were singing in his ear. The Muses are
how he remembers. And *what* they remember is all that it is his business to
know in order to be that indispensable member of his society, a poet—bard,
historian, keeper of the past, who knows who his people are and where
they have been, what they have done and suffered, what significances that
action and suffering can bear. The Muses remember through the music
that bears their name. They *sing*—that is, they put sounds and sounding
meanings into an order that can please the ear, light the imagination, and

accommodate the memory, so that they can reach the mind and heart and lodge there.

It is through the Daughters of Memory that Homer remembers how to make a sacrifice, how to launch a ship—those word patterns that repeat over and over again through the *Iliad* and the *Odyssey*. Thousands of bits of information are kept accessible through the Muses' rhythmic eloquence. Whatever society has a need for, the Muses are the means of remembering. Through the Muses the bard transmits the genealogies of gods and men, and the myths and legends that embody the existential and moral understanding of the culture. Through the Muses he transmits the proverbial wisdom. And the Muses are preservers of real historical knowledge too, for those who know how to listen: Clio, too, is a Muse. In Homer's own time the Mycenaean greatness he sang was long past. He himself was probably an Ionian Greek from the islands, who had never seen Greece. But Homer's Muses know the names of Bronze Age towns all over the Greek mainland, complete with details of their topography and agriculture. *The meadows of Haliartos. Arne of the vineyards.* I could not tell over the arguments about the historicity of the Homeric poems, not if I had ten tongues and ten mouths and a heart of brass within me. Not everyone agrees with Denys Page, who argues that the Muses' formulas preserve the names, even the characteristics, of a real Agamemnon and a real Achilles who led a real expedition and destroyed a real city. Not everyone trusts Clio; the Muses themselves told Hesiod that they knew how to sing false things as well as true. Schliemann dug for Troy and found walls under the hill of Hissarlik, but scoffers can point out that the gold beads he dug up were not King Priam's treasure, as he thought they were; that the Troy he found was a mere five acres in extent; and that the gold mask of Mycenae could never have been Agamemnon's. Nevertheless, Schliemann went where he went and dug where he dug because the Muses told him to, and but for their testimony the gold of Mycenae, and the shaft graves, and the burned city of Troy VII, would still be underground.

When Homer talks of the Muses, he has nothing to say about Inspiration. Certainly he knows about it. What poet does not? Hesiod, who if later than Homer was not very much later, describing that visit of the Muses which made him a poet, says that they "breathed into" him—literally *inspired* him with—the power of song, mysterious and divine, so that he might sing of things past and to come. The Muses are goddesses, and their dealings with men are inexplicable and silent; they are daughters of Zeus, and what else can that mean? That understood, there is nothing more to be said about Inspiration. It happens—who knows how? But in order for it to happen—that's where the Muses need their mother. Hesiod says just the one word about Inspiration; Homer not that. But he tells a terrible story of a bard who boasted that he could compete with the Muses in a singing contest and win. Myth after myth tells what happens to humans who make *that* kind of boast. It happened this time too. But the Muses didn't kill him, though the gods often did that to mortals who overstepped. Instead, they "in their anger struck him maimed, and the voice of wonder / they took away, and made him a singer *without memory.*" A stroke, we'd call it. They didn't dry up the springs of Inspiration; they didn't afflict him with singer's block. All they had to do was to take away that which made him a poet, his memory. He couldn't sing any more after that; he had neither the means nor the materials. With nothing in his head, what good could Inspiration do him?

But this is just an old tale, out of the long ago. It is different for us, of course. Because we can write. The Homeric bard couldn't, or didn't, so of course he needed his memory. But we can, and what a difference that makes!

What a difference indeed. Let's skip some four hundred and fifty years and listen in on one of those intellectual conversations that the Athenians delighted in, that Plato spent his life recreating, and that we call dialogues. Plato could write, of course, and did; and in his time the transition from a culture of singers, speakers, and listeners to a culture of readers and writers had begun, although it was not so far advanced that the word for uneducated had become *a-gram-matikos*—illiterate—but was still *a-mousikos*—unmusical, deaf to the Muses. In the *Phaedrus,* Plato makes the definitive statement about writing's effect on memory. Socrates is telling his young friend Phaedrus a story:

> At Naukratis in Egypt, there was one of the old gods there named Theuth. . . . He was the inventor of number and calculation and geometry and astronomy, and checkers and dice, but especially letters. The god Thamuz was then the king of all Egypt, ruling from that great city of Upper Egypt which the Hellenes called Egyptian Thebes. . . . Theuth came to him and showed him his inventions, and said that they should be given to the other Egyptians. Thamuz asked about the use of each of them, approving of some and disapproving others. It would take a long time to go through what Thamuz said to Theuth about each of the various inventions, but when they came to letters, "This," said Theuth, "will make the Egyptians wiser and give them better memories, for it is a specific both for memory and intelligence." Thamuz replied, "Most ingenious Theuth, he who gives birth to an invention is not the one to judge of the harm or benefit it can bring to the user. For you, the father of letters, out of paternal affection are claiming for them just the opposite of what they will do. This discovery will create forgetfulness in the learners' souls, because they will not use their memories, they will trust to the external written characters, and not remember of them-

selves. You have found a specific not for memory but for reminding. You give your disciples not truth, but the *appearance* of wisdom; they will be hearers of many things without in fact learning them; will appear to be omniscient and will generally know nothing: they will be hard to be with, seeming to be wise when they are not."

We all recognize the phenomenon. And rereading this passage in the last of the many educational institutions through which I have passed, learning and teaching, reading and forgetting, how well I know the feeling. Hearers of many things—the easy appearance of omniscience—students and teachers, here we stand together. Someone has defined man as the only animal that buys more books than he can read.

So Socrates asks: "Isn't there another kind of word . . . far better and more powerful than this one? . . . one which is written . . . in the soul of the learner, able to defend itself and knowing whom to speak to and when to be silent?" and Phaedrus answers: "You mean the living word of knowledge which has a soul, and of which the written word is properly only an image."

It is in this context that we must understand what we have all heard: that Socrates wrote nothing, that all his extraordinary influence came through the living, spoken word. When Plato came to set down his version of the words that had meant so much to him—in writing, of course, an irony of which he was not unaware—he used all the art he possessed to communicate not mere abstract arguments but the sense of conversation, of the living human word, rooted in history and personality, contingent, supple, even contradictory. He was able to do it—to save the past alive—because, fortunately for us, and despite his opinion of poetry, he was dear to the Muses.

"The living word of knowledge which has a soul." Socrates' young friend Phaedrus understands very well what Socrates means. The story of Theuth's invention comes at the end of their conversation, but Phaedrus has come for a walk expressly to tell Socrates about a fine speech he's heard someone give about love. He doesn't want to forget it; he's been rehearsing it, and is almost ready to go through it when Socrates comes along. Socrates expects him to repeat it by heart—doubtless that is what *he* could have done at Phaedrus's age—unless, he says, it is "unusually long." But Phaedrus begs off: how can his unpracticed memory do justice to such a fine work? He offers to give, not the actual words, but a point-by-point summary by headings. But Socrates catches sight of something hidden under his cloak. Young Phaedrus has been working not from memory but from the written copy; he's brought the scroll along with him. Socrates makes him read it, since he's got it, and Phaedrus doesn't have to use his memory at all. At the end of the *Phaedrus,* in his myth of

Theuth's great invention, Plato comments on the transition from an oral to a written culture; he has already dramatized it at the beginning. Of course we shouldn't be too hard on Phaedrus. Today we should be well satisfied if a student could rehearse a speech point by point. And the speech was in prose, which is much harder to memorize than poetry. Like the *bourgeois gentilhomme*, people have always spoken prose—but only the use of writing made it possible to preserve it, and took away from the rhythms of poetry their practical necessity. The process of converting the Muses from powerful and essential goddesses into pretty ladies had already begun.

Yet Phaedrus certainly knew plenty of poetry by heart. A hundred years before him there had been no significant literature in prose. Agricultural know-how, scientific observations, philosophical speculations, all were preserved in verse. How else could they be remembered? Even in Plato's time, memory was still at the center of education. The living word written in the soul of the learner was still the primary method—poetry above all, which was why Plato was so fussy about what poetry he allowed into his Republic. But as poetry gave way to prose, means were found to memorize that too. Young Phaedrus, after all, has only had the speech a couple of hours; he hasn't had time to get it word-perfect. But with his summary by headings he's well on his way. There are plenty to encourage him; the Sophists who teach young men to compose speeches also have been developing an art of memory to help them deliver them, for who would be persuaded by a mere reading? Nor do many people have the money to acquire individual handmade copies, or imported papyrus to make notes on, while anything you jot down on a wax tablet is temporary.

It is the spoken word that lodges in the memory. Few people even today are so naturally oriented to written symbols that they can readily commit to memory a text seen merely as a text. Eidetic memory, the ability to recall a page of writing exactly as seen, is extremely rare. It is true that classical memory techniques worked by visual images: if you had a complex sequence of ideas to remember, you converted each of them into a vivid visual image and disposed them, in imagination, at specific locations in the room of a building you knew so well that you could instantly call it to mind. But the classical texts differentiate memory for subject matter from memory for words. Visual methods will keep your arguments straight, but to learn the exact words, says Quintilian, you should say them, "that the memory may derive assistance from the double effort of speaking and listening."

We do not realize how long it took—not just hundreds of years, more like a thousand—for the word even to begin its separation from its sound in the ear and its feel in the mouth. Eric Havelock describes how slowly "the new habits of literacy" penetrated a wholly oral culture; Plato's relation to writing, Havelock says, was more like Homer's than like ours. There was no speed-reading of manuscripts in which there were no capital and lowercase letters, no separations between words, no marks of punctuation—all introduced in postclassical times. Only the living voice could translate the marks on stone or wax or papyrus back into the words they signified and bridge the abyss between marks and meaning. We take for granted that writing implies not a speaker but a reader. But it was not always so.

"Among the Greeks," writes Moses Hadas, literature was "something to be listened to in public rather than scanned silently in private." Even after books and private reading became more common, "the regular method of publication was by public recitation." Not only Plato's dialogues, then, or the exchanges of Greek drama, but "all classic literature . . . is conceived of as a conversation with, or an address to, an audience." Herodotus recited his history—at the Olympic Games, no less—for more publicity. Horace tells us that he "recites to no one except friends, and then under constraint; not just anywhere or in the presence of just anyone"; on the other hand, Ovid complains that in his Black Sea exile he can't find the kind of audience that would appreciate him. Roman prose writers recited too. The Emperor Claudius "gave constant recitals through a professional reader." Philosophers complained of audiences who shouted and swayed, "impassioned by the charm . . . and rhythm of the words," but paid no attention to the philosophy.

But we are, after all, familiar enough with lectures and poetry readings. We know that in the Hellenistic and Roman worlds booksellers grew common. We know of libraries, including the great library at Alexandria, and we think we know how the private individual reads for his own purposes. Silently, how else? Only clods move their lips. But listen to Saint Augustine describe an extraordinary sight—his master, Saint Ambrose, reading. It is A.D. 384. Augustine is thirty years old, a well-known teacher of rhetoric, versed in all literature of his day. He has studied and taught for years in the great intellectual centers of Carthage and of Rome. *And he has never before seen a man read silently.* When Saint Ambrose read, "his eyes glided over the pages, and his heart searched out their meaning, but his voice and tongue were at rest." It's hard to explain such a phenomenon. "We thought perhaps he was afraid if the author he was reading had expressed things obscurely that it would be necessary to explain it for some perplexed but eager listener, and if his time were used up in such tasks, he would be able to read fewer books than he wished to. However, the need to save his voice, which easily grew hoarse, was perhaps the truer reason for his reading to himself. But with whatever intention he did it," says Augustine, still a bit suspicious, "in such a man it was good."

From Homer to Plato, by our impressionistic dating, is some four hundred and fifty years; from Plato to Augustine, some seven hundred and fifty more. More than a millennium of writing, and the word was still living in the mouth. It is in the sixteen hundred years *since* Augustine that the real change has taken place. It took a long time, but Theuth's invention, writing, has fundamentally changed the conception of literature, starting with the word itself, in which the word for "letters," *litterae,* is so embedded that we do not question its presence. Enamored of the text, we are scarcely able to imagine what Augustine's anecdote makes plain: that all classical literature, Thucydides and Cicero and Caesar as well as Sophocles and Sappho and Catullus, though it was transmitted in writing, existed in the sound of the human voice. That means Euclid too, and Aristotle, uneuphonious as we may think them. Why not? Augustine had seen people reading philosophy and mathematics too.

I don't know when silent reading became common. It's clear from his description that Augustine himself didn't imitate Saint Ambrose, even after he had observed him. But I suppose that if Saint Ambrose could do it, Saint Thomas did, nine hundred years later; and when I imagine Dante poring over his manuscript of Virgil, in the classical Latin that at first he found so hard to understand, I should imagine him studying in silence. But once he got the hang of it, I'm not going to imagine him *reading* it in silence. Being a poet, he didn't read it any faster than he could say it. I imagine that he said it *as* he read it, as we still exhort the freshmen to do, knowing full well that they aren't going to do any such thing. For Dante says he knows the whole of the *Aeneid, tutta quanta,* which must certainly mean "by heart." It is not such a feat if you love the words and value their meaning; I myself knew a blind man who knew by heart the whole *Divine Comedy.* But it can't be done through disembodied congress between page and mind. To get a passage by heart, of poetry or prose either, requires the aid of tongue, mouth, and ear, a full synesthetic response to meaning and sound and feel and rhythm, the gifts of the Muses.

I'm only guessing, of course. I don't know how Dante read, or Chaucer, or how much of what they knew they knew by heart. Nor do I know what people did with Shakespeare's "sugared sonnets" as they passed them about in manuscript or read them in the first printed copies—whether they read them aloud and how rapidly, whether they moved their lips. But we do know how much of the Elizabethan lyric poetry that we read in our anthologies, silently and too fast, was truly, literally *lyric*—written to be sung.

> Come unto these yellow sands,
> And then take hands.

[handwritten margin notes:] Shakespeare understood out straightens grammar speaking more easily read aloud when revise phrasing

> Curtsied when you have, and kissed
> (The wild waves whist),
> Foot it featly here and there,
> And sweet sprites, the burden bear.

How can we *read* these lines, least of all silently? And the songs are the least of it. Throughout Shakespeare's life his plays existed primarily in the mouths and memories of actors. And we remember Prince Hamlet himself, who told the players that he had heard that speech about Hecuba only once. He would like to hear it again; he asks the player, "If it live in your memory, begin at this line." But in fact it's Hamlet himself who begins, groping at first, then coming out with a line: "The rugged Pyrrhus, like th' Hyrcanian beast—." But that's not right. "'Tis not so, it begins with Pyrrhus"—then he gets it: "The rugged Pyrrhus, he whose sable arms, / Black as his purpose, did the night resemble. . . ."

Hamlet carries it on for thirteen lines; he stops only when Polonius interrupts him, to praise, not his memory, but his delivery. If it seemed plausible to an Elizabethan audience that Hamlet could speak off an indefinite number of lines he'd heard only once, years before, how much poetry—speeches, fragments of speeches, floating lines—did the Elizabethan playgoer himself carry around with him, preserved by that powerful gift of the sixteenth-century British Muse, blank verse?

But we know that actors memorize their lines even if we don't; we expect drama to be spoken. But epic? *Arma virumque cano*: "Arms and the man I sing." Virgil, and Dante after him, talked about how they sang; but they wrote their epics. They composed for the speaking voice, but they did not compose orally. When Milton invoked his Heav'nly Muse, not quite sixty years after *Hamlet,* the old bards we began with, who carried the whole culture of a people in their heads, were long gone. Homer, the first great European oral poet, was also nearly the last—and Homer was more than two thousand years in the past in 1658. Yet Milton, too, was an oral poet. It seems obvious enough, yet it is exactly the obvious that is most likely to escape us: like Homer, who also, tradition has it, was blind, Milton *wrote* not one of the 10,564 lines of *Paradise Lost.* All were first communicated to the ear, dictated to him, as he says, by the Heav'nly Muse, his Christian Urania, she who inspired Moses and whose "Voice divine" will lead Milton above Olympus, above the achievements of Homer and Virgil into the Heav'n of Heav'ns.

> Descend from Heav'n Urania, by that name
> If rightly thou art call'd, whose Voice divine
> Following, above th' Olympian Hill I soare,
> Above the flight of Pegasean wing.

> The meaning, not the Name I call; for thou
> Nor of the Muses nine, nor on the top
> Of old Olympus dwell'st, but Heav'nly born,
> Before the Hills appeared, or Fountain flow'd,
> Thou with Eternal Wisdom didst converse,
> Wisdom thy Sister, and with her didst play
> In presence of th' Almighty Father, pleas'd
> With thy Celestial Song. . . .

Blind though he is, and "fall'n on evil days, / In darkness and with dangers compass'd round," Milton is a poet still; his Heav'nly Muse visits him unimplored; she dictates to him nightly and inspires Easy his unpremeditated verse. In the morning he himself dictates it to the waiting amanuensis, who copies it down, preserving his pauses and special pronunciations in the punctuation and spelling of the printed edition, which of course Milton never saw. So we can hear Milton's own voice and know that those who still say "heighth" for "height" speak with Milton's seventeenth-century authority.

Certainly, if we call "the meaning not the name," the Muse is Milton's Inspiration. She is his poetic skill too—and, like her classical avatars, she too is Memory's daughter. Can we imagine how stocked Milton's mind was, had to be, with what he needed to make his poem—stocked with the Bible, whose words are everywhere recognizable in *Paradise Lost*; stocked with names, ideas, facts, images, references; with all the materials of his astonishing erudition—in order for his song to well up, easy and unpremeditated, by night? Lucky for him that the cultivation of memory was still, in the Renaissance, an essential part of education—as it has been in every time and place until the advent of today's sophisticated eye-and-print culture. Those old enough to remember know how things have changed. My mother read to her sisters while they sewed; they didn't mind setting in the sleeves and she did. Even I had a college friend whose father still read the family a chapter of Dickens every night as they sat around the dinner table. For all the Gutenberg revolution and the spread of literacy, it's within our lifetimes that Socrates' prediction has been fully justified, and that poetry has moved out of its ancient and accustomed locus—ears, mouth, and gut—and into the place where D. H. Lawrence thought sex ought not to be—the head.

I suspect I'm not the only person over fifty-five who can sing along with these lines:

> Then up spake brave Horatius,
> The keeper of the gate;
> "To every man upon the earth
> Death cometh soon or late.

> And how can man die better
> Than facing fearful odds
> For the ashes of his fathers
> And the altars of his gods?"

And certainly this:

> Breathes there a man with soul so dead,
> Who never to himself hath said,
>   This is my own, my native land!
> Whose heart hath ne'er within him burned
> As home his footsteps he hath turned
>   From wand'ring on a foreign strand?
> If such there be, go, mark him well;
> For him no minstrel raptures swell.
> High though his power, mighty his fame,
> Boundless his wealth as wish could claim,
> For all his pride of power and pelf,
> The wretch, concentred all in self,
> Living, shall forfeit fair renown,
> And, doubly dying, shall go down
> To the vile dust from whence he sprung,
> Unwept, unhonored, and unsung.

I may not have those lines quite right; I've never seen them in print. For years I didn't know who wrote them. I heard them before I was old enough to read poems in books, and when I faltered, trying to recall them, an older colleague was able to supply the lines—from memory. They reached me entirely through oral tradition, as poetry still could in that age of innocence—not as literary *Ding an sich,* still less as a "text," but as what all poetry was once: sound artfully patterned, a familiar, nourishing rumble.

Full many a flower is born to blush unseen. Man is born to sorrow as the sparks fly upward. The Assyrian came down like a wolf on the fold. Say not the struggle naught availeth. This above all, to thine own self be true. I am the master of my fate, I am the captain of my soul. The moving finger writes, and having writ. . . . My grandmother, from whom I first heard most of these lines, never went to college. She was no better educated than the average gentlewoman born in 1856. But lines like these were part of her common speech; they lay in her consciousness, a rich, undiscriminating cultural humus, the verbal deposits of a lifetime. Those to whom literature was really important could do much better; they carried whole anthologies in their heads, as we are told that Borges did—blind, like Milton and Homer. The central place still held by the spoken word ensured that most people who had been to school, and many who had only been to church, possessed a stock of words, figures, phrases, sentences, that deviated satisfyingly from everyday speech but with which they felt at home—portable, personal, usable belongings.

"Every student in the class was required . . . to memorize and recite long poems and chapters from the Bible." James Earl Carter is describing the educational methods current in his boyhood in Plains, Georgia, and paying tribute to Miss Julia Coleman, a "superlative teacher," he calls her, who "heavily influenced" his life. I will not, I suppose, make many converts by calling on Jimmy Carter's Muses. We have left that kind of education behind, and we have made real gains in doing so. It did not require understanding; it did not invite questioning; it did not insist on a discriminating response—though we are wrong if we think that it precluded these good things. But it did make elevated language a familiar possession. In December 1979 Jimmy Carter had a grave matter to talk about on television: an embassy attacked, citizens held hostage. So he dredged up two lines of poetry from the long ago, and spoke them with unusual feeling:

> God is not dead, nor does He sleep;
> The right is strong, and shall prevail. . . .

Not the first lines of Longfellow's poem, not particularly famous, and so not likely to be the contribution of a speech writer—Miss Julia's legacy, rather, waiting in the memory bank.

Certainly it's not our kind of poem; it's a shade inspirational for our tastes. Miss Julia's poems, like my grandmother's, tended to be like that. It's poetry, though—and I would argue that there is a sounder, more genuine relationship to poetry attending the natural use of these two lines than in all the elaborate and self-conscious presidential noticing of poets that began with John Kennedy. We need the words, we reach for them, they are there, we use them. Should poetry be useful? Why not? "Art for art's sake" was born yesterday. The classical dictum was that poetry should profit and delight—both together. Homer was so useful that Greek education was based on his poems for hundreds of years. Milton considered *Paradise Lost* to be of the greatest utility; he wrote it to justify the ways of God to men. Dante told his patron explicitly that he wrote his *Comedy* for a practical purpose: to lead souls from darkness into light. These are grand uses. My grandmother had small ones, though perhaps the human need for capsule inspiration or comfort is not entirely insignificant. It takes all kinds. And it's true that those who use poetry naturally will naturally misuse is—get it wrong, misunderstand it, or misapply it—as Socrates "misused" Homer when he quoted, three days before his death, Achilles' words, "On the third day you shall reach fertile Phthia," though Achilles clearly wasn't thinking of death at all. But Socrates was, and at the time it was *his* poem.

Our own relationship to poetry is much more respectful. More anxious, too; we have been made aware that poetry has many pitfalls, that we can get things wrong, and that most of us will. One of the more interesting dates of literary history must surely be the date when someone was first graded on his reading of a poem. It certainly wasn't in my grandmother's time. For me it wasn't until graduate school in the late 1940s, though I. A. Richards must have been putting his students through it years before that. The method works, and works well; it made two generations of students—and teachers—better readers. Grading concentrates the mind wonderfully, as Dr. Johnson said of hanging. We learned, in those years, to respect the poem, to read it for itself, in itself, to value it for itself, and not for what we wanted it to do for us. This was an immense gain. But it was a loss too. In truly secure relationships, respect and easy intimacy are compatible, between person and person and between person and poem, too. But that kind of security is hard-earned; few of our students attain it. In most relationships, respect entails a certain distance. We may respect poetry too much, treat it too carefully. If we do, it is no longer fully our own.

I do not suggest that today's readers do not value poetry. Today the Muses frequent colleges, indeed are seldom found outside them. And our colleges have done their work well. There are as many people as ever, perhaps more than ever, for whom poetry exists, and exists with a freighted seriousness my grandmother and Miss Julia never imagined. But even for these it exists only partially. We teach from the printed text, inculcating attentiveness and accuracy, analyzing structures, exploring metaphors, searching out hidden linkages, conscientiously attending to tone. Tone? That's a word I didn't hear even in graduate school; now it's such a necessary concept that we teach it to freshmen. "Descriptions of tone," we tell them (I quote from the *Norton Introduction to Literature*), "try to characterize the way the words of the poem are (or should be) spoken when one sensitively reads the poem aloud."

Aloud—the sound of the human voice is unexpectedly recalled. But now the important thing is not to speak the poem ourselves or listen to it, but to learn to characterize in writing how it should be spoken. It's not easy, for the freshmen or for us. The limits of the English adverb are quickly reached. "Playfully"? "Seriously"? "Sarcastically"? (The freshmen love that word, though they don't know what it means.) "Ironically," most treacherous of all? It's surprising how well we manage, when you consider the difficulty of the task and how little time is left to spend actually saying the poems. So gifted senior English majors, who read with a depth and intelligence that was never asked of me in an undergraduate

English course, can still stun me by asking what I mean when I say a line doesn't scan. There are brilliant graduates of fine doctoral programs in English, lovers of poetry, who know less poetry by heart than Jimmy Carter, and who possess, therefore, texts, or intellectual-emotional reconstructions, or paraphrases, but no poems. A paraphrase is not a poem; English teachers work very hard to teach exactly that. But without memory we grope for "That time of year thou mayst in me behold" or J. Alfred Prufrock's mermaids—but they slip away, and all we are left holding are our ungainly paraphrases. Which is why some of us are now surprising our students by asking them to memorize poetry.

There is a memory for fact, of course, and memory for language. Homer's Muses did not distinguish them, and I have mixed them up cavalierly here and left no space to sort them out. But they do connect, in our time as well as Homer's. Creative thinking of any kind requires more than just knowing where to look things up; you have to know they're there before you know you need them. The mind is the greatest of computers, and it works its marvels best when well stored—with facts: names, dates, places, events, sequences—and also with language: words, phrases, sentences, the tongues of men and of angels. Perhaps language is the most important of all. We all notice the contraction in the range of reference of the young. But facts can be looked up, that's true, and if we get a grant, our servants can do that for us. What's harder to acquire—in adulthood hard indeed—is that intimacy with language, that sense for different ways of using it, which grows naturally when we carry Shakespeare and the Bible, Jefferson and Lincoln, Eliot and Yeats, Edward Lear and P. G. Wodehouse in our heads. In our heads or, better, in another part of the body, where we "learn by heart"—in the unconscious, where the Muses sing to us darkling, and all the richness of what we know and value can come together in unexpected, unheard-of combinations. Memory is not the enemy of Inspiration, or of thought either. Today, as always, it is the essential prerequisite of both.

from *Remembrance of Things Past*

Marcel Proust   (1871–1922)

Remembrance of Things Past "is the story of how a little boy became a writer. That is the first—and last—simple statement that can be made about it." So says Howard Moss, poet and long-time poetry editor of *The New Yorker,* at the outset of *The Magic Lantern of Marcel Proust,* his concise study of Marcel Proust; and he goes on to say, "A truer definition is impossibly complicated: it is the biography of a novelist written by its subject, who has decided to write a novel instead of an autobiography, and whose only novel is the biography he is writing. . . . The narrator of Proust's novel is named Marcel, but he is not Proust." In explaining the reason for such a seeming deception, Moss remarks,

> In the original complication of having the narrator and the author of *Remembrance of Things Past* bear the same Christian name, Proust begins the process of merging appearance and reality in order that he may, ultimately, separate them. This doubling of names makes us aware that we are reading a novel that is, in some way, based on fact; it warns us simultaneously that appearances can be deceiving. The strange duality, connecting and yet severing the "I" of the book from the "I" of its creator, suggests its theme: it is nothing less than the rescuing of the self from the oblivion of time. There is an "I" that needs to be rescued; there is an "I" that does the rescuing. In so far as each successfully acts out his role, the "Marcel" of Proust's narrator more cleverly disguises himself than any other name possibly could. The fictional Marcel only becomes aware of the need of salvation as he turns into the Marcel that creates him. And it is in the process of that creation that salvation exists.

Memory, of course, connects the two Marcels, and is the agency of that salvation. To illustrate the value that Proust found in memory, I have chosen a passage mentioned by nearly all commentators on his long novel. It comes toward the end of Proust's final volume, *Time Regained,* as "the fictional Marcel" is turning "into the Marcel that creates him"; certainly the division of memory by the fictional character into the voluntary and involuntary categories (with the latter representing the ability of memory to reach beyond time and to find the essential reality whose perception provides the happiness so crucial both to art and to life) is the view of the author. The joy and certitude that return to the fictional Marcel have their source in his involuntary memories, and are necessary for the lengthy book he is about to write—the same book that the author himself is now beginning to conclude.

As the selection opens, the fictional Marcel, suffering from both physical and psychical ailments, has recently returned to Paris, following a stay of unspecified length at a sanitorium. He is about to attend a party at the mansion of a

circles

family—the Guermantes—whose very name held for him, as a child, an aristo-cratic allure that now has quite vanished. Marcel has reached that point in his own life in which he has ceased to desire, for hope has vanished, perhaps forever; paradoxically, his very passivity permits him to be unusually responsive to random events (the first is his staggering upon some uneven paving-stones) that recall earlier experiences, earlier moments of recall; the major motifs of the novel—the tasting of a madeleine, a musical phrase by Vinteuil, and so on—return, bringing every joy attached to them. Memory can put us in touch with "the essence of things," with what is beyond time itself. In this passage, we see the importance of imagination to memory, the intertwining of the two that makes the memory of an event superior to the event itself; and the reason that "the true paradises are the paradises we have lost." The meditation on these matters continues beyond the passage I have excerpted, and the interested reader might wish to turn to the novel itself.

I got out of my cab a second time just before it reached the house of the Princesse de Guermantes and I began once more to reflect upon the mood of lassitude and boredom in which I had attempted, the previous day, to note the characteristics of that line which, in a countryside reputed one of the loveliest of France, had separated upon the trunks of the trees the shadow from the light. Certainly the reasoned conclusions which I had drawn at the time did not cause me so much pain to-day. They were unchanged; but at this moment, as on every occasion when I found myself torn from my habits—in a new place, or going out at an unaccustomed hour—I was feeling a lively pleasure. The pleasure seemed to me to-day a purely frivolous one, that of going to an afternoon party given by Mme de Guermantes. But since I knew now that I could hope for nothing of greater value than frivolous pleasures, what point was there in depriving myself of them? I told myself again that I had felt, in attempting the description, not a spark of that enthusiasm which, if it is not the sole, is one of the first criteria of talent. I tried next to draw from my memory other "snapshots," those in particular which it had taken in Venice, but the mere word "snapshot" made Venice seem to me as boring as an exhibition of photographs, and I felt that I had no more taste, no more talent for describing now what I had seen in the past, than I had had yesterday for describing what at that very moment I was, with a meticulous and melancholy eye, actually observing. In a few minutes a host of friends whom I had not seen for years would probably ask me to give up being a recluse and devote my days to them. And what reason had I to refuse their request, now that I possessed the proof that I was useless and that literature could no longer give me any joy whatever, whether this was my fault, through my not having enough talent, or the fault of literature itself, if it were true that literature was less charged with reality than I had once supposed?

When I thought of what Bergotte had said to me: "You are ill, but one cannot pity you for you have the joys of the mind," how mistaken he had been about me! How little joy there was in this sterile lucidity! Even if sometimes perhaps I had pleasures (not of the mind), I sacrificed them always to one woman after another; so that, had fate granted me another hundred years of life and sound health as well, it would merely have added a series of extensions to an already tedious existence, which there seemed to be no point in prolonging at all, still less for any great length of time. As for the "joys of the intelligence," could I call by that name those cold observations which my clairvoyant eye or my power of accurate ratiocination made without any pleasure and which remained always unfertile?

[handwritten margin note: *lack of emotion makes world colorless*]

[handwritten note after "unfertile?": *process of being rational*]

But it is sometimes just at the moment when we think that everything is lost that the intimation arrives which may save us; one has knocked at all the doors which lead nowhere, and then one stumbles without knowing it on the only door through which one can enter—which one might have sought in vain for a hundred years—and it opens of its own accord. Revolving the gloomy thoughts which I have just recorded, I had entered the courtyard of the Guermantes mansion and in my absentminded state I had failed to see a car which was coming towards me; the chauffeur gave a shout and I just had time to step out of the way, but as I moved sharply backwards I tripped against the uneven paving-stones in front of the coach-house. And at the moment when, recovering my balance, I put my foot on a stone which was slightly lower than its neighbour, all my discouragement vanished and in its place was that same happiness which at various epochs of my life had been given to me by the sight of trees which I had thought that I recognised in the course of a drive near Balbec, by the sight of the twin steeples of Martinville, by the flavour of a madeleine dipped in tea, and by all those other sensations of which I have spoken and of which the last works of Vinteuil had seemed to me to combine the quintessential character. Just as, at the moment when I tasted the madeleine, all anxiety about the future, all intellectual doubts had disappeared, so now those that a few seconds ago had assailed me on the subject of the reality of my literary gifts, the reality even of literature, were removed as if by magic. I had followed no new train of reasoning, discovered no decisive argument, but the difficulties which had seemed insoluble a moment ago had lost all importance. The happiness which I had just felt was unquestionably the same as that which I had felt when I tasted the madeleine soaked in tea. But if on that occasion I had put off the task of searching for the profounder causes of my emotion, this time I was determined not to resign myself to a failure to understand them. The emotion was the same; the difference, purely material, lay in the images evoked: a profound azure intoxicated my eyes, impressions of coolness, of dazzling light, swirled round me and in my desire to seize them—as afraid to move as I had been on the earlier occasion when I had continued to savour the taste of the madeleine while I tried to draw into my consciousness whatever it was that it recalled to me—I continued, ignoring the evident amusement of the great crowd of chauffeurs, to stagger as I had staggered a few seconds ago, with one foot on the higher paving-stone and the other on the lower. Every time that I merely repeated this physical movement, I achieved nothing; but if I succeeded, forgetting the Guermantes party, in recapturing what I had felt when I first placed my feet on the ground in this way, again the dazzling and indistinct vision fluttered near me, as if to say: "Seize me as I pass if you can, and try to solve the riddle of happiness which I set you." And almost at once I recognised the vision: it was Venice, of which my efforts to describe it and the supposed snapshots taken by my memory had never told me anything, but which the sensation which I had once experienced as I stood upon two uneven stones in the baptistery of St. Mark's had, recurring a moment ago, restored to me complete with all the other sensations linked on that day to that particular sensation, all of which had been waiting in their place—from which with imperious suddenness a chance happening had caused them to emerge—in the series of forgotten days. In the same way the taste of the little madeleine had recalled Combray to me. But why had the images of Combray and of Venice, at these two different moments, given me a joy which was like a certainty and which sufficed, without any other proof, to make death a matter of indifference to me?

Still asking myself this question, and determined to-day to find the answer to it, I entered the Guermantes mansion, because always we give precedence over the inner task that we have to perform to the outward role which we are playing, which was, for me at this moment, that of guest. But when I had gone upstairs, a butler requested me to wait for a few minutes in a little sitting-room used as a library, next to the room where the refreshments were being served, until the end of the piece of music which was being played, the Princess having given orders for the doors to be kept shut during its performance. And at that very moment a second intimation came to reinforce the one which had been given to me by the two uneven paving-stones and to exhort me to persevere in my task. A servant, trying unsuccessfully not to make a noise, chanced to knock a spoon against a plate and again that same species of happiness which had come to me from the uneven paving-stones poured into me; the sensation was again of great heat, but entirely different: heat combined

flashbacks

*senses bringing back
extraordinarily strong
memories*

with a whiff of smoke and relieved by the cool smell of a forest background; and I recognised that what seemed to me now so delightful was that same row of trees which I had found tedious both to observe and to describe but which I had just now for a moment, in a sort of daze—I seemed to be in the railway carriage again, opening a bottle of beer—supposed to be before my eyes, so forcibly had the identical noise of the spoon knocking against the plate given me, until I had had time to remember where I was, the illusion of the noise of the hammer with which a railwayman had remedied some defect on a wheel of the train while we stopped near the little wood. And then it seemed as though the signs which were to bring me, on this day of all days, out of my disheartened state and restore to me my faith in literature, were thronging eagerly about me, for, a butler who had long been in the service of the Prince de Guermantes having recognised me and brought to me in the library where I was waiting, so that I might not have to go to the buffet, a selection of *petits fours* and a glass of orangeade, I wiped my mouth with the napkin which he had given me; and instantly, as though I had been the character in the *Thousand and One Nights* who unwittingly accomplishes the very rite which can cause to appear, visible to him alone, a docile genie ready to convey him to a great distance, a new vision of azure passed before my eyes, but an azure that this time was pure and saline and swelled into blue and bosomy undulations, and so strong was this impression that the moment to which I was transported seemed to me to be the present moment: more bemused than on the day when I had wondered whether I was really going to be received by the Princesse de Guermantes or whether everything round me would not collapse, I thought that the servant had just opened the window on to the beach and that all things invited me to go down and stroll along the promenade while the tide was high, for the napkin which I had used to wipe my mouth had precisely the same degree of stiffness and starchedness as the towel with which I had found it so awkward to dry my face as I stood in front of the window on the first day of my arrival at Balbec, and this napkin now, in the library of the Prince de Guermantes's house, unfolded for me—concealed within its smooth surfaces and its folds—the plumage of an ocean green and blue like the tail of a peacock. And what I found myself enjoying was not merely these colours but a whole instant of my life on whose summit they rested, an instant which had been no doubt an aspiration towards them and which some feeling of fatigue or sadness had perhaps prevented me from enjoying at Balbec but which now, freed from what is necessarily imperfect in external perception, pure and disembodied, caused me to swell with happiness.

The piece of music which was being played might end at any moment, and I might be obliged to enter the drawing-room. So I forced myself to try as quickly as possible to discern the essence of the identical pleasures which I had just experienced three times within the space of a few minutes, and having done so to extract the lesson which they might be made to yield. The thought that there is a vast difference between the real impression which we have had of a thing and the artificial impression of it which we form for ourselves when we attempt by an act of will to imagine it did not long detain me. Remembering with what relative indifference Swann years ago had been able to speak of the days when he had been loved, because what he saw beneath the words was not in fact those days but something else, and on the other hand the sudden pain which he had been caused by the little phrase of Vinteuil when it gave him back the days themselves, just as they were when he had felt them in the past, I understood clearly that what the sensation of the uneven paving-stones, the stiffness of the napkin, the taste of the madeleine had reawakened in me had no connexion with what I frequently tried to recall to myself of Venice, Balbec, Combray, with the help of an undifferentiated memory; and I understood that the reason why life may be judged to be trivial although at certain moments it seems to us so beautiful is that we form our judgment, ordinarily, on the evidence not of life itself but of those quite different images which preserve nothing of life—and therefore we judge it disparagingly. At most I noticed cursorily that the differences which exist between every one of our real impressions—differences which explain why a uniform depiction of life cannot bear much resemblance to the reality—derive probably from the following cause: the slightest word that we have said, the most insignificant action that we have performed at any one epoch of our life was surrounded by, and coloured by the reflection of, things which logically had no connexion with it and which later have been separated from it by our intellect which could make nothing of fun or its own rational purposes, things, however, in the midst of which—here the pink reflection of the evening upon the flower-covered wall of a country restaurant, a feeling of hunger, the desire for women, the pleasure of luxury; there the blue volutes of the morning sea and, enveloped in them, phrases of music half emerging like the shoulders of water-nymphs—the simplest act or gesture remains immured as within a thousand sealed vessels, each one of them filled with things of a colour, a scent, a temperature that are absolutely different one from another, vessels, moreover, which being disposed over the whole range of our years, during which we have never ceased to change if only in our dreams and our thoughts, are situated at the most various moral altitudes and give us the sensation of extraordinarily diverse atmospheres. It is true that we have accomplished these changes imperceptibly; but between the memory which brusquely returns to us and our present state, and no less between two memories of different years, places, hours, the distance is such that it alone, even without any specific originality, would make it impossible to compare one with the other. Yes: if, owing to the work of oblivion, the returning memory can throw no bridge, form no connecting link between itself and the present minute, if it remains in the context of its own place and date, if it keeps its distance, its isolation in the hollow of a valley or upon the highest peak of a mountain summit, for this very reason it causes us suddenly to breathe a new air, an air which is new precisely because we have breathed it in the past, that purer air which the poets have vainly tried to situate in paradise and which could induce so profound a sensation of renewal only if it has been breathed before, since the true paradises are the paradises that we have lost.

And I observed in passing that for the work of art which I now, though I had not yet reached a conscious resolution, felt myself ready to undertake, this distinctness of different events would entail very considerable difficulties. For I should have to execute the successive parts of my work in a succession of different materials; what would be suitable for mornings beside the sea or afternoons in Venice would be quite wrong if I wanted to depict those evenings at Rivebelle when, in the dining-room that opened on to the garden, the heat began to resolve into fragments and sink back into the ground, while a sunset glimmer still illumined the roses on the walls of the restaurant and the last water-colours of the day were still visible in the sky—this would be a new and distinct material, of a transparency and a sonority that were special, compact, cool after warmth, rose-pink.

Over all these thoughts I skimmed rapidly, for another inquiry demanded my attention more imperiously, the inquiry, which on previous occasions I had postponed, into the cause of this felicity which I had just experienced, into the character of the certitude with which it imposed itself. And this cause I began to divine as I compared these diverse happy impressions, diverse yet with this in common, that I experienced them at the present moment and at the same time in the context of a distant moment, so that the past was made to encroach upon the present and I was made to doubt whether I was in the one or the other. The truth surely was that the being within me which had enjoyed these impressions had enjoyed them because they had in them something that was common to a day long past and to the present, because in some way they were extra-temporal, and this being made its appearance only when, through one of these identifications of the present with the past, it was likely to find itself in the one and only medium in which it could exist and enjoy the essence of things, that is to say: outside time. This explained why it was that my anxiety on the subject of my death had ceased at the moment when I had unconsciously recognised the taste of the little madeleine, since the being which at that moment I had been was an extra-temporal

196

[handwritten: memory makes one ageless and immortal]

being and therefore unalarmed by the vicissitudes of the future. This being had only come to me, only manifested itself outside of activity and immediate enjoyment, on those rare occasions when the miracle of an analogy had made me escape from the present. And only this being had the power to perform that task which had always defeated the efforts of my memory and my intellect, the power to make me rediscover days that were long past, the Time that was Lost.

And perhaps, if just now I had been disposed to think Bergotte wrong when he spoke of the life of the mind and its joys, it was because what I thought of at that moment as "the life of the mind" was a species of logical reasoning which had no connexion with it or with what existed in me at this moment—an error like the one which had made me find society and life itself tedious because I judged them on the evidence of untrue recollections, whereas now, now that three times in succession there had been reborn within me a veritable moment of the past, my appetite for life was immense.

A moment of the past, did I say? Was it not perhaps very much more: something that, common both to the past and to the present, is much more essential than either of them? So often, in the course of my life, reality had disappointed me because at the instant when my senses perceived it my imagination, which was the only organ that I possessed for the enjoyment of beauty, could not apply itself to it, in virtue of that ineluctable law which ordains that we can only imagine what is absent. And now, suddenly, the effect of this harsh law had been neutralised, temporarily annulled, by a marvellous expedient of nature which had caused a sensation—the noise made both by the spoon and by the hammer, for instance—to be mirrored at one and the same time in the past, so that my imagination was permitted to savour it, and in the present, where the actual shock to my senses of the noise, the touch of the linen napkin, or whatever it might be, had added to the dreams of the imagination the concept of "existence" which they usually lack, and through this subterfuge had made it possible for my being to secure, to isolate, to immobilise—for a moment brief as a flash of lightning—what normally it never apprehends: a fragment of time in the pure state. The being which had been reborn in me when with a sudden shudder of happiness I had heard the noise that was common to the spoon touching the plate and the hammer striking the wheel, or had felt, beneath my feet, the unevenness that was common to the paving-stones of the Guermantes courtyard and to those of the baptistery of St. Mark's, this being is nourished only by the essences of things, in these alone does it find its sustenance and delight. In the observation of the present, where the senses cannot feed it with this food, it languishes, as it does in the consideration of a past made arid by the intellect or in the anticipation of a future which the will constructs with fragments

[handwritten marginal note, right side: imagination matches to present, matches to past, that is not necessarily connected]

[margin: emotions / senses much / more important / and evocative / than purely / intellectual / thoughts]

of the present and the past, fragments whose reality it still further reduces by preserving of them only what is suitable for the utilitarian, narrowly human purpose for which it intends them. But let a noise or a scent, once heard or once smelt, be heard or smelt again in the present and at the same time in the past, real without being actual, ideal without being abstract, and immediately the permanent and habitually concealed essence of things is liberated and our true self which seemed—had perhaps for long years seemed—to be dead but was not altogether dead, is awakened and reanimated as it receives the celestial nourishment that is brought to it. A minute freed from the order of time has re-created in us, to feel it, the man freed from the order of time. And one can understand that this man should have confidence in his joy, even if the simple taste of a madeleine does not seem logically to contain within it the reasons for this joy, one can understand that the word "death" should have no meaning for him; situated outside time, why should he fear the future?

But this species of optical illusion, which placed beside me a moment of the past that was incompatible with the present, could not last for long.

[margin: purely / emotional / memory / totally / spontaneous]

The images presented to us by the voluntary memory can, it is true, be prolonged at will, for the voluntary memory requires no more exertion on our part than turning over the pages of a picture-book. On the day, for instance, long ago, when I was to visit the Princesse de Guermantes for the first time, I had from the sun-drenched courtyard of our house in Paris idly regarded, according to my whim, now the Place de l'Eglise at Combray, now the beach at Balbec, as if I had been choosing illustrations for that particular day from an album of water-colours depicting the various places where I had been; and with the egotistical pleasure of a collector, I had said to myself as I catalogued these illustrations stored in my memory: "At least I have seen some lovely things in my life." And of course my memory had affirmed that each one of these sensations was quite unlike the others, though in fact all it was doing was to make varied patterns out of elements that were homogeneous. But my recent experience of the three memories was something utterly different. These, on the contrary, instead of giving me a more flattering idea of myself, had almost caused me to doubt the reality, the existence of that self. And just as on the day when I had dipped the madeleine in the hot tea, in the setting of the place where I happened at the time to be—on that first day my room in Paris, today at this moment the library of the Prince de Guermantes, a few minutes earlier the courtyard of his house—there had been, inside me and irradiating a little area outside me, a sensation (the taste of the madeleine dipped in the tea, a metallic sound, a step of a certain kind) which was common both to my actual surroundings and also to another place (my aunt Léonie's bedroom, the railway carriage, the baptistery of St. Mark's). And now again, at the very moment when I was making these reflections, the shrill noise of water running through a pipe, a noise exactly like those long-drawn-out whistles which sometimes on summer evenings one heard the pleasure-steamers emit as they approached Balbec from the sea, made me feel—what I had once before been made to feel in Paris, in a big restaurant, by the sight of a luxurious dining-room, half-empty, summery and hot—something that was not merely a sensation analogous to the one I used to have at the end of the afternoon in Balbec when, the tables already laid and glittering with linen and silver, the vast window-bays still open from one end to the other on to the esplanade without a single interruption, a single solid surface of glass or stone, while the sun slowly descended upon the sea and the steamers in the bay began to emit their cries, I had, if I had wished to join Albertine and her friends who were walking on the front, merely to step over the low wooden frame not much higher than my ankle, into a groove in which the whole continuous range of windows had been wound down so that the air could come into the hotel. (The painful recollection of having loved Albertine was, however, absent from my present sensation. Painful recollections are always of the dead. And the dead decompose rapidly, and there remains even in the proximity of their tombs nothing but the beauty of nature, silence, the purity of the air.) It was no mere analogous sensation nor even a mere echo or replica of a past sensation that I was made to feel by the noise of the water in the pipe, it was that past sensation itself. And in this case as in all the others, the sensation common to past and present had sought to re-create the former scene around itself, while the actual scene which had taken the former one's place opposed with all the resistance of material inertia this incursion into a house in Paris of a Normandy beach or a railway embankment. The marine dining-room of Balbec, with its damask linen prepared like so many altar-cloths to receive the setting sun, had sought to shatter the solidity of the Guermantes mansion, to force open its doors, and for an instant had made the sofas around me sway and tremble as on another occasion it had done to the tables of the restaurant in Paris. Always, when these resurrections took place, the distant scene engendered around the common sensation had for a moment grappled, like a wrestler, with the present scene. Always the present scene had come off victorious, and always the vanquished one had appeared to me the more beautiful of the two, so beautiful that I had remained in a state of ecstasy on the uneven paving-stones or before the cup of tea, endeavouring to prolong or to reproduce the momentary appearances of the Combray or the Balbec or the Venice which invaded only to be driven back, which rose up only at once to abandon me in the midst of the new scene which somehow, nevertheless, the past had been able to permeate. And if the present scene had not very quickly been victorious, I believe that I should have lost consciousness; for so complete are these resurrections of the past during the second that they last, that they not only oblige our eyes to cease to see the room which is near them in order to look instead at the railway bordered with trees or the rising tide, that even force our nostrils to breathe the air of places which are in fact a great distance away, and our will to choose between the various projects which those distant places suggest to us, they force our whole self to believe that it is surrounded by these places or at least to waver doubtfully between them and the places where we now are, in a dazed uncertainty such as we feel sometimes when an indescribably beautiful vision presents itself to us at the moment of our falling asleep.

Fragments of existence withdrawn from Time: these then were perhaps what the being three times, four times brought back to life within me had just now tasted, but the contemplation, though it was of eternity, had been fugitive. And yet I was vaguely aware that the pleasure which this contemplation had, at rare intervals, given me in my life, was the only genuine and fruitful pleasure that I had known. The unreality of the others is indicated clearly enough—is it not?—either by their inability to satisfy us, as is the case with social pleasures, the only consequence of which is likely to be the discomfort provoked by the ingestion of unwholesome food, or with friendship, which is a simulacrum, since, for whatever moral reasons he may do it, the artist who gives up an hour of work for an hour of conversation with a friend knows that he is sacrificing a reality for something that does not exist (our friends being friends only in the light of an agreeable folly which travels with us through life and to which we readily accommodate ourselves, but which at the bottom of our hearts we know to be no more reasonable than the delusion of the man who talks to the furniture because he believes that it is alive), or else by the sadness which follows their satisfaction, a sadness which I had felt, for instance, on the day when I had been introduced to Albertine, at having taken pains (not even in fact very great pains) in order to achieve something—getting to know this girl—which seemed to me trivial simply because I had achieved it. And even a more profound pleasure, like the pleasure which I might have hoped to feel when I was in love with Albertine, was in fact only experienced inversely, through the anguish which I felt when she was not there, for when I was sure that she would soon be with me, as on the day when she had returned from the Trocadéro, I had seemed to experience no more than a vague dissatisfaction, whereas my exaltation and my joy grew steadily greater as I probed more and more deeply into the noise of the spoon on the plate or the taste of the tea which had brought into my bedroom in Paris the bedroom of my aunt Léonie and in its train all Combray and the two ways of our walks.

To this contemplation of the essence of things I had decided therefore that in future I must attach myself, so as somehow to immobilise it.

"Memory and Imagination"

Patricia Hampl (1946–)

Patricia Hampl, a poet and memoirist, has written, among other works, *A Romantic Education,* an account of her growing-up years in St. Paul that captures her half-Czech heritage. The nature of memory obviously matters to her, as it has to generations of philosophers, poets, and other seekers of knowledge and whatever passes for truth among humans. In "Memory and Imagination," she answers as frankly and as honestly as she can some difficult questions that have long been asked: What causes us to remember images? What accounts for our apparent falsifications about the past? What is "the congruence between stored images and hidden emotion"? The "real job" of the memoirist, she says, is to find the answer to the final question, and to connect that answer to the more abstract issues that underlie life itself. To do so requires reflection and the necessary invention that turns an image into a symbol—in other words, imagination must be added, if memoir is to create a viable version of the past.

Is autobiographical writing, with its necessary repetitions of "I," narcissistic and self-serving? In another essay, "The Need to Remember" (included in *The Writer on Her Work,* vol. II), Hampl says that the narrator of the successful memoir is never a hero, only a protagonist; the "I" is a "minion of memory" belonging "not only to the personal world, but to the public realm." "Memory and Imagination" complements that insight by saying that in the memoirist's "act of remembering, the personal environment expands, resonates beyond itself, beyond its 'subject,' into the endless and tragic recollection that is history." My own long concern with the meanings and value of memory has led me to consider imagination less as a separate faculty than as a quality, or dimension, of memory itself—a view that these remarks seem to support.

When I was seven, my father, who played the violin on Sundays with a nicely tortured flair which we considered artistic, led me by the hand down a long, unlit corridor in St. Luke's School basement, a sort of tunnel that ended in a room full of pianos. There many little girls and a single sad boy were playing truly tortured scales and arpeggios in a mash of troubled sound. My father gave me over to Sister Olive Marie, who did look remarkably like an olive.

Her oily face gleamed as if it had just been rolled out of a can and laid on the white plate of her broad, spotless wimple. She was a small, plump woman; her body and the small window of her face seemed to interpret the entire alphabet of olive: her face was a sallow green olive placed upon the jumbo ripe olive of her black habit. I trusted her instantly and smiled, glad to have my hand placed in the hand of a woman who made sense, who provided the satisfaction of being what she was: an Olive who looked like an olive.

My father left me to discover the piano with Sister Olive Marie so that one day I would join him in mutually tortured piano-violin duets for the edification of my mother and brother who sat at the table meditatively spooning in the last of their pineapple sherbet until their part was called for: they put down their spoons and clapped while we bowed, while the sweet ice in their bowls melted, while the music melted, and we all melted a little into each other for a moment.

But first Sister Olive must do her work. I was shown middle C, which Sister seemed to think terribly important. I stared at middle C and then glanced away for a second. When my eye returned, middle C was gone, its slim finger lost in the complicated grasp of the keyboard. Sister Olive struck it again, finding it with laughable ease. She emphasized the importance of middle C, its central position, a sort of North Star of sound. I remember thinking, "Middle C is the belly button of the piano," an insight whose originality and accuracy stunned me with pride. For the first time in my life I was astonished by metaphor. I hesitated to tell the kindly Olive for some reason; apparently I understood a true metaphor is a risky business, revealing of the self. In fact, I have never, until this moment of writing it down, told my first metaphor to anyone.

Sunlight flooded the room; the pianos, all black, gleamed. Sister Olive, dressed in the colors of the keyboard, gleamed; middle C shimmered with meaning and I resolved never—never—to forget its location: it was the center of the world.

Then Sister Olive, who had had to show me middle C twice but who seemed to have drawn no bad conclusions about me anyway, got up and went to the windows on the opposite wall. She pulled the shades down, one after the other. The sun was too bright, she said. She sneezed as she stood at the windows with the sun shedding its glare over her. She sneezed and sneezed, crazy little convulsive sneezes, one after another, as helpless as if she had the hiccups.

"The sun makes me sneeze," she said when the fit was over and she was back at the piano. This was odd, too odd to grasp in the mind. I associated sneezing with colds, and colds with rain, fog, snow and bad weather. The sun, however, had caused Sister Olive to sneeze in this wild way, Sister Olive who gleamed benignly and who was so certain of the location of the center of the world. The universe wobbled a bit and became unreliable. Things were not, after all, necessarily what they seemed. Appearance deceived: here was the sun acting totally out of character, hurling this woman into sneezes, a woman so mild that she was named, so it seemed, for a bland object on a relish tray.

I was given a red book, the first Thompson book, and told to play the first piece over and over at one of the black pianos where the other children were crashing away. This, I was told, was called practicing. It sounded alluringly adult, practicing. The piece itself consisted mainly of middle C, and I excelled, thrilled by my savvy at being able to locate that central note amidst the cunning camouflage of all the other white keys before me. Thrilled too by the shiny red book that gleamed, as the pianos did, as Sister Olive did, as my eager eyes probably did. I sat at the formidable machine of the piano and got to know middle C intimately, preparing to be as tortured as I could manage one day soon with my father's violin at my side.

But at the moment Mary Katherine Reilly was at my side, playing something at least two or three lessons more sophisticated than my piece. I believe she even struck a chord. I glanced at her from the peasantry of single notes, shy, ready to pay homage. She turned toward me, stopped playing, and sized me up.

Sized me up and found a person ready to be dominated. Without introduction she said, "My grandfather invented the collapsible opera hat."

I nodded, I acquiesced, I was hers. With that little stroke it was decided between us—that she should be the leader, and I the side-kick. My job was admiration. Even when she added, "But he didn't make a penny from it. He didn't have a patent"—even then, I knew and she knew that this was not an admission of powerlessness, but the easy candor of a master, of one who can afford a weakness or two.

With the clairvoyance of all fated relationships based on dominance and submission, it was decided in advance: that when the time came for us to play duets, I should always play second piano, that I should spend my allowance to buy her the Twinkies she craved but was not allowed to have, that finally, I should let her copy from my test paper, and when confronted by our teacher, confess with convincing hysteria that it was I, I who had cheated, who had reached above myself to steal what clearly belonged to the rightful heir of the inventor of the collapsible opera hat. . . .

There must be a reason I remember that little story about my first piano lesson. In fact, it isn't a story, just a moment, the beginning of what could perhaps become a story. For the memoirist, more than for the fiction writer, the story seems already *there,* already accomplished and fully achieved in history ("in reality," as we naively say). For the memoirist, the writing of the story is a matter of transcription.

That, anyway, is the myth. But no memoirist writes for long without experiencing an unsettling disbelief about the reliability of memory, a hunch that memory is not, after all, *just* memory. I don't know why I remembered this fragment about my first piano lesson. I don't, for instance, have a single recollection of my first arithmetic lesson, the first time I studied Latin, the first time my grandmother tried to teach me to knit. Yet these things occurred too, and must have their stories.

It is the piano lesson that has trudged forward, clearing the haze of forgetfulness, showing itself bright with detail more than thirty years after the event. I did not choose to remember the piano lesson. It was simply there, like a book that has always been on the shelf, whether I ever read it or not, the binding and title showing as I skim across the contents of my life. On the day I wrote this fragment I happened to take that memory, not some other, from the shelf and paged through it. I found more detail, more event, perhaps a little more entertainment than I had expected, but the memory itself was there from the start. Waiting for me.

Or was it? When I reread what I had written just after I finished it, I realized that I had told a number of lies. I *think* it was my father who took me the first time for my piano lesson—but maybe he only took me to meet my teacher and there was no actual lesson that day. And did I even know then that he played the violin—didn't he take up his violin again much later, as a result of my piano playing, and not the reverse? And is it even remotely accurate to describe as "tortured" the musicianship of a man who began every day by belting out "Oh What a Beautiful Morning" as he shaved?

More: Sister Olive Marie did sneeze in the sun, but was her name Olive? As for her skin tone—I would have sworn it was olive-like; I would have been willing to spend the better part of an afternoon trying to write the exact description of imported Italian or Greek olive her face suggested: I wanted to get it right. But now, were I to write that passage over, it is her intense black eyebrows I would see, for suddenly they seem the central fact of that face, some indicative mark of her serious and patient nature. But the truth is, I don't remember the woman at all. She's a sneeze in the sun and a finger touching middle C. That, at least, is steady and clear.

Worse: I didn't have the Thompson book as my piano text. I'm sure of that because I remember envying children who did have this wonderful book with its pictures of children and animals printed on the pages of music.

As for Mary Katherine Reilly. She didn't even go to grade school with me (and her name isn't Mary Katherine Reilly—but I made that change on purpose). I met her in Girl Scouts and only went to school with her later, in high school. Our relationship was not really one of leader and follower; I played first piano most of the time in duets. She certainly never copied anything from a test paper of mine: she was a better student, and cheating just wasn't a possibility with her. Though her grandfather (or someone in her family) did invent the collapsible opera hat and I remember that she was proud of that fact, she didn't tell me this news as a deft move in a chidish power play.

So, what was I doing in this brief memoir? Is it simply an example of the curious relation a fiction writer has to the material of her own life? Maybe. That may have some value in itself. But to tell the truth (if anyone still believes me capable of telling the truth), I wasn't writing fiction. I was writing memoir—or was trying to. My desire was to be accurate. I wished to embody the myth of memoir: to write as an act of dutiful transcription.

Yet clearly the work of writing narrative caused me to do something very different from transcription. I am forced to admit that memoir is not a matter of transcription, that memory itself is not a warehouse of finished stories, not a static gallery of framed pictures. I must admit that I invented. But why?

Two whys: why did I invent, and then, if a memoirist must inevitably invent rather than transcribe, why do I—why should anybody—write memoir at all?

I must respond to these impertinent questions because they, like the bumper sticker I saw the other day commanding all who read it to QUESTION AUTHORITY, challenge my authority as a memoirist and as a witness.

It still comes as a shock to realize that I don't write about what I know: I write in order to find out what I know. Is it possible to convey to a reader the enormous degree of blankness, confusion, hunch and uncertainty lurking in the art of writing? When I am the reader, not the writer, I too fall into the lovely illusion that the words before me (in a story by Mavis Gallant, an essay by Carol Bly, a memoir by M. F. K. Fisher), which *read* so inevitably, must also have been *written* exactly as they appear, rhythm and cadence, language and syntax, the powerful waves of the sentences laying themselves on the smooth beach of the page one after another faultlessly.

But here I sit before a yellow legal pad, and the long page of the preceding two paragraphs is a jumble of crossed-out lines, false starts, confused order. A mess. The mess of my mind trying to find out what it wants to say. This is a writer's frantic, grabby mind, not the poised mind of a reader ready to be edified or entertained.

I sometimes think of the reader as a cat, endlessly fastidious, capable, by turns, of mordant indifference and riveted attention, luxurious, recumbent, and ever poised. Whereas the writer is absolutely a dog, panting and moping, too eager for an affectionate scratch behind the ears, lunging frantically after any old stick thrown in the distance.

The blankness of a new page never fails to intrigue and terrify me. Sometimes, in fact, I think my habit of writing on long yellow sheets comes from an atavistic fear of the writer's stereotypic "blank white page."

At least when I begin writing, my page isn't utterly blank; at least it has a wash of color on it, even if the absence of words must finally be faced on a yellow sheet as truly as on a blank white one. Well, we have our ways of whistling in the dark.

If I approach writing from memory with the assumption that I know what I wish to say, I assume that intentionality is running the show. Things are not that simple. Or perhaps writing is even more profoundly simple, more telegraphic and immediate in its choices than the grating wheels and chugging engine of logic and rational intention. The heart, the guardian of intuition with its secret, often fearful intentions, is the boss. Its commands are what a writer obeys—often without knowing it. Or, I do.

That's why I'm a strong adherent of the first draft. And why it's worth pausing for a moment to consider what a first draft really is. By my lights, the piano lesson memoir is a first draft. That doesn't mean it exists here exactly as I first wrote it. I like to think I've cleaned it up from the first time I put it down on paper. I've cut some adjectives here, toned down the hyperbole there, smoothed a transition, cut a repetition—that sort of housekeeperly tidying-up. But the piece remains a first draft because I haven't yet gotten to know it, haven't given it a chance to tell me anything. For me, writing a first draft is a little like meeting someone for the first time. I come away with a wary acquaintanceship, but the real friendship (if any) and genuine intimacy—that's all down the road. Intimacy with a piece of writing, as with a person, comes from paying attention to the revelations it is capable of giving, not by imposing my own preconceived notions, no matter how well-intentioned they might be.

I try to let pretty much anything happen in a first draft. <u>A careful first draft is a failed first draft.</u> That may be why there are so many inaccuracies in the piano lesson memoir: I didn't censor, I didn't judge. I kept moving. But I would not publish this piece as a memoir on its own in its present state. It isn't the "lies" in the piece that give me pause, though a reader has a right to expect a memoir to be as accurate as the writer's memory can make it. No, it isn't the lies themselves that makes the piano lesson memoir a first draft and therefore "unpublishable."

The real trouble: the piece hasn't yet found its subject; it isn't yet about what it wants to be about. Note: what *it* wants, not what I want. The difference has to do with the relation a memoirist—any writer, in fact—has to unconscious or half-known intentions and impulses in composition.

Now that I have the fragment down on paper, I can read this little piece as a mystery which drops clues to the riddle of my feelings, like a culprit who wishes to be apprehended. My narrative self (the culprit who has invented) wishes to be discovered by my reflective self, the self who wants to understand and make sense of a half-remembered story about a nun sneezing in the sun. . . .

We only store in memory images of value. The value may be lost over the passage of time (I was baffled about why I remembered that sneezing nun, for example), but that's the implacable judgment of feeling: *this,* we say somewhere deep within us, is something I'm hanging on to. And of course, often we cleave to things because they possess heavy negative charges. Pain likes to be vivid.

Over time, the value (the feeling) and the stored memory (the image) may become estranged. Memoir seeks a permanent home for feeling and image, a habitation where they can live together in harmony. Naturally, I've had a lot of experiences since I packed away that one from the basement of St. Luke's School; that piano lesson has been effaced by waves of feeling for other moments and episodes. I persist in believing the event has value—after all, I remember it—but in writing the memoir I did not simply relive the experience. Rather, I explored the mysterious relationship between all the images I could round up and the even more impacted feelings that caused me to store the images safely away in memory. Stalking the relationship, seeking the congruence between stored image and hidden emotion—that's the real job of memoir.

By writing about that first piano lesson, I've come to know things I could not know otherwise. But I only know these things as a result of reading this first draft. While I was writing, I was following the images, letting the details fill the room of the page and use the furniture as they wished. I was their dutiful servant—or thought I was. In fact, I was the faithful retainer of my hidden feelings which were giving the commands.

I really did feel, for instance, that Mary Katherine Reilly was far superior to me. She was smarter, funnier, more wonderful in every way—that's how I saw it. Our friendship (or she herself) did not require that I become her vassal, yet perhaps in my heart that was something I wanted; I wanted a way to express my feelings of admiration. I suppose I waited until this memoir to begin to find the way.

Just as, in the memoir, I finally possess that red Thompson book with the barking dogs and bleating lambs and winsome children. I couldn't (and still can't) remember what my own music book was, so I grabbed the name and image of the one book I could remember. It was only in reviewing the piece after writing it that I saw my inaccuracy. In pondering this "lie," I came to see what I was up to: I was getting what I wanted. At last.

The truth of many circumstances and episodes in the past emerges for the memoirist through details (the red music book, the fascination with a nun's name and gleaming face), but these details are not merely information, not flat facts. Such details are not allowed to lounge. They must work. Their work is the creation of symbol. But it's more accurate to call it the *recognition* of symbol. For meaning is not "attached" to the detail by the memoirist; meaning is revealed. That's why a first draft is important. Just as the first meeting (good or bad) with someone who later becomes the beloved is important and is o ften reviewed for signals, meanings, omens and indications.

orientation

Now I can look at that music book and see it not only as "a detail," but for what it is, how it *acts*. See it as the small red door leading straight into the dark room of my childhood longing and disappointment. That red book *becomes* the palpable evidence of that longing. In other words, it becomes symbol. There is no symbol, no life-of-the-spirit in the general or the abstract. Yet a writer wishes—indeed all of us wish—to speak about profound matters that are, like it or not, general and abstract. We wish to talk to each other about life and death, about love, despair, loss, and innocence. We sense that in order to live together we must learn to speak of peace, of history, of meaning and values. Those are a few.

We seek a means of exchange, a language which will renew these ancient concerns and make them wholly and pulsingly ours. Instinctively, we go to our store of private images and associations for our authority to speak of these weighty issues. We find, in our details and broken and obscured images, the language of symbol. Here memory impulsively reaches out its arms and embraces imagination. That is the resort to invention. It isn't a lie, but an act of necessity, as the innate urge to locate personal truth always is.

All right. Invention is inevitable. But why write memoir? Why not call it fiction and be done with all the hashing about, wondering where memory stops and imagination begins? And if memoir seeks to talk about "the big issues," about history and peace, death and love—why not leave these reflections to those with expert and scholarly knowledge? Why let the common or garden variety memoirist into the club? I'm thinking again of that bumper sticker: why Question Authority?

My answer, of course, is a memoirist's answer. Memoir must be written because each of us must have a created version of the past. Created: that is, real, tangible, made of the stuff of a life lived in place and in history. And the down side of any created thing as well: we must live with a version that attaches us to our limitations, to the inevitable subjectivity of our points of view. We must acquiesce to our experience and our gift to transform experience into meaning and value. You tell me your story, I'll tell you my story.

If we refuse to do the work of creating this personal version of the past, someone else will do it for us. That is a scary political fact. "The struggle of man against power," a character in Milan Kundera's novel *The Book of Laughter and Forgetting* says, "is the struggle of memory against forgetting." He refers to willful political forgetting, the habit of nations and those in power (Question Authority!) to deny the truth of memory in order to disarm moral and ethical power. It's an efficient way of controlling masses of people. It doesn't even require much bloodshed, as long as people are entirely willing to give over their personal memories. Whole histories can be rewritten. As Czeslaw Milosz said in his 1980 Nobel Prize lecture, the number of books published that seek to deny the existence of the Nazi death camps now exceeds one hundred.

What is remembered is what *becomes* reality. If we "forget" Auschwitz, if we "forget" My Lai, what then do we remember? And what is the purpose of our remembering? If we think of memory naively, as a simple story, logged like a documentary in the archive of the mind, we miss its beauty but also its function. The beauty of memory rests in its talent for rendering detail, for paying homage to the senses, its capacity to love the particles of life, the richness and idiosyncrasy of our existence. The function of memory, on the other hand, is intensely personal and surprisingly political.

Our capacity to move forward as developing beings rests on a healthy relation with the past. Psychotherapy, that widespread method of mental health, relies heavily on memory and on the ability to retrieve and organize images and events from the personal past. We carry our wounds and perhaps even worse, our capacity to wound, forward with us. If we learn not only to tell our stories but to listen to what our stories tell us—to write the first draft and then return for the second draft—we are doing the work of memoir.

Memoir is the intersection of narration and reflection, of storytelling and essay-writing. It can present its story *and* reflect and consider the meaning of the story. It is a peculiarly open form, inviting broken and incomplete images, half-recollected fragments all the mass (and mess) of detail. It offers to shape this confusion—and in shaping, of course it necessarily creates a work of art, not a legal document. But then, even legal documents are only valiant attempts to consign the truth, the whole truth and nothing but the truth to paper. Even they remain versions.

Locating touchstones—the red music book, the olive Olive, my father's violin playing—is deeply satisfying. Who knows why? Perhaps we all sense that we can't grasp the whole truth and nothing but the truth of our experience. Just can't be done. What can be achieved, however, is a version of its swirling, changing wholeness. A memoirist must acquiesce to selectivity, like any artist. The version we dare to write is the only truth, the only relationship we can have with the past. Refuse to write your life and you have no life. At least, that is the stern view of the memoirist.

Personal history, logged in memory, is a sort of slide projector flashing images on the wall of the mind. And there's precious little order to the slides in the rotating carousel. Beyond that confusion, who knows who is running the projector? A memoirist steps into this darkened room of flashing, unorganized images and stands blinking for a while. Maybe for a long while. But eventually, as with any attempt to tell a story, it is necessary to put something first, then something else. And so on, to the end. That's a first draft. Not necessarily the truth, not even *a* truth sometimes, but the first attempt to create a shape.

The first thing I usually notice at this stage of composition is the appalling inaccuracy of the piece. Witness my first piano lesson draft. Invention is screamingly evident in what I intended to be transcription. But here's the further truth: I feel no shame. In fact, it's only now that my interest in the piece truly quickens. For I can see what isn't there, what is shyly hugging the walls, hoping not to be seen. I see the filmy shape of the next draft. I see a more acute version of the episode or—this is more likely—an entirely new piece rising from the ashes of the first attempt.

The next draft of the piece would have to be a true re-vision, a new seeing of the materials of the first draft. Nothing merely cosmetic will do—no rouge buffing up the opening sentence, no glossy adjective to lift a sagging line, nothing to attempt covering a patch of gray writing. None of that. I can't say for sure, but my hunch is the revision would lead me to more writing about my father (why was I so impressed by that ancestral inventor of the collapsible opera hat? Did I feel I had nothing as remarkable in my own background? Did this make me feel inadequate?) I begin to think perhaps Sister Olive is less central to this business than she is in this draft. She is meant to be a moment, not a character.

And so I might proceed, if I were to undertake a new draft of the memoir. I begin to feel a relationship developing between a former self and me.

And, even more compelling, a relationship between an old world and me. Some people think of autobiographical writing as the precious occupation of a particularly self-absorbed person. Maybe, but I don't buy that. True memoir is written in an attempt to find not only a self but a world.

The self-absorption that seems to be the impetus and embarrassment of autobiography turns into (or perhaps always was) a hunger for the world. Actually, it begins as hunger for *a* world, one gone or lost, effaced by time or a more sudden brutality. But in the act of remembering, the personal environment expands, resonates beyond itself, beyond its "subject," into the endless and tragic recollection that is history.

We look at old family photographs in which we stand next to black, boxy Fords and are wearing period costumes, and we do not gaze fascinated because there we are young again, or there we are standing, as we never will again in life, next to our mother. We stare and drift because there we are . . . historical. It is the dress, the black car that dazzle us now and draw us beyond our mother's bright arms which once caught us. We reach into the attractive impersonality of something more significant than ourselves. We write memoir, in other words. We accept the humble position of writing a version rather than "the whole truth."

I suppose I write memoir because of the radiance of the past—it draws me back and back to it. Not that the past is beautiful. In our communal memoir, in history, the death camps *are* back there. In intimate life too, the record is usually pretty mixed. "I could tell you stories . . ." people say and drift off, meaning terrible things have happened to them.

But the past is radiant. It has the light of lived life. A memoirist wishes to touch it. No one owns the past, though typically the first act of new political regime, to grab the past and make it over so the end comes out right. So their power looks inevitable.

No one owns the past, but it is a grave error (another age would have said a grave sin) not to inhabit memory. Sometimes I think it is all we really have. But that may be a trifle melodramatic. At any rate, memory possesses authority for the fearful self in a world where it is necessary to have authority in order to Question Authority.

There may be no more pressing intellectual need in our culture than for people to become sophisticated about the function of memory. The political implications of the loss of memory are obvious. The authority of memory is a personal confirmation of selfhood. To write one's life is to live it twice, and the second living is both spiritual and historical, for a memoir reaches deep within the personality as it seeks its narrative form and also grasps the life-of-the-times as no political treatise can.

Our most ancient metaphor says life is a journey. Memoir is travel writing, then, notes taken along the way, telling how things looked and what thoughts occurred. But I cannot think of the memoirist as a tourist. This is the traveller who goes on foot, living the journey, taking on mountains, enduring deserts, marveling at the lush green places. Moving through it all faithfully, not so much a survivor with a harrowing tale to tell as a pilgrim, seeking, wondering.

"Memory, Creation, and Writing"

Toni Morrison (1931-)

Toni Morrison is the second American woman, and the only African American, to have been awarded the Nobel Prize in literature. She has used the very exclusions and injustices placed upon blacks to transcend these severe handicaps—indeed, her particular gift, entwined as it is with her knowledge of the importance of memory, lies in a breadth of vision that makes her work inclusive rather than exclusive for all readers, regardless of race or sex. Of her novels, *Beloved* is the one in which memory is so important that it becomes, indeed, subject. Beloved, the title character, is created out of memory itself—the memory of a mother, escaped from slavery, who cannot forget the enormity of her own offense, the killing of her infant daughter. Such a murder is as inevitable as any in Greek tragedy: it is an act of love, the consequence of the institution of slavery itself, committed to prevent the baby from being taken from her into the death-in-life of bondage. Is Beloved, the young woman who years later enters the mother's house and life, an apparition or an actual person? In a sense, the question is unimportant: the mother's need is so great that the daughter is clearly there. The novel has such integrity and dramatic intensity that no excerpt can properly represent its use of memory; to indicate Morrison's concern with that faculty, I have selected "Memory, Creation and Writing," a brief essay she wrote after the publication of *Tar Baby,* the novel that immediately precedes *Beloved.* The essay makes references to the use of memory in her past novels but is just as relevant to the novels yet to come.

In "Memory, Creation, and Writing," Morrison says she has always "wanted to write literature that was irrevocably, indisputably Black"; if her fiction "is faithfully to reflect the aesthetic tradition of Afro-American culture, it must make conscious use of the characteristics of its art forms and translate them into print." Personal memory is crucial to her task "because it ignites some process of invention" and "because I cannot trust the literature and the sociology of other people to help me know the truth of my own cultural sources." In discussing her use of memory, she refers to an aspect about remembering not sufficiently emphasized elsewhere in this anthology: the "entire galaxy of feeling and impression" that accompanies, say, the memory of a particular person. What Morrison remembers from her young childhood of a woman named Hannah Peace is not a visual image but the atmosphere of her presence—a "galaxy of emotions." (I know that in remembering somebody, particularly a person for whom I feel affection, I recall a pervasive grouping of qualities before I can capture a facial image; I imagine this is true for most of us—not only in our recollections of a family member or friend, but in our apprehension of the nature of a fictional character.)

For Morrison, such a remembered "galaxy of emotions" can be the "seed" that sets her creative process as novelist into motion. The seed is a recollected piece, which attracts other recollected pieces, and they coalesce into a part.

She says it is important to distinguish between pieces and parts; the latter (so I judge, from the listing of the parts of *Tar Baby* at the end of the essay) are the combinations crucial to structure and meaning: creation itself is the discovery of those parts. That memory is central to the entire creative act, from seed to completed work, is apparent from a number of references in the essay. At one point, Morrison remarks, "Memory, then, no matter how small the piece remembered, demands my respect, my attention, and my trust." And, at another point, she refers to her present activity (the composition of *Beloved*, perhaps) as a "process" of "trusting memory and culling from it theme and structure."

It is not enough for a work of art to have ordered planes and lines. If a stone is tossed at a group of children, they hasten to scatter. A regrouping, an action, has been accomplished. This is composition. This regrouping, presented by means of color, lines, and planes, is an artistic and painterly motif.

—Edvard Munch

I like that quotation, as I do many of the remarks painters make about their work, because it clarifies for me an aspect of creation that engages me as a writer. It suggests how that interior part of the growth of a writer (the part that is both separate and indistinguishable from craft) is connected not only to some purely local and localized sets of stimuli but also to memory: the painter can copy or reinterpret the stone—its lines, planes, or curves—but the stone that causes something to happen among children he must remember, because it is done and gone. As he sits before his sketchbook he remembers how the scene looked, but most importantly he remembers the specific milieu that accompanies the scene. Along with the stone and the scattered children is an entire galaxy of feeling and impression—the motion and content of which may seem arbitrary, even incoherent, at first.

Because so much in public and scholarly life forbids us to take seriously the milieu of buried stimuli, it is often extremely hard to seek out both the stimulus and its galaxy and to recognize their value when they arrive. Memory is for me always fresh, in spite of the fact that the object being remembered is done and past.

Memory (the deliberate act of remembering) is a form of willed creation. It is not an effort to find out the way it really was—that is research. The point is to dwell on the way it appeared and why it appeared in that particular way.

I once knew a woman named Hannah Peace. I say *knew*, but nothing could be less accurate. I was perhaps four years old when she was in the town where I lived. I don't know where (or even if) she is now, or to whom she was related then. She was not even a visiting friend. I couldn't describe her in a way that would make her known in a photograph, nor would I recognize her if she walked into this room. But I have a memory of her, and it's like this: the color of her skin—the mat quality of it. Something purple around her. Also eyes not completely open. There emanated from her an aloofness that seemed to me kindly disposed. But most of all I remember her name—or the way people pronounced it. Never Hannah or Miss Peace. Always Hannah Peace. And more: something hidden—some awe perhaps, but certainly some forgiveness. When they pronounced her name they (the women and the men) forgave her something.

That's not much, I know: half-closed eyes, an absence of hostility, skin powdered in lilac dust. But it was more than enough to evoke a character—in fact, any more detail would have prevented (for me) the emergence of a fictional character at all. What is useful—definitive—is the galaxy of emotion that accompanied the woman as I pursued my memory of her, not the woman herself. (I am still startled by the ability—even the desire—to "use" acquaintances or friends or enemies as fictional characters. There is no yeast for me in a real-life person, or else there is so much it is not useful—it is done-bread, already baked.)

The pieces (and only the pieces) are what begin the creative process for me. And the process by which the recollections of these pieces coalesce into a part (and knowing the difference between a piece and a part) is creation. Memory, then, no matter how small the piece remembered, demands my respect, my attention, and my trust.

I depend heavily on the ruse of memory (and in a way it does function as a creative writer's ruse) for two reasons. One, because it ignites some process of invention, and two, because I cannot trust the literature and the sociology of other people to help me know the truth of my own cultural sources. It also prevents my preoccupations from descending into sociology. Since the discussion of Black literature in critical terms is unfailingly sociology and almost never art criticism, it is important for me to shed those considerations from my work at the outset.

In the examples I have given of Hannah Peace it was the having-been-easily-forgiven that caught my attention, not growing up Black; and that quality, that "easily forgiveness" that I believe I remember in connection with a shadow of a woman my mother knew, is the theme of *Sula*. The women forgive each other—or learn to. Once that piece of the galaxy became apparent, it dominated the other pieces. The next step was to discover what there is to be forgiven among women. Such things must now be raised and invented because I am going to tell about feminine forgiveness in story form. The things to be forgiven are grave errors and violent misdemeanors, but the point is less the thing to be forgiven than the nature and quality of forgiveness among women—which is to say friendship among women. What one puts up with in a friendship is determined by the emotional value of the relationship. But *Sula* is not simply about friendship among women, but among Black women, a qualifying term the artistic responsibilities of which I will touch upon in a moment.

I want my fiction to urge the reader into active participation in the nonnarrative, nonliterary experience of the text, which makes it difficult for the reader to confine himself to a cool and distant acceptance of data. When one looks at a very good painting, the experience of looking is deeper than the data accumulated in viewing it. The same, I think, is true in listening to good music. Just as the literary value of a painting or a musical composition is limited, so too is the literary value of literature limited. I sometimes think how glorious it must have been to have written drama in sixteenth-century England, or poetry in ancient Greece, or religious narrative in the Middle Ages, when literature was need and did not have a critical history to constrain or diminish the writer's imagination. How magnificent not to have to depend on the reader's literary associations—his literary experience—which can be as much an impoverishment of the reader's imagination as it is of a writer's. It is important that what I write not be merely literary. I am most self-conscious about making sure that I don't strike literary postures. I avoid, too studiously perhaps, name-dropping, lists, literary references, unless oblique and based on written folklore. The choice of a tale or folklore in my work is tailored to the character's thoughts or actions in a way that flags him or her and provides irony, sometimes humor.

Milkman, about to meet the oldest Black woman in the world, the mother of mothers who has spent her life caring for helpless others, enters her house thinking of a European tale, Hansel and Gretel, a story about parents who abandon their children to a forest and a witch who makes a diet of them. His confusion at that point, his racial and cultural ignorance, is flagged. Equally marked is Hagar's bed, described as Goldilocks' choice, partly because of Hagar's preoccupation with hair, and partly because, like Goldilocks, a house-breaker if ever there was one, she is greedy for things, unmindful of property rights or other people's space. Hagar is emotionally selfish as well as confused.

This deliberate avoidance of literary references has become a firm if boring habit with me, not only because they lead to poses, not only because I refuse the credentials they bestow, but also because they are inappropriate to the kind of literature I wish to write, the aims of that literature, and the discipline of the specific culture that interests *me*. Literary references in the hands of writers I love can be extremely revealing, but they can also supply a comfort I don't want the reader to have because I want him to respond on the same plane as an illiterate or preliterate reader would. I want to subvert his traditional comfort so that he may experience an unorthodox one: that of being in the company of his own solitary imagination.

My beginnings as a novelist were very much focused on creating this discomfort and unease in order to insist that the reader rely on another body of knowledge. However weak those beginnings were in 1965, they nevertheless pointed me toward the process that engages me in 1984: trusting memory and culling from it theme and structure. In *The Bluest Eye* the recollection of what I felt and saw upon hearing a child my own age say she prayed for blue eyes provided the first piece. I then tried to distinguish between a piece and a part—in the sense that a piece of a human body is different from a part of a human body.

As I began developing parts out of pieces, I found that I preferred them unconnected—to be related but not to touch, to circle, not line up—because the story of this prayer was the story of a shattered, fractured perception resulting from a shattered, splintered life. The novel turned out to be a composition of parts circling each other, like the galaxy accompanying memory. I fret the pieces and fragments of memory because too often we want the whole thing. When we wake from a dream we want to remember all of it, although the fragment we are remembering may be, and very probably is, the most important piece in the dream. Chapter and Part designations, as conventionally used in novels, were never very much help to me in writing. Nor are outlines. I permit their use for the sake of the designer and for ease in talking about the book. They are usually identified at the last minute.

There may be play and arbitrariness in the way memory surfaces, but none in the way the composition is organized, especially when I hope to recreate play and arbitrariness in the way narrative events unfold. The form becomes the exact interpretation of the idea the story is meant to express. There is nothing more traditional than that—but the sources of the images are not the traditional novelistic or readerly ones. The visual image of a splintered mirror, or the corridor of split mirrors in blue eyes, is the form as well as the content of *The Bluest Eye*.

Narrative is one of the ways in which knowledge is organized. I have always thought it was the most important way to transmit and receive knowledge. I am less certain of that now—but the craving for narrative has never lessened, and the hunger for it is as keen as it was on Mt. Sinai or Calvary or in the middle of the fens. Even when novelists abandon or grow tired of it as an outmoded mimetic form, historians, journalists, and performing artists take up the slack. Still, narrative is not and never has been enough, just as the object drawn on a canvas or a cave wall is never simply mimetic.

My compact with the reader is not to reveal an already established reality (literary or historical) that he or she and I agree upon beforehand. I don't want to assume or exercise that kind of authority. I regard that as patronizing, although many people regard it as safe and reassuring. And because my métier is Black, the artistic demands of Black culture are such that I cannot patronize, control, or pontificate. In the Third World cosmology as I perceive it, reality is not already constituted by my literary predecessors in Western culture. If my work is to confront a reality unlike that received reality of the West, it must centralize and animate information discredited by the West—discredited not because it is not true or useful or even of some racial value, but because it is information held by discredited people, information dismissed as "lore" or "gossip" or "magic" or "sentiment."

If my work is faithfully to reflect the aesthetic tradition of Afro-American culture, it must make conscious use of the characteristics of its art forms and translate them into print: antiphony, the group nature of art, its functionality, its improvisational nature, its relationship to audience performance, the critical voice which upholds tradition and communal values and which also provides occasion for an individual to transcend and/or defy group restrictions.

Working with those rules, the text, if it is to take improvisation and audience participation into account, cannot be the authority—it should be the map. It should make a way for the reader (audience) to participate in the tale. The language, if it is to permit criticism of both rebellion and tradition, must be both indicator and mask, and the tension between the two kinds of language is its release and its power. If my work is to be functional to the group (to the village, as it were) then it must bear witness and identify that which is useful from the past and that which ought to be discarded; it must make it possible to prepare for the present and live it out, and it must do that not by avoiding problems and contradictions but by examining them; it should not even attempt to solve social problems, but it should certainly try to clarify them.

Before I try to illustrate some of these points by using *Tar Baby* as an example, let me hasten to say that there are eminent and powerful, intelligent, and gifted Black writers who not only recognize Western literature as part of their own heritage but who have employed it to such an advantage that it illuminates both cultures. I neither object to nor am indifferent to their work or their views. I relish it, in precisely the way I relish a world of literature from other cultures. The question is not legitimacy or the "correctness" of a point of view, but the difference between my point of view and theirs. Nothing would be more hateful to me than a monolithic prescription for what Black literature is or ought to be. I simply wanted to write literature that was irrevocably, indisputably Black, not because its characters were, or because I was, but because it took as its creative task and sought as its credentials those recognized and verifiable principles of Black art.

In the writing of *Tar Baby*, memory meant recollecting the *told* story. I refused to read a modern or Westernized version of the story, selecting out instead the pieces that were disturbing or simply memorable: fear, tar, the rabbit's outrage at a failing in traditional manners (the tar baby does not speak). Why was the tar baby formed, to what purpose, what was the farmer trying to protect, and why did he think the doll would be attractive to the rabbit—what did he know, and what was his big mistake? Why does the tar baby cooperate with the farmer, and do the things the farmer wishes to protect wish to be protected? What makes his job more important than the rabbit's, why does he believe that a briar patch is sufficient punishment, what does the briar patch represent to the rabbit, to the tar baby, and to the farmer?

Creation meant putting the above pieces together in parts, first of all concentrating on tar as a part. What is it, and where does it come from? What are its holy uses and its profane uses—consideration of which led to a guiding motif: ahistorical earth and historical earth. That theme was translated into the structure in these steps:

1. Coming out of the sea (that which was there before earth) is both the beginning and the end of the book—in both of which Son emerges from the sea in a section that is not numbered as a chapter.

2. The earth that came out of the sea, its conquest by modern man, and the pain caused to the conquered life forms, as they are viewed by fishermen and clouds.

3. Movement from the earth into the household: its rooms, its quality of shelter. The activity for which the rooms were designed: eating, sleeping, bathing, leisure, etc.

4. The house disrupted precisely as the earth was disrupted. The chaos of the earth duplicated in the house designed for order. The disruption caused by the man born out of the womb of the sea accompanied by ammonia odors of birth.

5. The conflict that follows between the ahistorical (the pristine) and the historical (or social) forces inherent in the uses of tar.

6. The conflict, further, between two kinds of chaos: civilized chaos and natural chaos.

7. The revelation, then, is the revelation of secrets. Everybody, with one or two exceptions, has a secret: secrets of acts committed (as with Margaret and Son), and secrets of thoughts unspoken but driving nonetheless (as with Valerian and Jadine). And then the deepest and earliest secret of all: that *just as we watch other life, other life watches us.*

from *One Writer's Beginnings*

Eudora Welty (1909–)

Eudora Welty, that radiant figure in the literature of our past half-century or so, gave a series of three lectures—"Listening," "Learning to See," and "Finding a Voice"—at Harvard University in 1983 that link her writing with her life. Published as *One Writer's Beginnings,* this highly selective account—as much of an autobiography as the writer has permitted herself—became widely read, a rare example of a work of spiritual integrity as a best seller.

One Writer's Beginnings emphasizes journeys as important both to life and writing. "Learning to See," like "Finding a Voice," opens with a marvelous evocation of what traveling means, to a child; indeed, travel provides the frame in "Learning to See." In this section, Welty's memories of her grandparents on her father's side, at their Ohio farm; and of her grandmother and her five sons (Welty's uncles) on her mother's side, at their mountain-top home above the Elk River in West Virginia, are presented within the context of the trips she took as a child with her parents to see their respective families. Her West Virginia memories are the richer ones, and were transformed into the memory of Laurel, the central figure of her most recent novel, *The Optimist's Daughter.* "It took the mountain top," Welty says in *One Writer's Beginnings,* "to give me the sensation of independence"; also, the West Virginia relatives are important to her as a unified family group, as a clan of the generations, much given to talk and music. At Grandpa Welty's house, she remarks, no other family members ever showed up, and—an equally telling observation—"there wasn't much talking and no tales were told, even for the first time."

Any reader of Welty's fiction recognizes the importance of memory to her characters—as well as to the underlying value of the story she is constructing. "Writing fiction," she says, "has developed in me an abiding respect for the unknown in a human lifetime and a sense of where to look for the threads, how to follow, how to connect, find in the thick of the tangle what clear line persists. The strands are all there: to the memory nothing is lost." And she speaks of memory as "that most wonderful interior vision."

I have excerpted three sections from *One Writer's Beginnings.* Two of them form the frame of "Learning to See"; the first is the description of traveling by car to the homes of her grandparents, the second—a comment on those summer trips—discusses the affinity between journeys and the shape of fiction as well as the significance that memory discloses from our experiences. The third, and most important, comes at the end of "Finding a Voice," and it includes a passage that comes from another conclusion, that of *The Optimist's Daughter.* In this passage, Laurel, who has returned home to be with her father during the illness that precedes his death (he is the third to die of those whom she loves best: the other deaths are those of her husband, Phil, and her mother), is about to leave again. She dreams of—and then consciously remembers—a train trip during which she and Phil had shared a view of the confluence of the Ohio and

219

Mississippi Rivers as they were crossing the waters on a high trestle. That Welty would conclude both the novel and this autobiographical account with a moving tribute to confluence demonstrates how highly she regards the implications of that "wonderful word"; her own final comments in the autobiography link it to the power of "interior vision" to unify, to merge—for "the greatest confluence of all is that which makes up the human memory."

When we set out in our five-passenger Oakland touring car on our summer trip to Ohio and West Virginia to visit the two families, my mother was the navigator. She sat at the alert all the way at Daddy's side as he drove, correlating the AAA Blue Book and the speedometer, often with the baby on her lap. She'd call out, "All right, Daddy: '86-point-2, crossroads. Jog right, past white church. Gravel ends.'—And there's the church!" she'd say, as though we had scored. Our road always became her adversary. "This doesn't surprise me at all," she'd say as Daddy backed up a mile or so into our own dust on a road that had petered out. "I could've told you a road that looked like that had little intention of going anywhere."

"It was the first one we'd seen all day going in the right direction," he'd say. His sense of direction was unassailable, and every mile of our distance was familiar to my father by rail. But the way we set out to go was popularly known as "through the country."

My mother's hat rode in the back with the children, suspended over our heads in a pillowcase. It rose and fell with us when we hit the bumps, thumped our heads and batted our ears in an authoritative manner when sometimes we bounced as high as the ceiling. This was 1917 or 1918; a lady couldn't expect to travel without a hat.

Edward and I rode with our legs straight out in front of us over some suitcases. The rest of the suitcases rode just outside the doors, strapped on the running boards. Cars weren't made with trunks. The tools were kept under the back seat and were heard from in syncopation with the bumps; we'd jump out of the car so Daddy could get them out and jack up the car to patch and vulcanize a tire, or haul out the tow rope or the tire chains. If it rained so hard we couldn't see the road in front of us, we waited it out, snapped in behind the rain curtains and playing "Twenty Questions."

My mother was not naturally observant, but she could scrutinize; when she gave the surroundings her attention, it was to verify something—the truth or a mistake, hers or another's. My father kept his eyes on the road, with glances toward the horizon and overhead. My brother Edward periodically stood up in the back seat with his eyelids fluttering while he played the harmonica, "Old Macdonald had a farm" and "Abdul the Bulbul Amir," and the baby slept in Mother's lap and only woke up when we crossed some rattling old bridge. "*There's* a river!" he'd crow to us all. "Why, it certainly *is*," my mother would reassure him, patting him back to sleep. I rode as a hypnotic, with my set gaze on the landscape that vibrated past at twenty-five miles an hour. We were all wrapped by the long ride into some cocoon of our own.

The journey took about a week each way, and each day had my parents both in its grip. Riding behind my father I could see that the road had him by the shoulders, by the hair under his driving cap. It took my mother to make him stop. I inherited his nervous energy in the way I can't stop writing on a story. It makes me understand how Ohio had him around the heart, as West Virginia had my mother. Writers and travelers are mesmerized alike by knowing of their destinations.

And all the time that we think we're getting there so fast, how slowly we do move. In the days of our first car trip, Mother proudly entered in her log, "Mileage today: 161!" with an exclamation mark.

"A Detroit car passed us yesterday." She always kept those logs, with times, miles, routes of the day's progress, and expenses totaled up.

That kind of travel made you conscious of borders; you rode ready for them. Crossing a river, crossing a county line, crossing a state line—especially crossing the line you couldn't see but knew was there, between the South and the North—you could draw a breath and feel the difference.

The Blue Book warned you of the times for the ferries to run; sometimes there were waits of an hour between. With rivers and roads alike winding, you had to cross some rivers three times to be done with them. Lying on the water at the foot of a river bank would be a ferry no bigger than somebody's back porch. When our car had been driven on board—often it was down a roadless bank, through sliding stones and runaway gravel, with Daddy simply aiming at the two-plank gangway—father and older children got out of the car to enjoy the trip. My brother and I got barefooted to stand on wet, sun-warm boards that, weighted with your car, seemed exactly on the level with the water; our feet were the same as in the river. Some of these ferries were operated by a single man pulling hand over hand on a rope bleached and frazzled as if made from cornshucks.

I watched the frayed rope running through his hands. I thought it would break before we could reach the other side.

"No, it's not going to break," said my father. "It's never broken before, has it?" he asked the ferry man.

"No sirree."

"You see? If it never broke before, it's not going to break this time."

His general belief in life's well-being worked either way. If you had a pain, it was "Have you ever had it before? You have? It's not going to kill you, then. If you've had the same thing before, you'll be all right in the morning."

My mother couldn't have more profoundly disagreed with that.

"You're such an optimist, dear," she often said with a sigh, as she did now on the ferry.

"You're a good deal of a pessimist, sweetheart."

"I certainly *am*."

And yet I was well aware as I stood between them with the water running over my toes, he the optimist was the one who was prepared for the worst, and she the pessimist was the daredevil: he the one who on our trip carried chains and a coil of rope and an ax all upstairs to our hotel bedroom every night in case of fire, and she the one—before I was born—when there *was* a fire, had broken loose from all hands and run back—on crutches, too—into the burning house to rescue her set of Dickens which she flung, all twenty-four volumes, from the window before she jumped out after them, all for Daddy to catch.

"I make no secret of my lifelong fear of the water," said my mother, who on ferry boats remained inside the car, clasping the baby to her—my brother Walter, who was destined to prowl the waters of the Pacific Ocean in a minesweeper.

As soon as the sun was beginning to go down, we went more slowly. My father would drive sizing up the towns, inspecting the hotel in each, deciding where we could safely spend the night. Towns little or big had beginnings and ends, they reached to an edge and stopped, where the country began again as though they hadn't happened. They were intact and to themselves. You could see a town lying ahead in its whole, as definitely formed as a plate on a table. And your road entered and ran straight through the heart of it; you could see it all, laid out for your passage through. Towns, like people, had clear identities and your imagination could go out to meet them. You saw houses, yards, fields, and people busy in them, the people that had a life where they were. You could hear their bank clocks striking, you could smell their bakeries. You would know those towns again, recognize the salient detail, seen so close up. Nothing was blurred, and in passing along Main Street, slowed down from twenty-five to twenty miles an hour, you didn't miss anything on either side. Going somewhere "through the country" acquainted you with the whole way there and back.

My mother never fully gave in to her pleasure in our trip—for pleasure every bit of it was to us all—because she knew we were traveling with a loaded pistol in the pocket on the door of the car on Daddy's side. I doubt if my father fired off any kind of gun in his life, but he could not have carried his family from Jackson, Mississippi to West Virginia and Ohio through the country, unprotected.

Back on Congress Street, when my father unlocked the door of our closed-up, waiting house, I rushed ahead into the airless hall and stormed up the stairs, pounding the carpet of each step with both hands ahead of me, and putting my face right down into the cloud of the dear dust of our long absence. I was welcoming ourselves back. Doing likewise, more methodically, my father was going from room to room re-starting all the clocks.

I think now, in looking back on these summer trips—this one and a number later, made in the car and on the train—that another element in them must have been influencing my mind. The trips were wholes unto themselves. They were stories. Not only in form, but in their taking on direction, movement, development, change. They changed something in my life: each trip made its particular revelation, though I could not have found words for it. But with the passage of time, I could look back on them and see them bringing me news, discoveries, premonitions, promises—I still can; they still do. When I did begin to write, the short story was a shape that had already formed itself and stood waiting in the back of my mind. Nor is it surprising to me that when I made my first attempt at a novel, I entered its world—that of the mysterious Yazoo-Mississippi Delta—as a child riding there on a train: "From the warm window sill the endless fields glowed like a hearth in firelight, and Laura, looking out, leaning on her elbows with her head between her hands, felt what an arriver in a land feels—that slow hard pounding in the breast."

The events in our lives happen in a sequence in time, but in their significance to ourselves they find their own order, a timetable not necessarily—perhaps not possibly—chronological. The time as we know it subjectively is often the chronology that stories and novels follow: it is the continuous thread of revelation.

Through learning at my later date things I hadn't known, or had escaped or possibly feared realizing, about my parents—and myself—I glimpse our whole family life as if it were freed of that clock time which spaces us apart so inhibitingly, divides young and old, keeps our living through the same experiences at separate distances.

It is our inward journey that leads us through time—foreward or back, seldom in a straight line, most often spiraling. Each of us is moving, changing, with respect to others. As we discover, we remember; remembering, we discover; and most intensely do we experience this when our separate journeys converge. Our living experience at those meeting points is one of the charged dramatic fields of fiction.

I'm prepared now to use the wonderful word *confluence,* which of itself exists as a reality and a symbol in one. It is the only kind of symbol that for me as a writer has any weight, testifying to the pattern, one of the chief patterns, of human experience.

Here I am leading to the last scenes in my novel, *The Optimist's Daughter.*

She had slept in the chair, like a passenger who had come on an emergency journey in a train. But she had rested deeply.

She had dreamed that she *was* a passenger, and riding with Phil. They had ridden together over a long bridge.

Awake, she recognized it: it was a dream of something that had really happened. When she and Phil were coming down from Chicago to Mount Salus to be married in the Presbyterian Church, they came on the train. Laurel, when she travelled back and forth between Mount Salus and Chicago, had always taken the sleeper. She and Phil followed the route on the day train, and she saw it for the first time.

When they were climbing the long approach to a bridge after leaving Cairo, rising slowly higher until they rode above the tops of bare trees, she looked down and saw the pale light widening and the river bottoms opening out, and then the water appearing, reflecting the low, early sun. There were two rivers. Here was where they came together. This was the confluence of the waters, the Ohio and the Mississippi.

They were looking down from a great elevation and all they saw was at the point of coming together, the bare trees marching in from the horizon, the rivers moving into one, and as he touched her arm she looked up with him and saw the long, ragged, pencil-faint line of birds within the crystal of the zenith, flying in a V of their own, following the same course down. All they could see was sky, water, birds, light, and confluence. It was the whole morning world.

And they themselves were a part of the confluence. Their own joint act of faith had brought them here at the very moment and matched its occurrence, and proceeded as it proceeded. Direction itself was made beautiful, momentous. They were riding as one with it, right up front. It's our turn! she'd thought exultantly. And we're going to live forever.

Left bodiless and graveless of a death made of water and fire in a year long gone, Phil could still tell her of her life. For her life, any life, she had to believe, was nothing but the continuity of its love.

She believed it just as she believed that the confluence of the waters was still happening at Cairo. It would be there the same as it ever was when she went flying over it today on her way back—out of sight, for her, this time, thousands of feet below, but with nothing in between except thin air.

Of course the greatest confluence of all is that which makes up the human memory—the individual human memory. My own is the treasure most dearly regarded by me, in my life and in my work as a writer. Here time, also, is subject to confluence. The memory is a living thing—it too is in transit. But during its moment, all that is remembered joins, and lives—the old and the young, the past and the present, the living and the dead.

As you have seen, I am a writer who came of a sheltered life. A sheltered life can be a daring life as well. For all serious daring starts from within.

The instructor said,

> *Go home and write*
> *a page tonight.*
> *And let that page come out of you—*
> *Then, it will be true.*

I wonder if it's that simple?
I am twenty-two, colored, born in Winston-Salem.
I went to school there, then Durham, then here
to this college on the hill above Harlem.
I am the only colored student in my class.
The steps from the hill lead down into Harlem,
through a park, then I cross St. Nicholas,
Eighth Avenue, Seventh, and I come to the Y,
the Harlem Branch Y, where I take the elevator
up to my room, sit down, and write this page:

It's not easy to know what is true for you or me
at twenty-two, my age. But I guess I'm what
I feel and see and hear, Harlem, I hear you:
hear you, hear me—we two—you, me, talk on this page.
(I hear New York, too.) Me—who?

Well, I like to eat, sleep, drink, and be in love.
I like to work, read, learn, and understand life.
I like a pipe for a Christmas present,
or records—Bessie, bop, or Bach.
I guess being colored doesn't make me *not* like
The same things other folks like who are other races.
So will my page be colored that I write?

Being me, it will not be white.
But it will be
a part of you, instructor.
You are white—
yet a part of me, as I am a part of you.
That's American.
Sometimes perhaps you don't want to be a part of me.

Nor do I often want to be a part of you.
But we are, that's true!
As I learn from you,
I guess you learn from me—
although you're older—and white—
and somewhat more free.

This is my page for English B.

—Langston Hughes, "Theme for English B"

Memory, Culture, and Identity

"Theme for English B" was written at a time in which racial discrimination in America was more blatant than it is now—and yet a time in which the solution to racial problems seemed possible of attainment in the foreseeable future. From the present perspective, the young black male who writes this "theme" for a college class may strike us as naive. Still, his assumption of the human bond underlying color differences remains so valid—it is, after all, a physical as well as a moral truth—that the poem carries for us today an almost unbearable poignancy. Everything that follows in this introduction can be read as a meditation on Hughes' poem.

The modern nation-state developed from the earliest groupings of individuals into families and tribes, and continues to reflect the virtues and defects of its origins. Tribes and nations alike engender cooperation among their members for many reasons beneficial to survival. A major reason, the one with the darkest implications, is to repel the predations and larger aggressions of other groups—and often to initiate acts of hostility, through either threatening gestures or organized combat instituted in the name of a specific belief-system. As political structures reflecting the wish and need for human solidarity, both tribe and nation are (in any comprehensive sense) incomplete expressions of a desire, since they find their definition as entities through the exclusion of other entities. For the much more complex nation-state, that emphasis on solidarity through difference extends inwardly as well as outwardly, leading to cultural distinctions based on social and economic standing, ethnic origins, and skin color.

Our personal identities are a consequence not only of personal experience and genetic heritage but of the very culture that surrounds us from birth—its traditions and language, its particular knowledge and values, its biases. Essays by scientists in the opening section of this anthology refer to the importance of collective or cultural memory. In this section, the question of one's cultural identity is a central concern—made so by the writers' own keen awareness of it, an awareness brought about by their cultural dislocation.

The section opens with contributions by two Native Americans—the first is a short story about the quandary of identity that clearly is shaped by personal experience, and the second consists of excerpts from an autobiography. Three essays—the largest block—are the work of African Americans. These are followed by individual essays by a Chinese American, a Mexican American, and a Japanese American. Without exception, the selections in this section could have been included in the next one, which is devoted to the insights and perspective that one's personal memory can provide. I have grouped them here because they illuminate the significance of cultural identity against the encompassing background of shared human identity.

The categories one makes in editing an anthology such as *The Anatomy of Memory* say much about the editor's own assumptions or leanings, a matter I am particularly conscious of in selecting the material for this section. Why have I limited my selections to offerings by American citizens? Why have I relegated to the following section the essays by Vladimir Nabokov, Fyodor Dostoevsky, and Primo Levi, all of whom have suffered serious cultural dislocation through repression, imprisonment, or exile? The most persuasive reason I can offer is that American citizens who are nonwhite (or who, whether white or not, have encountered discrimination because of their sex) are especially aware of the contrast between the cultural assumptions underlying their nation—particularly the assumption of the equality of all of its members—and the prejudicial treatment accorded them. Nabokov and Dostoevsky demonstrate no sense that their personal worth has been compromised by the attitudes or ideology of the dominant culture or hierarchy; the revolution that sent Nabokov into exile managed, if anything, to intensify his sense of personal worth. Levi, an Italian Jew who survived Auschwitz, is a special case: his sense of himself so transcended his own Jewish heritage that he identified himself with the whole human race and the horrors it is capable of.

No doubt there are further reasons—including the stress that America's economic system as well as its democratic and egalitarian beliefs place upon individual achievement—that the members of minority groups in this nation are particularly conscious of the effect of culture upon identity. As an American myself, one belonging by the accident of birth to the cultural majority, I find that my reading of these essays by members of various American minorities helps my appreciation of the indignities and injustices they have endured. That reading also strengthens my awareness that all of us live as mortal creatures on a small globe in an indifferent and frighteningly vast universe, and that what we share far exceeds differences in skin pigmentation, gender, social class, ethnic origin, and cultural assumptions. But what we as individuals may recognize as an essential truth has yet to be transcribed adequately into the knowledge and actions of our social and political institutions.

"The Hyatt, the Maori, and the Yanamamo"

Irvin Morris (1958–)

"The Hyatt, the Maori, and the Yanamamo," a story by a promising young Native American writer, intrigues me by its obvious use of the writer's own memories and the collective memories—the sacred beliefs and historical events—of his Navajo tribe. I admire the story's sensitivity to the implications of language and to the indications of racial inequities, social stress and general decline currently threatening not only Native Americans but the larger civilization in which they are entangled.

The narrative thread concerns the search for an elderly woman (referred to as "Grandmother" in English, as "Shimi sani" in the Navajo language) of increasing senility who lives with her daughter Grace and her son-in-law Frank; as she has done in the past, she has wandered out of the house to become lost somewhere in the landscape of the reservation as dark descends. The family can't find her that night, but at dawn the next morning Frank discovers her in a culvert where she had safely spent the intervening hours.

Though the story is about caring and responsibility within a family and has a happy resolution, its meaning is more complex; the dilemma of Native Americans caught in, and affected by, the dominant culture has no apparent resolution. The opening paragraphs establish the antithetical nature of the two cultures within which these Native Americans, including the youthful narrator, exist. Watching the sunset from his porch steps, the narrator perceives (in the thunderheads above the mountains) the Holy People of his native beliefs "come in answer to our prayers once again, bringing nothing less than life itself," and imagines the canyon filled with the Ancient Ones—the Anaa'sazi—dancing: "Prayer in motion," he thinks. Entering the house, he notices the trinkets, replicas of artifacts from a variety of cultures (and no doubt representative of K-Mart commercial multiculturalism) on the windowsill, before turning on the television to a talk show in which "thunderous applause" and "hysterical laughter" are replaced by "tight faces as Eddie Murphy began talking about black and white."

Such an antithesis runs throughout the story. Grandmother herself, whatever her tribal memories of atrocities against her people, whatever the resilience and responsibility that may be her inheritance from the past, was influenced in her youth by images—no doubt from films and magazines—of white fashion. All of the members of this family remember a time before the present shattering of the old ways: once the Native American families stayed together, in unified support. Now, though, the members of the family are dependent upon the dominant culture that has nearly vanquished their own; Frank, who gains some income from his livestock, lost his job when the uranium mine closed (the deadly irony is not stressed); Grace, to help support the family, takes "an hour commute" each day to her job in Gallup, and her sisters have left the reservation for positions elsewhere. Frank and Grace alike feel guilt that they cannot be at home to give responsible care to Grandmother. Given the demands upon them all, shouldn't the family put the old woman in a nursing home?

The question, of course, echoes one frequently made in the white culture, which has experienced a similar shattering of family solidarity. The most affecting portion of this little story—and the one that most suggests the degree of Native American entrapment within that dominant culture—comes with the family's wholly conscious use of all the white clichés to explain and justify their shared predicament: "Soon we were whooping and snorting at the absurdity of us flopping helpless as hooked fish in the [English] language," the narrator says.

At the very end, the story reaches beyond the reservation to comment upon social chaos, racial unrest, and signs of structural collapse in America and elsewhere on the globe; but, for the moment, Grandmother is safe and this family, fragile though it is, endures—and the narrator (as apparently is his daily ritual) goes "out to greet the dawn with prayer and pollen."

After supper, I cut a slice of watermelon and sat on the porch steps, spitting seeds and watching the shadow of the mountains behind my home stretch across the valley. As they touched the horizon, there was a final smolder of color. The pale cliffs of Chaco Canyon gleamed like inlays of mica on the edge of the world. Gray thunderheads tinged with orange and pink glowed over Torréon and the Sierra Nacimiento. They were Holy People come from the south, dressed in icy robes of water. They had come in answer to our prayers once again, bringing nothing less than life itself.

"Anaa'sazi." I imagined the canyon sacred with the jingle of copper bells, vibrant with voices, bright with parrot feathers. The Ancient Ones dancing. Prayer in motion. The plaza at Pueblo Bonito awash with firelight and the thunder of drums rolling like waves through the canyon. Far to the east, a rainbow glowed in the last light.

"Ahalaanee," I thought. How better to express the joy and awe?

I sank into the deep cushions of the sofa and the indigo landscape outside dropped below the cluttered sill. A gilded dragon. Brass elephants. A pair of rosy-cheeked youth, a boy and girl caught in mid-stride, a wooden bucket held between them. They had been on their way back from the well when the ceramist froze them for all time. I aimed the remote and the television came alive, hissing.

Thunderous applause. Hysterical laughter. Then tight faces as Eddie Murphy began talking about black and white. The dog barked. I punched the mute button and the gate hinges squeaked twice. There was a knock on the door. I flicked on the porch light and Frank, my neighbor and in-law, squinted in the sudden glare. He stepped quickly into the room, trailing a faint wake of rain-scented air. His expression was grim. "Don't tell me," I said. "Is she . . ."

"She is," he nodded. "Again."

While I rummaged for flashlights in the kitchen drawers, he told me that he had just got back from pulling a cow out of the mud at the watering hole. "That took all afternoon, and then I come home to this mess," he said, shaking his head. "Dammit." He'd left the oldest girl in charge, but she'd been too busy gabbing on the phone to notice anything.

The last time the old lady had disappeared, they found her huddled in a clump of saltbush, cold, hungry, and nearly dehydrated.

A knotted cord, images and emotions, slipped through my mind: The old lady—my grandfather's sister—crawling on hands and knees through the furnace heat of a summer day. Over scorching sand, through fields of tumbleweeds, over anthills, under barbed wire fences, across arroyos and the busy bus road. I pictured the thick calluses on her palms, and her face, darkened by the sun, seamed with wrinkles like the eroded foothills to the west. Her failing eyes, clouded and blinking behind thick glasses. Gray hair, once glossy black, in disarray, loosened in wisps from the woolen hair tie. And carrying on conversations with men and women long dead. One time I had come across her crouching in a shallow ditch, cowering in terror. "Yiiya, shiyazhi," she'd whispered. "Naakaai dashooltse'lago." There hadn't been any Mexican horsemen in the area for over three hundred years.

We walked slowly, swinging the beams of our flashlights back and forth. Voices called out now and then. "Shima sani! Shima sani!" Grandmother, grandmother. Some of the children whispered and giggled, but an adult voice hushed them. We might not see her, you carrying on like that! It was impossible to see anything besides the stars overhead and the flashlights bobbing in the darkness. In a few minutes, a pair of headlights swung out from the cluster of our houses and bounced toward us. There was no road so the vehicle maneuvered around sandhills and clumps of rabbitbrush. The long beams lit up the rugged slopes of the foothills a mile away.

"There she is!" someone shouted.

"Shima sani!"

"You dorks, it's just a piece of roofing paper!"

From the top of a low outcrop of clay, the headlights reached across the plain. The vehicle backed up slowly and swept its beams over the land. Then it descended and came toward us. In time, Grace, who was Frank's wife and my aunt, pulled up next to me in their truck. She rolled down her window and motioned to me. I went over, but she didn't say anything for a while. She stared out the windshield.

"You must think I'm awful," she said.
"No, Grace, I don't."

The truth was that I didn't, really. I understood more than she seemed
to suppose. I waited. A burrowing owl called out, predicting more warm
weather. A movement to the side caught my eye. "This flashlight of yours
burned out," Frank said, handing me the cold object. I clicked it on and
the filament in the bulb glowed a dull orange.

"I don't think we'll find her tonight," Frank said. "Best thing's to start
again in the morning. Right now, she's holed up somewhere. We won't
find her like that."

"You sure?" I asked, but I knew he was right. She would be too afraid
to move. She would hide.

Grace sighed and pulled a tissue from the box on the dashboard. "It's
sure as hell not easy," she said, her eyes glittering in the dim light of the
instrument panel. Frank shifted uneasily and looked away. He leaned
against the cab. I excused myself to tell the others. As I walked away, I
heard the truck door open.

"Sometimes I feel like quitting my job, but . . ." Grace said back at her
house, waving her hand vaguely about the room as she poured coffee.
I knew all about their situation and I could sympathize. Splinters and
stone—that was rez life. Many families had gone to find better times in
the cities, and those who stayed behind were left with the weight of
holding things together. Frank and Grace had seven mouths to feed. And
if that wasn't enough, the old lady had gone steadily downhill for a couple
of years.

She'd cut quite a figure in her youth—a term I once heard her use—the
first local woman to pluck her eyebrows and wear lipstick. Faux pearls.
In one hand-tinted photograph she wore a fur stole, bobbed hair and a
Garbo-esque hat. Her acid wit had meant her dealings with men went
strictly by her terms.

I once saw a tree fall. The feeling was like that. Within the past year,
she had taken to the worrisome habit of leaving her house and crawling
about outside, never mind the time or weather. It wasn't that she was
deliberately neglected, however. The trouble was that she had to be watched
constantly. The minute you turned your back, she was out the door. The
responsibility could wear anyone down.

"I'm sick of the hour commute to Gallup, and then *this* happens,"
Grace said, sitting down across from me at the table. "I suppose I'll have
to call in."

"No, don't do that," Frank told her. "I'll saddle up first thing in the
morning. I'll find her."

Frank stood in the kitchen doorway, holding their youngest daughter Faith who was fast asleep. He carried her into the other room and Grace sighed looking after them. She glanced at me, and I knew what she was thinking. Frank had been unemployed for over three years now, ever since the uranium mines had closed. He'd gone around town with references from the employment office, but finally he had stopped knocking on doors. He never said anything about it, but I knew. It was easier to stay away from town than face the humiliation. And you didn't have to see the wealth and the way they treated people.

We walked a razor's edge. What else could we do? Every day we faced the theft, the lies, and the hate. And there weren't too many things to do about it. Either you smiled and pretended it didn't matter, withdrew to where they couldn't reach you, or kissed ass. Or you went under. Half the boys I'd known in grade school were dead. The list was long: Despair. Self-hate. Alcohol. No work and plenty of time to stew. How would any man feel? He didn't have to tell me why he didn't meet the gaze of the rednecks in town, the tourists who asked to take his picture, or the contemptuous social workers who didn't understand.

"It's totally crazy," Grace said. Frank came back and sat next to her. "They're asleep," he said, indicating the children in the next room with a nod of his head.

"It's a dirty shame," said Frank. "In the old days, old folks stayed with family to the end."

"That's the old days," sighed Grace.

"Dead and buried," said Frank, shaking his head.

"Gone with the buffalo," I said.

Frank looked at me. He grinned. "Belly up," he said, holding out his hand and wiggling his fingers.

"A bum deal," I said.

"The shits."

"A crying shame."

"Honestly, you guys," Grace said.

"Just awful," said Frank, and eyed her sideways.

Grace made a funny sound and her shoulders began to jerk up and down. I thought she was crying, but she wasn't. "Utter tragedy," she gasped, and her throaty laugh swept us up. Soon we were whooping and snorting at the absurdity of us flopping helpless as hooked fish in the language.

After we calmed down, Grace brought more coffee and a plate of muffins. "Amazing, isn't it?" she said. "It started with Dick-and-Jane. Now, it's ship-the-old-lady-off-to-the-home."

"The Golden Years," Frank said.

"Shady Pines," I said.

"Okay, you two, that's enough," said Grace. "Let's get serious."

"If your sisters weren't such hang-around-the-fort Indians, you would have some help," Frank said.

"Now, Hon," Grace smiled. "They're making good money. You know they can't get that kind of lab work around here. And they'll help with the cost too, you know."

"I wish I could do something." Frank leaned back and ran his hand through his hair.

"You have the cattle to look after. I don't know what we would do if we didn't have the calves to sell in the fall. Besides, you look after the little ones when there's no sitter. How can I expect you to do all that and watch her too?"

As I sat listening to them, I smelled the sharp odor of drying roots and wool. I heard the roof creak with the force of the wind. It was midwinter and I was about five years old. Shima sani stood by the woodstove stirring something in a pot. The room was steamy and warm. She spoke in quiet voice, describing in our language how her grandmother had told of surviving the forced march to Fort Sumner, three hundred miles to the east. A hundred years after it had happened, the tragedy was fresh in her mind. "It was cold like that," she'd said, pointing with her lips toward the window to indicate the freezing wind outside. "The people walked the whole distance at gunpoint. Many bad things happened. If anyone paused to rest, they were shot. A woman who had stopped to give birth was impaled on a sword. Old people were abandoned and babies were clubbed. Vultures followed them all the way."

I drowsed on her lap, the crackle of the fire inside the iron stove lulling me within the womb-like embrace of her arms. The kerosene lamp cast a soft light on the log walls of her house.

There was a loom by her bed and she spent long hours each day weaving precious inches onto the rugs she made to sell. I played around her, making roads for my toy cars on the dirt floor. I stayed with her while my mother was at the hospital, a mysterious place I knew nothing about. After a while, she carried me to the bed and covered me with a quilt. Then she blew out the lamp and I went to sleep.

Now, her loom stood idle.

I saw what I had to do. "It's really for the best," I lied. "I mean, it's not doing her any good being out there. Think about winter, the storms, the hot stove. And you won't be the first ones to do it."

The words scraped my throat. Can you believe it, I thought. But these were modern times. The stars had shifted, my grandfather once said, and he didn't know what it meant.

The sink made a gurgling noise. We turned. The small panes of the window above the counter fractured our faces into a strange mosaic.

"Remember last month when she almost picked up that baby rattler?" Frank said. "At least she'll be safe in Chinle."

"Safe," Grace sighed. "Who would have thought that one day I would be the one? That she would turn into a child and that I would be the parent?"

"We have to do it, Grace. There's no choice." Frank touched her hand. A surge of anger rose inside me. They would never stop. The changes. The meddling. We were all affected, the men, the women, the children, and now, the elders.

I glanced up and saw Frank and Grace looking at me. I shrugged.

"Dammit," Grace said.

I studied the veins on the back of my hands.

The alarm rang at four. I rolled out of bed and quickly got dressed. I went out to greet the dawn with prayer and pollen. Then I put on the coffee and watched the all night news on TV while I waited for sunrise. In New York City, blacks were protesting the killing of one of their young men by bat-wielding skinheads. The body of an undercover drug agent had been discovered in a shallow grave in Mexico. Outside, the rooster crowed and the clouds to the east slowly turned orange and pink.

The dog gruffed once and the gate hinges squeaked. Frank opened the door and came in. He rubbed his hands together and grinned.

"I found her," he said. "She was in that culvert under the bus road. Shit, I passed by there twice yesterday and didn't think to look inside it. She's home now, sipping coffee and munching warm tortillas like nothing happened." He laughed and shook his head. "That old lady is really something. . . ." He looked out the window.

I couldn't help but smile.

I poured two cups of coffee and we watched the rest of the newscast. A suspended walkway in the atrium of Kansas City Hyatt Regency had collapsed, killing several people and trapping scores of others under tons of steel and concrete. In Brazil, the Yanamamo were protesting the destruction of their forest homeland. On the other side of the world, the Maori were threatening to disrupt a visit by the Queen.

from *The Names*

N. Scott Momaday (1934–)

"The storyteller Pohd-lohk gave me the name Tsoai-talee," the Native American writer N. Scott Momaday says in the preface to *The Names*. "He believed that a man's life proceeds from his name, in the way that a river proceeds from its source." In the Kiowa language, that name means "Rock-Tree Boy"; it refers to what in English is known as Devil's Tower in Wyoming. Before the Kiowa moved eastward, they inhabited those regions that now include Wyoming, and this particular volcanic shaft was sacred in their creation myths. To Momaday, this name—not the one on his birth certificate—defines his identity: "My name is Tsoai-talee. I am, therefore, Tsoai-talee; therefore I am."

The Names is Momaday's autobiographical account of his childhood among the Kiowa in Oklahoma but chiefly among the Navajo in New Mexico and Arizona—for, despite a number of returns to Oklahoma, his childhood was spent primarily near or on the Navajo reservation, where his parents were employed as teachers at the Jemez Day School. If I understand Momaday correctly, childhood represents for him less an idyllic and lost past than a movement by stages from self-confusion to a regained knowledge of identity. As a child, he knew simply, without thought, that "[t]he past and the future were simply the contingencies of a given moment; they bore upon the present and gave it shape. One does not pass through time, but time enters upon him, in his place"; and such knowledge makes him later aware that "an idea of one's ancestry and posterity is really an idea of the self." Language, especially its function in naming, is crucial in the development of his "idea" of himself, since (as we know not only from this memoir but from his novel, *House Made of Dawn*) the Kiowa believe the divine spirit of things is to be found in their names, which participate in, and follow from, the sacred Word, the original Name—a belief crucial to Momaday's sense of himself as Tsoai-talee.

I have selected four brief passages from *The Names* that help to define Momaday's views on the related issues of memory, language, and naming. The first passage, apparently one of his earliest memories, concerns a terrifying and unwilled imaginative construct or fantasy that could be explained if only a word, a name, could be found. The second deals with the power of words to establish a name, an identity (even if it is not yet that of Tsoai-talee), as time journeys past the boy. The third is a memory of a festival day at Jemez Pueblo that suggests the continuing value of a past environment upon the adult; and the last is the episode that concludes his childhood. About to enter white culture, he holds within himself many sustaining names.

Memory begins to qualify the imagination, to give it another formation, one that is peculiar to the self. I remember isolated, yet fragmented and

236

confused, images—and images, shifting, enlarging, is the word, rather than moments or events—which are mine alone and which are especially vivid to me. They involve me wholly and immediately, even though they are the disintegrated impressions of a young child. They call for a certain attitude of belief on my part now; that is, they must mean something, but their best reality does not consist in meaning. They are not stories in that sense, but they are storylike, mythic, never evolved but evolving ever. There are such things in the world: it is in their nature to be believed; it is not necessarily in them to be understood. Of all that must have happened to and about me in those my earliest days, why should these odd particulars alone be fixed in my mind? If I were to remember other things, I should be someone else.

There is a room full of light and space. The walls are bare; there are no windows or doors of which I am aware. I am inside and alone. Then gradually I become aware of another presence in the room. There is an object, something not extraordinary at first, something of the room itself—but what I cannot tell. The object does not matter at first, but at some point—after a moment? an hour?—it moves, and I am unsettled. I am not yet frightened; rather I am somewhat surprised, vaguely anxious, fascinated, perhaps. The object grows; it expands farther and farther beyond definition. It is no longer an object but a mass. It is so large now that I am dwarfed by it, reduced almost to nothing. And *now* I am afraid, nearly terrified, and yet I have no will to resist; I remain attentive, strangely curious in proportion as I am afraid. The huge, shapeless mass is displacing all of the air, all of the space in the room. It swells against me. It is soft and supple and resilient, like a great bag of water. At last I am desperate, desperately afraid of being suffocated, lost in some dimple or fold of this vague, enormous thing. I try to cry out, but I have no voice.

RESTORE MY VOICE FOR ME

How many times has this memory been nearly recovered, the definition almost realized! Again and again I have come to that awful edge, that one word, perhaps, that I cannot bring from my mouth. I sometimes think that it is surely a name, the name of someone or something, that if only I could utter it, the terrific mass would snap away into focus, and I should see and recognize what it is at once; I should have it then, once and for all, in my possession.

Children trust in language. They are open to the power and beauty of language, and here they differ from their elders, most of whom have come to imagine that they have found words out, and so much of magic is lost upon them. Creation says to the child: Believe in this tree, for it has a name.

The Anatomy of Memory

If you say to a child, "The day is almost gone," he will take you at your word and will find much wonder in it. But if you say this to a man whom the world has disappointed, he will be bound to doubt it. *Almost* will have no precision for him, and he will mistake your meaning. I can remember that someone held out his hand to me, and in it was a bird, its body broken. *It is almost dead.* I was overcome with the mystery of it, that the dying bird should exist entirely in its dying. J. V. Cunningham has a poem, "On the Calculus":

> From almost nought to almost all I flee,
> And *almost* has almost confounded me;
> Zero my limit, and infinity.

I can almost see into the summer of a year in my childhood. I am again in my grandmother's house, where I have come to stay for a month or six weeks—or for a time that bears no common shape in my mind, neither linear nor round, but it is a deep dimension, and I am lonely in it. Earlier in the day—or in the day before, or in another day—my mother and father have driven off. Somewhere on a road, in Texas, perhaps, they are moving away from me, or they are settled in a room away, away, thinking of me or not, my father scratching his head, my mother smoking a cigarette and holding a little dog in her lap. There is a silence between them and between them and me. I am thoughtful. I see into the green, transparent base of a kerosene lamp; there is a still circle within it, the surface of a deeper transparency. Do I bring my hands to my face? Do I turn or nod my head? Something of me has just now moved upon the metal throat of the lamp, some distortion of myself, nonetheless recognizable, and I am distracted. I look for my image then in the globe, rising a little in my chair, but I see nothing but my ghost, another transparency, glass upon glass, the wall beyond, another distortion. I take up a pencil and set the point against a sheet of paper and define the head of a boy, bowed slightly, facing right. I fill in quickly only a few details, the line of the eye, the curve of the mouth, the ear, the hair—all in a few simple strokes. Yet there is life and expression in the face, a conjugation that I could not have imagined in these markings. The boy looks down at something that I cannot see, something that lies apart from the picture plane. It might be an animal, or a leaf, or the drawing of a boy. He is thoughtful and well-disposed. It seems to me that he will smile in a moment, but there is no laughter in him. He is contained in his expression—and fixed, as if the foundation upon which his flesh and bones are set cannot be shaken. I like him certainly, but I don't know who or where or what he is, except that he is the inscrutable reflection of my own vague certainty. And then I write, in my child's hand, beneath the drawing, "This is someone. Maybe this is Mammedaty. This is Mammedaty when he was a boy." And I wonder at the words. *What are they?* They stand, they lean and run upon the page of a manuscript—I have made a manuscript, rude and illustrious. The page bears the likeness of a boy—so simply crude the likeness to some pallid shadow on my blood—and his name consists in the letters there, the words, the other likeness, the little, jumbled drawings of a ritual, the nominal ceremony in which all homage is returned, the legend of the boy's having been, of his going on. I have said it; I have set it down. I trace the words; I touch myself to the words, and they stand for me. My mind lives among them, moving ever, ever going on:

On the first of August, at dusk, the Pecos bull ran through the streets of Jemez, taunted by the children, chased by young boys who were dressed in outlandish costumes, most in a manner which parodied the curious white Americans who came frequently to see the rich sights of Jemez on feast days. This "bull" was a man who wore a mask, a wooden framework on his back covered with black cloth and resembling roughly a bull, the head of which was a crude thing made of horns, a sheepskin, and a red cloth tongue which wagged about. It ran around madly, lunging at the children; and they in turn were delighted with it, pretending great alarm. All this was played out amid much shouting and laughter. And then in the plaza appeared briefly another mask, the little horse of Pecos. This, too, was a man; he wore about his waist a covered framework in the shape of a horse, and he danced to the accompaniment of a drum, the drummer close by his side. But this mask is very different in character from that of the bull. It is indeed one of the most beautiful and dramatic figures in Jemez ceremony, a thing in which fine art and the elements of the sacred are brought together in a whole and profound expression. From the first time I saw the Pecos horse it has been fixed in my imagination, as if it had come to be there long before I knew it; such things are beheld, and in the same moment they are recognized, and they do not pass from the mind. The little head, with its delicate ears and black mane, was finely made. The frame of its body, draped round with a beautiful kilt, suggested perfectly its fine limbs, its temperament high-strung and imperative, its little round rump bunched and bouncing, its tail not flowing but shimmying. The man appeared to be mounted on the little horse, and he, too, was a beautiful and dramatic thing to see, a strange and almost ominous aspect of the mask, a black veil over his head, under a black hat. And all the while he danced to the high, hectic rattle of the drum, virtually in place, his motion translated into the pure illusion of the horse, the centaur quivering. And in the last light a holy man came out of one of the holy houses and sprinkled meal on the horse's head. Sometimes you look at a thing and see only that it is opaque, that it cannot be looked into. And this opacity is its essence, the very truth of the matter. So it was, for me, with the little Pecos horse mask. The man inside was merely motion, and he had no face, and his name was the name of the mask itself. Had I lifted the veil beneath the hat, there should have been no one and nothing to see.

The masks of the bull and the horse, along with an old statue of Our Lady of the Angels, are said to have been brought to Jemez by the survivors of Pecos, which place is now a ruin that lies some eighty miles to the south and east. The pueblo of Pecos was destroyed by a plague about 1840. The survivors, eighteen or twenty souls in all, came to Jemez and were taken in. From that time the blood of these two peoples has been mingled, and there are many Pecos elements now in Jemez tradition, including this observance, on August second, of the Feast of Our Lady of the Angels, who is called Porcingula.

The next day, after mass, the little statue Porcingula was borne in procession to the plaza and placed in a bower of evergreens there, and through the afternoon there was dancing and feasting, feasting in the homes of the Pecos descendants. I came to love this "Old Pecos Day," as it is called, above other feast days at Jemez. Perhaps it was because I, too, like those old immigrants, came there with my masks and was taken in.

And throughout the year there were ceremonies of many kinds, and some of these were secret dances, and on these holiest days guards were posted on the roads and no one was permitted to enter the village. My parents and I kept then to ourselves, to our reservation of the day school, and in this way, through the tender of our respect and our belief, we earned the trust of the Jemez people, and we were at home there.

Now as I look back on that long landscape of the Jemez Valley, it seems to me that I have seen much of the world. And I have been glad to see it, glad beyond the telling. But what I see now is this: If I should hear at evening the wagons on the river road and the voices of children playing in the cornfields, or if in the sunrise I should see the long shadows running out to the west and the cliffs flaring up in the light ascending, or if riding out on an afternoon cool with rain I should see in the middle distance the old man Francisco with his flock, standing deep in the colors and patterns of the plain, it would again be all that I could hold in my heart.

At Jemez I came to the end of my childhood. There were no schools within easy reach. I had to go nearly thirty miles to school at Bernalillo, and one year I lived away in Albuquerque. My mother and father wanted me to have the benefit of a sound preparation for college, and so we read through many high school catalogues. After long deliberation we decided that I should spend my last year of high school at a military academy in Virginia.

The day before I was to leave I went walking across the river to the red mesa, where many times before I had gone to be alone with my thoughts. And I had climbed several times to the top of the mesa and looked among the old ruins there for pottery. This time I chose to climb the north end, perhaps because I had not gone that way before and wanted to see what it was. It was a difficult climb, and when I got to the top I was spent. I lingered among the ruins for more than an hour, I judge, waiting for my strength to return. From there I could see the whole valley below, the fields, the river, and the village. It was all very beautiful, and the sight of it filled me with longing.

I looked for an easier way to come down, and at length I found a broad, smooth runway of rock, a shallow groove winding out like a stream. It appeared to be safe enough, and I started to follow it. There were steps along the way, a stairway, in effect. But the steps became deeper and deeper, and at last I had to drop down the length of my body and more. Still it seemed convenient to follow in the groove of rock. I was more than halfway down when I came upon a deep, funnel-shaped formation in my path. And there I had to make a decision. The slope on either side was extremely steep and forbidding, and yet I thought that I could work my way down on either side. The formation at my feet was something else. It was perhaps ten or twelve feet deep, wide at the top and narrow at the bottom, where there appeared to be a level ledge. If I could get down through the funnel to the ledge, I should be all right; surely the rest of the way down was negotiable. But I realized that there could be no turning back. Once I was down in that rocky chute I could not get up again, for the round wall which nearly encircled the space there was too high and sheer. I elected to go down into it, to try for the ledge directly below. I eased myself down the smooth, nearly vertical wall on my back, pressing my arms and legs outward against the sides. After what seemed a long time I was trapped in the rock. The ledge was no longer there below me; it had been an optical illusion. Now, in this angle of vision, there was nothing but the ground, far, far below, and jagged boulders set there like teeth. I remember that my arms were scraped and bleeding, stretched out against the walls with all the pressure that I could exert. When once I looked down I saw that my legs, also spread out and pressed hard against the walls, were shaking violently. I was in an impossible situation: I could not move in any direction, save downward in a fall, and I could not stay beyond another minute where I was. I believed then that I would die there, and I saw with a terrible clarity the things of the valley below. They were not the less beautiful to me. It seemed to me that I grew suddenly very calm in view of that beloved world. And I remember nothing else of that moment. I passed out of my mind, and the next thing I knew I was sitting down on the ground, very cold in the shadows, and looking up at the rock where I had been within an eyelash of eternity. That was a strange thing in my life, and I think of it as the end of an age. I should never again see the world as I saw it on the other side of that moment, in the bright reflection of time lost. There are such reflections, and for some of them I have the names.

"Stranger in the Village"
James Baldwin (1924–1987)

James Baldwin wrote "Stranger in the Village" in 1953, when he was not quite thirty and much of his reputation (and financial security) as a major American writer still lay before him. This essay concludes *Notes of a Native Son,* a collection that has been reprinted many times since its original publication in 1955. In "Autobiographical Notes," which serves as a kind of preface to that volume, he comments, "I have not written about being a Negro at such length because I expect that to be my only subject, but only because it was the gate I had to unlock before I could hope to write about anything else." Nevertheless, it remained his crucial subject; given what he says in "Stranger in the Village" about racial relationships in America, it is hardly surprising that this would be the case.

In "Autobiographical Notes," Baldwin says that "the most crucial time in my own development came when I was forced to recognize that I was a kind of bastard of the West"—the underlying theme of "Stranger in the Village." He wrote the essay during his second stay in an isolated Swiss hamlet, a location that gave him the necessary distance from social affairs (a distance every writer needs, as he also says in "Autobiographical Notes") to see that even these inhabitants of a remote mountain village were part of Western civilization, with its cultural artifacts and traditions—its collective memory—in a way that he was not. The descendants of slaves in America have no memory of the forms and customs of an earlier life; in their attempt to discover the past from which they came, they are "abruptly arrested by the signature on the bill of sale which served as the entrance paper" for any ancestor. (I have been told by several African American scholars that Baldwin overstates the case: evidence continues to grow of African customs and beliefs transmitted orally—in speech and song— from the first generation of slaves to their descendants.)

I doubt that the perspective provided by his stay in the Swiss village is necessary for Baldwin's awareness that America's belief in democracy is at odds with its idea of "white supremacy," for such a conflict (as he notices) has been apparent at least since the Civil War. The distance, though, gives him his central theme, and probably contributes to some further insights contained within the essay. While acknowledging that both democracy and white supremacy are part of the heritage that America received from Europe, he observes that in America the conflict is most pronounced, since blacks from the beginning have been "an inescapable part of the social fabric" in the United States. "At the root of the American Negro problem," Baldwin remarks, "is the necessity of the American white man to find a way of living with the Negro in order to be able to live with himself." And he adds that "the interracial drama acted out on the American continent has not only created a new black man, it has created a new white man, too. . . . The world is white no longer, and it will never be white again."

From all available evidence no black man had ever set foot in this tiny Swiss village before I came. I was told before arriving that I would probably be a "sight" for the village; I took this to mean that people of my complexion were rarely seen in Switzerland, and also that city people are always something of a "sight" outside of the city. It did not occur to me—possibly because I am an American—that there could be people anywhere who had never seen a Negro.

It is a fact that cannot be explained on the basis of the inaccessibility of the village. The village is very high, but it is only four hours from Milan and three hours from Lausanne. It is true that it is virtually unknown. Few people making plans for a holiday would elect to come here. On the other hand, the villagers are able, presumably, to come and go as they please—which they do: to another town at the foot of the mountain, with a population of approximately five thousand, the nearest place to see a movie or go to the bank. In the village there is no movie house, no bank, no library, no theater; very few radios, one jeep, one station wagon; and at the moment, one typewriter, mine, an invention which the woman next door to me here had never seen. There are about six hundred people living here, all Catholic—I conclude this from the fact that the Catholic church is open all year round, whereas the Protestant chapel, set off on a hill a little removed from the village, is open only in the summertime when the tourists arrive. There are four or five hotels, all closed now, and four or five *bistros,* of which, however, only two do any business during the winter. These two do not do a great deal, for life in the village seems to end around nine or ten o'clock. There are a few stores, butcher, baker, *épicerie,* a hardware store, and a money-changer—who cannot change travelers' checks, but must send them down to the bank, an operation which takes two or three days. There is something called the *Ballet Haus,* closed in the winter and used for God knows what, certainly not ballet, during the summer. There seems to be only one schoolhouse in the village, and this for the quite young children; I suppose this to mean that their older brothers and sisters at some point descend from these mountains in order to complete their education—possibly, again, to the town just below. The landscape is absolutely forbidding, mountains towering on all four sides, ice and snow as far as the eye can reach. In this white wilderness, men and women and children move all day, carrying washing, wood, buckets of milk or water, sometimes skiing on Sunday afternoons. All week long boys and young men are to be seen shoveling snow off the rooftops, or dragging wood down from the forest in sleds.

The village's only real attraction, which explains the tourist season, is the hot spring water. A disquietingly high proportion of these tourists are cripples, or semi-cripples, who come year after year—from other parts of Switzerland, usually—to take the waters. This lends the village, at the height of the season, a rather terrifying air of sanctity, as though it were a lesser Lourdes. There is often something beautiful, there is always something awful, in the spectacle of a person who has lost one of his faculties, a faculty he never questioned until it was gone, and who struggles to recover it. Yet people remain people, on crutches or indeed on deathbeds; and wherever I passed, the first summer I was here, among the native villagers or among the lame, a wind passed with me—of astonishment, curiosity, amusement, and outrage. That first summer I stayed two weeks and never intended to return. But I did return in the winter, to work; the village offers, obviously, no distractions whatever and has the further advantage of being extremely cheap. Now it is winter again, a year later, and I am here again. Everyone in the village knows my name, though they scarcely ever use it, knows that I come from America—though this, apparently, they will never really believe: black men come from Africa— and everyone knows that I am the friend of the son of a woman who was born here, and that I am staying in their chalet. But I remain as much a stranger today as I was the first day I arrived, and the children shout *Neger! Neger!* as I walk along the streets.

It must be admitted that in the beginning I was far too shocked to have any real reaction. In so far as I reacted at all, I reacted by trying to be pleasant—it being a great part of the American Negro's education (long before he goes to school) that he must make people "like" him. This smile-and-the-world-smiles-with-you routine worked about as well in this situation as it had in the situation for which it was designed, which is to say that it did not work at all. No one, after all can be liked whose human weight and complexity cannot be, or has not been, admitted. My smile was simply another unheard-of phenomenon which allowed them to see my teeth—they did not, really, see my smile and I began to think that, should I take to snarling, no one would notice any difference. All of the physical characteristics of the Negro which had caused me, in America, a very different and almost forgotten pain were nothing less than miraculous—or infernal—in the eyes of the village people. Some thought my hair was the color of tar, that it had the texture of wire, or the texture of cotton. It was jocularly suggested that I might let it all grow long and make myself a winter coat. If I sat in the sun for more than five minutes some daring creature was certain to come along and gingerly put his fingers on my hair, as though he was afraid of an electric shock, or put his hand on my hand, astonished that the color did not rub off. In all of this, in which it must be conceded there was the charm of genuine wonder and

245

in which there were certainly no element of intentional unkindness, there was yet no suggestion that I was human: I was simply a living wonder.

I knew that they did not mean to be unkind, and I know it now; it is necessary, nevertheless, for me to repeat this to myself each time that I walk out of the chalet. The children who shout *Neger!* have no way of knowing the echoes this sound raises in me. They are brimming with good humor and the more daring swell with pride when I stop to speak them. Just the same, there are days when I cannot pause and smile, when I have no heart to play with them; when, indeed, I mutter sourly to myself, exactly as I muttered on the streets of a city these children have never seen, when I was no bigger than these children are now: *Your mother was a nigger.* Joyce is right about history being a nightmare—but it may be the nightmare from which no one can awaken. People are trapped in history and history is trapped in them.

There is a custom in the village—I am told it is repeated in many villages—of "buying" African natives for the purpose of converting them to Christianity. There stands in the church all year round a small box with a slot for money, decorated with a black figurine, and into this box the villagers drop their francs. During the *carnaval* which precedes Lent, two village children have their faces blackened—out of which bloodless darkness their blue eyes shine like ice—and fantastic horsehair wigs are placed on their blond heads; thus disguised, they solicit among the villagers for money for the missionaries in Africa. Between the box in the church and the blackened children, the village "bought" last year six or eight African natives. This was reported to me with pride by the wife of one of the *bistro* owners and I was careful to express astonishment and pleasure at the solicitude shown by the village for the souls of black folks. The *bistro* owner's wife beamed with a pleasure far more genuine than my own and seemed to feel that I might now breathe more easily concerning the souls of at least six of my kinsmen.

I tried not to think of these so lately baptized kinsmen, of the price paid for them, or the peculiar price they themselves would pay, and said nothing about my father, who having taken his own conversion too literally never, at bottom, forgave the white world (which he described as heathen) for having saddled him with a Christ in whom, to judge at least from their treatment of him, they themselves no longer believed. I thought of white men arriving for the first time in an African village, strangers there, as I am a stranger here, and tried to imagine the astounded populace touching their hair and marveling at the color of their skin. But there is a great difference between being the first white man to be seen by Africans and being the first black man to be seen by whites. The white man takes the astonishment as tribute, for he arrives to conquer and to convert the natives, whose inferiority in relation to himself is not even to be questioned;

whereas I, without a thought of conquest, find myself among a people whose culture controls me, has even, in a sense, created me, people who have cost me more in anguish and rage than they will ever know, who yet do not even know of my existence. The astonishment with which I might have greeted them, should they have stumbled into my African village a few hundred years ago, might have rejoiced their hearts. But the astonishment with which they greet me today can only poison mine.

And this is so despite everything I may do to feel differently, despite my friendly conversations with the *bistro* owner's wife, despite their three-year-old son who has at last become my friend, despite the *saluts* and *bonsoirs* which I exchange with people as I walk, despite the fact that I know that no individual can be taken to task for what history is doing, or has done. I say that the culture of these people controls me—but they can scarcely be held responsible for European culture. America comes out of Europe, but these people have never seen America, nor have most of them seen more of Europe than the hamlet at the foot of their mountain. Yet they move with an authority which I shall never have; and they regard me, quite rightly, not only as a stranger in their village but as a suspect latecomer, bearing no credentials, to everything they have—however unconsciously—inherited.

For this village, even were it incomparably more remote and incredibly more primitive, is the West, the West onto which I have been so strangely grafted. These people cannot be, from the point of view of power, strangers anywhere in the world; they have made the modern world, in effect, even if they do not know it. The most illiterate among them is related, in a way that I am not, to Dante, Shakespeare, Michelangelo, Aeschylus, Da Vinci, Rembrandt, and Racine; the cathedral at Chartres says something to them which it cannot say to me, as indeed would New York's Empire State Building, should anyone here ever see it. Out of their hymns and dances comes Beethoven and Bach. Go back a few centuries and they are in their full glory—but I am in Africa, watching the conquerors arrive.

The rage of the disesteemed is personally fruitless, but it is also absolutely inevitable; this rage, so generally discounted, so little understood even among the people whose daily bread it is, is one of the things that makes history. Rage can only with difficulty, and never entirely, be brought under the domination of the intelligence and is therefore not susceptible to any arguments whatever. This is a fact which ordinary representatives of the *Herrenvolk,* having never felt this rage and being unable to imagine, quite fail to understand. Also, rage cannot be hidden, it can only be dissembled. This dissembling deludes the thoughtless, and strengthens rage and adds, to rage, contempt. There are, no doubt, as many ways of coping with the resulting complex of tensions as there are black men in the world, but no black man can hope ever to be entirely liberated from this internal warfare—rage, dissembling, and contempt having inevitably accompanied his first realization of the power of white men. What is crucial here is that, since white men represent in the black man's world so heavy a weight, white men have for black men a reality which is far from being reciprocal; and hence all black men have toward all white men an attitude which is designed, really, either to rob the white man of the jewel of his naïveté, or else to make it cost him dear.

The black man insists, by whatever means he finds at his disposal, that the white man cease to regard him as an exotic rarity and recognize him as a human being. This is a very charged and difficult moment, for there is a great deal of will power involved in the white man's naïveté. Most people are not naturally reflective any more than they are naturally malicious, and the white man prefers to keep the black man at a certain human remove because it is easier for him thus to preserve his simplicity and avoid being called to account for crimes committed by his forefathers, or his neighbors. He is inescapably aware, nevertheless, that he is in a better position in the world than black men are, nor can he quite put to death the suspicion that he is hated by black men therefore. He does not wish to be hated, neither does he wish to change places, and at this point in his uneasiness he can scarcely avoid having recourse to those legends which white men have created about black men, the most usual effect of which is that the white man finds himself enmeshed, so to speak, in his own language which describes hell, as well as the attributes which lead one to hell, as being as black as night.

Every legend, moreover, contains its residuum of truth, and the root function of language is to control the universe by describing it. It is of quite considerable significance that black men remain, in the imagination, and in overwhelming numbers in fact, beyond the disciplines of salvation; and this despite the fact that the West has been "buying" African natives for centuries. There is, I should hazard, an instantaneous necessity to be divorced from this so visibly unsaved stranger, in whose heart, moreover, one cannot guess what dreams of vengeance are being nourished; and, at the same time, there are few things on earth more attractive than the idea of the unspeakable liberty which is allowed the unredeemed. When, beneath the black mask, a human being begins to make himself felt one cannot escape a certain awful wonder as to what kind of human being it is. What one's imagination makes of other people is dictated, of course, by the laws of one's own personality and it is one of the ironies of black-white relations that, by means of what the white man imagines the black man to be, the black man is enabled to know who the white man is.

I have said, for example, that I am as much a stranger in this village today as I was the first summer I arrived, but this is not quite true. The villagers wonder less about the texture of my hair than they did then, and wonder rather more about me. And the fact that their wonder now exists on another level is reflected in their attitudes and in their eyes. There are the children who make those delightful, hilarious, sometimes astonishingly grave overtures of friendship in the unpredictable fashion of children; other children, having been taught that the devil is a black man, scream in genuine anguish as I approach. Some of the older women never pass without a friendly greeting, never pass, indeed, if it seems that they will be able to engage me in conversation; other women look down or look away or rather contemptuously smirk. Some of the men drink with me and suggest that I learn how to ski—partly, I gather, because they cannot imagine what I would look like on skis—and want to know if I am married, and ask questions about my *métier*. But some of the men have accused *le sale nègre*—behind my back—of stealing wood and there is already in the eyes of some of them that peculiar, intent, paranoiac malevolence which one sometimes surprises in the eyes of American white men when, out walking with their Sunday girl, they see a Negro male approach.

There is a dreadful abyss between the streets of this village and the streets of the city in which I was born, between the children who shout *Neger!* today and those who shouted *Nigger!* yesterday—the abyss is experience, the American experience. The syllable hurled behind me today expresses, above all, wonder: I am a stranger here. But I am not a stranger in America and the same syllable riding on the American air expresses the war my presence has occasioned in the American soul.

For this village brings home to me this fact: that there was a day, and not really a very distant day, when Americans were scarcely Americans at all but discontented Europeans, facing a great unconquered continent and strolling, say, into a marketplace and seeing black men for the first time. The shock this spectacle afforded is suggested, surely, by the promptness with which they decided that these black men were not really men but cattle. It is true that the necessity on the part of the settlers of the New World of reconciling their moral assumptions with the fact—and the necessity—of slavery enhanced immensely the charm of this idea, and it is also true that this idea expresses, with a truly American bluntness, the attitude which to varying extents all masters have had toward all slaves.

But between all former slaves and slave-owners and the drama which begins for Americans over three hundred years ago at Jamestown, there are at least two differences to be observed. The American Negro slave could not suppose, for one thing, as slaves in past epochs had supposed and often done, that he would ever be able to wrest the power from his master's hands. This was a supposition which the modern era, which was to bring about such vast changes in the aims and dimensions of power, put to death; it only begins, in unprecedented fashion, and with dreadful implications, to be resurrected today. But even had this supposition persisted with undiminished force, the American Negro slave could not have used it to lend his condition dignity, for the reason that this supposition rests on another: that the slave in exile yet remains related to his past, has some means—if only in memory—of revering and sustaining the forms of his former life, is able, in short, to maintain his identity.

This was not the case with the American Negro slave. He is unique among the black men of the world in that his past was taken from him, almost literally, at one blow. One wonders what on earth the first slave found to say to the first dark child he bore. I am told that there are Haitians able to trace their ancestry back to African kings, but any American Negro wishing to go back so far will find his journey through time abruptly arrested by the signature on the bill of sale which served as the entrance paper for his ancestor. At the time—to say nothing of the circumstances—of the enslavement of the captive black man who was to become the American Negro, there was not the remotest possibility that he would ever take power from his master's hands. There was no reason to suppose that his situation would ever change, nor was there, shortly, anything to indicate that his situation had ever been different. It was his necessity, in the words of E. Franklin Frazier, to find a "motive for living under American culture or die." The identity of the American Negro comes out of this extreme situation, and the evolution of this identity was a source of the most intolerable anxiety in the minds and the lives of his masters.

For the history of the American Negro is unique also in this: that the question of his humanity, and of his rights therefore as a human being, became a burning one for several generations of Americans, so burning a question that it ultimately became one of those used to divide the nation. It is out of this argument that the venom of the epithet *Nigger!* is derived. It is an argument which Europe has never had, and hence Europe quite sincerely fails to understand how or why the argument arose in the first place, why its effects are frequently disastrous and always so unpredictable, why it refuses until today to be entirely settled. Europe's black possessions remained—and do remain—in Europe's colonies, at which remove they represented no threat whatever to European identity. If they posed any problem at all for the European conscience it was a problem which remained comfortingly abstract: in effect, the black man, as a *man*, did not exist for Europe. But in America, even as a slave, he was an inescapable part of the general social fabric and no American could escape having an attitude toward him. Americans attempt until today to make an abstraction of the Negro, but the very nature of these abstractions reveals the tremendous effect the presence of the Negro has had on the American character.

When one considers the history of the Negro in America it is of the greatest importance to recognize that the moral beliefs of a person, or a people, are never really as tenuous as life—which is not moral—very often causes them to appear; these create for them a frame of reference and a necessary hope, the hope being that when life has done its worst they will be enabled to rise above themselves and to triumph over life. Life would scarcely be bearable if this hope did not exist. Again, even when the worst has been said, to betray a belief is not by any means to have put oneself beyond its power; the betrayal of a belief is not the same thing as ceasing to believe. If this were not so there would be no moral standards in the world at all. Yet one must also recognize that morality is based on ideas and that all ideas are dangerous—dangerous because ideas can only lead to action and where the action leads no man can say. And dangerous in this respect: that confronted with the impossibility of remaining faithful to one's beliefs, and the equal impossibility of becoming free of them, one can be driven to the most inhuman excesses. The ideas on which American beliefs are based are not, though Americans often seem to think so, ideas which originated in America. They came out of Europe. And the establishment of democracy on the American continent was scarcely as radical a break with the past as was the necessity, which Americans faced, of broadening this concept to include black men.

This was, literally, a hard necessity. It was impossible, for one thing, for Americans to abandon their beliefs, not only because these beliefs alone seemed able to justify the sacrifices they had endured and the blood that they had spilled, but also because these beliefs afforded them their only bulwark against a moral chaos as absolute as the physical chaos of the continent it was their destiny to conquer. But in the situation in which Americans found themselves, these beliefs threatened an idea which, whether or not one likes to think so, is the very warp and woof of the heritage of the West, the idea of white supremacy.

Americans have made themselves notorious by the shrillness and the brutality with which they have insisted on this idea, but they did not invent it; and it has escaped the world's notice that those very excesses of which Americans have been guilty imply a certain, unprecedented uneasiness over the idea's life and power, if not, indeed, the idea's validity. The idea of white supremacy rests simply on the fact that white men are the creators of civilization (the present civilization, which is the only one that matters; all previous civilizations are simply "contributions" to our own) and are therefore civilization's guardians and defenders. Thus it was impossible for Americans to accept the black man as one of themselves, for to do so was to jeopardize their status as white men. But not so to accept him was to deny his human reality, his human weight and complexity, and the strain of denying the overwhelmingly undeniable forced Americans into rationalizations so fantastic that they approached the pathological.

At the root of the American Negro problem is the necessity of the American white man to find a way of living with the Negro in order to be able to live with himself. And the history of this problem can be reduced to the means used by Americans—lynch law and law, segregation and legal acceptance, terrorization and concession—either to come to terms with this necessity, or to find a way around it, or (most usually) to find a way of doing both these things at once. The resulting spectacle, at once foolish and dreadful, led someone to make the quite accurate observation that "the Negro-in-America is a form of insanity which overtakes white men."

In this long battle, a battle by no means finished, the unforeseeable effects of which will be felt by many future generations, the white man's motive was the protection of his identity; the black man was motivated by the need to establish an identity. And despite the terrorization which the Negro in America endured and endures sporadically until today, despite the cruel and totally inescapable ambivalence of his status in his country, the battle for his identity has long ago been won. He is not a visitor to the West, but a citizen there, an American; as American as the Americans who despise him, the Americans who fear him, the Americans who love him—the Americans who became less than themselves, or rose to be greater than themselves by virtue of the fact that the challenge he represented was inescapable. He is perhaps the only black man in the world whose relationship to white men is more terrible, more subtle, and more meaningful than the relationship of bitter possessed to uncertain possessors. His survival depended, and his development depends, on his ability to turn his peculiar status in the Western world to his own advantage and, it may be, to the very great advantage of that world. It remains for him to fashion out of his experience that which will give him sustenance, and a voice.

The cathedral at Chartres, I have said, says something to the people of this village which it cannot say to me; but it is important to understand that this cathedral says something to me which it cannot say to them. Perhaps they are struck by the power of the spires, the glory of the windows; but they have known God, after all, longer than I have known him, and in a different way, and I am terrified by the slippery bottomless well to be found in the crypt, down which heretics were hurled to death, and by the obscene, inescapable gargoyles jutting out of the stone and seeming to say that God and the devil can never be divorced. I doubt that the villagers think of the devil when they face a cathedral because they have never been identified with the devil. But I must accept the status which myth, if nothing else, gives me in the West before I can hope to change the myth.

Yet, if the American Negro has arrived at his identity by virtue of the absoluteness of his estrangement from his past, American white men still nourish the illusion that there is some means of recovering the European innocence, of returning to a state in which black men do not exist. This is one of the greatest errors Americans can make. The identity they fought so hard to protect has, by virtue of that battle, undergone a change: Americans are as unlike any other white people in the world as it is possible to be. I do not think, for example, that it is too much to suggest that the American vision of the world—which allows so little reality, generally speaking, for any of the darker forces in human life, which tends until today to paint moral issues in glaring black and white—owes a great deal to the battle waged by Americans to maintain between themselves and black men a human separation which could not be bridged. It is only now beginning to be borne in on us—very faintly, it must be admitted, very slowly, and very much against our will—that this vision of the world is dangerously inaccurate, and perfectly useless. For it protects our moral high-mindedness at the terrible expense of weakening our grasp of reality. People who shut their eyes to reality simply invite their own destruction, and anyone who insists on remaining in a state of innocence long after that innocence is dead turns himself into a monster.

The time has come to realize that the interracial drama acted out on the American continent has not only created a new black man, it has created a new white man, too. No road whatever will lead Americans back to the simplicity of this European village where white men still have the luxury of looking on me as a stranger. I am not, really, a stranger any longer for any American alive. One of the things that distinguishes Americans from other people is that no other people has ever been so deeply involved in the lives of black men, and vice versa. This fact faced, with all its implications, it can be seen that the history of the American Negro problem is not merely shameful, it is also something of an achievement. For even when the worst has been said, it must also be added that the perpetual challenge posed by this problem was always, somehow, perpetually met. It is precisely this black-white experience which may prove of indispensable value to us in the world we face today. This world is white no longer, and it will never be white again.

from *I Know Why the Caged Bird Sings*

Maya Angelou   (1928–)

Given the psychic and physical injuries inflicted upon her in childhood, it is remarkable that Maya Angelou went on to become an accomplished poet, writer, actor, theater director, lecturer, and university professor. One of her major writing projects is a continuing autobiography, of which the first volume is *I Know Why the Caged Bird Sings*. Covering as it does her formative years from early childhood through the pregnancy and birth that made her a mother while she was still a high school student, it is the book that reveals the spiritual resilience, determination, and growing self-confidence that underlie Angelou's later achievements.

For a brief period during her grammar school years, Maya and her brother Bailey lived in St. Louis, first with the grandmother on her mother's side and then with her mother and her mother's current lover—who raped the young girl. Rarely has such an account been written so frankly and with such integrity by an adult woman remembering her sexual victimization as a child. Maya's parents were separated some years before that event, and she saw her father so infrequently that he seemed a stranger to her. She grew to know her mother better, living with her not only in St. Louis but during her high school years in San Francisco, and came to appreciate, especially in San Francisco, her mother's affection and help as well as the vitality of her personality; but it is clear enough that the mother treated her children in their early years with a kind of grand insouciance—leaving them for most of these years in the capable care of her husband's mother, who owned a store and other properties in the black section of Stamps, Arkansas. So fully did the Arkansas grandmother serve the role of mother that she becomes "Momma" for both Maya and Bailey. (Angelou, whose first name actually is Marguerite, became "Maya" for life while still an infant; her three-year-old brother addressed her as "Mya Sister" before further shortening the phrase.)

The racially prejudiced atmosphere of Stamps during roughly the period of the Depression permeates much of *I Know Why the Caged Bird Sings*; to be more precise, Stamps is the center of a prejudicial atmosphere that moves out from this small Arkansas town to reach St. Louis and, though apparently thinner, extends to San Francisco during the early years of World War II. The book contains many episodes that dramatize this atmosphere at its center in Stamps. I have chosen an almost self-contained chapter to exemplify it. The chapter describes Maya's graduation from the eighth grade, the final grade of her grammar school. It dramatizes the response of her race as well as that of the protagonist herself to the white attitudes surrounding their segregated enclave, and ends with a moving tribute (from the adult Angelou) to the black poets—all of the creative spirits—who have sustained her people in their struggle against oppression.

That tribute demonstrates the dual perspective which underlies the whole autobiography. While Angelou is reconstructing, as faithfully as she can, actual experiences from her childhood, her memories necessarily are shaped by the maturity—the knowledge—of her later years; at the time of the writing, she is a woman of about forty looking back over the decades. This particular chapter is as moving as it is not only because we see in it the expectations of the students being crushed by the brutal insensitivity of the white politician who briefly appears to make a graduation speech that reveals his bigotry but because it marks the emergence, in Angelou and her classmates, of pride in themselves, as members of "the wonderful, beautiful Negro race," and is wholly in keeping with Angelou's mature awareness of the spiritual equality of all individuals—a moral awareness that makes the struggle to overcome racial animosities a struggle to liberate both oppressor and victim.

The children in Stamps trembled visibly with anticipation. Some adults were excited too, but to be certain the whole young population had come down with graduation epidemic. Large classes were graduating from both the grammar school and the high school. Even those who were years removed from their own day of glorious release were anxious to help with preparations as a kind of dry run. The junior students who were moving into the vacating classes' chairs were tradition-bound to show their talents for leadership and management. They strutted through the school and around the campus exerting pressure on the lower grades. Their authority was so new that occasionally if they pressed a little too hard it had to be overlooked. After all, next term was coming, and it never hurt a sixth grader to have a play sister in the eighth grade, or a tenth-year student to be able to call a twelfth grader Bubba. So all was endured in a spirit of shared understanding. But the graduating classes themselves were the nobility. Like travelers with exotic destinations on their minds, the graduates were remarkably forgetful. They came to school without their books, or tablets or even pencils. Volunteers fell over themselves to secure replacements for the missing equipment. When accepted, the willing workers might or might not be thanked, and it was of no importance to the pre-graduation rites. Even teachers were respectful of the now quiet and aging seniors, and tended to speak to them, if not as equals, as beings only slightly lower than themselves. After tests were returned and grades given, the student body, which acted like an extended family, knew who did well, who excelled, and what piteous ones had failed.

Unlike the white high school, Lafayette County Training School distinguished itself by having neither lawn, nor hedges, nor tennis court, nor climbing ivy. Its two buildings (main classrooms, the grade school and home economics) were set on a dirt hill with no fence to limit either its boundaries or those of bordering farms. There was a large expanse to the left of the school which was used alternately as a baseball diamond or a basketball court. Rusty hoops on the swaying poles represented the permanent recreational equipment, although bats and balls could be borrowed from the P. E. teacher if the borrower was qualified and if the diamond wasn't occupied.

Over this rocky area relieved by a few shady tall persimmon trees the graduating class walked. The girls often held hands and no longer bothered to speak to the lower students. There was a sadness about them, as if this old world was not their home and they were bound for higher ground. The boys, on the other hand, had become more friendly, more outgoing. A decided change from the closed attitude they projected while studying for finals. Now they seemed not ready to give up the old school, the familiar paths and classrooms. Only a small percentage would be continuing on to college—one of the South's A & M (agricultural and mechanical) schools, which trained Negro youths to be carpenters, farmers, handymen, masons, maids, cooks, and baby nurses. Their future rode heavily on their shoulders, and blinded them to the collective joy that had pervaded the lives of the boys and girls in the grammar school graduating class.

Parents who could afford it had ordered new shoes and ready-made clothes for themselves from Sears and Roebuck or Montgomery Ward. They also engaged the best seamstresses to make the floating graduating dresses and to cut down secondhand pants which would be pressed to a military slickness for the important event.

Oh, it was important, all right. Whitefolks would attend the ceremony, and two or three would speak of God and home, and the Southern way of life, and Mrs. Parsons, the principal's wife, would play the graduation march while the lower-grade graduates paraded down the aisles and took their seats below the platform. The high school seniors would wait in empty classrooms to make their dramatic entrance.

In the Store I was the person of the moment. The birthday girl. The center. Bailey had graduated the year before, although to do so he had had to forfeit all pleasures to make up for his time lost in Baton Rouge.

My class was wearing butter-yellow piqué dresses, and Momma launched out on mine. She smocked the yoke into tiny crisscrossing puckers, then shirred the rest of the bodice. Her dark fingers ducked in and out of the lemony cloth as she embroidered raised daisies around the hem. Before she considered herself finished she had added a crocheted cuff on the puff sleeves, and a pointy crocheted collar.

I was going to be lovely. A walking model of all the various styles of fine hand sewing and it didn't worry me that I was only twelve years old and merely graduating from the eighth grade. Besides, many teachers in Arkansas Negro schools had only that diploma and were licensed to impart wisdom.

The days had become longer and more noticeable. The faded beige of former times had been replaced with strong and sure colors. I began to see my classmates' clothes, their skin tones, and the dust that waved off pussy willows. Clouds that lazed across the sky were objects of great concern to me. Their shiftier shapes might have held a message that in my new happiness and with a little bit of time I'd soon decipher. During that period I looked at the arch of heaven so religiously my neck kept a steady ache. I had taken to smiling more often, and my jaws hurt from the unaccustomed activity. Between the two physical sore spots, I suppose I could have been uncomfortable, but that was not the case. As a member of the winning team (the graduating class of 1940) I had outdistanced unpleasant sensations by miles. I was headed for the freedom of open fields.

Youth and social approval allied themselves with me and we trammeled memories of slights and insults. The wind of our swift passage remodeled my features. Lost tears were pounded to mud and then to dust. Years of withdrawal were brushed aside and left behind, as hanging ropes of parasitic moss.

My work alone had awarded me a top place and I was going to be one of the first called in the graduating ceremonies. On the classroom blackboard, as well as on the bulletin board in the auditorium, there were blue stars and white stars and red stars. No absences, no tardiness, and my academic work was among the best of the year. I could say the preamble to the Constitution even faster than Bailey. We timed ourselves often: "WethepeopleoftheUnitedStatesinordertoformamoreperfectunion . . ." I had memorized the Presidents of the United States from Washington to Roosevelt in chronological as well as alphabetical order.

My hair pleased me too. Gradually the black mass had lengthened and thickened, so that it kept at last to its braided pattern, and I didn't have to yank my scalp off when I tried to comb it.

Louise and I had rehearsed the exercises until we tired out ourselves. Henry Reed was class valedictorian. He was a small, very black boy with hooded eyes, a long, broad nose and an oddly shaped head. I had admired him for years because each term he and I vied for the best grades in our class. Most often he bested me, but instead of being disappointed I was pleased that we shared top places between us. Like many Southern Black children, he lived with his grandmother, who was as strict as Momma and as kind as she knew how to be. He was courteous, respectful and soft-spoken to elders, but on the playground he chose to play the roughest games. I admired him. Anyone, I reckoned, sufficiently afraid or sufficiently dull could be polite. But to be able to operate at a top level with both adults and children was admirable.

His valedictory speech was entitled "To Be or Not to Be." The rigid tenth-grade teacher had helped him write it. He'd been working on the dramatic stresses for months.

The weeks until graduation were filled with heady activities. A group of small children were to be presented in a play about buttercups and daisies and bunny rabbits. They could be heard throughout the building practicing their hops and their little songs that sounded like silver bells. The older girls (nongraduates, of course) were assigned the task of making refreshments for the night's festivities. A tangy scent of ginger, cinnamon, nutmeg and chocolate wafted around the home economics building as the budding cooks made samples for themselves and their teachers.

In every corner of the workshop, axes and saws split fresh timber as the woodshop boys made sets and stage scenery. Only the graduates were left out of the general bustle. We were free to sit in the library at the back of the building or look in quite detachedly, naturally, on the measures being taken for our event.

Even the minister preached on graduation the Sunday before. His subject was, "Let your light so shine that men will see your good works and praise your Father, Who is in Heaven." Although the sermon was purported to be addressed to us, he used the occasion to speak to backsliders, gamblers and general ne'er-do-wells. But since he had called our names at the beginning of the service we were mollified.

Among Negroes the tradition was to give presents to children going only from one grade to another. How much more important this was when the person was graduating at the top of the class. Uncle Willie and Momma had sent away for a Mickey Mouse watch like Bailey's. Louise gave me four embroidered handkerchiefs. (I gave her three crocheted doilies.) Mrs. Sneed, the minister's wife, made me an underskirt to wear for graduation, and nearly every customer gave me a nickel or maybe even a dime with the instruction "Keep on moving to higher ground," or some such encouragement.

Amazingly the great day finally dawned and I was out of bed before I knew it. I threw open the back door to see it more clearly, but Momma said, "Sister, come away from that door and put your robe on."

I hoped the memory of that morning would never leave me. Sunlight was itself still young, and the day had none of the insistence maturity would bring it in a few hours. In my robe and barefoot in the backyard, under cover of going to see about my new beans, I gave myself up to the gentle warmth and thanked God that no matter what evil I had done in my life He had allowed me to live to see this day. Somewhere in my fatalism I had expected to die, accidentally, and never have the chance to walk up the stairs in the auditorium and gracefully receive my hard-earned diploma. Out of God's merciful bosom I had won reprieve.

Bailey came out in his robe and gave me a box wrapped in Christmas paper. He said he had saved his money for months to pay for it. It felt like a box of chocolates, but I knew Bailey wouldn't save money to buy candy when we had all we could want under our noses.

He was as proud of the gift as I. It was a soft-leather-bound copy of a collection of poems by Edgar Allan Poe, or, as Bailey and I called him, "Eap." I turned to "Annabel Lee" and we walked up and down the garden rows, the cool dirt between our toes, reciting the beautifully sad lines.

Momma made a Sunday breakfast although it was only Friday. After we finished the blessing, I opened my eyes to find the watch on my plate. It was a dream of a day. Everything went smoothly and to my credit. I didn't have to be reminded or scolded for anything. Near evening I was too jittery to attend to chores, so Bailey volunteered to do all before his bath.

Days before, we had made a sign for the Store, and as we turned out the lights Momma hung the cardboard over the doorknob. It read clearly: CLOSED. GRADUATION.

My dress fitted perfectly and everyone said that I looked like a sunbeam in it. On the hill, going toward the school, Bailey walked behind with Uncle Willie, who muttered, "Go on, Ju." He wanted him to walk ahead with us because it embarrassed him to have to walk so slowly. Bailey said he'd let the ladies walk together, and the men would bring up the rear. We all laughed, nicely.

Little children dashed by out of the dark like fireflies. Their crepe-paper dresses and butterfly wings were not made for running and we heard more than one rip, dryly, and the regretful "uh uh" that followed.

The school blazed without gaiety. The windows seemed cold and unfriendly from the lower hill. A sense of ill-fated timing crept over me, and if Momma hadn't reached for my hand I would have drifted back to Bailey and Uncle Willie, and possibly beyond. She made a few slow jokes about my feet getting cold, and tugged me along to the now-strange building.

Around the front steps, assurance came back. There were my fellow "greats," the graduating class. Hair brushed back, legs oiled, new dresses and pressed pleats, fresh pocket handkerchiefs and little hand-bags, all homesewn. Oh, we were up to snuff, all right. I joined my comrades and didn't even see my family go in to find seats in the crowded auditorium.

The school band struck up a march and all classes filed in as had been rehearsed. We stood in front of our seats, as assigned, and on a signal from the choir director, we sat. No sooner had this been accomplished than the band started to play the national anthem. We rose again and sang the song, after which we recited the pledge of allegiance. We remained standing for a brief minute before the choir director and the principal signaled to us, rather desperately I thought, to take our seats. The command was so unusual that our carefully rehearsed and smooth-running machine was thrown off. For a full minute we fumbled for our chairs and bumped into each other awkwardly. Habits change or solidify under pressure, so in our state of nervous tension we had been ready to follow our usual assembly pattern: the American national anthem, then the pledge of allegiance, then the song every Black person I knew called the Negro National Anthem. All done in the same key, with the same passion and most often standing on the same foot.

Finding my seat at last, I was overcome with a presentiment of worse things to come. Something unrehearsed, unplanned, was going to happen, and we were going to be made to look bad. I distinctly remember being explicit in the choice of pronoun. It was "we," the graduating class, the unit, that concerned me then.

The principal welcomed "parents and friends" and asked the Baptist minister to lead us in prayer. His invocation was brief and punchy, and for a second I thought we were getting back on the high road to right action. When the principal came back to the dais, however, his voice had changed. Sounds always affected me profoundly and the principal's voice was one of my favorites. During assembly it melted and lowed weakly into the audience. It had not been in my plan to listen to him, but my curiosity was piqued and I straightened up to give him my attention.

He was talking about Booker T. Washington, our "late great leader," who said we can be as close as the fingers on the hand, etc. . . . Then he said a few vague things about friendship and the friendship of kindly people to those less fortunate than themselves. With that his voice nearly faded, thin, away. Like a river diminishing to a stream and then to a trickle. But he cleared his throat and said, "Our speaker tonight, who is also our friend, came from Texarkana to deliver the commencement address, but due to the irregularity of the train schedule, he's going to, as they say, 'speak and run.'" He said that we understood and wanted the man to know that we were most grateful for the time he was able to give us and then something about how we were willing always to adjust to another's program, and without more ado—"I give you Mr. Edward Donleavy."

Not one but two white men came through the door offstage. The shorter one walked to the speaker's platform, and the tall one moved over to the center seat and sat down. But that was our principal's seat, and already occupied. The dislodged gentleman bounce around for a long breath or two before the Baptist minister gave him his chair, then with more dignity than the situation deserved, the minister walked off the stage.

Donleavy looked at the audience once (on reflection, I'm sure that he wanted only to reassure himself that we were really there), adjusted his glasses and began to read from a sheaf of papers.

He was glad "to be here and to see the work going on just as it was in the other schools."

At the first "Amen" from the audience I willed the offender to immediate death by choking on the word. But Amens and Yes, sir's began to fall around the room like rain through a ragged umbrella.

He told us the wonderful changes we children in Stamps had in store. The Central School (naturally, the white school was Central) had already been granted improvements that would be in use in the fall. A well-known artist was coming from Little Rock to teach art to them. They were going to have the newest microscopes and chemistry equipment for their laboratory. Mr. Donleavy didn't leave us long in the dark over who made these improvements available to Central High. Nor were we to be ignored in the general betterment scheme he had in mind.

He said that he had pointed out to people at a very high level that one of the first-line football tacklers at Arkansas Agricultural and Mechanical College had graduated from good old Lafayette County Training School. Here fewer Amen's were heard. Those few that did break through lay dully in the air with the heaviness of habit.

He went on to praise us. He went on to say how he had bragged that "one of the best basketball players at Fisk sank his first ball right here at Lafayette County Training School."

The white kids were going to have a chance to become Galileos and Madame Curies and Edisons and Gauguins, and our boys (the girls weren't even in on it) would try to be Jesse Owenses and Joe Louises.

Owens and the Brown Bomber were great heroes in our world, but what school official in the white-goddom of Little Rock had the right to decide that those two men must be our only heroes? Who decided that for Henry Reed to become a scientist he had to work like George Washington Carver, as a bootblack, to buy a lousy microscope? Bailey was obviously always going to be too small to be an athlete, so which concrete angel glued to what country seat had decided that if my brother wanted to become a lawyer he had to first pay penance for his skin by picking cotton and hoeing corn and studying correspondence books at night for twenty years?

The man's dead words fell like bricks around the auditorium and too many settled in my belly. Constrained by hard-learned manners I couldn't look behind me, but to my left and right the proud graduating class of

1940 had dropped their heads. Every girl in my row had found something new to do with her handkerchief. Some folded the tiny squares into love knots, some into triangles, but most were wadding them, then pressing them flat on their yellow laps.

On the dais, the ancient tragedy was being replayed. Professor Parsons sat, a sculptor's reject, rigid. His large, heavy body seemed devoid of will or willingness, and his eyes said he was no longer with us. The other teachers examined the flag (which was draped stage right) or their notes, or the windows which opened on our now-famous playing diamond.

Graduation, the hush-hush magic time of frills and gifts and congratulations and diplomas, was finished for me before my name was called. The accomplishment was nothing. The meticulous maps, drawn in three colors of ink, learning and spelling decasyllabic words, memorizing the whole of *The Rape of Lucrece*—it was for nothing. Donleavy had exposed us.

We were maids and farmers, handymen and washerwomen, and anything higher that we aspired to was farcical and presumptuous.

Then I wished that Gabriel Prosser and Nat Turner had killed all whitefolks in their beds and that Abraham Lincoln had been assassinated before the signing of the Emancipation Proclamation, and that Harriet Tubman had been killed by that blow on her head and Christopher Columbus had drowned in the *Santa María*.

It was awful to be Negro and have no control over my life. It was brutal to be young and already trained to sit quietly and listen to charges brought against my color with no chance of defense. We should all be dead. I thought I should like to see us all dead, one on top of the other. A pyramid of flesh with the whitefolks on the bottom, as the broad base, then the Indians with their silly tomahawks and teepees and wigwams and treaties, the Negroes with their mops and recipes and cotton sacks and spirituals sticking out of their mouths. The Dutch children should all stumble in their wooden shoes and break their necks. The French should choke to death on the Louisiana Purchase (1803) while silkworms ate all the Chinese with their stupid pigtails. As a species, we were an abomination. All of us.

Donleavy was running for election, and assured our parents that if he won we could count on having the only colored paved playing field in that part of Arkansas. Also—he never looked up to acknowledge the grunts of acceptance—also, we were bound to get some new equipment for the home economics building and the workshop.

He finished, and since there was no need to give any more than the most perfunctory thank-you's, he nodded to the men on the stage, and the tall white man who was never introduced joined him at the door.

They left with the attitude that now they were off to something really important. (The graduation ceremonies at Lafayette County Training School had been a mere preliminary.) The ugliness they left was palpable. An uninvited guest who wouldn't leave. The choir was summoned and sang a modern arrangement of "Onward, Christian Soldiers," with new words pertaining to graduates seeking their place in the world. But it didn't work. Elouise, the daughter of the Baptist minister, recited "Invictus," and I could have cried at the impertinence of "I am the master of my fate, I am the captain of my soul." My name had lost its ring of familiarity and I had to be nudged to go and receive my diploma. All my preparations had fled. I neither marched up to the stage like a conquering Amazon, nor did I look in the audience for Bailey's nod of approval. Marguerite Johnson, I heard the name again, my honors were read, there were noises in the audience of appreciation, and I took my place on the stage as rehearsed.

I thought about colors I hated: ecru, puce, lavender, beige and black.

There was shuffling and rustling around me, then Henry Reed was giving his valedictory address, "To Be or Not to Be." Hadn't he heard the whitefolks? We couldn't *be,* so the question was a waste of time. Henry's voice came out clear and strong. I feared to look at him. Hadn't he got the message? There was no "nobler in the mind" for Negroes because the world didn't think we had minds, and they let us know it. "Outrageous fortune"? Now, that was a joke. When the ceremony was over I had to tell Henry Reed some things. That is, if I still cared. Not "rub," Henry, "erase." "Ah, there's the erase." Us.

Henry had been a good student in elocution. His voice rose on tides of promise and fell on waves of warnings. The English teacher had helped him to create a sermon winging through Hamlet's soliloquy. To be a man, a doer, a builder, a leader, or to be a tool, an unfunny joke, a crusher of funky toadstools. I marveled that Henry could go through with the speech as if we had a choice.

I had been listening and silently rebutting each sentence with my eyes closed; then there was a hush, which in an audience warns that something unplanned is happening. I looked up and saw Henry Reed, the conservative, the proper, the A student, turn his back to the audience and turn to us (the proud graduating class of 1940) and sing, nearly speaking,

> "Lift ev'ry voice and sing
> Till earth and heaven ring
> Ring with the harmonies of Liberty . . ."

It was the poem written by James Weldon Johnson. It was the music composed by J. Rosamond Johnson. It was the Negro national anthem. Out of habit we were singing it.

Our mothers and fathers stood in the dark hall and joined the hymn of encouragement. A kindergarten teacher led the small children onto the stage and the buttercups and daisies and bunny rabbits marked time and tried to follow:

> "Stony the road we trod
> Bitter the chastening rod
> Felt in the days when hope, unborn, had died.
> Yet with a steady beat
> Have not our weary feet
> Come to the place for which our fathers sighed?"

Every child I knew had learned that song with his ABC's and along with "Jesus Love Me This I Know." But I personally had never heard it before. Never heard the words, despite the thousands of times I had sung them. Never thought they had anything to do with me.

On the other hand, the words of Patrick Henry had made such an impression on me that I had been able to stretch myself tall and trembling and say, "I know not what course others may take, but as for me, give me liberty or give me death."

And now I heard, really for the first time:

> "We have come over a way that with tears
> has been watered,
> We have come, treading our path through
> the blood of the slaughtered."

While echoes of the song shivered in the air, Henry Reed bowed his head, said "Thank you," and returned to his place in the line. The tears that slipped down many faces were not wiped away in shame.

We were on top again. As always, again. We survived. The depths had been icy and dark, but now a bright sun spoke to our souls. I was no longer simply a member of the proud graduating class of 1940; I was a proud member of the wonderful beautiful Negro race.

Oh, Black known and unknown poets, how often have your auctioned pains sustained us? Who will compute the lonely nights made less lonely by your songs, or by the empty pots made less tragic by your tales?

If we were a people much given to revealing secrets, we might raise monuments and sacrifice to the memories of our poets, but slavery cured us of that weakness. It may be enough, however, to have it said that we survive in exact relationship to the dedication of our poets (include preachers, musicians and blues singers).

"A Death in the Family"

Kenneth McClane (1951–   )

Walls is a collection of essays by a black poet who turned to autobiographical prose as a medium for expressing his feelings in a more direct way than his poetry would allow. The title is a reference to all the barriers separating humans from each other. Certain walls are imposed by society in its exclusions and prejudices and its conjoined desires for safety and denial: prisons are one example. Others are interior walls erected by individuals so damaged, so vulnerable, that they wish to separate themselves from their own families, refusing the nurture that conceivably could lead to their recovery. And then there are walls that are unconsciously built by those who want no walls at all, barricades constructed out of anger and frustration and guilt at all the surrounding fortifications.

In "A Death in the Family" and the other essays in his collection, Kenneth McClane is aware of all these barriers to understanding and mutuality; the book is his attempt to break through at least those walls that are of his own making. In writing of the death of his brother, Paul, two years younger than he, McClane *does* free emotions that have been pent up. Like their father, a doctor who for many decades practiced in Harlem, McClane has made for himself a successful professional career, as college professor as well as poet; but Paul, a talented musician, seems to have preferred his destruction in the walls of the ghetto to any promise of middle-class respectability. Paul withdrew from his family, finding solace in sex and drugs—primarily alcohol.

Paul died in 1983, from the effects of severe alcoholism; the essay, written two years later, reconstructs McClane's difficult relationship with his brother through memories, including one moment in which he is a mirror of Paul's own bitter hatred. The essay also faces up to the angers and resentments among other members of the family that were occasioned by Paul's inexorable movement toward self-destruction. But memory is also the redemptive agent, permitting the ultimate awareness of the love that always has bound together the members of the family, even as it has been connected to the intensities of anger and terror.

He was a kid of about the same age as Rufus, from some insane place like Jersey City or Syracuse, but somewhere along the line he had discovered that he could say it with a saxophone. He had a lot to say. He stood there, wide-legged, humping the air, filling his barrel chest, shivering in the rags of his twenty-odd years, and screaming through the horn Do you love me? Do you love? Do you me? *And, again,* Do you love me? Do you love me? Do you love me?

—James Baldwin, *Another Country*

I recall how difficult it was for me to realize that my brother loved me. He was always in the streets, doing this and that, proverbially in trouble, in a place, Harlem, where trouble indeed was great. At times we would even come to blows, when, for example, drunk as he could be, he wished to borrow my car and I had visions of his entrails splayed over the city. I remember one incident as if it were yesterday: Paul, my younger brother, physically larger than me, his hand holding a screwdriver, poised to stab me, his anger so great that his brother, the college professor, wouldn't let him drive his "lady" home, even though he could barely walk. I can still see him chiding me about how I had always done the right thing, how I was not his father, how I was just a poor excuse for a white man, the last statement jeweled with venom. And from his place, this was certainly true: I had done what I was expected to do; and the world, in its dubious logic, had paid me well. I was a college teacher; I had published a few collections of poems; I had a wonderful girlfriend; and what suffering I bore, at least to my brother's eyes, centered around my inability to leave him alone. Luckily, this confrontation ended when my father rushed in on us, our distress exceeded only by the distress in his eyes. Later, my brother would forget the events of that evening, but not the fact that I had not lent him the car. For my part, I would never forget how we were both so angry, so hate-filled. I, too, that night, might have killed my brother.

As children we were often at each other's throat. The difference in our ages, just two years, was probably a greater bridge than either of us welcomed. And so we often went for each other's pressure points: the greater discomfort enacted, the more skillful our thrust. But this was child's play, in a child's world. On that November might when my brother and I confronted each other with hate and murder in our eyes, I realized I had mined a new intensity, full of terror and, though I didn't know it then, of love.

Though he was incredibly angry (bitter, some might say), I always admired my brother's honesty and self-love. It seemed that everything he thrust into his body was a denial of self—alcohol, smoke, cocaine—yet his mind and his quick tongue demanded that he be heard. In a world full of weakness, he was outspoken, never letting anyone diminish him. When he was at the wheel of that torturous abandon euphemistically called "city driving," he invariably would maneuver abreast of a driver who had somehow slighted him, and tell him, in no uncertain language, where he could go with utmost dispatch. Paul never cared how big, crazy, or dangerous this other driver might be. When I cautioned him, reliving again and again the thousand headlines of "Maniac Kills Two over Words," he would just shrug. "He's a bastard, needs to know it." I remember how scared I became when he would roll down the window—scared and yet proud.

My brother was unable to ride within the subway, moving immediately to the small catwalk between the cars, where the air might reach him. He complained that he was always too hot, that the people were too close; indeed, as soon as he entered the train, sweat began to cascade off him, as if he had just completed a marathon. Later this image would remain with me: my brother, feet apart, sweat pouring from his body, trying to keep his delicate balance between the two radically shifting platforms, while always maintaining that he was fine. "Bro, I'm just hot." I would later learn that these manifestations were the effects of acute alcoholism; I would later learn much about my brother.

Like the day's punctuation, Paul would make his numerous runs to the *bodega*, bringing in his small brown paper bags, then quickly returning to his room, where he would remain for hours. Some days you would barely see him; my father could never coax him out. Paul saw my father as the establishment—"fat man," he would call him, though this too was somewhat playful. With Paul play and truth were so intermeshed that they leased the same root. One had to be forever careful of traveling with a joke only to find that no joke was intended. Or, just as often, finding sympathy with something Paul said, one was startled to see him break out in the most wondrous smile, amusement everywhere. In this spectacle, one thing was enormously clear: Paul was a difficult dancer. And, as with all artists, his mastery was also, for the rest of us, cause for contempt. We enjoyed his flights; but we also sensed, and poignantly, that they were had at our expense. Clearly we had failed as listeners, for Paul had not sought to befuddle us; but we, as the majority, were in the position of power and could always depend on it as our last defense. And power, arguments to the contrary, is rarely generous.

My brother would stay in his room for hours, watching the box, playing his drums, talking to his endless friends who, until he was just about to die, came to sit and talk and smoke. Paul inevitably would be holding court; he knew where the parties were, could get anyone near anything, had entrée with the most beautiful girls, who sensed something in his eyes that would not betray them. Many of his friends would later become doctors, a few entertainers, all of them by the most incomprehensible and torturous of routes. The black middle class—if it can really be termed that—is a class made up of those who are either just too doggedly persistent or too stupid to realize that, like Fitzgerald's America, their long-sought-after future remains forever beckoning and endlessly retreating. And Paul's friends, who sensed his demise well before we did, as only the doomed or the near-doomed can, were as oddly grafted to class—or even the promise of respectability—as it is humanly possible to imagine. Like Paul, they sat waiting for the warden, knowing only that the walls exist, that the sentence is real. Indeed, if the crime were lack of understandable passion, they were guilty a hundredfold. But it is not understanding, alas, that the world is interested in. And the world—they rightfully sensed—was certainly not interested in them.

Paul was no saint. Like most of us, he exhibited the confusions and the possibilities that intermittently set us on our knees or loose with joy. He wasn't political in the established way; his body, in its remoteness, was political. It said that the state of the world was nothing he cared to be involved with. Fuck it, he'd say.

In the language of the street, Paul was a "lover." And like all lovers he believed that the pounding of the bed frame testified to something that "his woman" best understood. And in the logic of his bed and of those who shared it, women's lib to the contrary, there seemed to be no complaints. Often I wondered about his use of the term "my woman," the possessiveness of it, the language that brought to mind the auction block and a brutal history that had profited neither of us. But Paul's woman was like his life: if I had my job and my poems, he had his woman. Feminists might complain of this uneasy pairing—I certainly share their concern—but within the brutal reward structure of the ghetto, where one's life is often one's only triumph, such a notion is understandable. My brother's woman was his only bouquet, the one thing that testified that he was not only a man, but a man whom someone wanted. Arguments notwithstanding, no manner of philosophy or word play can alter the truth. My brother loved his woman in the most profound sense of the word, since his love centered on the greatest offering he could give, the sharing of himself. And I do not mean to be coy here. For when you are, in Gwendolyn Brooks's terms, "all your value and all your art," the gift of yourself is an unprecedented one.

But this is a brother's testimony; it is a way of a brother living with a brother dead. It doesn't have the violence of unknowing—the great violence that kept me for so long feeling guilty, which still makes the early morning the most difficult time. I remember how Paul volunteered to watch our cats when Rochelle and I, living for a three-month exile in Hartsdale, New York, had to be away. Max, the large white one, hell-bent on intercourse with the hardly possible, hid within the wall, and Paul went nearly crazy, looking here and there, wondering if he should call, afraid that disaster had no shores. Strange how I recall this; it certainly isn't important. But Paul was scared—scared more so because he loved animals, saw in their pain more than he saw in ours, in his.

In July, my father called to say that I had best come to New York. Paul was ill. Very ill. He would probably die. The whole thing was incredible. My father has the nagging desire to protect those he loves from the worrisome. What this tends to create, however, is the strangest presentiment: when he does finally communicate something, it is always at the most dire stage, and the onlooker can barely understand how something has become so involved, so horrible, so quickly; or is thrown, similarly, into the uncomfortable position of confronting the possibility that one failed to acknowledge something so momentous occurring. In either case, one is completely unprepared for revelation, and no matter what my father's heroic designs (and they were that), one's horror at not being allowed to participate in the inexorable outdistances any possible feeling of gratitude. Although pain cannot be prepared for, neither can it be denied. But on this day, my father's voice was that of cold disbelief—the doctor without any possible placebo. And I was in the air in a few hours.

At that time I was involved in teaching summer school, and the day before one of my students had suggested that we read Baldwin's *Sonny's Blues*. I had read the story some years before and had been favorably impressed, though I couldn't remember any of its particulars. Well, at six-fifteen I got on the airplane, armed with a few clothes and Baldwin. Little did I know that this story would save my life, or at least make it possible to live with.

Sonny's Blues is about an older brother's relationship with his younger brother, Sonny, who happens to be a wonderful jazz pianist and a heroin addict. The story, obviously, is about much more: it involves love, denial, and the interesting paradox by which those of us who persist in the world may in fact survive, not because we understand anything but because we consciously exclude things. Sonny's older brother teaches algebra in a Harlem high school, where algebra is certainly not the only education the students are receiving. There are drugs, dangers, people as hell-bent on living as they are fervent on dying. But most importantly, *Sonny's Blues* is about the ways in which we all fail; the truth that love itself cannot save someone; the realization that there are unreconcilable crises in the world; and, most importantly, the verity that there are people among us, loved ones, who, no matter what one may do, will perish.

Now, I read this story on the plane, conscious, as one is only when truly present at one's distress, of the millions of things going on about me. The plane was headed to Rochester, a course only capitalism can explain, for Rochester is west of Ithaca; and New York, my destination, is east of Ithaca, my place of origin. Clearly this makes no sense, but neither does serving gin and tonic at six-fifteen A.M. And I was thankful for that.

The hospital was located in central Manhattan, some five blocks from my father's newly acquired office. My father had just moved from his long-held office at 145th Street because he had routinely been robbed; the most recent robbery had taken on a particularly brutal nature, when the intruders placed a huge, eight-hundred-pound EKG machine atop him to pin him to the floor. Robberies in this neighborhood were not unusual; my father had been robbed some eight times within the previous four years. But with the escalation of the dope traffic, and the sense that every doctor must have a wonderful stash, doctors, even when they, like my father, had no narcotics at all, became prime targets. My father loved is office; he had been there since he first came to New York in 1941. Although he could have made much more money in Midtown, he remained by choice in Harlem. As a child I could not understand this. I wanted him to be among the skyscrapers, with the Ben Caseys. Little did I know then that his forsaking all these things was the highest act of selflessness. As he once quietly stated, probably after a bout of my pestering, "Black people need good doctors, too." I imagine my father would have remained in his office until a bullet found his head had not my mother finally put her foot down and declared, "Honey, I know thirty-five years is a long time, but you've got to move."

I walked past my father's new office and headed into the intensive care unit of Roosevelt Hospital. There I met my father and the attending physician—two doctors, one with a son—and listened to the prognosis. Medicine, as you know, has wonderful nomenclature for things: the most horrible things and something as slight as hiccups have names that imply the morgue. But the litany of my brother—septicemia, pneumonia—had the weight, rehearsed in my father's face, of the irreconcilable. My brother was *going* to die. The doctor said my brother was *going to die.* They would try like hell, but the parameters (the word *parameters* had never before been so important to me) left little in the way of hope.

It is difficult enough to be a parent and have a twenty-nine-year-old child dying of alcoholism, his gut enlarged, his eyes red, lying in a coma. It is even more difficult, however, when you are a parent and also a doctor. For you have a dual obligation, one to a profession, a way of seeing, and one to nature, a rite of loving. As a doctor, my father knew what was medically possible—as surely as did any well-trained specialist—in my brother's precarious situation; he certainly knew what the parameters dictated. But as a parent, hoping like any parent that his child might live, he knew nothing, hope being a flight from what is known to the fanciful. And so these two extremes placed my father in a country rarely encountered, a predicament where I could sense, even then, his distress, but a place from which no on could save him.

In the two weeks that would follow, my mother, in grief, would ask my father what were Paul's chances. And he—doctor, parent, and husband—would be placed in that country again and again. As a parent, every slight twitching of Paul, a slight movement of the lips, a small spasm of the hand, would move him to joy, to speculation—was that an attempt at words, was Paul reaching out? But as a doctor, he knew the terrible weight of parameters—how a word, no matter how strange its sound or source, does involve meaning. So, often he was placed in the terrible paradox of stating what he least wanted to hear. That yes, it was possible that Paul was reaching for us; but the parameters, the this test and the that test, suggested that Paul was still critical, very critical. And we never pressed him further, probably sensing that he would have to announce that these small skirmishes with the inevitable, like water pools just before turning to ice, could not remove the fact, no matter how much we or he would wish it so, that Paul was going to die. Moreover, for us, this dalliance with hope was a temporary way station so that we could harden our own tools for the coming onslaught. My father did not have this privilege; he was, like all the greatest heroes, the angel without the hope of heaven.

In many ways the third factor in my father's difficult situation now came most into play: that of husband. My mother, like all of us, clung to hope; but more, she clung to her son. There is no way to detail the sense of a mother's love. In substance, a mother protects her son from the world, which, she rightly senses, is unceasingly bent on his destruction. Yet, in my house, since Paul was an artist—and so remote—my mother, in a sense, defended a phantom, defending him in much the way one supports the constitutional right of due process. For my mother, Paul was to be protected in theory: he was an artist; he was sensitive; he was silent. This identification with him and with those of his facets the world was bound not to respect—and indeed never did—made her involvement with Paul all the more intense, for he was not only the issue of her womb but the wellspring of her imagination.

My father certainly understood some of this, yet his way of reacting to any ostensible conundrum was conditioned by his medical school training. If there was a problem, he maintained, it could be reasonably addressed. And so he hoped that Paul would descend from his room and tell him what the problem was, why he wasn't finishing college, why he continued to drink so heavily, what, in God's name, he did up in that room. And as it became obvious that the Socratic method demanded an interchange between two consenting mentors, my father became increasingly concerned and distressed. (The problem with any axiom is that it is valuable only as long as it works: my father's belief in reason had served him happily heretofore; yet now he was encountering an unforeseen circumstance. And he, like all of us when confronting Paul, had little in the bank.)

In any event, my father, in the hospital, was forced continually to grapple with three very difficult responsibilities all somehow connected. My mother, as Paul miraculously showed slight signs of rallying (the doctors had originally stated that he had a ten-percent chance of surviving), continued to find reasons, as all of us did, for hope. I recall how my wife and I visited one day and Paul actually extended his wobbling hand—and I, relating this later to my father, actually did press him, asking if he thought Paul could possibly make it. My father, caught between a brother's hope and the sense that miracles do happen, and possibly even to him, said, "Yes, I think he could; but the parameters *(again that word)* are inconclusive." (Now I know that he didn't believe that Paul could live—the doctor in him didn't believe, that is.)

But the most difficult moments for my father came, I think, when he had to explain to my mother, his wife, what he saw, trying always to remember that she was a grieving mother and a hopeful one; and no matter what was happening, might happen, he had to remain a source of strength for her, as she had so often been for him. In this difficult barter, my father also had to worry about my mother's natural inclination to believe the impossible, for hope would make us all immortal, while at the same time protecting that part of her which would permit her to bear this thing, no matter what the outcome. My father continued to caution my mother about the dire state of my brother. The word *parameter* became as palpable to my family as my brother's breath. And the boundaries, no matter what my brother's outward appearance, remained the same. It was enough to drive one crazy. With the weather, when the sun rises and the skin feels warm, the thermometer registers one's sense of new heat. Yet with my brother it seemed that our senses were at war with the medical reality. What, then, in this place, were cause and effect?

During the last week of my brother's life, my mother became increasingly angry with my father, blurting out, "You sound as if you want your son to die." Clearly this was an outburst culled out of anguish, frustration, and grief. And yet it adequately gave language to my father's paradox. Never have I seen the mind and the heart so irrefutably at odds.

My brother died after five coronaries at two A.M. thirteen nights after he was admitted to intensive care. His funeral took place some 250 miles from New York, on lovely Martha's Vineyard, where Paul and the family had spent our happiest years. The funeral was a thrown-together affair: 90 percent grief and the rest dogged persistence that something had to be done. The service was a plain one, with an Episcopal minister reading from the dreary Book of Common Prayer. My mother had hoped that someone could better eulogize my brother, someone who might get beyond the ashes-to-ashes bit and talk about the stuff of him, possibly so that we, his family, might finally get to know the person who had slowly drained away from us. The one reverend who knew my brother begged off, with the excuse that Paul had traveled a great distance from when he knew him. And that, to say the least, was the profoundest ministry that man had ever preached.

Although the funeral was a hasty affair, with little notice—and though we hardly knew many of Paul's friends—somehow a large contingent gathered, coming from Vermont, New York, and elsewhere, many of them for the first time at a funeral of one of their peers. I can't adequately describe the motley assemblage. Suffice it to say that these were the Lord's children, the ones who had tasted the bread of his world and waited, still, for manna. One young woman said a few words, choked them out, and then the sobbing began.

I think this meditation aptly ends with his friends, for they knew him and loved him as we did. In Baldwin's *Another Country,* one of the characters, Vivaldo, is described as feeling that "love is a country he knew nothing about." With the death of my brother, I learned about love: my love for him; my love for my parents; their love for each other; my love for those thin-shelled children who gathered on that small hillside to pay witness to one of theirs who didn't make it, who evidenced in his falling that death indeed is a possibility, no matter how young one is or how vigorous. I can't say that I know who my brother was, but I know that I miss him, more now than ever. And love, yes, is a country that I know something about.

from *The Woman Warrior:*
Memoirs of a Girlhood Among Ghosts
Maxine Hong Kingston   (1940–   )

The daughter of emigrants from China, Maxine Hong Kingston was born in California in 1940. Near the beginning of "No Name Woman," the initial memoir of her *The Woman Warrior,* she says that she and other Chinese Americans "in the first American generations have had to figure out how the invisible world the emigrants built around our childhoods fit in solid America." That "invisible world" consists of the spirits of dead ancestors, the gods who would curse or abet the living, the myths and legends recounted in "talk story" by emigrants to each other and (at bedtime) to their children, and unmentionable family secrets. Disparate as they are, the five memoirs that make up the volume are an attempt by Kingston to know herself, as a Chinese American. The autobiographical thread, if we extricate it from this assemblage of legends, dreams, adolescent sexual fears, and tales whose factual truth is uncertain, is the account of the development of her own Chinese American identity, a development that requires her to overcome the most crippling aspect of the Chinese heritage—the relegation of women to an inferior status, to servitude and slavery, their lowly position intimately connected to (if not the result of) a cultural attitude that forbade any mention of sexual desires: "No one talked sex, ever."

"No Name Woman" is Kingston's attempt to resurrect, at least in memory, an aunt whom her family has tried to expunge by "deliberately forgetting her." That aunt brought disgrace to the family and to the Chinese village to which the family belonged; she drowned herself and her newborn illegitimate child in the well following a ritual act of destruction and despoliation of family property by the villagers as punishment against all the family members for the aunt's transgression of the sexual code. As a child who has just "started to menstruate," Maxine is told by her mother of the aunt's fate as a kind of warning, to prevent the child from a repetition of sexual behavior that could once again so "humiliate" the family that she, too, would be "forgotten as if you had never been born." Instructed by her mother never to mention what she had just revealed about the aunt, Kingston waited twenty years before she violated that injunction by writing this essay. How reliable, how faithful to the aunt's actual life and personality, is it? The mother's version is itself a subjective one; and upon its details Kingston, now perhaps nearly the age of the mother who told it to her, constructs a couple of versions of her own—in the first, the aunt is a victim of rape and male domination; in the second, the aunt is motivated by her own sexual desires.

"No Name Woman" is an example, then, of the interplay between a recalled story and imagined interpretations of it—with imagination in this particular case inserting opposing explanations in accordance both with Kingston's later experiences as an adult American and her childhood knowledge of Chinese customs and beliefs. Such interplay, I assume, is essential to the establishment of her identity—indeed, of her freedom—as a person and as a Chinese American. The memoir is cautionary in a way quite opposite to her mother's intention: for silence about sex—a willful forgetting of the aggressions, the desires, the romanticizing it arouses—serves simply to reinforce female bondage, psychological anxiety, sexual fears. (In a later memoir from her childhood, the hostility and aggression that the young Maxine demonstrates to another Chinese American girl, a handicapped child who can't or won't speak, is surely to be read against all the injunctions of silence that have been imposed upon her.)

"You must not tell anyone," my mother said, "what I am about to tell you. In China your father had a sister who killed herself. She jumped into the family well. We say that your father has all brothers because it is as if she had never been born.

"In 1924 just a few days after our village celebrated seventeen hurry-up weddings—to make sure that every young man who went 'out on the road' would responsibly come home—your father and his brothers and your grandfather and his brothers and your aunt's new husband sailed for America, the Gold Mountain. It was your grandfather's last trip. Those lucky enough to get contracts waved good-bye from the decks. They fed and guarded the stowaways and helped them off in Cuba, New York, Bali, Hawaii. 'We'll meet in California next year,' they said. All of them sent money home.

"I remember looking at your aunt one day when she and I were dressing; I had not noticed before that she had such a protruding melon of a stomach. But I did not think, 'She's pregnant,' until she began to look like other pregnant women, her shirt pulling and the white tops of her black pants showing. She could not have been pregnant, you see, because her husband had been gone for years. No one said anything. We did not discuss it. In early summer she was ready to have the child, long after the time when it could have been possible.

"The village had also been counting. On the night the baby was to be born the villagers raided our house. Some were crying. Like a great saw, teeth strung with lights, files of people walked zigzag across our land, tearing the rice. Their lanterns doubled in the disturbed black water, which drained away through the broken bunds. As the villagers closed in, we could see that some of them, probably men and women we knew well, wore white masks. The people with long hair hung it over their faces. Women with short hair made it stand up on end. Some had tied white bands around their foreheads, arms, and legs.

"At first they threw mud and rocks at the house. Then they threw eggs and began slaughtering our stock. We could hear the animals scream their deaths—the roosters, the pigs, a last great roar from the ox. Familiar

<u>wild heads</u> flared in our night windows; the villagers encircled us. Some of the faces stopped to peer at us, their eyes rushing like searchlights. The hands flattened against the panes, framed heads, and left red prints.

"The villagers broke in the front and the back doors at the same time, even though we had not locked the doors against them. Their knives dripped with the blood of our animals. They smeared blood on the doors and walls. One woman swung a chicken, whose throat she had slit, splattering blood in red arcs about her. We stood together in the middle of our house, <u>in the family hall with the pictures and tables of the ancestors around us</u>, and looked straight ahead.

"At that time the house had only two wings. When the men came back, we would build two more to enclose our courtyard and a third one to begin a second courtyard. The villagers pushed through both wings, even your grandparents' rooms, to find your aunt's, which was also mine until the men returned. From this room a new wing for one of the younger families would grow. They ripped up her clothes and shoes and broke her combs, grinding them underfoot. They tore her work from the loom. They scattered the cooking fire and rolled the new weaving in it. We could hear them in the kitchen breaking our bowls and banging the pots. They overturned the great waist-high earthenware jugs; duck eggs, pickled fruits, vegetables burst out and mixed in acrid torrents. The old woman from the next field swept a broom through the air and loosened the spirits-of-the-broom over our heads. 'Pig.' 'Ghost.' 'Pig,' they sobbed and scolded while they ruined our house.

"When they left, they took sugar and oranges to bless themselves. They cut pieces from the dead animals. Some of them took bowls that were not broken and clothes that were not torn. Afterward we swept up the rice and sewed it back up into sacks. But the smells from the spilled preserves lasted. Your aunt gave birth in the pigsty that night. The next morning when I went for the water, I found her and the baby plugging up the family well."

"Don't let your father know that I told you. He denies her. Now that you have started to menstruate, what happened to her could happen to you. Don't humiliate us. <u>You wouldn't like to be forgotten as if you had never been born.</u> The villagers are watchful." *ancestor worship/ memory/ erasure*

Whenever she had to warn us about life, my mother told stories that ran like this one, a story to grow up on. She tested our strength to establish realities. Those in the emigrant generations who could not reassert brute survival died young and far from home. Those of us in the first American generations have had to figure out how this invisible world the emigrants built around our childhoods fits in solid America.

The emigrants confused the gods by diverting their curses, misleading them with crooked streets and false names. They must try to confuse their offspring as well, who, I suppose, threaten them in similar ways—always trying to get things straight, always trying to name the unspeakable. The Chinese I know hide their names; sojourners take new names when their lives change and guard their real names with silence.

Chinese-Americans, when you try to understand what things in you are Chinese, how do you separate what is peculiar to childhood, to poverty, insanities, one family, your mother who marked your growing with stories, from what is Chinese? What is Chinese tradition and what is the movies?

If I want to learn what clothes my aunt wore, whether flashy or ordinary, I would have to begin, "Remember Father's drowned-in-the-well sister?" I cannot ask that. My mother has told me once and for all the useful parts. She will add nothing unless powered by Necessity, a riverbank that guides her life. She plants vegetable gardens rather than lawns; she carries the odd-shaped tomatoes home from the fields and eats food left for the gods.

Whenever we did frivolous things, we used up energy; we flew high kites. We children came up off the ground over the melting cones our parents brought home from work and the American movie on New Year's Day—*Oh, You Beautiful Doll* with Betty Grable one year, and *She Wore a Yellow Ribbon* with John Wayne another year. After the one carnival ride each, we paid in guilt; our tired father counted his change on the dark walk home.

Adultery is extravagance. Could people who hatch their own chicks and eat the embryos and the heads for delicacies and boil the feet in vinegar for party food, leaving only the gravel, eating even the gizzard lining—could such people engender a prodigal aunt? To be a woman, to have a daughter in starvation time was a waste enough. My aunt could not have been the lone romantic who gave up everything for sex. Women in the old China did not choose. Some man had commanded her to lie with him and be his secret evil. I wonder whether he masked himself when he joined the raid on her family.

Perhaps she had encountered him in the fields or on the mountain where the daughters-in-law collected fuel. Or perhaps he first noticed her in the marketplace. He was not a stranger because the village housed no strangers. She had to have dealings with him other than sex. Perhaps he worked an adjoining field, or he sold her the cloth for the dress she sewed and wore. His demand must have surprised, then terrified her. She obeyed him; she always did as she was told.

When the family found a young man in the next village to be her husband, she had stood tractably beside the best rooster, his proxy, and promised before they met that she would be his forever. She was lucky that he was her age and she would be the first wife, an advantage secure now. The night she first saw him, he had sex with her. Then he left for America. She had almost forgotten what he looked like. When she tried to envision him, she only saw the black and white face in the group photograph the men had taken before leaving.

The other man was not, after all, much different from her husband. They both gave orders: she followed. "If you tell your family, I'll beat you. I'll kill you. Be here again next week." No one talked sex, ever. And she might have separated the rapes from the rest of living if only she did not have to buy her oil from him or gather wood in the same forest. I want her fear to have lasted just as long as rape lasted so that the fear could have been contained. No drawn-out fear. But women at sex hazarded birth and hence lifetimes. The fear did not stop but permeated everywhere. She told the man, "I think I'm pregnant." He organized the raid against her.

On nights when my mother and father talked about their life back home, sometimes they mentioned an "outcast table" whose business they still seemed to be settling, their voices tight. In a commensal tradition, where food is precious, the powerful older people made wrongdoers eat alone. Instead of letting them start separate new lives like the Japanese, who could become samurais and geishas, the Chinese family, faces averted but eyes glowering sideways, hung on to the offenders and fed them leftovers. My aunt must have lived in the same house as my parents and eaten at an outcast table. My mother spoke about the raid as if she had seen it, when she and my aunt, a daughter-in-law to a different household, should not have been living together at all. Daughters-in-law lived with their husbands' parents, not their own; a synonym for marriage in Chinese is "taking a daughter-in-law." Her husband's parents could have sold her, mortgaged her, stoned her. But they had sent her back to her own mother and father, a mysterious act hinting at disgrace not told me. Perhaps they had thrown her out to deflect the avengers.

She was the only daughter; her four brothers went with her father, husband, and uncles "out on the road" and for some years because western men. When the goods were divided among the family, three of the brothers took land, and the youngest, my father, chose an education. After my grandparents gave their daughter away to her husband's family, they had dispensed all the adventure and all the property. They expected her alone to keep the traditional ways, which her brothers, now among the barbarians, could fumble without detection. The heavy, deep-rooted women were to maintain the past against the flood, safe for returning. But the rare urge west had fixed upon our family, and so my aunt crossed boundaries not delineated in space.

The work of preservation demands that the feelings playing about in one's guts not be turned into action. Just watch their passing like cherry blossoms. But perhaps my aunt, my forerunner, caught in a slow life, let dreams grow and fade and after some months or years went toward what persisted. Fear at the enormities of the forbidden kept her desires delicate, wire and bone. She looked at a man because she liked the way the hair was tucked behind his ears, or she liked the question-mark line of a long torso curving at the shoulder and straight at the hip. For warm eyes or a soft voice or a slow walk—that's all—a few hairs, a line, a brightness, a sound, a pace, she gave up family. She offered us up for a charm that vanished with tiredness, a pigtail that didn't toss when the wind died. Why, the wrong lighting could erase the dearest thing about him.

It could very well have been, however, that my aunt did not take subtle enjoyment of her friend, but, a wild woman, kept rollicking company. Imagining her free with sex doesn't fit, though. I don't know any women like that, or men either. Unless I see her life branching into mine, she gives me no ancestral help.

To sustain her being in love, she often worked at herself in the mirror, guessing at the colors and shapes that would interest him, changing them frequently in order to hit on the right combination. She wanted him to look back.

On a farm near the sea, a woman who tended her appearance reaped a reputation for eccentricity. All the married women blunt-cut their hair in flaps about their ears or pulled it back in tight buns. No nonsense. Neither style blew easily into heart-catching tangles. And at their weddings they displayed themselves in their long hair for the last time. "It brushed the backs of my knees," my mother tells me. "It was braided, and even so, it brushed the backs of my knees."

At the mirror my aunt combed individuality into her bob. A bun could have been contrived to escape into black streamers blowing in the wind or in quiet wisps about her face, but only the older women in our picture album wear buns. She brushed her hair back from her forehead, tucking the flaps behind her ears. She looped a piece of thread, knotted into a circle between her index fingers and thumbs, and ran the double strand across her forehead. When she closed her fingers as if she were making a pair of shadow geese bite, the string twisted together catching the little hairs. Then she pulled the thread away from her skin, ripping the hairs out neatly, her eyes watering from the needles of pain. Opening her fingers she cleaned the thread, then rolled it along her hairline and the tops of her eyebrows. My mother did the same to me and my sisters and herself. I used to believe that the expression "caught by the short hairs" meant a captive held with a depilatory string. It especially hurt at the temples, but my mother said we were lucky we didn't have to have our feet bound when we were seven. Sisters used to sit on their beds and cry together, she said, as their mothers or their slaves removed the bandages for a few minutes each night and let the blood gush back into their veins. I hope that the man my aunt loved appreciated a smooth brow, that he wasn't just a tits-and-ass man.

Once my aunt found a freckle on her chin, at a spot that the almanac said predestined her for unhappiness. She dug it out with a hot needle and washed the wound with peroxide.

More attention to her looks than these pullings of hairs and picking at spots would have caused gossip among the villagers. They owned work clothes and good clothes, and they wore good clothes for feasting the new seasons. But since a woman combing her hair hexes beginnings, my aunt rarely found an occasion to look her best. Women looked like great sea snails—the corded wood, babies, and laundry they carried were the whorls on their backs. The Chinese did not admire a bent back; goddesses and warriors stood straight. Still there must have been a marvelous freeing of beauty when a worker laid down her burden and stretched and arched.

Such commonplace loveliness, however, was not enough for my aunt. She dreamed of a lover for the fifteen days of New Year's, the time for families to exchange visits, money, and food. She plied her secret comb. And sure enough she cursed the year, the family, the village, and herself.

Even as her hair lured her imminent lover, many other men looked at her. Uncles, cousins, nephews, brothers would have looked, too, had they been home between journeys. Perhaps they had already been restraining their curiosity, and they left, fearful that their glances, like a field of nesting birds, might be startled and caught. Poverty hurt, and that was their first reason for leaving. But another, final reason for leaving the crowded house was the never-said.

She may have been unusually beloved, the precious only daughter, spoiled and mirror gazing because of the affection the family lavished on her. When her husband left, they welcomed the chance to take her back from the in-laws; she could live like the little daughter for just a while longer. There are stories that my grandfather was different from other people, "crazy ever since the little Jap bayoneted him in the head." He used to put his naked penis on the dinner table, laughing. And one day he brought home a baby girl, wrapped up inside his brown western-style greatcoat. He had traded one of his sons, probably my father, the youngest, for her. My grandmother made him trade back. When he finally got a daughter of his own, he doted on her. They must have all loved her, except perhaps my father, the only brother who never went back to China, having once been traded for a girl.

Brothers and sisters, newly men and women, had to efface their sexual color and present plain miens. Disturbing hair and eyes, a smile like no other, threatened the ideal of five generations living under one roof. To focus blurs, people shouted face to face and yelled from room to room. The immigrants I know have loud voices, unmodulated to American tones even after years away from the village where they called their friendships out across the fields. I have not been able to stop my mother's screams in public libraries or over telephones. Walking erect (knees straight, toes pointed forward, not pigeon-toed, which is Chinese-feminine) and speaking in an inaudible voice, I have tried to turn myself American-feminine. Chinese communication was loud, public. Only sick people had to whisper. But at the dinner table, where the family members came nearest one another, no one could talk, not the outcasts nor any eaters. Every word that falls from the mouth is a coin lost. Silently they gave and accepted food with both hands. A preoccupied child who took his bowl with one hand got a sideways glare. A complete moment of total attention is due everyone alike. Children and lovers have no singularity here, but my aunt used a secret voice, a separate attentiveness.

She kept the man's name to herself throughout her labor and dying; she did not accuse him that he be punished with her. To save her inseminator's name she gave silent birth.

He may have been somebody in her own household, but intercourse with a man outside the family would have been no less abhorrent. All the village were kinsmen, and the titles shouted in loud country voices never let kinship be forgotten. Any man within visiting distance would have been neutralized as a lover—"brother," "younger brother," "older brother"—one hundred and fifteen relationship titles. Parents researched birth charts probably not so much to assure good fortune as to circumvent incest in a population that has but one hundred surnames. Everybody has eight million relatives. How useless then sexual mannerisms, how dangerous.

As if it came from an atavism deeper than fear, I used to add "brother" silently to boys' names. It hexed the boys, who would or would not ask me to dance, and made them less scary and as familiar and deserving of benevolence as girls.

But, of course, I hexed myself also—no dates. I should have stood up, both arms waving, and shouted out across libraries, "Hey, you! Love me back." I had no idea, though, how to make attraction selective, how to control its direction and magnitude. If I made myself American-pretty so that the five or six Chinese boys in the class fell in love with me, everyone else—the Caucasian, Negro, and Japanese boys—would too. Sisterliness, dignified and honorable, made much more sense.

Attraction eludes control so stubbornly that whole societies designed to organize relationships among people cannot keep order, not even when they bind people to one another from childhood and raise them together.

Among the very poor and the wealthy, brothers married their adopted sisters, like doves. Our family allowed some romance, paying adult brides' prices and providing dowries so that their sons and daughters could marry strangers. Marriage promises to turn strangers into friendly relatives—a nation of siblings.

In the village structure, spirits shimmered among the live creatures, balanced and held in equilibrium by time and land. But one human being flaring up into violence could open up a black hole, a maelstrom that pulled in the sky. The frightened villagers, who depended on one another to maintain the real, went to my aunt to show her a personal, physical representation of the break she had made in the "roundness." Misallying couples snapped off the future, which was to be embodied in true offspring. The villagers punished her for acting as if she could have a private life, secret and apart from them.

If my aunt had betrayed the family at a time of large grain yields and peace, when many boys were born, and wings were being built on many houses, perhaps she might have escaped such severe punishment. But the men—hungry, greedy, tired of planting in dry soil—had been forced to leave the village in order to send food-money home. There were ghost plagues, bandit plagues, wars with the Japanese, floods. My Chinese brother and sister had died of an unknown sickness. Adultery, perhaps only a mistake during good times, became a crime when the village needed food.

The round moon cakes and round doorways, the round tables of graduated sizes that fit one roundness inside another, round windows and rice bowls—these talismans had lost their power to warn this family of the law: a family must be whole, faithfully keeping the descent line by having sons to feed the old and the dead, who in turn look after the family. The villagers came to show my aunt and her lover-in-hiding a broken house. The villagers were speeding up the circling of events because she was too shortsighted to see that her infidelity had already harmed the village, that waves of consequences would return unpredictably, sometimes in disguise, as now, to hurt her. This roundness had to be made coin-sized so that she would see its circumference: punish her at the birth of her baby. Awaken her to the inexorable. People who refused fatalism because they could invent small resources insisted on culpability. Deny accidents and wrest fault from the stars.

After the villagers left, their lanterns now scattering in various directions toward home, the family broke their silence and cursed her. "Aiaa, we're going to die. Death is coming. Death is coming. Look what you've done. You've killed us. Ghost! Dead ghost! Ghost! You've never been born." She ran out into the fields, far enough from the house so that she could no longer hear their voices, and pressed herself against the earth, her own land no more. When she felt the birth coming, she thought that she had been hurt. Her body seized together. "They've hurt me too much," she thought. "This is gall, and it will kill me." With forehead and knees against the earth, her body convulsed and then relaxed. She turned on her back, lay on the ground. The black well of sky and stars went out and out and out forever; her body and her complexity seemed to disappear. She was one of the stars, a bright dot in blackness, without home, without a companion, in eternal cold and silence. An agoraphobia rose in her, speeding higher and higher, bigger and bigger; she would not be able to contain it; there would no end to fear.

Flayed, unprotected against space, she felt pain return, focusing her body. This pain chilled her—a cold, steady kind of surface pain. Inside, spasmodically, the other pain, the pain of the child, heated her. For hours she lay on the ground, alternately body and space. Sometimes a vision of normal comfort obliterated reality: she saw the family in the evening gambling at the dinner table, the young people massaging their elders' backs. She saw them congratulating one another, high joy on the mornings the rice shoots came up. When these pictures burst, the stars drew yet further apart. Black space opened.

She got to her feet to fight better and remembered that old-fashioned women gave birth in their pigsties to fool the jealous, pain-dealing gods, who do not snatch piglets. Before the next spasms could stop her, she ran to the pigsty, each step a rushing out into emptiness. She climbed over the fence and knelt in the dirt. It was good to have a fence enclosing her, a tribal person alone.

Laboring, this woman who had carried her child as a foreign growth that sickened her every day, expelled it at last. She reached down to touch the hot, wet, moving mass, surely smaller than anything human, and could feel that it was human after all—fingers, toes, nails, nose. She pulled it up on to her belly, and it lay curled there, butt in the air, feet precisely tucked one under the other. She opened her loose shirt and buttoned the child inside. After resting, it squirmed and thrashed and she pushed it up to her breast. It turned its head this way and that until it found her nipple. There, it made little snuffling noises. She clenched her teeth at its preciousness, lovely as a young calf, a piglet, a little dog.

She may have gone to the pigsty as a last act of responsibility: she would protect this child as she had protected its father. It would look after her soul, leaving supplies on her grave. But how would this tiny child without family find her grave when there would be no marker for her anywhere, neither in the earth nor the family hall? No one would give her a family hall name. She had taken the child with her into the wastes. At its birth the two of them had felt the same raw pain of separation, a wound that only the family pressing tight could close. A child with no descent line would not soften her life but only trail after her, ghostlike, begging her to give it purpose. At dawn the villagers on their way to the fields would stand around the fence and look.

Full of milk, the little ghost slept. When it awoke, she hardened her breasts against the milk that crying loosens. Toward morning she picked up the baby and walked to the well.

Carrying the baby to the well shows loving. Otherwise abandon it. Turn its face into the mud. Mothers who love their children take them along. It was probably a girl; there is some hope of forgiveness for boys.

"Don't tell anyone you had an aunt. Your father does not want to hear her name. She has never been born." I have believed that sex was unspeakable and words so strong and fathers so frail that "aunt" would do my father mysterious harm. I have thought that my family, having settled among immigrants who had also been their neighbors in the ancestral land, needed to clean their name, and a wrong word would incite the kinspeople even here. But there is more to this silence: they want me to participate in her punishment. And I have.

In the twenty years since I heard this story I have not asked for details nor said my aunt's name; I do not know it. People who can comfort the dead can also chase after them to hurt them further—a reverse ancestor worship. The real punishment was not the raid swiftly inflicted by the villagers, but the family's deliberately forgetting her. Her betrayal so maddened them, they saw to it that she would suffer forever, even after death. Always hungry, always needing, she would have to beg food from other ghosts, snatch and steal it from those whose living descendants give them gifts. She would have to fight the ghosts massed at crossroads for the buns a few thoughtful citizens leave to decoy her away from village and home so that the ancestral spirits could feast unharassed. At peace, they could act like gods, not ghosts, their descent lines providing them with paper suits and dresses, spirit money, paper houses, paper automobiles, chicken, meat, and rice into eternity—essences delivered up in smoke and flames, steam and incense rising from each rice bowl. In an attempt to make the Chinese care for people outside the family, Chairman Mao encourages us now to give our paper replicas to the spirits of outstanding soldiers and workers, no matter whose ancestors they may be. My aunt remains forever hungry. Goods are not distributed evenly among the dead.

My aunt haunts me—her ghost drawn to me because now, after fifty years of neglect, I alone devote pages of paper to her, though not origamied into houses and clothes. I do not think she always means me well. I am telling on her, and she was a spite suicide, drowning herself in the drinking water. The Chinese are always very frightened of the drowned one, whose weeping ghost, wet hair hanging and skin bloated, waits silently by the water to pull down a substitute.

from *Hunger of Memory*
Richard Rodriguez   (1944–   )

Having completed all the requirements for a doctorate at Berkeley except for his dissertation on Renaissance literature, Richard Rodriguez, a Mexican American, was besieged with job offers from Ivy League and other universities. He rejected them all and spent most of the next five years writing an autobiographical account that, as "the history of my schooling," is, at least in part, an explanation of that decision. "Many days I feared I had stopped living by committing myself to remember the past," he says about the loneliness he felt during those years of composition. "I feared that my absorption with events in my past amounted to an immature refusal to live in the present. I would tell myself otherwise. I would tell myself that the act of remembering is an act of the present."

As a political statement, *Hunger of Memory* has angered a number of minority activists, for it attacks affirmative action programs as well as demands for bilingual education. As a personal statement, it is a persuasive and moving document, one that shows the undeniable losses as well as the gains for a Mexican American who has chosen to find his public identification within the white English-speaking culture. Its argument is simple enough, relying largely on issues of language and conceptions of the self as "private" or "public." In his prologue, Rodriguez says, "Once upon a time, I was a 'socially disadvantaged' child. An enchantedly happy child. Mine was a childhood of intense family closeness. And extreme public alienation." His parents were supportive, always encouraging Rodriguez and his siblings to develop their abilities, to gain the education that would give them success in the outer world. Still, the solidarity felt by the Spanish-speaking family members within their own house is connected to their sense of separation from the world. Catholicism—and the Catholic schools at which the children were educated in the use of English—served both as a bridge connecting the private to the public and as a means of entrance into the dominant culture. (While Catholicism—particularly its rituals—has altered since his childhood, it remains a significant influence upon him; his long chapter on Catholicism is remarkably poignant.) For Rodriguez, an emphasis on ethnicity and bilingual education chiefly serves to intensify a separation from the English-speaking culture, hindering a member of a "disadvantaged" group from any assumption of equality in American citizenship and from taking advantage of the privileges—and the self-confidence—that such an assumption can bring.

In encouraging their children's education as they did, Rodriguez' parents inevitably brought about cultural differences between themselves and their children. Rodriguez is painfully aware of the losses that have come to him as a consequence both of his convictions and of his very achievements in the public or non-Hispanic world; his acknowledgment of them gives stature to his essential argument, which, after all, is made in the pursuit of an ideal of equality and justice. His convictions—and perhaps his pride—prevented his acceptance of an academic position offered him in consequence of affirmative action programs. By attempting to remedy the inequalities imposed by skin color rather than those imposed by social class, such programs contradict the leftist principles of those who most actively support them, he notes; the irony reminds me of George Orwell, a writer he admires. Too, the rewards bestowed by universities in the name of affirmative action are most likely to come to those who, like Rodriguez himself, don't really need them.

"Memory teaches me what I know of these matters; the boy reminds the adult," he says early in his first chapter, in reference to his indictment of bilingual education. The cohesion of American society has become more problematic than it was in Rodriguez' childhood—and the tendency toward fragmentation has intensified in the years since the publication of his book. *Hunger of Memory* strengthens my own sense that English should be the primary language of public education in America, so long as we continue to believe in the possibility of a cohesive social fabric, one strong enough to tolerate and respect differences.

I

I remember to start with that day in Sacramento—a California now nearly thirty years past—when I first entered a classroom, able to understand some fifty stray English words.

The third of four children, I had been preceded to a neighborhood Roman Catholic school by an older brother and sister. But neither of them had revealed very much about their classroom experiences. Each afternoon they returned, as they left in the morning, always together, speaking in Spanish as they climbed the five steps of the porch. And their mysterious books, wrapped in shopping-bag paper, remained on the table next to the door, closed firmly behind them.

An accident of geography sent me to a school where all my classmates were white, many the children of doctors and lawyers and business executives. All my classmates certainly must have been uneasy on that first day of school—as most children are uneasy—to find themselves apart from their families in the first institution of their lives. But I was astonished.

The nun said, in a friendly but oddly impersonal voice, "Boys and girls, this is Richard Rodriguez." (I heard her sound out: *Rich-heard Road-ree-guess.*) It was the first time I had heard anyone name me in English. "Richard," the nun repeated more slowly, writing my name down in her black leather book. Quickly I turned to see my mother's face dissolve in a watery blur behind the pebbled glass door.

Many years later there is something called bilingual education—a scheme proposed in the late 1960s by Hispanic-American social activists, later endorsed by a congressional vote. It is a program that seeks to permit non-

English-speaking children, many from lower-class homes, to use their family language as the language of school. (Such is the goal its supporters announce.) I hear them and am forced to say no: It is not possible for a child—any child—ever to use his family's language in school. Not to understand this is to misunderstand the public uses of schooling and to trivialize the nature of intimate life—a family's "language."

Memory teaches me what I know of these matters; the boy reminds the adult. I was a bilingual child, a certain kind—socially disadvantaged—the son of working-class parents, both Mexican immigrants.

In the early years of my boyhood, my parents coped very well in America. My father had steady work. My mother managed at home. They were nobody's victims. Optimism and ambition led them to a house (our home) many blocks from the Mexican south side of town. We lived among *gringos* and only a block from the biggest, whitest houses. It never occurred to my parents that they couldn't live wherever they chose. Nor was the Sacramento of the fifties bent on teaching them a contrary lesson. My mother and father were more annoyed than intimidated by those two or three neighbors who tried initially to make us unwelcome. ("Keep your brats away from my sidewalk!") But despite all they achieved, perhaps because they had so much to achieve, any deep feeling of ease, the confidence of "belonging" in public was withheld from them both. They regarded the people at work, the faces in crowds, as very distant from us. They were the others, *los gringos*. That term was interchangeable in their speech with another, even more telling, *los americanos*.

I grew up in a house where the only regular guests were my relations. For one day, enormous families of relatives would visit and there would be so many people that the noise and the bodies would spill out to the backyard and front porch. Then, for weeks, no one came by. (It was usually a salesman who rang the doorbell.) Our house stood apart. A gaudy yellow in a row of white bungalows. We were the people with the noisy dog. The people who raised pigeons and chickens. We were the foreigners on the block. A few neighbors smiled and waved. We waved back. But no one in the family knew the names of the old couple who lived next door; until I was seven years old, I did not know the names of the kids who lived across the street.

In public, my father and mother spoke a hesitant, accented, not always grammatical English. And they would have to strain—their bodies tense—to catch the sense of what was rapidly said by *los gringos*. At home they spoke Spanish. The language of their Mexican past sounded in counterpoint to the English of public society. The words would come quickly, with ease. Conveyed through those sounds was the pleasing, soothing, consoling reminder of being at home.

During those years when I was first conscious of hearing, my mother and father addressed me only in Spanish; in Spanish I learned to reply. By contrast, English *(inglés)*, rarely heard in the house, was the language I came to associate with *gringos*. I learned my first words of English overhearing my parents speak to strangers. At five years of age, I knew just enough English for my mother to trust me on errands to stores one block away. No more.

I was a listening child, careful to hear the very different sounds of Spanish and English. Wide-eyed with hearing, I'd listen to sounds more than words. First, there were English *(gringo)* sounds. So many words were still unknown that when the butcher or the lady at the drugstore said something to me, exotic polysyllabic sounds would bloom in the midst of their sentences. Often, the speech of people in public seemed to me very loud, booming with confidence. The man behind the counter would literally ask, "What can I do for you?" But by being so firm and so clear, the sound of his voice said that he was a *gringo*; he belonged in public society.

I would also hear then the high nasal notes of middle-class American speech. The air stirred with sound. Sometimes, even now, when I have been traveling abroad for several weeks, I will hear what I heard as a boy. In hotel lobbies or airports, in Turkey or Brazil, some Americans will pass, and suddenly I will hear it again—the high sound of American voices. For a few seconds I will hear it with pleasure, for it is now the sound of *my* society—a reminder of home. But inevitably—already on the flight headed for home—the sound fades with repetition. I will be unable to hear it anymore.

When I was a boy, things were different. The accent of *los gringos* was never pleasing nor was it hard to hear. Crowds at Safeway or at bus stops would be noisy with sound. And I would be forced to edge away from the chirping chatter above me.

I was unable to hear my own sounds, but I knew very well that I spoke English poorly. My words could not stretch far enough to form complete thoughts. And the words I did speak I didn't know well enough to make into distinct sounds. (Listeners would usually lower their heads, better to hear what I was trying to say.) But it was one thing for *me* to speak English with difficulty. It was more troubling for me to hear my parents speak in public: their high-whining vowels and guttural consonants; their sentences that got stuck with "eh" and "ah" sounds; the confused syntax; the hesitant rhythm of sounds so different from the way *gringos* spoke. I'd notice, moreover, that my parents' voices were softer than those of *gringos* we'd meet.

I am tempted now to say that none of this mattered. In adulthood I am embarrassed by childhood fears. And, in a way, it didn't matter very much that my parents could not speak English with ease. Their linguistic difficulties had no serious consequences. My mother and father made themselves understood at the county hospital clinic and at government offices. And yet, in another way, it mattered very much—it was unsettling to hear my parents struggle with English. Hearing them, I'd grow nervous, my clutching trust in their protection and power weakened.

There were many times like the night at a brightly lit gasoline station (a blaring white memory) when I stood uneasily, hearing my father. He was talking to a teenaged attendant. I do not recall what they were saying, but I cannot forget the sounds my father made as he spoke. At one point his words slid together to form one word—sounds as confused as the threads of blue and green oil in the puddle next to my shoes. His voice rushed through what he had left to say. And, toward the end, reached falsetto notes, appealing to his listener's understanding. I looked away to the lights of passing automobiles. I tried not to hear anymore. But I heard only too well the calm, easy tones in the attendant's reply. Shortly afterward, walking toward home with my father, I shivered when he put his hand on my shoulder. The very first chance that I got, I evaded his grasp and ran on ahead into the dark, skipping with feigned boyish exuberance.

But then there was Spanish. *Español*: my family's language. *Español*: the language that seemed to me a private language. I'd hear strangers on the radio and in the Mexican Catholic church across town speaking in Spanish, but I couldn't really believe that Spanish was a public language, like English. Spanish speakers, rather, seemed related to me, for I sensed that we shared—through our language—the experience of feeling apart from *los gringos*. It was thus a ghetto Spanish that I heard and I spoke. Like those whose lives are bound by a barrio, I was reminded by Spanish of my separateness from *los otros, los gringos* in power. But more intensely than for most barrio children—because I did not live in a barrio—Spanish seemed to me the language of home. (Most days it was only at home that I'd hear it.) It became the language of joyful return.

A family member would say something to me and I would feel myself specially recognized. My parents would say something to me and I would feel embraced by the sounds of their words. Those sounds said: *I am speaking with ease in Spanish. I am addressing you in words I never use with* los gringos. *I recognize you as someone special, close, like no one outside. You belong with us. In the family.*

(Ricardo.)

At the age of five, six, well past the time when most other children no longer easily notice the difference between sounds uttered at home and words spoken in public, I had a different experience. I lived in a world magically compounded of sounds. I remained a child longer than most; I lingered too long, poised at the edge of language—often frightened by the sounds of *los gringos,* delighted by the sounds of Spanish at home. I shared with my family a language that was startlingly different from that used in the great city around us. For me there were none of the gradations between public and private society so normal to a maturing child. Outside the house was public society; inside the house was private. Just opening or closing the screen door behind me was an important experience. I'd rarely leave home all alone or without reluctance. Walking down the sidewalk, under the canopy of tall trees, I'd warily notice the—suddenly—silent neighborhood kids who stood warily watching me. Nervously, I'd arrive at the grocery store to hear there the sounds of the *gringo*—foreign to me—reminding me that in this world so big, I was a foreigner. But then I'd return. Walking back toward our house, climbing the steps from the sidewalk, when the front door was open in summer, I'd hear voices beyond the screen door talking in Spanish. For a second or two, I'd stay, linger there, listening. Smiling, I'd hear my mother call out, saying in Spanish (words): "Is that you, Richard?" All the while her sounds would assure me: *You are home now; come closer; inside. With us.*

"Sí," I'd reply.

Once more inside the house I would resume (assume) my place in the family. The sounds would dim, grow harder to hear. Once more at home, I would grow less aware of that fact. It required, however, no more than the blurt of the doorbell to alert me to listen to sounds all over again. The house would turn instantly still while my mother went to the door. I'd hear her hard English sounds. I'd wait to hear her voice return to soft-sounding Spanish, which assured me, as surely as did the clicking tongue of the lock on the door, that the stranger was gone.

Plainly, it is not healthy to hear such sounds so often. It is not healthy to distinguish public words from private sounds so easily. I remained cloistered by sounds, timid and shy in public, too dependent on voices at home. And yet it needs to be emphasized: I was an extremely happy child at home. I remember many nights when my father would come back from work, and I'd hear him call out to my mother in Spanish, sounding relieved. In Spanish, he'd sound light and free notes he never could manage in English. Some nights I'd jump up just at hearing his voice. With *mis hermanos* I would come running into the room where he was with my mother. Our laughing (so deep was the pleasure!) became screaming. Like others who know the pain of public alienation, we transformed the knowledge of our public separateness and made it consoling—the reminder of intimacy. Excited, we joined our voices in a celebration of sounds. *We are speaking now the way we never speak out in public. We are alone—together,* voices sounded, surrounded to tell me. Some nights, no one seemed willing to loosen the hold sounds had on us. At dinner, we invented new words.

(Ours sounded Spanish, but made sense only to us.) We pieced together new words by taking, say, an English verb and giving it Spanish endings. My mother's instructions at bedtime would be lacquered with mock-urgent tones. Or a word like *sí* would become, in several notes, able to convey added measures of feeling. Tongues explored the edges of words, especially the fat vowels. And we happily sounded that military drum roll, the twirling roar of the Spanish *r*. Family language: my family's sounds. The voices of my parents and sisters and brother. Their voices insisting: *You belong here. We are family members. Related. Special to one another. Listen!* Voices singing and sighing, rising, straining, then surging, teeming with pleasure that burst syllables into fragments of laughter. At times it seemed there was steady quiet only when, from another room, the rustling whispers of my parents faded and I moved closer to sleep.

2

Supporters of bilingual education today imply that students like me miss a great deal by not being taught in their family's language. What they seem not to recognize is that, as a socially disadvantaged child, I considered Spanish to be a private language. What I needed to learn in school was that I had the right—and the obligation—to speak the public language of *los gringos*. The odd truth is that my first-grade classmates could have become bilingual, in the conventional sense of that word, more easily than I. Had they been taught (as upper-middle-class children are often taught early) a second language like Spanish or French, they could have regarded it simply as that: another public language. In my case such bilingualism could not have been so quickly achieved. What I did not believe was that I could speak a single public language.

Without question, it would have pleased me to hear my teachers address me in Spanish when I entered the classroom. I would have felt much less afraid. I would have trusted them and responded with ease. But I would have delayed—for how long postponed?—having to learn the language of public society. I would have evaded—and for how long could I have afforded to delay?—learning the great lesson of school, that I had a public identity.

Fortunately, my teachers were unsentimental about their responsibility. What they understood was that I needed to speak a public language. So their voices would search me out, asking me questions. Each time I'd hear them, I'd look up in surprise to see a nun's face frowning at me. I'd mumble, not really meaning to answer. The nun would persist, "Richard, stand up. Don't look at the floor. Speak up. Speak to the entire class, not just to me!" But I couldn't believe that the English language was mine to use. (In part, I did not want to believe it.) I continued to mumble. I resisted the teacher's demands. (Did I somehow suspect that once I learned public language my pleasing family life would be changed?) Silent, waiting for the bell to sound, I remained dazed, diffident, afraid.

Because I wrongly imagined that English was intrinsically a public language and Spanish an intrinsically private one, I easily noted the difference between classroom language and the language of home. At school, words were directed to a general audience of listeners. ("Boys and girls.") Words were meaningfully ordered. And the point was not self-expression alone but to make oneself understood by many others. The teacher quizzed: "Boys and girls, why do we use that word in this sentence? Could we think of a better word to use there? Would the sentence change its meaning if the words were differently arranged? And wasn't there a better way of saying much the same thing?" (I couldn't say. I wouldn't try to say.)

Three months. Five. Half a year passed. Unsmiling, ever watchful, my teachers noted my silence. They began to connect my behavior with the difficult progress my older sister and brother were making. Until one Saturday morning three nuns arrived at the house to talk to our parents. Stiffly, they sat on the blue living room sofa. From the doorway of another room, spying the visitors, I noted the incongruity—the clash of two worlds, the faces and voices of school intruding upon the familiar setting of home. I overheard one voice gently wondering, "Do your children speak only Spanish at home, Mrs. Rodriguez?" While another voice added, "That Richard especially seems so timid and shy."

That Rich-heard!

With great tact the visitors continued, "Is it possible for you and your husband to encourage your children to practice their English when they are home?" Of course, my parents complied. What would they not do for their children's well-being? And how could they have questioned the Church's authority which those women represented? In an instant, they agreed to give up the language (the sounds) that had revealed and accentuated our family's closeness. The moment after the visitors left, the change was observed. *"Ahora,* speak to us *en inglés,"* my father and mother united to tell us.

At first, it seemed a kind of game. After dinner each night, the family gathered to practice "our English." (It was still then *inglés,* a language foreign to us, so we felt drawn as strangers to it.) Laughing, we would try to define words we could not pronounce. We played with strange English sounds, often over-anglicizing our pronunciations. And we filled the smiling gaps of our sentences with familiar Spanish sounds. But that was cheating, somebody shouted. Everyone laughed. In school, meanwhile, like my brother and sister, I was required to attend a daily tutoring session. I needed a full year of special attention. I also needed my teachers to keep my attention from straying in class by calling out, *Rich-heard*—their English voices slowly prying loose my ties to my other name, its three notes, *Ri-car-do.* Most of all I needed to hear my mother and father speak to me in a moment of seriousness in broken—suddenly heartbreaking—English. The scene was inevitable: One Saturday morning I entered the kitchen where my parents were talking in Spanish. I did not realize that they were talking in Spanish however until, at the moment they saw me, I heard their voices change to speak English. Those *gringo* sounds they uttered startled me. Pushed me away. In that moment of trivial misunderstanding and profound insight, I felt my throat twisted by unsounded grief. I turned quickly and left the room. But I had no place to escape to with Spanish. (The spell was broken.) My brother and sisters were speaking English in another part of the house.

Again and again in the days following, increasingly angry, I was obliged to hear my mother and father: "Speak to us *en inglés.*" *(Speak.)* Only then did I determine to learn classroom English. Weeks after, it happened: One day in school I raised my hand to volunteer an answer. I spoke out in a loud voice. And I did not think it remarkable when the entire class understood. That day, I moved very far from the disadvantaged child I had been only days earlier. The belief, the calming assurance that I belonged in public, had at last taken hold.

Shortly after, I stopped hearing the high and loud sounds of *los gringos.* A more and more confident speaker of English, I didn't trouble to listen to *how* strangers sounded, speaking to me. And there simply were too many English-speaking people in my day for me to hear American accents anymore. Conversations quickened. Listening to persons who sounded eccentrically pitched voices, I usually noted their sounds for an initial few seconds before I concentrated on *what* they were saying. Conversations became content-full. Transparent. Hearing someone's *tone* of voice—angry or questioning or sarcastic or happy or sad—I didn't distinguish it from the words it expressed. Sound and word were thus tightly wedded. At the end of a day, I was often bemused, always relieved, to realize how "silent," though crowded with words, my day in public had been. (This public silence measured and quickened the change in my life.)

At last, seven years old, I came to believe what had been technically true since my birth: I was an American citizen.

But the special feeling of closeness at home was diminished by then. Gone was the desperate, urgent, intense feeling of being at home; rare was the experience of feeling myself individualized by family intimates. We remained a loving family, but one greatly changed. No longer so close; no longer bound tight by the pleasing and troubling knowledge of our public separateness. Neither my older brother nor sister rushed home after school anymore. Nor did I. When I arrived home there would often be neighborhood kids in the house. Or the house would be empty of sounds.

Following the dramatic Americanization of their children, even my parents grew more publicly confident. Especially my mother. She learned the names of all the people on our block. And she decided we needed to have a telephone installed in the house. My father continued to use the word *gringo*. But it was no longer charged with the old bitterness or distrust. (Stripped of any emotional content, the word simply became a name for those Americans not of Hispanic descent.) Hearing him, sometimes, I wasn't sure if he was pronouncing the Spanish word *gringo* or saying gringo in English.

Matching the silence I started hearing in public was a new quiet at home. The family's quiet was partly due to the fact that, as we children learned more and more English, we shared fewer and fewer words with our parents. Sentences needed to be spoken slowly when a child addressed his mother or father. (Often the parent wouldn't understand.) The child would need to repeat himself. (Still the parent misunderstood.) The young voice, frustrated, would end up saying, "Never mind"—the subject was closed. Dinners would be noisy with the clinking of knives and forks against dishes. My mother would smile softly between her remarks; my father at the other end of the table would chew and chew at his food, while he stared over the heads of his children.

My *mother!* My *father!* After English became my primary language, I no longer knew what words to use in addressing my parents. The old Spanish words (those tender accents of sound) I had used earlier—*mamá* and *papá*—I couldn't use anymore. They would have been too painful reminders of how much had changed in my life. On the other hand, the words I heard neighborhood kids call *their* parents seemed equally unsatisfactory. *Mother* and *Father; Ma, Papa, Pa, Dad, Pop* (how I hated the all-American sound of that last word especially)—all these terms I felt were unsuitable, not really terms of address for *my* parents. As a result, I never used them at home. Whenever I'd speak to my parents, I would try to get their attention with eye contact alone. In public conversations, I'd refer to "my parents" or "my mother and father."

My mother and father, for their part, responded differently, as their children spoke to them less. She grew restless, seemed troubled and anxious at the scarcity of words exchanged in the house. It was she who would question me about my day when I came home from school. She smiled at small talk. She pried at the edges of my sentences to get me to say something more. (What?) She'd join conversations she overheard, but her intrusions often stopped her children's talking. By contrast, my father seemed reconciled to the new quiet. Though his English improved some-what, he retired into silence. At dinner he spoke very little. One night his children and even his wife helplessly giggled at his garbled English pronunciation of the Catholic Grace before Meals. Thereafter he made his wife recite the prayer at the start of each meal, even on formal occasions, when there were guests in the house. Hers became the public voice of the family. On official business, it was she, not my father, one would usually hear on the phone or in stores, talking to strangers. His children grew so accustomed to his silence that, years later, they would speak routinely of his shyness. (My mother would often try to explain: Both his parents died when he was eight. He was raised by an uncle who treated him like little more than a menial servant. He was never encouraged to speak. He grew up alone. A man of few words.) But my father was not shy, I realized, when I'd watch him speaking Spanish with relatives. Using Spanish, he was quickly effusive. Especially when talking with other men, his voice would spark, flicker, flare alive with sounds. In Spanish, he expressed ideas and feelings he rarely revealed in English. With firm Spanish sounds, he conveyed confidence and authority English would never allow him.

The silence at home, however, was finally more than a literal silence. Fewer words passed between parent and child, but more profound was the silence that resulted from my inattention to sounds. At about the time I no longer bothered to listen with care to the sounds of English in public, I grew careless about listening to the sounds family members made when they spoke. Most of the time I heard someone speaking at home and didn't distinguish his sounds from the words people uttered in public. I didn't even pay much attention to my parents' accented and ungrammatical speech. At least not at home. Only when I was with them in public would I grow alert to their accents. Though, even then, their sounds caused me less and less concern. For I was increasingly confident of my own public identity.

I would have been happier about my public success had I not sometimes recalled what it had been like earlier, when my family had conveyed its intimacy through a set of conveniently private sounds. Sometimes in public, hearing a stranger, I'd hark back to my past. A Mexican farmworker approached me downtown to ask directions to somewhere. "*¿Hijito . . .?*" he said. And his voice summoned deep longing. Another time, standing beside my mother in the visiting room of a Carmelite convent, before the dense screen which rendered the nuns shadowy figures, I heard several Spanish-speaking nuns—their busy, singsong overlapping voices—assure us that yes, yes, we were remembered, all our family was remembered in their prayers. (Their voices echoed faraway family sounds.) Another day, a dark-faced old woman—her hand light on my shoulder—steadied herself against me as she boarded a bus. She murmured something I couldn't quite comprehend. Her Spanish voice came near, like the face of a never-before-seen relative in the instant before I was kissed. Her voice, like so many of the Spanish voices I'd hear in public, recalled the golden age of my youth. Hearing Spanish then, I continued to be a careful, if sad, listener to sounds. Hearing a Spanish-speaking family walking behind me, I turned to look. I smiled for an instant, before my glance found the Hispanic-looking faces of strangers in the crowd going by.

Today I hear bilingual educators say that children lose a degree of "individuality" by becoming assimilated into public society. (Bilingual schooling was popularized in the seventies, that decade when middle-class ethnics began to resist the process of assimilation—the American melting pot.) But the bilingualists simplistically scorn the value and necessity of assimilation. They do not seem to realize that there are *two* ways a person is individualized. So they do not realize that while one suffers a diminished sense of *private* individuality by becoming assimilated into public society, such assimilation makes possible the achievement of *public* individuality.

The bilingualists insist that a student should be reminded of his difference from others in mass society, his heritage. But they equate mere separateness with individuality. The fact is that only in private—with intimates—is separateness from the crowd a prerequisite for individuality. (An intimate draws me apart, tells me that I am unique, unlike all others.) In public, by contrast, full individuality is achieved, paradoxically, by those who are able to consider themselves members of the crowd. Thus it happened for me: Only when I was able to think of myself as an American, no longer an alien in *gringo* society, could I seek the rights and opportunities necessary for full public individuality. The social and political advantages I enjoy as a man result from the day that I came to believe that my name, indeed, is *Rich-heard Road-ree-guess*. It is true that my public society today is often impersonal. (My public society is usually mass society.) Yet despite the anonymity of the crowd and despite the fact that the individuality I achieve in public is often tenuous—because it depends on my being one in a crowd—I celebrate the day I acquired my new name. Those middle-class ethnics who scorn assimilation seem to me filled with decadent self-pity, obsessed by the burden of public life. Dangerously, they romanticize public separateness and they trivialize the dilemma of the socially disadvantaged.

My awkward childhood does not prove the necessity of bilingual education. My story discloses instead an essential myth of childhood—inevitable pain. If I rehearse here the changes in my private life after my Americanization, it is finally to emphasize the public gain. The loss implies the gain: The house I returned to each afternoon was quiet. Intimate sounds no longer rushed to the door to greet me. There were other noises inside. The telephone rang. Neighborhood kids ran past the door of the bedroom where I was reading my schoolbooks—covered with shopping-bag paper. Once I learned public language, it would never again be easy for me to hear intimate family voices. More and more of my day was spent hearing words. But that may only be a way of saying that the day I raised my hand in class and spoke loudly to an entire roomful of faces, my childhood started to end.

"Kubota"

Garrett Hongo (1951–)

Garrett Hongo's *Volcano* is an autobiographical work about the search for belonging on the part of a fourth-generation Japanese American. Unlike most accounts of such a quest, his gives at least as much emphasis to natural origins as it does to cultural antecedents. Near the conclusion of the book, he remarks that his search has been for "[a] way to belong that, at once, ties me to human culture and to a living earth that is itself without culture or care for human life." Hongo's descriptions of volcanic eruptions, as well as of the seemingly fragile and yet stubbornly enduring flora of his native Hawaii, constitute such a remarkable evocation of natural forces that the reader quickly understands them as the foundation underlying any definition we may obtain as members of any given culture.

"Kubota" is a self-standing chapter, one that emphasizes the effects of cultural bias on a member of a minority group. The chapter is named for Hongo's maternal grandfather; it is a sensitive tribute by a grandson who feels the obligation to be a witness for an older relative whose use of English is far less assured than his own. As opposed to the four years of camp detainment—accompanied, as we now know, by the loss of property as well as of jobs—that the war with Japan brought to mainland Americans of Japanese descent following the attack on Pearl Harbor, Hongo's grandfather on Oahu underwent only several days of confinement by federal agents, during which he was subjected to intense questioning. Though he was a widely respected store manager for a company in the sugar cane business, Kubota was suspected of espionage; "fishing was his obsession and passion," and the traditional torches he lit for nighttime fishing were thought to have been placed in the shallow waters to guide Japanese pilots on their strafing passes over a nearby airfield. Such a blow to Kubota's honor was one he was destined to forget only after Alzheimer's disease in his final years took away his memory completely. A mainly silent man, he was in his mid-sixties and living with Hongo's parents in Los Angeles before he chose Hongo, then just entering his teens, to hear his story over and over again, to bear witness for him. Writers—particularly those with the capacity for empathy that Hongo possesses—have a couple of advantages over psychiatrists as patient auditors of another's almost unbearable shame. The first is their lack of a professional predisposition to interpret what they hear into something other than the simple words, and the second is the fact that they are under no ethical compulsion to maintain secrecy about a personal account that requires (for the amelioration of private suffering) the hope of ultimate public exposure.

Hongo, known chiefly for his poetry before the publication of *Volcano*, is as fine a writer-witness as any relative could wish for; he transfers his grandfather's memories of degradation into his own life and memory, and in the lovely dream that concludes his memoir transforms those cruel memories into a blessing.

The Anatomy of Memory

For all that I had *not* been told about my family, there was yet one story that seemed to me always to have been told—a part of my upbringing, a telling that made it clear that I did come from some sort of emotional lineage, at least on my mother's side of things.

On December 8, 1941, the day after the Japanese attack on Pearl Harbor in Hawai'i, my maternal grandfather had barricaded himself with his family—my grandmother, my teenage mother, her two sisters and two brothers—inside of his home in Lā'ie, a sugar plantation village on O'ahu's North Shore. This was my mother's father, a man most villagers called by his last name—Kubota. It could mean either "Wayside Field" or else "Broken Dreams" depending on which ideograms he used. Kubota ran Lā'ie's general store, and the previous night, after a long day of bad news on the radio, some locals had come by, pounded on the front door, and made threats. One was said to have brandished a machete. They were angry and shocked, as was the whole nation, in the aftermath of the surprise attack. Kubota was one of the few Japanese Americans in the village and president of the local Japanese language school. He had become a target for their rage and suspicion. A wise man, he locked all his doors and windows and did not open his store the next day, but stayed closed and waited for news from some official.

He was a Kibei, a Japanese American born in Hawai'i (a U. S. territory then, so he was thus a citizen) but who was subsequently sent back by his father for formal education in Hiroshima, Japan—their home province. *Kibei* is written with two ideograms in Japanese—one is the word for "return" and the other is the word for "rice." Poetically, it means one who returns from America, known as "the Land of Rice" in Japanese (by contrast, Chinese immigrants called their new home "Mountain of Gold").

Kubota was graduated from a Japanese high school and then came back to Hawai'i as a teenager. He spoke English—and a Hawaiian creole version of it at that—with a Japanese accent. But he was well liked and good at numbers, scrupulous and hardworking like so many immigrants and children of immigrants. Castle and Cooke, a grower's company that ran the sugarcane business along the North Shore, first hired him as a stock boy and then appointed him to run one of its company stores. He did well, had the trust of management and labor—not an easy accomplishment in any day—married, had children, and had begun to exert himself in community affairs and excel in his own recreations. He put together a Japanese community organization that backed a Japanese-language school for children and sponsored teachers from Japan. Kubota boarded many of them, in succession, in his own home. This made dinners a silent affair for his talkative, Hawaiian-bred children, as their stern *sensei*, or "teacher," was nearly always at table and their own abilities in the Japanese language were as delinquent as their attendance. While Kubota and the *sensei* rattled on

300

about things Japanese, speaking Japanese, his children hurried through their suppers and tried to run off early to listen to the radio shows.

After dinner, while the *sensei* graded exams seated in a wicker chair in the spare room and his wife and children gathered around the radio in the front parlor, Kubota sat on the screened porch outside, reading the local Japanese newspapers. He finished reading about the same time that he finished the tea he drank for his digestion—a habit he'd acquired in Japan—and then he'd get out his fishing gear and spread it out on the plank floors. The wraps on his rods needed to be redone, the gears in his reels needed oil, and, once through with those tasks, he'd painstakingly wind on hundreds of yards of new line. Fishing was his hobby and his passion. He spent weekends camping along the North Shore beaches with his children, setting up umbrella tents, packing a rice pot and *hibachi* along for meals. And he caught fish. *Ulua* mostly, the huge surf-feeding fish known as the jack crevalle on the Mainland, but he'd go after almost anything in its season. In Kawela, a plantation-owned bay nearby, he fished for mullet with a throw-net, stalking the bottom-hugging, gray-backed schools as they gathered at the stream mouths and in the freshwater springs. In an outrigger out beyond the reef, he'd try for *aku*—the skipjack tuna prized for steaks and, sliced raw and mixed with fresh seaweed and cut onions, for *sashimi* salad. In Kahalu‘u and Ka‘a‘awa and on an offshore rock locals called Goat Island, he loved to go torching, stringing lanterns on bamboo poles stuck in the sand to attract *kūmū,* the red goatfish, as they schooled at night just inside the reef. But in Lā‘ie on Laniloa Point near Kahuku, the northernmost tip of O‘ahu, he cast twelve- and fourteen-foot surf rods for the huge varicolored and fast-swimming *ulua* as they pursued schools of squid and baitfish just beyond the biggest breakers and past the low sand flats wadable from the shore to nearly a half mile out. At sunset, against the western light, he looked as if he were walking on water as he came back, fish and rods slung over his shoulders, stepping along the rock and coral path just inches under the surface of a running tide.

When it was torching season, in December or January, he'd drive out the afternoon before and stay with old friends, the Tanakas or Yoshikawas, shopkeepers like him who ran stores near the fishing grounds. They'd have been preparing for weeks, selecting and cutting their bamboo poles, cleaning the hurricane lanterns, tearing up burlap sacks for the cloths they'd soak with kerosene and tie onto sticks they'd poke into the soft sand of the shallows. Once lit, touched off with a Zippo lighter, these would be the torches they'd use as beacons to attract the schooling fish. In another time, they might have made up a dozen paper lanterns of the kind mostly used for decorating the summer folk dances outdoors on the grounds of the Buddhist church during O-Bon, the Festival for the Dead. But now, wealthy and modern and efficient killers of fish, Tanaka and Kubota used rag torches and Colemans and cast rods with tips made of Tonkin bamboo and butts of American-spun fiberglass. After just one good night, they might bring back a prize bounty of a dozen burlap bags filled with scores of bloody, rigid fish delicious to eat and even better to give away as gifts to friends, family, and special customers.

It was a Monday night, the day after Pearl Harbor, and there was a rattling knock at the front door. Two FBI agents presented themselves, showed identification, and took my grandfather in for questioning in Honolulu. No one knew what had happened or what was wrong. But there was a roundup going on of all those in the Japanese American community suspected of sympathizing with the enemy and worse. My grandfather was suspected of espionage, of communicating with offshore Japanese submarines launched from the attack fleet days before war began. Torpedo planes and escort fighters, decorated with the insignia of the rising sun, had taken an approach route from northwest of O'ahu directly across Kahuku Point and on toward Pearl. They had strafed an auxiliary air station near the fishing grounds my grandfather loved and destroyed a small gun battery there, killing three men. Kubota was known to have sponsored and harbored Japanese nationals in his own home. He had a radio. He had wholesale access to firearms. Circumstances and an undertone of racial resentment had combined with wartime hysteria in the aftermath of the tragic naval battle to cast suspicion on the loyalties of my grandfather and all other Japanese Americans. The FBI reached out and pulled hundreds of them in for questioning in dragnets cast throughout the West Coast and Hawai'i.

My grandfather was lucky, he was let go after only a few days. But others were not as fortunate. Hundreds, from small communities in Washington, California, Oregon, and Hawai'i, were rounded up and, after what appeared to be routine questioning, shipped off under Justice Department orders to holding centers in Leupp on the Navajo Indian Reservation in Arizona, in Fort Missoula in Montana, and on Sand Island in Honolulu Harbor. There were other special camps on Maui in Ha'ikū and on Hawai'i—the Big Island—in my own home village of Volcano.

Many of these men—it was exclusively the Japanese American men suspected of ties to Japan who were initially rounded up—did not see their families again for over four years. Under a suspension of due process that was only after-the-fact ruled as warranted by military necessity, they were, if only temporarily, "disappeared" in Justice Department prison camps scattered in particularly desolate areas of the United States designated as militarily "safe." These were grim forerunners of the assembly centers and concentration camps for the 120,000 Japanese American evacuees that were to come later.

I am Kubota's eldest grandchild, and I remember him as a lonely, habitually silent old man who lived with us in our home near Los Angeles for most of my childhood and adolescence. It was the fifties, and my parents had emigrated from Hawai'i to the Mainland in the hope of a better life away from the old sugar plantation. They had left Volcano after losing the store and property, settling in Kahuku. In a few years, when I was five, my father came to study electronics at a trade school in Los Angeles. After a year of this, he got a regular job and was able to send for us, and we were a family again, living in apartments around midtown. Then, after some success, my parents were able to buy a suburban home and had sent for my maternal grandparents and taken them in too. And it was my grandparents who did the work of the household while my mother and father worked at their salaried city jobs. My grandmother cooked and sewed, washed our clothes, and knitted in the front room under the light of a huge lamp with a bright, three-way bulb. Kubota raised a flower garden, read up on soils and grasses in gardening books, and planted a zoysia lawn in front and a dichondra one in back. He planted a small patch near the rear block wall with green onions, eggplant, white Japanese radishes, and cucumber. While he hoed and spaded the loamless, clayey earth of Los Angeles, he sang particularly plangent songs in Japanese about plum blossoms and bamboo groves.

Sometime in the mid-sixties, after a dinner during which, as always, he had been silent while he worked away at a meal of fish and rice spiced with dabs of Chinese mustard and catsup thinned with soy sauce, Kubota took his own dishes to the kitchen sink and washed them up. He took a clean jelly jar out of the cupboard—the glass was thick and its shape squatty like an old-fashioned. He reached around to the hutch below, where he kept his bourbon. He made himself a drink and retired to the living room, where I was expected to join him for "talk story"—the Hawaiian idiom for chewing the fat.

I was a teenager and, though I was bored listening to stories I'd heard often enough before at holiday dinners, I was dutiful. I took my spot on the couch next to Kubota and heard him out. Usually, he'd tell me about his schooling in Japan, where he learned *jūdō* along with mathematics and literature. He'd learned the *soroban* there—the abacus which was the original pocket calculator of the Far East—and that, along with his strong, *jūdō*-trained back, got him his first job in Hawai'i. This was the moral. "Study *ha-ahd*," he'd say with pidgin emphasis. "Learn read good. Learn speak da kine *good* English." The message is the familiar one taught to any children of immigrants—succeed through education. And imitation.

But this time, Kubota reached down into his past and told me a different story. I was thirteen by then, and I suppose he thought me ready for it.

He told me about Pearl Harbor, how the planes flew in wing after wing of formations over his old house in Lāʻie in Hawaiʻi, and how, the next day, after Roosevelt had made his famous "Day of Infamy" speech about the treachery of the Japanese, the FBI agents had come to his door and taken him in, hauled him off to Honolulu for questioning and held him without charge. I thought he was lying. I thought he was making up a kind of horror story to shock me and give his moral that much more starch. But it was true. I asked around. I brought it up during history class in junior high school and my teacher, a Jew, after silencing me and taking me aside to the back of the room, told me that it was indeed so. I asked my mother and she said it was true. I asked my schoolmates, who laughed and ridiculed me for being so ignorant. We lived in a Japanese American community and the parents of most of my classmates were the Nisei who had been interned as teenagers all through the war. But there was a strange silence around all of this. There was a hush, as if one were invoking the ill powers of the dead. No one cared to speak about the evacuation and relocation for very long. It wasn't in our history books, though we were studying World War II at the time. It wasn't in the family albums of the people I knew and whom I'd visit while spending weekends with friends. And it wasn't anything that the family talked about or allowed me to keep bringing up either. I was given the facts, told sternly and pointedly that "it was war" and that "nothing could be done." *Shikata ga nai* is the phrase in Japanese, a kind of resolute and determinist pronouncement on how to deal with inexplicable tragedy. I was to know it but not to dwell on it. Japanese Americans were busy trying to forget it ever happened and were having a hard enough time building their new lives after "Camp." It was as if we had no history for four years and the relocation was something unspeakable.

But Kubota would not let it go. In session after session, for months it seemed, he pounded away at his story. He wanted to tell me the names of the FBI agents. He went over their questions and his responses again and again. He'd tell me how one would try to act friendly toward him, offering him cigarettes while the other, who hounded him with accusations and threats, left the interrogation room. *Good cop/bad cop,* I thought to myself, already superficially streetwise from having heard the stories black classmates told of the Watts riots and from having watched too many episodes of "Dragnet" and "The Mod Squad." But Kubota was not interested in my experiences. I was not made yet and he was determined that his stories be part of my making. He spoke quietly at first, mildly, but once he was into his narrative and after his drink was down, his voice would rise and quaver with resentment and he'd make his accusations. He gave his testimony to me and I held it at first cautiously in my conscience as if it were an heirloom too delicate to expose to strangers and anyone outside of the world Kubota made with his words. "I give you story now," he once said. "And you learn speak good, eh?" It was my job, as the disciple of his preaching I had then become, Ananda to his Buddha, to reassure him with a promise. "You learn speak good like the Dillingham," he'd say another time, referring to the wealthy scion of the grower family who had once run, unsuccessfully, for one of Hawai'i's first senatorial seats. Or he'd then invoke a magical name, the name of one of his heroes, a man he thought particularly exemplary and righteous. "Learn speak dah good Ing-rish like *Mistah Inouye*," Kubota shouted. "He *lick* dah Dillingham even in debate. I saw on *terre-bision* myself." He was remembering the debates before the first senatorial election just before Hawai'i was admitted to the Union as its fiftieth state. "You *tell* story," Kubota would end. And I had my injunction.

The town we settled in after the move from Hawai'i is called Gardena, the independently incorporated city south of Los Angeles and north of San Pedro Harbor. At its northern limit, it borders on Watts and Compton—black towns. To the southwest are Torrance and Redondo Beach—white towns. To the rest of L. A., Gardena is primarily famous for having legalized five-card-draw poker after the war. On Vermont Boulevard, its eastern border, there is a dingy little Vegas-like strip of card clubs with huge parking lots and flickering neon signs that spell out THE RAINBOW and THE HORSESHOE in timed sequences of varicolored lights. The town is only secondarily famous as the largest community of Japanese Americans in the United States outside of Honolulu, Hawai'i. When I was in high school there, it seemed to me that every Sansei kid I knew wanted to be a doctor, an engineer, or a pharmicist. Our fathers were gardeners or electricians or nurserymen or ran small businesses catering to other Japanese Americans. Our mothers worked in civil service for the city or as cashiers for Thrifty Drug. What the kids wanted was a good job, good pay, a fine home, and no troubles. No one wanted to mess with the law—from either side—and no one wanted to mess with language or art. They all talked about getting into the right clubs so that they could go to the right schools. There was a certain kind of sameness, an intensely enforced system of conformity.

We did well in chemistry and in math, no one who was Japanese but me spoke in English class or in History unless called upon, and no one talked about World War II. The day after Robert Kennedy was assassinated after winning the California Democratic primary, we worked on calculus and elected class coordinators for the prom, featuring the 5th Dimension. We avoided grief. We avoided government. We avoided strong feelings and dangers of any kind. Once punished, we tried to maintain a concerted emotional and social discipline and would not willingly seek to fall out of the narrow margin of protective favor again.

But when I was thirteen, in junior high, I'd not understood why it was so difficult for my classmates, those who were themselves Japanese American, to talk about the relocation. They had cringed too when I tried to bring it up during our discussions of World War II. I was Hawaiian-born. They were Mainland-born. Their parents had been in Camp, had been the ones to suffer the complicated experience of having to distance themselves from their own history and all things Japanese in order to make their way back and into the American social and economic mainstream. It was out of this sense of shame and a fear of stigma I was only beginning to understand that the Nisei had silenced themselves. And for their children, among whom I grew up, they wanted no heritage, no culture, no contact with a defiled history. I recall the silence very well. The Japanese American children around me were burdened in a way I was not. Their injunction was silence. Mine was to speak.

Away at college, in another protected world and in its own way as magical to me as the Hawai'i of my childhood, I dreamed about my grandfather. I would be tired from studying languages, practicing German conjugations or scripting an army's worth of Chinese ideograms on a single sheet of paper, and Kubota would come to me as I drifted off into sleep. Or, I would be walking across the newly mown ball field in back of my dormitory, cutting through a streetside phalanx of ancient eucalyptus trees on my way to visit friends off-campus, and I would think of him, his anger, and his sadness.

I don't know myself what makes someone feel that kind of need to have a story they've lived through be deposited somewhere, but I can guess. I think about *The Iliad, The Odyssey*, the *History of the Peloponnesian War* of Thucydides, and a myriad of other books I've studied. A character, almost a *topos* he occurs so often, is frequently the witness who gives personal testimony about an event the rest of his community cannot even imagine. The Sibyl is such a character. And Philomela, the maid whose tongue is cut out so that she will not tell that she has been raped by her own brother-in-law, the king of Thrace. There are the dime novels, the epic blockbusters Hollywood makes into miniseries, and then there are the plain, relentless stories of witnesses who have suffered through horrors major and minor that have marked and changed their lives. I haven't myself talked to Holocaust victims, but I've read their survival stories and their stories of witness and been revolted and moved by them. My father-in-law tells me his war stories again and again and I listen. A Mennonite who set aside the strictures of his own church in order to serve, he was a marine codeman in the Pacific during World War II, in the Signal Corps on Guadalcanal, Morotai, and Bougainville. He was part of the island-hopping maneuver MacArthur had devised to win the war in the Pacific. He saw friends killed when bombs exploded not ten yards away. When he was with the 298th Signal Corps attached to the Thirteenth Air Force, he saw plane after plane come in and crash, just short of the runway, killing their crews, setting the jungle ablaze with oil and gas fires. Emergency wagons would scramble, bouncing over newly bulldozed land men had used just the afternoon before for a football game. Every time we go fishing together, whether it's in a McKenzie boat drifting for salmon in Tillamook Bay or taking a lunch break from wading the riffles of a stream in the Cascades, my father-in-law tells me about what happened to him and the young men in his unit. One was a Jewish boy from Brooklyn. One was a foul-mouthed kid from Kansas. They died. And he *has* to tell me. And I *have* to listen. It's a ritual payment the young owe their elders who have survived. The evacuation and relocation is something like that.

Kubota, my grandfather, grew sick of life in Los Angeles and, without my grandmother, went home to Hawai'i before I graduated from high school. He wanted to be near the sea again. He missed his foods and his "talk story" sessions with the old-timers and the neighbors. He wrote me a few times, sent celebration money for my graduation. Once I was in college, my grandmother rejoined him there. Within only a few years, he fell ill with Alzheimer's disease and became strangely diminished in mind for some time before he died.

At the house he'd built on Kamehameha Highway in Hau'ula, a seacoast village just down the road from Lā'ie where he had his store, he'd wander out from the garage or greenhouse where he'd set up a workbench, and trudge down to the beach or up toward the line of pines he'd planted while employed by the Work Projects Administration during the thirties. Kubota thought he was going fishing. Or he thought he was back at work for Roosevelt planting pines as a wind- or soilbreak on the windward flank of the Ko'olau Mountains, emerald monoliths rising out of sea and canefields from Waialua to Kāne'ohe. When I visited, my grandmother would send me down to the beach to fetch him. Or I'd run down Kam Highway a quarter mile or so and find him hiding in the canefield by the roadside, counting stalks, measuring circumferences in the claw of his thumb and forefinger. The look on his face was confused or concentrated—I didn't know which. But I guessed he was going fishing again. I'd grab him and walk him back to his house on the highway. My grandmother would shut him in a room.

Within a few years, Kubota had a stroke and survived it, then he had another one and was completely debilitated. The family decided to put him in a nursing home in Kahuku, just set back from the highway, within a mile or so of Kahuku Point and the Tanaka Store where he'd had his first job as a stock boy. He lived there three years, and I visited him once with my aunt. He was like a potato that had been worn down by cooking. Everything on him—his eyes, his teeth, his legs and torso—seemed like it had been sloughed away. What he had been was mostly gone now and I was looking at the nub of a man. In a wheelchair, he grasped my hands and tugged on them—violently. His hands were still thick, and, I believed, strong enough to lift me out of my own seat into his lap. He murmured something in Japanese—he'd long ago ceased to speak any English. My aunt and I cried a little, and we left him.

I remember walking out on the black asphalt of the parking lot of the nursing home. It was heat-cracked and eroded already, and grass had veined itself into the interstices. There were coconut trees around, a canefield I could see across the street, and the ocean I knew was pitching a surf just beyond it. The green Koʻolaus came up behind us. Somewhere nearby, alongside the beach, there was an abandoned airfield in the middle of the canes. As a child, I'd come upon it while playing one day, and my friends and I kept returning to it, day after day, playing war or sprinting games or coming to fly kites. I recognize it even now when I see it on TV—it's used as a site for action scenes in the detective shows Hollywood always sets in the Islands: a helicopter chasing the hero racing away in a Ferrari, or gun dealers making a clandestine rendezvous on the abandoned runway. It was the old airfield strafed by Japanese planes the day the major flight attacked Pearl Harbor. It was the airfield the FBI thought my grandfather had targeted in his night-fishing and signaling with the long surf poles he'd stuck in the sandy bays near Kahuku Point.

Kubota died a short while after I visited him, but not, I thought, without giving me a final message. I was on the Mainland, in California studying for Ph.D. exams, when my grandmother called me with the news. It was a relief. He'd suffered from his debilitation a long time and I was grateful he'd gone. I went home for the funeral and gave the eulogy. My grandmother and I took his ashes home in a small, heavy metal box wrapped in a black *furoshiki*—a large silk scarf. She showed me the name the priest had given to him on his death, scripted with a calligraphy brush on a long, narrow talent of plain wood. Buddhist commoners, at death, are given priestly names, received symbolically into the clergy. The idea is that, in their next life, one of scholarship and leisure, they might meditate and attain the enlightenment the religion is aimed at. *Shaku Shūchi*, the ideograms read. It was Kubota's Buddhist name, incorporating characters from his family and given names. It meant "Shining Wisdom of the Law." He died on Pearl Harbor Day, December 8, 1983.

After years, after I'd finally come back to live in Volcano again, only once did I dream of Kubota, my grandfather. It was the same night I'd heard that H.R. 442, the redress bill for Japanese Americans, had been signed into law. In my dream that night, Kubota was torching, and he sang a Japanese song, a querulous and wavery folk ballad, as he hung paper lanterns on bamboo poles stuck into the sand in the shallow water of the lagoon behind the reef near Kahuku Point. Then he was at a worktable, smoking a hand-rolled cigarette, letting it dangle from his lips, Bogart style, as he drew, daintily and skillfully, with a narrow trim brush, ideogram after ideogram on a score of paper lanterns he had hung in a dark shed to dry. He had painted a talismanic mantra onto each lantern, the ideogram for the word "red" in Japanese, a bit of art blended with some superstition, a piece of sympathetic magic appealing to the magenta coloring on the rough skins of the schooling, night-feeding fish he wanted to attract to his baited hooks. He strung them from pole to pole in the dream then, hiking up his khaki worker's pants so his white ankles showed, and wading through the shimmering black waters of the sand flats and then the reef. "The moon is leaving, leaving," he sang in Japanese. "Take me deeper in the savage sea." He turned and crouched like an ice-racer then, leaning forward so that his unshaven face almost touched the light film of water. I could see the light stubble of beard like a fine gray ash covering the lower half of his face. I could see his gold-rimmed spectacles. He held a small wooden boat in his cupped hands and placed it lightly on the sea and pushed it away. One of his lanterns was on it and, written in small, neat rows like a sutra scroll, it had been decorated with the silvery names of all our dead.

Perspectives of Memory

To Vladimir Nabokov, "the supreme achievement of memory . . . is the masterly use it makes of innate harmonies when gathering to its fold the suspended and wandering tonalities of the past." Like Nabokov and Proust and many others, I have often thought of music as a metaphor for memory's ability to group together, from the fluidity of time, any number of images or events, each of which may be trivial in itself but which nevertheless carries an emotional coloration that relates it to the others: for memory, set in spiritual motion by a pungent aroma, an image, or simply an inexplicable and transient feeling, searches for all the past affinities to it as surely as, when set in motion by a concept or idea, memory pursues linkages of a more theoretical or intellectual sort.

We are always what we were; we know ourselves—to the degree that knowledge of the self is possible—through our ever-growing past. The point is self-evident, and won't be belabored here, except to note that memory gives us a double perspective: as this section illustrates, not only does the past inform the present, but the present informs the past. In other words, the understanding of our present selves that memory provides us is capable of returning the gift, enabling us to know our earlier selves in a manner that eluded us then.

And yet how memory alters, as it traces the arc of our existence! No doubt this difference has something to do with our changing conceptions of time: in early childhood, while the world is still fresh and our eyes focus on each new object, time moves (if it moves at all) with the speed of a slug, and our earliest memories are as iridescent and viscid as the trail this deliberate little creature leaves behind it on a sidewalk caught in the clear morning light of a spring day; as we age, the speed increases, with the ever-growing memories rising higher and spreading more widely behind us—like those of a jet trail caught in the softer radiance of a setting sun.

In organizing material for this section, I have tried to demonstrate both the constant and the changing nature of human memory, as it traces the arc of our individual journeys. Though some precocious children have recorded their memories, I have chosen to begin at a later stage, so that the double perspectives of memory can be indicated. The vantage points are the periods of middle and old age, with middle age given by far the greatest attention. (As befits a septuagenarian, I think of the middle years as a lengthy period of maturation, its borders with adolescence and old age too tenuous to be guarded by any alert sentry or rigid customs official; we do most of our living—and writing—in this span.)

I have separated the essays I have selected into three groups. The first (and most extensive) examines childhood and adolescence from the perspective of the middle years, and the selections are arranged in accordance with the age of the child remembered by the adult—the essays that describe the earliest memories serving to open the group. It strikes me (from my own life as well as from these essays) that the middle years, in particular their latter portion, provide the richest experiences, with the memories of childhood and youth serving to color, and often to buttress, everything we have come to know; but those years of our fullest engagement with life also contain events of a kind unknown to the child, and hence are resistant to the benign influence that a secure childhood might offer: such events include chaotic happenings, losses that nothing has prepared us for.

The middle years, I think, are the ones in which we are most sharply informed of the tragic dimension of life—and perhaps that tragic awareness is part of their very richness. (In one of the essays of the opening section of this anthology, Gerald Edelman offers the common enough observation that human individuals, unlike individuals of the other animal species, are "tragic, insofar as they can imagine their own extinction.") The second group of essays reflects this tragic dimension. It demonstrates how memory, even when devoid of support from childhood, works to sustain us in midlife.

The essays in the third group offer illustrations of what all of us, if we are lucky enough, may come to recognize and to accept—for these essays are examples of a graceful acquiescence to a knowledge dependent upon the memories from childhood and middle age alike.

Childhood and the Middle Years

> ... who would not give,
> If so he might, to duty and to truth
> the eagerness of an infantine desire?
> A tranquillizing spirit presses now
> On my corporeal frame, so wide appears
> The vacancy between me and those days,
> Which yet have such self-presence in my heart
> That sometimes when I think of them I seem
> Two consciousnesses—conscious of myself,
> And of some other being.
>
> —William Wordsworth, from "The Two-Part Prelude"

The "other being" that Wordsworth "sometimes" thinks of as separate from his adult consciousness is the one contained in memory from his early years; yet it is clear from this passage that feelings from childhood remain undiminished within the adult's mind.

The transcription of childhood experiences into adult consciousness and identity is a major burden of the present grouping of essays. By coincidence, I happened to be reading *Starting Points,* the 1994 report of the Carnegie Task Force on Meeting the Needs of Young Children, while still in the process of selecting essays for this segment. A sense of desperation, an awareness of the urgency of the matter, underlies that report, aimed as it is on the ever-increasing incidence of neglect and abuse suffered by infants and young children. To lend scientific support to the importance of prenatal care and of nurture during a child's first three years, the report summarizes recent research on brain development (studies similar to those referred to in the opening section of this volume). These studies show that "brain cell formation is virtually complete before birth," that in the months after birth "the formation of connections among these cells" that "allow[s] learning to take place . . . proceeds with astounding rapidity," and that "brain development is much more vulnerable to environmental influence than we had ever expected."

Instances of childhood neglect or sexual abuse are apparent in two of the selections that follow (those by Virginia Woolf and Tobias Wolff), but they appear, in the general context, as aberrations that have not handicapped either writer's innate talent. Indeed, those of us who have the leisure and the education necessary to read and to write and to contemplate the resources provided us by memory are not apt to be among those whose early development was stunted by extreme poverty, malnourishment, surroundings in which violence is a frequent occurrence, or fetal alcohol syndrome. Still, given the related facts that the brain is as fully formed as it is by age three, and that three is usually the age at which we begin to hold conscious memories, the influential material that we classify as belonging to the unconscious mind must include—for the disadvantaged and privileged alike—very early experiences, if in a form too fragmented and shadowy to be recognized.

I hope that the reader will gain a heightened awareness (such as came to me in collecting and assembling these essays) of the exceptional influence of childhood experiences upon the later stages of life. Such knowledge is important for self-insight, for the way we treat our children, and for the amelioration of those conditions which, impairing the mental and physical growth of so many children, are the cause of much of the current social decay.

from "A Sketch of the Past"

Virginia Woolf (1882–1941)

Two years before her death, Virginia Woolf, the English novelist and essayist, began writing her memoir, "A Sketch of the Past." To write about herself offered her release, as she says, from her work at hand, a biography of Robert Fry that had become tedious to her; and, as soon becomes apparent, release also from the anxieties she felt as World War II became ever more imminent. "A Sketch of the Past" was not written for publication, though indications exist in it that she thought it might be revised and developed into a fuller work—a possibility precluded by Woolf's suicide four months after she made her final entry in this uncompleted memoir.

Woolf's concept of human identity has its basis in feelings and responses that go as far back as one's earliest memories, as "A Sketch of the Past" clearly shows. For her, an individual's life is divided between "being" and "non-being." The latter state consists of all those hours and days during which we live routinely, doing the needed or expected things; she thinks of this large proportion of our lives as living within "cotton wool." On the other hand, our apprehension of "being" occurs during our much more receptive intervals, and permits us "exceptional moments"—insights or experiences that strike us with immediate force, but whose significance becomes apparent only through their hold on memory, which continues to reflect upon them. To the adult, any such moment is, or can be, "a token of some real thing behind appearances." Woolf feels that these moments can be recalled—relived—with absolute fidelity, and that to explain or describe them, to perceive the transcendent pattern within them, provides the rapture inherent in creative activity. Still, the self—the identity—is always in flux, the present altering the past even as the past informs the present. The self is a consequence not only of moments of being but of all the influences to be found within a society, a culture, a period of history. "Invisible presences," she calls these exterior pressures and forces—and for her, as she indicates at the ending of this excerpt, for years they included her mother, who died when Woolf was thirteen.

The explanatory footnotes are the work of the editor of this text, Jeanne Schulkind, whose introduction to it and other posthumous work by Woolf is exemplary. To abet readers unfamiliar with Woolf's life, I add a few further explanations here: Talland House is the house at St. Ives in Cornwall, where Woolf spent her childhood vacations; Vanessa is her sister, Thoby and Adrian her brothers. Like Gerald, George (who, as documents reveal, also, if at a later date, made unwanted sexual advances—to Vanessa as well as Virginia) is her half brother, and Stella her half sister; all three are children of her mother and her first husband, Herbert Duckworth.

The Anatomy of Memory

Two days ago—Sunday, 16th April 1939 to be precise—Nessa said that if I did not start writing my memoirs I should soon be too old. I should be eighty-five, and should have forgotten—witness the unhappy case of Lady Strachey.* As it happens that I am sick of writing Roger's life, perhaps I will spend two or three mornings making a sketch.† There are several difficulties. In the first place, the enormous number of things I can remember; in the second, the number of different ways in which memoirs can be written. As a great memoir reader, I know many different ways. But if I begin to go through them and to analyse them and their merits and faults, the mornings—I cannot take more than two or three at most—will be gone. So without stopping to choose my way, in the sure and certain knowledge that it will find itself—or if not it will not matter—I begin: the first memory.

This was of red and purple flowers on a black ground—my mother's dress; and she was sitting either in a train or in an omnibus, and I was on her lap. I therefore saw the flowers she was wearing very close; and can still see purple and red and blue, I think, against the black; they must have been anemones, I suppose. Perhaps we were going to St Ives; more probably, for from the light it must have been evening, we were coming back to London. But it is more convenient artistically to suppose that we were going to St Ives, for that will lead to my other memory, which also seems to be my first memory, and in fact it is the most important of all my memories. If life has a base that it stands upon, if it is a bowl that one fills and fills and fills—then my bowl without a doubt stands upon this memory. It is of lying half asleep, half awake, in bed in the nursery at St Ives. It is of hearing the waves breaking, one, two, one, two, and sending a splash of water over the beach; and then breaking, one, two, one, two, behind a yellow blind. It is of hearing the blind draw its little acorn across the floor as the wind blew the blind out. It is of lying and hearing this splash and seeing this light, and feeling, it is almost impossible that I should be here; of feeling the purest ecstasy I can conceive.

I could spend hours trying to write that as it should be written, in order to give the feeling which is even at this moment very strong in me. But I should fail (unless I had some wonderful luck); I dare say I should only succeed in having the luck if I had begun by describing Virginia herself.

---

*Lady Strachey, mother of Lytton, died at the age of eighty-nine, in 1928. In old age she wrote "Some Recollections of a Long Life" which were very short—less than a dozen pages in *Nation and Athenaeum*. This may indicate, as Michael Holroyd has suggested, that by the early 1920s she had forgotten more than she remembered.

†VW was at work on *Roger Fry: A Biography* (The Hogarth Press; London, 1940).

Here I come to one of the memoir writer's difficulties—one of the reasons why, though I read so many, so many are failures. They leave out the person to whom things happened. The reason is that it is so difficult to describe any human being. So they say: "This is what happened"; but they do not say what the person was like to whom it happened. And the events mean very little unless we know first to whom they happened. Who was I then? Adeline Virginia Stephen, the second daughter of Leslie and Julia Prinsep Stephen, born on 25th January 1882, descended from a great many people, some famous, others obscure; born into a large connection, born not of rich parents, but of well-to-do parents, born into a very communicative, literate, letter writing, visiting, articulate, late nineteenth century world; so that I could if I liked to take the trouble, write a great deal here not only about my mother and father but about uncles and aunts, cousins and friends. But I do not know how much of this, or what part of this, made me feel what I felt in the nursery at St Ives. I do not know how far I differ from other people. That is another memoir writer's difficulty. Yet to describe oneself truly one must have some standard of comparison; was I clever, stupid, good looking, ugly, passionate, cold—? Owing partly to the fact that I was never at school, never competed in any way with children of my own age, I have never been able to compare my gifts and defects with other people's. But of course there was one external reason for the intensity of this first impression: the impression of the waves and the acorn on the blind; the feeling, as I describe it sometimes to myself, of lying in a grape and seeing through a film of semi-transparent yellow—it was due partly to the many months we spent in London. The change of nursery was a great change. And there was the long train journey; and the excitement. I remember the dark; the lights; the stir of the going up to bed.

But to fix my mind upon the nursery—it had a balcony; there was a partition, but it joined the balcony of my father's and mother's bedroom. My mother would come out onto her balcony in a white dressing gown. There were passion flowers growing on the wall; they were great starry blossoms, with purple streaks, and large green buds, part empty, part full.

If I were a painter I should paint these first impressions in pale yellow, silver, and green. There was the pale yellow blind; the green sea; and the silver of the passion flowers. I should make a picture that was globular; semi-transparent. I should make a picture of curved petals; of shells; of things that were semi-transparent; I should make curved shapes, showing the light through, but not giving a clear outline. Everything would be large and dim; and what was seen would at the same time be heard; sounds would come through this petal or leaf—sounds indistinguishable from sights. Sound and sight seem to make equal parts of these first impressions. When I think of the early morning in bed I also hear the caw of rooks

317

falling from a great height. The sound seems to fall through an elastic, gummy air; which holds it up; which prevents it from being sharp and distinct.* The quality of the air above Talland House seemed to suspend sound, to let it sink down slowly, as if it were caught in a blue gummy veil. The rooks cawing is part of the waves breaking—one, two, one, two—and the splash as the wave drew back and then it gathered again, and I lay there half awake, half asleep, drawing in such ecstasy as I cannot describe.

The next memory—all these colour-and-sound memories hang together at St Ives—was much more robust; it was highly sensual. It was later. It still makes me feel warm; as if everything were ripe; humming; sunny; smelling so many smells at once; and all making a whole that even now makes me stop—as I stopped then going down to the beach; I stopped at the top to look down at the gardens. They were sunk beneath the road. The apples were on a level with one's head. The gardens gave off a murmur of bees; the apples were red and gold; there were also pink flowers; and grey and silver leaves. The buzz, the croon, the smell, all seemed to press voluptuously against some membrane; not to burst it; but to hum round one such a complete rapture of pleasure that I stopped, smelt; looked. But again I cannot describe that rapture. It was rapture rather than ecstasy.

The strength of these pictures—but sight was always then so much mixed with sound that picture is not the right word—the strength anyhow of these impressions makes me again digress. Those moments—in the nursery, on the road to the beach—can still be more real than the present moment. This I have just tested. For I got up and crossed the garden. Percy was digging the asparagus bed; Louie was shaking a mat in front of the bedroom door.† But I was seeing them through the sight I saw here—the nursery and the road to the beach. At times I can go back to St Ives more completely than I can this morning. I can reach a state where I seem to be watching things happen as if I were there. That is, I suppose, that my memory supplies what I had forgotten, so that it seems as if it were happening independently, though I am really making it happen. In certain favourable moods, memories—what one has forgotten—come to the top. Now if this is so, is it not possible—I often wonder—that things we have felt with great intensity have an existence independent of our minds; are in fact still in existence? And if so, will it not be possible, in time, that some device will be invented by which we can tap them? I see

---

*VW has written "made it seem to fall from a great height" above "prevents . . . distinct."
†The gardener and daily help, respectively, at Monks House, the country home of the Woolfs in Rodmell, Sussex from 1919.

it—the past—as an avenue lying behind; a long ribbon of scenes, emotions. There at the end of the avenue still, are the garden and the nursery. Instead of remembering here a scene and there a sound, I shall fit a plug into the wall; and listen in to the past. I shall turn up August 1890. I feel that strong emotion must leave its trace; and it is only a question of discovering how we can get ourselves again attached to it, so that we shall be able to live our lives through from the start.

But the peculiarity of these two strong memories is that each was very simple. I am hardly aware of myself, but only of the sensation. I am only the container of the feeling of ecstasy, of the feeling of rapture. Perhaps this is characteristic of all childhood memories; perhaps it accounts for their strength. Later we add to feelings much that makes them more complex; and therefore less strong; or if not less strong, less isolated, less complete. But instead of analysing this, here is an instance of what I mean—my feeling about the looking-glass in the hall.

There was a small looking-glass in the hall at Talland House. It had, I remember, a ledge with a brush on it. By standing on tiptoe I could see my face in the glass. When I was six or seven perhaps, I got into the habit of looking at my face in the glass. But I only did this if I was sure that I was alone. I was ashamed of it. A strong feeling of guilt seemed naturally attached to it. But why was this so? One obvious reason occurs to me— Vanessa and I were both what was called tomboys; that is, we played cricket, scrambled over rocks, climbed trees, were said not to care for clothes and so on. Perhaps therefore to have been found looking in the glass would have been against our tomboy code. But I think that my feeling of shame went a great deal deeper. I am almost inclined to drag in my grandfather—Sir James, who once smoked a cigar, liked it, and so threw away his cigar and never smoked another. I am almost inclined to think that I inherited a streak of the puritan, of the Clapham Sect.* At any rate, the looking-glass shame has lasted all my life, long after the tomboy phase was over. I cannot now powder my nose in public. Everything to do with dress—to be fitted, to come into a room wearing a new dress—still frightens me; at least makes me shy, self-conscious, uncomfortable. "Oh to be able to run, like Julian Morrell, all over the garden in a new dress," I thought not many years ago at Garsington; where Julian undid a parcel and put on a new dress and scampered round and round like a hare.† Yet femininity was very strong in our family. We were famous for our beauty—my mother's beauty, Stella's beauty, gave me as early as I can

---

*In marrying Jane Catherine Venn, James Stephen had allied himself with the very heart of the Clapham Sect.

†Julian Morrell was the daughter of Ottoline and Philip Morrell; Garsington Manor was their house in Oxfordshire.

remember, pride and pleasure. What then gave me this feeling of shame, unless it were that I inherited some opposite instinct? My father was spartan, ascetic, puritanical. He had I think no feeling for pictures; no ear for music; no sense of the sound of words. This leads me to think that my—I would say "our" if I knew enough about Vanessa, Thoby and Adrian—but how little we know even about brothers and sisters—this leads me to think that my natural love for beauty was checked by some ancestral dread. Yet this did not prevent me from feeling ecstasies and raptures spontaneously and intensely and without any shame or the least sense of guilt, so long as they were disconnected with my own body. I thus detect another element in the shame which I had in being caught looking at myself in the glass in the hall. I must have been ashamed or afraid of my own body. Another memory, also of the hall, may help to explain this. There was a slab outside the dining room door for standing dishes upon. Once when I was very small Gerald Duckworth lifted me onto this, and as I sat there he began to explore my body. I can remember the feel of his hand going under my clothes; going firmly and steadily lower and lower. I remember how I hoped that he would stop; how I stiffened and wriggled as his hand approached by private parts. But it did not stop. His hand explored my private parts too. I remember resenting,—disliking it—what is the word for so dumb and mixed a feeling? It must have been strong, since I still recall it. This seems to show that a feeling about certain parts of the body; how they must not be touched; how it is wrong to allow them to be touched; must be instinctive. It proves that Virginia Stephen was not born on the 25th January 1882, but was born many thousands of years ago; and had from the very first to encounter instincts already acquired by thousands of ancestresses in the past.

And this throws light not merely on my own case, but upon the problem that I touched on the first page; why it is so difficult to give any account of the person to whom things happen. The person is evidently immensely complicated. Witness the incident of the looking-glass. Though I have done my best to explain why I was ashamed of looking at my own face I have only been able to discover some possible reasons; there may be others; I do not suppose that I have got at the truth; yet this is a simple incident; and it happened to me personally; and I have no motive for lying about it. In spite of all this, people write what they call "lives" of other people; that is, they collect a number of events, and leave the person to whom it happened unknown. Let me add a dream; for it may refer to the incident of the looking-glass. I dreamt that I was looking in a glass when a horrible face—the face of an animal—suddenly showed over my shoulder. I cannot be sure if this was a dream, or if it happened. Was I looking in the glass one day when something in the background moved, and seemed to me alive? I cannot be sure. But I have always remembered the other face in the glass, whether it was a dream or a fact, and that it frightened me.

These then are some of my first memories. But of course as an account of my life they are misleading, because the things one does not remember are as important; perhaps they are more important. If I could remember one whole day I should be able to describe, superficially at least, what life was like as a child. Unfortunately, one only remembers what is exceptional. And there seems to be no reason why one thing is exceptional and another not. Why have I forgotten so many things that must have been, one would have thought, more memorable than what I do remember? Why remember the hum of bees in the garden going down to the beach, and forget completely being thrown naked by father into the sea? (Mrs Swanwick says she saw that happen.)*

This leads to a digression, which perhaps may explain a little of my own psychology; even of other people's. Often when I have been writing one of my so-called novels I have been baffled by this same problem; that is, how to describe what I call in my private shorthand—"non-being". Every day includes much more non-being than being. Yesterday for example, Tuesday the 18th of April, was [as] it happened a good day; above the average in "being". It was fine; I enjoyed writing these first pages; my head was relieved of the pressure of writing about Roger; I walked over to Mount Misery† and along the river; and save that the tide was out, the country, which I notice very closely always, was coloured and shaded as I like—there were the willows, I remember, all plumy and soft green and purple against the blue. I also read Chaucer with pleasure; and began a book—the memoirs of Madame de la Fayette—which interested me. These separate moments of being were however embedded in many more moments of non-being. I have already forgotten what Leonard and I talked about at lunch; and at tea; although it was a good day the goodness was embedded in a kind of nondescript cotton wool. This is always so. A great part of every day is not lived consciously. One walks, eats, sees things, deals with what has to be done; the broken vacuum cleaner; ordering dinner; writing orders to Mabel; washing; cooking dinner; bookbinding. When it is a bad day the proportion of non-being is much larger. I had a slight temperature last week; almost the whole day was non-being.

---

*Mrs Swanwick was the only daughter of Oswald and Eleanor Sickert. In her autobiography, *I Have Been Young* (London, 1935), she recalls having known Leslie Stephen at St Ives: "We watched with delight his naked babies running about the beach or being towed into the sea between his legs, and their beautiful mother."

†Two cottages on the down between Southease and Piddinghoe known locally as Mount Misery.

The real novelist can somehow convey both sorts of being. I think Jane Austen can; and Trollope; perhaps Thackeray and Dickens and Tolstoy. I have never been able to do both. I tried—in *Night and Day*; and in *The Years*. But I will leave the literary side alone for the moment.

As a child then, my days, just as they do now, contained a large proportion of this cotton wool, this non-being. Week after week passed at St Ives and nothing made any dint upon me. Then, for no reason that I know about, there was a sudden violent shock; something happened so violently that I have remembered it all my life. I will give a few instances. The first: I was fighting with Thoby on the lawn. We were pommelling each other with our fists. Just as I raised my fist to hit him, I felt: why hurt another person? I dropped my hand instantly, and stood there, and let him beat me. I remember the feeling. It was a feeling of hopeless sadness. It was as if I became aware of something terrible; and of my own powerlessness. I slunk off alone, feeling horribly depressed. The second instance was also in the garden at St Ives. I was looking at the flower bed by the front door; "That is the whole", I said. I was looking at a plant with a spread of leaves; and it seemed suddenly plain that the flower itself was a part of the earth; that a ring enclosed what was the flower; and that was the real flower; part earth; part flower. It was a thought I put away as being likely to be very useful to me later. The third case was also at St Ives. Some people called Valpy had been staying at St Ives, and had left. We were waiting at dinner one night, when somehow I overheard my father or my mother say that Mr Valpy had killed himself. The next thing I remember is being in the garden at night and walking on the path by the apple tree. It seemed to me that the apple tree was connected with the horror of Mr Valpy's suicide. I could not pass it. I stood there looking at the grey-green creases of the bark—it was a moonlit night—in a trance of horror. I seemed to be dragged down, hopelessly, into some pit of absolute despair from which I could not escape. My body seemed paralysed.

These are three instances of exceptional moments. I often tell them over, or rather they come to the surface unexpectedly. But now that for the first time I have written them down, I realise something that I have never realised before. Two of these moments ended in a state of despair. The other ended, on the contrary, in a state of satisfaction. When I said about the flower "That is the whole," I felt that I had made a discovery. I felt that I had put away in my mind something that I should go back [to], to turn over and explore. It strikes me now that this was a profound difference. It was the difference in the first place between despair and satisfaction. This difference I think arose from the fact that I was quite unable to deal with the pain of discovering that people hurt each other; that a man I had seen had killed himself. The sense of horror held me powerless. But in the case of the flower I found a reason; and was thus able to deal with the sensation. I was not powerless. I was conscious—if only at a distance—that I should in time explain it. I do not know if I was older when I saw the flower than I was when I had the other two experiences. I only know that many of these exceptional moments brought with them a peculiar horror and a physical collapse; they seemed dominant; myself passive. This suggests that as one gets older one has a greater power through reason to provide an explanation; and that this explanation blunts the sledge-hammer force of the blow. I think this is true, because though I still have the peculiarity that I receive these sudden shocks, they are now always welcome; after the first surprise, I always feel instantly that they are particularly valuable. And so I go on to suppose that the shock-receiving capacity is what makes me a writer. I hazard the explanation that a shock is at once in my case followed by the desire to explain it. I feel that I have had a blow; but it is not, as I thought as a child, simply a blow from an enemy hidden behind the cotton wool of daily life; it is or will become a revelation of some order; it is a token of some real thing behind appearances; and I make it real by putting it into words. It is only by putting it into words that I make it whole; this wholeness means that it has lost its power to hurt me; it gives me, perhaps because by doing so I take away the pain, a great delight to put the severed parts together. Perhaps this is the strongest pleasure known to me. It is the rapture I get when in writing I seem to be discovering what belongs to what; making a scene come right; making a character come together. From this I reach what I might call a philosophy; at any rate it is a constant idea of mine; that behind the cotton wool is hidden a pattern; that we—I mean all human beings—are connected with this; that the whole world is a work of art; that we are parts of the work of art. *Hamlet* or a Beethoven quartet is the truth about this vast mass that we call the world. But there is no Shakespeare, there is no Beethoven; certainly and emphatically there is no God; we are the words; we are the music; we are the thing itself. And I see this when I have a shock.

This intuition of mine—it is so instinctive that it seems given to me, not made by me—has certainly given its scale to my life ever since I saw the flower in the bed by the front door at St Ives. If I were painting myself I should have to find some—rod, shall I say—something that would stand for the conception. It proves that one's life is not confined to one's body and what one says and does; one is living all the time in relation to certain background rods or conceptions. Mine is that there is a pattern hid behind the cotton wool. And this conception affects me every day. I prove this, now, by spending the morning writing, when I might be walking, running a shop, or learning to do something that will be useful if war comes. I feel that by writing I am doing what is far more necessary than anything else. . . .
2nd May . . . Many bright colours; many distinct sounds; some human

beings, caricatures; comic; several violent moments of being, always including a circle of the scene which they cut out: and all surrounded by a vast space—that is a rough visual description of childhood. This is how I shape it; and how I see myself as a child, roaming about, in that space of time which lasted from 1882 to 1895. A great hall I could liken it to; with windows letting in strange lights; and murmurs and spaces of deep silence. But somehow into that picture must be brought, too, the sense of movement and change. Nothing remained stable long. One must get the feeling of everything approaching and then disappearing, getting large, getting small, passing at different rates of speed past the little creature; one must get the feeling that made her press on, the little creature driven on as she was by growth of her legs and arms, driven without her being able to stop it, or to change it, driven as a plant is driven up out of the earth, up until the stalk grows, the leaf grows, buds swell. That is what is indescribable, that is what makes all images too static, for no sooner has one said this was so, than it was past and altered. How immense must be the force of life which turns a baby, who can just distinguish a great blot of blue and purple on a black background, into the child who thirteen years later can feel all that I felt on May 5th 1895—now almost exactly to a day, forty-four years ago—when my mother died.

This shows that among the innumerable things left out in my sketch I have left out the most important—those instincts, affections, passions, attachments—there is no single word for them, for they changed month by month—which bound me, I suppose, from the first moment of consciousness to other people. If it were true, as I said above, that the things that ceased in childhood, are easy to describe because they are complete, then it should be easy to say what I felt for my mother, who died when I was thirteen. Thus I should be able to see her completely undisturbed by later impressions, as I saw Mr Gibbs and C. B. Clarke. But the theory, though true of them, breaks down completely with her. It breaks down in a curious way, which I will explain, for perhaps it may help to explain why I find it now so curiously difficult to describe both my feeling for her, and her herself.

Until I was in the forties—I could settle the date by seeing when I wrote *To the Lighthouse,* but am too casual here to bother to do it—the presence of my mother obsessed me.* I could hear her voice, see her, imagine what she would do or say as I went about my day's doings. She was one of the invisible presences who after all play so important a part in every life. This influence, by which I mean the consciousness of other

---

To the Lighthouse was begun in 1925 and published in 1927 when VW was forty-five.

groups impinging upon ourselves; public opinion; what other people say and think; all those magnets which attract us this way to be like that, or repel us the other and make us different from that; has never been analysed in any of those Lives which I so much enjoy reading, or very superficially. Yet it is by such invisible presences that the "subject of this memoir" is tugged this way and that every day of his life; it is they that keep him in position. Consider what immense forces society brings to play upon each of us, how that society changes from decade to decade; and also from class to class; well, if we cannot analyse these invisible presences, we know very little of the subject of the memoir; and again how futile life-writing becomes. I see myself as a fish in a stream; deflected; held in place; but cannot describe the stream.

To return to the particular instance which should be more definite and more capable of description than for example the influence on me of the Cambridge Apostles,* or the influence of the Galsworthy, Bennett, Wells school of fiction, or the influence of the Vote, or of the War—that is, the influence of my mother. It is perfectly true that she obsessed me, in spite of the fact that she died when I was thirteen, until I was forty-four. Then one day walking round Tavistock Square I made up, as I sometimes make up my books, *To the Lighthouse*; in a great, apparently involuntary, rush.† One thing burst into another. Blowing bubbles out of a pipe gives the feeling of the rapid crowd of ideas and scenes which blew out of my mind, so that my lips seemed syllabling of their own accord as I walked. What blew the bubbles? Why then? I have no notion. But I wrote the book very quickly; and when it was written, I ceased to be obsessed by my mother. I no longer hear her voice; I do not see her.

I suppose that I did for myself what psycho-analysts do for their patients. I expressed some very long felt and deeply felt emotion. And in expressing it I explained it and then laid it to rest. But what is the meaning of "explained" it? Why, because I described her and my feeling for her in that book, should my vision of her and my feeling for her become so much dimmer and weaker? Perhaps one of these days I shall hit on the reason; and if so, I will give it, but at the moment I will go on, describing what I can remember, for it may be true that what I remember of her now will weaken still further. (This note is made provisionally, in order

*The popular name for the semi-secret "Cambridge-Conversazione Society" which was founded in the 1820s. All the young men who formed the nucleus of "old Bloomsbury" belonged to it, except Clive Bell and Thoby Stephen.
†52 Tavistock Square was the London home of the Woolfs from 1924 to 1939.

to explain in part why it is now so difficult to give any clear description of her.)

Certainly there she was, in the very centre of that great Cathedral space which was childhood; there she was from the very first. My first memory is of her lap; the scratch of some beads on her dress comes back to me as I pressed my cheek against it. Then I see her in her white dressing gown on the balcony; and the passion flower with the purple star on its petals. Her voice is still faintly in my ears—decided, quick; and in particular the little drops with which her laugh ended—three diminishing ahs . . . "Ah—ah—ah . . ." I sometimes end a laugh that way myself. And I see her hands, like Adrian's, with the very individual square-tipped fingers, each finger with a waist to it, and the nail broadening out. (My own are the same size all the way, so that I can slip a ring over my thumb.) She had three rings; a diamond ring, an emerald ring, and an opal ring. My eyes used to fix themselves upon the lights in the opal as it moved across the page of the lesson book when she taught us, and I was glad that she left it to me (I gave it to Leonard). Also I hear the tinkle of her bracelets, made of twisted silver, given her by Mr Lowell, as she went about the house; especially as she came up at night to see if we were asleep, holding a candle shaded; this is a distinct memory, for, like all children, I lay awake sometimes and longed for her to come. Then she told me to think of all the lovely things I could imagine. Rainbows and bells . . . But besides these minute separate details, how did I first become conscious of what was always there—her astonishing beauty? Perhaps I never became conscious of it; I think I accepted her beauty as the natural quality that a mother—she seemed typical, universal, yet our own in particular—had by virtue of being our mother. It was part of her calling. I do not think that I separated her face from that general being; or from her whole body. Certainly I have a vision of her now, as she came up the path by the lawn at St Ives; slight, shapely—she held herself very straight. I was playing. I stopped, about to speak to her. But she half turned from us, and lowered her eyes. From that indescribably sad gesture I knew that Philips, the man who had been crushed on the line and whom she had been visiting, was dead. It's over, she seemed to say. I knew, and was awed by the thought of death. At the same time I felt that her gesture as a whole was lovely. Very early, through nurses or casual visitors, I must have known that she was thought very beautiful. But that pride was snobbish, not a pure and private feeling: it was mixed with pride in other people's admiration. It was related to the more definitely snobbish pride caused in me by the nurses who said one night talking together while we ate our supper: "They're very well connected . . ."

But apart from her beauty, if the two can be separated, what was she herself like? Very quick; very direct; practical; and amusing, I say at once off hand. She could be sharp, she disliked affectation. "If you put your head on one side like that, you shan't come to the party," I remember she said to me as we drew up in a carriage in front of some house. Severe; with a background of knowledge that made her sad. She had her own sorrow waiting behind her to dip into privately. Once when she had set us to write exercises I looked up from mine and watched her reading—the Bible perhaps; and, struck by the gravity of her face, told myself that her first husband had been a clergyman and that she was thinking, as she read what he had read, of him. This was a fable on my part; but it shows that she looked very sad when she was not talking.

But can I get any closer to her without drawing upon all those descriptions and anecdotes which after she was dead imposed themselves upon my view of her? Very quick; very definite; very upright; and behind the active, the sad, the silent. And of course she was central. I suspect the word "central" gets closest to the general feeling I had of living so completely in her atmosphere that one never got far enough away from her to see her as a person. (That is one reason why I see the Gibbses and the Beadles and the Clarkes so much more distinctly.) She was the whole thing; Talland House was full of her; Hyde Park Gate was full of her. I see now, though the sentence is hasty, feeble and inexpressive, why it was that it was impossible for her to leave a very private and particular impression upon a child. She was keeping what I call in my shorthand the panoply of life—that which we all lived in common—in being. I see now that she was living on such an extended surface that she had not time, nor strength, to concentrate, except for a moment if one were ill or in some child's crisis, upon me, or upon anyone—unless it were Adrian. Him she cherished separately; she called him "My Joy". The later view, the understanding that I now have of her position must have its say; and it shows me that a woman of forty with seven children, some of them needing grown-up attention, and four still in the nursery; and an eighth, Laura, an idiot, yet living with us; and a husband fifteen years her elder, difficult, exacting, dependent on her; I see now that a woman who had to keep all this in being and under control must have been a general presence rather than a particular person to a child of seven or eight. Can I remember ever being alone with her for more than a few minutes? Someone was always interrupting. When I think of her spontaneously she is always in a room full of people; Stella, George and Gerald are there; my father, sitting reading with one leg curled round the other, twisting his lock of hair; "Go and take the crumb out of his beard," she whispers to me; and off I trot. There are visitors, young men like Jack Hills who is in love with Stella; many young men, Cambridge friends of George's and Gerald's; old men, sitting round the tea table talking—father's friends, Henry James, Symonds,* (I see him peering up at me on the broad staircase at St Ives with his drawn yellow face and a tie made of a yellow cord with two plush balls on it); Stella's friends—the Lushingtons, the Stillmans; I see her at the head of the table underneath the engraving of Beatrice given her by an old governess and painted blue; I hear jokes; laughter; the clatter of voices; I am teased; I say something funny; she laughs; I am pleased; I blush furiously; she observes; someone laughs at Nessa for saying that Ida Milman is her B. F.; Mother says soothingly, tenderly, "Best friend, that means." I see her going to the town with her basket; and Arthur Davies goes with her; I see her knitting on the hall step while we play cricket; I see her stretching her arms out to Mrs. Williams when the bailiffs took possession of their house and the Captain stood at the window bawling and shying jugs, basins, chamber pots onto the gravel—"Come to us, Mrs Williams"; "No, Mrs Stephen," sobbed Mrs Williams, "I will not leave my husband."—I see her writing at her table in London and the silver candlesticks, and the high carved chair with the claws and the pink seat; and the three-cornered brass ink pot; I wait in agony peeping surreptitiously behind the blind for her to come down the street, when she has been out late the lamps are lit and I am sure that she has been run over. (Once my father found me peeping; questioned me; and said rather anxiously but reprovingly, "You shouldn't be so nervous, Jinny.") And there is my last sight of her; she was dying; I came to kiss her and as I crept out of the room she said: "Hold yourself straight, my little Goat." . . . What a jumble of things I can remember, if I let my mind run, about my mother; but they are all of her in company; of her surrounded; of her generalised; dispersed, omnipresent, of her as the creator of that crowded merry world which spun so gaily in the centre of my childhood. It is true that I enclosed that world in another made by my own temperament; it is true that from the beginning I had many adventures outside that world; and often went far from it; and kept much back from it; but there it always was, the common life of the family, very merry, very stirring, crowded with people; and she was the centre; it was herself. This was proved on May 5th 1895. For after that day there was nothing left of it. I leant out of the nursery window the morning she died. It was about six, I suppose. I saw Dr Seton walk away up the street with his head bent and his hands clasped behind his back. I saw the pigeons floating and settling. I got a feeling of calm, sadness, and finality. It was a beautiful blue spring morning, and very still. That brings back the feeling that everything had come to an end.

---

*John Addington Symonds, man of letters, was the father of Katherine who married the artist Charles Furse and Margaret (Madge) who married William Wyamar Vaughan.

from *Speak, Memory*

Vladimir Nabokov (1899–1977)

Speak, Memory is a chronological assemblage made by Vladimir Nabokov of fifteen previously published reminiscences from his early childhood in St. Petersburg (the first memories come from 1903) until his departure from Europe with his wife and child for the United States in 1940—less than a year after the beginning of the Second World War. That historical period was a chaotic one, for the rise of Nazism in Germany had been preceded by a war between Russia and Japan, the disturbances within Russia before the Russian Revolution, and the establishment of the Communist regime with the concomitant confiscation of property and flight from Russia of a majority of those who so far had escaped assassination or prison for their opposition to that regime.

Nabokov's parents were wealthy; they owned a country estate, Vyra, in the environs of St. Petersburg as well as a spacious home in the city, and employed a staff of fifty servants for the operation of both places. The memories that relate to Vyra (and to neighboring estates belonging to his mother's family) are at once the most detailed and the most loving of all the reminiscences in the autobiography. Patrician though he was, Nabokov's father was a Liberal, a supporter of democratic principles—a member, "by choice," the son writes, of "the great classless intelligentsia of Russia." The father's mother-in-law—the author's grandmother—had difficulty understanding why her son-in-law, "who, she knew, thoroughly appreciated all the pleasures of great wealth, could jeopardize its enjoyment by becoming a Liberal, thus helping to bring on a revolution that would, in the long run, as she correctly saw, leave him a pauper." (In 1922, an exile in Berlin, he was assassinated by Russian fascists.)

Toward the end of chapter 8, Nabokov tells us that "the supreme achievement of memory . . . is the masterly use it makes of innate harmonies when gathering to its fold the suspended and wandering tonalities of the past." The opening chapter, which follows, certainly makes us aware of such "innate harmonies." Time here is seen as a prison—though an awareness of time is also shown to be essential to human consciousness, so essential that the author holds a sharp memory of his first knowledge of time, a knowledge that marks "the birth of sentient life" within him. In addition to demonstrating primordial behavior in himself as a child (the references to it, as well as to the theory of recapitulation, are not, I think, fanciful—or not wholly so), Nabokov stresses the "first thrills" that the child remembers, thrills belonging "to the harmonious world of a perfect childhood" that can be recalled effortlessly. The chapter also contains an extraordinary apostrophe to human consciousness and recollection. Its concluding episode is for me a triumph of both art and memory. It foreshadows the chaos and revolution to come, it emphasizes time and mortality and the "two eternities of darkness" that precede and follow our lives, while yet suggesting (is it to be accomplished by art or memory, or both?) that a beloved father can endure, beyond death.

The cradle rocks above an abyss, and common sense tells us that our existence is but a brief crack of light between two eternities of darkness. Although the two are identical twins, man, as a rule, views the prenatal abyss with more calm than the one he is heading for (at some forty-five hundred heartbeats an hour). I know, however, of a young chronophobiac who experienced something like panic when looking for the first time at homemade movies that had been taken a few weeks before his birth. He saw a world that was practically unchanged—the same house, the same people—and then realized that he did not exist there at all and that nobody mourned his absence. He caught a glimpse of his mother waving from an upstairs window, and that unfamiliar gesture disturbed him, as if it were some mysterious farewell. But what particularly frightened him was the sight of a brand-new baby carriage standing there on the porch, with the smug, encroaching air of a coffin; even that was empty, as if, in the reverse course of events, his very bones had disintegrated.

Such fancies are not foreign to young lives. Or, to put it otherwise, first and last things often tend to have an adolescent note—unless, possibly, they are directed by some venerable and rigid religion. Nature expects a full-grown man to accept the two black voids, fore and aft, as stolidly as he accepts the extraordinary visions in between. Imagination, the supreme delight of the immortal and the immature, should be limited. In order to enjoy life, we should not enjoy it too much.

I rebel against this state of affairs. I feel the urge to take my rebellion outside and picket nature. Over and over again, my mind has made colossal efforts to distinguish the faintest of personal glimmers in the impersonal darkness on both sides of my life. That this darkness is caused merely by the walls of time separating me and my bruised fists from the free world of timelessness is a belief I gladly share with the most gaudily painted savage. I have journeyed back in thought—with thought hopelessly tapering off as I went—to remote regions where I groped for some secret outlet only to discover that the prison of time is spherical and without exits. Short of suicide, I have tried everything. I have doffed my identity in order to pass for a conventional spook and steal into realms that existed before I was conceived. I have mentally endured the degrading company of Victorian lady novelists and retired colonels who remembered having, in former lives, been slave messengers on a Roman road or sages under the willows of Lhasa. I have ransacked my oldest dreams for keys and clues—and let me say at once that I reject completely the vulgar, shabby, fundamentally medieval world of Freud, with its crankish quest for sexual symbols (something like searching for Baconian acrostics in Shakespeare's works) and its bitter little embryos spying, from their natural nooks, upon the love life of their parents.

Initially, I was unaware that time, so boundless at first blush, was a prison. In probing my childhood (which is the next best to probing one's eternity) I see the awakening of consciousness as a series of spaced flashes, with the intervals between them gradually diminishing until bright blocks of perception are formed, affording memory a slippery hold. I had learned numbers and speech more or less simultaneously at a very early date, but the inner knowledge that I was I and that my parents were my parents seems to have been established only later, when it was directly associated with my discovering their age in relation to mine. Judging by the strong sunlight that, when I think of that revelation, immediately invades my memory with lobed sun flecks through overlapping patterns of greenery, the occasion may have been my mother's birthday, in late summer, in the country, and I had asked questions and had assessed the answers I received. All this is as it should be according to the theory of recapitulation; the beginning of reflexive consciousness in the brain of our remotest ancestor must surely have coincided with the dawning of the sense of time.

Thus, when the newly disclosed, fresh and trim formula of my own age, four, was confronted with the parental formulas, thirty-three, and twenty-seven, something happened to me. I was given a tremendously invigorating shock. As if subjected to a second baptism, on more divine lines than the Greek Catholic ducking undergone fifty months earlier by a howling, half-drowned, half-Victor (my mother, through the half-closed door, behind which an old custom bade parents retreat, managed to correct the bungling archpresbyter, Father Konstantin Vetvenitski), I felt myself plunged abruptly into a radiant and mobile medium that was none other than the pure element of time. One shared it—just as excited bathers share shining seawater—with creatures that were not oneself but that were joined to one by time's common flow, an environment quite different from the spatial world, which not only man but apes and butterflies can perceive. At that instant, I became acutely aware that the twenty-seven-year-old being, in soft white and pink, holding my left hand, was my mother, and that the thirty-three-year-old being, in hard white and gold, holding my right hand, was my father. Between them, as they evenly progressed, I strutted, and trotted, and strutted again, from sun fleck to sun fleck, along the middle of a path, which I easily identify today with an alley of ornamental oaklings in the park of our country estate, Vyra, in the former Province of St. Petersburg, Russia. Indeed, from my present ridge of remote, isolated, almost uninhabited time, I see my diminutive self as celebrating, on that August day 1903, the birth of sentient life. If my left-hand-holder and my right-hand-holder had both been present before in my vague infant world, they had been so under the mask of a tender incognito; but now my father's attire, the resplendent uniform of the Horse Guards, with that smooth golden swell of cuirass burning upon his chest and back, came out like the sun, and for several years afterward I remained keenly interested in the age of my parents and kept myself informed about it, like a nervous passenger asking the time in order to check a new watch.

My father, let it be noted, had served his term of military training long before I was born, so I suppose he had that day put on the trappings of his old regiment as a festive joke. To a joke, then, I owe my first gleam of complete consciousness—which again has recapitulatory implications, since the first creatures on earth to become aware of time were also the first creatures to smile.

2

It was the primordial cave (and not what Freudian mystics might suppose) that lay behind the games I played when I was four. A big cretonne-covered divan, white with black trefoils, in one of the drawing rooms at Vyra rises in my mind, like some massive product of a geological upheaval before the beginning of history. History begins (with the promise of fair Greece) not far from one end of this divan, where a large potted hydrangea shrub, with pale blue blossoms and some greenish ones, half conceals, in a corner of the room, the pedestal of a marble bust of Diana. On the wall against which the divan stands, another phase of history is marked by a gray engraving in an ebony frame—one of those Napoleonic-battle pictures in which the episodic and the allegoric are the real adversaries and where one sees, all grouped together on the same plane of vision, a wounded drummer, a dead horse, trophies, one soldier about to bayonet another, and the invulnerable emperor posing with his generals amid the frozen fray.

With the help of some grown-up person, who would use first both hands and then a powerful leg, the divan would be moved several inches away from the wall, so as to form a narrow passage which I would be further helped to roof snugly with the divan's bolsters and close up at the ends with a couple of its cushions. I then had the fantastic pleasure of creeping through that pitch-dark tunnel, where I lingered a little to listen to the singing in my ears—that lonesome vibration so familiar to small boys in dusty hiding places—and then, in a burst of delicious panic, on rapidly thudding hands and knees I would reach the tunnel's far end, push its cushion away, and be welcomed by a mesh of sunshine on the parquet under the canework of a Viennese chair and two gamesome flies settling by turns. A dreamier and more delicate sensation was provided by another cave game, when upon awakening in the early morning I made a tent of my bedclothes and let my imagination play in a thousand dim ways with shadowy snowslides of linen and with the faint light that seemed to penetrate my penumbral covert from some immense distance, where I fancied that strange, pale animals roamed in a landscape of lakes. The recollection of my crib, with its lateral nets of fluffy cotton cords, brings back, too, the pleasure of handling a certain beautiful, delightfully solid, garnet-dark crystal egg left over from some unremembered Easter; I used to chew a corner of the bedsheet until it was thoroughly soaked and then wrap the egg in it tightly, so as to admire and re-lick the warm, ruddy glitter of the snugly enveloped facets that came seeping through with a miraculous completeness of glow and color. But that was not yet the closest I got to feeding upon beauty.

How small the cosmos (a kangaroo's pouch would hold it), how paltry and puny in comparison to human consciousness, to a single individual recollection, and its expression in words! I may be inordinately fond of my earliest impressions, but then I have reason to be grateful to them. They led the way to a veritable Eden of visual and tactile sensations. One night, during a trip abroad, in the fall of 1903, I recall kneeling on my (flattish) pillow at the window of a sleeping car (probably on the long-extinct Mediterranean Train de Luxe, the one whose six cars had the lower part of their body painted in umber and the panels in cream) and seeing with an inexplicable pang, a handful of fabulous lights that beckoned to me from a distant hillside, and then slipped into a pocket of black velvet: diamonds that I later gave away to my characters to alleviate the burden of my wealth. I had probably managed to undo and push up the tight tooled blind at the head of my berth, and my heels were cold, but I still kept kneeling and peering. Nothing is sweeter or stranger than to ponder those first thrills. They belong to the harmonious world of a perfect childhood and, as such, possess a naturally plastic form in one's memory, which can be set down with hardly any effort; it is only starting with the recollections of one's adolescence that Mnemosyne begins to get choosy and crabbed. I would moreover submit that, in regard to the power of hoarding up impressions, Russian children of my generation passed through a period of genius, as if destiny were loyally trying what it could for them by giving them more than their share, in view of the cataclysm that was to remove completely the world they had known. Genius disappeared when everything had been stored, just as it does with those other, more specialized child prodigies—pretty, curly-headed youngsters waving batons or taming enormous pianos, who eventually turn into second-rate musicians with sad eyes and obscure ailments and something vaguely misshapen about their eunuchoid hindquarters. But even so, the individual mystery remains to tantalize the memoirist. Neither in environment nor in heredity can I find the exact instrument that fashioned me, the anonymous roller that pressed upon my life a certain intricate watermark whose unique design becomes visible when the lamp of art is made to shine through life's foolscap.

3

To fix correctly, in terms of time, some of my childhood recollections, I have to go by comets and eclipses, as historians do when they tackle the fragments of a saga. But in other cases there is no dearth of data. I see myself, for instance, clambering over wet black rocks at the seaside while Miss Norcott, a languid and melancholy governess, who thinks I am following her, strolls away along the curved beach with Sergey, my younger brother. I am wearing a toy bracelet. As I crawl over those rocks, I keep repeating, in a kind of zestful, copious, and deeply gratifying incantation, the English word "childhood," which sounds mysterious and new, and becomes stranger and stranger as it gets mixed up in my small, overstocked, hectic mind, with Robin Hood and Little Red Riding Hood, and the brown hoods of old hunch-backed fairies. There are dimples in the rocks, full of tepid seawater, and my magic muttering accompanies certain spells I am weaving over the tiny sapphire pools.

The place is of course Abbazia, on the Adriatic. The thing around my wrist, looking like a fancy napkin ring, made of semitranslucent, pale-green and pink, celluloidish stuff, is the fruit of a Christmas tree, which Onya, a pretty cousin, my coeval, gave me in St. Petersburg a few months before. I sentimentally treasured it until it developed dark streaks inside which I decided as in a dream were my hair cuttings which somehow had got into the shiny substance together with my tears during a dreadful visit to a hated hairdresser in nearby Fiume. On the same day, at a waterside café, my father happened to notice, just as we were being served, two Japanese officers at a table near us, and we immediately left—not without my hastily snatching a whole *bombe* of lemon sherbet, which I carried away secreted in my aching mouth. The year was 1904. I was five. Russia was fighting Japan. With hearty relish, the English illustrated weekly Miss Norcott subscribed to reproduced war pictures by Japanese artists that showed how the Russian locomotives—made singularly toylike by the Japanese pictorial style—would drown if our Army tried to lay rails across the treacherous ice of Lake Baikal.

But let me see. I had an even earlier association with that war. One afternoon at the beginning of the same year, in our St. Petersburg house, I was led down from the nursery into my father's study to say how-do-you-do to a friend of the family, General Kuropatkin. His thickset, uni-form-encased body creaking slightly, he spread out to amuse me a handful of matches, on the divan where he was sitting, placed ten of them end to end to make a horizontal line, and said, "This is the sea in calm weather." Then he tipped up each pair so as to turn the straight line into a zigzag—and that was "a stormy sea." He scrambled the matches and was about to do, I hoped, a better trick when we were interrupted. His aide-de-camp, was shown in and said something to him. With a Russian, flustered grunt, Kuropatkin heavily rose from his seat, the loose matches jumping up on the divan as his weight left it. That day, he had been ordered to assume supreme command of the Russian Army in the Far East.

This incident had a special sequel fifteen years later, when at a certain point of my father's flight from Bolshevik-held St. Petersburg to southern Russia he was accosted while crossing a bridge, by an old man who looked like a gray-bearded peasant in his sheepskin coat. He asked my father for a light. The next moment each recognized the other. I hope old Kuropatkin, in his rustic disguise, managed to evade Soviet imprisonment, but that is not the point. What pleases me is the evolution of the match theme: those magic ones he had shown me had been trifled with and mislaid, and his armies had also vanished, and everything had fallen through, like my toy trains that, in the winter of 1904–05, in Wiesbaden, I tried to run over the frozen puddles in the ground of the Hotel Oranien. The following of such thematic designs through one's life should be, I think, the true purpose of autobiography.

4

The close of Russia's disastrous campaign in the Far East was accompanied by furious internal disorders. Undaunted by them, my mother, with her three children, returned to St. Petersburg after almost a year of foreign resorts. This was in the beginning of 1905. State matters required the presence of my father in the capital; the Constitutionalist Democratic Party, of which he was one of the founders, was to win a majority of seats in the First Parliament the following year. During one of his short stays with us in the country that summer, he ascertained, with patriotic dismay, that my brother and I could read and write English but not Russian (except KAKAO and MAMA). It was decided that the village schoolmaster should come every afternoon to give us lessons and take us for walks.

With a sharp and merry blast from the whistle that was part of my first sailor suit, my childhood calls me back into that distant past to have me shake hands again with my delightful teacher. Vasiliy Martinovich Zhernosekov had a fuzzy brown beard, a balding head, and china-blue eyes, one of which bore a fascinating excrescence on the upper lid. The first day he came he brought a boxful of tremendously appetizing blocks with a different letter painted on each side; these cubes he would manipulate as if they were infinitely precious things, which for that matter, they were (besides forming splendid tunnels for toy trains). He revered my father who had recently rebuilt and modernized the village school. In old-fashioned token of free thought, he sported a flowing black tie carelessly knotted in a bowlike arrangement. When addressing me, a small boy, he used the plural of the second person—not in the stiff way servants did, and not as my mother would do in moments of intense tenderness, when my temperature had gone up or I had lost a tiny train-passenger (as if the singular were too thin to bear the load of her love), but with the polite plainness of one man speaking to another whom he does not know well enough to use "thou." A fiery revolutionary, he would gesture vehemently on our country rambles and speak of humanity and freedom and the badness of warfare and the sad (but interesting, I thought) necessity of blowing up tyrants, and sometimes he would produce the then popular pacifist book *Doloy Oruzhie!* (a translation of Bertha von Suttner's *Die Waffen Nieder!*), and treat me, a child of six, to tedious quotations; I tried to refute them: at that tender and bellicose age I spoke up for bloodshed in angry defense of my world of toy pistols and Arthurian knights. Under Lenin's regime, when all non-Communist radicals were ruthlessly persecuted, Zhernosekov was sent to a hard-labor camp, but managed to escape abroad, and died in Narva in 1939.

To him, in a way, I owe the ability to continue for another stretch along my private footpath which runs parallel to the road of that troubled decade. When, in July 1906, the Tsar unconstitutionally dissolved the Parliament, a number of its members, my father among them, held a rebellious session in Viborg and issued a manifesto that urged the people to resist the government. For this, more than a year and a half later they were imprisoned. My father spent a restful, if somewhat lonesome, three months in solitary confinement, with his books, his collapsible bathtub, and his copy of J. P. Muller's manual of home gymnastics. To the end of her days, my mother preserved the letters he managed to smuggle through to her—cheerful epistles written in pencil on toilet paper (these I have published in 1965, in the fourth issue of the Russian-language review *Vozdushnïe puti,* edited by Roman Grynberg in New York). We were in the country when he regained his liberty, and it was the village schoolmaster who directed the festivities and arranged the bunting (some of it frankly red) to greet my father on his way home from the railway station, under archivolts of fir needles and crowns of bluebottles, my father's favorite flower. We children had gone down to the village, and it is when I recall that particular day that I see with the utmost clarity the sunspangled river; the bridge, the dazzling tin of a can left by a fisherman on its wooden railing; the linden-treed hill with its rosy-red church and marble mausoleum where my mother's dead reposed; the dusty road to the village; the strip of short, pastel-green grass, with bald patches of sandy soil, between the road and the lilac bushes behind which walleyed, mossy log cabins stood in a rickety row; the stone building of the new schoolhouse near the wooden old one; and, as we swiftly drove by, the little black dog with very white teeth that dashed out from among the cottages at a terrific pace but in absolute silence, saving his voice for the brief outburst he would enjoy when his muted spurt would at last bring him close to the speeding carriage.

5

The old and the new, the liberal touch and the patriarchal one, fatal poverty and fatalistic wealth got fantastically interwoven in that strange first decade of our century. Several times during a summer it might happen that in the middle of luncheon, in the bright, many-windowed, walnut-paneled dining room on the first floor of our Vyra manor, Aleksey, the butler, with an unhappy expression on his face, would bend over and inform my father in a low voice (especially low if we had company) that a group of villagers wanted to see the *barin* outside. Briskly my father would remove his napkin from his lap and ask my mother to excuse him. One of the windows at the west end of the dining room gave upon a portion of the drive near the main entrance. One could see the top of the honeysuckle bushes opposite the porch. From that direction the courteous buzz of a peasant welcome would reach us as the invisible group greeted my invisible father. The ensuing parley, conducted in ordinary tones, would not be heard, as the windows underneath which it took place were closed to keep out the heat. It presumably had to do with a plea for his mediation in some local feud, or with some special subsidy, or with the permission to harvest some bit of our land or cut down a coveted clump of our trees. If, as usually happened, the request was at once granted, there would be again that buzz, and then, in token of gratitude, the good *barin* would be put through the national ordeal of being rocked and tossed up and securely caught by a score or so of strong arms.

In the dining room, my brother and I would be told to go on with our food. My mother, a tidbit between her finger and thumb, would glance under the table to see if her nervous and gruff dachshund was there. *"Un jour ils vont le laisser tomber,"* would come from Mlle Golay, a primly pessimistic old lady who had been my mother's governess and still dwelt with us (on awful terms with our own governesses). From my place at the table I would suddenly see through one of the west windows a marvelous case of levitation. There, for an instant, the figure of my father in his wind-rippled white summer suit would be displayed, gloriously sprawling in midair, his limbs in a curiously casual attitude, his handsome, imperturbable features turned to the sky. Thrice, to the mighty heave-ho of his invisible tossers, he would fly up in this fashion, and the second time he would go higher than the first and then there he would be, on his last and loftiest flight, reclining, as if for good, against the cobalt blue of the summer noon, like one of those paradisiac personages who comfortably soar, with such a wealth of folds in their garments, on the vaulted ceiling of a church while below, one by one, the wax tapers in mortal hands light up to make a swarm of minute flames in the midst of incense, and the priest chants of eternal repose, and funeral lilies conceal the face of whoever lies there, among the swimming lights, in the open coffin.

from *This Boy's Life*

Tobias Wolff (1945–)

Tobias Wolff's *This Boy's Life* is an account of the personal confusions and problems that occur to a young person whose nature is yet to be discovered; his later experiences provide the perspective necessary to illuminate that chaotic period of amorphous, or at least uncertain, identity. Given Wolff's childhood, one might predict he would end up alienated, and perhaps in prison. What connects the younger self to the established writer is primarily a vivid imagination that permits the child to be so gifted a liar that he can transform the transgressions of others as well as himself into manifestations of ideal behavior.

In *This Boy's Life*, memory is rarely referred to as the agency that imposes meaning upon the past; and yet it is everywhere at work, doing precisely that. As a consequence, we understand the child in all of his rebellions, all of his attempts to escape various traps. Never does Wolff look back upon his childhood as idyllic. Early on his parents were divorced, his father taking the older son and marrying a woman with considerable income, his mother taking Tobias—and subjecting both of them to brutal and insensitive men. To escape one lover, Roy, she and Tobias leave Florida for Utah, but Roy follows them there; ultimately, she and Tobias leave Utah for Seattle, where she finds Dwight, an even more disagreeable lover, who during courtship conceals his desire for mastery. Dwight is a mechanic at an electricity plant in a power company's hamlet in the Cascade Mountains. While Toby's mother is trying to decide whether or not to marry him, Dwight takes Toby to live with him and his three children by a previous marriage. Ultimately, Toby's mother joins them; the majority of the memoir concerns the sufferings undergone by mother and son in their bondage to the frequently sadistic, always threatening, Dwight. Surprisingly, this tale is not so grim as it sounds. Given the detachment provided by the years, Wolff can look at his younger self with considerable irony and humor; and the love—the affectionate understanding—between mother and son remains a constant throughout their struggles.

In the excerpt that follows, Toby is in Utah, with Roy and his mother; over Toby's mother's objections, Roy has given him a Winchester .22 rifle, an emblem of power (and of the ideal he has constructed for himself) for the otherwise powerless boy. In writing this scene, Wolff remembers his own later experiences in Vietnam; but his own responses also foreshadow those of Dwight, and help make the latter more explicable to us. In the second excerpt, Toby is living with Dwight and his mother; he shares a bedroom with his stepbrother Skipper. Skipper has left for Mexico; Toby misses him less than he does both his actual brother and father. Momentarily, the story moves into the future; Wolff has become a father himself and is seeing his baby for the first time. An inept nurse is jabbing the infant with a needle for a blood sample; protectively holding the child at last, Wolff says that "something hard broke in me, and I knew that I was more alive than I had been before." But the pain inflicted upon his baby carries an analogy of the pain inflicted upon him by his own father, enabling him to cast aside his idealization of that father. This moment of adult self-understanding, one brought by memory, marks the crucial change within him; it provides a necessary corrective to his various childhood illusions—those false idealizations that have shielded him from himself—and permits Wolff the perspective his memoir requires.

Just after Easter Roy gave me the Winchester .22 rifle I'd learned to shoot with. It was a light, pump-action, beautifully balanced piece with a walnut stock black from all its oilings. Roy had carried it when he was a boy and it was still as good as new. Better than new. The action was silky from long use, and the wood of a quality no longer to be found.

The gift did not come as a surprise. Roy was stingy, and slow to take a hint, but I'd put him under siege. I had my heart set on that rifle. A weapon was the first condition of self-sufficiency, and of being a real Westerner, and of all acceptable employment—trapping, riding herd, soldiering, law enforcement, and outlawry. I needed that rifle, for itself and for the way it completed me when I held it.

My mother said I couldn't have it. Absolutely not. Roy took the rifle back but promised me he'd bring her around. He could not imagine anyone refusing him anything and treated the refusals he did encounter as perverse and insincere. Normally mute, he became at these times a relentless whiner. He would follow my mother from room to room, emitting one ceaseless note of complaint that was pitched perfectly to jelly her nerves and bring her to a state where she would agree to anything to make it stop.

After a few days of this my mother caved in. She said I could have the rifle if, and only if, I promised never to take it out or even touch it except when she and Roy were with me. Okay, I said. Sure. Naturally. But even then she wasn't satisfied. She plain didn't like the fact of me owning a rifle. Roy said he had owned several rifles by the time he was my age, but this did not reassure her. She didn't think I could be trusted with it. Roy said now was the time to find out.

For a week or so I kept my promises. But now that the weather had turned warm Roy was usually off somewhere, and eventually, in the dead hours after school when I found myself alone in the apartment, I decided that there couldn't be any harm in taking the rifle out to clean it. Only to clean it, nothing more. I was sure it would be enough just to break it down, oil it, rub linseed into the stock, polish the octagonal barrel and then hold it up to the light to confirm the perfection of the bore. But it wasn't enough. From cleaning the rifle I went to marching around the apartment with it, and then to striking brave poses in front of the mirror.

Roy had saved one of his army uniforms and I sometimes dressed up in this, together with martial-looking articles of hunting gear: fur trooper's hat, camouflage coat, boots that reached nearly to my knees.

The camouflage coat made me feel like a sniper, and before long I began to act like one. I set up a nest on the couch by the front window. I drew the shades to darken the apartment, and took up my position. Nudging the shade aside with the rifle barrel, I followed people in my sights as they walked or drove along the street. At first I made shooting sounds—kyoo! kyoo! Then I started cocking the hammer and letting it snap down.

Roy stored his ammunition in a metal box he kept hidden in the closet. As with everything else hidden in the apartment, I knew exactly where to find it. There was a layer of loose .22 rounds on the bottom of the box under shells of bigger caliber, dropped there by the handful the way men drop pennies on their dressers at night. I took some and put them in a hiding place of my own. With these I started loading up the rifle. Hammer cocked, a round in the chamber, finger resting lightly on the trigger, I drew a bead on whoever walked by—women pushing strollers, children, garbage collectors laughing and calling to each other, any-one—and as they passed under my window I sometimes had to bite my lip to keep from laughing in the ecstasy of my power over them, and at their absurd and innocent belief that they were safe.

But over time the innocence I laughed at began to irritate me. It was a peculiar kind of irritation. I saw it years later in men I served with, and felt it myself, when unarmed Vietnamese civilians talked back to us while we were herding them around. Power can be enjoyed only when it is recognized and feared. Fearlessness in those without power is maddening to those who have it.

One afternoon I pulled the trigger. I had been aiming at two old people, a man a woman, who walked so slowly that by the time they turned the corner at the bottom of the hill my little store of self-control was exhausted. I had to shoot. I looked up and down the street. It was empty. Nothing moved but a pair of squirrels chasing each other back and forth on the telephone wires. I followed one in my sights. Finally it stopped for a moment and I fired. The squirrel dropped straight into the road. I pulled back into the shadows and waited for something to happen, sure that someone must have heard the shot or seen the squirrel fall. But the sound that was so loud to me probably seemed to our neighbors no more than the bang of a cupboard slammed shut. After a while I sneaked a glance into the street. The squirrel hadn't moved. It looked like a scarf someone had dropped.

When my mother got home from work I told her there was a dead squirrel in the street. Like me, she was an animal lover. She took a cellophane bag off a loaf of bread and we went outside and looked at the squirrel. "Poor little thing," she said. She stuck her hand in the wrapper and picked up the squirrel, then pulled the bag inside out away from her hand. We buried it behind our building under a cross made of popsicle sticks, and I blubbered the whole time.

I blubbered again in bed that night. At last I got out of bed and knelt down and did an imitation of somebody praying, and then I did an imitation of somebody receiving divine reassurance and inspiration. I stopped crying. I smiled to myself and forced a feeling of warmth into my chest. Then I climbed back in bed and looked up at the ceiling with a blissful expression until I went to sleep.

Skipper and I shared the smallest room in the house. We used the same desk, the same dresser, the same closet. A space of five or six feet separated our beds. But I never felt cramped in there until Skipper left for Mexico. Because he took up so much room when he was home, I could not forget that he was gone, and that led me to think about him and his friend Ray out on the road, free as birds. And those thoughts made me feel cheated and confined. I believed that Skipper should have taken me instead of Ray. I had asked first and, after all, I was his brother. This meant something to me but I saw that it meant nothing to him. I hadn't always gotten along with my own brother, and we hadn't even seen each other in four years, but I still missed him and began to imagine how much better he would treat me.

I also missed my father. My mother never complained to me about him, but sometimes Dwight would make sarcastic comments about Daddy Warbucks and Lord High-and-Mighty. He meant to impugn my father for being rich and living far away and having nothing to do with me, but all these qualities, even the last, perhaps especially the last, made my father fascinating. He had the advantage always enjoyed by the inconstant parent, of not being there to be found imperfect. I could see him as I wanted to see him. I could give him sterling qualities and imagine good reasons, even romantic reasons, why he had taken no interest, why he had never written to me, why he seemed to have forgotten I existed. I made excuses for him long after I should have known better. Then, when I did know better, I resolved to put the fact of his desertion from my mind. I visited him on my way to Vietnam, and then again when I got back, and we became friends. He was no monster—he'd had troubles of his own. Anyway, only crybabies groused about their parents.

This way of thinking worked pretty well until my first child was born. He came three weeks early, when I was away from home. The first time I saw him, in the hospital nursery, a nurse was trying to take a blood sample from him. She couldn't find a vein. She kept jabbing him, and every time the needle went in I felt it myself. My impatience made her so clumsy that another nurse had to take over. When I finally got my hands on him I felt as if I had snatched him from a pack of wolves, and as I held him something hard broke in me, and I knew that I was more alive than I had been before. But at the same time I felt a shadow, a coldness at the edges. It made me uneasy, so I ignored it. I didn't understand what it was until it came upon me again that night, so sharply I wanted to cry out. It was about my father, ten years dead by then. It was grief and rage, mostly rage, and for days I shook with it when I wasn't shaking with joy for my son, and for the new life I had been given.

But that was still to come. As a boy, I found no fault in my father. I made him out of dreams and memories. One of these memories was of sitting in the kitchen of my stepmother's beautiful old house in Connecticut, where I had come for a visit, and watching him unload a box full of fireworks onto the table. It was all heavy ordnance, seriously life threatening and illegal. My stepmother was scolding him. She wanted to know what he planned to do with them. He pushed a bunch of cherry bombs over to me and said, "Blow 'em up, dear, blow 'em up."

"Once More to the Lake"

E. B. White (1899–1985)

From Scott Elledge's fine biography about him, I learn that E. B. White's long affection for the Belgrade lakes in Maine began at the age of six, and that in his early eighties he bought a canoe to paddle on Belgrade's Great Pond with a friend. Each August during White's childhood and youth, his father brought his family to Great Pond; it was a locale in which White could find some relief from the hay fever that afflicted him.

"Once More to the Lake" is an essay about his return to that area years later, in the company of his own son. The essay contains examples of Proust's valued "involuntary memory," in which a present sensation instantaneously returns one to the past, making of it a timeless reality. ("Summertime, oh summertime," White apostrophizes to that season, in a comment about its timelessness—a feeling about summer that a child of course *does* have, and which as an adult he now recaptures through this return, "pattern of life indelible, the fadeproof lake, the woods unshatterable, the pasture with the sweetfern and the juniper forever and ever, summer without end.") Connected with that sense of eternality (created alike by the recurring cycles of the natural world and the images of memory) is the illusion that his son has become him, even as he has become his father—a response that perhaps the father of every son has experienced at one time or another, and which, however disorienting it is, has validity for the impersonal operations of nature, in which generations matter more than individuals.

During the week that White spends with his son at the lake, he occasionally is forced into awareness of differences between past and present; the intrusive sound of outboard motors, for example, "would sometimes break the illusion and set the years moving." The conclusion of the essay, in which the son puts on his cold and soggy swimming trunks to swim during a rain, emphasizes both the generational timelessness and White's sudden awareness of his own mortality: the ending is an inspired use of "the small things of the day" (White elsewhere uses that phrase as an indication of the material he could best write about) to suggest the dual truths of continuation and death underlying all our lives. ("Life lives on," says Lucretius, in a passage that I have long held in my memory. "It is the lives, the lives, the lives that die.")

One summer, along about 1904, my father rented a camp on a lake in Maine and took us all there for the month of August. We all got ringworm from some kittens and had to rub Pond's Extract on our arms and legs night and morning, and my father rolled over in a canoe with all his clothes on; but outside of that the vacation was a success and from then on none of us ever thought there was any place in the world like that lake in Maine. We returned summer after summer—always on August 1st for one month. I have since become a salt-water man, but sometimes in summer there are days when the restlessness of the tides and the fearful cold of the sea water and the incessant wind which blows across the afternoon and into the evening makes me wish for the placidity of a lake in the woods. A few weeks ago this feeling got so strong I bought myself a couple of bass hooks and a spinner and returned to the lake where we used to go, for a week's fishing and to revisit old haunts.

I took along my son, who had never had any fresh water up his nose and who had seen lily pads only from train windows. On the journey over to the lake I began to wonder what it would be like. I wondered how time would have marred this unique, this holy spot—the coves and streams, the hills that the sun set behind, the camps and the paths behind the camps. I was sure that the tarred road would have found it out and I wondered in what other ways it would be desolated. It is strange how much you can remember about places like that once you allow your mind to return into the grooves which lead back. You remember one thing, and that suddenly reminds you of another thing. I guess I remembered clearest of all the early mornings, when the lake was cool and motionless, remembered how the bedroom smelled of the lumber it was made of and of the wet woods whose scent entered through the screen. The partitions in the camp were thin and did not extend clear to the top of the rooms, and as I was always the first up I would dress softly so as not to wake the others, and sneak out into the sweet outdoors and start out in the canoe, keeping close along the shore in the long shadows of the pines. I remembered being very careful never to rub my paddle against the gunwale for fear of disturbing the stillness of the cathedral.

The lake had never been what you would call a wild lake. There were cottages sprinkled around the shores, and it was in farming country although the shores of the lake were quite heavily wooded. Some of the cottages were owned by nearby farmers, and you would live at the shore and eat your meals at the farmhouse. That's what our family did. But although it wasn't wild, it was a fairly large and undisturbed lake and there were places in it which, to a child at least, seemed infinitely remote and primeval.

I was right about the tar: it led to within half a mile of the shore. But when I got back there, with my boy, and we settled into a camp near a farmhouse and into the kind of summertime I had known, I could tell that it was going to be pretty much the same as it had been before—I knew it, lying in bed the first morning, smelling the bedroom, and hearing the boy sneak quietly out and go off along the shore in a boat. I began to sustain the illusion that he was I, and therefore, by simple transposition, that I was my father. This sensation persisted, kept cropping up all the time we were there. It was not an entirely new feeling, but in this setting

it grew much stronger. I seemed to be living a dual existence. I would
be in the middle of some simple act, I would be picking up a bait box
or laying down a table fork, or I would be saying something, and suddenly
it would be not I but my father who was saying the words or making the
gesture. It gave me a creepy sensation.

We went fishing the first morning. I felt the same damp moss covering
the worms in the bait can, and saw the dragonfly alight on the tip of my
rod as it hovered a few inches from the surface of the water. It was the
arrival of this fly that convinced me beyond any doubt that everything
was as it always had been, that the years were a mirage and there had
been no years. The small waves were the same, chucking the rowboat
under the chin as we fished at anchor, and the boat was the same boat,
the same color green and the ribs broken in the same places, and under
the floor-boards the same fresh-water leavings and debris—the dead hell-
grammite, the wisps of moss, the rusty discarded fishhook, the dried blood
from yesterday's catch. We stared silently at the tips of our rods, at the
dragonflies that came and went. I lowered the top of mine into the water,
tentatively, pensively dislodging the fly, which darted two feet away,
poised, darted two feet back, and came to rest again a little farther up the
rod. There had been no years between the ducking of this dragonfly and
the other one—the one that was part of memory. I looked at the boy,
who was silently watching his fly, and it was my hands that held his rod,
my eyes watching. I felt dizzy and didn't know which rod I was at the
end of.

We caught two bass, hauling them in briskly as though they were
mackerel, pulling them over the side of the boat in a business-like manner
without any landing net, and stunning them with a blow on the back of
the head. When we got back for a swim before lunch, the lake was exactly
where we had left it, the same number of inches from the dock, and
there was only the merest suggestion of a breeze. This seemed an utterly
enchanted sea, this lake you could leave to its own devices for a few hours
and come back to, and find that it had not stirred, this constant and
trustworthy body of water. In the shallows, the dark, water-soaked sticks
and twigs, smooth and old, were undulating in clusters on the bottom
against the clean ribbed sand, and the track of the mussel was plain. A
school of minnows swam by, each minnow with its small individual
shadow, doubling the attendance, so clear and sharp in the sunlight. Some
of the other campers were in swimming, along the shore, one of them
with a cake of soap, and the water felt thin and clear and unsubstantial.
Over the years there had been this person with the cake of soap, this
cultist, and here he was. There had been no years.

Up to the farmhouse to dinner through the teeming, dusty field, the
road under our sneakers was only a two-track road. The middle track was

missing, the one with the marks of the hooves and the splotches of dried, flaky manure. There had always been three tracks to choose from in choosing which track to walk in; now the choice was narrowed down to two. For a moment I missed terribly the middle alternative. But the way it lay there in the sun reassured me; the tape had loosened along the backline, the alleys were green with plantains and other weeds, and the net (installed in June and removed in September) sagged in the dry noon, and the whole place steamed with midday heat and hunger and emptiness. There was a choice of pie for dessert, and one was blueberry and one was apple, and the waitresses were the same country girls, there having been no passage of time, only the illusion of it as in a dropped curtain—the waitresses were still fifteen; their hair had been washed, that was the only difference—they had been to the movies and seen the pretty girls with the clean hair.

Summertime, oh summertime, pattern of life indelible, the fadeproof lake, the woods unshatterable, the pasture with the sweetfern and the juniper forever and ever, summer without end; this was the background, and the life along the shore was the design, the cottages with their innocent and tranquil design, their tiny docks with the flagpole and the American flag floating against the white clouds in the blue sky, the little paths over the roots of the trees leading from camp to camp and the paths leading back to the outhouses and the can of lime for sprinkling, and at the souvenir counters at the store the miniature birchbark canoes and the post cards that showed things looking a little better than they looked. This was the American family at play, escaping the city heat, wondering whether the newcomers in the camp at the head of the cover were "common" or "nice," wondering whether it was true that the people who drove up for Sunday dinner at the farmhouse were turned away because there wasn't enough chicken.

It seemed to me, as I kept remembering all this, that those times and those summers had been infinitely precious and worth saving. There had been jollity and peace and goodness. The arriving (at the beginning of August) had been so big a business in itself, at the railway station the farm wagon drawn up, the first smell of the pine-laden air, the first glimpse of the smiling farmer, and the great importance of the trunks and your father's enormous authority in such matters, and the feel of the wagon under you for the long ten-mile haul, and at the top of the last long hill catching the first view of the lake after eleven months of not seeing this cherished body of water. The shouts and cries of the other campers when they saw you, and the trunks to be unpacked, to give up their rich burden. (Arriving was less exciting nowadays, when you sneaked up in your car and parked it under a tree near the camp and took out the bags and in five minutes it was all over, no fuss, no loud wonderful fuss about trunks.)

Peace and goodness and jollity. The only thing that was wrong now, really, was the sound of the place, an unfamiliar nervous sound of the outboard motors. This was the note that jarred, the one thing that would sometimes break the illusion and set the years moving. In those other summertimes all motors were inboard; and when they were at a little distance, the noise they made was a sedative, an ingredient of summer sleep. They were one-cylinder and two-cylinder engines, and some were make-and-break and some were jump-spark, but they all made a sleepy sound across the lake. The one-lungers throbbed and fluttered, and the twin-cylinder ones purred and purred, and that was a quiet sound too. But now the campers all had outboards. In the daytime, in the hot mornings, these motors made a petulant, irritable sound; at night, in the still evening when the afterglow lit the water, they whined about one's ears like mosquitoes. My boy loved our rented outboard, and his great desire was to achieve singlehanded mastery over it, and authority, and he soon learned the trick of choking it a little (but not too much), and the adjustment of the needle valve. Watching him I would remember the things you could do with the old one-cylinder engine with the heavy flywheel, how you could have it eating out of your hand if you got really close to it spiritually. Motor boats in those days didn't have clutches, and you would make a landing by shutting off the motor at the proper time and coasting in with a dead rudder. But there was a way of reversing them, if you learned the trick, by cutting the switch and putting it on again exactly on the final dying revolution of the flywheel, so that it would kick back against compression and begin reversing. Approaching a dock in a strong following breeze, it was difficult to slow up sufficiently by the ordinary coasting method, and if a boy felt he had complete mastery over his motor, he was tempted to keep it running beyond its time and then reverse it a few feet from the dock. It took a cool nerve, because if you threw the switch a twentieth of a second too soon you would catch the flywheel when it still had speed enough to go up past center, and the boat would leap ahead, charging bull-fashion at the dock.

We had a good week at the camp. The bass were biting well and the sun shone endlessly, day after day. We would be tired at night and lie down in the accumulated heat of the little bedrooms after the long hot day and the breeze would stir almost imperceptibly outside and the smell of the swamp drift in through the rusty screens. Sleep would come easily and in the morning the red squirrel would be on the roof, tapping out his gay routine. I kept remembering everything, lying in bed in the mornings—the small steamboat that had a long rounded stern like the lip of a Ubangi, and how quietly she ran on the moonlight sails, when the older boys played their mandolins and the girls sang and we ate doughnuts dipped in sugar, and how sweet the music was on the water in the shining

347

night, and what it had felt like to think about girls then. After breakfast we would go up to the store and the things were in the same place—the minnows in a bottle, the plugs and spinners disarranged and pawed over by the youngsters from the boys' camp, the fig newtons and the Beeman's gum. Outside, the road was tarred and cars stood in front of the store. Inside, all was just as it had always been, except there was more Coca-Cola and not so much Moxie and root beer and birch beer and sarsaparilla. We would walk out with a bottle of pop apiece and sometimes the pop would backfire up our noses and hurt. We explored the streams, quietly, where the turtles slid off the sunny logs and dug their way into the soft bottom; and we lay on the town wharf and fed worms to the tame bass. Everywhere we went I had trouble making out which was I, the one walking at my side, the one walking in my pants.

One afternoon while we were there at that lake a thunderstorm came up. It was like the revival of an old melodrama that I had seen long ago with childish awe. The second-act climax of the drama of the electrical disturbance over a lake in America had not changed in any important respect. This was the big scene, still the big scene. The whole thing was so familiar, the first feeling of oppression and heat and a general air around camp of not wanting to go very far away. In midafternoon (it was all the same) a curious darkening of the sky, and a lull in everything that had made life tick; and then the way the boats suddenly swung the other way at their moorings with the coming of a breeze out of the new quarter, and the premonitory rumble. Then the kettle drums, then the snare, then the bass drum and cymbals, then crackling light against the dark, and the gods grinning and licking their chops in the hills. Afterward the calm, the rain steadily rustling in the calm lake, the return of light and hope and spirits, and the campers running out in joy and relief to go swimming in the rain, their bright cries perpetuating the deathless joke about how they were getting simply drenched, and the children screaming with delight at the new sensation of bathing in the rain, and the joke about getting drenched linking the generations in a strong indestructable chain. And the comedian who waded in carrying an umbrella.

When the others went swimming my son said he was going in too. He pulled his dripping trunks from the line where they had hung all through the shower, and wrung them out. Languidly, and with no thought of going in, I watched him, his hard little body, skinny and bare, saw him wince slightly as he pulled up around his vitals the small, soggy, icy garment. As he buckled the swollen belt suddenly my groin felt the chill of death.

"Peasant Marey"

Fyodor Dostoevsky (1821–1881)

"Peasant Marey" is considered a story—for example, it is included in a collection translated into English called *The Short Stories of Dostoevsky*. If it indeed *is* a story, it is one that came to Dostoevsky as a gift of his memory. It is not a "fiction," one made up of imaginary elements; and for me the knowledge that its matter comes from the author's personal experiences, as a child on his family's estate and later as a political prisoner in Siberia, gives this tribute to a peasant—and to the value of memory—a greater authenticity and conviction than fiction would allow. The prison scene (with the redemptive memory that saves Dostoevsky from what seems nearly absolute despair) is a remembrance from his four years of convict labor. Dostoevsky was condemned to death in 1849 for his political activities; as he was awaiting the bullets of the firing squad, a courier brought an order from the czar commuting his sentence to four years of hard labor to be followed by lifetime service as a common soldier in the army. (Upon the accession of Czar Alexander II, and after Dostoevsky had spent ten years in exile, he was permitted to return home.)

Dostoevsky was in his mid-fifties when he wrote "Peasant Marey." In this story in which one memory encloses another, we are given a striking example of how durable and influential a childhood experience can be—for a span of forty-six years separates Dostoevsky at the time of composition from the child.

George Gibian, a specialist in Russian literature at Cornell, not only recommended "Peasant Marey" for inclusion in this anthology but composed a new translation for it; in addition, he prepared some biographical data about Dostoevsky of use to me in writing this headnote. A portion of that data clarifies the opening paragraph of the story:

> "Peasant Marey" was published for the first time in the February 1876 issue of the journal *Diary of a Writer*, which Fyodor Dostoevsky wrote, edited, and published single-handedly, cover to cover. The story was preceded by Dostoevsky's lengthy editorial comments entitled "About Love for the People. The Essential Contract with the People." (In the story, he refers to this article in the first line as *profession de foi* [declaration of one's belief] and a little later as a "treatise.") His remarks had been called forth by the opinions expounded by his friend Constantine Aksakov, who, in an article entitled "About the Human Beings of Our Times," had written that the simple Russian people (*narod*), despite its coarseness and ignorance, was nevertheless "enlightened" and educated spiritually.

All these *professions de foi* are, I think, boring to read. So I will tell an anecdote, actually not even an anecdote—only a very old, distant recollection, which for some reason I very much want to tell, precisely here and now, in conclusion of our treatise about the people. I was only nine years old at the time. But no, I had better start with what happened when I was twenty nine years old.

It was the second day of Holy Week. There was warmth in the air, the sky was blue, the sun stood high, "warm," bright, but in my heart it was very gloomy. I was wandering around behind the barracks. I looked at and counted the posts of the prison's stockade fence, but I did not really feel like counting them, although it was my habit to do that. It was already the second day of "feasting" in the prison. The prisoners were not convoyed out to work, there were many drunks, there was swearing, fights were breaking out everywhere all the time. Ugly, disgusting songs were sung, card games and gambling were going on under the bunks. A few prisoners, beaten half dead by the prisoners' own court, for especially violent misdeeds, lay on the bunks, covered by sheepskin coats, till they would regain consciousness and wake up. Knives had been drawn several times. All this, after two days of Easter, upset me till I felt sick. I was never able to endure without disgust the people's drunken debauchery, and particularly not here, in this place. During those days, even the authorities did not search the prison and did not look for liquor, understanding that once a year even these outcasts must be allowed to kick up their heels, otherwise things would become even worse. Finally I flared up in anger. I happened to meet the Pole M——tski, one of the political prisoners. He looked at me somberly, his eyes darkened, and his lips trembled. He gritted his teeth, said in a low voice, *"Je haïs ces brigands!"*, and walked past me.

I went back into the barracks, despite the fact that fifteen minutes before I had run out of them like someone half demented when six healthy, strong peasants had thrown themselves, all at the same time, on the drunken Tartar Gazin, in order to quiet him down, and had beaten him up. They beat him horrendously, one could have killed a camel with blows like that. But they knew that it was hard to kill that Hercules, and so they beat him without pulling their punches. Now, when I returned, I noticed Gazin, unconscious, at the end of the barracks, on the bunk in the corner, giving no signs of life. He lay there covered by a sheepskin coat. Everybody was walking around him in silence. They were firmly hoping that the next day towards morning he would come to, "but from blows like that, one never knows, a man could even die." I made my way to my place across from the window with iron bars, and lay there, face down, put my hands behind my head, and closed my eyes. I liked to lie like that. People leave you alone when you are sleeping, and you can dream and think. But I was not able to dream. My heart beat restlessly. In my ears I heard M——tski's words, *"Je haïs ces brigands!"* Anyway, what is the point of describing my impressions. Even now I dream of that time, at night, and those are the most agonizing of all my dreams. Perhaps my readers have noticed that until today, I have not once spoken in print about my life in prison. I wrote "Notes from the House of the Dead" fifteen years ago as if narrated by a fictional character, a criminal who was supposed to have murdered his wife. As a matter of fact, I will add this detail, since that time many people think about me and even now assert that I was sent into exile for the murder of my wife.

Bit by bit, I really did sink into unconsciousness and gradually became submerged in reminiscences. In the entire four years of my imprisonment I recalled uninterruptedly my entire past. It seems that in my memories I lived again through all my previous life. These recollections came of themselves. I seldom called them forth because I wanted to myself. It began from some point, some trait, sometimes an unnoticeable one, and then little by little it grew into an entire picture, into some strong and whole impression. I would analyze those impressions, add new traits to what I had experienced a long time before, and, most important, I corrected it. I corrected it ceaselessly, that was what all my pleasure consisted of. This time suddenly an insignificant moment from my earliest childhood, when I was only ten years old, came into my memory. A moment, it would seem, which I had completely forgotten. But at that time I loved especially memories from my very earliest childhood. I recalled August in our village, a dry and clear day, but somewhat cold and windy. The summer was drawing to its close, and soon we would have to go to Moscow, to be bored again all winter doing French lessons, and I felt so sorry to leave the country that I went out past the barns, and down into the ravine. I walked up to Losk, that was what we called the thick shrubs between the other side of the ravine and the woods. I pushed further into the bushes and I heard, as though from nearby, thirty steps away, in a clearing, one of our peasants, who was ploughing. I knew he was ploughing on a steep slope, and his horse was walking with difficulty. From time to time his shouts reached me, "Nu, nu!" I knew almost all our peasants. But I did not know which of them it was who was ploughing there. It was all the same to me; I was all preoccupied with what I was doing. I was busy, too. I was breaking off a twig from a nut-tree with which to whip frogs. Whips out of nut-trees twigs are so beautiful and elastic, much more so than birch tree ones. I was also paying attention to bugs and beetles. I collected them; there are some very beautiful ones. I also liked small, nimble, reddish-yellow lizards, with black spots, but I was afraid of snakes. Actually one ran across snakes much less often than lizards. There were few mushrooms there. One must go in the birch woods to find mushrooms, and I was planning to go there. There was nothing in my life that I loved as much as the woods with their mushrooms and wild berries, with their little bugs and birds, porcupines, squirrels with their humid smell of rotting leaves, which I was especially fond of. And even now, as I am writing this, I can smell the birch woods in our countryside. These impressions remain with one all one's life.

Suddenly, in the middle of the deep silence, I heard clearly and distinctly the shout: "There is a wolf!" I cried out. Beside myself with fear, shouting out loud, I ran into the clearing, directly to a peasant who was ploughing there.

It was our peasant Marey. I don't know if such a name exists, but everybody called him Marey. He was a fifty year old, thick-set, strapping peasant, with a lot of grey in his brown, broad, thick beard. I knew him, but before then I had almost never entered into a conversation with him. When he heard my cry, he stopped his horse, and when I ran up and seized his plough with one hand and his sleeve with the other, he realized how frightened I was.

"There is a wolf!" I shouted, out of breath.

He lifted up his head and involuntarily looked around. For a moment he almost believed me.

"Where is the wolf?"

"Somebody shouted . . . somebody just now shouted, 'There is a wolf!'" I babbled.

"Come on, come on, what wolf! It just seemed to you like that. What kind of wolf would be here," he muttered, cheering me up. But I was shaking all over and held on to his coat even more firmly. I must have been very pale. He looked at me with a worried smile, evidently fearing for me and worrying.

"Oh so you got scared, oh my," he shook his head. "Enough, my boy. No, no, boykin."

He reached out and suddenly stroked my cheek: "Enough, now, Christ be with you, cross yourself."

But I did not cross myself. The corners of my lips trembled, and it seemed that this particularly struck him. He reached out with his thick finger, slowly, and touched my shaking lips very quietly with his black finger-nail soiled with the earth. "Now now, oh," he smiled at me with a kind of motherly, long smile, "oh lord, what is this all about, oh come on, now."

Finally I understood that there was no wolf, and that I had only imagined that someone had shouted "wolf." The shout had really been very clear and distinct, but I had imagined such shouts (and not only about wolves) once or twice previously, and I was aware of that. (Later, after I grew out of childhood, these hallucinations disappeared.)

"Well, I'll go now," I said, looking at him questioningly and timidly.

"You go, and I will watch you. I'm not going to let the wolf get you," he added, still smiling in the same motherly way. "So Christ be with you, go, go now." He made the sign of the cross over me with his hand and crossed himself too. I went, looking back almost every ten steps. Marey stood next to his horse and looked at me as long as I was walking away. He nodded to me every time I looked around. I felt a little ashamed before him, I must confess, for having been so frightened, but I walked on, still very afraid of the wolf, until I had walked up the slope of the ravine, to the first barn. There my fright dropped off altogether, and there our dog Volchok [Little Wolf] appeared, out of nowhere, and jumped up at me. In Volchok's company, I cheered up completely, and turned towards Marey for one last time. I could no longer make out his face clearly, but I felt that he was still smiling at me tenderly in exactly the same way as before and that he was nodding to me. I waved to him with my hand, he waved to me also, and moved his horse along.

"Well, well," I heard him shouting in the distance. His horse was again pulling the plough.

All this arose at once in my memory, I don't know why, but in astonishingly precise detail. I regained consciousness suddenly and sat up on the bunk. I remember there was still a quiet smile of remembrance on my face. I went on reminiscing for another minute.

When I came home after having met Marey, that time, I did not tell anyone about my "adventure." What kind of adventure had it been anyway? I even very quickly forgot about Marey. Later I met him seldom. I never even talked with him, about the wolf or about anything else either. Now suddenly, twenty years later, in Siberia, I recalled our meeting with such absolute clarity, down to the last detail. It means it had sunk down into my mind imperceptably, all by itself, without my wanting this. And suddenly this meeting was recalled when it was needed. That tender, motherly smile of a poor serf was recalled, and the peasant, his signs of the cross, his nods, his "Oh well, boy, how frightened you are." And especially his thick finger dirtied with earth, with which he quietly, timidly, tenderly touched my shaking lips. Of course anybody would have cheered up a small boy, but that time in this isolated meeting it was as if something quite different took place. If I had been his own son, he could not have given me a look shining with clearer love. Who was forcing him to do it? He was a peasant serf who belonged to us, and I was his young master. Nobody would know how he comforted me, and nobody would reward him for it. Did he love little children so much? There are people like that. Our meeting took place in isolation, in an empty field, perhaps only God saw from above the deep and enlightened human feeling and delicate, almost womanly tenderness which can fill the heart of a coarse, bestially ignorant Russian peasant serf. He was not expecting or guessing at that time that he would be freed . . . Tell me, was it not this that Constantine Aksakov understood when he spoke of the high education of our people?

And when I got off the bunk and looked around me, I remember that I suddenly felt that I could look at those unhappy people with an altogether different attitude and that suddenly, through some miracle, all hatred and anger had disappeared from my heart. I walked on and looked deep into the faces I encountered. This peasant, his head shaved, dishonored, his face branded, drunk, roaring out his drunken, sleazy song, perhaps he is that same Marey. I cannot see into his heart. That evening I met again M——tski, too. Unhappy man! He could not have any memories of any Mareys. He could have no opinion of these people other than *"Je hais ces brigands."* No, these Poles suffered more than we did!

"The Girls and Ghouls of Memory"

Paul West (1930–)

In my reading for this anthology, I have come across a number of autobiographical references to the hallucinatory monsters of childhood—one such reference is to be found in an essay by N. Scott Momaday that is included elsewhere. The majority of humans probably carry in their memories vivid images of the terrors that stalked them from their early years into adolescence. How do we account for such frightening visions?

A prolific novelist and verbal gymnast who walks a high wire that often seems invisible, Paul West long has been attracted to the gothic elaborations that haunt the dark recesses of the human mind. The imaginative elaborations that characterize his thinking and hence his style make him an ideal writer to explore the significance of our private demons, the task he undertakes in "The Girls and Ghouls of Memory."

As might be expected, West gives far more emphasis to the ghouls of his title than to the girls. The ghouls include monsters of various sorts and sizes, from Areemayhew (a mental image that terrorized him as a child) through the gargoyles of European cathedrals (his descriptive listing of them, only a portion of which I have included here, indicates a loving obsession) to the figures in the paintings of the twentieth-century artist Francis Bacon. Playful though it often is, "The Girls and Ghouls of Memory" uses reminiscence to explore troubling issues with a long human history. West begins his discussion of mental monsters with the description of his youthful response to such a commonplace event as a childhood friend's need to wear glasses. That response—a "release of pent-up morbidity"—the adult author perceives as a consequence of "some excessive regard for natural beauty, or at least for God-given orthodoxy" that he felt in his pubescent years, causing him to react to "myths of mutilation" with a fascinated terror. In other words, beauty and ugliness constitute an antithesis in which the first term is a natural ideal or religious absolute; the second represents an awesome falling away from a desired perfection. (Like many other adolescents confused by their new yearnings, West conferred an ideal beauty upon adolescents of the other sex, the girls of his title.) Given that antithesis, which at least in part is socially sanctioned, we can understand the reason that actual facial disfigurements (at one end of the scale, a friend's glasses; at the other, his father's "unseeing left eye") can contribute to the spawning of Areemayhew, the monster within.

Rather than attempting to exorcize his demons, the older West accepts them as part of what humans are. One cannot separate beauty from those demons: "Beauty is," he remarks, "the cutting edge of terror." In fact, gargoyles, those constructions of illiterate medieval craftsmen, engross him as they do because they represent the upwelling of "the forces in us which make us frightened of ourselves." Hallucinatory creative works of the present as well as the past serve both as "metaphysical protest" against all the horrors imposed upon us (by disease-bearing bacteria, for example) and as a reminder of the hidden half of our divided natures. Indeed, we must be grateful "to those great creative invalids whose madness—in print, stone, paint, music, dance—forestalls and partly precludes our own."

Girls return at the essay's end, West's adolescent response to them adjusted to later insight. I end my own comment with a biographical fact that fits the bizarre mix of animal and human in the images described in this memoir: in 1987, West was named a Literary Lion by the New York Public Library.

Being fourteen corresponds to the role of the movie extra, secreted within the thorax of a fake triceratops which threshes about in automatic combat with yet another triceratops within whose thorax yet another extra earns the same pittance. The dumb alias promotes, but, watching the film of such a primeval encounter, the youth within may well feel failed: the death agony of the loser is colossal; the brute strut of the victor imbecilically huge; the blood, rich devil's-lava; the soundtrack, daunting feral thunder. Yet, one youth's tummy aches, the other's head. The mastodon masquerade cannot last for ever, or even for long. The bravura shrivels and the knowhow dies a natural death even as it impresses. At least, that was how I myself felt at such an age, when I fell short of heroic impostures expected of me, wishing I were instead an opossum. Bravely enough, no doubt, I tried to pass muster with bats and balls and the gear of other rigmaroles whose ancient honor ruled me along with millions; but dealing with girls was a surd altogether beyond me, calling for a masterful agility I never had and do not even pretend to now. I made the attempt, though, imperfectly rehearsed animal that I was, and just hoped against hope that *Homo sapiens* had been designed both first and last for books, airplanes, and chemistry experiments restricted to flasks, pipettes, and Bunsen burners. As I probe, the maladroitness of those wincing years stays put, at a convenient distance, does not come through entire. Something in me shrinks still from what I could not do, or, doing, did ditheringly wrong. Rose-cheeked Sylvia F., with whom I lay innocently in the deep spear grass during one clement English August, snaps out of view because a red ball has clicked against a fudge-brown bat. The delicate and hypnotic birthmark which, aslant her cheekbone, gave Betty G.'s green eyes a starry, catechistic elongation, vanishes into the pall under a bomber's cambered trunk. The double ping of the thumb-bell on June A.'s bicycle (which triggered off aortal tinnitus in me) drowns itself in drab black gunpowder on a round filter paper, no competition for sulfur, saltpeter, manganese dioxide, and potassium chloride (this last the stuff that made the bang).

Banned by pastimes I found vocational, these and other girls mix a fata morgana in my head, even now: lovely periphrases that call up Latin fairies and fates, Arabian coral (*margan*) and Greek pearl (*margarites*). The intense brooding I did on them in my tender years pays off now, fleshed as a heat-trembling frieze of tireless eidolons whose expression, a joint constant between winsome huff and roguish pout, eggs me on to make up for time not so much wasted as stilled. I was unspeakably slow in the accost, though with palpitating heart I did in the long run establish a regular movie date with Sylvia F., in ninepenny seats on the apocalyptic back row of the Rex cinema; go to Betty G.'s house on her birthday with, as gift, a record of Bob Crosby's Bobcats' raucous version of "The South Rampart Street Parade," which she detested on first hearing; and hold June A.'s magic bicycle for ten minutes while she entered the chemist's shop (in search of gruesome stuffs I pruriently thought a goddess should not need); we talked in blanks until she flashed off with a downthrust of her lissom thigh. They are all three still flashing away from me a quarter of a century later, seachanged into varicose viragoes (I guess), awaiting the first hot flash. Not that it matters: I long ago projected their hesitant elegance, if such it were, on to Keats's Grecian urn, that *ronde* of paradisal halts, and they abide at the ready, primed for an attention that has not come until this very moment.

Squeezing memory until it yields or snaps, I should be able to particularize these girls through talks or outings, but little or nothing sounds, recurs. With their physical immediacy unimpaired—Sylvia F.'s flushed calves (sign of poor circulation, doubtless), Betty G.'s small-stepped chopping gait, June A.'s habit of tossing her head back as if she had long instead of cropped hair—they nonetheless remain incomplete, have been definitely extruded thus by a memory that usually behaves much better. All three are silent, with no captions evincing their minds' movements, and I wonder if, here of all places, I have not a sample of what I remember only too well: an adolescence without conversation, when the answer to the throwaway question, *What's new?*, was always an unsaid, *Only what's ephemeral,* with no one half as eager as I to chat about such unfashionable "dry" things as Kinglake's *Eothen,* Maupassant's tales, Eliot's poems, compulsory reading that had switched on big searchlights to my moth of mind. Of course, my teachers, who after I reached fifteen were all women (because no self-respecting male taught arts or humanities), responded as best they could, and a brilliant, unstinting response it was, edged with repartee and spiced with an occasional cigarette in the teachers' common room. They were just too busy, teaching seven hours a day, to hear out the verbose importunities of their only male pupil (for, by the same token as the male teachers went, no self-respecting boy specialized in anything but sciences). Out on a limb of grimy *finesse,* while my peers hacked away at the trunk of the tree of knowledge, I developed a peculiar and incurable sense that the arts, literature, even philosophy, were disreputable distaff pursuits and that I was a nascent freak.

From that period, I recall only one conversation, keenly morbid on my part, with a boy named Gerald Roberts, who informed me that he was going to have to wear glasses. At once he became an object of endless conjecture, for all the world as if (to lard an anachronistic analogy into my recall) he were due for a heart transplant. His future looked invincibly prosthetic, deliciously marred; one of the limping wounded, he might soon be dead or at least insane, and with shuddering relish I envisioned myself likewise bespectacled—walled in by glass aureoles in ogive ribs tricked out with golden wires like a crudely repaired mannequin—and deemed it a fate worse than death. Obsessively, I questioned him about the testing he had undergone: the optician's card that shrank from bold-face roman capitals to quivering minuscules; the scalding eyedrops (which reminded me of the potion—quinine and phosphoric acid—fed into me for a month, a year or so previously, for my incessant nervous blinking); the selection of the frames and the tiny catafalque that held them safe. Did looking through the lenses hurt? Were the glasses heavy on the nose? Did he feel that people could less easily peer into his eyes and read his thoughts? Did he feel shielded? Unwittingly, Gerald Roberts, myopic rabbit to my Frankenstein appetite, had given a face and a name to an unthinkable abomination; it was like being affable with the condemned man while the hangman pinioned his wrists above the drop.

I still back away from the release of pent-up morbidity that boy set off. I must have been inordinately terrified by myths of mutilation, grounded no doubt in some excessive regard for natural beauty, or at least for God-given orthodoxy (a kind of Christian Science esthetics), and fomented by Saturday afternoon movie matinees in which, from behind a screen of ribbed protoplasm, The Clutching Hand came flexing out, sheathed in an eerie surgical mitten tipped with two cones of horn, on behalf of an owner—The Phantom of the C. H.—whose ruined face one never saw for a sort of sinus mask, with a cord trailing down. The Phantom of my callow psychodramas not only had an acid-eaten face and a rat-infested lair in the sewers; he had first twitched to composite life strapped to the operating table of Dr. Frankenstein-Jekyll-Moreau, who not only harnessed the lightning but rendered the final monster both vampiric and lupine, hunchbacked and intermittently invisible, Cyclopean and dragonish: in brief, a ghastly dysgenic collage which, at home, sent its carmine, serrated maw after me as I ran up the cellar steps with a jug of milk, and out and about waited for me in alleyways, trashcans, and derelict air-raid shelters with a live bat between its teeth.

A version of this *thing* still dogs me at the moment of falling asleep and even during the day whenever I allow my eyes to blur focus and so free the retinas for spontaneously generated ogres of a mind disjoint. Just as easily, innocuous images arise, free-floated from a cerebral marina which, if cut, would gleam softly like sodium: a pair of silent dogs, a setter and an Airedale, on a dim, brittle autumn afternoon, trotting through leaves in a steep woodland, like two itinerant seniors paroled from some canine mountain clinic; or a brain-damaged boy who whoops fiercely as he whirls through the air inside a tire roped to an overhanging bough that just must not break; or stratocumulus at sunset, when low water clouds of dark Indian red hem in what resembles a levitant ram of weathered chalcedony. These images I welcome unreservedly, uncaring what they mean. Observe, reader, how I have just flinched from setting down the features of my private demon, whom I long ago began to call Areemayhew, a verbal ricochet from my first years of speech when, I think, the word or phrase stood for something I soon learned not to mispronounce. Yet those four syllables lingered on, a gross quotient, a husk of lugubrious phonemes, reserved for the troll of my mind's eye, seen like this: enormous-pored tanned skin with white pig bristles jutting high from ruptured follicles; pupil-less lavender-blue irises in unlidded purulent whites flecked with blood like certain yolks; teeth the hue of wet straw and abominably rotten, like one of those mock-ups that dentists site within view of the chair. The entire head is wet (the white hair looks like dulled magnesium ribbon), whether with perspiration or rain I have no idea: it could be that of some dead and long-exposed forest ranger, or some Amerindian-Nordic feat of miscegenation. Less certainly, for I never have more than glimpses of certain other features, I think the nose is aquiline, the nostrils are capacious. Of ears, eyebrows, I see nothing, but the neck looks unhandsomely weathered.

Thus Areemayhew, whose manifestations forbode nothing, whose face corresponds to that of no human I remember, though it evokes hundreds. I have occasionally willed him to appear, and up he has lurched like a herald of plague or bloodcurdling delirium. The cremation of my father, in his seventy-fifth year, has come and gone, but it is not my father's face, although I suppose it could be read as an augury of that event, and certainly functions now as a vestige. In any event, before he went to sleep never again to wake, my father told my mother he had "just had a wonderful day, a marvelous day," and I cannot square that beautiful closing asseveration with my inscape's ghoul, to whom I attribute no consciousness at all. Areemayhew, warning of who knows what, replica of none, symbol of naught, I prefer to regard as the product of such a process as the block portrait which reduces the face of George Washington, or the Mona Lisa, to six hundred twenty-five squares, thus eliminating details that one may partially restore by viewing from twelve feet away, or making one's head tremble, or jiggling the picture, or by squinting just a little. I am more than willing to pigeonhole Areemayhew as what Thomas De Quincey called an involute, a compound experience incapable of being disentangled or forgotten, a perdurable enigma raised to exponential maximum, and all the more intimidating for being the face of *someone*. So far, it (I hover between *he* and *it*) has not literally petrified me or changed me into a salt monolith, dolmen, or menhir. If it is not Vincent van Gogh, seen by the light of an oil lamp, it must be a dead prospector in the Sierra Madre (Walter Huston, perhaps), with both of whom I have inchoate affinities. "He that fears leaves," runs one of Mallarmé's thousand *English Sentences to Learn By Heart*, "must not come into the wood"; but I was born therein; there is nothing to be done. Priggishly addicted to orthodox beauty, I subconsciously prepared for an appalling letdown by fixating on variants all the way from poor four-eyed Gerald Roberts to the long-armed, gloating Nosferatu of Max Schreck. I dolefully resented my mother's having to wear glasses: they made her more distant, more of a wire-and-plastic construct; I hated the spring-driven clop of her spectacle-case, and even the clammy fluff of the cleaning-pad beneath its lip.

Anyone diagnosing in this child a severe case of precocious perfectionism, a hyperesthesia beginning with an eye-maimed father created by an exploding shell in 1917, will have a point. Saved from a certain amount of shrapnel by the blood-soaked corpse of a man later identified as one Corporal Blood, my father no doubt instilled in me, through the hour-long war stories I foolishly never wrote down, a sense of the violence that can be done to man's flimsy symmetry. Apt pupil that I was, I held his dry, well-manicured hand, and tried to look into his unseeing left eye, where the wound's tiny white scar twirled in the dead iris like a worm.

Less dismal folk than I, or he, have invented much more horrible figures than Areemayhew. Medieval craftsmen, who could not read and had received no training except as apprentices in a stoneyard, fancied unconstrainedly in face of the incomprehensible, coming up with gargoyles that evince the forces in us which make us frightened of ourselves. That is why we have, and accept, these eidetic waterspouts, as if enacting century after century a line that Hermione utters in *The Winter's Tale:* "The bug that you would fright me with, I seek." Awesome phenomena of Nature personified, they originally took the form of dragons with live animals in their mouths (foxes, pigs, rabbits) or, as in the *papoire* of Amiens, a man inside a wicker effigy, operating monstrous jaws, or, as in the spiked and spine-serrated Tarasque of Tarascon, several men, who shot out fireworks. Such prototypes belong among ceremonies of blatant license, when sausages and dice rolled on high altars, priests wore grotesque masks, the laity dressed themselves as monks and nuns, asses came into church, and the congregation brayed. Amid such good humor (part of it, but not quite), folk burned cocks and hanged pigs, stretched all kinds of animals on the rack in order to read "confessions" in their cries. It was some eschatological levity that relished such an assortment as Virgil Tied-Up in a Basket, monsters under the mineral feet of depicted saints and bishops, both the presentation of dead souls as nudes (nudity being seldom used for other purposes) and of the damned as head-bellied, head-breasted, pelvic-winged, toad-vomiting epileptics. In those days, piety eructated, vice was a bit of a wag; beasts of the field knew right from wrong, and honest men sanctified their own dung. Since then, I think, we have become unjustifiedly simpler.

One's notion of gargoyles, at any rate, is almost always too strict. There are leaden and wooden ones as well as those of stone, symbolical ones and not. Some are not in the least bestial or even sarcastic. There are as many monks, nuns, pilgrims with staffs and wild men as there are animals and birds. According to Mrs. Jameson, they have their origins in prehistoric Silurian remains dug up in the Middle Ages, whereas others have discovered in them Isaiah 13:8, in which the sucking child plays on the hole of the asp and the weaned child sets his hand on the adder's lair, with equal safety; in Psalm 21's "mischievous device" and Psalm 22's gaping mouths and "I am poured out like water"; and in the bestiary of the constellations. Emile Male declares them of no symbolic force whatever, but of homely, spontaneous birth in the imaginations of housewives listening to primitive tales during the long winter watches. But, of course, there have been many who claim a church's every stone has a meaning and that gargoyles represent devils conquered by Light and enslaved for menial chores. Or they derive from processional animals or from those griffons of the East which, in ancient lore, stood guard over treasure. Call them what we will—all the way from those choked by molten lead from roofs in two world wars to the stunned cherub, Charles Laughton, among the "night-mares" on the towers of Notre Dame de Paris—they upset, provoke, fortify, and unquestionably display the dark (or dark-daft) side of man's presumed unconquerable mind. Even the drolleries on the misericordes do this, as much in the age of Dachau as in the Middle Ages. All very well for the Aristotles, Horaces, and Doctor Johnsons to inveigh with suety worthiness against freakish phantasmata: there is another view, less exclusive and more historical, which remembers how beauty is the cutting edge of terror, that art invites us to entertain childish responses we fight even as we indulge them, and that much of our gratitude goes to those great creative invalids whose madness—in print, stone, paint, music, dance—forestalls and partly precludes our own. After werewolves come Roger Bacon's talking head, *Titus Andronicus,* Walpole's *The Castle of Otranto,* Jack the Ripper, Bram Stoker's *Dracula,* Dr. Caligari, expressionists of all kinds of mutilatory persuasions, P. T. Barnum's Feejee Mermaid (a hoax monster, shriveled, a yard long, with hideous teeth and a fish body sewn to the head and hands of a monkey), and the yawning or screaming disemboweled (although also partly disembodied) figures of Francis Bacon the painter, who was never without a textbook entitled *Positioning in Radiography.* Our monsters will not save us, of course, but they tell us what in part we are, suffering on our behalf, turning night into day instead of the other way round. Adding enigmas, horrors, freaks, of our own making, to those inflicted upon us by the universe, we remedy nothing; but, in fighting back no matter how impotently, in rehearsing time and again this metaphysical protest, we deepen our sense of hubris. Or so I believe, being of the chimerical persuasion since a few years old. Only recently, I pasted a mask over the face of John F. Kennedy in my reproduction of Robert Rauschenberg's collage, *Buffalo II,* troubled by the cliché status of that face, which Rauschenberg put in before the assassination. The horror resides in the mask now, as in that overexposed face it no longer could. . . .

Among terms coined by military men as part of idiomatic anaesthesia, "god-botherer" for chaplain makes better sense than most. They reasonably (for them) suppose that one ought not to pretend one can pester inaccessible divinities; better by far to look after the men's welfare and provide the apprehensively dying with any kind of placebo. God-botherers bother everybody but God. I can see, now, how I might have become one, informally, by extending cosmic disappointment into divine accost, or rhetoric into putative influence, even to the point of saying to the First (or Subsequent) Cause, as if to a literary or a tennis acquaintance: "Do not so readily assume that whatever friendship there was between us has survived your recent crass behavior." Spurning such egregious mouthfuls, I know only what the gargoyles know, in all their miscellaneous stuntedness. Half-inclined to side with them (and Areemayhew) against all variants of heroism, all marriage-minded teenage girls (whether beautiful in hindsight or not), and all bacteria (given a job to do, they do it), I find myself doting on something lovely in the grotesque, whatever its forms: gargoyle, gurning, Halloween, the two Lon Chaneys mugging with violent humility, Max Ernst's railway compartment in *Une Semaine de Bonté,* in which ravaged-looking traveler looks away from both the bare-legged corpse on the floor and the great, spiny, glaring, overanimate Sphinx at the window. Beyond the straitened face of the norm there ripple the endlessly mobile features of initiative: Clio with an expressive set of masks.

Sylvia F. disappeared into a sanatorium, struck down by *Mycobacterium tuberculosis,* and for a month or two I walked about the village and the school inhaling mighty cliff-top breaths to quell whatever had been puffed across; I did not plan to die of any such thing, not with a chemistry set which, properly exploited, held the cure for every ill, although exactly how the Gershwin purple of potassium permanganate crystals would merge with the green ferrous sulfate and dusty pumice-gray lumps (strontium nitrate) that glowed in the dark, to make a panacea, I was unsure. To the purple salt that dyed, disinfected and deodorized, I added the green one that was both pigment, fertilizer, feed additive, and water-purifier, fervently willing that the addition of my third chemical (a mildly radioactive lava, after all) would transform the mixture from something that brought the color back into those cheeks and calves, massacred her minor germs, enhanced her aroma, made her at one stroke pregnant, voracious, and pure-watered, into something that necromantically besotted her with the young alchemist who pined, lovesick, over crucibles of acid burbling mud. All that remained, I thought, was to pass a current through the mixture, then send her a registered packet that held the precipitate: send it anonymously, "From an ardent admirer in the laboratory," labeled, with complacent pith, in unreadable "doctor"'s hand, "To be taken once only, before retiring." I never sent it, of course, part of my problem being the slapdash, generous mode of my chemistry and my word-builder's rather than scientist's attitude to formulas. I can recall one travesty, which went as follows: aluminum sulfate, plus tannic acid, plus ferrous oxide, or $Al_2 (SO_4)_3 + C_{76} H_{52} O_{46} + FeO$, which astonishingly yielded not a compound but a phrase: A FOOlS eCHO 3. Thus, even at thirteen and fourteen, I made puzzles of a low order out of Creation's building blocks, even as, a quarter of a century later, I find myself, sometimes whimsically, sometimes with an almost scientific impulsion, appropriating for my own fictional purposes the cosmic bizarreries called quasars, red shifts, and black holes. Sylvia F. declined in an unheated hospital full of scarlet blankets and inhaled an air cold enough to make her eyes pour.

Failing her recovery, through the ministrations of experts (I having withdrawn mine at the last moment in order to concentrate on the creation of a pyrotechnical device I might sum up as a radioactive roman candle), I would accompany June A. into the chemist's and there purchase, by the gross, provender of inhuman masculinity, so as to make things clear once and for all—and whoever wanted to could steal her unattended bicycle. As it happened, June A. disappeared too, into a domestic science college a hundred miles away, there to become proficient in meringues, Yorkshire pudding, and Scotch eggs: hardly a science, it was domestic enough to be learned at home. Exit June A., then, blithely pretentious, doomed to reappear in an ostentatiously colored college scarf, which she would flaunt around the village as if just down from Girton College, Cambridge. But, through some compensatory miracle, Betty G. became one of my mother's piano pupils at a shilling a lesson. With cramped-feeling chest, I watched her arrive each week at the front door, unseeably from my third-story window, then listened with almost servile approval to her scales and elementary pieces. When my mother rebuked her for some malfingered chord (which was not often), I froze, marveling how Mildred West, graduate of London's Royal Academy of Music, could be so undiscerning and cantankerous. At my boldest, I interrupted with a cup of tea my mother frowned at, needing none, while I blushed and redundantly hovered to catch Betty G.'s inflammatory eye, promising myself (oh, furtive voluptuary!) to nose the aroma of the padded throne she sat on before the next ivory-hammerer arrived. And it is with that vibrant nasal afterglow of hay, warm rubber, and silky asafoetida that she begins to go out of my life, a blissful damosel whose acorn-mind already knew how many infants she would have, what hue curtains in each of her house's rooms, which type of calendar (agricultural rather than Foreign Views) she wanted on the walls. In the year I went away, she won a gold medal in the Advanced Grade of the Royal College/Royal Academy examinations, a feat which gave my mother a long sustained smile like a twenty-four-hour bloom. But Betty G. did not like Bob Crosby's band, or being too near the sea or me, and I was happy to go away to fresh impostures.

Beauties in those days were like dandelion clocks: one blew their fluff away, muttering extinct formulas. Monsters became the most intimate companions of all: oneself at one's worst, in inspissated extremes, and Areemayhew gradually came into his own. As for the silence, it was like that before and after gigantic blasts of the Boston Light Ship's foghorn, a steam-drive diaphone that shatters downtown glass. At seventeen I found people to talk with: too many, in fact, for the good of my freshman studies. Out came the squashed-down romanticism. Minor exhibits on my chamber of horrors degenerated into the trivial: dancing, Christmas carols, schoolgirls with imitation engagement rings; puppy-love letters endorsed BOLTOP (meaning, of course, "Better on lips than on paper") or SWALK ("Signed with a loving kiss"); virility cults; the albino verse of P. B. Shelley; English damp, English coins, English fun. After six months of untidy bull sessions over coffee, beer, and cider, I realized that much of adolescence had dropped beyond recall, while its polarities—jussive abstractions of painful ecstasy and ravishing ugliness—stayed put, indispensable as systole and diastole.

Fatally afflicted with urbanity, I reckoned my very heartbeat allegorical and told myself that, at least until head grafts, things would stay this way. Extremes, not streams, of consciousness I envisioned as I ploughed into *Beowulf*, the poem with the Great Divide down its middle. All those half-lines evoked half-lives, contrapuntal opposites, Pisces (which folk jubilantly told me I was) swimming in two directions at once, purgatorial igloos whose under-halves accommodate no one at all. I was so glad to lift head above the pubertal compost that I almost forgot to strike up conversations with the nervous, industrious scholarship girls, whose mitigated simpers came straight out of Jane Austen's novels and their brains from the mint of heaven itself. Unbeautiful they may have been: box-jawed, myopic, mat-haired, stone-gaited, and nailbiters all, they nonetheless gave the morbid me a glimpse of self's yellowish rough diamond, just a touch lustrous in its blue kimberlite matrix.

from *A Walker in the City*

Alfred Kazin (1915–)

At various points in his life's journey, Alfred Kazin has stopped to assess in words the segment that now lies behind him. *A Walker in the City,* the first in his autobiographical series, takes him from his early childhood through his high school years in Brownsville, a New York Jewish ghetto inhabited by immigrants and their children. Readers of all sorts have a particular affection for this account, for in the sensuosity of its imagery as well as in its musical repetition of phrases—dual components of its lyricism—it captures much of the langorous longing, the pleasurable loneliness, and those moments both of fear and an almost incredible joy that represent a now-lost period in the lives of most of us. In Kazin's childhood, Brownsville was a crowded and impoverished district composed of decaying store fronts and tenements. His father was a house painter, his mother a seamstress. His parents, like all of the Jewish parents of the district, hoped that their children would escape into a better life—would escape, that is, into "the city," for Brownsville was a separate enclave, hopelessly removed from the world beyond. In his youth, Kazin made excursions out of the ghetto, to visit museums and libraries and so on; that he *did* escape in some larger sense is implied in the very title. *A Walker in the City* is the result of his return to Brownsville ten years after he made that escape; in walking its streets again, he remembers his ghetto years.

The excerpt that follows constitutes the concluding pages of the long chapter entitled "The Block and Beyond." Kazin, the adult, understands the confusions and longings of Alfred, the adolescent high school student—the boy of romantic temperament who wants to distance himself from Brownsville, who constructs lives for himself from the books he reads, who is drawn to the obviously cultured and widely traveled couple, the Soloveys, his new neighbors. The husband, a pharmacist, has taken over the drugstore, but his very manner—his aloofness, his arrogance, his untidiness—assures the failure of the business; it is as if he has assumed such a failure from the beginning. The wife is dreamy, a slender and blonde-haired wisp; the adolescent is drawn to this mother of two neglected and skinny children, and imagines a first name for her. The Soloveys speak Russian to each other, not the neighborhood Yiddish; to the boy, they are caught in a love-hate closeness that separates them from everybody else, a romantic attachment as hopeless as their very lives.

"I wanted," the adult Kazin says of his childhood self Alfred, "to bestow love that came from an idea," not the kind of love that issues from the solidarity of his own family, the love he shares with his mother. (Of that mother-son relationship, he says that "each of us bore some part of the other like a guarantee that the other would never die.") The most touching moment of this episode, the one that most fully reveals Mrs. Solovey's entrapment, comes in the description of Alfred's clumsy attempt to speak French with her. In love with the idea of love, he imagines her most frequently as a visitation of Anna Karenina into his actual life; but at the crowded funeral that follows Mrs. Solovey's suicide (to this extent, she does resemble Tolstoy's heroine), he desperately needs to find his mother. Art, we are often told, imitates—or is a representation of—an experienced reality; here is a gorgeous example of that statement in reverse.

The fruit and vegetable stand, the drygoods store, the luggage shop, the rummage shop that sold second-hand books. Only the corsetmaker's is left, his windows still lined with his old European diplomas and gold-sealed certificates of honor presented to him in 1906 at the Brussels Fair. Everywhere else—BARGAINS BARGAINS—the second-hand furniture stores have taken over our block, turning the old life out into the street. But walking past what had once been the candy store, I tasted all the old sweetness of malted milks on my tongue, breathed again the strong sweet fumes of the Murads and Helmars and Lord Salisburys our fathers smoked. Going past what had once been the rummage shop I could feel in my pocket the touch of all the hand-me-down Frank and Dick Merriwells I had bought there for a nickel each, and the copy of Edward Dowden's life of Browning I had read because it cost a dime, and the muddy paper-backed edition of *Great Poems in the English Language* where I first read Blake:

> *Little Lamb, I'll tell thee,*
> *Little Lamb, I'll tell thee:*

It is the old drugstore on the corner I miss most. All those maple beds in the window have made that store stupid; it has nothing to say to me now. Once it was the most exciting threshold I had ever crossed. In the windows glass urns of rose and pink and blue colored water hung from chains; in the doorway I took in the smell of camphor and mothballs and brown paper wardrobes whenever I earned three cents calling someone to the telephone; across from the telephone booths there hung over the black stippled wallpaper that large color picture, a present from a dye company, of General Israel Putnam on his horse riding up some stone steps just ahead of the British, but with his face turned back to me so that I could see it glorious with defiance.

Night after night in the winter, long after I had thrown my book on the kitchen floor and had pulled the string of the bulb in the ceiling, I would push myself as deep under the quilt as I could get, and lie there on the kitchen chairs near the stove thinking of Mrs. Solovey. And often in the middle of the night, I would be awakened by the sound of Negroes singing as they passed under our windows on their way back to Livonia

Avenue, and would pick up my book again as if to follow out to the end the phrase I had just heard. Then I seemed to confuse her blond hair with the long hair shining down the backs of the women in the placards on Mr. Solovey's counter advertising brilliantine. In those placards, their eyes wide open in adoration of their own richness, all women looked as if they were dreaming, too. Sometimes they had the hair of Blumka the madwoman, and sometimes the look of our unmarried cousin in her embroidered Russian blouse, long after she had gone away from us forever and I would sit on her bed staring miserably at the bookcase.

Under the quilt at night, I could dream even before I went to sleep. Yet even there I could never see Mrs. Solovey's face clearly, but still ran round and round the block looking for her after I had passed her kitchen window. It was an old trick, the surest way of getting to sleep: I put the quilt high over my head and lay there burrowing as deep into the darkness as I could get, thinking of her through the long black hair the women on the counter wore. Then I would make up dreams before going to sleep: a face behind the lattice of a summer house, half-hidden in thick green leaves; the hard dots sticking out of the black wallpaper below; the day my mother was ill and our cousin had taken me to school. The moment I felt myself drifting into sleep, my right knee jerked as if I had just caught myself from tripping over something in the gutter. Then I would start up in fright, and perfectly awake, watching the flames dance out from under the covers in the stove, would dream of the druggist's wife and of her blond hair. I had not seen many fair-haired people until I met Mrs. Solovey. There were the Polish "broads" from East New York, smoking cigarettes on someone's lap in the "Coney Island" dives across the street from school, the sheen down their calves and the wickedness of their painted lips what you expected of a blonde. There were the four daughters of our Russian Christian janitor, Mrs. Krylot, all of them with bright golden hair and faces deeply carved and immobile as a wood cut. But they did not count; they smelled of the salt butter the Gentiles used; their blondness seemed naive and uncouth. Mrs. Solovey's I had identified from the first with something direct and sinful.

The Soloveys had been very puzzling; from the day they had come to our tenement, taking over the small dark apartment on the ground floor next to his drugstore, no one had been able to make them out at all. Both the Soloveys had had an inaccessible air of culture that to the end had made them seem visitors among us. They had brought into our house and street the breath of another world, where parents read books, discussed ideas at the table, and displayed a quaint, cold politeness addressing each other. The Soloveys had traveled; they had lived in Palestine, France, Italy. They were "professional" people, "enlightened"—she, it was rumored, had even been a physician or "some kind of scientist," we could never discover which.

The greatest mystery was why they had come to live in Brownsville. We looked down on them for this, and suspected them. To come *deliberately* to Brownsville, after you had lived in France and Italy! It suggested some moral sickness, apathy, a perversion of all right feelings. The apathy alone had been enough to excite me. They were different!

Of course the Soloveys were extremely poor—how else could they even have thought of moving in among us? There were two drab little girls with Hebrew names, who went about in foreign clothes, looking so ill-nourished that my mother was indignant, and vowed to abduct them from their strange parents for an afternoon and feed them up thoroughly. Mrs. Solovey was herself so thin, shy, and gently aloof that she seemed to float away from me whenever I passed her in the hall. There was no doubt in our minds that the Soloveys had come to Brownsville at the end of their road. But what had they hoped to gain from us? If they had ever thought of making money in a Brownsville drugstore, they were soon disenchanted. The women on the block bought such drugs as they had to when illness came. But they did not go in for luxuries, and they had a hearty, familiar way of expecting credit as their natural right from a neighbor and fellow Jew that invariably made Mr. Solovey furious. That was only for the principle of the thing: he showed no interest in making money. He seemed to despise his profession, and the store soon became so clogged with dust and mothballs and camphor-smelling paper wardrobes and the shampoo ads indignantly left him by salesmen of beauty preparations which he refused to stock, that people hated to go in. They all thought him cynical and arrogant. Although he understood well enough when someone addressed him in Yiddish, he seemed to dislike the language, and only frowned, curtly nodding his head to show that he understood. The Soloveys talked Russian to each other, and though we were impressed to hear them going on this way between themselves, everyone else disliked them for it. Not to use our familiar neighborhood speech, not even the English expected of the "educated," meant that they wanted us not to understand them.

Mr. Solovey was always abrupt and ill-tempered, and when he spoke at all, it was to throw a few words out from under his walrus mustache with an air of bitter disdain for us all. His whole manner as he stood behind his counter seemed to say: "I am here because I am here, and I may talk to you if I have to! Don't expect me to enjoy it!" His business declined steadily. Everyone else on the block was a little afraid of him, for he would look through a prescription with such surly impatience that rumors spread he was a careless and inefficient pharmacist, and probably unsafe to use. If he minded, he never showed it. There was always an open book on the counter, usually a Russian novel or a work of philosophy; he spent most of his time reading. He would sit in a greasy old wicker armchair beside the telephone booths, smoking Murads in a brown-stained celluloid holder and muttering to himself as he read. He took as little trouble to keep himself clean as he did his store, and his long drooping mustache and black alpaca coat were always gray with cigarette ash. It looked as if he hated to be roused from his reading even to make a sale, for the slightest complaint sent him into a rage. "I'll never come back to you, Mr. Solovey!" someone would threaten. "Thanks be to God!" he would shout back. "Thanks God! Thanks God! It will be a great pleasure not to see you!" "A *meshúgener,*" the women on the block muttered to each other. "A real crazy one. Crazy to death."

The Soloveys had chosen to live in Brownsville when they could have lived elsewhere, and this made them mysterious. Through some unfathomable act of will, they had chosen us. But for me they were beyond all our endless gossip and speculation about them. They fascinated me simply because they were so different. There was some open madness in the Soloveys' relation to each other for which I could find no parallel, not even a clue, in the lives of our own parents. Whenever I saw the strange couple together, the gold wedding ring on his left hand thick as hers, I felt they were still lovers. Yet the Soloveys were not rich. They were poor as we were, even poorer. I had never known anyone like them. They were weary people, strange and bereft people. I felt they had floated into Brownsville like wreckage off the ship of foreignness and "culture" and the great world outside. And there was that visible tie between them, that wedding ring even a man could wear, some deep consciousness of each other, that excited me, it seemed so illicit. And this was all the more remarkable because, though lovers, they were so obviously unhappy lovers. Had they chucked each other on the chin, had they kissed in public, they would have seemed merely idiotic. No, they seemed to hate each other, and could often be heard quarreling in their apartment, which sent every sound out into the hallway and the street. These quarrels were not like the ones we heard at home. There were no imprecations, no screams, no theatrical sobs: "You're killing me! You're plunging the knife straight into my heart! You're putting me into an early grave! May you sink ten fathoms into the earth!" Such bitter accusations were heard among us all the time, but did not mean even that someone disliked you. In Yiddish we broke all the windows to let a little air into the house.

But in the Soloveys' quarrels there was something worse than anger; it was hopelessness. I felt such despair in them, such a fantastic need to confront each other alone all day long, that they puzzled me by not sharing their feelings with their children. *They* alone, the gruff ne'er-do-well husband and his elusive wife, were the family. Their two little girls did not seem to count at all; the lovers, though their love had been spent, still lived only for each other. And it was this that emphasized their strangeness for me—it was as strange as Mr. Solovey's books, as a Brownsville couple speaking Russian to each other, as strange as Mrs. Solovey's delightfully shocking blondness and the unfathomable despair that had brought them to us. In this severe dependence on each other for everything, there was a defiance of the family principle, of us, of their own poverty and apathy, that encouraged me to despise our values as crude and provincial. Only in movies and in *The Sheik* did people abandon the world for love, give themselves up to it—gladly. Yet there was nothing obviously immoral in the conduct of the Soloveys, nothing we could easily describe and condemn. It was merely that they were sufficient to each other; in their disappointment as in their love they were always alone. They left us out, they left Brownsville out; we were nothing to them. In the love despair of the Soloveys something seemed to say that our constant fight "to make sure" was childish, that we looked at life too narrowly, and that in any event, we did not count. Their loneliness went deeper than our solidarity.

And so I loved them. By now I, too, wanted to defy Brownsville. I did not know where or how to begin. I knew only that I could dream all day long while pretending to be in the world, and that my mind was full of visions as intimate with me as loneliness. I felt I was alone, that there were things I had to endure out of loyalty but could never accept, and that whenever I liked, I could swim out from the Brownsville shore to that calm and sunlit sea beyond where *great friends* came up from the deep. Every book I read re-stocked my mind with those great friends who lived out of Brownsville. They came into my life proud and compassionate, recognizing me by a secret sign, whispering through subterranean channels of sympathy: "Alfred! Old boy! What have they done to you!" Walking about, I learned so well to live with them that I could not always tell whether it was they or I thinking in me. As each fresh excitement faded, I felt myself being flung down from great peaks. Sometimes I was not sure which character I was on my walks, there were so many in my head at once; or how I could explain one to the other; but after an afternoon's reading in the "adults'" library on Glenmore Avenue, I would walk past the pushcarts on Belmont Avenue and the market women crying "Oh you darlings! Oh you pretty ones! Come! Come! Eat us alive! Storm us! Devour us! Tear us apart!"—proud and alien as Othello, or dragging my clubfoot after me like the hero *Of Human Bondage,* a book I had read to tatters in my amazement that Mr. W. Somerset Maugham knew me so well. In that daily walk from Glenmore to Pitkin to Belmont to Sutter I usually played out the life cycles of at least five imaginary characters. They did not stay in my mind very long, for I discovered new books every day; somewhere I felt them to be unreal, cut off by the sickening clean edge of the curb; but while they lived, they gave me a happiness that reverberated in my mind long after I had reached our street and had turned on the first worn step of our stoop for one last proud annihilating glance back at the block.

The Soloveys came into my life as the nearest of all the *great friends*. Everything which made them seem queer on the block deepened their beauty for me. I yearned to spend the deepest part of myself on someone close, someone I could endow directly with the radiant life of the brotherhood I joined in books. Passionately attached as I was to my parents, it had never occurred to me to ask myself what I thought of them as individuals. They were the head of the great body to which I had been joined at birth. There was nothing I could *give* them. I wanted some voluntary and delighted gift of emotion to rise up in me; something that would surprise me in the giving, that would flame directly out of me; that was not, like the obedience of our family love, a routine affair of every day. I wanted to bestow love that came from an idea. All day long in our kitchen my mother and I loved each other in measures of tribulation wellworn as the *Kol Nidre*. We looked to each other for support; we recognized each other with a mutual sympathy and irritation; each of us bore some part of the other like a guarantee that the other would never die. I stammered, she used to say, because she stammered; when she was happy, the air on the block tasted new. I could never really take it in that there had been a time, even in *der heym*, when she had been simply a woman alone, with a life in which I had no part.

Running around the block summer evenings, I always stopped in front of the Soloveys' windows and looked across the spiked iron fence above the cellar steps on the chance that I might see Mrs. Solovey moving around her kitchen. I still spent hours every afternoon hanging around the telephone; he simply refused to answer it; and sometimes I would sit in his greasy old wicker armchair outside the booths, excitedly taking in the large color picture of General Israel Putnam on his horse riding up the stone steps just ahead of the British, the hard dots that stuck out of the black stippled wallpaper, the ladies dreaming in the brilliantine ads on the counter, the mothballs and camphor and brown paper wardrobes that always smelled of something deep, secret, inside. I liked to watch Mr. Solovey as he sat there reading behind his counter, perfectly indifferent to everyone, glowering and alone, the last wet brown inch of cigarette gripped so firmly between his teeth that I could never understand why the smoke did not get into his eyes or burn the edges of his mustache. It excited me just to watch someone read like that.

But now, night after night as I lay on our kitchen chairs under the quilt, I found I could will some sudden picture of his wife, hospitable and grave in the darkness. Everything that now made her so lustrous to me—her air of not being quite placed in life, her gentle aloofness, her secret carnality—was missing in her husband's appearance. The store went from bad to worse, and he seemed to plant himself more and more in the back of it like a dead tree defying us to cut him down. He never even looked at me when I sat in his wicker armchair near the telephone booths, but barricaded himself behind his counter, where his Russian novels lay in a mound of dust and gradually displaced the brilliantine ads and the ten-cent toilet articles. Except in emergencies, or when I had someone to call to the telephone, hardly anyone now came into the store. Most people were afraid of him, and the boys on the block took a special delight in exasperating him by banging a handball just above his kitchen windows. Yet there was something indomitable in his bearing, and with it an ill-concealed contempt for us all, that made it impossible to feel sorry for him. His blazing eyes, his dirty alpaca jacket always powdered with a light dust of cigarette ash, the walrus mustache that drooped down the sides of his mouth with such an expression of disgust for us, for his life—everything seemed to say that he did not care how he lived or what we thought of him. Having determined to fail, his whole bearing told me he had chosen *us* to watch him; and he would fail just as he liked, shocking us as he went under, like a man drowning before our eyes whom our cries could not save. Perhaps he liked to shock us; perhaps our shame and incredulity at seeing him put back so far were things he viciously enjoyed, since the whole manner of his life as an assault on our own hopes and our plain sense of right and wrong. There was something positive in him that had chosen to die, that mocked all our admiration for success. We failed every day, but we fought our failure; we hated it; we measured every action by its help in getting us around failure. Mr. Solovey confused us. In some unspoken way, full of bitterness and scorn, he seemed to say that success did not matter.

I alone knew his secret; I, too, was in love with his wife. I was perfectly sure that all his misery came from the force and bafflement of his attachment to her. The hopeless love between them had scoured them clean of *normal* concerns, like getting money and "making sure" and being parents. The store went to pieces, the two little girls in their foreign clothes played jacks all afternoon long on the front steps, Mr. Solovey denounced us with his eyes, and Mrs. Solovey walked among us in her dream of a better life. But alone, I used to think every time I passed their door on my way upstairs, they glided up and down in their apartment like two goldfish in the same tank. This was the way I saw them; she was the only key I had to their mystery. I based it entirely on my incredulous delight in her.

It was her dreaminess, her air of not being quite related to anything around her, that pleased me most. She floated through our lives; in most ways she was never really with us. I saw her so seldom that afterward, whenever I summoned up her face a second before dropping off to sleep, I could never actually tell whether it was her face I remembered, or the face of another woman with blond hair who had once lived in our house. Under the quilt, all women with blond hair and gold wedding rings shining from behind the lattices of a summer house soon took on the same look as they comfortably placed one hand over my back, had the same wide-open dreamy smile as the women in the brilliantine ads on the counter. Only the name I had invented for Mrs. Solovey could bring *her* instantly back to me. I would say it over and over under my breath, just to hear the foreign syllables ring out—Elizavéta, Elizavéta, no name they ever gave a good Jewish woman; Elizavéta, Elizavéta, I was so astonished to think of Mrs. Solovey, a Jewish woman, speaking Russian every day; Elizavéta, Elizavéta, more accessible than any character I had ever found in a book, but as pliable; more real, but as deliciously unreal. There she was, only two flights of stairs below us, someone I might pass on the block every day, yet a woman like no other I had ever seen. Her blondness flashed out in our tenement, among our somber and dogged faces, with a smiling wantonness. *Die blonde! Die blonde!* In her blondness and langour I seemed to hear the comfortable rustle of nakedness itself.

One day she came into our kitchen, looking for my mother to make a dress for her. I was alone, doing my French lesson at the table. When she spoke to me in her timid, Russian-gruff accent, I felt myself flying back to *Anna Karenina*. There was a grandeur of suffering in her face, in the spindly thinness of her body in the old-fashioned dress, that immediately sent me to that world I had heard of all my life. I was glad my mother was out; I felt I could now enjoy Mrs. Solovey alone. She stood at the kitchen door smiling uneasily, deliberating with herself whether to wait, and when I pressed her, timidly sat down on the other side of the table. I had made so much of her that seeing her so close gave me a curious feeling of alarm. How would it turn out? How did you address your shameful secret love when she walked into a kitchen, and sat down with you, and smiled, smiled nervously, never fitting herself to the great design? Looking at her there, I scorned her mean role as a wife and mother, held to the wildly unhappy husband below, to the two little girls who were always playing jacks by themselves on the front steps. She was Anna, Tolstoy's and my Anna, the sensual and kindly and aristocratically aloof heroine who was unhappily married, who bewitched men's minds, who shocked everyone in St. Petersburg by the gentle power that welled up despite her gold wedding ring. She might have just walked in from a frosty afternoon's ride with her lover on the Nevsky Prospekt, swathed in furs, a mink toque on her head, shyly impervious to the stares and whispers of the envious crowd.

"You are perhaps going to school, young man?" Mrs. Solovey asked after a long silence.

I nodded.

"Do you, uh, do you like the going to school?"

I sighed. *She* would understand.

"Oh!" she said doubtfully. There was another long silence. Not knowing what else to do, I made a great show of studying my book.

"What are you reading, young man, so serious young man?" she smiled.

I turned the book around.

Surprise and delight showed in her face. "You study French? You already perhaps speak it? I call it my other language! From the time I was a girl in Odessa I study it with application and pleasure. How pleasing to speak French with you as I wait for your mother! We can converse?"

"Yes, Mrs. Solovey," I fumbled. "*Il . . . il me ferait? Il me ferait très heureux.*"

She laughed. "*Ferait? Pas du tout!* And you have not a suggestion of the true ac-cent!" Then I heard her say to me: "I suppose you are learning French only to read? The way you do everything! But that is a mistake, I can assure you! It is necessary to speak, to speak! Think how you would be happy to speak French well! To speak a foreign language is to depart from yourself. Do you not think it is tiresome to speak the same language all the time? *Their* language! To feel that you are in a kind of prison, where the words you speak every day are like the walls of your cell? To know with every word that you are the same, and no other, and that it is difficult to escape? But when I speak French to you I have the sensation that for a moment I have left, and I am happy."

I saw her timidly smile at me. "Come, young man, you will repeat your lesson to me?"

I read the exercise slowly from the book. "*Plus d'argent, donc plus d'amusement. N'importe; j'aime mieux ne pas m'amuser. Je n'ai dit mot à personne, et je n'en parlerai pas de ma vie. Ni moi non plus.*"

"*Et vous?*" she interrupted. "*Comment vous appelez-vous?*"

"Alfred."

"Al-fred! *Voilà un joli nom! Un nom anglais, n'est-ce pas? En connaissez-vous l'origine?*"

"What?"

She sighed. "You know the origin of your name?"
"*Je pense . . . pense . . . un roi d'Angleterre?*"
"*Bien sûr. Et la légende des petits gâteau?*"
"What?"
She tried again, very slowly.
I shook my head.
"But what is it they teach you in this American public school!"
"We're not up to irregular verbs."
"The old peasant woman, she asked the king to watch the cakes on the hearth. That they should not burn. But he thought and thought only of his poor country as he sat there, and he let them burn."
"*La vielle paysanne . . . était . . . était . . .*"
"*Fâchée! Ex-cel-lent!* She was very, very displeased. *Que c'est facile!* You must not stop now. Tell me something about yourself. *Quel âge avez-vous*"
"*Quinze.*"
"*Vous avez quinze ans.* My older girl, she is only nine. *Maintenant, dites-moi: qu'est-ce que vous aimez le mieux au monde?*"
"*J'aime . . . j'aime . . .*"
"You have not understood me at all! I must be more careful to speak slowly. *Quand-je-parle-comme-ceci-me-comprehenez-vous?*"
"*Oui.*"
"*Bien. Qu'est-ce que vous aimez le mieux au monde?*"
"*Livres.*"
"*Les livres!*" She laughed. "*Quel genre de livres?*"
"*Roman.*"
"*Le roman?*"
"*Poésie.*"
"*La poésie!*"
"*L'histoire. Les voyages.*"
"*Tout ça? Tout? Vous êtes un peu pédant.*"
"What?"
She sighed. "Does your mother come back very soon?"
"Soon! Soon!"
"Let us try again. What is it not books you like? *La mer?*"
"*Oui. J'aime la mer beaucoup.*"
"*J'aime beaucoup la mer. Encore.*"
"*J'aime beaucoup la mer.*"
"*Et puis?*"
"*Les montagnes.*"
"*Et ensuite?*"
"I know what I want to say, but don't know how to say it."
"*Le cinéma? Le sport? Les jeunes filles? Les jeunes filles ne vous déplaisent pas, naturellement?*"

"Yes," I said. "I like some girls very much. But . . . it's on the tip of my tongue . . ."

"*Pas en anglais!*"

"Well," I said, "I like summer."

"Summer! And the other seasons?"

"*Le printemps, l'automne, l'hiver?*"

"*Combien font trois fois trois?*"

"*Neuf.*"

"*Combien font quarante et vingt-six?*"

"*Soixante-six.*"

"*Pourquoi préférez-vous l'été?*"

"*La . . . la chaud?*" I gave it up. "The warmth . . . the evenness."

She stared at me silently, in gratitude. I distinctly heard her say: "I understand very well. I feel sympathy with your answer! I myself come from Odessa in the south of Russia. You know of Odessa? On the Black Sea. One of the most beautiful cities in all the world, full of sun. It is really a part of Greece. When I was a girl in Odessa, I would go down to the harbor every day and stare out across the water and imagine myself on a ship, a ship with blue sails, that would take me around the world."

"You have lived in many places."

"*Oui. Nous avons habité des pays différents. La Russie, la France, l'Italie, la Palestine.* Yes, many places."

"Why did you come *here?*" I asked suddenly.

She looked at me for a moment. I could not tell what she felt, or how much I had betrayed. But in some way my question wearied her. She rose, made a strange stiff little bow, and went out.

Occasionally I saw her in the street. She made no effort to continue my practice in French, and I did not know how to ask. For a long time I did not see her at all. We knew that Mr. Solovey had gone bankrupt, and was looking for someone to buy the fixtures. There were rumors on the block that once, in the middle of the night, he had beaten her so violently that people in the other tenement had been awakened by her screams. But there was nothing definite we knew about them, and after many weeks in which I vainly looked for her everywhere and once tried to get into their apartment from the yard, I almost forgot her. The store was finally sold, and Mr. Solovey became an assistant in a drugstore on Blake Avenue. They continued to live in the apartment on the ground floor. One morning, while her children were at school, and her husband was at work, Mrs. Solovey sealed all the doors and windows with adhesive tape, and sat over the open gas jets in the kitchen until she was dead. It was raining the day they buried her. Because she was a suicide, the rabbi was reluctant to say the necessary prayers inside the synagogue. But they prevailed upon him to come out on the porch, and looking down on the hearse as it waited in the street, he intoned the service over her coffin. It was wrapped in the blue and white flag with a Star of David at the head. There were hundreds of women in their shawls, weeping in the rain. Most of them had never seen Mrs. Solovey, but they came to weep out of pity for her children, and out of terror and awe because someone was dead. My mother was in the front line outside the synagogue, and I needed urgently to see her. But the crowd was so large that I could not find her, and I waited in the back until the service was over.

Other Dimensions

What is our innocence,
what is our guilt? All are
    naked, none is safe. And whence
is courage: the unanswered question,
the resolute doubt—
dumbly calling, deafly listening—that
in misfortune, even death,
        encourages others
        and in its defeat, stirs

    the soul to be strong? He
sees deep and is glad, who
    accedes to mortality
and in his imprisonment rises
upon himself as
the sea in a chasm, struggling to be
free and unable to be,
        in its surrendering
        finds its continuing.

    So he who strongly feels,
behaves. The very bird,
        grown taller as he sings, steels
his form straight up. Though he is captive,
his mighty singing
says, satisfaction is a lowly
thing, how pure a thing is joy.
        This is mortality,
        this is eternity.

—Marianne Moore, "What Are Years?"

Many affinities connect Marianne Moore's "What Are Years?" with Whitman's "Out of the Cradle Endlessly Rocking," a poem briefly discussed in the introduction to "The Memory of Nature." What separates them, I think, is more than a difference in restraint and control. Hers is a poem in which restraint masks an interior conflict, a disturbance that no mystical childhood experience can resolve; she brings to that disturbance the kind of questioning that a child—still free of any knowledge of her or his error-prone nature—could never ask. Perhaps she is making a passing reference to childhood, in her mention of the innocence that is part of her opening question; and no doubt the biblical garden is in her mind. She gets no comfort from any promise of ultimate safety predicated simply on moral behavior. We are fallible human beings who will experience misfortune and who will die. How can we counter, how can we defeat, such knowledge? Discussing this poem in a letter, Moore says, "The desperation attendant on moral fallibility is mitigated for me by admitting that the most willed and resolute vigilance may lapse, as with the Apostle Peter's denial that he could be capable of denial," and mitigated, too, by her knowledge "that failure, disgrace, and even death have now and again been redeemed into inviolateness by a sufficiently transfigured courage."

Courage is the underlying value explored in the three essays in this group. How does one gain the courage to face death, especially if one lacks faith in an afterlife? Montaigne's essay offers some calm and reasonable answers. Within the second essay by Primo Levi a much more difficult question can be found, one that requires a higher courage: how does one find reasons for living following the death of a beloved person killed during an epoch of pogroms and madness that implicates all of humanity? And a special kind of courage, one just as high and almost beyond telling, is required of a man who will make an affirmation of life despite the Job-like calamities—visited upon him not by God, but by the randomness of fate—which Andre Dubus describes in the final essay. (In Moore's poem, courage is more than a mere attitude; it is the deep feeling, the inner conviction, that leads to joy. Of the three essayists, only Dubus is aware of the need for this kind of courage: as spiritual ideal, it is necessary to his struggle.)

I might add that courage is also required of the reader, if he or she is to read these essays carefully enough to relive, in the imagination, the experiences that are written about, and to comprehend the understated suffering the second essayist seeks to oppose as well as the suffering so clearly evident in the third. A mitigation for such a painstaking reader may be the awareness of the help that memory can provide: the writers make specific references to such help, and beyond that, rely on memory to provide a release from itself through the very act of composition.

"Of Practice"

Michel de Montaigne (1533–1592)

Faced with the undeniable fact that death awaits all of us, a skeptic is denied the solace that religious belief can offer. Should we who have no final answers fear the finality that awaits us? In an age like ours—one in which the belief in a celestial kingdom is mainly asserted by a staunch and unyielding minority—the sense of our finite nature is a crucial component of our doubt in ourselves; do we have the courage to affirm the very meaning of life, despite the knowledge of our ultimate extinction? It ought to be of considerable interest to realize that others (going as far back as the classical age) have asked the same question. Using references to antiquity that are augmented by his own experiences, Montaigne about three hundred and fifty years ago provided some reasonable answers. In "Of Practice," he shows us how life itself can prepare us for its inevitable ending: something so natural—and so desired—as sleep prepares us, as does an accident severe enough that we approach the condition of death.

Life, then, can show us that we needn't fear its cessation. Montaigne's discussion of death is part of his spirited defense of his kind of writing; none of the later practitioners of autobiographical prose has given a better justification for their explorations of their own memories. To make the self subject of one's writings is not the narcissistic act that some accuse it of being—rather, if done properly, it is a method whereby one gains a necessary insight into his or her personal essence. "My trade and my art is living," Montaigne says: his writing, then, is practice in living. The precepts he gives us for writing about the self are ultimately moral in nature, for they all relate to the closest approximation to truth about ourselves that we can arrive at. "No particular quality will make a man proud who balances it against the many weaknesses and imperfections that are also in him, and, in the end, against the nullity of man's estate," he remarks in his conclusion, thus returning, with that reference to death as crucial to any honest self-assessment, to the subject with which he began.

Reasoning and education, though we are willing to put our trust in them, can hardly be powerful enough to lead us to action, unless besides we exercise and form our soul by experience to the way we want it to go; otherwise, when it comes to the time for action, it will undoubtedly find itself at a loss. That is why, among the philosophers, those who have wanted to gain some greater excellence have not been content to await the rigors of Fortune in shelter and repose, for fear she might surprise them inexperienced and new to the combat; rather they have gone forth to meet her and have flung themselves deliberately into the test of difficulties. Some of them have abandoned riches to exercise themselves in a voluntary poverty; others have sought labor and a painful austerity of life to toughen themselves against toil and trouble; others have deprived themselves of the most precious part of the body, such as sight and the organs of generation, for fear that their services, too pleasant and easy, might relax and soften the firmness of their soul.

But for dying, which is the greatest task we have to perform, practice cannot help us. A man can, by habit and experience, fortify himself against pain, shame, indigence, and such other accidents; but as for death, we can try it only once: we are all apprentices when we come to it.

In ancient times there were men who husbanded their time so excellently that they tried to taste and savor it even at the point of death, and strained their minds to see what this passage was; but they have not come back to tell us news of it:

> No man awakes
> Whom once the icy end of living overtakes.
> —Lucretius

Canius Julius, a Roman nobleman of singular virtue and firmness, after being condemned to death by that scoundrel Caligula, gave this among many prodigious proofs of his resoluteness. As he was on the point of being executed, a philosopher friend of his asked him: "Well, Canius, how stands your soul at this moment? What is it doing? What are your thoughts?" "I was thinking," he replied, "about holding myself ready and with all my powers intent to see whether in that instant of death, so short and brief, I shall be able to perceive any dislodgment of the soul, and whether it will have any feeling of its departure; so that, if I learn anything about it, I may return later, if I can, to give the information to my friends." This man philosophizes not only unto death, but even in death itself. What assurance it was, and what proud courage, to want his death to serve as a lesson to him, and to have leisure to think about other things in such a great business!

> Such sway he had over his dying soul.
> —Lucan

It seems to me, however, that there is a certain way of familiarizing ourselves with death and trying it out to some extent. We can have an experience of it that is, if not entire and perfect, at least not useless, and that makes us more fortified and assured. If we cannot reach it, we can approach it, we can reconnoiter it; and if we do not penetrate as far as its fort, at least we shall see and become acquainted with the approaches to it.

It is not without reason that we are taught to study even our sleep for the resemblance it was with death. How easily we pass from waking to sleeping! With how little sense of loss we lose consciousness of the light and of ourselves! Perhaps the faculty of sleep, which deprives us of all action and all feeling, might seem useless and contrary to nature, were it not that thereby Nature teaches us that she has made us for dying and living alike, and from the start of life presents to us the eternal state that she reserves for us after we die, to accustom us to it and take away our fear of it.

But those who by some violent accident have fallen into a faint and lost all sensation, those, in my opinion, have been very close to seeing death's true and natural face. For as for the instant and point of passing away, it is not to be feared that it carries with it any travail or pain, since we can have no feeling without leisure. Our sufferings need time, which in death is so short and precipitate that it must necessarily be imperceptible. It is the approaches that we have to fear; and these may fall within our experience.

Many things seem to us greater in imagination than in reality. I have spent a good part of my life in perfect and entire health; I mean not merely entire, but even blithe and ebullient. This state, full of verdure and cheer, made me find the thought of illnesses so horrible that when I came to experience them I found their pains mild and easy compared with my fears.

Here is what I experience every day: if I am warmly sheltered in a nice room during a stormy and tempestuous night, I am appalled and distressed for those who are then in the open country; if I am myself outside, I do not even wish to be anywhere else.

The mere idea of being always shut up in a room seemed to me unbearable. Suddenly I had to get used to being there a week, or a month, full of agitation, and weakness. And I have found that in time of health I used to pity the sick much more than I now think I deserve to be pitied when I am sick myself; and that the power of my apprehension made its object appear almost half again as fearful as it was in its truth and essence. I hope that the same thing will happen to me with death, and that it is not worth the trouble I take, the many preparations that I make, and all the many aids that I invoke and assemble to sustain the shock of it. But at all events, we can never be well enough prepared.

During our third civil war, or the second (I do not quite remember which), I went riding one day about a league from my house, which is situated at the very hub of all the turmoil of the civil wars of France. Thinking myself perfectly safe, and so near my home that I needed no better equipage, I took a very easy but not very strong horse. On my return, when a sudden occasion came up for me to use this horse for a service to which it was not accustomed, one of my men, big and strong, riding a powerful work horse who had a desperately hard mouth and was moreover fresh and vigorous—this man, in order to show his daring and get ahead of his companions, spurred his horse at full speed up the path behind me, came down like a colossus on the little man and little horse, and hit us like a thunderbolt with all his strength and weight, sending us both head over heels. So that there lay the horse bowled over and stunned, and I ten or twelve paces beyond, dead, stretched on my back, my face all bruised and skinned, my sword, which I had had in my hand, more than ten paces away, my belt in pieces, having no more motion or feeling than a log. It is the only swoon that I have experienced to this day.

Those who were with me, after having tried all the means they could to bring me round, thinking me dead, took me in their arms and were carrying me with great difficulty to my house, which was about half a French league from there. On the way, and after I had been taken for dead for more than two full hours, I began to move and breathe; for so great an abundance of blood had fallen into my stomach that nature had to revive its forces to discharge it. They set me up on my feet, where I threw up a whole bucketful of clots of pure blood, and several times on the way I had to do the same thing. In so doing I began to recover a little life, but it was bit by bit and over so long a stretch of time that my first feelings were much closer to death than to life:

> Because the shaken soul, uncertain yet
> Of its return, is still not firmly set.
>
> —Tasso

This recollection, which is strongly implanted on my soul, showing me the face and idea of death so true to nature, reconciles me to it somewhat.

When I began to see anything, it was with a vision so blurred, weak, and dead, that I still could distinguish nothing but the light,

> As one 'twixt wakefulness and doze,
> Whose eyes now open, now again they close.
>
> —Tasso

As for the functions of the soul, they were reviving with the same progress as those of the body. I saw myself all bloody, for my doublet was stained all over with the blood I had thrown up. The first thought that came to me was that I had gotten a harquebus shot in the head; indeed several were being fired around us at the time of the accident. It seemed to me that my life was hanging only by the tip of my lips; I closed my eyes in order, it seemed to me, to help push it out, and took pleasure in growing languid and letting myself go. It was an idea that was only floating on the surface of my soul, as delicate and feeble as all the rest, but in truth not only free from distress but mingled with that sweet feeling that people have who let themselves slide into sleep.

I believe that this is the same state in which people find themselves whom we see fainting with weakness in the agony of death; and I maintain that we pity them without cause, supposing that they are agitated by grievous pains or have their soul oppressed by painful thoughts. This has always been my view, against the opinion of many, and even of Étienne de la Boétie, concerning those whom we see thus prostrate and comatose as their end approaches, or overwhelmed by the length of the disease, or by a stroke of apoplexy, or by epilepsy—

> This do we often see:
> A man, struck, as by lightning, by some malady,
> Falls down all foaming at the mouth, shivers and rants;
> He moans under the torture, writhes his muscles, pants,
> And in fitful tossing exhausts his weary limbs
>
> —Lucretius

—or wounded in the head: When we hear them groan and from time to time utter poignant sighs, or see them make certain movements of the body, we seem to see signs that they still have some consciousness left; but I have always thought, I say, that their soul and body were buried in sleep.

> He lives, and is unconscious of his life.
>
> —Ovid

And I could not believe that with so great a paralysis of the limbs, and so great a failing of the senses, the soul could maintain any force within by which to be conscious of itself; and so I believed that they had no reflections to torment them, nothing able to make them judge and feel the misery of their condition, and that consequently they were not much to be pitied.

I can imagine no state so horrible and unbearable for me as to have my soul alive and afflicted, without means to express itself. I should say the same of those who are sent to execution with their tongue cut out, were it not that in this sort of death the most silent seems to be the most becoming, if it goes with a firm, grave countenance; and the same of those miserable prisoners who fall into the hands of the villainous murdering soldiers of these days, who torture them with every kind of cruel treatment to force them to pay some excessive and impossible ransom, keeping them meanwhile in a condition and in a place where they have no means whatever of expressing or signifying their thoughts and their misery.

The poets have portrayed some gods as favorable to the deliverance of those who thus drag out a lingering death:

> I bear to Pluto, by decree,
> This lock of hair, and from your body set you free.
>
> —Virgil

Nonetheless, the short and incoherent words and replies that are extorted from them by dint of shouting about their ears and storming at them, or the movements that seem to have some connection with what is asked them, are not evidence that they are alive, at least fully alive. So it happens to us in the early stages of sleep, before it has seized us completely, to sense as in a dream what is happening around us, and to follow voices with a blurred and uncertain hearing which seems to touch on only the edges of the soul; and following the last words spoken to us, we make answers that are more random than sensible.

Now I have no doubt, now that I have tried this out by experience, that I judged this matter rightly all along. For from the first, while wholly unconscious, I was laboring to rip open my doublet with my nails (for I was not in armor); and yet I know that I felt nothing in my imagination that hurt me; for there are many movements of ours that do not come from our will:

> And half-dead fingers writhe and seize the sword again.
>
> —Virgil

Thus those who are falling throw out their arms in front of them, by a natural impulse which makes our limbs lend each other their services and have stirrings apart from our reason:

> They say that chariots bearing scythes will cut so fast
> That severed limbs are writhing on the ground below
> Before the victim's soul and strength can ever know
> Or even feel the pain, so swift has been the hurt.
>
> —Lucretius

My stomach was oppressed with the clotted blood; my hands flew to it of their own accord, as they often do where we itch, against the intention of our will.

There are many animals, and even men, whose muscles we can see contract and move after they are dead. Every man knows by experience that there are parts that often move, stand up, and lie down, without his leave. Now these passions which touch only the rind of us cannot be called ours. To make them ours, the whole man must be involved; and the pains which the foot or the hand feel while we are asleep are not ours.

As I approached my house, where the alarm of my fall had already come, and the members of my family had met me with the outcries customary in such cases, not only did I make some sort of answer to what was asked me, but also (they say) I thought of ordering them to give a horse to my wife, whom I saw stumbling and having trouble on the road, which is steep and rugged. It would seem that this consideration must have proceeded from a wide-awake soul; yet the fact is that I was not there at all. These were idle thoughts, in the clouds, set in motion by the sensations of the eyes and ears; they did not come from within me. I did not know, for all that, where I was coming from or where I was going, nor could I weigh and consider what I was asked. These are slight effects which the senses produce of themselves, as if by habit; what the soul contributed was in a dream, touched very lightly, and merely licked and sprinkled, as it were, by the soft impression of the senses.

Meanwhile my condition was, in truth, very pleasant and peaceful; I felt no affliction either for others or for myself; it was a langour and an extreme weakness, without any pain. I saw my house without recognizing it. When they had put me to bed, I felt infinite sweetness in this repose, for I had been villainously yanked about by those poor fellows, who had taken the pains to carry me in their arms over a long and very bad road, and had tired themselves out two or three times in relays. They offered me many remedies, of which I accepted none, holding it for certain that I was mortally wounded in the head. It would, in truth, have been a very happy death; for the weakness of my understanding kept me from having any judgment of it, and that of my body from having any feeling of it. I was letting myself slip away so gently, so gradually and easily, that I hardly ever did anything with less of a feeling of effort.

When I came back to life and regained my powers,

> When my senses at last regained their strength,
>
> —Ovid

which was two or three hours later, I felt myself all of a sudden caught up again in the pains, my limbs being all battered and bruised by my fall; and I felt so bad two or three nights after that I thought I was going to die all over again, but by a more painful death; and I still feel the effect of the shock of that collision.

I do not want to forget this, that the last thing I was able to recover was the memory of this accident; I had people repeat to me several times where I was going, where I was coming from, at what time it had happened to me, before I could take it in. As for the manner of my fall, they concealed it from me and made up other versions for the sake of the man who had been the cause of it. But a long time after, and the next day, when my memory came to open up and picture to me the state I had been in at the instant I had perceived that horse bearing down on me (for I had seen him at my heels and thought I was a dead man, but that thought had been so sudden that I had no time to be afraid), it seemed to me that a flash of lightning was striking my soul with a violent shock, and that I was coming back from the other world.

This account of so trivial an event would be rather pointless, were it not for the instruction that I have derived from it for myself; for in truth, in order to get used to the idea of death, I find there is nothing like coming close to it. Now as Pliny says, each man is a good education to himself, provided he has the capacity to spy on himself from close up. What I write here is not my teaching, but my study; it is not a lesson for others, but for me.

And yet it should not be held against me if I publish what I write. What is useful to me may also by accident be useful to another. Moreover, I am not spoiling anything, I am using only what is mine. And if I play the fool, it is at my expense and without harm to anyone. For it is a folly that will die with me, and will have no consequences. We have heard of only two or three ancients who opened up this road, and even of them we cannot say whether their manner in the least resembled mine, since we know only their names. No one since has followed their lead. It is a thorny undertaking, and more so than it seems, to follow a movement so wandering as that of our mind, to penetrate the opaque depths of its innermost folds, to pick out and immobilize the innumerable flutterings that agitate it. And it is new and extraordinary amusement, which withdraws us from the ordinary occupations of the world, yes, even from those most recommended.

It is many years now that I have had only myself as object of my thoughts, that I have been examining and studying only myself; and if I study anything else, it is in order promptly to apply it to myself, or rather within myself. And it does not seem to me that I am making a mistake if—as is done in the other sciences, which are incomparably less useful—I impart what I have learned in this one, though I am hardly satisfied with the progress I have made in it. There is no description equal in difficulty, or certainly in usefulness, to the description of oneself. Even so one must spruce up, even so one must present oneself in an orderly arrangement, if one would go out in public. Now, I am constantly adorning myself, for I am constantly describing myself.

Custom has made speaking of oneself a vice, and obstinately forbids it out of hatred for the boasting that seems always to accompany it. Instead of blowing the child's nose, as we should, this amounts to pulling it off.

Flight from a fault will lead us into crime.

—Horace

I find more harm than good in this remedy. But even if it were true that it is presumptuous, no matter what the circumstances, to talk to the public about oneself, I still must not, according to my general plan, refrain from an action that openly displays this morbid quality, since it is in me; nor may I conceal this fault, which I not only practice but profess. However, to say what I think about it, custom is wrong to condemn wine because many get drunk on it. We can misuse only things which are good. And I believe that the rule against speaking of oneself applies only to the vulgar form of this failing. Such rules are bridles for calves, with which neither the saints, whom we hear speaking so boldly about themselves, nor the philosophers, nor the theologians curb themselves. Nor do I, though I am none of these. If they do not write about themselves expressly, at least when the occasion leads them to it they do not hesitate to put themselves prominently on display. What does Socrates treat of more fully than himself? To what does he lead his disciples' conversation more often than to talk about themselves, not about the lesson of their book, but about the essence and movement of their soul? We speak our thoughts religiously to God, and to our confessor, as our neighbors do to the whole people. But, someone will answer, we speak only our self-accusations. Then we speak everything: for our very virtue is faulty and fit for repentance.

My trade and my art is living. He who forbids me to speak about it according to my sense, experience, and practice, let him order the architect to speak of buildings not according to himself but according to his neighbor; according to another man's knowledge, not according to his own. If it is vainglory for a man himself to publish his own merits, why doesn't Cicero proclaim the eloquence of Hortensius, Hortensius that of Cicero?

Perhaps they mean that I should testify about myself by works and deeds, not by bare words. What I chiefly portray is my cogitations, a shapeless subject that does not lend itself to expression in actions. It is all I can do to couch my thoughts in this airy medium of words. Some of the wisest and most devout men have lived avoiding all noticeable actions. My actions would tell more about fortune than about me. They bear witness to their own part, not to mine, unless it be by conjecture and without certainty: they are samples which display only details. I expose myself entire: my portrait is a cadaver on which the veins, the muscles, and the tendons appear at a glance, each part in its place. One part of what I am was produced by a cough, another by a pallor or a palpitation of the heart—in any case dubiously. It is not my deeds that I write down; it is myself, it is my essence.

I hold that a man should be cautious in making an estimate of himself, and equally conscientious in testifying about himself—whether he rates himself high or low makes no difference. If I seemed to myself good and wise or nearly so, I would shout it out at the top of my voice. To say less of yourself than is true is stupidity, not modesty. To pay yourself less than you are worth is cowardice and pusillanimity, according to Aristotle. No virtue is helped by falsehood, and truth is never subject to error. To say more of yourself than is true is not always presumption; it too is often stupidity. To be immoderately pleased with what you are, to fall therefore into an undiscerning self-love, is in my opinion the substance of this vice. The supreme remedy to cure it is to do just the opposite of what those people prescribe who, by prohibiting talking about oneself, even more strongly prohibit thinking about oneself. The pride lies in the thought; the tongue can have only a very slight share in it.

It seems to them that to be occupied with oneself means to be pleased with oneself, that to frequent and associate with oneself means to cherish oneself too much. That may be. But this excess arises only in those who touch themselves no more than superficially; who observe themselves only after taking care of their business; who call it daydreaming and idleness to be concerned with oneself, and making castles in Spain to furnish and build oneself; who think themselves something alien and foreign to themselves.

If anyone gets intoxicated with his knowledge when he looks beneath him, let him turn his eyes upward toward past ages, and he will lower his horns, finding there so many thousands of minds that trample him underfoot. If he gets into some flattering presumption about his valor, let him remember the lives of the two Scipios, so many armies, so many nations, all of whom leave him so far behind them. No particular quality will make a man proud who balances it against the many weaknesses and imperfections that are also in him, and, in the end, against the nullity of man's estate.

Because Socrates alone had seriously digested the precept of his god—to know himself—and because by that study he had come to despise himself, he alone was deemed worthy of the name *wise*. Whoever knows himself thus, let him boldly make himself known by his own mouth.

from *The Periodic Table*

Primo Levi (1919–1987)

As Frances A. Yates tells us in another essay in this anthology, the Greek poet Simonides, founder of the art of memory, recommends that we stash away whatever we wish to recall by visualizing it in an actual location, such as a room in a house. By what method, though, do we find the right rooms for the infinite number of experiences that memory holds onto whether we want them to be there or not? How do we give order to our past—especially if that past reflects a disorder beyond personal control, a disorder so vast and brutal that it threatens the very idea of a human meaning?

To such questions the Italian writer and chemist Primo Levi found an original answer, one that brought his two professions together. In *The Periodic Table*, he uses the chart of the chemical elements—familiar to anybody who has taken a high school chemistry class—to organize fragments of his life, many of them from his bleakest and most tragic period. (He was a Jew who managed to survive Italian fascism and the Nazi concentration camps.) He has written extensively about Auschwitz: in his chapter in *The Periodic Table* on "Chromium," the one reprinted here, he says simply, in referring back to his own imprisonment there, "The things I had seen and suffered were burning inside of me; I felt closer to the dead than the living, and felt guilty at being a man, because men had built Auschwitz, and Auschwitz had gulped down millions of human beings, and many of my friends, and a woman who was dear to my heart."

As we first begin to read it, "Chromium" seems no more than a pleasantly digressive essay on the general topic of customs or habits so ingrained in us that we continue with them long after their meaning or purpose has been lost: another example, perhaps, of our human absurdity. Though it returns to that topic at the end, the essay shows the link between chromium and the restoration, however precarious it may be, of Levi's spiritual health. It is an essay of recovery from depression and suffering, and has much to say (concise though the remarks are) about the effect of the present upon the past as well as the effect of the past upon the present; it speaks, too, of the therapy that writing can provide. Finally, it contains a detective story about chemistry. The book uses twenty other chemical elements as chapter titles; in nearly every case, memory, with the aid of a chosen element, distills its own dark holdings. All the essays are limpid; "Chromium," though, is the only tranquil one—the one to be treasured for its victory over all that still was "burning inside" him.

In April 1987, following his completion of yet another Auschwitz book, Levi died—a death that almost at once was considered a suicide, though lately the verdict has come under review.

The entrée was fish, but the wine was red. Versino, head of maintenance, said that it was all a lot of nonsense, provided the wine and fish were good; he was certain that the majority of those who upheld the orthodox view could not, blindfolded, have distinguished a glass of white wine from a glass of red. Bruni, from the Nitro Department, asked whether somebody knew why fish goes with white wine: various joking remarks were made but nobody was able to answer properly. Old man Cometto added that life is full of customs whose roots can no longer be traced: the color of sugar paper, the buttoning from different sides for men and women, the shape of a gondola's prow, and the innumerable alimentary compatibilities and incompatibilities, of which in fact the one in question was a particular case: but in any event, why were pig's feet obligatory with lentils, and cheese on macaroni.

I made a rapid mental review to be sure that none of those present had as yet heard it, then I started to tell the story of the onion in the boiled linseed oil. This, in fact, was a dining room for a company of varnish manufacturers, and it is well known that boiled linseed oil has for many centuries constituted the fundamental raw material of our art. It is an ancient art and therefore noble: its most remote testimony is in Genesis 6:14, where it is told how, in conformity with a precise specification of the Almighty, Noah coated (probably with a brush) the Ark's interior and exterior with melted pitch. But it is also a subtly fraudulent art, like that which aims at concealing the substratum by conferring on it the color and appearance of what it is not: from this point of view it is related to cosmetics and adornment, which are equally ambiguous and almost equally ancient arts (Isaiah 3:16). Given therefore its pluri-millenial origins, it is not so strange that the trade of manufacturing varnishes retains in its crannies (despite the innumerable solicitations it modernly receives from kindred techniques) rudiments of customs and procedures abandoned for a long time now.

So, returning to boiled linseed oil, I told my companions at table that in a prescription book published about 1942 I had found the advice to introduce into the oil, toward the end of the boiling, two slices of onion, without any comment on the purpose of this curious additive. I had spoken about it in 1949 with Signor Giacomasso Olindo, my predecessor and teacher, who was then more than seventy and had been making varnishes for fifty years, and he, smiling benevolently behind his thick white mustache, had explained to me in actual fact, when he was young and boiled the oil personally, thermometers had not yet come into use: one judged the temperature of the batch by observing the smoke, or spitting into it, or, more efficiently, immersing a slice of onion in the oil on the point of a skewer; when the onion began to fry, the boiling was finished. Evidently, with the passing of the years, what had been a crude measuring operation had lost its significance and was transformed into a mysterious and magical practice.

Old Cometto told of an analogous episode. Not without nostalgia he recalled his good old times, the times of copal gum: he told how once boiled linseed oil was combined with these legendary resins to make fabulously durable and gleaming varnishes. Their fame and name survive now only in the locution "copal shoes," which alludes precisely to a varnish for leather at one time very widespread that has been out of fashion for at least the last half century. Today the locution itself is almost extinct. Copals were imported by the British from the most distant and savage countries, and bore their names, which in fact distinguished one kind from another: copal of Madagascar or Sierra Leone or Kauri (whose deposits, let it be said parenthetically, were exhausted along about 1967), and the very well known and noble Congo copal. They are fossil resins of vegetable origin, with a rather high melting point, and in the state in which they are found and sold in commerce are insoluble in oil: to render them soluble and compatible they were subjected to a violent, semi-destructive boiling, in the course of which their acidity diminished (they decarboxylated) and also the melting point was lowered. The operation was carried out in a semi-industrial manner by direct fire in modest, mobile kettles of four or six hundred pounds; during the boiling they were weighed at intervals, and when the resin had lost 16 percent of its weight in smoke, water vapor, and carbon dioxide, the solubility in oil was judged to have been reached. Along about 1940, the archaic copals, expensive and difficult to supply during the war, were supplanted by phenolic and maleic resins, both suitably modified, which, besides costing less, were directly compatible with the oils. Very well: Cometto told us how, in a factory whose name shall not be uttered, until 1953 a phenolic resin, which took the place of the Congo copal in a formula, was treated exactly like copal itself—that is, by consuming 16 percent of it on the fire, amid pestilential phenolic exhalations—until it had reached that solubility in oil which the resin already possessed.

Here at this point I remembered that all languages are full of images and metaphors whose origin is being lost, together with the art form which they were drawn: horsemanship having declined to the level of an expensive sport, such expressions as "belly to the ground" and "taking the bit in one's teeth" are unintelligible and sound odd; since mills with superimposed stones have disappeared, which were also called millstones, and in which for centuries wheat (and varnishes) were ground, such a phrase as "to eat like four millstones" sounds odd and even mysterious today. In the same way, since Nature too is conservative, we carry in our coccyx what remains of a vanished tail.

Bruni told us about an episode in which he himself had been involved, and as he told the story, I felt myself invaded by sweet and tenuous sensations which later I will try to explain. I must say first of all that Bruni worked from 1955 to 1965 in a large factory on the shores of a lake, the same one in which I had learned the rudiments of the varnish-making trade during the years 1946–47. So he told us that, when he was down there in charge of the Synthetic Varnishes Department, there fell into his hands a formula of a chromate-based anti-rust paint that contained an absurd component: nothing less than ammonium chloride, the old, alchemical sal ammoniac of the temple of Ammon, much more apt to corrode iron than preserve it from rust. He had asked his superiors and the veterans in the department about it: surprised and a bit shocked, they had replied that in that formulation, which corresponded to at least twenty or thirty tons of the product a month and had been in force for at least ten years, that salt "had always been in it," and that he had his nerve, so young in years and new on the job, criticizing the factory's experience, and looking for trouble by asking silly hows and whys. If ammonium chloride was in the formula, it was evident that it had some sort of use. What use it had nobody any longer knew, but one should be very careful about taking it out because "one never knows." Bruni is a rationalist, and he took all this very badly; but he is a prudent man, and so he accepted the advice, according to which in that formulation and in that lakeshore factory, unless there have been further developments, ammonium chloride is still being put in; and yet today it is completely useless, as I can state from firsthand experience because it was I who introduced it into the formula.

The episode cited by Bruni, the rustproof formula with chromates and ammonium chloride, flung me back in time, all the way to the freezing cold January of 1946, when meat and coal were still rationed, nobody had a car, and never in Italy had people breathed so much hope and so much freedom.

But I had returned from captivity three months before and was living badly. The things I had seen and suffered were burning inside of me; I felt closer to the dead than the living, and felt guilty at being a man, because men had built Auschwitz, and Auschwitz had gulped down millions of human beings, and many of my friends, and a woman who was dear to my heart. It seemed to me that I would be purified if I told its story, and I felt like Coleridge's Ancient Mariner, who waylays on the street the wedding guests going to the feast, inflicting on them the story of his misfortune. I was writing concise and bloody poems, telling the story at breakneck speed, either by talking to people or by writing it down, so much so that gradually a book was later born: by writing I found peace for a while and felt myself become a man again, a person like everyone else, neither a martyr nor debased nor a saint: one of those people who form a family and look to the future rather than the past.

Since one can't live on poetry and stories, I looked feverishly for work and found it in the big lakeshore factory, still damaged from the war, and during those months besieged by mud and ice. Nobody was much concerned with me: colleagues, the director, and workers had other things to think about—the son who wasn't returning from Russia, the stove without wood, the shoes without soles, the warehouses without supplies, the windows without panes, the freezing cold which split the pipes, inflation, famine, and the virulent local feuds. I had been benignly granted a lame-legged desk in the lab, in a corner full of crashing noise, drafts, and people coming and going carrying rags and large cans, and I had not been assigned a specific task. I, unoccupied as a chemist and in a state of utter alienation (but then it wasn't called that), was writing in a haphazard fashion page after page of the memories which were poisoning me, and my colleagues watched me stealthily as a harmless nut. The book grew under my hands, almost spontaneously, without plan or system, as intricate and crowded as an anthill. Every so often, impelled by a feeling of professional conscience, I would ask to see the director and request some work, but he was much too busy to worry about my scruples. I should read and study; when it came to paints and varnishes I was still, if I didn't mind his saying so, an illiterate. I didn't have anything to do? Well, I should praise God and sit in the library; if I really had the itch to do something useful, well, look, there were articles to translate from German.

One day he sent for me and with an oblique glint in his eyes announced that he had a little job for me. He took me to a corner of the factory's yard, near a retaining wall: piled up at random, the lowest crushed by the highest, were thousands of square blocks of a bright orange color. He told me to touch them: they were gelatinous and softish; they had the disagreeable consistency of slaughtered tripes. I told the director that, apart from the color, they seemed to me to be livers, and he praised me: that's just how it was described in the paint manuals! He explained that the phenomenon which had produced them was called just that in English, "livering"; under certain conditions certain paints turned from liquids into solids, with the consistency precisely of the liver or lungs, and must be thrown out. These parallelpiped shapes had been cans of paint: the paint had livered, the cans had been cut away, and the contents had been thrown on the garbage dump.

That paint, he told me, had been produced during the war and immediately after; it contained a basic chromate and alkyd resin. Perhaps the chromate was too basic or the resin too acidic: these were exactly the conditions under which a "livering" can take place. All right, he made me the gift of that pile of old sins; I should think about it, make tests and examinations, and try to say with precision why the trouble had occurred, what should be done so that it was not repeated, and if it were possible to reclaim the damaged goods.

Thus set forth, half chemistry and half police work, the problem attracted me: I was reconsidering it that evening (it was Saturday evening) as one of the sooty, freezing freight trains of that period lugged me to Turin. Now it happened that the next day destiny reserved for me a different and unique gift: the encounter with a woman, young and made of flesh and blood, warm against my side through our overcoats, gay in the humid mist of the avenues, patient, wise and sure as we were walking down streets still bordered with ruins. In a few hours we knew that we belonged to each other, not for one meeting but for life, as in fact has been the case. In a few hours I felt reborn and replete with new powers, washed clean and cured of a long sickness, finally ready to enter life with joy and vigor; equally cured was suddenly the world around me, and exorcized the name and face of the woman who had gone down into the lower depths with me and had not returned. My very writing became a different adventure, no longer the dolorous itinerary of a convalescent, no longer a begging for compassion and friendly faces, but a lucid building, which now was no longer solitary: the work of a chemist who weighs and divides, measures and judges on the basis of assured proofs, and strives to answer questions. Alongside the liberating relief of the veteran who tells his story, I now felt in the writing a complex, intense, and new pleasure, similar to that I felt as a student when penetrating the solemn order of differential calculus. It was exalting to search and find, or create, the right word, that is, commensurate, concise, and strong; to dredge up events from my memory and describe them with the greatest rigor and the least clutter. Paradoxically, my baggage of atrocious memories became a wealth, a seed; it seemed to me that, by writing, I was growing like a plant.

In the freight train of the following Monday, squeezed in a sleepy crowd bundled in scarfs, I felt full of joy and alert as never before or after. I was ready to challenge everything and everyone, in the same way that I had challenged and defeated Auschwitz and loneliness: disposed, especially, to engage in joyous battle with the clumsy pyramid of orange livers that awaited me on the lakeshore.

It is the spirit that dominates matter, is that not so? Was it not this that they had hammered into my head in the Fascist and Gentile *liceo*? I threw myself into the work with the same intensity that, at not so distant a period, we had attacked a rock wall; and the adversary was still the same, the not-I, the Button Molder, the *hyle*: stupid matter, slothfully hostile as human stupidity is hostile, and like it strong because of its obtuse passivity. Our trade is to conduct and win this interminable battle: a livered paint is much more rebellious, more refractory to your will than a lion in its mad pounce; but, let's admit it, it's also less dangerous.

The first skirmish took place in the archives. The two partners, the two fornicators from whose embrace had sprung our orange-colored monsters, were the chromate and the resin. The resin was fabricated on the spot: I found the birth certificate of all the batches, and they did not offer anything suspicious; the acidity was variable, but always inferior to 6, as prescribed. One batch that was found to have a pH of 6.2 had been dutifully discarded by an inspector with a flowery signature. In the first instance the resin could not be faulted.

The chromate had been purchased from different suppliers, and it too had been duly inspected batch by batch. According to Purchase Specification 480/0 it should have contained not less than 28 percent of chromium oxide in all; and now here, right before my eyes I had the interminable list of tests from January 1942 until today (one of the least exciting forms of reading imaginable), and all the values satisfied the specification, indeed were equal among themselves: 29.5 percent, not one percent more, not one less. I felt my inner being as a chemist writhe, confronted by that abomination; in fact, one should know that the natural oscillations in the method of preparation of such a chromate, added to the inevitable analytical errors, make it extremely improbable that the many values found in different batches and on different days could coincide so exactly. How come nobody had gotten suspicious? But in fact at that time I did not yet know the frightening anesthetic power of company papers, their capacity to hobble, douse, and dull every leap of intuition and every spark of talent. It is well known to the scholarly that all secretions can be harmful or toxic: now under pathological conditions it is not rare that the paper, a company secretion, is reabsorbed to an excessive degree, and puts to sleep, paralyzes, or actually kills the organism from which it has been exuded.

The story of what had happened began to take shape. For some reason, some analyst had been betrayed by a defective method, or an impure reagent, or an incorrect habit; he had diligently totted up those so obviously suspicious but formally blameless results; he had punctiliously signed each analysis, and his signature, swelling like an avalanche, had been consolidated · by the signatures of the lab chief, the technical director, and the general director. I could see him, the poor wretch, against the background of those difficult years: no longer young, since all the young men were in the military services; perhaps chivied by the Fascists, perhaps himself a Fascist being looked for by the partisans; certainly frustrated, because being an analyst is a young man's job; on guard in his lab within the fortress of his minuscule specialty, since the analyst is by definition infallible; and derided and regarded with a hostile eye outside the lab just because of his virtues as an incorruptible guardian, a severe, pedantic, unimaginative little judge, a stick poked in the wheels of production. To judge from the anonymous, neat handwriting, his trade must have exhausted him and at the same time brought him to a crude perfection, like a pebble in a mountain stream that has been twirled over and over all the way to the stream's mouth. It was not surprising that, with time, he had developed a certain insensitivity to the real significance of the operations he was performing and the notes he was writing. I planned to look into his particular case but nobody knew anything more about him; my questions were met with discourteous or absentminded replies. Moreover, I was beginning to feel around me and my work a mocking and malevolent curiosity: who was this Johnny-come-lately, this pipsqueak earning 7,000 lire a month, this maniac scribbler who was disturbing the nights of the guest quarters typing away at God knows what, and sticking his nose into past mistakes and washing a generation's dirty linen? I even had the suspicion that the job that had been assigned me had the secret purpose of getting me to bump into something or somebody; but by now this matter of the livering absorbed me body and soul, *tripes et boyaux*—in short, I was enamored of it almost as of that aforementioned girl, who in fact was a little jealous of it.

It was not hard for me to procure, besides the Purchase Specification (the PS), also the equally inviolable CS, the Checking Specifications: in a drawer in the lab there was a packet of greasy file cards, typewritten and corrected several times by hand, each of which contained the way to carry out a check of a specific raw material. The file card on prussian blue was stained with blue, the file card on glycerine was sticky, and the file card on fish oil smelled like sardines. I took out the file card on chromate, which due to long use had become the color of a sunrise, and read it carefully. It was all rather sensible and in keeping with my not-so-far-off scholastic notions; only one point seemed strange to me. Having achieved the disintegration of the pigment, it prescribed adding twenty-three drops of a certain reagent. Now, a drop is not so definite a unit as to entail so definite a numerical coefficient; and besides, when all is said and done, the prescribed dose was absurdly high: it would have flooded the analysis, leading in any case to a result in keeping with the specification. I looked at the back of the file card: it bore the date of the last review, January 4, 1944; the birth certificate of the first livered batch was on the succeeding February 22.

At this point I began to see the light. In a dusty archive I found the CS collection no longer in use, and there, lo and behold, the preceding edition of the chromate file card bore the direction to add "2 or 3" drops, not "23": the fundamental "or" was half erased and in the next transcription had gotten lost. The events meshed perfectly: the revision of the file card had caused a mistake in transcription, and the mistake had falsified all succeeding analyses, concealing the results on the basis of a fictitious value due to the reagent's enormous excess and thus bringing about the acceptance of shipments of pigment which should have been discarded; these, being too basic, had brought about the livering.

But there is trouble in store for anyone who surrenders to the temptation of mistaking an elegant hypothesis for a certainty: the readers of detective stories know this quite well. I got hold of the sleepy man in charge of the storeroom, requested from him all the samples of all the shipments of chromate from January 1944 on, and barricaded myself behind a workbench for three days in order to analyze them according to the incorrect and correct methods. Gradually, as the results lined up in a column on the register, the boredom of repetitive work was being transformed into nervous gaiety, as when as children you play hide and seek and discover your opponent clumsily squatting behind a hedge. With the mistaken method you constantly found the fateful 29.5 percent; with the correct method, the results were widely dispersed, and a good quarter, being inferior to the prescribed minimum, corresponded to the shipments which should have been rejected. The diagnosis was confirmed, the pathogenesis discovered: it was now a matter of defining the therapy.

This was found pretty soon, drawing on good inorganic chemistry, that distant Cartesian island, a lost paradise, for us organic chemists, bunglers, "students of gunks": it was necessary to neutralize in some way, within the sick body of that varnish, the excess of basicity due to free lead oxide. The acids were shown to be noxious from other aspects: I thought of ammonium chloride, capable of combining stably with lead oxide, producing an insoluble and inert chloride and freeing the ammonia. Tests on a small scale gave promising results: now quick, find the chloride, come to an agreement with the head of the Milling Department, slip into a small ball mill two of the livers disgusting to see and touch, add a weighed quantity of the presumed medicine, start the mill under the skeptical eyes of the onlookers. The mill, usually so noisy, started almost grudgingly, in a silence of bad omen, impeded by the gelatinous mass which stuck to the balls. All that was left was to go back to Turin to wait for Monday, telling the patient girl in whirlwind style the hypotheses arrived at, the things understood at the lakeshore, the spasmodic waiting for the sentence that the facts would pronounce.

The following Monday the mill had regained its voice: it was in fact crunching away gaily with a full, continuous tone, without that rhythmic roaring that in a ball mill indicates bad maintenance or bad health. I stopped it and cautiously loosened the bolts on the manhole; there spurted out with a hiss an ammoniacal puff, as it should. Then I took off the cover. Angels and ministers of grace!—the paint was fluid and smooth, completely normal, born again from its ashes like the Phoenix. I wrote out a report in good company jargon and the management increased my salary. Besides, as a form of recognition, I received the assignment of two tires for my bike.

Since the storeroom contained several shipments of perilously basic chromate, which must also be utilized because they had been accepted by the inspection and could not be returned to the supplier, the chloride was officially introduced as an antilivering preventive in the formula of that varnish. Then I quit my job: ten years went by, the postwar years were over, the deleterious, too basic chromates disappeared from the market, and my report went the way of all flesh: but formulas are as holy as prayers, decree-laws, and dead languages, and not an iota in them can be changed. And so my ammonium chloride, the twin of a happy love and a liberating book, by now completely useless and probably a bit harmful, is religiously ground into the chromate anti-rust paint on the shore of that lake, and nobody knows why anymore.

"Broken Vessels"

Andre Dubus (1936–   )

In autobiographical writing, the ability of memory to impose value on daily life usually is displayed in a clearly defined retrospective way, sometimes years after a specific event. Such is the case with a number of the essays in Andre Dubus' *Broken Vessels,* including the marvelous "Under the Lights," an account from his childhood experiences as a ball boy for the Lafayette, Louisiana, baseball team in which the crucial event is a home run hit by the most unlikely power hitter on the roster: "We never saw the ball start its descent, its downward arc to earth. For me, it never has. It is rising white over the lights high above the right field fence, a bright and vanishing sphere of human possibility soaring into the darkness beyond our vision."

The title essay is darker, much longer, and more convoluted than that. I have chosen it because it is a rare example of a memory not yet given the grace of time's passage; rather, it shows memory at work on tragic concerns of the present and the immediate past—at work, that is, when the help it can bring is almost indistinguishable from anguish. Long before dawn on a morning in July 1986, Dubus was permanently crippled—he lost one leg, as well as the use of the other—by a passing car that unaccountably swerved toward him and the two people he had stopped to assist, having seen that their car was disabled. One of those two was killed, the other saved by Dubus' instinctive act of tossing her from danger: memory was to give him the solace of that. At the time of the accident, Dubus' wife—the marriage was his third—was pregnant, and the couple already had a young child. By June 1988, Dubus' wife had left him and was given through court order the major custody of their children. The older, Cadence, was six, and Madeleine, the one born after Dubus was injured, seventeen months.

One might think that any essay produced from such material would be a justifiable exercise in self-pity, but Dubus' is anything but that. One reason is his clear awareness (and he gives harrowing evidence for it) that the "victim of injuries like mine is not always the apparent one"; he realizes the degree to which his wife and older daughter "were the true victims." A second reason is that the writing of this essay, begun not long after the children were taken from him, is of essence in his struggle to regain spiritual strength, to offset his wish to die.

"Broken Vessels" has not one but at least two present moments for its telling: we are given the date of July 6, 1988, for one of them, and August 29 of the same year for another. The essay, though, was completed the following year. All the events from the summer of 1986 onward exist in a kind of continuum, in which specific dates, important as they are, can be presented without any consideration of chronology. At the close of the essay, the wish for death has been overcome for some months—by those who have helped him (friends, therapists, doctors, grown children of a previous marriage as well as the young ones of the last), by faith in God (despite, Dubus says in an address to the latter, the "sometimes incomprehensible, sometimes seemingly lethal way that You give"), by a human truth confirmed in literature, and (most surprisingly, perhaps) by responses first gained during his Marine Corps training.

for Suzanne

On the twenty-third of June, a Thursday afternoon in 1988, I lay on my bed and looked out the sliding glass doors at blue sky and green poplars and I wanted to die. I wanted to see You and cry out to You: *So You had three years of public life which probably weren't so bad, were probably even good most of the time, and You suffered for three days, from Gethsemane to Calvary, but You never had children taken away from You.* That is what I wanted to do when I died, but it is not why I wanted to die. I wanted to die because my little girls were in Montauk on Long Island, and had been there since Wednesday, and would be till Sunday; and I had last seen and held and heard them on Tuesday. Cadence is six, and Madeleine is seventeen months.

I wanted to die because it was summer again, and all summer and fall of 1987 I had dreaded the short light and long dark of winter, and now it was June: summer, my favorite season since boyhood, one of less clothes and more hours in the sun: on the beach and the fishing boats and at Fenway Park and on the roads I used to run then walk, after twenty-five years of running; and the five-mile conditioning walks were so much more pleasurable that I was glad I lost running because of sinus headaches in my forties. It was summer again and I wanted to die because last summer I was a shut-in, but with a wife and two daughters in the house, and last August I even wrote. Then with the fall came the end of the family, so of writing; and now the long winter is over and I am shut in still, and without my children in the house; and unable to write, as I have been nearly all the days since the thirteenth of November 1987 when, five days after the girls' mother left me, she came with a court order and a kind young Haverhill police officer, and took Cadence and Madeleine away.

On Tuesday evening, the twenty-first of June in 1988, I ate pizza and Greek salad with my girls and Jack Herlihy, who lives with me, who moved into my basement in January of 1988 to help me pay the mortgage; to help me. But Wednesday and Thursday I could not eat, or hardly could, as though I were not the same man who had lived on Tuesday: in early afternoon, with my son Andre helping me, I had worked out with bench presses and chin-ups in the dining room, where Andre had carried the bench and bar and plates from the library. He rested the chinning bar on its holders on the sides of the kitchen doorway and stood behind me and helped me pull up from the wheelchair, then he pushed the chair ahead of me, and after sets of chin-ups I pulled the chair back under me with my right leg and my stump, and he held me as I lowered my body into it. This was after I had shadowboxed in my chair on the sundeck, singing with Louis Armstrong on cassette, singing for deep breathing with my stomach, and to bring joy to a sitting workout that took me most of the summer of 1987 to devise, with gratitude to my friend Jane Strüss, who taught me in voice lessons in the winter and spring of 1984 that I had spent my adult life breathing unnaturally. The shadowboxing while singing gives me the catharsis I once gained from the conditioning walks and, before those, the running that I had started when I was nineteen, after celebrating or, more accurately, realizing that birthday while riding before dawn with a busload of officer candidates to the rifle range at Quantico, Virginia, during my first six weeks of Marine Corps Platoon Leaders' Class, in August of 1955.

I came home from training to my sophomore year at McNeese State College in Lake Charles, Louisiana; and to better endure the second six weeks of Platoon Leaders' Class in 1957, then active duty as an officer after college, I ran on the roads near my home for the next three years, a time in America when no one worked out, not even athletes in their off-seasons, and anyone seen running on a road had the look of either a fugitive or a man gone mad in the noonday sun. When I left the Marines in 1964 I kept running, because it—and sometimes it alone—cleared my brain and gave peace to my soul. I never exercised for longevity or to have an attractive body and, strangely, my body showed that: I always had a paunch I assumed was a beer gut until the early spring of 1987 when my right leg was still in a cast, as it was for nearly eight months, and I drank no beer, only a very occasional vodka martini my wife made me, and I could not eat more than twice a day, but with Andre's help on the weight-lifting bench I started regaining the forty or so pounds I had lost in the hospital, and my stomach spread into its old mound and I told my physical therapist, Mary Winchell, that it never was a beer gut after all. Mary came to the house three times a week and endured with me the pain of nearly every session, and the other pain that was not of the body but the spirit: that deeper and more deleterious pain that rendered me on the twenty-second and twenty-third of June 1988 not the same man at all who, after my workout on the twenty-first of June, waited for Cadence and Madeleine to come to my house.

When they did, Jack was home doing his paperwork from the Phoenix Bookstore, and he hosed water into the plastic wading pool I had given Cadence for her sixth birthday on the eleventh of June. The pool is on the sundeck, which I can be on this summer because in March David

Novak and a young man named Justin built ramps from the dining room to the sunken living room, and from the living room to the sundeck. I wanted to be with Cadence, so Jack placed the feet of the wooden chaise longue in the pool and I transferred from my chair to the chaise, then lowered myself into the cold water. I was wearing gym shorts, Cadence was in her bathing suit, and I had taken off Madeleine's dress, and rubbed sun screen on her skin, and in diapers and sandals she walked smiling on the sundeck, her light brown and curly hair more blonde now in summer; but she did not want to be in the water. Sometimes she reached out for me to hold her, and I did, sitting in the pool, and I kept her feet above water till she was ready to leave again, and turned and strained in my arms, and said *Eh,* to show me she was. But she watched Cadence and me playing with a rubber Little Pony that floated, her long mane and tail trailing, and a rubber tiger that did not float, and Madeleine's small inflatable caramel-colored bear Cadence had chosen for her at The Big Apple Circus we had gone to in Boston on the fourth of June, to begin celebrating Cadence's birthday: Jack and Cadence and me in one car, and Madeleine with my grown daughter Suzanne and her friend Tom in another.

Cadence is tall and lithe, and has long red hair, and hazel eyes that show the lights of intelligence. Always she imagines the games we play. I was the Little Pony and she was the tiger; we talked for the animals, and they swam and dived to the bottom and walked on my right leg that was a coral reef, and had a picnic with iced tea on the plastic bank. There was no tea, no food. Once Madeleine's bear was bad, coming over the water to kill and eat our pony and tiger, and they dispatched him by holding a rubber beach ball on the bottom of the pool and releasing it under the floating bear, driving him up and over the side, onto the sundeck. Lynda Novak, young friend and daughter of dear friends, was with us, watching Madeleine as Cadence and I sat in the water under a blue sky, in dry but very warm air, and the sun of late June was hot and high.

I had planned to barbecue pork chops, four of them, center cut, marinating since morning in sauce in the refrigerator. When Cadence and I tired of the sun and the pool and the games in it, we went inside to watch a National Geographic documentary on sharks, a video, and while Lynda and Cadence started the movie, and Madeleine walked about, smiling and talking with her few words, and the echolalia she and usually Cadence and sometimes Lynda and I understood, I wheeled up the ramp to the dining room, and toward the kitchen, but did not get there for the chops, and the vegetables, frozen ones to give me more time with the girls. A bottle of basil had fallen from the work table my friend Bill Webb built against the rear wall of the dining room; he built it two days after Christmas because, two days before Christmas, he came to see me, and I was sitting in the dining room, in my wheelchair, and chopping turkey giblets on a small cutting board resting across my lap. *You like to cook,* he said, *and you can't do a Goddamn thing in that little kitchen of yours; you need a work bench.* The basil was on the floor, in my path; I leaned down, picked it up, flipped it into my lap as I straightened, and its top came off and basil spread and piled on my leg and stump and lap and chair.

Nothing: only some spilled basil, but Cadence was calling: *Daddy, come see the great white,* and I was confronting not basil but the weekend of 17–19 June, one of my two June weekends with Cadence and Madeleine. So I replaced the top on the jar, and with a paper towel picked up the mounds of basil, and with a sponge wiped off the rest of it. Then on the phone (*The phone is your legs,* a friend said to me once) I ordered pizza and Greek salad to be delivered, and joined my girls and Lynda in the living room to watch sharks, and Valerie Taylor of Australia testing a steel mesh shark-proof suit by letting a shark bite her arm. The pizza and salad arrived when Jack had come home from the bookstore, and he and the girls and Lynda and I ate on the sundeck.

On Friday the seventeenth of June I had had Delmonico steaks, potatoes, and snap beans. Jack was picking up the girls on his way home from the store, at about six-thirty, so at five forty-five I started scrubbing potatoes in the kitchen sink, and snapping the ends off beans and washing them. I had just finished shadowboxing on the sundeck, and I believed I could have the potatoes boiling, the beans ready, and also shower and shave before six-thirty. Too often, perhaps most days and nights, my body is still on biped time, and I wheel and reach and turn the chair to the sink or stove and twist in the chair to reach and learn yet again what my friend David Mix said last January. David lost his left leg, below the knee, to a Bouncing Betty that did not bounce, and so probably saved his life, on the first of August in 1967, while doing his work one morning as a Marine lieutenant in Vietnam. His novel, *Intricate Scars,* which I read in manuscript, is the most tenderly merciful and brutal war novel I have ever read. Last winter he said to my son Andre: *There comes a time in the life of an amputee when he realizes that everything takes three times as long.*

He was precise. That Friday night I stopped working in the kitchen long enough to shower, sitting on the stool, using Cadence's hand mirror to shave beneath and above my beard; I dried myself with a towel while sitting and lying on my bed, then wrapped my stump with two ace bandages, and pulled over it a tight stump sleeve to prevent edema. Twenty, maybe even thirty minutes, to shave and shower and shampoo and bandage and dress, yet we sat at the table for steak and boiled potatoes and snap beans and a salad of cucumbers and lettuce at nine-fifteen. And Jack was helping, from the time he got home till the meal was ready; but the kitchen is very small, and with the back of my wheelchair against the sink, I can reach the stove and nearly get food from the refrigerator to my right. I occupied all the cooking space; Jack could only set the table and be with the girls. Cadence was teaching Madeleine to seesaw in the hall, and often she called for me to come see Madeleine holding on and grinning and making sounds of delight, and I wheeled out of the kitchen and looked at the girls on the seesaw, then backed into the kitchen and time moved, as David Mix said, three times as fast as the action that once used a third of it.

Saturday's dinner was easy: I simply had to heat the potatoes and beans left over from Friday, and finish frying the steaks we had partially fried then, before we realized we had more than we needed, and the only difficulty was wheeling back and forth from the dining room table to the kitchen, holding dishes and glasses and flatware in my lap, a few at a time, then squirming and stretching in my chair to rinse them in the sink behind me, and place them in the dishwasher between the sink and refrigerator behind me. After dinner Cadence went to a dance concert with Suzanne and Tom.

I bathed Madeleine in the sink. She was happy in the bubbles from dish soap, and I hugged and dried her with a towel, and powdered her body and put a diaper on her, then buckled my seat belt around her and took her down the ramp to the living room. The late June sun was setting in the northwest, beyond the wide and high glass at the front of the house. I put her on the couch and got on it beside her, and Jack sat in a rocking chair at its foot, and we watched *Barfly* on VCR while Madeleine sat on my chest, smiling at me, pulling my beard and lower lip, her brown eyes deep, as they have been since she was a baby, when she would stare at each person who entered the house, would appear to be thinking about that man, that woman, would seem to be looking into their souls. She is my sixth child, and I have never seen a baby look at people that way. She still does.

That night on the couch she sometimes lay on my chest, her fleshy little arms hugging my neck, her soft and sweet-smelling cheek against mine. I felt her heart beating, and felt from her chest the sounds she made at my face, a series of rising and falling *oohs,* in the rhythm of soothing: *oohoohoohooh.* . . . After sunset, in the cooling room beneath the fan, she puckered her lips and smacked them in a kiss, as Suzanne had taught her, then leaned toward my face, her eyes bright, and kissed me; over and over; then she turned and reached behind her toward Jack, pointing her right hand, with its shortened forefinger. The top knuckle was severed in the sprocket of an exercise bicycle when she was a year and twenty-one days old; she has a tiny stump that Cadence says she got so that when she is older she will understand my stump. I told her to give Jack a kiss, and lifted her to her feet and held her arms as she stepped off my chest, onto the couch, and followed it back to the arm, where Jack's arms and face waited for her: she puckered and smacked as she walked, then she kissed her godfather. During most of the movie, before she grew sleepy and I put her in the chair with me and buckled the seat belt around her and took her up the ramp and to the refrigerator for her bottle of orange juice, then to the crib and sang "Smoke Gets in Your Eyes," while hers closed, she stayed on my chest, and I held her, drew from her little body and loving heart peace and hope, and gratitude for being spared death that night on the highway, or a brain so injured it could not know and love Madeleine Elise. I said: *Madeleine, I love you*; and she smiled and said: *I luh you.*

Once I paused the movie, and lifted her from me and got onto my chair and went past the television and down the short ramp to the sundeck, and I wheeled to the front railing to piss between its posts, out in the night air, under the stars. Madeleine followed me, with Jack behind her, saying: *She's coming after you, Brother.* I turned to see her coming down the ramp, balancing well, then she glanced up and saw what I had not; and still descending, her face excited, she pointed the stump of her finger to the northwest and said: *Moon.*

I looked ahead of me and up at a new moon, then watched her coming to me, pointing, looking skyward, saying: *Moon. Moon. Moon.*

About the next day, Sunday the nineteenth, I remember very little, save that I was tired, as if the long preparing of the meal on Friday had taken from me some energy that I suspect was spiritual, and that I did not regain. Suzanne spent the afternoon with me and the girls. At five o'clock, in accordance with the court order, she took them to their mother's.

Today, the sixth of July 1988, I read chapter nine of St. Luke. Since starting to write this, I have begun each day's work by reading a chapter of the New Testament. Today I read: *"If anyone wishes to come after me let him deny himself, and take up his cross daily, and follow me."* And: *"took a little child and set him at his side, and said to them: 'Whoever receives this little child for my sake, receives me'."*

In June of 1987 I graduated from physical therapy at home with Mary Winchell: she taught me to transfer from my wheel chair to the passenger seat of a car, meaning the Visiting Nurses Association and Blue Cross and Blue Shield would no longer pay her to come work with me. But it was time: for the physical therapy clinic at Hale Hospital in Haverhill; for Judith Tranberg, called Mrs. T by herself and almost everyone who knows her: a lady who worked at Walter Reed with amputees from the Korean War, a lady whose lined, brown, merry and profound face and hazel eyes and deep tobacco voice I loved at once. On the twenty-second of July I wheeled into her clinic and said to her: *They've always told me my left leg is my best one,* and she said: *Why did they tell you your left leg is your best one? I* said: *I like you. I had my spirit till June, then the surgeon took off the cast and I saw my right leg and I started listening to my body. But now my spirit is back.* Mrs. T said: *I never listen to the body; only the spirit.*

My right leg looked like one found on a battlefield, perhaps a day after its severance from the body it had grown with. Except it was not bloated. It was very thin and the flesh had red and yellow hues and the foot was often purple and nearly always the big toe was painful. I do not know why. On the end of my stump was what people thought then was a blister, though it was a stitch which would become infected and, a year later, require surgery, a debridement. So Mrs. T told me not to use the artificial leg. She started me on parallel bars with the atrophied right leg, whose knee probably bent thirty-two degrees, and was never supposed to bend over forty-five, because of the shattered femur and the scar tissue in my thigh muscles, and the hole under my knee where a bone is now grafted. The tibia was also shattered, and part of my calf muscle is grafted to the top of my shin. Because of muscle and nerve damage, my surgeon, Fulton Kornack, and Mary Winchell told me my leg would never hold my foot in a neutral position, and it still does not: without a brace, from the sole and heel up my calf, my foot droops, and curls. But Mary never gave up on the knee, nor has Mrs. T, nor have I, and it can now bend sixty-three degrees.

The best person for a crippled man to cry with is a good female physical therapist, and the best place to do that crying is in the area where she works. One morning in August of 1987, shuffling with my right leg and the walker, with Mrs. T in front of me and her kind younger assistants, Kathy and Betty, beside me, I began to cry. Moving across the long therapy room with beds, machines, parallel bars, and exercise bicycles, I said through my weeping: *I'm not a man among men anymore and I'm not a man among women either.* Kathy and Betty gently told me I was fine. Mrs. T said nothing, backing ahead of me, watching my leg, my face, my body. We kept working. I cried and talked all the way into the small room with two beds that are actually leather-cushioned tables with a sheet and pillow on each, and the women helped me onto my table, and Mrs. T went to the end of it, to my foot, and began working on my ankle and toes and calf with her gentle strong hands. Then she looked up at me. Her voice has much peace whose resonance is her own pain she has moved through and beyond. *It's in Jeremiah,* she said. *The potter is making a pot and it cracks. So he smashes it, and makes a new vessel. You can't make a new vessel out of a broken one. It's time to find the real you.*

Her words and their images rose through my chest like a warm vapor, and in it was the man shattering clay, and me at Platoon Leaders' Class at Quantico, a boy who had never made love, not when I turned nineteen there, not when I went back for the second six weeks just before becoming twenty-one; and memories of myself after my training at Quantico, those times in my life when I had instinctively moved toward action, to stop fights, to help the injured or stricken, and I saw myself on the highway that night, and I said: *Yes. It makes sense. It started as a Marine, when I was eighteen; and it ended on a highway when I was almost fifty years old.*

In the hospital one night when I was in very bad shape, I woke from a dream. In the dream I was in the hospital at Camp Pendleton, California, and I was waiting for Major Forrest Joe Hunt, one of the best commanding officers I ever served with, to come and tell me where I must go now, and what I must do. But when I woke I was still at Camp Pendleton and the twenty-nine years since I left there to go on sea duty did not exist at all and I was a lieutenant waiting for Major Hunt. I asked the nurse if we were at Camp Pendleton and it took her a long time to bring me back to where and who I was. Some time later my old friend, Mark Costello, phoned me at the hospital; Mark and I met on the rifle range in Officers' Basic School at Quantico in 1958. I told him about the dream, and he said: *Marine Corps training is why you were on the highway that night.* I said I knew that, and he told me he had pulled a drowning man from the surf one summer at Mazatlan and that a Mexican man on the beach would not help him, would not go out in the water with him, and he said: *Civilian training is more conservative.* I had known that too, and had believed for a long time that we too easily accuse people of apathy or callousness when they do not help victims of assault or accidents or other disasters. I believe most people want to help, but are unable to because they have not been trained to act. Then, afterward, they think of what they could have done and they feel like physical or moral cowards or both. They should not. When I came home from the hospital a state trooper came to visit me; he told me that doctors, nurses, and paramedics were usually the only people who stopped at accidents. Sadly, he told me that people do stop when the state troopers are there; they want to look at the bodies. I am sure that the trooper's long experience has shown him a terrible truth about our species; and I am also sure that the doctors and nurses and paramedics who stop are not the only compassionate people who see an accident, but the only trained ones. *Don't just stand there, Lieutenant* they told us again and again at Officers' Basic School; *Do something, even if it's wrong.*

Until the summer and fall of 1987 I still believed that Marine training taught us to control our natural instincts to survive. But then, writing a long letter to a friend, night after night, I began to see the truth: the Marine Corps develops our natural instincts to risk ourselves for those we truly love, usually our families, for whom many human beings would risk or knowingly sacrifice their lives, and indeed many have. In a world whose inhabitants from their very beginning turned away from rather than toward each other, chose self over agape, war was a certainty; and soldiers learned that they could not endure war unless they loved each other. So I now believe that, among a species which has evolved more selfishly than lovingly, thus making soldiers an essential body of a society, there is this paradox: in order to fight wars, the Marine Corps develops in a recruit at Boot Camp, an officer candidate at Quantico, the instinct to surrender oneself for another; expands that instinct beyond families or mates or other beloveds to include all Marines. It is a Marine Corps tradition not to leave dead Marines on the battlefield, and Marines have died trying to retrieve those dead. This means that after his training a young Marine has, without words, taken a vow to offer his life for another Marine. Which means, sadly, that the Marine Corps, in a way limited to military action, has in general instilled more love in its members than Christian churches have in theirs. The Marine Corps does this, as all good teachers do, by drawing from a person instincts that are already present, and developing them by giving each person the confidence to believe in those instincts, to follow where they lead. A Marine crawling under fire to reach a wounded Marine is performing a sacrament, an action whose essence is love, and the giving and receiving of grace.

The night before the day I cried with Mrs. T for the first time (I would cry many times during physical therapy that fall and winter and spring of 1987 and 1988, and she teases me about it still, her eyes bright and her grin crinkling her face), my wife took me to a movie. She sat in an aisle seat and I sat in my wheelchair beside her, with my plastic urinal on the floor beneath my chair leg that held my right foot elevated for better circulation of blood. Two young couples in their late teens sat directly in front of us. One of the boys was talking before the movie, then when it began he was still talking and he did not stop; the other three were not silent either, but he was the leader, the loud one. In my biped days, I was the one who asked or told people to be quiet. But in my chair I felt helpless, and said nothing. There was no rational cause for feeling that way. When you ask or tell people to be quiet in movies, they do not come rushing out of their seats, swinging at you. But a wheelchair is a spiritually pervasive seat. My wife asked the boy to please stop talking. He turned to her, looking over his left shoulder, and patronizingly harassed her, though without profanity. I said, *Cool it.* He looked at me as though he had not seen me till then; and maybe, indeed, he had not. Then he turned to the screen, and for the rest of the movie he and his friends were quiet.

I was not. I made no sounds, but I felt them inside of me. As the movie was ending, I breathed deeply and slowly with adrenaline, and relaxed as much as I could the muscles I meant to use. I would simply look at his eyes as he left his seat and turned toward me to walk around my chair and up the aisle. If he insulted me I would pull him down to me and punch him. During the closing credits he and his date and the other couple stood and left their row of seats. I watched him; he did not turn his eyes to mine. He stepped into the aisle and turned to me but did not face me; he looked instead at the carpet as he walked past me, then was gone. The adrenaline, the edge, went out of me, and seven demons worse than the first came in: sorrow and shame.

So next day, weeping, lying on my back on the table while Mrs. T worked on my body, I told her the story and said: *If you confront a man from a wheelchair you're bullying him. Only a coward would hit a man in a chair.*

That is part of what I told her; I told her, too, about making love: always on my back, unable to kneel, and if I lay on my stomach I could barely move my lower body and had to keep my upper body raised with a suspended pushup. I did not tell her the true sorrow of lovemaking but I am certain that she knew: it made me remember my legs as they once were, and to feel too deeply how crippled I had become.

You can't make a new vessel out of a broken one. I can see her now as she said it, hear her voice, soft but impassioned with certainty, as her face and eyes were. *It's time to find the real you.*

I was working on a novella in August, but then in September, a beautiful blue September with red and orange and yellow leaves, I could not work on it any longer, for I knew that soon my wife would leave. So did Cadence. We played now on my bed with two small bears, Papa Bear and Sister Bear. She brought them to the bed, and their house was my lap; Cadence had just started kindergarten, and Sister Bear went to school, at a spot across the bed, and came home, where she and Papa Bear cooked dinners. They fished from my right leg, the bank of a river, and walked in the forest of my green camouflage Marine poncho liner, and climbed the pillows and the headboard that were mountains. I knew the mother bear was alive, but I did not ask where she was, and Cadence never told me.

But what did she see, in her heart that had already borne so much? Her fourth birthday was on the eleventh of June 1986, then on the twenty-third of July the car hit me and I was in the hospital for nearly two months, her mother coming to see me from one in the afternoon till eight at night every day save one when I told her to stay home and rest, and Cadence was at play school and with a sitter or friends until her mother came home tired at nine o'clock or later at night.

Her mother had waked her around one-thirty in the morning of the twenty-third, to tell her Daddy had been in an accident and her brother Jeb, my younger grown son, was taking Mommy to the hospital and Jeb's friend Nickie would spend the night with her, and she had cried with fear, or terror: that sudden and absolute change in a child's life, this one

coming at night too, the worst of times, its absence of light in the sky
and on trees and earth and manmade objects rendering her a prisoner of
only what she could see: the lighted bedroom, the faces of her mother
and brother and the young woman, and so a prisoner of her imagination
that showed her too much of danger and death and night. Her four years
of life forced her physically to be passive, unable to phone the hospital or
friends, unable even to conceive of tomorrow and tomorrow and tomorrow, of life and healing and peace. Over a year later, on a September
afternoon in the sun, she told me of the first time her mother brought
her to see me, in intensive care: *The little room,* she said, *with all the machines.
I kept that in mind,* she said. *You had that thing in your mouth and it was hard
for me to kiss you. What was it for?* I told her it was probably to let me
breathe. Then she said: *I thought you were dead till then.* And I said that
surely Mommy told her I was alive; she said: *Yes. But I thought you were
dead till I saw you.*

She came to the hospital for short visits with her mother, then friends
took her home; I talked to her on the phone from the hospital bed, and
she was only with her mother in the morning and late at night. She did
not mind that my leg would be cut off; *he'll be asleep and he won't feel it,*
she told a friend who was with her for an afternoon in Boston while her
mother sat with me. *When Daddy comes home,* she told her mother, *I'm
going to help him learn to walk.* At the hospital her mother sat with me, and
watched the clock with me, for the morphine that, twenty minutes after
the injection, would ease the pain. Then I was home in a rented hospital
bed in the library adjacent to our bedroom, and through its wide door I
looked at the double bed, a mattress and boxsprings on the floor, where
Cadence and her mother slept. In the mornings Cadence woke first and
I woke to her voice and face, sitting up in the bed, on the side where I
used to sleep, and looking out the glass door to the sundeck, looking out
at the sky, the morning; and talking. That fall and winter she often talked
about the baby growing in her mother's body; and one night, when she
and I were on the couch in the living room, she said: *Once upon a time
there was a father and mother and a little girl and then they had a baby and
everything went crazy.*

She was only four. That summer of 1986 her mother and I believed
Cadence would only have to be four and worry about a baby coming
into her life, perhaps believing the baby would draw her parents' love
away from her, or would simply be in the way. And her mother and I
believed that, because I had a Guggenheim grant from June of 1986 to
June of 1987, we would simply write and pay the bills and she would
teach her fiction workshop at home on Wednesday nights and I would
try to recover from burning out as a teacher, then becoming so tired
visiting colleges for money from January till July of 1986 that I spent a

night in intensive care at Montpelier, Vermont, on the fourth of July, with what the cardiologist thought was a heart attack but was exhaustion; and we would have a child.

Madeleine grew inside of my wife as she visited the hospital, then as she cared for me at home, changing bandages as they taught her in the hospital, emptying urinals, bringing food to the hospital bed in the library, and juice and water, and holding my leg when I transferred from bed to chair to couch and back again; Madeleine growing inside of her as she soothed the pain in my body and soul, as she put the bed pan under me then cleaned me and it, and she watched with me as the Red Sox beat the Angels in the playoffs and lost to the Mets in the World Series, sacrifice enough for her, to watch baseball till late at night, pregnant and caring for a four-year-old energetic girl and a crippled man. But she sacrificed more: for some time, I don't know how much time, maybe two weeks or three, because it remains suspended in memory as an ordeal that broke us, or broke part of us anyway and made laughter more difficult, I had diarrhea, but not like any I had ever had before. It not only flowed from me without warning, but it gave me no sign at all, so that I did not even know when it flowed, and did not know after it had, and for some reason we could not smell it either. So when a game ended she would stand over me on the couch and turn my body toward hers, and look, and always I was foul, so foul that it took thirty minutes to clean me and get me from the couch to the bed, after midnight then, the pregnant woman going tired and unheld to bed with Cadence, who would wake her in the morning.

Which would begin with cleaning me, and that remained such a part of each day and night that I remember little else, and have no memory of the Red Sox losing the seventh game I watched from the couch. *They saved your life and put you back together,* she said, *and they can't cure this.* Gene Harbilas, my doctor and friend here, cured it, and that time was over, and so was something else: a long time of grace given us in the hospital and at home, a time of love near death and with crippling, a time when my body could do little but lie still and receive, and when her every act was of the spirit, for every act was one of love, even the resting at night for the next long day of driving to and from the hospital to sit there; or, later, waking with me at home, to give me all the sustenance she could. In the fall, after the diarrhea, she was large with Madeleine, and exhaustion had its hold on her and would not let her go again, would not release her merely to gestate and give birth, and nurse and love her baby. The victim of injuries like mine is not always the apparent one. All that year I knew that she and Cadence were the true victims.

Cadence cried often. On a night in January, while Andre was staying with us for the month of Madeleine's birth, having come up from New York to take care of Cadence and mostly me (yes: the bed pan: my son)

Cadence began loudly crying and screaming. She was in her bedroom. I was no longer in the hospital bed but our new one in the bedroom, and they brought her there: her eyes were open but she did not act as though she were awake. She was isolate, screaming with terror, and she could not see or hear us; or, if she could, whatever we did and said was not strong enough to break what held her. Andre called Massachusetts General Hospital and spoke to a pediatrician, a woman. He told her what Cadence was doing and she asked whether Cadence had been under any stress. He said her father was hit by a car in July and was in the hospital for two months and they cut off his leg, and her mother just had a baby and Cadence had chicken pox then so she couldn't visit her mother in the hospital, where she stayed for a week because she had a cesarean. The doctor gasped. Then she told Andre it was night terrors. I do not remember what she told us to do, because nothing we did soothed Cadence; she kept crying and screaming, and I lay helpless on my back, wanting to rise, and hold her in my arms, and walk with her, and I yelled at the ceiling, the night sky above it: *You come down from that cross and give this child some peace!* Then we played the cassette of *Porgy and Bess* by Louis Armstrong and Ella Fitzgerald that she often went to sleep to, and she was quiet and she lay beside me and slept.

In late spring of 1987 Cadence talked me into her room, in my wheel-chair; I had not been able to do it till then, but she encouraged and directed me through the series of movements, forward and back and short turns, then I was there, beside her bed on the floor. After that I could go in and read to her. One night, still in the spring, I went into her room, where she sat on the bed. I looked at her face just below mine and said: "I want to tell you something. You're a very brave and strong girl. Not many four-year-olds have had the kind of year you've had. Some children have to be lied to sometimes, but Mommy and I never had to lie to you."

"What do you mean?"

"We could always tell you the truth. We could tell you they were going to cut off my leg, and that the right one wouldn't be good, and you understood everything, and when you felt happy you were happy, and when you felt sad, you cried. You always let us know how you felt and what was wrong. You didn't see Mommy much for two months while I was in the hospital, and then she was gone for a week to have Madeleine and you only saw her for a couple of minutes at the hospital till the nurse saw your chicken pox and said you had to leave. Then Mommy came home with a baby sister. Most little girls don't go through all of that. All this year has been harder on you than on anybody else, and when you grow up, somebody will have to work awfully hard to make you unhappy, because you're going to be a brave, strong woman."

Tears flowed down her cheeks, but she was quiet and her eyes were shining, and her face was like a woman's receiving love and praise.

Then in the summer and early fall of 1987, we did lie to her, but she knew the truth anyway, or the part of it that gave her pain and demanded, again, resilience; and she brought to my bed only the two bears, the father and the daughter; and her days must have drained her: she woke with the fear of kindergarten and the other fear and sorrow she must have escaped only in sleep and with new children and work at kindergarten, and with familiar friends at play school, in the same way adults are absorbed long enough by certain people and actions to gain respite from some deep fear or pain at the center of their lives. I could no longer work. When the house was empty I phoned Jack at the Phoenix Bookstore and asked for his prayers and counsel and comfort, and I went to physical therapy three times a week, going there and back in a wheelchair van, three hours each session with Mrs. T, and the physical work and pain gave me relief, and I prayed for patience and strength and love, and played with Cadence and Madeleine, and waited for the end.

The girls' mother left on the eighth of November, a Sunday night; and people who love us helped me care for my girls until after dark, around six o'clock, on Friday the thirteenth, when she came with the court order and the Haverhill police officer. That afternoon Cadence and I were lying on my bed. Beside her was her pincher, a strip of grey cloth from the apron of her first Raggedy Ann doll, before she was a year old. She goes to sleep with it held in her fist, her thumb in her mouth. When she is tired or sad she holds it and sucks her thumb, or simply holds it; and she holds it too when she rides in a car or watches cartoons. She held it that afternoon after my lawyer phoned; his name is Scotty, he is an old friend, and he was surprised and sad as he told me of my wife's lawyer calling from the courthouse, to say my wife was coming for my daughters. I wheeled from the kitchen phone, down the short hall to my bedroom where Cadence and I had been playing, where for nearly a year we had played with stuffed animals. I also played the giant who lay on his back, and had lost a leg, and his right one was in a cast. The giant has a deep voice, and he loves animals. Cadence is the red-haired giant, but we usually talk about her in the third person, the animals and I, for Cadence is the hearts and voices of animals with the giant; when Madeleine could sit up and be with me, she became the baby giant, cradled in my arm. Most days in the first year Cadence brought to the games an animal with a missing or wounded limb, an animal who needed healing and our love.

Next to the bed I braked the wheelchair and moved from it to my place beside Cadence. She was sitting. I sat close to her and put my left arm around her and told her that judges were people who made sure everyone was protected by the law, even little children, and Mommy had gone to see one because she believed it was better for Cadence and Madeleine not to be with me, and Mommy was coming now with a policeman, to take her and Madeleine. I told her Mommy was not doing anything wrong, she was doing what she felt was right, like a good Momma Bear. Cadence held her pincher and looked straight ahead and was quiet. Her body was taut.

"I don't want to go in the car with them."

"Who's them, sweetie?"

"The judge and the police."

"No, darling. The judge won't be in the car. Neither will the policeman. It'll just be Mommy."

One of our animals we had played with since I came home from the hospital on the seventeenth of September 1986 is Oatmeal, a blond stuffed bear with pink ears and touches of pink on his cheeks and the top of his head and the back of his neck. On my birthday on the eleventh of August 1987, Cadence gave me shells and seaweed from the beach, and a prayer for a Japanese gingko tree she gave me with her mother, and Oatmeal. I am his voice; it is high. I am also the voice of his wife, Koala Bear; but after the marriage ended, Cadence stopped bringing Koala Bear to our games, save for one final night in December, while Madeleine was asleep and Cadence and I were playing in the dining room, and she said Oatmeal and Koala Bear were breaking up but maybe if Koala Bear had a baby they would love each other again; then she got a small bear from her room and put it with Koala Bear and Oatmeal and said they had a baby now and loved each other again. Then we watched Harry Dean Stanton as an angel in *One Magic Christmas*. After my birthday I kept Oatmeal on my bed; Cadence and I understand that he is a sign from her to me, when she is not here.

That afternoon she gazed in front of her; then quickly she moved: her face and upper body turned to me, her eyes darkly bright with grief and anger; and her arms and hands moved, one hand holding the pincher still, and she picked up Oatmeal and swung him backhanded into my lap. Then she turned away from me and was off the bed, circling its foot, and I watched the pallid right side of her face. When she turned at the bed's end and walked toward the hall, I saw her entire face, her right thumb in her mouth, the grey pincher hanging, moving with her strides; and in her eyes were tears. Her room is adjacent to mine, where I had slept with her mother, where I had watched all the seasons through the glass sliding door that faced northwest. Cadence walked past me, out my door, and into hers. She closed it.

My friend Joe Hurka and my oldest daughter Suzanne were in the house; Joe had been with us all week, driving back and forth, an hour and ten minutes each way, to his job in Peterborough, New Hampshire. I called to Cadence: "Sweetie? Do you want me in your room with you?"

I had never heard her voice from behind a door and a wall as well; always her door was open. Her voice was too old, too sorrowful for five; it was soft because she is a child, but its sound was that of a woman, suffering alone: "No."

I moved onto the wheelchair and turned it toward the door, the hall, her room. I wheeled at an angle through her doorway: she lay above me in her bunk on the left side of the room. She was on her back and sucking her right thumb and holding the pincher in her fist; she looked straight above her, and if she saw anything palpable it was the ceiling. She was pale, and tears were in her right eye, but not on her cheek. I moved to the bunk and looked up at her.

The bunk was only a few months old and, before that, she had a low bed and when she lay on it at night and I sat above her in my chair, she could not see the pictures in the books I read aloud. So we lay on my bed to read. But from the bunk she could look down over my shoulder at the pictures. She climbed a slanted wooden ladder to get on it, and I had told Mrs. T I wanted to learn to climb that ladder. *Not yet, Mr. Andre,* she had said; *not yet.* In that moment in Cadence's room, looking at her face, I said in my heart: *Fuck this cripple shit,* and I pushed the two levers that brake the wheels, and with my left hand I reached up and held the wooden side of the bunk and with my right I pushed up from the arm of the chair. I had learned from Mrs. T not to think about a new movement, but simply to do it. I rose, my extended right arm taking my weight on the padded arm of the chair, and my left trying to straighten, to lift my body up and to pivot onto the mattress beside Cadence. I called Joe and he came quickly down the hall and, standing behind me, he held me under my arms and lifted, and I was on the bunk. Cadence was sitting now, and blood colored her face; her wet eyes shone, and she was grinning.

"Daddy. You got *up* here."

Joe left us, and I lay beside her, watching her face, listening to her voice raised by excitement, talking about me on the bunk. I said now we knew I could lie on the bunk at night and read to her. She crawled to the foot of the bed and faced me. Beyond her, two windows showed the grey sky in the southeast and the greyish white trunks of poplars without leaves. Cadence lowered her head and somersaulted, and her long bent legs arced above us, her feet struck the mattress, and her arms rose toward me, ahead of her face and chest. Her eyes were bright and dry, looking into mine, and she was laughing.

We were on the bunk for an hour or more. We did not talk about our sorrow, but Cadence's face paled, while Suzanne and Joe waited with Madeleine in the dining room for the car to come. When it did, Suzanne called me, and Joe came and stood behind the wheelchair and held my upper body as I moved down from the bunk. In the dining room Madeleine was in her high chair; Suzanne was feeding her cottage cheese. I talked with the young police officer, then hugged and kissed Madeleine and Cadence goodbye.

In Salem District Court I got shared but not physical custody. The girls would be with me two weekends a month, Thursday afternoons and alternate Monday afternoons through dinner, half a week during the week-long vacations from school, and two weeks in the summer. *That's a lot of time,* people say. Until I tell them it is four nights a month with my two daughters, except for the two weeks in summer, and ask them if their own fathers spent only four nights a month with them when they were children (of course many say yes, or even less); or until I tell them that if I were making a living by traveling and earning a hundred thousand a year and spent only four nights a month with my family I would not be a good father. The family court system in Massachusetts appears to define a father as a sperm bank with a checkbook. But that is simply the way they make a father feel, and implicit in their dealings is an admonishment to the father to be grateful for any time at all with his children. The truth is that families are asunder, so the country is too, and no one knows what to do about this, or even why it is so. When the court receives one of these tragedies it naturally assigns the children to the mother's house, and makes the father's house a place for the children to visit. This is not fatherhood. My own view is that one house is not a home; our home has now become two houses.

On the tenth of January 1988, Madeleine was a year old. It was a Sunday, and one of my weekends with the girls, and we had balloons and a cake and small presents, and Cadence blew out the candle for her sister. During that time in winter I was still watching Cadence for signs of pain, as Suzanne and Andre and Jack were, and Marian and David Novak, and Joe Hurka and Tom. Madeleine was sometimes confused or frightened in her crib at night, but never for long. She is a happy little girl, and Cadence and Suzanne and Jack and I learned during the days of Christmas that "Silent Night" soothes her, and I sing it to her still, we all do, when she is troubled; and she stops crying. Usually she starts singing at *holy night, all is calm,* not with words but with the melody, and once this summer she sang the melody to Cadence when she was crying. We all knew that Madeleine, only ten months old when the family separated, was least touched, was the more fortunate of the children, if indeed anything about this can be fortunate for one of the children. So we watched Cadence, and let her be sad or angry, and talked with her; and we hugged and kissed Madeleine, and played with her, fed her, taught her words, and sang her to sleep.

The fifth of February was a Friday in 1988, and the first night of a weekend with the girls. Suzanne brought them into the house shortly after six o'clock in the evening; I was in the shower, sitting on the stool, and she brought them to the bathroom door to greet me. When I wheeled out of the bathroom into the dining room, a towel covering my lap, Cadence was in the living room, pedaling my exercise bicycle. A kind woman had given it to me when she saw me working on one at physical therapy, and learned from Mrs. T that I did not have the money to buy one. With my foot held by the pedal strap I could push the pedal down and pull it up, but my knee would not bend enough for me to push the wheel in a circle. In February I did not have the long ramp to the living room, against its rear wall, but a short steep one going straight down from the dining room and I could not climb or descend it alone, because my chair would turn over. Madeleine was in the dining room, crawling, and Suzanne stood behind me, in the doorway between the dining room and kitchen, talking on the phone and looking at the girls. I was near the ramp, and Cadence was saying: *Watch this, Daddy,* and was standing on the right pedal with her right foot, stretching her left leg up behind her, holding with both hands the grip on the right end of the handlebar, and pushing the pedal around and around.

Then she was sitting on the seat and pedaling and Madeline crawled down the ramp and toward her and the bicycle, and Cadence said: *Madeleine, no,* as Madeleine reached with her right hand to the chain guard at the wheel and her index finger went into a notch I had never seen, and a tooth of the sprocket cut her with a sound distinct among those of the moving chain and spinning wheel and Suzanne's voice: a *thunk,* followed at once by the sound of Madeline's head striking the floor as she fell back from the pain, and screamed. She did not stop. Cadence's face was pale and frightened and ashamed, and I said: *She'll be all right, darling. Is it her head or her finger?* and Cadence said: *It's her finger and it's bleeding,* and Suzanne was there, bending for Madeleine, reaching for her, saying: *It is her finger and it's cut* off. Three of my four daughters, and I see their faces now: the oldest bravely grieving, the youngest red with the screams that were as long as her breathing allowed, and above them the five-year-old, pale with the horror of the bleeding stump she saw and the belief that she alone was responsible.

Then Suzanne was rising with Madeleine in her arms and saying: *I have to find the finger, they can sew it back on,* and bringing Madeleine up the ramp to me. She was screaming and kicking and writhing and I held her and looked at her tiny index and middle fingers of her right hand: the top knuckle of her index finger was severed, and so was the inside tip of her middle finger, at an angle going up and across her fingernail. In months, that part of her middle finger would grow back. Suzanne told Cadence to stop the chain because Madeleine's finger could be stuck in it, and she dialed 911, and the police officer told her to put the dismembered piece in ice. Cadence came up the ramp; I was frightened of bleeding and shock, and had only a towel, which does not stop bleeding. I said to Cadence: *Go get me a bandana.* She turned and sprinted down the hall toward my room, and I called after her: *In the second drawer of my chest,* and she ran back with a clean bandana she held out to me. Suzanne was searching the bicycle chain and the living room, and Cadence watched me wrap Madeleine's fingers. I held her kicking legs up but she did not go into shock and she did not stop screaming, while Suzanne found the rest of her finger lying on the floor, and wrapped it in ice and put it in the refrigerator, and twice I told Cadence it was not her fault and she must never think it was.

But she did not hear me. I imagine she heard very little but Madeleine's screaming, and perhaps her own voice saying *Madeleine, no,* before either Suzanne or I could see what was about to happen, an instant before that sound of the sprocket tooth cutting through flesh and bone; and she probably saw, besides her sister's screaming and tearful face and bandaged bleeding hand, and the blood on Madeleine's clothes and on the towel and chair and me, her own images: her minutes of pleasure on the bicycle before Madeleine crawled down the ramp toward her and then once again, and so quickly again, her life became fear and pain and sorrow, already and again demanding of her resilience and resolve. When a police officer and two paramedics arrived, she said she wanted to go in the ambulance with Madeleine and Suzanne.

By then Tom and Jack were there, and I was drying and dressing. The police officer found the small piece of Madeleine's middle finger in the chain and ran outside with it, and gave it to the paramedics before they drove to Lawrence General Hospital, because Hale Hospital has no trauma center. I asked Jack to phone David Novak, and by the time I dressed and gave the officer what he needed for his report, David was in the house. I phoned Andre at work and Jeb at home, then David and Tom and Jack and I drove in David's Bronco to the hospital, twenty-five minutes away. I had put into my knapsack what I would need to spend the night in the hospital with Madeleine. Her mother was in Vermont, to ski. But in the car, talking to David, I knew that Cadence would need me more.

In the ambulance Madeleine stopped screaming, and began the sounds she made that winter when she was near sleep: *ah* ah *ah* ah. . . . At the hospital she cried steadily, because of the pain, but now she was afraid too and that was in her voice, even more than pain. A nurse gave her to me and I held her cheek to mine and sang "Silent Night," then Jeb was there. At Lawrence General they could not work on Madeleine's finger: they phoned Massachusetts General Hospital in Boston, then took her there. Suzanne rode with her, and Jeb and Tom followed. Suzanne dealt with the surgeons and, on the phone, reported to me; I talked to the girls' mother in Vermont; and Suzanne and Jeb and Tom stayed at the hospital until the operation was over, and Madeleine was asleep in bed. The surgeon could not sew on the part of Madeleine's finger, because of the angle of its amputation. Early next morning her mother drove to the hospital and brought her to my house; her hand was bandaged and she felt no pain; her mother had asked on the phone in Vermont if she could spend the weekend with Madeleine, and Cadence went with them for the afternoon, then in the evening her mother brought her back to me for the rest of the weekend.

When David and Jack and Cadence and I got home from Lawrence General, I put Cadence on my lap and wheeled to my bedroom and lifted her to my bed. She lay on her back and held her pincher and sucked her thumb. She watched me as I told her she had been very good when Madeleine was hurt, that she had not panicked; she asked me what that meant, and I told her, and said that some children and some grown-ups would not have been able to help Suzanne and me, and that would be very normal for a child, but I only had to tell her to get me a bandana and she had run down the hall to the drawer in my chest before I could even tell her which drawer to look in. She turned to me: "I heard you when I was running down the hall. You said the second drawer, but I already knew and I was running to it."

I told her that was true courage, that to be brave you had to be afraid, and I was very proud of her, and of Suzanne, because we were all afraid and everyone controlled it and did what had to be done. She said: "*You* were afraid?"

"Yes. That's why I was crying."

She looked at the ceiling as I told her she must never blame herself for Madeleine's finger, that no one had seen the notch in the chain guard, the bicycle had looked safe, and she had tried to stop Madeleine, had said *Madeleine, no,* and two grown-ups were right there watching and it happened too fast for anyone to stop it. She looked at me. "I started pedaling backwards when I saw her reaching for the wheel."

Then she looked up again, and I said she had done all she could to keep Madeleine from getting hurt, and it was very important for her never to feel responsible, never to blame herself, because that could hurt her soul, and its growth; and if she ever felt that way she must tell me or

Mommy or Suzanne or Andre or Jeb. Her thumb was in her mouth and her pincher lay across her fingers, so part of it was at her nose, giving her the scent she loves. Finally I said: "Is there anything you want to ask me?" Still gazing straight up, she lowered her thumb and said: "I only have one question. Why does it always happen to me? First you got hurt. Now Madeleine is hurt. Maybe next Mommy will get hurt. Or I will."

I closed my eyes and waited for images, for words, but no words rose from my heart; I saw only Cadence's face for over a year and a half now, suffering and enduring and claiming and claiming cheer and joy and harmony with her body and spirit, and so with her life, a child's life with so very few choices. I opened my eyes.

"I don't know," I said. "But you're getting awfully good at it."

It is what she would tell me now; or encourage me to do.

Today is the twenty-ninth of August 1988, and since the twenty-third of June, the second of two days when I wanted to die, I have not wanted my earthly life to end, have not wanted to confront You with anger and despair. I receive You in the Eucharist at daily Mass, and look at You on the cross, but mostly I watch the priest, and the old deacon, a widower, who brings me the Eucharist; and the people who walk past me to receive; and I know they have all endured their own agony, and prevailed in their own way, though not alone but drawing their hope and strength from those they love, those who love them; and from You, in the sometimes tactile, sometimes incomprehensible, sometimes seemingly lethal way that You give.

A week ago I read again *The Old Man and the Sea,* and learned from it that, above all, our bodies exist to perform the condition of our spirits: our choices, our desires, our loves. My physical mobility and my little girls have been taken from me; but I remain. So my crippling is a daily and living sculpture of certain truths: we receive and we lose, and we must try to achieve gratitude; and with that gratitude to embrace with whole hearts whatever of life that remains after the losses. No one can do this alone, for being absolutely alone finally means a life not only without people or God or both to love, but without love itself. In *The Old Man and the Sea,* Santiago is a widower and a man who prays; but the love that fills and sustains him is of life itself: living creatures, and the sky, and the sea. Without that love, he would be an old man alone in a boat.

One Sunday afternoon in July, Cadence asked Jack to bring up my reserve wheelchair from the basement, and she sat in it and wheeled about the house, and moved from it onto my bed and then back to the chair, with her legs held straight, as I hold my right one when getting on and off the bed. She wheeled through the narrow bathroom door and got onto the toilet, her legs straight, her feet above the floor, and pushed her pants down; and when she pulled them up again she said it was hard to do, sitting down. She went down and up the ramp to the living room, and the one to the sundeck. *Now I know what it's like to be you,* she said. When she was ready to watch a VCR cartoon, she got onto the living room couch as I do, then pushed her chair away to make room for mine, and I moved onto the couch and she sat on my stump and nestled against my chest; and Madeleine came, walking, her arms reaching for me, and I lifted her and sat her between my leg and stump, and with both arms I held my girls.

Insights of Old Age

An aged man is but a paltry thing,
A tattered coat upon a stick, unless
Soul clap its hand and sing, and louder sing
For every tatter in its mortal dress . . .

—William Butler Yeats, from "Sailing to Byzantium"

From a myriad of possibilities, I have chosen four essays to represent the insights of our final years. Two of these essays—as simple as they are brief, both by the same woman—color small moments in the past with present knowledge. The other essays offer a summing up—one by a man who in his eighties has just concluded an arduous search for an elusive truth; the other by a woman who examines her entire past in pursuit of what finally matters. Each of these people is alone; the mate is gone, the children elsewhere. The major tragedies are in the past, as are the moments of fulfillment. Major ambitions have been either realized or dismissed, and the fear of dying has long since vanished. ("Old age should burn and rave at the close of day," Dylan Thomas says, in a poem that may have the example of Lear in mind; the advice, while ostensibly addressed to his dying father, probably reflects his own wish to oppose the inevitable.)

If one's life has been dismal, there well may be rage and resentment at its end—either that, or silence. If life has been rewarding—as is the case with the three essayists presented here—the final song will include acceptance, a spiritual requirement beyond the power of most younger people.

from *To Begin Again: Stories and Memoirs, 1908–1929*

M. F. K. Fisher (1908–1992)

M. F. K. Fisher, who died at the age of eighty-three, is known for her deft prose about the pleasures of food; among her eighteen books are *The Art of Eating* and *The Gastronomical Me*. In "Grandmother's Nervous Stomach," one of the essays included in *To Begin Again*, published shortly after Fisher's death, she remembers the years of her childhood when her grandmother lived with her family. A woman of rigorous religious observance, the grandmother imposed upon the family the blandness of the diet that was one of the corollaries of her creed. Only when the grandmother was on a trip—to a religious convention or a dietary retreat—did the family enjoy good cheer (and good food) at mealtimes. In rebellion against her grandmother's sense of joyless duty, Fisher, at the age of five, began some theorizing about food that led to the development of her own sense of obligation: "Increasingly," she writes, "I saw, felt, understood the importance, especially between people who love and trust one another, of a full sharing of one of our three main hungers, which are for food, for love, and for shelter. We must satisfy them in order to survive as creatures. It is our duty, having been created."

The shared enjoyment of food, though, is not a central preoccupation of the selections contained in her posthumous book; indeed, a couple of years before the publication of *To Begin Again*, she was quoted in the *New York Times* as saying about her advanced years, "I'm not hungry anymore." The best of these last essays emphasize, in place of bodily satisfactions, a spiritual acceptance—the kind of wisdom that luckily comes to some of us in our elderly years, as memory, using all that it has gained through the decades, sees our past nature against present knowledge. I have selected two brief pieces that communicate this dimension of memory, "The Jackstraws" and "Tally." In the former, Fisher, sitting on her California veranda "as day slips into night," acknowledges at last the value of the jackstraws that her grandfather long ago, and somewhat clumsily, crafted for her; in the latter, she remembers the "invisible friends" that both she and her brother David were comforted by—David as a young child, Fisher as a young woman. The "warm hand" of the invisible presence beneath her bed has long since vanished, though as an old woman the need for the availability of help is obvious. Why has that guardian left her? "Well, it is plain that he is needed more somewhere else," she says briskly; adding, at the end of the essay, that it "is good to know" that "he and Tally [the latter the name of David's also departed invisible companion] are somewhere." Now, she can be "very thankful that for a long time I knew I was not alone."

THE JACKSTRAWS (1922)

Every thinking man is prone, particularly as he grows older, to feel waves large or small of a kind of cosmic regret for what he let go past him. He wonders helplessly—knowing how futile it would be to feel any active passion—how he could have behaved as he did or let something or other happen without acknowledging it.

The only salve to this occasional wound, basically open until death, no matter how small and hidden—is to admit that there is potential strength in it: not only in recognizing it as such but in accepting the long far ripples of understanding and love that most probably spread out from its beginning.

A good time for me to contemplate such personal solutions, or whatever they may be, is when day slides into night. In almost all weather I can sit for a few minutes or an hour or so on my veranda, looking west-southwest and letting a visceral realization flow quietly through me of what other people have given me that I can only now understand.

A clear one, tonight, was of the jackstraws my Grandfather Kennedy whittled for my siblings and me in perhaps 1922 or before. It was never pointed out to me, as I now think it should have been, that an old man had spent long hours making something to please us. I blame my mother for this: she was constitutionally opposed to in-laws, and her whole attitude was that they must perforce be equally antagonistic toward her as the bride who robbed their roost of a fine cock and as a person of higher social station. This was unfortunate for all of us, and my mother lost the most by it and realized it much too late.

Meanwhile, whatever Grandfather Kennedy did was put into limbo in a subtly mocking way, and as far as I can remember we laughed a little at the clumsy set of jackstraws and pushed them into the back of the game closet, tempted by glossier packaged things like a new set of Parcheesi and even the baby stuff Tiddlywinks.

I still have a couple of the jackstraws. They are made of fine dry hardwood, and I think that some at the first had been stained faintly with green and red—dyes Grandmother may have brewed for her dotty husband, grinning sardonically as she prophesied in silence about the obvious end to the caper. One of the straws (were there a hundred in each set, with one hook to be passed around among the players?) is shaped like a crude mace. There were others like arrows, daggers. . . . Each one, according to its shape and then its color, was worth a certain number of points.

I cannot find the rules anywhere in my otherwise somewhat gamey shelves, but I know that the person chosen to be "first" held all the jack-straws firmly in his one or two fists, depending on his age and the length of his fingers, with the hook or perhaps the king straw in the middle, and then twisted them while everybody held his breath around the table. Then the hand or little fists let go, and the pile fell into a contrived heap on the table. And then—yes, the hook was kept out, apart, in order to start the trembling battle, and it *was* the king straw we'd left in the middle!—then we took turns and delicately plucked out one straw, then another if we had not jiggled anything, no straw at all if we had, always aiming for the main glorious one so deftly buried under the little heap. The hook was passed around. Whoever got out the prize won the game, and unless it was time for bed we had another game, drunk with the taste of deliberate skill and *kill:* after all, if you have dug down to that king straw and tweaked it out smilingly, you are yourself king—no matter what your sex—for at least twenty-three seconds!

This sounds competitive, a boring word to me. It is: competitive and therefore boring and probably to be frowned upon by now. But it is a game that was played very quietly, over and over, by men like my midwestern grandfather no matter what his age, and he handed it on to us. It was a silent game, except for occasional shudderings and little groans from the younger ones, quickly snubbed as weak. Grandfather sat like a giant prophet behind his silvery beard, which we knew in a completely disinterested way (at that age!) had been grown to hide his beauty from a horde of young ladyloves, and with an enormous bony brown hand he plucked one jackstraw and then, when his turn came around again, another from the wicked pile. We watched him like hypnotized chickens and tried to do likewise. If one of us missed, there may have been a quiet moan from the others but never a chuckle: we were taught not to *gloat* in public.

Outside the quiet house there was, as far as I remember, no sound, except toward morning an occasional coyote. Of course, there were wild rabbits and moles and mice, but we paid them no heed. Inside, the game was as intense as in any elegant casino, although that connection would have outraged Grandfather: he did not believe in gambling, yet he practiced it every night of his life with jackstraws, Parcheesi, and later crossword puzzles that he transposed into Latin. He would never say "bet," but he would say "wager"; he never said, "My little mare is twice as good as yours," but rather "She is better, I believe." His differences were semantic as well as religious.

So we picked delicately and passionately at the pile of whittled sticks, with their faint colorings, when we played in Grandfather's house. It was *quiet* there on his ranch near La Puente, in southern California. At ours, the game fell flat. He was not there. I see now that such was the reason, although then I thought, if I thought at all, that it was a silly *kid* thing, to be played patiently and politely with an old man. And as I now remember it, I barely thanked my grandfather for the set he had so carefully whittled for us. I had grown past all that. I was in another environment, another age in my own rapid transit from here to there. He was, in a way, stopped at what I hope was the enjoyment of sitting at a table in soft light and watching young people fix their eyes and lick their upper lips and control their fingers to pluck one nicely carved stick from underneath another, in order to edge toward the king itself.

I wish that I had told my grandfather then, in all the hurly-burly of Christmas when he presented the little box of jackstraws to us after such lengthy whittlings and colorings, that I realized what he had done. But I did not. I had no actual physical conception, much less a spiritual one, of what his gift meant. He was an old person and I was a young one. I knew nothing of patience, pain, all that. He could not possibly have tried to tell me about it. So he made a set of jackstraws, and here and now I wish to state that I finally know how to accept them. (At least, I *think* I do.)

It is too bad that my mother waited so long to slough off her conditioned reactions to being related by marriage to people who, in spite of everything she did, were better educated than her own parents but not as affluent. She held us away, willy-nilly, from much warmth, and knowledge, and all that. I don't blame her now. I simply regret it, as I do the fact that I cannot tell Grandfather Kennedy how much I love the two faded pieces of the jackstraw set that he made, and that we casually pushed aside, and that I still have.

TALLY (1923, 1928–1953)

No doubt there is a rich lode of written information about the invisible companions who sometimes walk beside us, or warm our chilly hearts, or wait timelessly to take our groping hands. Sometimes they have been called guardian angels and sung about and painted and made into statues and music. Probably students of the human mind and heart have made charts and lists and even diagrams of their appearance, of when and why they manifest themselves and to which human beings. Probably I should try to find out about all this, since surely records have been kept for our scientific if not spiritual edification. For I feel muddled, as I try to think about the reason why I slept for about twenty-five years with my hand hanging over the edge of any bed I lay in.

Until this night, perhaps a couple of hours ago, it had never occurred to me to wonder why I did this with such a warm feeling of trust and confidence, such an unquestioning surety that if ever the moment was right, my hand would be held in a strong warm other hand.

It is not a usual thing for a child to live with an invisible companion, but neither is it considered very rare, as far as I know. My brother David, who was eleven years younger than I, had a friend none of us ever saw, named Tally, and we seemed to take it for granted that although Tally was not visible to us, he was closer to David than any of us and was therefore our important friend. David and his sister Norah, two years older, were deeply attached to each other, more like twins than plain siblings, but I don't think Norah ever played with Tally, and I am not aware that she ever felt any jealousy. It is part of our general family acceptance, probably, that I have never thought to ask her.

When my next-younger sister Anne and I would come home from school and ask where were the kids, the little ones, Mother would say, "David's upstairs reading with Norah," or "Oh, he's been out all afternoon in the walnut tree with Tally." And on Sundays, when Father did not publish the *News* and we sat longer at table, he would ask David, "How's Tally these days?" David would say, "He's fine, I think. He cut his finger, though. It's all right." Then we would talk about other things, but not deliberately changing the subject. It was all very simple.

When David was perhaps eight, though, Father asked him one day at lunch how Tally was, and David said in a clear flat voice, not looking at any of us, "Tally has gone away." We did not speak for a minute, which may have been filled with shock or even horror. Mother made a little sound, finally, a kind of muffled *oh,* and Father said something like "That's too bad!" and we never mentioned Tally again, at least not to David and indeed almost never otherwise. It would have been rude or something like that.

As I think about all this, for the first time in perhaps half a century or even a thousand years, it seems improbable, but certainly the general acceptance of my little brother's companion was as real as everything else was then—as real as all our voices, and the smell of the old walnut tree, and the long dusty walks home from school, and the Sunday lunches. Now I wonder: Tally was invisible to us, but did David see him, as they played together for long fine hours? I remember that David read and talked aloud a lot to him and that he answered many questions that we never heard. It seems strange, now, that although Norah must have known more about Tally than any of us did, we never felt indiscreet enough to ask her what we knew we must not ask David.

And now I am trying to put into satisfactory words a description of another such visitor as Tally: the nameless, faceless, shapeless spirit who for about twenty-five years stayed under my bed, nearest to me while I slept.

Today a friend, whose left foot must feel wooden for a few months after a hardened artery was repaired, wrote that she was letting her leg dangle over the edge of the bed at midnight. It felt naked and silly, she said. And suddenly I was remembering about my companion, the ancient man who stayed so long nearby in case I needed reassurance. (Of course, I often did, but never enough to ask him for it, like putting off taking two aspirins in case you may need them more later than you do now.)

The person under my bed was a man, all right, and it seems strange that I never questioned or bothered about that nor about the fact that he was indeed somebody. I knew all this without any wondering at all, as a small child may understand without words or worry that someone loves and will care for him. The old man must have been tiny, because it did not matter if I slept on a real bed or on a pallet on bare boards: I simply let my left hand stay trustingly over the edge of whatever I lay on, even if I lay close to a dear lover or a sweet little child. And it did not matter if my hand hung sweaty in the tropics, or carefully escaping from heavy warmth in a snowland, or even from a high sterile hospital bed: I knew that when I most needed it, the old man there, tiny as a pea or big as a skinny child perhaps, would reach out and clasp it confidently in his own strong clean hand.

This comforter or friend or whatever he might be called was never named, at least by me, and indeed I seldom gave him a thought, consciously anyway. If anyone had asked me what he might look like, so faithful there beneath wherever I slept, I would have said something vague about tiny-bones-long-nose-wise-eyes-white-beard, perhaps. Mostly, I am sure, I would have got rid of the whole intrusiveness with a shrug and dismissing smile. I don't think I have ever told any human being about him, which as I write this now seems very odd. Certainly I was not embarrassed. It was simply that it seemed unnecessary, the way it was unnecessary to ask about what Tally did when he was with young David.

And now that I think about it, the strangest thing is that I do not remember when I stopped needing to put my left hand down over whatever I lay on, knowing that he would hold it if need be. (Once, I remember, I was lying on a bed of wild garlic in a Swiss forest!)

Certainly I need help now—or at least the assumption of its availability—as much as I ever did and perhaps more. But all I can do, at this stage in my life game, is feel very thankful that for a long time I knew that I was not alone. As I try to remember the hows and whys of this strange certainty, I feel truly puzzled about the whole silly business. All I know is that the tiny old man was there, if ever I needed anything more than my unspoken and largely unfelt belief that indeed he was. And I like to think that such presences, the kind that come and go without question or mockery or indeed even recognition, will stay near all of us. Tally was much more a part of my little brother David's life than my old man was of mine. He had a name, and perhaps, for David anyway, a recognizable image. My own guardian was nameless, unseen. But I know that the firm grip of his hand would be there if ever I called silently for it, or even if *he* knew that it was time to take the hand I left out for him.

Sometime now when I am between sleep and wakefulness, I wish that he were still down there, underneath the bed or the blades of grass between me and the earth. Once in a hospital I felt actively hurt, or at least baffled, that he was gone. Why had he left? I wondered irritably, half-amused at my childishness.

Well, it is plain that he is needed more somewhere else. I suppose David knew that about Tally, too, philosophically. And clinically, I doubt that my leaving my left hand free for a warm reassuring grasp from an invisible and nameless and formless presence was at all like spending long agreeable hours with a friend, as my brother did. My old man, who could be either bent into a bundle two feet tall under a real bedstead or tiny as a pea in the grass—but whose hand was always ready to hold mine—may not even have been one of the "invisible playmates" that child psychiatrists write books about. For one thing, I was too old: I think that I was about twenty when I first knew that he was there, all right. (That was in Dijon, under a high ancient French bed where I slept with my first husband. Need for any other comfort was not in my conscious mind, certainly, and yet that is when the little old man first took up his watch-and-wait station.)

As for his leaving me, I was not aware of it until a long time later (I've said twenty-five years, but it may have been much more) when I realized that I no longer put my hand outside the covers and down over the edge to tell him that I was there.

When did I stop? Speaking dispassionately, I would say that I need his warm strong hand in mine now more than ever, but he is not there. My hand, left out, would grow cold and awkward. He is gone. But he and Tally are somewhere, of course, and that is good to know.

from *Young Men and Fire*

Norman Maclean   (1902–1990)

The publisher's note to *Young Men and Fire* tells us that Norman Maclean "did not start work on this book until his seventy-fourth year, after publication of *A River Runs Through It and Other Stories*," and that it was unfinished at his death in 1990, "at the age of eighty-seven." Perhaps his advanced age gives him the wry detachment as well as the compassion for young people that enables him to keep a steady view on an exterior event—here, the final minutes before death took thirteen youthful Forest Service Smokejumpers during an explosive fire in Mann Gulch, Montana—while also permitting him to explore his memories and his feelings. Obsessions are subjective by definition, and surely Maclean's lengthy investigations of that 1949 tragedy are obsessive; indeed, his intense interest in the Mann Gulch blowup goes back to his own youth, to his own fright as a fifteen-year-old firefighter scrambling to escape a large fire—a memory whose haunting imagery causes him, decades later, to visit Mann Gulch soon after the tragedy there. But Maclean's obsession, whatever its origins in his past, is to gain an external truth that may help him find an internal one.

   The latter half of *Young Men and Fire* is, as Maclean tells us, "the quest to find the full story of the Mann Gulch fire, to find what of it was once known and was then scattered and buried, to discover the parts so far missing because fire science had not been able to explain the behavior of the blowup or the 'escape fire,' and to imagine the last moments of those who went to their crosses unseen and alone." (The "escape fire," set by R. Wagner Dodge, foreman of the crew, saved his life; one of only three to survive, he was to be accused by the grieving father of one of the dead as bringing death to the others through his secondary blaze. The most enthralling portion of the book is the detective work undertaken by Maclean and a friend in the Forest Service, Laird Robinson, that exonerates Dodge through physical proof that the two other survivors, Walter Rumsey and Robert Sallee, had incorrectly identified the crevice in the reef that had afforded them escape. The identification of the true crevice permits other evidence to fall in place.) Related to his search for truth is Maclean's own quest to know himself—to see himself in relationship to those who died in the conflagration; to understand the tragic implications of human life, implications necessary for human compassion; and to voice (without sentimentality) those spiritual affirmations that remain applicable to all of us.

   Following is the final chapter, a meditation on what he has learned from his exploration of the past.

It would be natural to near the end to try to divest the fire of any personal liability to those who died in it and to become for a moment a distant and detached spectator. It might be possible then, if ever, to see fire in something like total perspective as it became total conflagration. If you had known something about wildfire, you already would have seen spot fires twisting themselves into fire swirls and fire swirls converging upon themselves. But viewing total conflagration is literally blinding, as sight becomes sound and the roar of the fire goes out of the head of the gulch and away and beyond, far away. The last you saw of the ground was a mole coming out of the smoke, a little more terrified than you, debating which way to go and ending the argument with itself forever by turning back into the impenetrable fire. So it is, when you cannot see the fire because of the smoke, sight becomes sound. You hear the fire as a roar of an animal without the animal or as an attacking army blown up by the explosion of its own ammunition dump.

Pictures, then, of a big fire are pictures of many realities, designed so they change into each other and fit ultimately into a single picture of one monster becoming another monster. The pictures and the monsters are untroubled by mathematics. The monster becomes one as it extends itself simultaneously as a monster and a real animal or more likely just as a part of a real animal—after it disgorges itself, all that can be seen of it from afar are its fried gray intestines. Oddly, as destruction comes close to being total, destruction erects for brief moments into the sexual and quickly sinks back again into destruction. Intestines stretch out all the way to the curvatures of the brain. The two don't look much different, and they aren't and they are.

Thus, pictures which wildfire creates of itself are at least bi-visual, part of the fire's process of procreating its meanings. So, as the fire at the top of the ridge slithered through the rocks, it stretched itself out into a snake rearing its head to see that it was on course and using its tongue as a torch to cut through obstructions. So, too, a little lower on the hillside, when the main fire paused for a moment in front of the escape fire, the red flames crowded together until they became ravaging military monsters enraged by the precocity of an obstacle in front of them; then for a moment these deranged military monsters, blocked in their advance, raged sideways up and down the line looking for a way to pass—small fires were left behind as the phalanx of flame threw torches ahead, jumped the line, and left something like a smoldering monster in ruins.

Because of their many meanings, wildfires can be tri-visual or more. Some of what even a seasoned firefighter sees never seems real.

After its deranged military front had passed, pieces of the main fire remained burning fiercely in clutches of timber. Dead standing trees, especially Ponderosa pine full of resin, became giant candles burning for the dead. Then one would explode, disappearing from the air where it stood, detonated by its own heat. The disappearance of the tree would not be visible; it would be a theological disappearance; immediately after the explosion, its falling would be transubstantiated into spreading waves of earth generated by its own earthquake, and after its waves had swelled and broken and passed over and under and on, it would return as sound and terminate in echoes of its earthquake rumbling out of the sides and head of the gulch. The world then was more than ever theological, and the nuclear was never far off.

By now, if not sooner, the fire had become total—it was below, above, behind, and now also in front at the head of the gulch. Spot fires must have been burning there, started in the grass by burning cones and ashes blown from the approaching fires. Suddenly in the semigloom they would pop out of the ground, bi-visual as little poisonous mushrooms. The bi-visual mushrooms bred instantly, swelled with impregnation underground and aboveground into a vast bulbous head with a giant stalk. The vast wildfire continued on its bi-visual way—sometimes the bulbous mushroom looked like a bulbous mushroom impregnated by a snake in the grass and sometimes like gray brains boiling out of the crevice of the earth. Then the brains themselves became bi-visual and changed again into suffering gray intestines.

The atomic mushroom has become for our age the outer symbol of our inner fear of the explosive power of the universe. It is the symbol of a whole age, and it took an artist to express the meaning the mushroom has for us. Henry Moore, one of our age's most expressive sculptors, commemorated the occasion that led to the Atomic Age—the first self-sustained nuclear reaction—on the site at the University of Chicago where it occurred. His bronze atomic mushroom, with its hollow eyes, is intentionally bi-visual from every point of view. Wherever you stand, the bronze looks like both an atomic mushroom and a skull, and is meant to.

When the blowup rose out of Mann Gulch and its smoke merged with the jet stream, it looked much like an atomic explosion in Nevada on its cancerous way to Utah. When last seen, the tri-visual figure had stretched out and was on its way, far, far, far away, looking like death and looking back at its dead and looking forward to its dead yet to come. Perhaps it could see all of us.

No one could know the power of it. It stretched until it became particles on the horizon, where it may have joined the company of Sky Spirits as particles, knowing what we do not know, probably something nuclear.

Now, almost forty years later, small trees have just started to grow along the bottoms of dry finger gulches on the hillside in Mann Gulch, where moisture from rain and snow are retained underground. Since even now these little evergreens are only six or eight inches high, the grass has to be parted to find them, but I look for such things. I see better what happens in grass than on the horizon. Most of us do, and probably it is just as well, but what's found buried in grass doesn't tell us how to get out of the way.

At the end, our point of view of the fire changes radically so that we no longer look down from the distant horizon and see in the blinding smoke only pictures composed of our primitive history and our nuclear future. Instead, now at the end we stay as close to the ground as we can, are guided by our compassion, and accompany highly select young men who never once realized that they could be mortal on their way to the obliterating earth. We should hope, though, in trying to identify ourselves with them that we will be able to retain our own identity, for their sake as well as ours. Because we are much older than they were ever to be and have lived in a time more advanced scientifically than theirs, we should know much that they did not know but that should be of value in this journey of compassion. In a journey of compassion what we have ultimately as our guide is whatever understanding we may have gained along the way of ourselves and others, chiefly those close to us, so close to us that we have lived daily in their sufferings. From here on, then, in the blinding smoke it is no longer a "seeing world" but a "feeling world"—the pain of others and our compassion for them.

Things moved rapidly to the end after the crew left the foreman at his escape fire. It makes no difference whether the crew could not understand in the roaring of the main fire what Dodge was trying to say to them or whether they thought his idea of lying down in the hot ashes of his own fire was crazy. Either way they were entering No Man's Land, lonely in the boiling semidarkness of the main fire, which by now must have been less than fifty yards behind them. Rumsey and Sallee, ahead of them, testified that the smoke parted enough for them to see the top of the ridge only two or three times. If we have difficulty seeing the rest of the men, they had difficulty seeing themselves. Heat and loneliness were becoming the only remaining properties. Their loneliness loomed up suddenly—they were young and not used to being alone, and as Smokejumpers they were not allowed to be alone, except in that perilous moment after they jumped from the sky and before they landed on earth.

It has been said since tragedy was first analyzed that it is governed by the emotions of fear and pity. As the Smokejumpers went up the hill after leaving Dodge it was like a great jump backwards into the sky—they were suddenly and totally without command and suddenly without structure and suddenly free to disintegrate and free finally to be afraid. The evidence is that they were not afraid before this moment, but now great fear suddenly possessed the empty places.

Beyond the world of sight and soon even beyond fear, the nonhuman elements of heat and toxic gases were becoming the only two elements, and soon heat was even burning out fear. To find a place that was cool was all that was left of human purpose. Knowing at least this much about fire and mortality, we can guess why most of the dead young men were found in depressions on the hillside; there it was thought to be cooler, so it was there that most of them went before they fell.

From our knowledge of others close to us we may learn something about how it felt this near the end. In the spring of the year my wife died from cancer of the esophagus, she remarked to me, "I feel as if I had spent all winter with my head under water." Later, when I asked a doctor what he thought it must be like to die in a fire, not from the burning but from the suffocation and lack of oxygen, he replied, "It is not terrible," and then added, but not as an afterthought, "It is something like drowning." If you compare my wife's remark to this more scientific attempt to speak of death by suffocation, you can see how careful my wife was, when she allowed herself to speak of such matters, to speak with precision.

It was not, therefore, for most of them, a terrible death. Many of the bodies were terribly burned when they were found, so much so that later it was discovered the caskets should not have been brought into the funeral chapel. Even so, they did not die of burning. The burning came afterwards.

To project ourselves into their final thoughts will require feelings about a special kind of death—the sudden death in fire of the young, elite, unfulfilled, and seemingly unconquerable. As the elite of young men, they felt more surely than most who are young that they were immortal. So if we are to feel with them, we must feel that we are set apart from the rest of the universe and safe from fires, all of which are expected to be put out by ten o'clock the morning after Smokejumpers are dropped on them. As to what they felt about sudden death, we can start by feeling what the unfulfilled always feel about it, and, since the unfulfilled are many, the Book of Common Prayer cries out for all of them and us when it begs that we all be delivered from sudden death.

Good Lord, deliver us.

From lightning and tempest; from earthquake, fire, and flood; from plague, pestilence, and famine; from battle and murder, and from sudden death,

Good Lord, deliver us.

One thing is certain about these final thoughts—there was not much size to them. Time and place did not permit even superior young men dying suddenly "to see their whole lives pass in review," although books portray people preparing to die as seeing a sort of documentary movie of their lives. Everything, however, gets smaller on its way to becoming eternal. It is also probable that the final thoughts of elite young men dying suddenly were not seeing or scenic thoughts but were cries or a single cry of passion, often of self-compassion, justifiable if those who cry are justly proud. The two living survivors of the Mann Gulch fire have told me that, as they went up the last hillside, they remember thinking only, "My God, how could you do this to me? I cannot be allowed to die so young and so close to the top." They said they could remember hearing their voices saying this out loud.

Of the two great tragic emotions this close to the end, fear had been burned away and pity was in sole possession. Not only is it heat that burns fear away; the end of tragedy purifies itself of it. Before the end of a tragedy the most famous of tragic heroes can stand in fear before ghosts and can shake in front of apparitions of those they have murdered, but by the end the same tragedy has purged these same tragic heroes of fear, as is made immortally clear by the last lines of one of the most famous of these tragic heroes: "Lay on, Macduff, / And damn'd be him that first cries, 'Hold, enough!'"

The pity that remains is perhaps the last and only emotion felt if it is the young and unfulfilled who suffer the tragedy. It is pity in the form of self-pity, but the compassion felt for themselves by the tragic young is self-pity transformed into some divine bewilderment, one of the few emotions in which the young and the universe are the only characters. Although divine bewilderment addresses its grief to the universe, it only cries out to it. It has to find its answer, if at all, in its own final act. It is not to be found among the answers God gave to Job in a whirlwind.

The most eloquent expression of this cry was made by a young man who came from the sky and returned to it and who, while on earth, knew he was alone and beyond all other men, and who, when he died, died on a hill: "About the ninth hour he cried with a loud voice, Eli, Eli, lama sabachthani?" ("My God, my God, why has thou forsaken me?")

Although we can enter their last thoughts and feelings only by indirection, we are sure of the final act of many of them. Dr. Hawkins, the physician who went in with the rescue crew the night the men were burned, told me that, after the bodies had fallen, most of them had risen again, taken a few steps, and fallen again, this final time like pilgrims in prayer, facing the top of the hill, which on that slope is nearly east. Ranger Jansson, in charge of the rescue crew, independently made the same observation.

The evidence, then, is that at the very end beyond thought and beyond fear and beyond even self-compassion and divine bewilderment there remains some firm intention to continue doing forever and ever what we last hoped to do on earth. By this final act they had come about as close as body and spirit can to establishing a unity of themselves with earth, fire, and perhaps the sky.

This is as far as we are able to accompany them. When the fire struck their bodies, it blew their watches away. The two hands of a recovered watch had melted together at about four minutes to six. For them, that may be taken as the end of time.

It was 6:10 by Dodge's watch when he rose from the ashes of his own fire. From then on, Dodge had his own brief tragedy to lead, which in some ways also must be considered a part of this tragedy.

We leave the dead on the hillside with a promise made to me at the Office of Air Operations and Fire Management of Region One of the United States Forest Service that their crosses will always be renewed.

I, an old man, have written this fire report. Among other things, it was important to me, as an exercise for old age, to enlarge my knowledge and spirit so I could accompany young men whose lives I might have lived on their way to death. I have climbed where they climbed, and in my time I have fought fire and inquired into its nature. In addition, I have lived to get a better understanding of myself and those close to me, many of them now dead. Perhaps it is not odd, at the end of this tragedy where nothing much was left of the elite who came from the sky but courage struggling for oxygen, that I have often found myself thinking of my wife on her brave and lonely way to death.

from *Images and Shadows: Part of a Life*

Iris Origo (1902–1988)

Though born in America, Iris Origo spent most of her life in Europe. Even as a young child, when her residence was still in the United States, she spent summers in the country house of her grandparents in Ireland; following the death of her father during a trip her family took to Egypt when Origo was seven, she lived with her mother in Fiesole, above Florence; and, after her marriage to the Italian Antonio Origo, she and her husband settled in La Foce, a Tuscan villa and farm in the Val d'Orcia. La Foce became her permanent home, but she was frequently in England and America, and traveled about the world with her husband. Hers was, as she says in the introduction to her autobiography, *Images and Shadows*, "a life of privilege," her awareness of that fact giving her "a discomfort which increases as I get older." (Privileged or not, the years of fascism in Italy, particularly during World War II, were not without hardship and danger, as one knows from reading her earlier *War in Val D'Orcia*, as well as the references to this period in *Images and Shadows*.)

Origo was sixty-eight when she completed *Images and Shadows* in 1970. Perhaps because she was so cosmopolitan, the work emphasizes specific places; its very structure is imposed by the houses most important in her life—country houses in the United States and Ireland, the villa in Fiesole, the farm in the Val d'Orcia. (The "walls of a house," she muses, "sometimes become imbued with the nature of its inhabitants.") From a number of loci of which these are the central ones, she constructs her "fragmentary account of what it has been like to live in three totally distinct periods of civilisation: first briefly, and partly through hearsay, in the pre-war world of 1914; then in the world between two wars; and finally in the present time, which is so rapidly taking on new shapes both intellectually and materially, that I have found myself unwillingly becoming, in some aspects at least, a spectator rather than a participator."

In her opening paragraph, Origo remarks, "The brilliant talk I heard at I Tatti [the estate of the art historian Bernard Berenson near Florence] in my youth, in Bloomsbury in the thirties, in New York and Rome in later years, has lost some of its glitter. . . . All that is left to me of my past life that has not faded into mist has passed through the filter, not of my mind, but of my affections. What was not warmed by them is now for me as if it has never been." For Origo as for Proust, then, feelings, not reason, are crucial to memory, revivifying the past; and it is affection—affection for people, affection for place—which gives *Images and Shadows* its modesty and its hold upon the reader.

The effect of the book is cumulative; I find it difficult to make a selection that satisfactorily communicates it. Instead, I have excerpted two portions of Origo's "Epilogue." The first is concerned with the nature of memory itself, particularly its ability to filter out the significant from the ordinary, providing the former with a greater intensity than perhaps the original experience produced and managing to reveal the essence of what constitutes our lives; the second excerpt, a longer one, reaches out from the two events—the death of her father and the death of her son Gianni (a victim of tubercular meningitis when he was only seven)—of greatest import to her life in her first thirty years. In this passage, Origo discusses the "very vivid sense of the continuity of love" provided by memory, despite the deaths that occur, and then explores the spiritual beliefs that personal experience, as contained in memory, have provided her.

> *"I don't know where to go."*
> *"Neither do I. Let's go together."*
>
> —Ignazio Silone

The pattern is set now—though not all set down—and I am looking back upon my life. What do I see? For every life is not only a string of events: it is also a myth.

First of all, perhaps, one should ask: is it possible to see one's own life? "What the devil then am I?" cried Carlyle at the age of eighty, as he was drying his old bones after his bath. "After all these eighty years I know nothing at all about it."

To "see" one's life (though the end is lacking—and perhaps that is why it is so difficult: perhaps, when the end has come, the pieces may fall into place and form a pattern) one should surely try to look back upon it with as much detachment as if it were someone else's. Humboldt, I think, was saying something of this kind when he spoke of history as "a landscape of clouds." "The man who is within it, can see nothing. It is only by looking at it from some way off, that he can perceive how clear and various it is." It is the experience of the traveller whose plane has broken through a bank of clouds and who looks down upon a vast, billowy sea, constantly changing its shape, forming new valleys and new peaks.

A friend of mine whom I asked if he could look back as detachedly as this upon his life replied that he had succeeded in doing so in regard to every part of it except the immediate past. He vividly remembered both what he saw and felt up to a few years ago, but could no longer identify himself with his own past emotions, any more than if they had belonged to a character in a novel or a play: "The stage setting is still there, but the lights have gone out."

I do not think that I could say quite the same, at least not yet, though it would be true of many parts of my life. The child riding her donkey on the Nubian sands; the schoolgirl reading the *Iliad* with Monti; the self-conscious débutante in the English country-house—they are me and they are no longer me. "We are like the relict garment of a Saint," said Keats, "the same and not the same: for the careful Monks patch it and patch it:

440

till there's not a thread of the original garment left, and still they show it for St. Anthony's shirt."

Yet there is something that remains. If I think back, I can sometimes recapture certain intense moments of feeling: the hour beside the Nile when I saw that my father's tent had been taken up and suddenly knew that he was dead; the evening on which I read, on the terrace of the Villa Medici, the letter from Antonio which, after six months of separation, renewed our engagement and determined the course of our life; the night, forty-four years ago, on which, immediately after Gianni's birth, I heard the Florentine bells ring out and saw the sky lit up with fireworks for St. John's Eve, and felt happiness sweep over me. Proust, who cultivated the art of memory as perhaps no-one else has ever done, would say that these recollections have always been part of me. He wrote in *Du Coté de Chez Swann* that in later life he was able again to hear certain sounds which "in reality had never stopped", the sobs which had shaken him at a certain moment of his childhood. "It is only because life is now growing silent about me," he wrote, "that I hear them afresh, like convent bells which one might believe were not rung nowadays, because during the day they are drowned by the city hubbub, but which may be heard clearly enough in the stillness of the evening."

If Proust is right, I am carrying within me (in spite of all the changes that have taken place) the *whole* of my life, from the day when "the arable field of events" first lay before me, until the moment in which the typewriter is tapping out these words. And certainly it is also true that some of the memories I can now summon up have a greater intensity than the events themselves seemed to possess at the time, or rather—since memory has a filter of its own, sometimes surprising in what it suppresses or retains, but always significant—some of them stand out in disproportionate clarity to the rest.

Bernard Berenson once said in his old age that if he were a beggarman on a street corner, he would stretch out his hand to every passer-by, begging for "more time, more time!" I do not agree with him. I should like, of course—for I enjoy living—to have a few more years (provided all my faculties remained) in which to watch my grandchildren growing up, to see a little more of the world and of the overwhelming changes that are taking place in it and, above all, to see a little more clearly into myself. But the time I would really beg for, at any street corner, would be *time in the past,* time in which to comfort, to complete and to re-pair—time wasted before I knew how quickly it would slip by.

Most of us, however well we may know that remorse is fruitless, carry in our memories some heavy burdens, and perhaps at least one so poignant that we can hardly bear to look back on it: a weight of sadness and regret, a knowledge that we have failed even those who needed us most—especially those, since with other people one is not upon that plane at all. Nor is it of much consolation to realise that almost everyone, while life is actually going on, is constantly being distracted by irrelevances. Just as, in travel, one may miss seeing the sunset because one cannot find the ticket-office or is afraid of missing the train, so in even the closest human relationships a vast amount of time and of affection is drained away in minor misunderstandings, missed opportunities, and failures in consideration or understanding. It is only in memory that the true essence remains.

And now we are back where we started. If life is indeed "a perpetual allegory", if what we seek in it is awareness, understanding, then the small stream of events I have set down here has only been a means—a means to what? I seem to have been diverted a long way from my original inquiry, but perhaps it has not really been so very far, since it has only been through my affections that I have been able to perceive, however imperfectly, some faint "intimations of immortality", a foretaste, perhaps, granted to the short-sighted of another, transcendental love.

Looking back at the first thirty years of my life, two events have an outstanding significance: my father's death, when I was seven and a half, and Gianni's, when he was the same age that I was then. And both of these events are significant for the same reason—that neither of them was an ending. I do not mean of course that there was not the pain of *parting*—but that separation did not prevent my father's personality from pervading my childhood, as Gianni's has pervaded the rest of my life. Since then, a few years ago, there has been the death of Elsa, the closest companion of my middle age, and the same has been true about her. I am not speaking now about an orthodox belief in "another life"—nor am I entering upon the complex question of the survival of personality. All that I can affirm is what I know of my own experience: that though I have never ceased to miss my father, child and friend, I have also never lost them. They have been to me, at all times, as real as the people I see every day, and it is this, I think, that has conditioned my whole attitude both to death and to human affections.

It is very easy, on this subject, to become sentimental or woolly, or to say more than one really means. I think I am only trying to say something very simple: that my own personal experience has given me a very vivid sense of the continuity of love, even after death, and that it has also left me believing in the truth of Burke's remark that society—or I should prefer to say, life itself—is "a partnership not only between those who are living, but between those who are living, those who are dead, and those who are to be born". Not only are we not alone, but we are not living only in a bare and chilly now. We are irrevocably bound to the past—and no less irrevocably, though the picture is less clear to us, to the future. It is this feeling that has made death seem to me not less painful, never that—for there is no greater grief than that of parting—but not, perhaps, so very important, and has caused affection, in its various forms, to be the guiding thread of my life.

At the time of Gianni's death, I received a letter from George Santayana (who in his later years to some extent returned, at least in feeling, to his Spanish, Catholic origins) which expresses, far better than I ever could, my feelings upon this subject.

> . . . We have no claim to any of our possessions. We have no claim to exist; and, as we have to die in the end, so we must resign ourselves to die piecemeal, which really happens when we lose somebody or something that was closely intertwined with our existence. It is like a physical wound; we may survive, but maimed and broken in that direction; dead there.
>
> Not that we can, or ever do at heart, renounce our affections. Never that. We cannot exercise our full nature all at once in every direction; but the parts that are relatively in abeyance, their centre lying perhaps in the past or the future, belong to us inalienably. We should not be ourselves if we cancelled them. I don't know how literally you may believe in another world, or whether the idea means very much to you. As you know, I am not myself a believer in the ordinary sense, yet my *feeling* on this subject is like that of believers, and not at all like that of my fellow-materialists. The reason is that I disagree utterly with that modern philosophy which regards *experience* as fundamental. Experience is a mere whiff or rumble, produced by enormously complex and ill-deciphered causes of experience; and in the other direction, experience is a mere peephole through which glimpses come down to us of eternal things. These are the only things that, in so far as we are spiritual beings, we can find or can love at all. All our affections, when clear and pure and not claims to possession, transport us to another world; and the loss of contact, here or there, with those eternal beings is merely like closing a book which we keep at hand for another occasion.

About more orthodox beliefs, I am very hesitant to write, for fear of saying a little more or less than I mean or than is true. I have spent a good deal of my life in various forms of wishful thinking—trying to persuade myself, in one way or another, that things were a little better than they really were: my feelings or convictions deeper, and situations pleasanter or clearer, than was in fact the case—and I think it is time to stop. For this is what Plato called "the true lie", the lie in the soul, "hated by gods and men", of which the lie in words is "only a kind of imitation and shadowy image".

Yet it is also true that all my life (though not steadily, but rather in fitful waves) I have been seeking a meaning, a framework, a goal—I should say, more simply, God. *"Tu ne me chercherais pas si tu ne m'avais trouvé,"* was Pascal's reply—but is this not too easy a way out for a fitful purpose and a vacillating mind? I remember a passage in Julian Green's *Journal*: *"Je lis les mystiques comme on lit les récits des voyageurs qui reviennent de pays lointains ou l'on sait bien que l'on n'ira jamais. On voudrait visiter la Chine, mais quel voyage! Et pourtant je crois que jusqu'à la fin de mes jours je conververai ce déraisonnable espoir."*

That "unreasonable hope" is always latent: one should perhaps open the door to it more often. Someone to whom I once spoke about these matters suggested that instead of nourishing a sense of guilt for what one cannot comprehend or fully accept, it would be better to start by dwelling upon what one honestly can believe. I think the advice is good, and have tried to ask myself that question.

I have seen and believe in goodness: the indefinable quality which is immediately and unhesitatingly recognised by the most different kinds of men: the simple goodness of an old nurse or the mother of a large family; the more complex and costly goodness of a priest, a doctor or a teacher. When such people are also believers, their beliefs are apt to be *catching*—or so I myself, at least, have found. It is the Eastern principle of the *guru* and his disciples: goodness and faith conveyed (or perhaps evil and disbelief dispelled) by an actual, living presence.

The outstanding instance in our lifetime has been that of Pope John XXIII. I do not think that anyone—believer or agnostic—who was present in St. Peter's Square during the Mass said for him as he lay dying could fail to have a sense of what was meant by "the communion of the faithful", or to receive a dim apprehension of his own vision of "one flock and one shepherd", of the love of mankind as a whole. And if, since then, the realisation of this dream has been full of complexities, and many minds have been disturbed and confused by conflicts, upheavals and innovations, the vision still endures.

I believe in the dependence of people upon each other. I believe in the light and warmth of human affection, and in the disinterested acts of kindness and compassion of complete strangers. I agree with Simone Weil that "charity and faith, though distinct, are inseparable"—and I share her conviction "whoever is capable of a movement of pure compassion (which incidentally is very rare) towards an unhappy man, possesses, implicitly but truly, faith and the love of God".

I believe, not theoretically, but from direct personal experience, that very few of the things that happen to us are purposeless or accidental (and this includes suffering and grief—even that of others), and that sometimes one catches a glimpse of the link between these happenings. I believe—even when I am myself being blind and deaf, or even indifferent—in the existence of a mystery.

Beyond this, I still do not know—nor do I feel inclined to examine here—how far I can go. Yet I derive comfort, at times, from a passage in one of Dom John Chapman's letters. "There is worry and anxiety and trouble and bewilderment, and there is also an unfelt, yet real acquiescence in being anxious, troubled and bewildered, and a consciousness that the *real* self is at peace, while the anxiety and worry are unreal. It is like a peaceful lake, whose surface reflects all sorts of changes, because it is calm."

A still lake, ruffled only upon the surface: a world of clouds, through which it is possible to break to the light—are these indeed metaphors more true than I can yet fully perceive?

> Man is one world, and hath
> Another to attend him.

I went to the summit and stood in the high nakedness:
the wind tore about this
way and that in confusion and its speech could not
get through to me nor could I address it:
still I said as if to the alien in myself
    I do not speak to the wind now:
for having been brought this far by nature I have been
brought out of nature
and nothing here shows me the image of myself:
for the word *tree* I have been shown a tree
and for the word *rock* I have been shown a rock,
for stream, for cloud, for star
this place has provided firm implication and answering
    but where here is the image for *longing:*
so I touched the rocks, their interesting crusts:
I flaked the bark of stunt-fir:
I looked into space and into the sun
and nothing answered my word *longing:*
    goodbye, I said, goodbye, nature so grand and
reticent, your tongues are healed up into their own
element
and as you have shut up you have shut me out: I am
as foreign here as if I had landed, a visitor:
so I went back down and gathered mud
and with my hands made an image for *longing:*
    I took the image to the summit: first
I set it here, on the top rock, but it completed
nothing: then I set it there among the tiny firs
but it would not fit:
so I returned to the city and built a house to set
the image in
and men came into my house and said
    that is an image for *longing*
and nothing will ever be the same again.

                       —A. R. Ammons, "For Harold Bloom"

Beyond Memory

This final section of *The Anatomy of Memory* is a brief collection of dreams, desires, and visions. It makes dominant a motif or musical theme—that is to say, a feeling or a tonality—heard in the selection that opens the book. The theme emerges again in the second section, "The Memory of Nature," and appears elsewhere, perhaps most consistently in "Memory and Creativity," which emphasizes the seemingly innate ability of human memory to search for analogies, for likenesses, for syntheses.

This theme is the human soul, a subject so contested—perhaps so abstract—that I will approach it here in a circumscript way, through references to two other themes that also recur in the anthology, intermingling with each other and with this one. If music—as is suggested in the introduction to the previous section—serves as a metaphor for memory's achievements, the three themes, each carrying its own elusive meanings or coloration but mingling with the others, constitute memory's melodic structure. For the moment, I will withhold comment on the motif given its fullest expression in this section, permitting its description to be revealed through a discussion of the other two.

One of these themes is the human unconscious. Previous essays refer to it in a variety of ways, sometimes with competing illustrations of what it does, either to or for us. The unconscious, it would seem, is connected to our beginnings within the natural world, to our genetic memories; it represents the deeper part of the self, that spiritual part which links all of humanity; it is a component of our dream world and serves to explain our psychology, particularly the neuroses that afflict us; it is essential to inspiration and creativity; it motivates whole societies into irrational actions, including the possible annihilation of those or other societies; for better or worse, it is a repository of early experiences that conscious memory cannot recall. In short, the human unconscious is a vast category into which we put all that remains mysterious about our responses and behavior, all that eludes rationality.

The second theme is human identity, as reflected in personality and selfhood. According to all we have come to know about the matter, both personality (which has a social dimension) and selfhood (the inner sense of who we are) have their source in memories contained in the unconscious as well as the conscious mind. If this is true, memory is the source not only of our emotions and quirks but of our spiritual desires. Memory itself expresses, I believe, a wanting: a desire to make sense of one's life and of the phenomenal world. Of all the sentient life on this planet, humans (so far as any human can tell) are the only species to know this kind of wanting. It is a hunger as emotional as it is intellectual, and no doubt has its source in our distant past, lurking with other hungers existing in the unconscious. As we've seen, particularly in the last section, memory searches for connections between present and past experiences in its desire to know, to evaluate, to make sense of life; and it searches as well for connections among the properties of phenomena in the objective world. Ultimately, though, it comes up against a barrier, beyond which it cannot go.

To mention that barrier is to introduce the word *soul,* at least as I would define it. In a secular age, it's still possible to consider the soul as the principle of thought, or as synonymous with mind; but to define it in a purely spiritual or metaphysical way seems hopelessly quaint to many of us today. Still, I claim to possess a soul in this sense, and find indications of its possession in everybody I know. Like the unconscious mind, like personality and selfhood, it is not an entity but a quality. As I conceive of that quality, the soul is desire—memory's desire for a holy synthesis, especially as it is challenged by that barrier to ultimate knowledge.

Whether their scope is vast or small, the selections in this section either contain, or are strongly colored by, this desire; and through the wantings they express, these selections carry in varying degrees an intimation of what may lie beyond the barrier. Whatever that unknown reality is, it is sacred (and will remain so, until—an unlikely possibility—we discover its secret); it is very still, our present awareness of it coming from whatever apprehension of silence our buzzing consciousness permits; and it unites us with everything else in the universe. My temerity in making such a generalizing claim is bolstered by a lifetime of reading, finding in the writing of others an abundance of support for it, whether in tantalizing clues or in visionary illuminations. Some of that support can be seen in the material that follows.

This introduction is preceded by a poem that is a purer and more haunting expression of the motif explored in this section than anything that my prose is capable of achieving. Ammons' poem communicates the sense of a final barrier to our quest for unity and self-knowledge through nature as well as the longing that is the inevitable consequence, the longing that marks us as human and connects us one to the other. I began this anthology with a brief selection from Augustine's *Confessions,* and end it with a visionary passage from that spiritual autobiography. The penultimate selection is a story by Anton Chekhov, its conclusion bearing what I take to be a somewhat analogous vision. Lacking the support of a specific religious belief, it may strike some readers as darker, more somber, than Augustine's; and yet both imply a transcendent unity to be achieved only through the vanquishing of personal identity, of the sense of self. I can give no valid reason, chronological or otherwise, for the ordering of the other material in this conclusion of the anthology; like E. M. Forster, I believe that the human soul remains constant enough for us to visualize all of these writers as sitting together in the same room, taking turns—in a manner as informal as it is random—as they speak to us.

from *Maps to Anywhere*

Bernard Cooper (1951–)

Bernard Cooper's collection of autobiographical essays, *Maps to Anywhere,* is such an assemblage of fragments that one is apt to classify his sensibility as postmodern. *Postmodern* is a slippery term in literature and other art forms, since it gets its definition from its separation from the equivocal *modern.* To the degree that *modern,* at least in its conventional usage, refers to the present—a period in time always to be replaced by another present—*postmodern* has a certain foreboding quality about it, as if survivors of the modern period were only going through the motions, the human game being in some ultimate sense already over. Indeed, some postmodern literature *is* suffused beneath an apocalyptic atmosphere. In most of the literary examples of postmodernism I can think of, human nature has lost the spiritual basis that once provided meaning, character definition, and narrative direction. If the old human game is up, postmodern writers are free to invent games of their own—self-consciousness can rule, and writers can enjoy the artifice of their constructions.

The fragmentary nature of Cooper's writing and the self-consciousness that marks it (including the game-playing) suggest postmodernism. The longer essays—the major thread of one is a brother's slow dying of leukemia; of another, the growing affection between Cooper and his father in the father's old age—are arrangements of fragments that are grasping toward a solidity that finally dissipates into apparition and mist, into wind. But to read this lovely book several times makes one aware of how misleading the word *postmodern* can be, for beneath the fragments lie all the old desires of memory, however ironically they may be treated: the desires for a unity which is indistinguishable from submergence, for a wholeness beyond rationality or time, for silence itself. We translate such desires, as a number of the essays demonstrate, into visions of utopia, models of new houses, an envisioned Tomorrowland made from plastic. Causality may be absent from the text, each fragment a discrete element—but nearly every fragment is like a jewel that reflects facets common to them all. In the longer pieces, as in the book as a whole, the art lies not only in the crafting of the individual segments but in their combinations and arrangements.

I have chosen some smaller pieces so that the facets of one can be compared with those of others. One of them—"Capiche?"—is composed, we learn, of lies, and verges toward fiction in the writer's attempt to capture an "untranslatable truth" which invests the random events and sounds of any day with strangeness and possibility. "All I had was the glass of language to blow into a souvenir," he says in his final sentence, an apt metaphor for the brilliance of his gift to turn language into crystals of memory.

ATLANTIS

How did the barber pole originate? When did its characteristic stripes become kinetic, turning hypnotically, driven by a hidden motor, giving the impression of red and blue forever twining, never slowing? No matter. No icon or emblem, no symbol or sign, still or revolving, lit from within or lit from without, could in any way have prepared me for that haircut at Nick's Barber Shop, or for Nick himself. His thick Filipino accent obscured meaning, though the sound was mellifluous, and the sense, translated in the late afternoon light, was expressed in the movements of Nick's hands. He flourished a comb he never dropped, a soundless scissors, a razor which revealed, gently, gently, the nape of my neck, now so smooth, attuned to the wind and the wool of my collar.

After our initial exchange of misunderstood courtesies, Nick nudged me toward a wall, museum bright, on which hung a poster depicting the "Official Haircuts for Men and Boys" from 1955. I understood immediately that I was to choose from among the Brush Cut, the Ivy League, the Flat Top with Fenders. To insure sanctity and a sense of privacy, Nick turned off the fan for a moment, lowered his head, and even the dust stopped drifting in abeyance. Above me, in every phase from profile to full front, were heads of hair, luxuriant, graphic, lacquer-black: outmoded curls like scrolls on entablature, sideburns rooted in the past, strands and locks in arrested motion, cresting waves styled into hard edges, like Japanese prints of typhoons.

None of the heads contained a face. One simply interjected his own face. These oval vessels waited to be filled again and again by men's imaginations. For decades, they absorbed the eyes and noses and lips of customers who stood on the checkerboard of old linoleum, or sat in salmon-pink chairs next to wobbling tables stacked with magazines featuring bikinis and ballgames.

The haircut was over in no time. (Nick did a stint in the army, where expedience is everything.) I kept my eyes closed. But aware of strange and lovely afterimages—ghostly pay phone, glowing push broom—I seemed to be submerged in the rapture of the deep. The drone of the fan, the minty and intoxicating scent of Barbasol pressed upon me; phosphene shimmered like minnows in the dark corners of my vision, and I found that this world, cigar stained, sergeant striped, basso profundo, was the lost world of my father, who could not love me. So when Nick kneaded my shoulders and pressed my temples (free scalp manipulation with every visit), I unconsciously grazed him like a cat in Atlantis. His fingers flowed over my forehead like water. I began to smile imperceptibly and see barber poles aslant like sunken columns and voluptuous mermaids in salmon-pink bikinis and bubbles the size of baseballs rising to the surface and bursting with snippets of Filipino small talk.

I can't tell you how odd it was when, restored by a splash of astringent tonic, I finally opened my eyes and saw a clump of my own hair, blown by the fan, skitter across the floor like a cat. For a moment the mirrors were unbearably silver, and the hand-lettered signs, reflected in reverse, seemed inscriptions in a long-forgotten language.

Indeed I looked better, contented. Older too in the ruddy light of sunset. And all of this, this seminal descent to the floor of the sea, this inundation of two paternal hands, this sudden maturation in the mirror, for only four dollars and fifty cents. But my debt of gratitude, beyond the dollar-fifty tip, will be paid here, in the form of Nick's actual telephone number, area code (213) 660-4876. Even his business card, adorned with a faceless haircut holding a phone, says, "Call any time!" Nick means any time. He means day or night. I've driven by and glimpsed him asleep in the barber chair, his face turned toward the street, his combs soaking in blue medicinal liquid, the barber pole softly aglow like a nightlight, the stripes cascading endlessly down, rivulets running toward a home in the ocean.

CAPICHE?

In Italy, the dogs say bow-bow instead of bow-wow, and my Italian teacher, Signora Marra, is not quite sure why this should be. When we tell her that here in America the roosters say cock-a-doodle-do, she throws back her head like a hen drinking raindrops and laughs uncontrollably, as if we were fools to believe what our native red rooster says, or ignoramuses not to know that Italian roosters scratch and clear their gullets before reciting Dante to the sun.

In Venice there is a conspicuous absence of dogs and roosters, but all the pigeons on the planet seem to roost there, and their conversations are deafening. When the city finally sinks, only a thick dark cloud of birds will be left to undulate over the ocean, birds kept alive by pure nostalgia and a longing to land. And circulating among them will be stories, reminiscences, anecdotes of all kinds to help pass the interminable days. Even when this voluble cloud dissipates, the old exhausted birds drowning in the sea, the young bereft birds flying away, the sublime and untranslatable tale of the City of Canals will echo off the oily water, the walls of vapor, the nimbus clouds.

There were so many birds in front of Café Florian's, and mosquitoes sang a piercing song as I drank my glass of wine. Waving them away, I inadvertently beckoned Sandro, a total stranger. With great determination, anxious to know me, he bounded around tables of tourists.

The Piazza San Marco holds many noises within its light-bathed walls, sounds that clash, are superimposed or densely layered like torte. Within that cacophony of words and violins, Sandro and I struggled to communicate. Something unspoken suffered between us. We were, I think, instantly in love, and when he offered me, with his hard brown arms, a blown glass ashtray shaped like a gondola, all I could say, all I could recall of Signora Marra's incanting and chanting (she believed in saturating students in rhyme), was "No capiche." I tried to inflect into that phrase every modulation of meaning, the way different tonalities of light had changed the meaning of that city.

But suddenly this adventure is over. Everything I have told you is a lie. Almost everything. There is no lithe and handsome Sandro. I've never learned Italian or been to Venice. Signora Marra is a feisty fiction. But lies are filled with modulations of untranslatable truth, and early this morning when I awoke, birds were restless in the olive trees. Dogs tramped through the grass and growled. The local rooster crowed fluently. The Chianti sun was coming up, intoxicating, and I was so moved by the strange, abstract trajectories of sound that I wanted to take you with me somewhere, somewhere old and beautiful, and I honestly wanted to offer you something, something like the prospect of sudden love, or color postcards of chaotic piazzas, and I wanted you to listen to me as if you were hearing a rare recording by Enrico Caruso. All I had was the glass of language to blow into a souvenir.

UTOPIA

Today I was going to borrow some books about mankind's concepts of utopia, but the downtown library was destroyed by fire a couple of months ago and now there is only a charred hull, stepped like a ziggurat, cordoned off at a busy intersection, soot seeping from its broken windows, the whole block reeking of smoke. I thought of going to another library, but that would involve negotiating unfamiliar streets, and I'm a man entrenched in routine. I travel the city like a needle coursing through grooves of a record. Work, market, home. Work, market, home. You visit the same places often enough and each day is like the refrain of Old Black Magic—"Round and round I go, in a spin, loving that spin I'm in . . ."

When I look back at childhood, my breakfast bowl was like the curved congress building in the South American capital of Brasilia, a city whose stark architecture was eventually overrun with clotheslines and curtains and chickens plodding through lobbies. The spotless glass-topped bureau where my mother and father kept cologne and lint brushes and shoehorns was a lot like Le Corbusier's Radiant City, egalitarian, rational, based upon the symmetry of His and Hers. Except that my parents filed for divorce. Except that Corbu's schematic plans are nothing now but a blur of monoliths rendered in pencil. Our yard was like a small model of Frank Lloyd Wright's Broadacre City; the faulty fountain, wooden birdhouse, and sparse vegetable garden were as absurd as Wright's metropolis where each resident, living in a mile-high apartment complex, would own an individual plot of farmland which they could fly to in a compact helicopter adorned with geometric designs.

Anyway, I ended up staying at home today, crossing the carpet on journeys to the window and desk and back, staring at tract houses which cover the hills like ice plant or ivy, redundant and dense. As a boy, I used to visit a local subdivision every Sunday and wander through the model home. The foyer was filled with piped-in music. I'd swing back a medicine cabinet mirror to reveal the pristine enamel, the green tiers of glass. Nubby synthetic curtains, clamped tight against the view, created a dim monastic light just right for contemplation. One need only pull a cord to, swoosh, be blinded by the wall of a neighbor, shadowless and absolute across a dusty abyss. Even the brochure's abbreviations—2 bdrm., 2 ba., fully equip. kit.—sounded primal, percussive, melodic as a conga. Late at night the tract homes twinkled, windows burnished by the television's glow, pool lights bluing the air, electric garage doors yawning. And I would have given anything to be the boy in my illustrated school book, walking up to a typical house that contained a family, open-armed, ebullient with the usual greeting.

My home life resisted perfection, and I vented my frustration on Plasticville, an HO-scale community consisting of a fire station, hospital, airport, market, post office, school, ranch house, and cottage. I'd orchestrate train wrecks in the heart of town, or instigate earthquakes, just to see the microcosm topple, to force walls to shake from foundations, to cause bright pieces to fall where they may. But this was nothing compared to the documentary I'd seen of a house in the Nevada desert where Mr. and Mrs. Mannequin and their kids waited in a living room to test the effects of a nuclear blast. Those splintering chairs, that melting hair, those bodies blown like dust from erasers . . .

I can't possibly go about my business day in and day out, parting the curtain of space before me, with any greater sense of apocalypse than I already have. Why, just a few days ago I watched this program on TV where an archaeologist who had unearthed more bodies in Pompeii pulled out trays of remains she actually had pet names for. "Octavia," she said, waving a clavicle. And then she rummaged through the rest of the bones in much the same way that I used to rummage through the puzzle pieces of an autumn landscape searching for the red parts of the barn.

For years, I loved the lightest, most makeshift of shelters: the tent of a linen sheet that sifted the afternoon light; the dining table's underworld with its pillars of living legs. This was long before I'd heard of Buckminster Fuller's comprehensive-anticipatory-design-science, or laid eyes upon a geodesic dome, a habitat of facets as complex as a diamond, though not as enduring. This was before the advent of megastructures composed of lightweight, prefabricated, single-family units which were piled into place by stupendous cranes. This was before the international housing shortage when major urban areas were left to decay and bands of adolescents with shaved heads and black jackets would rasp lyrics like, "Home is where the heart is. Home is so remote. Home is just emotion sticking in my throat."

Morning after morning I listen to music. This morning I played a record of Debussy's "The Sunken Cathedral." For eight minutes and twenty-two seconds, those subaquatic octaves formed in my mind a conception of refuge so sweet, I felt as though I were living in Atlantis; treble and bass had the tensile strength of lintels and beams; the grand piano hammered chords that rose up higher and higher. And as the finale filled the room, sound waves pummeled the plaster walls, molecules tumbling down by the billions.

CHILDLESS

So I was talking to this guy who's the photo editor of *Scientific American,* and he told me he was having trouble choosing a suitable photograph of coral sperm for an upcoming issue. I was stunned because I'd always thought of coral as inanimate matter, a castle of solidified corpses, though corpses of what I wasn't sure. Of course, I had to find out what coral sperm looks like, and he told me it's round and fuchsia. I could see it perfectly, or so I supposed, as if through an electron microscope, buoyant and livid, pocked like golf balls, floating like dust motes. Still, I couldn't visualize the creature who constitutes female coral, as distinct from male, toward whom one seminal ball went bouncing, like a bouncing ball over lyrics to a song. It was kind of sad to think that, for all its flamboyant fans, osseous reefs, gaudy turrets, coral was one more thing, or species of thing, about which I knew almost nothing, except that it generates sperm, round, fuchsia.

The funny thing about being a man who is childless and intends to stay that way is that you almost never think of yourself as possessing spermatazoa. Semen, yes; but not those discrete entities, tadpoles who frolic in the microcosm of your aging anatomy, future celebrities who enter down a spiral staircase of deoxyribonucleic acid, infinitesimal relay runners who lug your traits, coloration, and surname from points remote and primitive. Certainly you don't believe that the substance you spill when you huff and heave in a warm tantrum of onanism could ever, given a million years and a Petri dish and an infrared lamp, could ever come to resemble you. It would be like applauding wildly at a Broadway play and then worrying that you hurt the mites who inhabit the epidermis of your hands. Death is all around us, and we sometimes assist.

Anyway, there are so many varieties of life, and hardly enough Sunday afternoons to watch all those educational programs that teach you about the reproductive mechanisms of albino mountain goats with antlers that branch off and thin away like thoughts before you fall asleep. And sloths who move so slowly they never dry off from morning dew and so possess emerald coats of mold. And yonic orchids housing pools of perfume in which bees drink and wade and drown.

The first time I was alone in the wilderness, I walked through a field that throbbed with song and wondered whether crickets played their wings or their legs. My footfalls, instead of causing the usual thud, caused spreading pools of solemn silence. Sound stopped wherever I walked. And I walked and walked to hush the world, leaving silence like spoor.

from *Let Us Now Praise Famous Men*

James Agee   (1909–1955)

Let Us Now Praise Famous Men, James Agee's best-known work, is an account of what Agee learned while living with three impoverished tenant families in Alabama during the summer of 1936. The photographer Walker Evans, whose photographs of members of those families precede Agee's words, sometimes stayed with them, too. The book, which evades all categories, is more than a cry for social justice. Agee's indignation at what we do to each other as well as his view of our individual value depends upon his awareness of our relationship to the natural world and the universe surrounding our little globe. Early on, he tells us, in rhythmic phrases reminiscent of biblical passages in the King James version,

> Each [person] is intimately connected with the bottom and the extremest reach of time:
>
> Each is composed of substances identical with the substance of all that surrounds him, both the common objects of his disregard, and the hot centers of stars:
>
> All that each person is, and experiences, and shall never experience, in body and in mind, all these things are differing expressions of himself and of one root, and are identical: and not one of these things nor one of these persons is ever quite to be duplicated, nor replaced, nor has it ever quite had precedent: but each is a new and incommunicably tender life, wounded in every breath, and almost as hardly killed as easily wounded: sustaining, for a while, without defense, the enormous assaults of the universe . . . .

Let Us Now Praise Famous Men is so personal, and frequently so idiosyncratic, that a reader can say, with some justice, that it is more concerned with Agee's own guilt and love than it is with his ostensible subjects, the tenant farmers. Yet he would, if he could, get beyond his own ego, get beyond the self-consciousness and other limitations of art itself. Interspersed through the book are interconnected sections called "On the Porch," each of those titles preceded by a parenthesis that has no concluding bracket, suggesting (perhaps) that what is perceived from that position is a part of a limitless vista. (I have deleted that opening bracket from my references, to avoid the confusion that would also be created if I didn't follow this sentence with one.) The porch stands in front of one of the tenant houses. "On the Porch: 2" tells us that sometimes Agee and Evans slept there, one lying on the rear seat of a Chevrolet sedan normally used as a kind of settee, the other on a makeshift pallet—a piece of quilting that once had been the seat of a divan.

"On the Porch: 3," the conclusion of the book, which is excerpted here, describes two complementary voices that Agee and Evans listened to, one night on that porch. These cold and distant voices probably are those of foxes calling to each other, but Agee doesn't want so to delimit them. They represent—they are—a communion of joy and anguish, two nonhuman voices existing like the auditory equivalent (the analogy is mine) of the Neoplatonic emanation from the divine source. The passage represents the attempt to communicate what lies beyond communication.

From these woods a good way out along the hill there now came a sound that was new to us.

All the darkness in near range of the earth as far as we were able to hear was strung with noises that were all one noise, and to this we had become so accustomed that this new sound came out of silence, and left an even more powerful silence behind it, so that with each return it, and the ensuing silence, gave each other more and more value, like the exchanges of two mirrors laid face to face.

Whereas we had been silent before, this sound immediately stiffened us into much more intense silence. Without exchange of word or glance we each received communication of a new opening of delight: but chiefly we now engaged in mutual listening and in analysis of what we heard, so strongly, that in all the body and in the whole range of mind and memory, each of us became all one hollowed and listening ear.

It was perhaps most nearly like the noise hydrogen makes when a match flame is passed across the mouth of a slanted test-tube. It was about the same height as this sound: soprano, with a strong alto illusion. It was colder than this sound, though: as cold and as chilling as the pupil of a goat's eye, or a low note of the clarinet. It ran eight identical notes to a call or stanza, a little faster than allegretto, in this rhythm and accent:

— — – – : – – : – — :

Every note was sharply, dryly, and cleanly accented, just short of staccato; and each was driven out with such strictness and restraint that there was in the short silence between each note an extreme tightness and mutual, organically shared tension. Each of the first seven notes was given exactly the same force; the seventh, hit harder, splayed open a fraction, and out of two things, the extra, hammer hardness it was hit with, and a barely discernible trailing-down at its end, gave the illusion of being a higher note.

This sound, then, started up, with great dramatic suddenness, at some indeterminable distance from us, a distance which in time became a little more determinable, though it was never at all possible accurately to locate it; for the ear always needs the help of the eye. It was from somewhere in the woods out to the left of the house at the bottom of our hill; and a little later it became clear that it was not in the low woods, but somewhere up the opposite slope; and after a little we got it in range within say twenty degrees of the ninety on the horizontal circle which at first could have occupied any part of. It became clear that it would be between an eighth and a quarter mile away; and this became remarkable to us because at that considerable distance we could nevertheless hear, or rather by some equivalent to radioactivity strongly feel, the motions and tensions of the throat and body, the very tilt of the head, that discharged it.

Soon we were helped in locating it (as a second point in any geometry always is helpful, whereas one point alone can run you crazy) by the opening-up of a second call. This call was identical with the first but, coming from a good deal farther away, seemed higher, hollower, and thinner: scarcely more, yet very definitely more, than a loud clear echo.

Which of these calls seemed more mysterious, it is not possible to say. Their quality was very different by virtue both of their difference in distance and of a distinct though indefinable difference in the personality of the callers. At one moment the more distant call was more exciting simply in its distance and because, by its secondary appearance and by its distance beyond the first caller in relation to us, we got the illusion that it was the thing sought by the other; the next, the nearer call took all the honors from it, by nearness; by having become the searcher with whom we had identified ourselves and taken sides and by having yet at the same time remained so entirely itself, without regard for us, no part of us, more alien to us, because it was alive and conscious and within our near perspective of kinship, than any stone or star. The fact is of course that these two series of calls, when they had been set going, enhanced each other quite as richly as each enhanced and received enhancement from its own, and the other's, interventions of silence, and a little later from its participation in, yet aristocratic distinction from, that plebeian, unanimous ringing of the air which had at no time ceased or diminished and which, now that we were listening so intently, became once more a part of the reality of hearing.

By use only of silences, without changing their stanzaic structure, these two calls went through any number of rhythmic-dramatic devices of delays in question and answer, of overlappings, of tricks of delay by which each pretended to show that it had signed off for the night or, actually, that it no longer even existed. There is an old, not specially funny vaudeville act in which the whole troupe builds up and burlesques a dramatic situation simply by different vocal and gesticulative colorations of the word "you." I thought of that now: but its present use was any amount better because the artists were subtler and what they had to say was more enigmatic and more exciting to the audience. Neither of them changed a note or a beat of his call; and if either allowed himself any change of tone or color whatever, it was so delicate that it is impossible to assign it to the callers save through the changefulness and human sentimentality of us who were listening and making what we could of it. But certainly, one way or the other, its meanings changed. One time it would be sexual; another, just a casual colloquy; another, a challenge; another, a signal or warning; another, a comment on us; another, some simple and desperate effort at mutual location; another, most intense and masterful irony; another, laughter; another, triumph; another, a masterpiece of parody of any one, any combination, or all of these assigned or implicit tones: but at all times it was beyond even the illusion of full apprehension, and was noble, frightening and distinguished: a work of great, private and unambitious art which was irrelevant to audience.

We were trying hardest of all to make out what animal or bird was making these sounds, but we had no clue, no anchorage in knowledge through whose help we might by comparative projections have taken it. I cannot even try to say how in the long run we concluded (perhaps in part through its sharpness, tightness out of the throat, and carnivorous timbre) that it was the voice of a fur-bearing animal and that the animal was on the small side and that he might most likely, then that he must, be a fox. It is this sort of mystery we should run against in all casual experience if we found ourselves without warning possessed of a new sense.

Now this is one of a universe of things which should be accepted and recorded for its own sake. The first entrance of this call was as perfect a piece of dramatic or musical structure as I know of: the context perfectly prepared, the entrance of the mysterious principal completely unforeseen yet completely casual, with none of the quality of studiousness in its surprise which hurts for instance some of the music of Brahms; and from its first entrance on, the whole world was frozen and fixed under its will as by the introduction of a precipitant; so that the identical entrance of the second voice carried with it an excitement almost beyond what is possible to bear.

When this second voice had spoken, the first did not answer, but froze just as we and our world had frozen. That which had called was listening intently too. And that which had called the caller was waiting and listening. And now after a long space of more and more tremendous silence (into which there arose, but very faintly, loosely, as natural and common as dew, the ramified ringing of frogs, insects, and night birds), after this long space of silence had extended itself beyond any degree of natural endurance, the second voice spoke a second time, identically, yet, because of the silence, the lack of answer, more imperious-sounding than at first.

Then there was a wait, in whose first part the call repeated itself on the ear's memory silently yet keenly as print, and in whose latter expansion once again we were intense with waiting; and then, by some rhythmic genius a little, but only a very little, off-beat, off the beat of eccentrics our ear had of the sum of the calls computed, a very little before it was quite possible to expect it, there came the voice of the first creature; and it was with the breaking open of this voice that we too broke open, silently, our whole bodies broke open into a laughter that destroyed and restored us more even than the most absolute weeping ever can. This is a laughter I have experienced only rarely: listening to the genius of Mozart at its angriest and cleanest, most masculine fire; the sudden memory of some line of Shakespeare, "Nymph, in thine orisons be all my sins remembered"; walking in streets or driving in country; watching negroes; or in that delicate stage of love when a girl, serious and scarcely tinged with smiling, her eyes muted and her head poised most immaculately, first begins, not in pleasure alone, but in a kind of fear and deep gentleness, to use her light, slow, frank hands upon your head and body: a phase so unassailably beyond any meaning of tenderness and of trust, so like the opening of first living upon the shining of the young earth in its first morning, that an overwhelming knowledge of God and of his non-existence fight in you and, all in this same quietness, you feel it impossible that you can look into her eyes one more moment and not be so distended by incredulous joy that you are of one size and ignorance and fleshlessness with space itself.[1]

And this phase of love, to anyone who holds love in the utmost esteem that is its due, must be beyond all comparison the cruelest and bitterest thing in human experience. Even within its own moments it draws you both irresistibly into those desperate battlings of the body which only in their first few seconds seem the greater joy they are not, and which so soon blunt and blind the delicate munificence of your exchange into their own beautiful but violent, charcoal-drawn terms. Out of this violence of flesh and of total mutual confidence it is not possible many times to withdraw into that quieter sphere of apposition in which the body, brain and spirit of each of you is all one perfectly focused lens and in which these two lenses devour, feed, enrich and honor each other; it is not possible because the violence blurs, feathers and distorts the essential constituency of the lens. And it is then, living in flushes of memory of a thing more excellent than you may much hope to share between you again, that with scarcely conscious bravery and sorrow, and with measureless compassion, love must assume itself to be established and alive between you. There will be goodness and joy between you again, with wisdom and luck a

---

[1] The essences of anguish and of joy are thus identical: they are the explosion or incandescence resulting from the incontrovertible perception of the incredible.

great deal, more than enough, but not all the kind regard nor all the love within the scope of existence will ever restore you what for a while, and only that you might lose it in the blind service of nature, you had.

In the sound of these foxes, if they were foxes, there was nearly as much joy, and less grief. There was the frightening joy of hearing the world talk to itself, and the grief of incommunicability. In that grief I am now as then, with the small yet absolute comfort of knowing that communication of such a thing is not only beyond possibility but irrelevant to it; whereas in love, where we find ourselves so completely involved, so completely responsible and so apparently capable, and where all our soul so runs out to the loveliness, strength, and defenseless mortality, plain, common, salt and muscled toughness of human existence of a girl[1] that the desire to die for her seems the puniest and stingiest expression of your regard which you can, like a proud tomcat with a slain fledgling, lay at her feet; in love the restraint in focus and the arrest and perpetuation of joy seems entirely possible and simple, and its failure inexcusable, even while we know it is beyond the power of all biology and even while, like the fading of flowerlike wonder out of a breast to which we are becoming habituated, that exquisite joy lies, fainting through change upon change, in the less and less prescient palm of the less and less godlike, more and more steadily stupefied, human, ordinary hand.

And so though this incident of the calling of two creatures should by rights be established at very least as a poem, or a piece of music, and though, even, I know that a more gifted human being, and even I myself, could come nearer giving it, I do not relinquish the ultimately hopeless effort with entire grief: simply because that effort would be, above most efforts, so useless.

This calling continued, never repeating a pattern, and always with what seemed infallible art, for perhaps twenty minutes. It was thoroughly as if principals had been set up, enchanted, and left like dim sacks at one side of a stage as enormous as the steadfast tilted deck of the earth, and as if onto this stage, accompanied by the drizzling confabulation of nocturnal-pastoral music, two masked characters, unforetold and perfectly irrelevant to the action, had with catlike aplomb and noiselessness stept and had sung, with sinister casualness, what at length turned out to have been the most significant, but most unfathomable, number in the show; and had then in perfect irony and silence withdrawn.

It was after the ending of this that we began a little to talk. Ordinarily we enjoyed talking and of late, each absorbed throughout most of the day

---

[1] I would presume this to be quite as possible, and of no less dignity and valor, in homosexual as well as in heterosexual love.

in subtle and painful work that made even the lightest betrayal of our full reactions unwise, we had found the fragments of time we were alone, and able to give voice to them and to compare and analyze them, valuable and necessary beyond comparison of cocaine. But now in this structure of special exaltation it was, though not unpleasant, thoroughly unnecessary, and obstructive of more pleasing usage. Our talk drained rather quickly off into silence and we lay thinking, analyzing, remembering, in the human and artist's sense praying, chiefly over matters of the present and of that immediate past which was a part of the present; and each of these matters had in that time the extreme clearness, and edge, and honor, which I shall now try to give you; until at length we too fell asleep.

"Waves"

Edwin J. Kenney, Jr. (1942–1992)

For the last fifteen years of his life, Edwin J. Kenney, Jr., struggling against a rare form of cancer, continued to find fulfillment as dedicated teacher (he was a professor of English at Colby College), as husband and father, and as sailor of his small boat in Penobscot Bay. In 1990, his mother suffered a recurrence of breast cancer. In his last visit with her before her death, he saw in her "drawn, waxen, olive-skinned, skull-like face" a foreshadowing of his own fate. In the clear and beautifully controlled prose of "Waves," Kenney tells us, "I think now that perhaps this powerful seeing of myself in my mother is what we all must see in the suffering and dying of others: ourselves, all of us who, being human, will suffer, become ill, and die. But only by seeing this in those we love, who have loved us all of our lives, whose features resemble our own, do we permit ourselves—because we really cannot defend against it—to be overcome by this recognition."

Preoccupied as we are with our own sufferings and pleasures, aware on some level of the fact of our personal mortality, we might want to resist reading about such painful experiences—much as we might want, at first, to resist those described by Andre Dubus in his "Broken Vessels." The objectivity with which Kenney examines himself at this moment, though, suggests that he has gained a perspective, a self-knowledge, that will enable him to transcend this grief for himself and a beloved mother. Actually, this essay builds toward such a transcendence, implicit in the concluding visionary insight Kenney experiences while sailing alone in his boat.

This essay, which deals with life at one of its two extremities, is as concise—and as convincing—a statement of the value of memory as any I have come across. It appeals, at any rate, to my own belief that memory (whatever else it is) is our major spiritual faculty. In "Waves," a series of gestures of farewell are linked not only with the motion of water but with that moment at the end of the essay in which Kenney perceives the people waving at him from the shore first as possessing the perfection and beauty of a painting and then as a part of a living tableau—a vision of human unity that includes him. The wave of the major figure on the shore becomes "not a wave of good-bye, signifying death or estrangement, or loss, but a welcome, beckoning me back into the life of the world."

"My illness and my sailing," Kenney says, as part of his preparation for this conclusion, "have been inextricably bound up with one another. . . . I love the concentration that being out there by myself requires, the complete and necessary attention to the act that can paradoxically render things of the world so precisely and luminously, which has always given me an extraordinary sense of well-being while at the same time abolishing my sense of self." I am reminded by the unitary experience at the end of this essay of that of Augustine at Ostia, of that of Agee on the front porch of the house of the Alabama tenant farmers, and of related spiritual experiences of others aware of the crucial role that memory plays in their lives. The happiness—the joy—of such unitary experiences seems always to require the transcendence of one's own anxieties, of one's own conscious self. In such cases, memory leads the individual to its vanishing point of union; afterward, it returns, investing life with the knowledge and happiness of that moment.

Kenney died four months after he completed this essay.

In July of 1990, after complaining of persistent chest and back pain, my mother told me that she had been diagnosed with a recurrence of breast cancer. Sixteen years earlier, she had had a radical mastectomy which not only took her whole breast but also part of her lymph system, so that her right arm became significantly and permanently swollen. Although she enjoyed many good years, following her mastectomy my mother was hampered by the swelling and the awkwardness, discomfort, and pain that it caused. She wore an elastic sleeve on her arm every day, tried to keep it elevated at night when she slept, and "milked" it with a machine that through pressure and vibration attempted to move the fluid out of her arm and into her circulatory system. But the arm stayed swollen and even increased in size and weight so that my mother's five-foot frame was actually dragged down on her right side by it. Even though she feared surgery, my mother gamely underwent two experimental operations, an unsuccessful attempt to repair the lymph system and then a painful but moderately successful effort to de-bulk the arm, which, however, left her with a long scar running from her armpit to her wrist.

This physical disfigurement did not cause, but to my eyes greatly exaggerated, a peculiar physical characteristic of my mother's. When she waved good-bye her arm and hand always seemed oddly out of sync with one another, as though her hand were not properly attached to her arm. I remember her down the years since her mastectomy, waving good-bye to me and my family as we left after a visit to return to our home in Maine, where my wife and I taught at a small college. She would stand at the sliding glass doors or the raised deck on the house she and my father bought in Shark River Hills, New Jersey in 1981, her enlarged forearm going in one direction while her hand, inexplicably and preposterously, went in the other. The gesture seemed to express my mother's great energy and vitality, her love of the social amenities, as well as a certain lack of attention or control that my eldest sister, Joyce, has always called "ditsy."

My mother's recurrence had an especially powerful and disturbing effect on me, for I, too, had been treated for cancer, a rare form called malignant pheochromocytoma. Since 1977, I had had two major operations, chemo-therapy, and I had just recently concluded radiation treatment. Although I had long ago intellectually accepted that there is no justice evident in the distribution of illness and other misfortunes, I found myself feeling angry that this should have happened to my mother, because she didn't deserve anything like this after all she had been through. But I also felt disappointed and oddly let down, as well as angry, that my mother was sick again. I asked myself "What have I been doing all this for?" and caught myself out in the mostly unconscious heroic inflation that the reason I had been sick and undergoing all these various treatments and anxieties was so that others, most of all those I loved, would not have to. Underlying these feelings, however, was an even deeper, more pervasive feeling of despair. I felt that something was taking my mother away from me, beyond the reach of my love. My mother's recurrence overwhelmed me with the feeling that no matter what we do or how well we do, the disease is inexorably persistent and will get us in the end—that it is out of our control. We do not cause nor can we cure our illness. We can only live with it, make what life we can within the arc of its demands on us, and see what it may teach us.

The conventional hormonal therapy for metastatic breast cancer had no effect at all, and by September, my mother's pain was increasing and she was discussing harsher chemotherapy with her doctors. I had become so traumatized by my two years of chemotherapy that simply going to the hospital for any reason made me nauseated as soon as I walked in the door. I was saddened and frightened of even talking about this with my mother, but I tried to be careful not to project my fears onto her or, by anything I said or did, to encourage her to share them.

We all spent Thanksgiving together at my younger sister's new house on the water at Packanack Lake, New Jersey. Although Mom was suffering from nausea and diarrhea caused by chemotherapy and therefore was somewhat subdued, she looked good, got around with some of her old energy, enjoyed seeing my sister's new place and being together with all of us. We were all relieved to see her at least holding her own, and regarded all this as a good sign. There was, however, one unavoidable and ominous note. My mother had always been a superb and confident cook. She made excellent pies from scratch, any kind of pie we liked—ap-ple, pumpkin, lemon meringue, coconut custard, chocolate cream—and we always looked forward to these homemade pies at all our family gatherings. But this Thanksgiving there simply were none. She and my father arrived for dinner with several pies in cardboard store boxes. Embar-rassed and ashamed to the point of tears, my mother admitted that at the last minute, her own "just didn't turn out," so she had sent my father to the supermarket to buy pies for our dessert. Quietly horrified, we commented on how good they were for "store-bought," and let it go at that, just as we all continued to take a willfully optimistic view of her chances.

According to my sisters, Christmas was her last good day. By this time, she had begun another chemotherapy protocol and was taking medication for pain. She was uncharacteristically neglecting how she or her house looked, and seemed to have difficulty focusing on what was going on around her. But she rallied for the day and the big meal prepared by my sisters. After this, whenever I called my mother on the phone, she was in bed, immobilized by the pain and her disorientation from it and the drugs. Once she said to me, "I never thought it would be this bad." The antecedent of "it" was unclear. Did she mean chemo? pain? cancer? dying? Two weeks later, on January 9, 1991, my parents called to wish me a happy 49th birthday, and I could hear the fear in my father's voice. Up until now he had always been deliberately putting the best face on everything, not only because if he didn't, my mother might hear what he really felt, but also, I think now, because he wanted to protect me from what he might well have sensed were my own difficulties in dealing with my mother's illness. When my mother got on the phone I asked her how she was feeling, and she said she was not doing very well. Her voice sounded weak, and she was having difficulty breathing. There was a prolonged silence, and then she said, "I have . . . I have . . . oh, what is it?" Then she called out to my father: "Dad, what is it that I have?" I heard his voice in the background but couldn't make out what he was saying. Then my mother's voice came back with some note of surprise at having discovered what she was looking for: "I have cancer. That's what it is, cancer."

After trying yet another chemotherapy protocol, the doctors decided toward the end of January to discontinue treating my mother. As they put it, the cancer had "outrun" the treatment. They estimated that my mother had between a couple of weeks and a couple of months to live. Now bedridden most of the time, unable to cook or look after the house, or even take care of herself adequately, heavily medicated for pain, my mother seemed really to be going further and further away from us and to live more and more on what we called the "other side." She was oblivious to most activity immediately around her, as though she were instead deeply engaged in some conversation in her mind set way back in another time, in another place. The family arranged for my mother to be cared for at home professionally during the day, for my father was visibly shaken by his inability to care for her alone and obviously worn down by having spent so much time watching her decline so rapidly.

From the moment I first started chemotherapy I strove never to miss work unless I had to; indeed, I had developed a tendency to take on more work around the college than I probably should have. I don't think this was some simple compensatory gesture to prove my manhood; it was more the feeling that teaching was my chosen profession, my vocation, that this was my life, and that I wanted to stay with it and do as much of it as I could while I was still able. I did not want to lose the atmosphere, the rhythm, the energy of the classroom, for even when I did not feel well physically, it gave me a spiritual sense of well-being. But as I worried about my mother, about not being with her and my father and sisters, and about my own disease, I bore down so hard on teaching every day of the January term, determined not to miss a day, to make everything seem "all right" for myself and others that I became increasingly inaccessible myself. I was anxious, tense, and depressed.

I was obviously not an easy person to live with during this time, and part of the reason was that I tried to keep most of my strongest feelings to myself because I considered them too awful, too depressing to share with others. But this strategy failed me, or I failed to execute it, for I would, often inappropriately and irrationally, express my worst fears and anxieties to my wife, who was naturally upset both by my being silent and withdrawn and then uncontrollably morbid, fearful, angry, and resentful. Having lived with me through the chronic maintenance of my disease and the many frightening crises it caused, Susie was struggling to preserve herself and her life from being completely taken over by my illness. The main form this effort at self-preservation took was her going away to do research for her next book, to give readings, and to be a guest teacher at other institutions. This year she was on sabbatical and so she was away even more often than usual. Because I did not understand at the time as well as I think I do now what Susie was seeking, I was often hurt by her absences and found our many leave-takings hard. But, typically, I did not reveal my feelings or talk them through with her. Instead, I masked them by a parodic military ceremony in our driveway as she took off in the car. I would stand at mock attention and give a grotesquely rigid salute as she backed out and headed down the road. My vision of her became focused on her small arm, delicate wrist, and tiny fingers slowly forming a little cupped wave of the hand as she left me there alone. This gesture of hers seemed so perfunctory, almost absent-minded, that I felt as though she were already gone away, living a life of her own, apart from me.

During this month of January I felt emotionally alone and isolated, and what strikes me now as I look back on it is the way this experience with Susie was also repeated with my daughter. Our older child, James, was away at college, our younger at home, a senior in high school. When Susie would go away, my daughter Anne and I would be home alone together. This arrangement, though not always easy or fun, did serve to bring us closer together. Anne was busy at school and active in many extracurricular activities, but we shopped and cooked and ate together, shared accounts of our days, and generally connected in an authentic and often intense way. Anne always wanted to know what was going on with my disease, and she was sympathetic to how I felt about what was going on with me and my mother. Without being intrusive or even asking a lot of questions, she was able to pick up on how I was feeling and respond in an empathetic way. But, every weekend during the winter Anne left to go to Sugarloaf Mountain to pursue her love of snowboarding and to visit with the family of a young man to whom she was very attached. Maybe she, too, just needed to get away for a time. Perhaps because she knew of my good-byes to Susie in the driveway, she parodied the mock-military ceremony through a raucous leave-taking of her own. She would honk the horn loudly and repeatedly as she backed down the driveway and headed up the road. She would also either roll down her window, or, preferably, if the roof of her car was not covered with snow, open the sun roof, stick her arm up through it and wave vigorously. This was Anne: dramatic, spirited, funny. But I missed her too, and I dreaded the prospect of her going off to college in the fall, leaving me without her bright presence. When she and Susie were both gone during those winter weekends, I would be left alone with the dog to listen to my collection of female jazz singers from Billie Holiday through Ella Fitzgerald and Sarah Vaughn to Diane Schurr.

At the end of January, I left to see my mother for what I knew would be the last time. When I arrived on Thursday evening, Mom looked strangely ethereal to me. My sister Joyce had helped prepare her for my visit, and she was sitting up in bed with her hair combed, wearing lipstick, a nice sweater over her nightgown, and the special earrings we had given her for her 75th birthday in her pierced ears. In these superficial ways she looked very much like herself. But she had lost weight and hair; her face was much thinner; her skin was waxen, clearly showing the shape of her skull. Most of the time she seemed to be living psychically in another world. Everything we did seemed to reach her as though across a great distance. A person walking into her room to bring her medication, something to eat or drink, or just say hello, all came as a surprise to her, almost an intrusion.

Yet she was so obedient, so compliant, when we tried to move her or asked her to help us help her. Her questions were plaintive, childlike. She asked me, clearly suffering, "What do I have? What is wrong with me?"

Then, before I could answer, she said, "You can't say. You don't know." When I told her she had cancer, she lapsed back into the trance her life had become, as though she were already gone. We could not seem to connect with her in the present moment, in the actual circumstances of her disease and dying.

Memories seemed to shoot across her mind. When I came in to eat my breakfast cereal with her the next morning, she blurted out, "Oh, I remember that!" When I asked her what it was that she remembered, she said, "Where I used to eat at your house."

She did occasionally issue commands. On Saturday morning, after getting her up out of bed to pee at 5:30 and 7:30, I was in the kitchen letting my parents' chubby and indulged Sheltie out, and my mother called for me urgently. When I got into the bedroom, she was calling "Ed, little Ed." Then, when she was sure I was there and she had my attention, she said, "Get me into the hospital, *please.*" I asked why she wanted to go and she said, "They can do more for me there." Given her state of mind, I was unclear whether she meant that they could make her more comfortable, or that, not consciously knowing that she was dying, she believed they could still treat her disease in some beneficial way. But the idea of her now physically removing herself from the house with which she was so identified seemed yet another attempt to go away from us.

We had a long family conference about whether to hire a private 24-hour nurse and keep Mom at home or to go along with her wish to be put in the hospital. It took a long time, but my father finally told us not only that he was worried about caring for her at home, even with the assistance of a professional nurse, but also that he did not want her to die at home. He had witnessed enough of her dying in this house. We decided to send Mom to the hospital the next day, the day I was to leave to go back to Maine.

My mother rarely drank. She would have a glass of wine as part of the ceremony of her meals, but that was it. Later that day, when I joked with her, as I often did, about having a drink with us before dinner, she looked directly at me and smiled just like her old self. "Are you *kidding* me?" she said. In her voice was the familiar tone of mock exasperation and delight that appeared whenever she caught us out in an effort to fool her. In this fleeting moment she was herself again, and those were the last words she addressed directly to me, acknowledging the playful nature of our adult relationship.

The next morning we called the doctor, who was out of town, waited for his partner to call back, called the ambulance, and waited for it to arrive. My sisters and I paced up and down the deck, looking out at the

Shark River, waiting for the ambulance. It was clear and sunny, with little wind, the temperature setting a record for that day by reaching into the 60s. Finally I went in by myself and got Mom up and to the portable commode and gave her some Italian ice with her pain medication, crying the whole time and telling her I loved her. She seemed not to notice, and I was just as glad, for even now I am not sure whether I was mourning only for my mother, not only because I was her first child and only son and she my mother and I loved her and could not tolerate her suffering and could not imagine life without her, but also because I, too, was a cancer patient with an incurable, progressive disease that in the past few months had seemed to be speeding up. In her drawn, waxen, olive-skinned, skull-like face, whose features so resembled mine, her helpless body, and untethered mind, I saw myself in the all-too-immediate future. I think now that perhaps this powerful seeing of myself in my mother is what we all must see in the suffering and dying of others: ourselves, all of us who, being human, will suffer, become ill, and die. But only by seeing this in those we love, who have loved us all of our lives, whose features resemble our own, do we permit ourselves—because we really cannot defend against it—to be overcome by this recognition.

My mother was taken out of the house on a stretcher, through the kitchen, out the side door, and down the side steps of the wrap-around deck. My sisters were to ride with her to the hospital, and I would soon begin the long drive home. At the bottom of the stairs I stopped the progress of the ambulance crew and kissed my mother for what I knew was the last time. As they continued their procession toward the driveway and the waiting ambulance again, my mother weakly raised her swollen right arm against the restraints holding her securely on the stretcher and waved good-bye to me for the last time, her hand oddly out of sync with her arm.

After my mother's death, after the burial mass, and after the end of spring term, my repeat CT scan showed what the medical profession calls with unintended metaphorical accuracy "increased tumor burden." I had only one damaged kidney so I was reluctant to risk it in further treatment, at least as long as I was feeling as well as I did. Nor was there sufficient data to demonstrate that any of what my doctor calls the "industrial strength" chemotherapies remaining to me would do any good against my strange disease. So the questions of whether to undergo treatment, what kind, when, and for how long, all remained. As my doctor said to me, "These are not just medical questions, Ed; they are ultimate, existential questions."

For the moment, I decided to leave them hanging, to wait and see, and to continue the familiar struggle not to let my knowledge of my disease, or the fear caused by the knowledge, interfere with my living of my life in the present moment. In the summer months since my first operation in 1977, this for me has always involved sailing on the coast of Maine. My illness and my sailing have been inextricably bound up with one another. So when I returned from the hospital in Michigan in late May, I uncovered, prepared, and launched my boat. Although my children are more willing to sail now that they are older and I do sometimes take friends who enjoy being out on the water, I most often sail alone. I love the concentration that being out there by myself requires, the complete and necessary attention to the act that can paradoxically render things of the world so precisely and luminously, which has always given me an extraordinary sense of well-being while at the same time abolishing my sense of self.

And so it was that one day, sailing by myself in Penobscot Bay out from Castine toward Parker Cove on the northeast side of Isleboro, I found myself once again completely absorbed in the atmospheric tension of wind and wave.

Near land it is sunny, clear, and bright. With winds building from the southeast, the light shatters on the waves, and takes on their motion, while giving them in return a sharp, shimmering, prismatic brilliance. But out in the bay there is thick fog, which the sun's light illumines as though from the inside, only occasionally and briefly revealing its presence above in the sky. There is a strangely disorienting merger of the elements of water, fog, sunlight, and sky so that, moved silently by the wind in the sails through the motion of the sea, I feel transported not simply from one place to another but into a whole other plane of existence.

As I emerge from the fog in the middle of the East Bay toward Parker Cove, I am approaching a large house elevated on a point with a tall flagpole, the flag blown straight out and fluttering. The flag, combined with the sharp quality of the light, which had the effect of showing all objects in their full roundness and stolidity, reminds me of Monet's *Terrace at Le Havre*. As I continue close into shore, the shapes and bits of color compose themselves into people eating and drinking on the porch and the steps leading down from it and children playing on the lawn in front of them. Because it is just before high tide at 1:15, I can go in close to the rocky shore and, as I do, I notice a woman get up quickly and run into the house. She emerges from another door with binoculars, to look at me. When she gets me in sight, while holding the binoculars in her left hand, she gives me a big wave, her right arm fully extended and moving energetically in a wide arc. Then all the people, adults and children, wave to me. I wave back, come about smartly and wave again, now going away from Parker's Cove back out into the bay and the mixture of light and fog.

This was all deeply moving to me at the time. Before I even realized what was happening, my eyes filled with tears and I was sobbing loudly. The vision had seemed at first like a painting because everything in it was so composed and beautiful, so perfect. But then it all came alive; the people were real and alive in the moment and so was I. No longer subject and object, we were participants in the moment together. And I was there for it, fully present and focused.

And the moment remains in my mind; it endures. I often look up and see again in my mind's eye the figure of the woman, waving to me. Because I did not have my binoculars in the cockpit when I saw her, I do not know whether she was young or old, beautiful or plain; her actual features remain elusive. In the absence of them, I can project onto her the face of my mother, my wife, or my daughter. But this seems a limitation on the significance of this experience for me. Even though I cannot explain it, I derive from this visionary moment a deeply abiding sense of peace and assurance and joy. When it recurs, I can feel the light and the fog and wind on the water and my boat moving through it, and when I again see the figure of the woman waving to me across the distance I know intuitively that this is not a wave good-bye, signifying death, or estrangement, or loss, but a welcome, beckoning me back into the life of the world. And whatever my disease and its treatment may bring, whatever I may decide to do, in this recurring and abiding moment I am riding the wave of mystery that is my life, and I fully know it.

"Teaching a Stone to Talk"

Annie Dillard (1945–)

In compiling material for the various sections of this anthology, I frequently have been tempted to include an essay by Annie Dillard—something from her *Pilgrim at Tinker Creek* in "The Memory of Nature," for example, or a generous excerpt from her *An American Childhood* in the childhood portion of "Perspectives of Memory." In willing myself to exclude a segment of that latter book from a section in which it would have been wholly appropriate, I came to a partial understanding of the withdrawal problems of a recovering addict—and, much like a wise addict, rewarded myself for the loss with a promise, in my case the promise of having "Teaching a Stone to Talk" in this final section.

The essay is about silence—about the absence of God's voice from nature, ever since we willed God to silence. "We are here to bear witness," Dillard says. "There is nothing else to do with those mute materials we do not need." Central to the essay are two visits that she made to the Galápagos Islands, and central to these visits is the role of memory in dismissing certain responses and images, in selecting others (here, the *palo santo* trees) for the larger meaning they contain. This essay, with its celebration of trees whose passivity and lack of vitality is more apparent than real, with its celebration of a silence in which God somehow must reside, is in such harmony with my own soul and body that it makes me happy, every time I read it.

The island where I live is peopled with cranks like myself. In a cedar-shake shack on a cliff—but we all live like this—is a man in his thirties who lives alone with a stone he is trying to teach to talk.

Wisecracks on this topic abound, as you might expect, but they are made as it were perfunctorily, and mostly by the young. For in fact, almost everyone here respects what Larry is doing, as do I, which is why I am protecting his (or her) privacy, and confusing for you the details. It could be, for instance, a pinch of sand he is teaching to talk, or a prolonged northerly, or any one of a number of waves. But it is, in fact, I assure you, a stone. It is—for I have seen it—a palm-sized oval beach cobble whose dark gray is cut by a band of white which runs around and, presumably, through it; such stones we call "wishing stones," for reasons obscure but not, I think, unimaginable.

He keeps it on a shelf. Usually the stone lies protected by a square of untanned leather, like a canary asleep under its cloth. Larry removes the cover for the stone's lessons, or more accurately, I should say, for the ritual or rituals which they perform together several times a day.

473

No one knows what goes on at these sessions, least of all myself, for I know Larry but slightly, and that owing only to a mix-up in our mail. I assume that like any other meaningful effort, the ritual involves sacrifice, the suppression of self-consciousness, and a certain precise tilt of the will, so that the will becomes transparent and hollow, a channel for the work. I wish him well. It is a noble work, and beats, from any angle, selling shoes.

Reports differ on precisely what he expects or wants the stone to say. I do not think he expects the stone to speak as we do, and describe for us its long life and many, or few, sensations. I think instead that he is trying to teach it to say a single word, such as "cup," or "uncle." For this purpose he has not, as some have seriously suggested, carved the stone a little mouth, or furnished it in any way with a pocket of air which it might then expel. Rather—and I think he is wise in this—he plans to initiate his son, who is now an infant living with Larry's estranged wife, into the work, so that it may continue and bear fruit after his death.

II

Nature's silence is its one remark, and every flake of world is a chip off that old mute and immutable block. The Chinese say that we live in the world of the ten thousand things. Each of the ten thousand things cries out to us precisely nothing.

God used to rage at the Israelites for frequenting sacred groves. I wish I could find one. Martin Buber says: "The crisis of all primitive mankind comes with the discovery of that which is fundamentally not-holy, the a-sacramental, which withstands the methods, and which has no 'hour,' a province which steadily enlarges itself." Now we are no longer primitive; now the whole world seems not-holy. We have drained the light from the boughs in the sacred grove and snuffed it in the high places and along the banks of sacred streams. We as a people have moved from pantheism to pan-atheism. Silence is not our heritage but our destiny; we live where we want to live.

The soul may ask God for anything, and never fail. You may ask God for his presence, or for wisdom, and receive each at his hands. Or you may ask God, in the words of the shopkeeper's little gag sign, that he not go away mad, but just go away. Once, in Israel, an extended family of nomads did just that. They heard God's speech and found it too loud. The wilderness generation was at Sinai; it witnessed there the thick darkness where God was: "and all the people saw the thunderings, and the lightnings, and the noise of the trumpet, and the mountain smoking." It scared them witless. Then they asked Moses to beg God, please, never speak to them directly again. "Let not God speak with us, lest we die." Moses took the message. And God, pitying their self-consciousness, agreed. He agreed not to speak to the people anymore. And he added to Moses, "Go say to them, Get into your tents again."

III

It is difficult to undo our own damage, and to recall to our presence that which we have asked to leave. It is hard to desecrate a grove and change your mind. The very holy mountains are keeping mum. We doused the burning bush and cannot rekindle it; we are lighting matches in vain under every green tree. Did the wind use to cry, and the hills shout forth praise? Now speech has perished from among the lifeless things of earth, and living things say very little to very few. Birds may crank out sweet gibberish and monkeys howl; horses neigh and pigs say, as you recall, oink oink. But so do cobbles rumble when a wave recedes, and thunders break the air in lightning storms. I call these noises silence. It could be that wherever there is motion there is noise, as when a whale breaches and smacks the water—and wherever there is stillness there is the still small voice, God's speaking from the whirlwind, nature's old song and dance, the show we drove from town. At any rate, now it is all we can do, and among our best efforts, to try to teach a given human language, English, to chimpanzees.

In the forties an American psychologist and his wife tried to teach a chimp actually to speak. At the end of three years the creature could pronounce, in a hoarse whisper, the words "mama," "papa," and "cup." After another three years of training she could whisper, with difficulty, still only "mama," "papa," and "cup." The more recent successes at teaching chimpanzees American Sign Language are well known. Just the other day a chimp told us, if we can believe that we truly share a vocabulary, that she had been sad in the morning. I'm sorry we asked.

What have we been doing all these centuries but trying to call God back to the mountain, or, failing that, raise a peep out of anything that isn't us? What is the difference between a cathedral and physics lab? Are not they both saying: Hello? We spy on whales and on interstellar radio objects; we starve ourselves and pray till we're blue.

IV

I have been reading comparative cosmology. At this time most cosmologists favor the picture of the evolving universe described by Lemaître and Gamow. But I prefer a suggestion made years ago by Valéry—Paul Valéry. He set forth the notion that the universe might be "head-shaped."

The mountains are great stone bells; they clang together like nuns. Who shushed the stars? There are a thousand million galaxies easily seen in the Palomar reflector; collisions between and among them do, of course, occur. But these collisions are very long and silent slides. Billions of stars sift among each other untouched, too distant even to be moved, heedless as always, hushed. The sea pronounces something, over and over, in a hoarse whisper; I cannot quite make it out. But God knows I have tried.

At a certain point you say to the woods, to the sea, to the mountains, the world, Now I am ready. Now I will stop and be wholly attentive. You empty yourself and wait, listening. After a time you hear it: there is nothing there. There is nothing but those things only, those created objects, discrete, growing or holding, or swaying, being rained on or raining, held, flooding or ebbing, standing, or spread. You feel the world's word as a tension, a hum, a single chorused note everywhere the same. This is it: this hum is the silence. Nature does utter a peep—just this one. The birds and insects, the meadows and swamps and rivers and stones and mountains and clouds: they all do it; they all don't do it. There is a vibrancy to the silence, a suppression, as if someone were gagging the world. But you wait, you give your life's length to listening, and nothing happens. The ice rolls up, the ice rolls back, and still that single note obtains. The tension, or lack of it, is intolerable. The silence is not actually suppression; instead, it is all there is.

V

We are here to witness. There is nothing else to do with those mute materials we do not need. Until Larry teaches his stone to talk, until God changes his mind, or until the pagan gods slip back to their hilltop groves, all we can do with the whole inhuman array is watch it. We can stage our own act on the planet—build our cities on its plains, dam its rivers, plant its topsoils—but our meaningful activity scarcely covers the terrain. We do not use the songbirds, for instance. We do not eat many of them; we cannot befriend them; we cannot persuade them to eat more mosquitoes or plant fewer weed seeds. We can only witness them—whoever they are. If we were not here, they would be songbirds falling in the forest. If we were not here, material events like the passage of seasons would lack even the meager meanings we are able to muster for them. The show would play to an empty house, as do all those falling stars which fall in the daytime. That is why I take walks: to keep an eye on things. And that is why I went to the Galápagos islands.

All this becomes especially clear on the Galápagos islands. The Galápagos islands are just plain here—and little else. They blew up out of the ocean, some plants blew in on them, some animals drifted aboard and evolved weird forms—and there they all are, whoever they are, in full swing. You can go there and watch it happen, and try to figure it out. The Galápagos are a kind of metaphysics laboratory, almost wholly uncluttered by human culture or history. Whatever happens on those bare volcanic rocks happens in full view, whether anyone is watching or not.

What happens there is this, and precious little it is: clouds come and go, and the round of similar seasons; a pig eats a tortoise or doesn't eat a tortoise; Pacific waves fall up and slide back; a lichen expands; night follows day; an albatross dies and dries on a cliff; a cool current upwells from the ocean floor; fishes multiply, flies swarm, stars rise and fall, and diving birds dive. The news, in other words, breaks on the beaches. And taking it all in are the trees. The *palo santo* trees crowd the hillsides like any outdoor audience; they face the lagoons, the lava lowlands, and the shores.

I have some experience of these *palo santo* trees. They interest me as emblems of the muteness of the human stance in relation to all that is not human. I see us all as *palo santo* trees, holy sticks, together watching all that we watch, and growing in silence.

In the Galápagos, it took me a long time to notice the *palo santo* trees. Like everyone else, I specialized in sea lions. My shipmates and I liked the sea lions, and envied their lives. Their joy seemed conscious. They were engaged in full-time play. They were all either fat or dead; there was no halfway. By day they played in the shallows, alone or together, greeting each other and us with great noises of joy, or they took a turn offshore and body-surfed in the breakers, exultant. By night on the sand they lay in each other's flippers and slept. Everyone joked, often, that when he "came back," he would just as soon do it all over again as a sea lion. I concurred. The sea lion game looked unbeatable.

But a year and a half later, I returned to those unpeopled islands. In the interval my attachment to them had shifted, and my memories of them had altered, the way memories do, like particolored pebbles rolled back and forth over a grating, so that after a time those hard bright ones, the ones you thought you would never lose, have vanished, passed through the grating, and only a few big, unexpected ones remain, no longer unnoticed but now selected out for some meaning, large and unknown.

Such were the *palo santo* trees. Before, I had never given them a thought. They were just miles of half-dead trees on the red lava sea cliffs of some deserted islands. They were only a name in a notebook: "*Palo santo*—those strange white trees." Look at the sea lions! Look at the flightless cormorants, the penguins, the iguanas, the sunset! But after eighteen months the wonderful cormorants, penguins, iguanas, sunsets, and even the sea lions, had dropped from my holey heart. I returned to the Galápagos to see the *palo santo* trees.

They are thin, pale, wispy trees. You walk among them on the lowland deserts, where they grow beside the prickly pear. You see them from the water on the steeps that face the sea, hundreds together, small and thin and spread, and so much more pale than their red soils that any black-and-white photograph of them looks like a negative. Their stands look like blasted orchards. At every season they all look newly dead, pale and bare as birches drowned in a beaver pond—for at every season they look leafless, paralyzed, and mute. But in fact, if you look closely, you can see during the rainy months a few meager deciduous leaves here and there on their brittle twigs. And hundreds of lichens always grow on their bark in mute, overlapping explosions which barely enlarge in the course of the decade, lichens pink and orange, lavender, yellow, and green. The *palo santo* trees bear the lichens effortlessly, unconsciously, the way they bear everything. Their multitudes, transparent as line drawings, crowd the cliffsides like whirling dancers, like empty groves, and look out over cliff-wrecked breakers toward more unpeopled islands, with their freakish lizards and birds, toward the grieving lagoons and the bays where the sea lions wander, and beyond to the clamoring seas.

Now I no longer concurred with my shipmates' joke; I no longer wanted to "come back" as a sea lion. For I thought, and I still think, that if I came back to life in the sunlight where everything changes, I would like to come back as a *palo santo* tree, one of thousands on a cliffside on those godforsaken islands, where a million events occur among the witless, where a splash of rain may drop on a yellow iguana the size of a dachshund, and ten minutes later the iguana may blink. I would like to come back as a *palo santo* tree on the weather side of an island, so that I could be, myself, a perfect witness, and look, mute, and wave my arms.

VI

The silence is all there is. It is the alpha and the omega. It is God's brooding over the face of the waters; it is the blended note of the ten thousand things, the whine of wings. You take a step in the right direction to pray to this silence, and even to address the prayer to "World." Distinctions blur. Quit your tents. Pray without ceasing.

"Gusev"

Anton Chekhov (1860–1904)

In 1890, Anton Chekhov sought release from a bitter form of depression—a sense of alienation unusual for him—by undertaking a strenuous, 6,500-mile overland journey from Moscow across Siberia to the penal island of Sakhalin. The adventure was therapeutic; and surely he escaped his own sense of self-imprisonment in meeting with, and attempting to assist, convicts undergoing an almost unimaginable suffering. He returned homeward by sea; during the journey, a typhoon nearly capsized his ship. Two passengers died during the voyage; their bodies, after a brief ceremony, were given in their canvas shrouds to the sea. Before the ship docked, Chekhov wrote "Gusev." I think of this story—in which certain of his homeward experiences are transformed by the larger experience of the whole journey—as a record of what he has learned.

Though Chekhov was not religious in the customary sense—he considered Christianity enervated, a superstition—his two characters, Gusev and Pavel Ivanych, are reminiscent, in their oppositions, of the old antithesis between soul and body. In Chekhov's translation of those oppositions, "soul" is selflessness and acceptance; "body" is self-regard and an intellectual concentration on differences and division. As representations of separate qualities usually inter-twined in all of us, Gusev and Pavel Ivanych nearly become figures in allegory; as fictional embodiments of qualities recently out of balance in Chekhov, they demonstrate, I think, his new-found distance from the depression that had plagued him.

Were it not for Gusev's unreasoning hatred of all Chinese, a reader would be hard put to define him, so accepting is this simple peasant of everything else in the social and natural realms. In his longing for his cold homeland, where children play in the snow, the dying Gusev is expressing the longing for freedom that marks Chekhov himself, accounting for the appeal that vast natural vistas—of steppes and mountains, of sea and sky—always held for him; a longing that he also had observed in the convicts at the penal colony. On the other hand, Pavel Ivanych takes pride in his intellect, which dissects rather than unifies. His railing at political oppression and social injustice has nothing to do with any belief in human equality or kinship. He suffers from hubris, from a belief of his superiority to others (including the ignorant Gusev) as well as to the natural processes themselves. In constructing his embittered intellectual, Chekhov may be con-sciously commenting upon a kind of radical intellectual common enough in his day (and not unknown in our own) but he also is describing, consciously or not, his own alienation and anger at the start of his journey. And yet how laconically, how casually, the deaths of these two people are treated! It is as if we are seeing these deaths from a detached viewpoint, almost as if this is how Nature itself would view human death, if Nature had a viewpoint.

The detachment is most pronounced in the final section of this story, which strikes me as a visionary insight offered Chekhov by memory from any number of experiences during the entirety of his journey and perhaps from his earlier life. I find a terrifying beauty in the description first of Gusev's body sinking ever deeper into the sea and then of the sky at sunset. Sky and water merge into a miraculous unity at the end—into those "tender, joyous, passionate colors for which it is hard to find a name in the language of man" because they are indifferent to him, as indifferent to the mortality and appetites of his body as they are to the desires of his soul. The use of the pathetic fallacy—of giving human characteristics to natural phenomena—is a conscious attempt on Chekhov's part to humanize a natural order that has no concern for any individual's fate. For much the same reason, he refers to the downward-settling corpse again and again as "Gusev"; it is as if the author himself is reluctant to accept the clear truth of his vision, to relinquish the name that gives life to his simple peasant, that separates him from the cosmos into which his body is dissolving. If these are impurities in what seems otherwise an almost perfect detachment, they signify a human consciousness using language as best it can to communicate an intuited unitary vision beyond the limits either of language or of normal consciousness itself.

It is already dark, it will soon be night.

Gusev, a discharged private, half rises in his bunk and says in a low voice:

"Do you hear me, Pavel Ivanych? A soldier in Suchan was telling me: while they were sailing, their ship bumped into a big fish and smashed a hole in its bottom."

The individual of uncertain social status whom he is addressing, and whom everyone in the ship infirmary calls Pavel Ivanych, is silent as though he hasn't heard.

And again all is still. The wind is flirting with the rigging, the screw is throbbing, the waves are lashing, the bunks creak, but the ear has long since become used to these sounds, and everything around seems to slumber in silence. It is dull. The three invalids—two soldiers and a sailor—who were playing cards all day are dozing and talking deliriously.

The ship is apparently beginning to roll. The bunk slowly rises and falls under Gusev as though it were breathing, and this occurs once, twice, three times . . . Something hits the floor with a clang: a jug must have dropped.

"The wind has broken loose from its chain," says Gusev, straining his ears.

This time Pavel Ivanych coughs and says irritably:

"One minute a vessel bumps into a fish, the next the wind breaks loose from its chain . . . Is the wind a beast that it breaks loose from its chain?"

"That's what Christian folks say."

"They are as ignorant as you . . . They say all sorts of things. One must have one's head on one's shoulders and reason it out. You have no sense."

Pavel Ivanych is subject to seasickness. When the sea is rough he is usually out of sorts, and the merest trifle irritates him. In Gusev's opinion there is absolutely nothing to be irritated about. What is there that is strange or out of the way about that fish, for instance, or about the wind breaking loose from its chain? Suppose the fish were as big as the mountain and its back as hard as a sturgeon's, and supposing, too, that over yonder at the end of the world stood great stone walls and the fierce winds were chained up to the walls. If they haven't broken loose, why then do they rush all over the sea like madmen and strain like hounds tugging at their leash? If they are not chained up what becomes of them when it is calm?

Gusev ponders for a long time about fishes as big as a mountain and about stout, rusty chains. Then he begins to feel bored and falls to thinking about his home, to which he is returning after five years' service in the Far East. He pictures an immense pond covered with drifts. On one side of the pond is the brick-colored building of the pottery with a tall chimney and clouds of black smoke; on the other side is a village. His brother Alexey drives out of the fifth yard from the end in a sleigh; behind him sits his little son Vanka in big felt boots, and his little girl Akulka also wearing felt boots. Alexey has had a drop, Vanka is laughing, Akulka's face cannot be seen, she is muffled up.

"If he doesn't look out, he will have the children frostbitten," Gusev reflects. "Lord send them sense that they may honor their parents and not be any wiser than their father and mother."

"They need new soles," a delirious sailor says in a bass voice. "Yes, yes!"

Gusev's thoughts abruptly break off and suddenly without rhyme or reason the pond is replaced by a huge bull's head without eyes, and the horse and sleigh are no longer going straight ahead but are whirling round and round, wrapped in black smoke. But still he is glad he has had a glimpse of his people. In fact, he is breathless with joy, and his whole body, down to his fingertips, tingles with it. "Thanks be to God we have seen each other again," he mutters deliriously, but at once opens his eyes and looks for water in the dark.

He drinks and lies down, and again the sleigh is gliding along, then again there is the bull's head without eyes, smoke, clouds . . . And so it goes till daybreak.

II

A blue circle is the first thing to become visible in the darkness—it is the porthole; then, little by little, Gusev makes out the man in the next bunk, Pavel Ivanych. The man sleeps sitting up, as he cannot breathe lying down.

His face is gray, his nose long and sharp, his eyes look huge because he is terribly emaciated, his temples are sunken, his beard skimpy, his hair long. His face does not reveal his social status: you cannot tell whether he is a gentleman, a merchant, or a peasant. Judging from his expression and his long hair, he may be an assiduous churchgoer or a lay brother, but his manner of speaking does not seem to be that of a monk. He is utterly worn out by his cough, by the stifling heat, his illness, and he breathes with difficulty, moving his parched lips. Noticing that Gusev is looking at him he turns his face toward him and says:

"I begin to guess . . . Yes, I understand it all perfectly now."

"What do you understand, Pavel Ivanych?"

"Here's how it is . . . It has always seemed strange to me that terribly ill as you fellows are, you should be on a steamer where the stifling air, the heavy seas, in fact everything, threatens you with death; but now it is all clear to me . . . Yes . . . The doctors put you on the steamer to get rid of you. They got tired of bothering with you, cattle . . . You don't pay them any money, you are a nuisance, and you spoil their statistics with your deaths . . . So, of course, you are just cattle. And it's not hard to get rid of you . . . All that's necessary is, in the first place, to have no conscience or humanity, and, secondly, to deceive the ship authorities. The first requirement need hardly be given a thought—in that respect we are virtuosos, and as for the second condition, it can always be fulfilled with a little practice. In a crowd of four hundred healthy soldiers and sailors, five sick ones are not conspicuous; well, they got you all onto the steamer, mixed you with the healthy ones, hurriedly counted you over, and in the confusion nothing untoward was noticed, and when the steamer was on the way, people discovered that there were paralytics and consumptives on their last legs lying about the deck . . ."

Gusev does not understand Pavel Ivanych; thinking that he is being reprimanded, he says in self-justification:

"I lay on the deck because I was so sick; when we were being unloaded from the barge onto the steamer, I caught a bad chill."

"It's revolting," Pavel Ivanych continues. "The main thing is, they know perfectly well that you can't stand the long journey and yet they put you here. Suppose you last as far as the Indian Ocean, and then what? It's horrible to think of . . . And that's the gratitude for your faithful, irreproachable service!"

Pavel Ivanych's eyes flash with anger. He frowns fastidiously and says, gasping for breath, "Those are the people who ought to be given a drubbing in the newspapers till the feathers fly in all directions."

The two sick soldiers and the sailor have waked up and are already playing cards. The sailor is half reclining in his bunk, the soldiers are sitting near by on the floor in most uncomfortable positions. One of the soldiers has his right arm bandaged and his wrist is heavily swathed in wrappings that look like a cap, so that he holds his cards under his right arm or in the crook of his elbow while he plays with his left. The ship is rolling heavily. It is impossible to stand up, or have tea, or take medicine.

"Were you an orderly?" Pavel Ivanych asks Gusev.

"Yes, sir, an orderly."

"My God, my God!" says Pavel Ivanych and shakes his head sadly. "To tear a man from his home, drag him a distance of ten thousand miles, then wear him out till he gets consumption and . . . and what is it all for, one asks? To turn him into an orderly for some Captain Kopeykin or Midshipman Dyrka! How reasonable!"

"It's not hard work, Pavel Ivanych. You get up in the morning and polish the boots, start the samovars going, tidy the rooms, and then you have nothing more to do. The lieutenant drafts plans all day, and if you like, you can say your prayers, or read a book or go out on the street. God grant everyone such a life."

"Yes, very good! The lieutenant drafts plans all day long, and you sit in the kitchen and long for home . . . Plans, indeed! . . . It's not plans that matter but human life. You have only one life to live and it mustn't be wronged."

"Of course, Pavel Ivanych, a bad man gets no break anywhere, either at home or in the service, but if you live as you ought and obey orders, who will want to wrong you? The officers are educated gentlemen, they understand . . . In five years I have never once been in the guard house, and I was struck, if I remember right, only once."

"What for?"

"For fighting. I have a heavy hand, Pavel Ivanych. Four Chinks came into our yard; they were bringing firewood or something, I forget. Well, I was bored and I knocked them about a bit, the nose of one of them, damn him, began bleeding . . . The lieutenant saw it all through the window, got angry, and boxed me on the ear."

"You are a poor, foolish fellow . . ." whispers Pavel Ivanych. "You don't understand anything."

He is utterly exhausted by the rolling of the ship and shuts his eyes; now his head drops back, now it sinks forward on his chest. Several times he tries to lie down but nothing comes of it: he finds it difficult to breathe.

"And what did you beat up the four Chinks for?" he asks after a while.

"Oh, just like that. They came into the yard and I hit them."

There is silence . . . The card-players play for two hours, eagerly, swearing sometimes, but the rolling and pitching of the ship overcomes them, too; they throw aside the cards and lie down. Again Gusev has a vision: the big pond, the pottery, the village . . . Once more the sleigh is gliding along, once more Vanka is laughing and Akulka, the silly thing, throws open her fur coat and thrusts out her feet, as much as to say: "Look, good people, my felt boots are not like Vanka's, they're new ones.'"

"Going on six, and she has no sense yet," Gusev mutters in his delirium. "Instead of showing off your boots you had better come and get your soldier uncle a drink. I'll give you a present."

And here is Andron with a flintlock on his shoulder, carrying a hare he has killed, and behind him is the decrepit old Jew Isaychik, who offers him a piece of soap in exchange for the hare; and here is the black calf in the entry, and Domna sewing a shirt and crying about something, and then again the bull's head without eyes, black smoke . . .

Someone shouts overhead, several sailors run by; it seems that something bulky is being dragged over the deck, something falls with a crash. Again some people run by. . . . Has there been an accident? Gusev raises his head, listens, and sees that the two soldiers and the sailor are playing cards again; Pavel Ivanych is sitting up and moving his lips. It is stifling, you haven't the strength to breathe, you are thirsty, the water is warm, disgusting. The ship is still rolling and pitching.

Suddenly something strange happens to one of the soldiers playing cards. He calls hearts diamonds, gets muddled over his score, and drops his cards, then with a frightened, foolish smile looks round at all of them.

"I shan't be a minute, fellows . . ." he says, and lies down on the floor.

Everybody is nonplussed. They call to him, he does not answer.

"Stepan, maybe you are feeling bad, eh?" the soldier with the bandaged arm asks him. "Perhaps we had better call the priest, eh?"

"Have a drink of water, Stepan . . ." says the sailor. "Here, brother, drink."

"Why are you knocking the jug against his teeth?" says Gusev angrily. "Don't you see, you cabbage-head?"

"What?"

"What?" Gusev mimicks him. "There is no breath in him, he's dead! That's what! Such stupid people, Lord God!"

III

The ship has stopped rolling and Pavel Ivanych is cheerful. He is no longer cross. His face wears a boastful, challenging, mocking expression. It is as though he wants to say: "Yes, right away I'll tell you something that will make you burst with laughter." The round porthole is open and a soft breeze is blowing on Pavel Ivanych. There is a sound of voices, the splash of oars in the water . . . Just under the porthole someone is droning in a thin, disgusting voice; must be a Chinaman singing.

"Here we are in the harbor," says Pavel Ivanych with a mocking smile. "Only another month or so and we shall be in Russia. M'yes, messieurs of the armed forces! I'll arrive in Odessa and from there go straight to

Kharkov. In Kharkov I have a friend, a man of letters. I'll go to him and say, 'Come, brother, put aside your vile subjects, women's amours and the beauties of Nature, and show up the two-legged vermin . . . There's a subject for you."

For a while he reflects, then says:

"Gusev, do you know how I tricked them?"

"Tricked who, Pavel Ivanych?"

"Why, these people . . . You understand, on this steamer there is only a first class and a third class, and they only allow peasants, that is, the common herd, to go in the third. If you have got a jacket on and even at a distance look like a gentleman or a bourgeois, you have to go first class, if you please. You must fork out five hundred rubles if it kills you. 'Why do you have such a regulation?' I ask them. 'Do you mean to raise the prestige of the Russian intelligentsia thereby?' 'Not a bit of it. We don't let you simply because a decent person can't go third class; it is too horrible and disgusting there.' 'Yes, sir? Thank you for being so solicitous about decent people's welfare. But in any case, whether it's nasty there or nice, I haven't got five hundred rubles. I didn't loot the Treasury, I didn't exploit the natives, I didn't traffic in contraband, I flogged nobody to death, so judge for yourselves if I have the right to occupy a first class cabin and even to reckon myself among the Russian intelligentsia.' But logic means nothing to them. So I had to resort to fraud. I put on a peasant coat and high boots, I pulled a face so that I looked like a common drunk, and went to the agents: 'Give us a little ticket, your Excellency,' said I—"

"You're not of the gentry, are you?" asked the sailor.

"I come of a clerical family. My father was a priest, and an honest one; he always told the high and mighty the truth to their faces and, as a result, he suffered a great deal."

Pavel Ivanych is exhausted from talking and gasps for breath, but still continues:

"Yes, I always tell people the truth to their faces. I'm not afraid of anyone or anything. In this respect, there is a great difference between me and all of you, men. You are dark people, blind, crushed; you see nothing and what you do see, you don't understand . . . You are told that the wind breaks loose from its chain, that you are beasts, savages, and you believe it; someone gives it to you in the neck—you kiss his hand; some animal in a racoon coat robs you and then tosses you a fifteen-kopeck tip and you say: 'Let me kiss your hand, sir.' You are outcasts, pitiful wretches. I am different, my mind is clear. I see it all plainly like a hawk or an eagle when it hovers over the earth, and I understand everything. I am protest personified. I see tyranny—I protest. I see a hypocrite—I protest, I see a triumphant swine—I protest. And I cannot be put down, no Spanish Inquisition can silence me. No. Cut out my tongue and I will protest with gestures. Wall me up in a cellar—I will shout so that you will hear me half a mile away, or will starve myself to death, so that they may have another weight on their black consciences. Kill me and I will haunt them. All my acquaintances say to me: 'You are a most insufferable person, Pavel Ivanych.' I am proud of such a reputation. I served three years in the Far East and I shall be remembered there a hundred years. I had rows there with everybody. My friends wrote to me from Russia: 'Don't come back,' but here I am going back to spite them . . . Yes . . . That's life as I understand it. That's what one can call life."

Gusev is not listening; he is looking at the porthole. A junk, flooded with dazzling hot sunshine, is swaying on the transparent turquoise water. In it stand naked Chinamen, holding up cages with canaries in them and calling out: "It sings, it sings!"

Another boat knocks against it; a steam cutter glides past. Then there is another boat: a fat Chinaman sits in it, eating rice with chopsticks. The water sways lazily, while sea gulls languidly hover over it.

"Would be fine to give that fat fellow one in the neck," reflects Gusev, looking at the stout Chinaman and yawning.

He dozes off and it seems to him that all nature is dozing too. Time flies swiftly by. Imperceptibly the day passes. Imperceptibly darkness descends . . . The steamer is no longer standing still but is on the move again.

IV

Two days pass. Pavel Ivanych no longer sits up but is lying down. His eyes are closed, his nose seems to have grown sharper.

"Pavel Ivanych," Gusev calls to him. "Hey, Pavel Ivanych."

Pavel Ivanych opens his eyes and moves his lips.

"Are you feeling bad?"

"No . . . It's nothing . . ." answers Pavel Ivanych gasping for breath. "Nothing, on the contrary . . . I am better . . . You see, I can lie down now . . . I have improved . . ."

"Well, thank God for that, Pavel Ivanych."

"When I compare myself to you, I am sorry for you, poor fellows. My lungs are healthy, mine is a stomach cough . . . I can stand hell, let alone the Red Sea. Besides, I take a critical attitude toward my illness and the medicines. While you—Your minds are dark . . . It's hard on you, very, very hard!"

The ship is not rolling, it is quiet, but as hot and stifling as a Turkish bath; it is hard, not only to speak, but even to listen. Gusev hugs his knees, lays his head on them and thinks of his home. God, in this stifling heat, what a relief it is to think of snow and cold! You're driving in a sleigh; all of a sudden, the horses take fright at something and bolt. Careless of the road, the ditches, the gullies, they tear like mad things right through the village, across the pond, past the pottery, across the open fields. "Hold them!" the pottery hands and the peasants they meet shout at the top of their voices. "Hold them!" But why hold them? Let the keen cold wind beat in your face and bite your hands; let the lumps of snow, kicked up by the horses, slide down your collar, your neck, your chest; let the runners sing, and the traces and the whippletrees break, the devil take them. And what delight when the sleigh upsets and you go flying full tilt into a drift, face right in the snow, and then you get up, white all over with icicles on your mustache, no cap, no gloves, your belt undone . . . People laugh, dogs bark . . .

Pavel Ivanych half opens one eye, fixes Gusev with it and asks softly:

"Gusev, did your commanding officer steal?"

"Who can tell, Pavel Ivanych? We can't say, we didn't hear about it."

And after that, a long time passes in silence. Gusev broods, his mind wanders, and he keeps drinking water: it is hard for him to talk and hard for him to listen, and he is afraid of being talked to. An hour passes, a second, a third; evening comes, then night, but he doesn't notice it; he sits up and keeps dreaming of the frost.

There is a sound as though someone were coming into the infirmary, voices are heard, but five minutes pass and all is quiet again.

"The kingdom of Heaven be his and eternal peace," says the soldier with a bandaged arm. "He was an uneasy chap."

"What?" asks Gusev. "Who?"

"He died, they have just carried him up."

"Oh, well," mutters Gusev, yawning, "the kingdom of Heaven be his."

"What do you think, Gusev?" the soldier with the bandaged arm says after a while. "Will he be in the kingdom of Heaven or not?"

"Who do you mean?"

"Pavel Ivanych."

"He will . . . He suffered so long. Then again, he belonged to the clergy and priests have a lot of relatives. Their prayers will get him there."

The soldier with the bandage sits down on Gusev's bunk and says in an undertone:

"You too, Gusev, aren't long for this world. You will never get to Russia."

"Did the doctor or the nurse say so?" asks Gusev.

"It isn't that they said so, but one can see it. It's plain when a man will die soon. You don't eat, you don't drink, you've got so thin it's dreadful to look at you. It's consumption, in a word. I say it not to worry you, but because maybe you would like to receive the sacrament and extreme unction. And if you have any money, you had better turn it over to the senior officer."

"I haven't written home," Gusev sighs. "I shall die and they won't know."

"They will," the sick sailor says in a bass voice. "When you die, they will put it down in the ship's log, in Odessa they will send a copy of the entry to the army authorities, and they will notify your district board or somebody like that."

Such a conversation makes Gusev uneasy and a vague craving begins to torment him. He takes a drink—it isn't that; he drags himself to the porthole and breathes the hot, moist air—it isn't that; he tries to think of home, of the frost—it isn't that . . . At last it seems to him that if he stays in the infirmary another minute, he will certainly choke to death.

"It's stifling, brother," he says. "I'll go on deck. Take me there, for Christ's sake."

"All right," the soldier with the bandage agrees. "You can't walk, I'll carry you. Hold on to my neck."

Gusev puts his arm around the soldier's neck, the latter places his uninjured arm round him and carries him up. On the deck, discharged soldiers and sailors are lying asleep side by side; there are so many of them it is difficult to pass.

"Get down on the floor," the soldier with the bandage says softly. "Follow me quietly, hold on to my shirt."

It is dark, there are no lights on deck or on the masts or anywhere on the sea around. On the prow the seaman on watch stands perfectly still like a statue, and it looks as though he, too, were asleep. The steamer seems to be left to its own devices and to be going where it pleases.

"Now they'll throw Pavel Ivanych into the sea," says the soldier with the bandage, "in a sack and then into the water."

"Yes, that's the regulation."

"At home, it's better to lie in the earth. Anyway, your mother will come to the grave and shed a tear."

"Sure."

There is a smell of dung and hay. With drooping heads, steers stand at the ship's rail. One, two, three—eight of them! And there's a pony. Gusev puts out his hand to stroke it, but it shakes its head, shows its teeth, and tries to bite his sleeve.

"Damn brute!" says Gusev crossly.

The two of them thread their way to the prow, then stand at the rail, peering. Overhead there is deep sky, bright stars, peace and quiet, exactly as at home in the village. But below there is darkness and disorder. Tall waves are making an uproar for no reason. Each one of them as you look at it is trying to rise higher than all the rest and to chase and crush its neighbor; it is thunderously attacked by a third wave that has a gleaming white mane and is just as ferocious and ugly.

The sea has neither sense nor pity. If the steamer had been smaller, not made of thick iron plates, the waves would have crushed it without the slightest remorse, and would have devoured all the people in it without distinguishing between saints and sinners. The steamer's expression was equally senseless and cruel. This beaked monster presses forward, cutting millions of waves in its path; it fears neither darkness nor the wind, nor space, nor solitude—it's all child's play for it, and if the ocean had its population, this monster would crush it, too, without distinguishing between saints and sinners.

"Where are we now?" asks Gusev.

"I don't know. Must be the ocean."

"You can't see land . . ."

"No chance of it! They say we'll see it only in seven days."

The two men stare silently at the white phosphorescent foam and brood. Gusev is first to break the silence.

"There is nothing frightening here," he says. "Only you feel queer as if you were in a dark forest; but if, let's say, they lowered the boat this minute and an officer ordered me to go fifty miles across the sea to catch fish, I'll go. Or, let's say, if a Christian were to fall into the water right now, I'd jump in after him. A German or a Chink I wouldn't try to save, but I'd go in after a Christian."

"And are you afraid to die?"

"I am. I am sorry about the farm. My brother at home, you know, isn't steady; he drinks, he beats his wife for no reason, he doesn't honor his father and mother. Without me everything will go to rack and ruin, and before long it's my fear that my father and old mother will be begging their bread. But my legs won't hold me up, brother, and it's stifling here. Let's go to sleep."

V

Gusev goes back to the infirmary and gets into his bunk. He is again tormented by a vague desire and he can't make out what it is that he wants. There is a weight on his chest, a throbbing in his head, his mouth is so dry that it is difficult for him to move his tongue. He dozes and talks in his sleep and, worn out with nightmares, with coughing and the stifling heat, towards morning he falls into a heavy sleep. He dreams that they have just taken the bread out of the oven in thebarracks and that he has climbed into the oven and is having a steam bath there, lashing himself with a besom of birch twigs. He sleeps for two days and on the third at noon two sailors come down and carry him out of the infirmary. He is sewn up in sailcloth and to make him heavier, they put two gridirons in with him. Sewn up in sailcloth, he looks like a carrot or a radish: broad at the head and narrow at the feet. Before sunset, they carry him on deck and put him on a plank. One end of the plank lies on the ship's rail, the other on a box placed on a stool. Round him stand the discharged soldiers and the crew with heads bared.

"Blessed is our God," the priest begins, "now, and ever, and unto ages of ages."

"Amen," three sailors chant.

The discharged men and the crew cross themselves and look off at the waves. It is strange that a man should be sewn up in sailcloth and should soon be flying into the sea. Is it possible that such a thing can happen to anyone?

The priest strews earth upon Gusev and makes obeisance to him. The men sing "Memory Eternal."

The seaman on watch duty raises the end of the plank, Gusev slides off it slowly and then flying, head foremost, turns over in the air and—plop! Foam covers him, and for a moment, he seems to be wrapped in lace, but the instant passes and he disappears in the waves.

He plunges rapidly downward. Will he reach the bottom? At this spot the ocean is said to be three miles deep. After sinking sixty or seventy feet, he begins to descend more and more slowly, swaying rhythmically as though in hesitation, and, carried along by the current, moves faster laterally than vertically.

And now he runs into a school of fish called pilot fish. Seeing the dark body, the little fish stop as though petrified and suddenly all turn round together and disappear. In less than a minute they rush back at Gusev, swift as arrows and begin zigzagging round him in the water. Then another dark body appears. It is a shark. With dignity and reluctance, seeming not to notice Gusev, as it were, it swims under him; then while he, moving downward, sinks upon its back, the shark turns, belly upward, basks in the warm transparent water and languidly opens its jaws with two rows of teeth. The pilot fish are in ecstasy; they stop to see what will happen next. After playing a little with the body, the shark nonchalantly puts his jaws under it, cautiously touches it with his teeth and the sailcloth is ripped the full length of the body, from head to foot; one of the gridirons falls out, frightens the pilot fish and striking the shark on the flank, sinks rapidly to the bottom.

Meanwhile, up above, in that part of the sky where the sun is about to set, clouds are massing, one resembling a triumphal arch, another a lion, a third a pair of scissors. A broad shaft of green light issues from the clouds and reaches to the middle of the sky; a while later, a violet beam appears alongside of it and then a golden one and a pink one . . . The heavens turn a soft lilac tint. Looking at this magnificent enchanting sky, the ocean frowns at first, but soon it, too, takes on tender, joyous, passionate colors for which it is hard to find a name in the language of man.

from *Confessions*

St. Augustine (354–430)

Book VIII of St. Augustine's *Confessions* is the crucial or pivotal one in his autobiography, for it is the one in which he describes how he overcame his own inner tension—a conflict of opposing wills that in modern terms would be called neurotic, resulting in psychosomatic symptoms—to be confirmed as a Christian. The autobiography demonstrates Augustine's insight into his own psychological nature, documenting, among other matters, the effect of past experience—of habit—upon personality; in large measure, we are what we were. For full acceptance of Christianity, Augustine believed, he had to overcome his own sexual desires (in Book VIII, he confesses that as a youth he had prayed to God, "Give me chastity and continence, but not yet"). He had a mistress, by whom he had a child, Adeodatus, whom he deeply loved; he was considering marriage to another woman, barely more than a child herself. For that full acceptance (and for Augustine it was all or nothing) he had also to give up his profession as teacher of rhetoric, work that he disliked but which offered him a livelihood and a certain prominence, as well as much else in the physical and social worlds that he was drawn to. Book VIII concludes with his total acquiescence in God's will through a denial of his own. The epiphany—in later literature, from Joyce onward, the term is adapted to secular use, as a sudden illumination or awakening, a key moment akin to Wordsworth's earlier use of "spots of Time"—takes place in a Milan garden, and is described in a way that gives it a psychological as well as a spiritual credibility.

In Book IX, Augustine discusses some of the changes that have occurred to him in consequence of his confirmation and baptism. But his mother, Monica, is given the greatest emphasis in the book. Augustine openly discusses the relationship between his parents. His father, Patricius, was unfaithful to Monica. He was hot-tempered; Monica saved herself from physical abuse through her patient acceptance of verbal abuse. (Feminists today are not alone in their indignation toward religious beliefs like Monica's that hold marriage to be a contract binding women in uncomplaining servitude to their husbands.) Following the death of Patricius, Monica lived for a time in Rome. She became ill, and Augustine decided to accompany her back to her native home in Africa. They were detained in Ostia, then Rome's seaport, by the "barbarians" in control of the Mediterranean—a foreshadowing of the sack of Rome by Alaric and the Goths two decades later. While at Ostia, Monica died.

I have selected from Book IX a segment that includes Augustine's memory of his parents and the enforced stay of mother and son at Ostia. The passage lucidly describes a visionary experience shared by the two, an experience of touching "the eternal Wisdom" through silence and the abnegation of self and even of beloved human relationships—to Augustine, divine understanding is to be reached through a recognition of everything that is not. That is to say, the phenomenal world and those memories that constitute personal identity within

491

it must be overcome to apprehend the Truth—the "state of blessed happiness" which, as he says in the following book, we were granted some memory of, however dim it may be, at birth, and have ever since desired. This passage also gives Monica's response to her coming death, and Augustine's grief that follows the dying.

One of the many distinguishing qualities of the *Confessions* is its integrity. A reader might assume that following his conversion Augustine (as a bishop destined, he felt, for further importance in his Church) would demonstrate, at least in his public pronouncements, the steadfastness to be found in faith, the unbending strength of his convictions; but in Book IX—and later—he shows us the human difficulty, if not the impossibility, of such resolute behavior. The grief is poignant and real.

∞

You, O God, who bring men of one mind to live together, brought a young man from our own town, named Evodius, to join our company. He had been converted and baptized before us, while he was employed as a government officer, but he had given up the service of the State and entered upon yours. He remained with us and we intended to live together in the devout life which we proposed to lead. We discussed where we could most usefully serve you and together we set out to return to Africa. While we were at Ostia, at the mouth of the Tiber, my mother died.

There are many things which I do not set down in this book, since I am pressed for time. My God, I pray you to accept my confessions and also the gratitude I bear you for all the many things which I pass over in silence. But I will omit not a word that my mind can bring to birth concerning your servant, my mother. In the flesh she brought me to birth in this world: in her heart she brought me to birth in your eternal light. It is not of her gifts that I shall speak, but of the gifts you gave to her. For she was neither her own maker nor her own teacher. It was you who made her, and neither her father nor her mother knew what kind of woman their daughter would grow up to be. It was by Christ's teaching, by the guidance of your only Son, that she was brought up to honour and obey you in one of those good Christian families which form the body of your Church. Yet she always said that her good upbringing had been due not so much to the attentiveness of her mother as to the care of an aged servant, who had carried my grandfather on her back when he was a baby, as older girls do with small children. Her master and mistress, out of gratitude for her long service and respect for her great age and unexceptionable character, treated her as an honoured member of their Christian household. This was why they placed their daughters in her care. She was conscientious in attending to her duties, correcting the children when necessary with strictness, for the love of God, and teaching them to lead wise and sober lives. Except at the times when they ate their frugal meals at their parents' table she would not allow them to drink even water, however great their thirst, for fear that they might develop bad habits. She used to give them this very good advice: "Now you drink water because you are not allowed to have wine. But when you are married and have charge of your own larders and cellars, you will not be satisfied with water, but the habit of drinking will be too strong for you." By making rules of this sort and using her influence she was able to keep the natural greediness of childhood within bounds and teach the girls to control their thirst as they ought, so that they no longer wanted what it was not correct for them to have.

Yet in spite of this, as your servant my mother used to tell me herself, she developed a secret liking for wine. Her parents, believing her to be a good and obedient child, used to send her to draw wine from the cask, as was the custom. She used to dip the cup through the opening at the top of the barrel, and before pouring the wine into the flagon she would sip a few drops, barely touching it with her lips, but no more than this, because she found the taste disagreeable. She did this, not because she had any relish for the liquor and its effects, but simply from the exuberant high spirits of childhood, which find their outlet in playful escapades and are generally kept in check by the authority of older people. Each day she added a few more drops to her daily sip of wine. But *little things despise, and little by little you shall come to ruin.* It soon became a habit, and she would drink her wine at a draught, almost by the cupful. Where then was that wise old woman? What use were her strict prohibitions? Could there have been any remedy for this secret disease except your healing power, O Lord, which always watches over us? Even when our fathers and mothers and those who have charge of us in childhood are not with us, you are there, you who created us, you who call us to come to you, you who also use those who are placed over us to help us to save our souls. What did you do then, my God? How did you look after my mother and cure her disease? Was it not you who, from another soul, brought harsh words of rebuke, as though the sharp taunt were a surgeon's knife drawn from your secret store, with which you cut away the gangrene at one stroke? For my mother used to go to the cellar with a servant-girl. One day when they were alone, this girl quarrelled with her young mistress, as servants do, and intending it as a most bitter insult, called my mother a drunkard. The word struck home. My mother realized how despicable her fault had been and at once condemned it and renounced it. Our enemies can often correct our faults by their disparagement, just as the flattery of friends can corrupt us. But you, O Lord, reward them, not according to the ends which you achieve by using them, but according to the purpose which they have in mind. For the girl had lost her temper and wanted to provoke her young mistress, not to correct her. She did it when they were alone, either because the quarrel happened to take place at a time when no one else was present, or because she may have been afraid of being punished for not having mentioned the matter earlier. But you, O Lord, Ruler of all things in heaven and on earth, who make the deep rivers serve your purposes and govern the raging tide of time as it sweeps on, you even used the anger of one soul to cure the folly of another. Let this be a warning, so that none of us may ascribe it to our own doing if we find that others, whose ways we wish to see reformed, are corrected by the words we speak.

In this way my mother was brought up in modesty and temperance. It was you who taught her to obey her parents rather than they who taught her to obey you, and when she was old enough, they gave her in marriage to a man whom she served as her lord. She never ceased to try to gain him for you as a convert, for the virtues with which you had adorned her, and for which he respected, loved, and admired her, were like so many voices constantly speaking to him of you. He was unfaithful to her, but her patience was so great that his infidelity never became a cause of quarrelling between them. For she looked to you to show him mercy, hoping that chastity would come with faith. Though he was remarkably kind, he had a hot temper, but my mother knew better than to say or do anything to resist him when he was angry. If his anger was unreasonable, she used to wait until he was calm and composed and then took the opportunity of explaining what she had done. Many women, whose faces were disfigured by blows from husbands far sweeter-tempered than her own, used to gossip together and complain of the behaviour of their menfolk. My mother would meet this complaint with another—about the women's tongues. Her manner was light but her meaning serious when she told them that ever since they had heard the marriage deed read over to them, they ought to have regarded it as a contract which bound them to serve their husbands, and from that time onward they should remember their condition and not defy their masters. These women knew well enough how hot-tempered a husband my mother had to cope with. They used to remark how surprising it was that they had never heard, or seen any marks to show, that Patricius had beaten his wife or that there had been any domestic disagreement between them, even for one day. When they asked her, as friends, to tell them the reason, she used to explain the rule which I have mentioned. Those who accepted it found it a good one: the others continued to suffer humiliation and cruelty.

Her mother-in-law was at first prejudiced against her by the tale-bearing of malicious servants, but she won the older woman over by her dutiful attentions and her constant patience and gentleness. In the end her mother-in-law complained of her own accord to her son and asked him to punish the servants for their meddlesome talk, which was spoiling the peaceful domestic relations between herself and her daughter-in-law. Patricius, who was anxious to satisfy his mother as well as to preserve the good order of his home and the peace of his family, took the names of the offenders from his mother and had them whipped as she desired. She then warned them that anyone who told tales about her daughter-in-law, in the hope of pleasing her, could expect to receive the same reward. After this none of them dared to tell tales and the two women lived together in wonderful harmony and mutual goodwill.

There was another great gift which you had given to your good servant in whose womb you created me, O God, my Mercy. Whenever she could, she used to act the part of the peacemaker between souls in conflict over some quarrel. When misunderstanding is rife and hatred raw and undigested, it often gives vent, in the presence of a friend, to spite against an absent enemy. But if one woman launched a bitter tirade against another in my mother's hearing, she never repeated to either what the other had said, except for such things as were likely to reconcile them. I should not regard this as especially virtuous, were it not for the fact that I know from bitter experience that a great many people, infected by this sin as though it were some horrible, widespread contagion, not only report to one disputant what the other has said, but even add words that were never spoken. And yet a man who loves his own kind ought not to be satisfied merely to refrain from exciting or increasing enmity between other men by the evil that he speaks: he should do his best to put an end to their quarrels by kind words. This was my mother's way, learned in the school of her heart, where you were her secret teacher.

In the end she won her husband for you as a convert in the very last days of his life on earth. After his conversion she no longer had to grieve over those faults which had tried her patience before he was a Christian. She was also the servant of your servants. Those of them who knew her praised you, honoured you, and loved you in her, for they could feel your presence in her heart and her holy conversation gave rich proof of it. *She had been faithful to one husband, had made due returns to those who gave her birth. Her own flesh and blood had had first claim on her piety, and she had a name for acts of charity.* She had brought up her children and had been *in travail afresh* each time she saw them go astray from you. Finally, O Lord, since by your gift you allow us to speak as your servants, she took good care of all of us when we had received the grace of your baptism and were living as companions before she fell asleep in you. She took good care of us, as though she had been the mother of us all, and served each one as though she had been his daughter.

495

Not long before the day on which she was to leave this life—you knew which day it was to be, O Lord, though we did not—my mother and I were alone, leaning from a window which overlooked the garden in the courtyard of the house where we were staying at Ostia. We were waiting there after our long and tiring journey, away from the crowd, to refresh ourselves before our sea-voyage. I believe that what I am going to tell happened through the secret working of your providence. For we were talking alone together and our conversation was serene and joyful. *We had forgotten what we had left behind and were intent on what lay before us.* In the presence of Truth, which is yourself, we were wondering what the eternal life of the saints would be like, that life which *no eye has seen, no ear has heard, no human heart conceived.* But we laid the lips of our hearts to the heavenly stream that flows from your fountain, *the source of all life* which is *in you,* so that as far as it was in our power to do so we might be sprinkled with its waters and in some sense reach an understanding of this great mystery.

Our conversation led us to the conclusion that no bodily pleasure, however great it might be and whatever earthly light might shed lustre upon it, was worthy of comparison, or even of mention, beside the happiness of the life of the saints. As the flame of love burned stronger in us and raised us higher towards the eternal God, our thoughts ranged over the whole compass of material things in their various degrees, up to the heavens themselves, from which the sun and the moon and the stars shine down upon the earth. Higher still we climbed, thinking and speaking all the while in wonder at all that you have made. At length we came to our own souls and passed beyond them to that place of everlasting plenty, where you feed Israel for ever with the food of truth. There life is that Wisdom by which all these things that we know are made, all things that ever have been and all that are yet to be. But that Wisdom is not made: it is as it has always been and as it will be for ever—or, rather, I should not say that it *has been* or *will be,* for it simply *is,* because eternity is not in the past or in the future. And while we spoke of the eternal Wisdom, longing for it and straining for it with all the strength of our hearts, for one fleeting instant we reached out and touched it. Then with a sigh, leaving *our spiritual harvest* bound to it, we returned to the sound of our own speech, in which each word has a beginning and an ending—far, far different from your Word, our Lord, who abides in himself for ever, yet never grows old and gives new life to all things.

And so our discussion went on. Suppose, we said, that the tumult of a man's flesh were to cease and all that his thoughts can conceive, of earth, of water, and of air, should no longer speak to him; suppose that the heavens and even his own soul were silent, no longer thinking of itself but passing beyond; suppose that his dreams and the visions of his imagination spoke no more and that every tongue and every sign and all that is transient grew silent—for all these things have the same message to tell, if only we can hear it, and their message is this: We did not make ourselves, but he who abides for ever made us. Suppose, we said, that after giving us this message and bidding us listen to him who made them, they fell silent and he alone should speak to us, not through them but in his own voice, so that we should hear him speaking, not by any tongue of the flesh or by an angel's voice, not in the sound of thunder or in some veiled parable, but in his own voice, the voice of the one whom we love in all these created things; suppose that we heard him himself, with none of these things between ourselves and him, just as in that brief moment my mother and I had reached out in thought and touched the eternal Wisdom which abides over all things; suppose that this state were to continue and all other visions of things inferior were to be removed, so that this single vision entranced and absorbed the one who beheld it and enveloped him in inward joys in such a way that for him life was eternally the same as that instant of understanding for which we had longed so much—would not this be what we are to understand by the words *Come and share the joy of your Lord?* But when is it to be? Is it to be when *we all rise again, but not all of us will undergo the change?*

This was the purport of our talk, though we did not speak in these precise words or exactly as I have reported them. Yet you know, O Lord, that as we talked that day, the world, for all its pleasures, seemed a paltry place compared with the life that we spoke of. And then my mother said, "My son, for my part I find no further pleasure in this life. What I am still to do or why I am here in the world, I do not know, for I have no more to hope for on this earth. There was one reason, and one alone, why I wished to remain a little longer in this life, and that was to see you a Catholic Christian before I died. God has granted my wish and more besides, for I now see you as his servant, spurning such happiness as the world can give. What is left for me to do in this world?"

I scarcely remember what answer I gave her. It was about five days after this, or not much more, that she took to her bed with a fever. One day during her illness she had a fainting fit and lost consciousness for a short time. We hurried to her bedside, but she soon regained consciousness and looked up at my brother and me as we stood beside her. With a puzzled look she asked "Where was I?" Then watching us closely as we stood there speechless with grief, she said "You will bury your mother here." I said nothing, trying hard to hold back my tears, but my brother said something to the effect that he wished for her sake that she would die in her own country, not abroad. When she heard this, she looked at him anxiously and her eyes reproached him for his worldly thoughts. She turned to me and said, "See how he talks!" and then, speaking to both of us, she went on, "It does not matter where you bury my body. Do not let that worry you! All I ask of you is that, wherever you may be, you should remember me at the altar of the Lord."

Although she hardly had the strength to speak, she managed to make us understand her wishes and then fell silent, for her illness was becoming worse and she was in great pain. But I was thinking of your gifts, O God. Unseen by us you plant them like seeds in the hearts of your faithful and they grow to bear wonderful fruits. This thought filled me with joy and I thanked you for your gifts, for I had always known, and well remembered now, my mother's great anxiety to be buried beside her husband's body in the grave which she had provided and prepared for herself. Because they had lived in the greatest harmony, she had always wanted this extra happiness. She had wanted it to be said of them that, after her journeyings across the sea, it had been granted to her that the earthly remains of husband and wife should be joined as one and covered by the same earth. How little the human mind can understand God's purpose! I did not know when it was that your good gifts had borne their full fruit and her heart had begun to renounce this vain desire, but I was both surprised and pleased to find that it was so. And yet, when we talked at the window and she asked, "What is left for me to do in this world?", it was clear that she had no desire to die in her own country. Afterwards I also heard that one day during our stay at Ostia, when I was absent, she had talked in a motherly way to some of my friends and had spoken to them of the contempt of this life and the blessings of death. They were astonished to find such courage in a woman—it was your gift to her, O Lord—and asked whether she was not frightened at the thought of leaving her body so far from her own country. "Nothing is far from God," she replied, "and I need have no fear that he will not know where to find me when he comes to raise me to life at the end of the world."

And so on the ninth day of her illness, when she was fifty-six and I was thirty-three, her pious and devoted soul was set free from the body.

I closed her eyes, and a great wave of sorrow surged into my heart. It would have overflowed in tears if I had not made a strong effort of will and stemmed the flow, so that the tears dried in my eyes. What a terrible struggle it was to hold them back! As she breathed her last, the boy Adeodatus began to wail aloud and only ceased his cries when we all checked him. I, too, felt that I wanted to cry like a child, but a more mature voice within me, the voice of my heart, bade me keep my sobs in check, and I remained silent. For we did not think it right to mark my mother's death with weeping and moaning, because such lamentations are the usual accompaniment of death when it is thought of as a state of misery or as total extinction. But she had not died in misery nor had she wholly died. Of this we were certain, both because we knew what a holy life she had led and also because our faith was real and we had sure reasons not to doubt it.

What was it, then, that caused me such deep sorrow? It can only have been because the wound was fresh, the wound I had received when our life together, which had been so precious and so dear to me, was suddenly cut off. I found comfort in the memory that as I did what I could for my mother in the last stages of her illness, she had caressed me and said that I was a good son to her. With great emotion she told me that she could not remember ever having heard me speak a single hard or disrespectful word against her. And yet, O God who made us both, how could there be any comparison between the honour which I showed to her and the devoted service she had given me? It was because I was now bereft of all the comfort I had had from her that my soul was wounded and my life seemed shattered, for her life and mine had been as one.

When we had succeeded in quieting Adeodatus, Evodius took up a psaltery and began to sing the psalm *Of mercy and justice my song shall be; a psalm in thy honour, Lord,* and the whole house sang the responses. On hearing what was happening many of our brothers in the faith and many pious women came to us, and while those whose duty it was made arrangements for the funeral, I remained in another room, where I could talk without irreverence, and conversed with friends on matters suitable to the occasion, for they did not think it right to leave me to myself. These words of truth were the salve with which I soothed my pain. You knew, O Lord, how I suffered, but my friends did not, and as they listened intently to my words, they thought that I had no sense of grief. But in your ears, where none of them could hear, I blamed myself for my tender feelings. I fought against the wave of sorrow and for a while it receded, but then it swept upon me again with full force. It did not bring me to tears and no sign of it showed in my face, but I knew well enough what I was stifling in my heart. It was misery to feel myself so weak a victim of these human emotions, although we cannot escape them, since they are the natural lot of mankind, and so I had the added sorrow of being grieved by my own feelings, so that I was tormented by a twofold agony.

When the body was carried out for burial, I went and returned without a tear. I did not weep even during the prayers which we recited while the sacrifice of our redemption was offered for my mother and her body rested by the grave before it was laid in the earth, as is the custom there. Yet all that day I was secretly weighed down with grief. With all my heart I begged you to heal my sorrow, but you did not grant my prayer. I believe that this was because you wished to impress upon my memory, if only by this one lesson, how firmly the mind is gripped in the bonds of habit, even when it is nourished on the word of truth. I thought I would go to the baths, because I had been told that the Latin name for them was derived from the Greek βαλανειον, so called because bathing rids the mind of anxiety. And I acknowledge your mercy in this too, O Father of orphans, for I went to the baths and came back in the same state as before. Water could not wash away the bitter grief from my heart. Then I went to sleep and woke up to find that the rest had brought me some relief from my sorrow. As I lay alone in bed, I remembered the verses of your servant Ambrose and realized the truth of them:

Deus, Creator omnium,	Maker of all things! God most high!
polique Rector, vestiens	Great Ruler of the starry sky!
diem decoro lumine,	Who, robing day with beauteous light,
noctem sopora gratia,	Hast clothed in soft repose the night,
Artus solutos ut quies	That sleep may wearied limbs restore,
reddat laboris usui,	And fit for toil and use once more;
mentesque fessas allevet,	May gently soothe the careworn breast,
luctusque solvat anxios.	And lull our anxious griefs to rest.

—from Saint Ambrose's 'Evening Hymn', trs. J. D. Chambers, 1854

Then little by little, my old feelings about your handmaid came back to me. I thought of her devoted love for you and the tenderness and patience she had shown to me, like the holy woman that she was. Of all this I found myself suddenly deprived, and it was a comfort to me to weep for her and for myself and to offer my tears to you for her sake and for mine. The tears which I had been holding back streamed down, and I let them flow as freely as they would, making of them a pillow for my heart. On them it rested, for my weeping sounded in your ears alone, not in the ears of men who might have misconstrued it and despised it.

And now, O Lord, I make you my confession in this book. Let any man read it who will. Let him understand it as he will. And if he finds that I sinned by weeping for my mother, even if only for a fraction of an hour, let him not mock at me. For this was the mother, now dead and hidden awhile from my sight, who had wept over me for many years so that I might live in your sight. Let him not mock at me but weep himself, if his charity is great. Let him weep for my sins to you, the Father of all the brothers of your Christ.

Now that my soul has recovered from that wound, in which perhaps I was guilty of too much worldly affection, tears of another sort stream from my eyes. They are tears which I offer to you, my God, for your handmaid.

They flow from a spirit which trembles at the thought of the dangers which await every soul that *has died with Adam*. For although she was alive in Christ even before her soul was parted from the body, and her faith and the good life she led resounded to the glory of your name, yet I cannot presume to say that from the time when she was reborn in baptism no word contrary to your commandments ever fell from her lips. Your Son, the Truth, has said: *Any man who says to his brother, You fool, must answer for it in hell fire,* and however praiseworthy a man's life may be, it will go hard with him if you lay aside your mercy when you come to examine it. But you do not search out our faults ruthlessly, and because of this we hope and believe that one day we shall find a place with you. Yet if any man makes a list of his deserts, what would it be but a list of your gifts? If only men would know themselves for what they are! If only *they who boast would make their boast in the Lord!*

And so, my Glory and my Life, God of my heart, I will lay aside for a while all the good deeds which my mother did. For them I thank you, but now I pray to you for her sins. Hear me through your Son, who hung on the cross and now *sits at your right hand and pleads for us,* for he is the true medicine of our wounds. I know that my mother always acted with mercy and that she forgave others with all her heart when they trespassed against her. Forgive her too, O Lord, if ever she trespassed against you in all the long years of her life after baptism. Forgive her, I beseech you; *do not call her to account. Let your mercy give your judgement an honourable welcome,* for your words are true and you have promised mercy to the merciful. If they are merciful, it is by your gift; and *you will show pity on those whom you pity; you will show mercy where you are merciful.*

I believe that you have already done what I ask of you, but, *Lord, accept these vows of mine.* For on the day when she was so soon to be released from the flesh she had no care whether her body was to be buried in a rich shroud or embalmed with spices, nor did she wish to have a special monument or a grave in her own country. These were not the last wishes she passed on to us. All she wanted was that we should remember her at your altar, where she had been your servant day after day, without fail. For she knew that at your altar we receive the holy Victim, who *cancelled the decree made to our prejudice,* and in whom we have triumphed over the enemy who reckons up our sins, trying to find some charge to bring against us, yet can find no fault in him in whom we conquer. Who shall restore to him his innocent blood? Who shall take us from him by repaying him the price for which he bought us? By the strong ties of faith your handmaid had bound her soul to this sacrament for our redemption. Let no one tear her away from your protection. Let not the devil, who is *lion and serpent* in one, bar her way by force or by guile. For she will not answer that she has no debt to pay, for fear that her cunning accuser should prove her wrong and win her for himself. Her reply will be that her debt has been paid by Christ, to whom none can repay the price which he paid for us, though the debt was not his to pay.

Let her rest in peace with her husband. He was her first husband and she married no other after him. She served him, *yielding you a harvest*, so that in the end she also won him for you. O my Lord, my God, inspire your servants my brothers—they are your sons and my masters, whom I serve with heart and voice and pen—inspire those of them who read this book to remember Monica, your servant, at your altar and with her Patricius, her husband, who died before her, by whose bodies you brought me into this life, though how it was I do not know. With pious hearts let them remember those who were not only my parents in this light that fails, but were also my brother and sister, subject to you, our Father, in our Catholic mother the Church, and will be my fellow citizens in the eternal Jerusalem for which your people sigh throughout their pilgrimage, from the time when they set out until the time when they return to you. So it shall be that the last request that my mother made to me shall be granted in the prayers of the many who read my confessions more fully than in mine alone.

Acknowledgments

Acknowledgments

Kingston, Maxine Hong: "No Name Woman" from *The Woman Warrior* by Maxine Hong Kingston. Copyright © 1975, 1976 by Maxine Hong Kingston. Reprinted by permission of Alfred A. Knopf, Inc. and Picador.

Landretti, John: "On Waste Lonely Places" by John Landretti first appeared in *Orion,* Summer 1994. Copyright © 1994 by John Landretti. Reprinted by permission of the author.

Levi, Primo: "Chromium" from *The Periodic Table* (pp. 147–159) by Primo Levi, trans. by Raymond Rosenthal. Translation copyright © 1984 by Schocken Books Inc. Copyright © Giulio Einaudi Editore s.p.a. Turin, 1975. Reprinted by permission of Schocken Books, published by Pantheon Books, a division of Random House, Inc. and Michael Joseph Ltd.

Maclean, Norman: From *Young Men and Fire* by Norman Maclean. Copyright © 1992 by The University of Chicago. Reprinted by permission of The University of Chicago Press.

McClane, Kenneth: "A Death in the Family" by Kenneth McClane first appeared in the *Antioch Review,* Vol. 43, No. 2, Spring 1985. Copyright © 1985 by the Antioch Review, Inc. Reprinted by permission of the Editors.

Momaday, N. Scott: From *The Names* by N. Scott Momaday. Published by Harper & Row, 1976. Copyright © 1976 by N. Scott Momaday. Reprinted by permission of the author. "On the Calculus" by J. V. Cunningham from *The Collected Poems and Epigrams of J. V. Cunningham* published by Swallow Press. Copyright © 1971. Reprinted by permission of Jessie C. Cunningham.

Montaigne, Michel de: "Of Practice" from *The Complete Essays of Montaigne,* translated by Donald M. Frame. Copyright © 1958 by the Board of Trustees of the Leland Stanford Junior University. Reprinted with the permission of the publisher, Stanford University Press.

Moore, Marianne: "What Are Years?" by Marianne Moore from *Collected Poems of Marianne Moore.* Copyright 1941 and renewed 1969 by Marianne Moore. Published in the British Commonwealth, except Canada, as *Complete Poems of Marianne Moore.* Reprinted with permission of the publishers Simon & Schuster, Inc. and Faber & Faber Ltd.

Morris, Irvin: "The Hyatt, the Maori, and the Yanamamo" from *Akwe:kon Journal,* Vol. 9, No. 3, Fall 1992. Reprinted by permission of Akwe:kon Press.

Morrison, Toni: "Memory, Creation, and Writing" by Toni Morrison first appeared in *Thought: A Journal of Culture and Ideas,* December 1984, Vol. 59, #235. Copyright © 1984 by Toni Morrison. Reprinted by permission of International Creative Management, Inc.

Nabokov, Vladimir: From *Speak, Memory* by Vladimir Nabokov. Copyright © 1989 by the Estate of Vladimir Nabokov. Reprinted by permission of Vintage Books, a division of Random House, Inc.

Origo, Iris: From *Images and Shadows* by Iris Origo. Reprinted by permission of John Murray (Publishers) Ltd. Excerpt from letter by George Santayana is from *The Letters of George Santayana,* edited by Danniel Cory, published by The MIT Press.

Park, Clara Claiborne: "The Mother of the Muses: In Praise of Memory" by Clara Claiborne Park first appeared in *The American Scholar,* Winter 1980–1981 and later in *Rejoining the Common Reader* by Clara Claiborne Park. Reprinted by permission of the publisher, Northwestern University Press.

Acknowledgments

Poincaré, Henri: "Mathematical Creation" from *The Foundations of Science* by Henri Poincaré, translated by George Bruce Halstead. Reprinted by permission of L. Pearce Williams.

Proust, Marcel: From *Time Regained* from Vol III of *Remembrance of Things Past* by Marcel Proust, translated by C. K. Scott Moncrieff and Terence Kilmartin. Vol. III's *Time Regained* translated by Andreas Mayor. Translation copyright © 1981 by Random House, Inc. and Chatto & Windus. Reprinted by permission of Random House, Inc. Rights in the British Commonwealth administered by Random House UK Ltd. Grateful acknowledgment is made to the Estate of the author, the Estate of C. K. Scott Moncrieff, and the publisher, Chatto & Windus.

Rodriguez, Richard: From *Hunger of Memory* by Richard Rodriguez. Copyright © 1982 by Richard Rodriguez. Reprinted by permission of David R. Godine, Publisher, Inc.

Rose, Steven: From *The Making of Memory: From Molecules to Mind* by Steven Rose. Copyright © 1993 by Steven Rose. Used by permission of Doubleday, a division of Bantam Doubleday Dell Publishing Group, Inc. and Sheil Land Associates Ltd.

Stafford, Kim R.: "A Walk in Early May" from *Having Everything Right* by Kim R. Stafford. Copyright © 1986 by Kim R. Stafford. Reprinted by permission of Confluence Press, Inc. at Lewis-Clark State College, Lewiston, Idaho.

Thomas, Lewis: "On Societies as Organisms," copyright © 1971 by The Massachusetts Medical Society and "Information," copyright © 1972 by The Massachusetts Medical Society, from *The Lives of a Cell* by Lewis Thomas. Used by permission of Viking Penguin, a division of Penguin Books USA Inc. and the Darhansoff & Verrill Literary Agency.

Warner, Esther: "This Old and Thingless World" from *The Crossing Fee* by Esther Warner. Copyright © 1968 by Esther Warner. Reprinted by permission of Houghton Mifflin Co. and John Hawkins & Associates, Inc. as agent for the author. All Rights Reserved.

Welty, Eudora: From *One Writer's Beginnings* by Eudora Welty, Cambridge, Mass.: Harvard University Press. Copyright © 1983, 1984 by Eudora Welty. Reprinted by permission of the publisher. The excerpt from *The Optimist's Daughter* by Eudora Welty is copyright © 1969, 1972 by Eudora Welty. Reprinted by permission of Random House, Inc. and Virago Press.

West, Paul: "The Girls and Ghouls of Memory" from *New Directions International Anthology*, edited by James Laughlin, Issue #42. Copyright © 1981 by Paul West. All rights reserved by the author. Reprinted by permission of Paul West c/o Elaine Markson Literary Agency, Inc.

White, E. B.: "Once More to the Lake," from *One Man's Meat* by E. B. White. Copyright 1941 by E. B. White. Reprinted by permission of HarperCollins Publishers, Inc.

Wolff, Tobias: From *This Boy's Life* by Tobias Wolff. Copyright © 1989 by Tobias Wolff. Published in the U.S. by Grove/Atlantic, Inc. and by Bloomsbury Publishing PLC in London, April 1989. Used by permission of the publishers.

Woolf, Virginia: From "A Sketch of the Past" from *Moments of Being* by Virginia Woolf. Copyright © 1976 by Quentin Bell and Angelica Garnett. Reprinted by permission of Harcourt Brace & Company, the Estate of the author, and Chatto & Windus.

Acknowledgments

Yates, Frances A.: From *The Art of Memory* by Frances A. Yates. Copyright © 1966 by Frances A. Yates. Reprinted by permission of the University of Chicago Press and Routledge, Chapman & Hall Ltd.

Yeats, William Butler: "Leda and the Swan" and selected lines from "Sailing to Byzantium" are reprinted from *The Poems of W. B. Yeats: A New Edition,* edited by Richard J. Finneran. Copyright 1928 by Macmillan Publishing Company, renewed 1956 by Georgie Yeats. Reprinted with permission of Simon & Schuster, Inc.

Author Index